The H

The House of Vines

Lauren K. Nixon

Jan —
 Be wary of books that try
 to read you back!

 [signature]

The House of Vines

Copyright © 2017 Lauren. K. Nixon

All rights reserved.

ISBN: 1979929548

ISBN-13: 978-1979929547

The House of Vines

For Niall, who actually likes this one!

Other Titles

From The Mysterium:

Echoes of the Light
The Fox and the Fool

With The Superstars:

Title Not Included
Some Assembly Required

A good bookshop is just a genteel Black Hole that knows how to read.
Terry Pratchett

And above all, watch with glittering eyes the whole world around you because the greatest secrets are always hidden in the most unlikely places. Those who don't believe in magic will never find it.
Roald Dahl

The House of Vines

PROLOGUE

He could understand why, now that he held it in his shaking hands. He had never fully comprehended the lure, the power of the thing. Now, with its wrappings coiling across his knees and the cool, enticing Chalice in his grip he fancied that he could hear it calling to him.

He shuddered, involuntarily.

Almost without meaning to, he caressed the artefact, running his bitten fingertips over the strange, seductive designs adorning its surface.

It wanted him.

He could feel it.

But he wouldn't make that mistake, not where countless others had before. He had seen what had happened to them, through the myopic lens of history, glimpsed the smoking ruins of their lives – seen, in minute detail the potential power within. He had already lost too much.

He would not let it destroy anyone else's family, as it had his own.

Ignoring its delicious temptation, he wrapped it once again in its plain, linen bindings, and nestled it, reverently, amongst the straw.

The infernal thing had caused so much pain, bred so much hatred. It was a state of affairs that could not be allowed to continue.

He remembered the night – such a long, bleak night – that he had tried to destroy it, and he had wept as the flames licked at the Chalice, the core of his – and so many others' desires. But no matter how the flames had leapt and crackled, no matter how the tinder smoked and smouldered, no matter how much fuel he had stoked around the thing, it would not burn, would not even blacken.

That had been a terrible, dreadful confirmation – if he hadn't already had enough proof. Something so wicked that it could not be touched by flame: it had to be the work of the Devil himself.

With the certainty that he was safeguarding the young and enterprising fools of the future, he sealed the box and concealed it deep in the shadows. For a long moment, he gazed at it.

Think, it seemed to say.

Think of what we could do, you and I. Together.

He compressed his lips in distaste, and touched the hollow in the wall. He waited until the grinding cacophony of stone on stone ceased, and inspected his work. Satisfied that his hiding place betrayed no crack, no sign of itself, he turned and walked purposefully away.

He would not look back, he had sworn that to himself, and that promise, at least, he would keep.

No matter how it whispered to him.

Face pale under the waxing moon, and feeling curiously lighter now that his burden had been laid down, he closed the great oak doors with the softest of clicks.

Some things were better left buried.

ooo

Henri Petitjean stumbled home in the false dark of the city, pointedly ignoring the man throwing up in the mouth of a nearby alley. One more glass and he might have been joining him.

He reeled cheerfully along the winding street he lived above and swung himself through the basement window, startling the enormous white cat that had been snoozing languidly on the sill.

Stupid thing, he thought, aiming a lazy kick in its general direction. The cat gave a lethargic yowl that was really more of a yawn and settled back down on the windowsill, where it purred lethargically.

Henri shook his head at it and crept to the door at the top of the basement steps.

He could hear Madame Plamondon's television, voices drifting from her lair along the hall.

He held the bottles in the pocket of his great-coat to stop them clanging together and made a dash for the stairs, pausing on the landing above to make sure she hadn't heard him. Content that the old dragon had been evaded, he made his way upstairs, telling himself that he really ought to replace the front door key he had lost months before.

Henri was ultimately certain that he never would. Sneaking in made him feel young again – and it was too much damn' fun.

"Hey, Luca," he called, as he reached his landing, confident that Mme Plamondon wouldn't hear him now over her American soap operas. "Move yourself!" He clinked the bottles together jubilantly. "It is a good day," he called, through the door. "We both were lucky – you met your rich client and I –" he rattled the bottles together – "won two bottles of Port at the club!"

He frowned when his brother didn't burst out of their apartment, his habitual cloud of cigarette smoke curling around him.

"Luca?" he called, much less certainly. He tightened his grip on the necks of the port bottles and sidled over to the fire escape, careful not to make any more noise. Swiftly, he slammed the fire escape door, crossed the hall and flattened himself against the wall.

He heard the tell-tale creak of the loose floorboard by the door: someone was looking through the peephole.

Henri held his breath as whoever it was satisfied themselves that the hallway was empty of loud-mouthed drunks; the person moved away from the door, the wood protesting beneath them.

Henri crept closer to the door, hoping desperately that his brother wasn't in there; he pressed his ear to the wall, straining to hear. He could make out hushed voices behind the wall: there were at least two people in his apartment, and neither of them sounded like his brother.

Maybe Luca had walked out – to the café on the corner, perhaps – and these men had broken in while he was out.

Yes, Henri thought, desperately. *He's at the café, and I should get out of this place, wake Mme Plamondon, who is undoubtedly asleep in her chair, and march her and that stupid cat of hers out to the café to join him. Then we can call the Sûreté and watch the show...*

Inside the apartment, something fell over and someone swore in English.

Henri closed his eyes and sent a prayer to the God that he usually ignored. He couldn't take the chance that Luca was in there and needed his help. He'd never be able to live with himself if –

Henri squared his shoulders, refusing to follow that particular train of thought, and barged through the door, roaring.

Two men froze in a ghastly tableau in front of him and the roar died in his throat. An enormous man with dark skin had paused in the act of rifling through his brother's desk; papers and manuscripts were strewn across the apartment. The other man – a shorter, wirier, paler sort – was crouching over Luca.

Henri forced himself to look at his brother: his outstretched arm seemed to be reaching towards him, searching for comfort, his eyes glazed and dull in death.

Henri lost it, lunging at the closest man; his friend at the desk was quicker. He moved so fast that Henri hadn't even seen what he threw, but whatever it was hit him square in the chest and he flew backwards, winded.

He struggled to his feet just as they slipped out of the window, the edge of one of their coats flapping in the cold Paris air. Enraged, he hurtled to the window, hurling abuse and bottles of Port after them as they pelted down the street and out of sight.

Then he turned back to the room and saw his brother, sprawled amongst his beloved manuscripts. Henri fell to his knees beside him and pulled him into his arms, rocking him back and forth as the tears fell into his dark, greying hair.

Mme Plamondon's rotund and generally unthreatening form filled the doorway, rendered ferocious by fear. She brandished a poker but dropped it when her eyes fell on the brothers.

She rushed to help, but it was clearly too late for Luca.

"Henri..." she murmured, a hand on his shoulder as she plugged numbers into her phone.

"They went out the window," he sobbed. He was aware that Mme Plamondon had moved to look out of it, probably wondering, as he had, how anyone could have dropped three storeys of sheer stone wall without breaking their legs.

"Yes," she said into her phone, watching the shadows across the street, "I need the police – there's been a murder..."

1
DOWN AND OUT

It had been another bad day in a series of bad days.

He had risen hideously early, walked into the small town from the tiny, filth-encrusted flat that he called home, and arrived at the shopping centre just in time to be informed that, since he had taken so many days off sick (six, in the last two months), the manager found his continued employment 'untenable'. After quite a heated argument – not on his part, it had to be said, largely just on the manager's – he had returned his uniform and made a hasty exit from the building, his manager's angry roar of indignation ringing in his ears.

At least the staff of the Records Office had been sorry to see him go; they had clubbed together (that morning, it seemed, as soon as they had found out he was going), and bought him a small cake and a leaving card. They had stood around, awkwardly, for a few minutes, trying to give comfort and advice before drifting back to their jobs, secure in the knowledge that they were safe, for now. He had felt their eyes on him as he'd walked despondently away, and a few of them had waved. He had appreciated the effort.

They had almost made him feel human.

It had been a long walk back to his dingy little flat in the seedier end of Brindleford. He dropped his keys in the bowl by the door and collapsed into the incredibly uncomfortable armchair, generally feeling sorry for himself and wondering where the hell he was going to find this month's rent. He had just been about to reach for the cake as a substitute for real food when his landlord had banged on his door.

He could tell the man was approaching, even before registering his distinctive knock (he was of the 'attempt to take the door off its hinges so that the tenant will have to replace it' school of thought). His landlord stank.

Not long after moving in, Christopher had realised he could close his eyes and track the odious man around the neighbourhood, by stench alone. It was a many layered smell, a bizarre mix of sweat, wet dog, decay and *Brut* – and a strange, fruity, tang that he would rather not identify. It had almost taken on a life of its own, and Christopher was mildly concerned that he might meet it down a dark alley on a dark night.

With a sinking heart (and having taken a deep breath of comparatively fresher air), he opened the door and surveyed the man, trying not to gag.

He was an oddly round man: nature had cruelly provided him with not enough body and a proliferation of neck. As usual, he was bright red – either from the exertion of climbing all those stairs, or from anger, Christopher was never sure – and his grubby string vest clung to his gelatinous body, possibly in an attempt to become one with it. He had a bent, half-smoked cigarette jammed behind his right ear and, unusually, he was grinning. This wasn't what had captured Christopher's attention, however. No, the thing that Christopher found most interesting on this occasion was that the man had a shotgun pointed at his chest.

He stared at it for a few moments, as the man's stench wandered past him and made itself at home in the room behind him, the metallic notes of the gun barely permeating the dreadful odour.

Christopher swallowed.

"Hello Mr Johnson," he managed, not taking his eyes off the end of the gun. "What can I do f-" he faltered as Viv Johnson waved the barrels at him.

"You shut up," he growled. "I knows what you are, boy, no use pretending."

Christopher raised his eyes to Johnson's face, trying to gauge precisely what it was that he thought was going on.

"You do?" he asked, weakly.

"Yus," the man grunted. "I knew there wus something dodgy about you from the start. Thought maybe you wus one of them rent boys or something, but know I knows, don't I?"

Christopher, rather taken aback that anyone would mistake him for a prostitute, of all things, took a step backwards as Johnson advanced with the shotgun and poked him in the chest.

"Now I knows," he went on, "that you are *unnatural*. You's one of them dark 'uns."

Christopher swallowed.

"I am?" he asked, weakly.

"You's a werewolf."

He opened his mouth, ran through several vocal options – including abject denial and screaming like a madman – and shut it again, horribly aware of the gun barrels pressing against his shirt.

Contrary to popular belief, you don't need silver bullets to kill a werewolf, particularly in human form. True, they might heal faster than other humans, and if you piss one off by shooting at it, you're really in trouble, but if you, say, shoot one at point blank range with an illegal shotgun, you're probably going to be scraping dark creature off the walls and carpet.

Johnson gave him a long look, as if he were considering doing just that. Apparently deciding that the cleaning bill would be too pricey, he prodded him once more with the gun and narrowed his eyes at him.

"I wants you out," he growled. "*Now*."

Mutely, Christopher managed to nod, while Johnson leaned against the door frame, gun still levelled at his soon-to-be-former tenant.

Christopher, incredibly aware of those twin metal tubes glaring at him across the room, forwent the usual discretion he used around maniacal landlords, and started to pack using magic.

Johnson watched, fascinated, as Christopher's belongings folded themselves, wrapping themselves and whizzing into his backpack, carryall, suitcase and solitary cardboard box.

When he was finished, Johnson gave a low whistle.

"The Missus'll never believe –" he regained his internal balance and thrust the shotgun at Christopher as he heaved the pack onto his shoulders, picked up the carry-all and suitcase in one hand and balanced the cardboard box in the other. "*Out.*"

ooo

That had been an hour ago, and he had gone to the one place that he knew he wouldn't be turned away.

The Rose and Crown was a dingy, ancient pub, hidden in one of the back streets of Brindleford, which smelled largely of stale beer. Too grimy to be of historic importance, and too unnoticeable to attract more than the most observant tourists, it was a particularly depressing place. It catered for a few local people, too old, lazy, or stubborn to find an alternative watering hole, but mostly it specialised in people who were... *different.*

Charlie, the landlord, was half Troll (Christopher really didn't want to know the story behind that), and not a bad sort, even if he was eight-foot-something, about as wide as a door frame, and kept a big-stick-with-nails-on under the bar. He was understanding about things like evictions, and had a bit of a soft spot when it came to Christopher. Like most magical people, he had a strong dislike for werewolves, generally, but Christopher's situation had the trappings of a potential romantic adventure, and Charlie liked that a lot. Christopher had once caught him reading a Catherine Cookson novel in the tap-room, and had been sworn to the utmost secrecy.

Most of his patrons assumed that he couldn't read at all.

He had taken one look at Christopher as he trudged through the door to the empty pub, sighed, and opened the door to the kitchen so that he could dump his stuff.

He'd let him have a cup of something approaching tea, and Christopher had shared his cake with him, trying desperately to think of somewhere that would take him without an income.

Charlie didn't like to take lodgers, mostly on the basis that some of them might try to eat him while he slept and he didn't like cleaning up the mess, and partly, he'd confided to Christopher, because he didn't want anyone to see his Mills and Boon collection. As Christopher had filed that under 'never needed to know', Charlie had gone on to explain that if he took one person in, everyone would want to stay.

He had a little money saved, in a cunning puzzle box that his sister had given him for his eighteenth birthday. Perhaps it would be enough for a deposit.

Christopher sighed, his breath raising tiny clouds of multi-coloured dust on the counter. He had taken up his usual position behind the door, looking out through the dingy stained glass into the street outside. The rippled glass made everyone passing the window into strange and fantastic shapes, and he liked that. It made him feel less isolated.

Tiredly, he ran his eyes over the crumpled paper in his hand. It was his latest letter from Rachel, telling him how happy she was about him settling into Brindleford at last.

He missed his sister.

A couple of years his junior, he had always felt protective of Rachel, especially as she got older and more beautiful, and began attracting the attentions of the wrong sort of boys – and, as far as he was concerned, they were *all* the wrong sort of boy. She had borne his stern glares at her admirers with commendable patience, and had simply laughed at him when he told her that she needed to be more careful. Looking back, he could see her point; she had never had the proclivity to randomly jump into something without thinking. Unlike him.

They had both been so excited when he'd been accepted at the University of his dreams, and she had even caught the train with him on the day he moved into the Halls of Residence, their parents letting them do this alone as a rite of passage.

That had been the last time he had seen her, waving goodbye from a train window as she sped back home, as eager to start her A-Levels as he was to start his Degree. She wrote to him that very week, and her letter had made him laugh so much that he had immediately written back, initiating a flurry of correspondence that kept him grounded as he got used to living away from home. His Mum and Dad would ring, occasionally, to check on him and to gossip about work and the neighbours, usually catching him as he was dashing out of the door to the pub, or dozing in the library.

Student life suited him down to the ground and he had loved every minute of it, studying, drinking, reading, drinking, making new friends, drinking some more – looking back now, it seemed idyllic.

He had become used to the student haunts, often staying late and drinking heavily with his friends. Which was when it had all gone wrong.

They had been out on the town that night, he and his friends, celebrating his birthday. If he was honest, he couldn't remember most of it, other than a strange, blurred cacophony of laughter, alcohol and loud music, but at some point he had decided that he needed to get some fresh air, and had stumbled and weaved his way out of the busy bar, and into the dark, moonlit street beyond.

It was stupid, really, but he had looked up at the moon that night, and remembered all the stories that his parents had told him as a child, about staying indoors on full moons, and not walking down blind alleys – about being careful who you annoyed – and he had laughed to himself. As if anything like that could happen here! Out in the countryside, maybe, but not in the middle of the city. It was just too unlikely. So, when he turned to see the looming shadow behind him, he had cheerfully said 'hello', instead of running for his life.

The head of the university ice-hockey club, the Polar Bears: a bad tempered final year student who was built like a bear and had a reputation for getting into fights.

Christopher, who had thus far managed to avoid any arguments with the man, had simply grinned drunkenly at him, expecting to pass the time of day. He hadn't even known his name, though he *did* know that everyone called him 'Frosty', for some reason.

'Frosty', as it turned out, had a girlfriend whose favourite hobby was watching him fight other, less fortunate souls... dimly – and far, *far* too late – Christopher had recalled the stunning, leggy redhead who had been draping herself all over him all night, and had been about to try to explain when 'Frosty' had leapt, from a standing position, directly towards him, transforming into a great, snarling wolf as he flew.

Christopher had watched these developments with a kind of numb and fascinated detachment that lasted right up until the point where 'Frosty's' teeth had ripped through his shoulder.

He didn't remember screaming, but he must have, and as his drunken and confused friends spilled out of the bar to his aid, the creature that had been 'Frosty' had disappeared off into the night.

His friends hadn't known what to do; he found out later that several of them had simply been sick and left, but two of them had picked him up and bundled him into a taxi. He didn't remember much of the ride to A&E, other than the pain.

It had seemed to him to be a physical thing, sitting atop his chest and pounding at his shoulder and lungs. He had blacked out several times, and he could dimly remember one of his mates desperately trying to stop the bleeding with a screwed up t-shirt. He had been aware of something else, too; a dark thing, cackling at him in the gloom when he closed his eyes. He had been sure that he had been hallucinating then, but later...

He had woken up in hospital to two very concerned, suddenly very sober, rugby players and twenty-seven stitches, a triage nurse peering down at him over the top of her spectacles. She had given him a barrage of injections, including one for Rabies, since everyone had seen 'Frosty' run off, however indistinctly, and told him that he had been very lucky.

Christopher, who remembered his attack quite clearly, seriously doubted this, but he'd kept his mouth shut. His friends had escorted him home that night, and he had thanked them profusely, forcing them to take some of his surplus alcohol as payment.

That first night had been particularly bad.

The wound itched and burned as he moved, and more than once he had the unsettling sensation that something was bubbling beneath his skin. Every time he took the pain medication the nurse had given him, he was violently sick and was eventually forced to give up, shivering and weak as the coils of a dreadful fever wracked through his body. It felt like his shoulder was on fire, the flames spreading out until they consumed his whole being.

In his fevered imagination, the dark thing that had taunted him in the taxi had returned, whispering to him and cackling as he writhed and sweated; he realised later that it had been the curse, taking a form in his mind as it consumed his body.

After a night tortured by pain and heat, he had slept for nearly two whole days, waking, finally, to bright autumnal sunshine and the very pressing need to eat. He had struggled out of his room to find the Halls strangely quiet and empty. Padding into the kitchen and finding it curiously tidy he realised that he must have slept his way into reading week, so far out of it that he hadn't heard the tell-tale slamming of doors and whoops of excitement as his housemates had departed.

Luckily, someone had abandoned a full loaf of bread and he ate the lot, buttering each slice and eating it as the next one toasted. He was still hungry, he realised, once he'd finished – ravenous in fact – and had gone through four boxes of left over takeaway and two frozen pizzas before he stopped and thought about what he was doing.

That had been the first time that he had noticed the smell. Well, *smells*.

Everything smelled.

Him, the food, the bins, the mysterious and migratory pile of clothing his flatmate had abandoned in the hall – even the detergents in the bathroom, three doors away. It was as if each odour had taken on a solid form, a colour. He could almost *see* them, vividly swirling about him in a violent, vibrant cacophony. It had all been a little too much for him, and he had once again been forced to empty his stomach, bewildered and overwrought.

It hadn't been until he had showered (and discovered that his usual shower gel smelled unpleasantly synthetic and chemical) and had glanced at his reflection in the mirror that he had remembered the bite.

He had been bitten by a *werewolf*.

Forcing himself not to panic, he had peeled back the bandage and examined the wound in the tiny, scratched mirror above his sink, noticing with startled curiosity that some of the stitches the nurse had given him only three days before had started to work their way out of his skin.

His skin: *which had already healed.*

Where there should have been an open wound, held together with surgical suture, was a jagged, dark red line, broken by oval marks where the teeth had pierced his skin.

He was a werewolf.

In that moment he had fully comprehended his predicament for the first time, and he had simply stared numbly at himself for a full ten minutes, refusing to believe the evidence of his own senses.

He was a *werewolf*.

Eventually, he had to move, and as he did he uttered a single, terrified noise; it had startled him, until he had recognised it as his own voice.

He was a werewolf, and he knew what that meant.

Sternly, he had made himself walk back to his room and dig out the metal first-aid box that his mother had insisted he take with him when he left. His mother... His hands shook until he could push the memory of saying goodbye to her away. He had never imagined it would be the last time.

Carefully, he had removed the stitches, having to painfully dig a few of them out with a needle as his flesh had knit so tightly about them – no mean feat when you're working on your own shoulder, using a mirror. Then, he made himself eat, more slowly this time, not allowing himself to think until he had finished.

He remembered packing his things slowly and carefully, using a trick that his father had taught him to make everything fit into only a couple of bags.

He kept Rachel's letters, and the photographs of his family that he had brought with him, putting them safely between the books that he intended to take away. He removed the storage from all of his electronic devices one by one; he would find a way to get the pictures off them later. The rest he could sell. After all, what use would he have for a computer, now?

Finally, he had taken out his ID and laid it on the bed, next to the school books that he was leaving for his friends, the random assortment of useless free stuff that he had picked up at the Fresher's Fayre, and a letter addressed to his parents. It was a forlorn collection of things.

He had tried long and hard to think of what to tell his mum and dad: they would be so upset.

But he knew what would happen to the family of a werewolf. They would lose their jobs, Rachel her place in school, her prospects – they would have to move, over and over again, going to a new town every time someone found out about him.

The way people would look at them.

He couldn't bear it.

In the end he had settled for simply: 'I love you, and I'm sorry.' God only knew what they might infer from that.

He had been about to leave when the phone had begun to ring. He stared at it for a long moment before turning to go, the sound of it following him out of the Halls and into the darkening world.

He had taken what was left of his student loan out of the bank, dropped his borrowed books back at the Library and caught the first train away from the city.

That had been nearly a decade ago, and he had never gone back, finding it depressingly easy to disappear. It had taken him nearly six months for him to work up the courage to write to his sister, taking care not to give too much away about his location, and telling her that he was alright, and to let his mum and dad know.

He had written again, around Christmas, and had included a post office where she might write back to him – if she promised not to tell the rest of the family, or come looking for him. Rachel had readily agreed, scolding him for leaving without a word, begging him to come home, demanding why he would do this to them.

It had taken her a while, and an avalanche of stationery, but she had eventually wheedled the story out of him, and promised to keep his secret – as long as he continued to write to her.

He sighed, heavily. He would have to write to her again, now, to tell her his new address. Assuming that he found somewhere.

He glared despondently into his cup of tea. Well, he supposed that it was tea. He swirled it around the mug a few times, considering its tea-like properties: it was certainly liquid, and sort of brownish, but really, there the similarity ended. It was weak, not particularly milky, and didn't really smell of anything except hot tin – a product, he suspected, of its recent incarceration in the big tea-urn in the kitchen.

Christopher sighed and put the cup carefully back down on its cracked saucer. He should be grateful, really, that Charlie let him steal the odd cup.

Wearily resigned to his predicament, he pushed himself away from the counter. This wasn't getting him anywhere. Depositing his cup of – by now – stone cold proto-tea on the bar and nodding to Charlie in a despondent kind of way, he turned to the pub's shabby notice board. It was usually covered in torn and ragged bits of paper, the CAMRA symbol the only splash of respectability on a matted collage of things that had been made into posters when woodcuts were still popular.

There were always a couple of adverts for lodgers, which generally led to unsavoury or just plain bizarre housemates, and Christopher had tried them all. Apparently, no matter how many bloodstains were on the rug or who you liked to grind down and use in your spells, you were always less unsavoury than a werewolf. One of the adverts, a beautifully penned card that Christopher had watched a tiny old lady in a massive pink cardigan pin up, he had very nearly answered; Charlie had warned him off, however. Apparently lodgers taken in by the Widow Shaw were seldom seen again.

To his surprise, there was a new card today. Not for accommodation, as he had hoped, but for a job. It was rather succinct:

'Experienced book wrangler required.
Good wage, decent hours.
Must be polite, punctual, and unconcerned by the macabre.
Non-Practitioners, or those with
only rudimentary skills, need not apply.'

Christopher scratched the back of his neck contemplatively. It was a funny kind of advert, without any contact details, or further instructions. He turned to ask Charlie about it but the man, in view of the lack of paying customers, had disappeared into the tap-room, and was probably engrossed in his latest paperback by now.

Turning back to the board, he read the advertisement through again. There were still no directions.

Carefully, he prised the slim piece of card away from the board and examined the back. Nothing. Just intricate patterns.

He turned it over again.

Who would put up an advert that no one could answer? he thought. Deciding that the answer to this was probably 'no-one', he leaned against the grubby bar and turned the card over and over in his hands, troubles forgotten. He loved puzzles. His whole family did – his mother had once remarked that it must be a genetic predisposition.

He wracked his brains, staring at the gold filigree decoration on the back of the card. Frowning, he closed his eyes, trying to remember what his father had told him about the magical properties of gold.

It could be used to cure eye problems, he recalled, though rubbing a lump of metal in your eye had always seemed to him to be a little counterproductive if you wanted it to stop hurting. It was a good base for Glamours, particularly ones that made the wearer more beautiful.

He shook his head and opened his eyes once more. Mostly, what he could remember about gold was the maniacal search for its creation, and Alchemy had never been his strong suit.

For a long moment he peered at the card until it hit him. It *was* a Glamour. A very subtle and craftily constructed Glamour, but a Glamour nonetheless – and on an inanimate object!

Christopher was impressed.

Quietly, he collected his thoughts, and began to concentrate on the swirling, gold embossed patterns, looking for an edge, a fault, a way in.

Minutes passed, and nothing happened – sweat broke out on his forehead as his eyes bored into the ink: finally, just when he had been about to give up, the lines began to move and twist, and he pushed just a little harder, buoyant with triumph. The sinuous pattern resolved into an address – just on the other side of town.

> *'Zarrubabel and Barraclough,*
> *Purveyors of Fine Books,*
> *7a Market Plaza,*
> *Brindleford.'*

Sore-eyed and grinning, Christopher hurried into the tap-room. Charlie was lounging, feet up on a barrel, deeply engrossed in a brightly coloured book; Christopher's sudden appearance made him jump to his feet.

"Don't do that, boy!" he said, taking in his friend's manic expression and slightly red eyes. "What?"

"I need to head out for a bit," he said, fingering the card. "Can I leave my stuff here for a little while?"

"If you must," he grunted. "But don't go thinking you can move in."

"I won't, don't worry – I think I may have found a job – or at least one I'd like to do, for a change."

"Well," grunted Charlie, who was a man of few words. "Good luck then."

ooo

She watched him in the silvered mirror, prowling about her bedroom like a cat: sleek and possessive. He was beautiful, and Candace Crawley loved beautiful things.

She had built her life around them: her gallery, her business, this apartment. She pinned back her white-blonde hair and put the finishing touches to her make-up. She would look perfect at the benefit that evening, she knew, and he would look perfect on her arm.

Carefully, she smoothed the pale pink silk of her dress and considered her options. He wanted something – that was easy enough to see: he wouldn't be here if he didn't.

As attractive as she undoubtedly was, she hadn't been

his first choice when he had stalked into her New York gallery two days before. He had had his eye on the collection of antiquities in the studio, the exclusive little parlour where she showed off her most sought after items.

The current fashion was for Medieval European trinkets, and Candace always paid attention to fashion. It was how she made her money, after all.

The precisely appointed display cases were full of jewel-encrusted specimens this month, survivors of several centuries of avarice. Few of the artefacts were what Candace would call elegant, but they were popular and expensive, and she didn't have to take them home with her.

He had spent several hours in the studio, and she had kept a calculating eye on him while he did. Even rich, handsome young men could be thieves – particularly rich, handsome young men, in fact, and she had no intention of letting him make her play the fool.

He had set out to charm her that evening, probably in an effort to secure a discount – or worse, a tab. He would be sorely disappointed when he realised that Candace had no intention of granting him either. In the meantime, however, she was content to encourage his seduction. It had been a decadent way to spend a weekend, but she made a point of never mixing business with pleasure.

Her eyes followed him as he sauntered across the floor towards her. "You have something I want," he said silkily.

"You just bet I do," she purred, raising her icy blue eyes to his exquisite face.

"I don't take refusal well," he murmured, resting his fingers lightly on her perfect neck.

Candace smiled indulgently. She liked it when men thought they could control her. She enjoyed disabusing them of their misconceptions.

"Tomorrow," she said, and for a moment it seemed as though his grip had tightened, ever so slightly.

"Whatever you say," he said, removing his hands. He picked up her shawl and offered her his arm.

"Always is, darlin'," she purred, rising and taking his proffered arm. "Always is."

2
First Impressions

Christopher sheltered miserably beneath a statue of a swooping angel. The otherwise sweltering August weather had suddenly and unexpectedly turned into a monsoon. Fat, enormous raindrops were splashing with extraordinary force onto him and his surroundings, making the pavements slick with water and drenching his rather dismal – and only – suit.

He had wanted to make a good impression when he turned in the card, and had spent some time digging through his possessions to find the suit (which he had first worn at his cousin's wedding, over a decade previously) and making sure that he looked presentable and professional, particularly as the address was in the posh part of town.

Now, however, he looked like a drowned rat.

He shivered, glaring up at the sky and trying to will the clouds away. They loomed overhead, unconcerned. Glancing up at the big clock across the square, he huffed: it was already half-past four – if he didn't get to the shop soon, he'd have to wait until tomorrow.

Screwing up his face against the rain he hurried across the square and through a strange little alley that had been created by the proximity of the Town Hall and a fishing supplies shop. He paused in the lee of the larger building for a moment and squinted down at the card.

'7a Market Plaza'.

This was the place, though it was hard to make any of the signs out in the rain. Shoving the rectangle of card back into his pocket, he strode into the middle of the plaza and peered at the ornate signs above the windows:

There, in between '*Roxy's Pet Palace*', and '*Everything but the Cook*' was an elegant painted sign, gold leaf on wood:

*'Zarrubabel and Barraclough,
Purveyors of Fine Books.'*

Underneath it, someone had carefully added, in silver this time:

'Prints and Maps also Available, Enquire Within.'

Its dark wooden frame looked magnificently out of place amongst the terrible 1960s architecture, and that alone made Christopher smile, despite the rain. Running his hand through his rebellious, sopping wet hair in a defiant but rather futile rebuff to the weather, he went in, momentarily spilling the warm internal light onto the puddles on the pavement.

The bright jingling of a shop bell sounded above his head as he closed the door behind him, and someone called out from the depths of the shop: "Just a moment!"

Christopher looked around him. There were books everywhere: on the shelves, on the floor, even on the window-ledge. Every available space had been taken up by them, and by the stacks of papers strewn about the room. It looked a little like a small hurricane had meandered its way through the shop, leaving a strangely ordered trail of destruction in its wake.

It smelled fantastic: of old paper, and good cloth, and the deep, spicy scent of the leather. It reminded him a little of the Records Office store-room, although that had also occasionally smelled disturbingly of nothingness, because of the air filters they used to reduce the risk of mould.

He inhaled deeply. There were other scents here, too, like tea, and rosemary, and wool: these must, he reasoned, belong to the muffled voices coming from the room behind the counter. Whoever it was appeared to be having an argument.

Christopher surveyed the room: it was a friendly mix of dark woods and warm, yellow light. He reached out and brushed his fingers over the spines of the books nearest to him: they felt warm to the touch.

Well, that explains the job description of 'Wrangler',

he thought. *These books are clearly alive.*

The moment he thought it, a strange rustling passed around the room, as if the books had *heard* him.

He smiled, slightly, and bent to pick up one of the fallen volumes on the floor; it stopped rustling the moment he touched it, as if it were pleased to be being handled – or at least, happy to no longer be on the floor.

Gently, he laid it down on the only remaining surface – an old-fashioned writing desk, kept clear, presumably, for customers to use. The moment he had, the rustling began again, this time coming exclusively from the books on the floor.

"Oh, you want me to rescue you too, do you?" he chuckled to himself, and began to gather them up, piling them atop the first book on the writing desk.

As he put the last one down, it fell open, seemingly at random. He scanned the spine: it was a herbarium index, and beautifully penned.

He flicked through the pages in sheer admiration before turning back to the page the book had opened to him.

He gasped.

Aconite!

The book had opened at *Aconite*.

He closed it with a snap, staring at its cover as if he had been burned.

"They won't thank you for that, young man," said a crisp voice from behind him. Christopher spun around, and found an elderly gentleman watching him from behind the counter. He was everything the owner of an arcane bookshop ought to be: from the slightly dilapidated brown, wool suit to the wispy white hair and arresting pale blue eyes, peering at him from behind a monocle. He was the very picture of respectable eccentricity, and smelled a good deal like the books in his care.

The only thing missing, Christopher thought, was the slightly insane laughter.

"They prefer to be treated with respect," he continued,

giving Christopher and the pile of stacked books beside him an appraising look. "Which you appear to do, some of the time." He frowned at him. "May I help you with something specific, young man? Only it *is* getting close to closing time and any detailed search of my resources will have to wait until morning."

"Oh – er – no," Christopher stammered. Nervously, he produced the card, now a little squashed and damp from being in his pocket all afternoon.

The gentleman behind the counter took it and peered myopically at it through his monocle.

"Well now," he said, and looked up at Christopher. "Joanna," he called. "Joanna! Come and look at this!"

"Give me a moment, Morton," said a thin, reedy, voice from the room behind him; after a couple of moments and an unexpectedly colourful stream of muffled oaths, a small, round older lady emerged. Her rather primlooking spectacles had been knocked askew by something, and she was engaged in re-buttoning her peach-coloured, fluffy cardigan.

"Really, Morton, Hector is getting quite out of hand! Why, one of these days, I'll –" she paused, upon noticing Christopher. "Oh, I do beg your pardon, sir, I had a slight disagreement with our colleague."

She glanced at Morton, awaiting some form of explanation; he handed her the card, not taking his eyes off Christopher.

He wished that he would stop staring at him like that; it was really quite unnerving.

Joanna, looking up from the card with an expression of surprise on her face, joined her husband's scrutiny.

"But I only put this up this morning," she said.

"I..." He coughed. "I found it this afternoon," he said. "In the *Rose and Crown*," he added, helpfully.

"Indeed?" Morton asked him.

"Er, yes..." replied Christopher, a little baffled. "I came about the job."

"Yes, of course you did," said Morton, surprised. "But –"

But he didn't find out what, because at that moment, Christopher sneezed. It wasn't one of those little, manageable sneezes, either, but a proper, honking, body-squeezing sneeze.

"Gods bless you," said Morton.

"Oh, you poor chap, you're soaked through!" cried Joanna. "*Where* are our manners? Come on," she ordered, taking his arm and dragging him into the back room. She was surprisingly strong, for a little old lady, and completely ignored his and her husband's protests as she forced him into a chair and bustled about, making tea. The back room was much like the rest of the shop, only much smaller and with more desks. There were two faded, elderly armchairs either side of the old range about which Joanna was tinkering, clanging the kettle down and pulling cups out of a battered old cupboard beside it.

"Really, I'm fine," he said, weakly. "It's just a bit of a cold."

"Nonsense!" she cried. "You look positively peaky!"

"But –"

Morton clapped him on the shoulder.

"You'd best leave her to it, lad – once she has a bee in her bonnet about something, she won't do anything else until it's been sorted out," he chuckled, fondly. "In the meantime – Professor Morton Barraclough, at your service," he said, extending a hand, which Christopher shook damply.

"Christopher Porter," he replied.

"And this is my darling wife, Joanna," Barraclough indicated, as the aforementioned lady advanced upon them with a loaded tray.

"There you go," said Joanna, putting down a steaming mug of tea in front of him. "Get that down you, boy."

Christopher gratefully acquiesced; unlike the watery mess that he had tried to drink at the Rose and Crown, this was proper tea, with that homely, oaky aroma, and the sense that as soon as he had one sip, all would be right with the world.

He felt the heat of it spreading through his body and relaxed a little, feeling some of the colour return to his face.

"That's better," said Joanna.

"Thank you," Christopher managed, between sips.

"You're more than welcome," she said, with a smile. "Now, you're going to tell us how you deciphered our little puzzle so quickly."

Morton nodded, and they both peered at him, expectantly.

"Oh, that," said Christopher, setting down his mug. "Well, I'll admit it had me stumped at first, a job advert with no information on it, but that just seemed insanely unlikely, so I knew it had to be a trick." Joanna nodded, impressed, and he carried on. "So I tried to think of all the things that could be changed on the card: there didn't appear to be anything particularly unusual about the ink –"

"How could you tell?" asked Morton, curiously.

"It didn't – er, that is, it looked fairly normal to me. A *good* ink, but just ink, when you get right down to it."

Morton nodded, thoughtfully. Christopher was extremely glad that he had stopped himself from saying 'It didn't smell odd'; he suspected that that particular admission might not have gone down too well.

"I tried to see if there were any flaws to the card – hidden charms, trigger points, hollow enchantments, that kind of thing, but there wasn't anything."

"Well, there wouldn't be," said Joanna, matter-of-factly. "That would have been too simple."

Christopher smiled at her.

"So then I thought about the constituent parts of the card: the paper, the ink and the gold leaf," he continued. "And I'd already eliminated the ink, so that left the paper and the gold. Paper is used in a lot of spells, but not generally spells of concealment, so I concentrated on the gold. It took a while, but then I realised that it was a Glamour – a really good one, too – and once I'd undone it, the address appeared, and I came straight here," he finished, with a touch of pride.

"But *how* did you undo, it?" pressed Morton.

"Well, you just sort of look for the edges of the spell and, well, *push*," Christopher explained. "Don't you?"

He looked at them, suddenly aware that they were both peering at him with slightly more attention than he liked.

"Ye-es," said Morton, slowly. "I suppose you could call it that..." He looked at him, closely. "I can see that you have *some* magical talent," he began, and was apparently kicked under the table by Joanna, as he squawked.

"I'd say more than 'some', wouldn't you laddie?" she beamed at Christopher, and he blushed.

"Yes, well, you have talent," Morton repeated, grumpily rubbing his shin. "My point is, you haven't studied, have you?"

"N-no sir," Christopher stammered, knowing that he meant magic. "But my whole family are Practitioners, to some degree."

Morton nodded again, thoughtfully.

"Wait here a moment," he instructed, and headed off into the depths of the stacks.

"Did I do something wrong?" Christopher asked, and Joanna shook her head.

"No, dearie, you're just a little perplexing, is all," she took off her spectacles and began to polish them. "It should have taken you days to solve that little puzzle of ours."

Christopher was shocked – it had seemed so easy.

"Days? Really?" he asked. "But... I suppose it's all the practice I used to get at home – all my family love solving puzzles, it's what we do to relax."

"Yes, I suppose that makes sense," said Joanna, but Christopher couldn't shake the feeling that she was just being polite.

"Are your family local?" Morton asked, returning with a stack of books and papers.

"No," said Christopher, truthfully.

"I didn't think I recognised the name," said Morton.

"And I think we would have heard of you, with talent like that – you would have attended the Brightwell Academy I expect. We're on the Board of Governors, don't you know."

"I've not heard of it, sir, I'm afraid."

"Definitely not a local lad then," Morton chuckled. "Now, what do you make of *this*?"

He presented Christopher with the uppermost paper, an exquisitely decorative scroll, every inch of which was covered, either with the lavishly ornate first letter, or the tiny inked script.

The Professor, he noted, wasn't touching the paper directly, but had on a pair of white, cotton gloves.

"Um... May I have some?" he asked, gesturing to the other man's hands. "If there are any spare – I wouldn't want to damage anything."

Joanna passed a second pair over, with a small smile. Apparently he had passed this first test.

Fully gloved, he reached for the parchment, pausing before his fingers grazed the page. There was something off, here – *something* was emanating from the material. It was faint, but definitely there.

Hmm.

Taking care not to touch it, he leaned closer, reading the Latin inscription.

After a few moments, he sat back, a small, satisfied smile on his lips.

"It's a contract," he said. "With a particularly nasty Binding spell on it – a contact trigger too, I think. It must have caused quite a bit of mayhem in the past – I wouldn't want to be under terms like those."

Morton and Joanna exchanged a look.

"And this one?" Joanna asked, pushing a leather-bound book across the table.

Having learned caution from the first document, he hovered his hand over the bindings, but felt nothing. He resisted the urge to sniff the air – the book smelled old, curiously so.

The ink of the title had long since faded from the cover

and the spine, but the embossing was still intact. Thoughtfully, he ran his fingertips over the title: it was a little difficult to make out.

"The *Leicester Codex!*" he breathed, and looked up quickly.

Morton and Joanna were smiling, surprised.

"May I?" he asked, and to his absolute delight, they nodded.

He laughed, feeling a thrill of excitement as he reverently opened the book.

"This is – I mean – the *Leicester Codex!*" he stammered, excitedly. "My Dad told me about this when I was a kid, but I never thought – wow! Wow." A thought crossed his mind. "But I thought all the copies were destroyed in the seventeenth century, during the Great Purge?"

"Not *all* of them," Morton smiled, smugly. "And of course, there were inferior copies made, some of which still exist."

Christopher stared at him.

"Now this," said Joanna, carefully lifting the Codex away; he watched it go with hungry eyes.

Reluctantly, he turned his attention back to the book in front of him.

It was a slim volume, bound in black silk with red trim.

"Very gothic," he murmured, and chuckled, as he read the title on the spine. "Dracula – well, it would be..."

Carefully, he examined the book for any discernible trace of enchantments, any latent charms, but there were none. Carefully, he opened the volume and read a few passages: nothing. He leaned closer and risked a surreptitious sniff.

The ink smelled slightly metallic, meaning that it had been printed in the mid-part of the last century. He ran a gloved finger along the edge of one of the leaves: the paper was normal too: good quality, but perfectly mundane.

He frowned, running his fingers over the text, which

stood slightly proud of the smooth paper. Nothing unusual there.

Closing his eyes, he prodded the book with his mind, the way his mother had taught him, all those years ago. It responded sluggishly, like a sleeping thing. He tried again – and again –

Nothing.

Frustrated, he opened his eyes and glared at it. Just as he was about to give up, he had a thought. Head slightly to one side, he picked the book up, flicked through the pages at random, and tried again, exploring each facet of the volume's construction with his mind.

Absolutely nothing.

He placed the book back down onto the table and looked up at the Professor and his wife, feeling triumphant.

"It's perfectly mundane," he announced. "A beautiful copy, mid-twentieth century, I think."

"Hmm," said Joanna, with a glance at her husband, who nodded, and replaced the book with another.

This one was smaller and fatter, bound in cheap and faded red leather with gold edged pages.

He looked at it with mild distaste.

There *were* signs of magic in this book, more than the usual background level displayed by the previous volume. He picked it up, cautiously.

It wasn't the binding, or the edges, despite their gilding. He opened it to see pages slightly reddened with age and residual magic. Whatever spell had been used on this book was decaying, and taking the paper with it.

He read a few lines of tawdry poetry and paused, surprised: the words, a poor choice on the poet's part, had sparked the most fantastical visions. He could almost taste the wine being described.

Interesting.

It *had* to be the ink, surely?

He held the book up, so that the pages were level with his eyes. Sure enough, there was the faintest of glimmers.

"Enchanted ink?" he asked. "Not a particularly good enchantment," he remarked, on Morton's nod.

Joanna snorted, in a very un-ladylike fashion.

"Not particularly good poetry, either," she observed. "Penned by Edwin Harcastle in the late eighteenth century. Bit of a bugger for sousing up his otherwise dreary prose with badly constructed enchantments. Makes the books rot from the inside out."

The three of them shared an expression that suggested that the man would have met a sticky end for his crimes against the written word, if they had got their hands on him.

"Last one," said Morton, presenting Christopher with a children's atlas.

It *looked* unremarkable, covered in brightly coloured maps and the politically correct images of various cultures, but something about it bothered him. For a start, it smelled wrong, like a great, confused mass of sensations all bundled up into one – but he couldn't say that, it would make his condition too obvious.

He prodded it with his mind, and it glittered like fireworks at midnight.

Biting his lip, he recalled how, as a child, Rachel had always been fascinated by maps, gazing at them for hours and planning out the spectacular adventures that she was sure that she and Christopher would have one day. It had been adorable, an innocuous past-time that his parents had indulged.

But *this* atlas...

This atlas was dangerous. The enchantments on it were seductive, begging him to open the pages and take a look inside.

He resisted, but only just – a child would have been completely taken in. He had never felt anything like it, or even heard about something like it. He frowned up at his silent audience.

"I don't know," he said. "It's dangerous – enticing too, like it wants me to pick it up and look through it... but I don't know what it could do. I've never seen magic like this before."

Professor Barraclough took it away again, and stacked it against the wall.

Christopher let out a breath that he hadn't realised he had been holding.

"That one is particularly powerful, and particularly nasty," the Professor said. "It contains a plethora of portal spells. They only activate at random points, and leave their victims – generally young children – in inhospitable places with no means of return. And their poor parents..."

"Who would do that?" Christopher asked, appalled, thinking of his sister.

Joanna looked at him for a moment. "There are a great many unpleasant people in this world," she said, quietly.

Morton nodded, soberly, and there was quiet in the tiny office for a moment.

"Anyway," said Joanna, clapping her hands together in a business-like manner. "That's quite enough of that kind of talk. I have to say, young man, that that was quite an impressive performance."

"Indeed," said the Professor, as Christopher blushed, hotly. "What experience do you have of magical texts?"

"Er – only what I picked up at home," he said, embarrassed. "As I said, my family love puzzles – and I studied history for a little while too." He broke off, thinking sadly of his abandoned studies. "There were a few arcane documents at the Records Office, where I used to work, but nothing particularly lively – or dangerous," he added, on their looks.

"This is the first magical bookshop you have ever been in?" Joanna asked, surprised.

"Not the first. My dad took me and Rachel – my sister – to one in London when we were little," he smiled at the recollection. "It was wonderful."

"Hmm..." said Professor Barraclough, again. "But you *do* have experience with mundane documents – and a fine mind for conundrums, it would seem." He exchanged a look with his wife. "I think you might be the right chap for the job," he said, finally, and Christopher had to fight the urge to hug the man. "It would be full time – my wife and I would like to step away from the business a little more, now we're older."

"We're no spring chickens," added Joanna, cheerfully.

"And you'll have to work Saturdays, if that's not a problem?"

Christopher, amazed at how calm he was managing to appear, indicated that it was not.

"You'll get another day off, of course. How does Thursday seem?" Morton asked. "Good. Erm, your wage – yes... We've had to start using that infernal machine in the shop –"

"He means the PIN machine," Joanna put in. "You can use one, can you? Oh good," she smiled, on his nod.

"– so we will be paying you using the electronic bank system. You'll need to bring in your details, of course, as and when – and I could do with a character reference, if you have one. It's a fairly competitive wage, I think you'll agree," he said, playing the typical British gent, and passing Christopher a slip of paper with a series of numbers on it.

Christopher stared at it and felt himself go numb. It was more money than he had seen in his adult life.

He nodded, mutely.

"You'll be on probation to start with, of course, as you learn the ropes, and we get used to you," Joanna said, with a smile. "Shall we say: three months?"

"That sounds great," Christopher managed, shell shocked. He *would* keep this job.

He had to.

Professor Barraclough nodded. "Do you have Insignia, by the way?" he asked. "For the books."

Insignia were a form of magical identification, almost like a fingerprint; you designed your own when you came of age, if you wanted one. Not everyone did, and Christopher had stopped using his as soon as he'd been turned. His family could use it to track him, and he had no intention of his parents' names being dragged through the muck because of him.

"No," he lied, confidently.

"Right. Well, I think that leaves just one more thing," said Professor Barraclough, slowly. "I think it would be only fair if I introduced you to my business partner."

Already a little suspicious of the wary look that Joanna was giving him, and the fact that he couldn't smell a third person in the shop, Christopher steeled himself for the unexpected; it was rather a good thing that he did.

"Hector!" called Barraclough. "Come and meet our new employee!"

There was the sound of tearing paper, as a stack of books upended themselves off one of the shelves. Sat atop the bottom-most book was the shockingly distinct figure of a middle-aged man.

He had a pair of pince-nez balanced on his long nose, and an extremely unpleasant expression on his face. Every part of him, from his balding head and practical woollen suit, to his glinting watch-chain and leather-clad toes, was a shade of grey-green.

Christopher was momentarily overwhelmed by the strong smell of mouldering paper, before it dimmed to mere mustiness.

The apparition coughed, phlegmatically.

"You went and hired a new employee?" it demanded in a petulant tone. "Against my wishes? You are a beast, Morton! A *beast!*"

He turned his narrow eyes on to Christopher, and curled his lip in distaste.

"That him?" he snarled. "What a useless lump of a human being! Get rid of him this instant! Out of my sight! *Out of my sight!*" he cried.

"Oh, be quiet, you old devil," said Joanna, impatiently. "He's a good boy, and he's passed every test we could think of."

"Well clearly you didn't think hard enough!" he snarled. "And *you*, Joanna! Didn't you think of my feelings at all?"

"It would be difficult not to, the way you carry on," she retorted.

"Now, now," said Professor Barraclough, in a placating fashion. "That's quite enough from both of you, particularly in front of our young friend."

Christopher stared between the three of them, thoroughly nonplussed.

"*That* is *not* my friend," said the ghost, petulantly, distaste dripping from every syllable.

"Well, he's *our* friend," said Joanna, hotly, "and he's coming to work for us whether you like it or not!"

"Why you impudent old hag!" he cried. "I should –"

Barraclough put a hand on Christopher's shoulder as the ghost and his wife set upon one another.

"We'd better leave them to it," he said, leading him back into the shop, proper.

"They don't appear to get on," remarked Christopher, weakly.

"Like cats and dogs," agreed Barraclough, cheerfully. "They were always that way – always had one another's backs though. They're brother and sister, you know."

"Gosh," said Christopher.

"Indeed. My esteemed colleague, Professor Hector Zarrubabel... he's always been somewhat acerbic –"

Christopher nodded at what had to be the understatement of the century.

"– but these days he's much worse. Bitter about his untimely demise."

"He was murdered?" Christopher asked, and Barraclough laughed at his expression.

"No, I wasn't particularly surprised, either," he nodded, and then gave him a close look. "Not having second thoughts?" he asked.

Christopher thought he could detect a note of worry in the old wizard's voice.

"No, sir," he said, truthfully. "It sounds like an excellent job," he continued, as the both of them ignored the crashing sounds emanating from the office. "Challenging."

Again, Barraclough chuckled.

"That sense of humour will come in handy," he smiled, and clapped Christopher on the back. "Well, we'll see you on Monday, yes? And don't worry so much about the suit. As long as you don't look like the moths have had a better lunch than you have it'll be fine."

"Thanks, sir," said Christopher, gratefully. "I'll see you on Monday then."

The rain had stopped now, making the pavement gleam with borrowed light. His heart a hundred times lighter than it had been only hours before, he set off down the street, whistling to himself, and wondering whether Charlie might be persuaded to provide him with a reference.

Perhaps he would even let him sleep in the bar.

Things were looking up.

ooo

Back in the shop, Professor Morton Barraclough gazed at the door through which Christopher had exited.

"A promising young man, I thought," he said, almost to himself.

"Yes," said Joanna, joining him as the crashing in the room behind them subsided. "He seemed like a nice boy. Clever, too. Clever enough not to get eaten by the books."

"Something not quite right about him though."

His wife nodded, contemplatively. "Might be none of our business," she offered. "After all, we were hiding Hector – it may be as simple as that."

"Maybe," said Barraclough, thoughtfully. "Didn't seem threatening, at any rate."

"No."

They were quiet for a moment.

"Although," said the Professor. He strode over to the pile of books on the desk. "I would be interested to see what made him take against *Culpepper*."

3
Aconite

He very nearly overslept, which wouldn't have made a particularly good impression on his first day.

Christopher and Charlie had spent much of the evening before moving his belongings into the tiny, dingy flat that he had found in the paper. It was small, damp and smelled a bit like incontinent cats, but he was a tenant of the Council now, and the fact that it would never smell like Viv Johnson more than made up for that. The fact that it was Council run had the added benefit of making eviction marginally less likely. Although the hope of his more unusual qualities falling under their Equal Opportunities policy was comically unlikely, they probably didn't have the right form for 'Eviction due to Lycanthropy', either.

Charlie, delighted at the prospect of having a friend in the book trade, had been more than happy for Christopher to sleep in the bar for two nights, and had even provided him with a slightly musty blanket and as many pork-scratchings as he could eat. The blanket had had little pink bunnies on it.

For the first time in years, Christopher had treated himself to a Chinese takeout, and he and Charlie had spent a companionable evening talking about nothing at all. It had been nearly midnight when the half-Troll had wandered home, muttering something about early morning brewery deliveries, and Christopher had set about making the place slightly more homely.

It was quite a challenge.

But at least he had a bed, even if it was a little lumpy, and a reasonably sound roof over his head – and the view wasn't half bad.

From his grimy, slightly cracked window he could see across the river and up to the other side of the valley, where the lights of the town began to dwindle. Part of him was mildly concerned that the river had been a good deal more swollen and closer to his building than it should have been when he was moving in, but the flats had been here for a long time, and would probably be here long after he left. After all, beggars couldn't be choosers, and if he managed to keep his job at the bookshop, he would be able to save up and move somewhere with hot water and quieter neighbours.

As it had turned out, he only ignored his alarm clock for ten minutes, and had just enough time to walk briskly up the hill and across town – although he *had* skipped breakfast.

His stomach rumbled angrily at him as he arrived in the shop, causing Joanna to give him the kind of look that he associated with his mother, when she thought that someone wasn't eating properly. He gave her what he hoped was a smile, but given how excited he was it was probably more like a manic grin.

She ushered him into the back room and sat him down at one of the desks.

"Morton will be along in a moment," she said, putting the kettle on to boil. "You have the documents?"

"Oh, yes," he said, pulling a slim, rather battered folder out of his ancient backpack. "Those are the bank details, and this is my character reference."

He passed the relevant bits of paper to her and enjoyed her expression as she read the name at the bottom of the character reference.

"Charlie Greaves, eh?" she asked, with a raised eyebrow. "Interesting. Not known for his generosity, generally. You must have made quite the impression on him."

"He's not as bad as he likes everyone to think," Christopher said, with a small smile.

"No, indeed," said Joanna. "Ah," she said, as her husband came in. "Here bright and early, as predicted," she said and smiled at Christopher.

"Excellent," cried Morton, clapping his hands together. "We'll get started in a moment – need to show you how the back room operates first. Will you take care of his documents, Joanna?"

"Already am, you daft old thing," she said, polishing her spectacles on her cardigan (plum-coloured, this morning).

"Is er..." he lowered his voice to a conspiratorial whisper. "*Is he sleeping?*"

Christopher presumed that he meant Professor Zarrubabel, and his suspicions were confirmed when Joanna glared at the stack of books from which he had erupted a few days previously. He could just make out the spine of the book that he'd been sitting on at the bottom of the pile.

"He was sulking something rotten," she said, in an undertone. "So I stacked the Post Office Directories on top of him in the hopes that he would drop off for a bit. It's not that he doesn't like you, you understand," she said, turning to reassure Christopher. "It's just that he thinks we're abandoning him – we've all three of us spent so long in this shop. I suppose he always thought that we would just carry on as we always have, but he fails to take into account that, unlike him, we age."

"Don't know what he'll do with himself when we finally pop our clogs," said the Professor. "I considered having his book put in a museum so that he could pop out and frighten people, but I'm not sure I could do that to anyone else."

Despite his first-day nerves, Christopher chuckled.

"Right," said Morton, rubbing his hands together. "Let's get started – how much do you know about cataloguing?"

ooo

It had been quite a tiring morning, what with learning a new classification system, navigating his way through the Professor's apparently random filing system and nearly drowning in the sheer volume of tea that Joanna considered necessary for a successful working day.

He had also had to fend off the flurries of paperwork

that Zarrubabel had thrown at him (and, to be fair, everyone else) when he had worked out that he had been duped. It was extraordinary, really, how many papercuts you could get from projectile stationery.

He sucked his fingers.

The woman behind the counter at the sandwich shop kept looking at him oddly.

"I'm, er, cutting down a rose-bush," he said, by way of an explanation, and she nodded in sympathy.

Christopher ate his disappointing sandwich in the park, and watched the ducks swimming about on the river. It was strange, he reflected, as he picked out the last unasked for gherkin, just how much you could miss disappointing sandwiches, when you had nothing at all.

He threw the gherkins on the riverbank for the ducks, and watched them investigate the possibility of pickles for a few minutes before setting off back to the shop. It was nice to think that there was somewhere permanent to go back to, and he was really looking forward to getting into the work proper, once they'd got past all of the basics.

As tedious as the filing was, he was still the happiest he had been in years.

If he could just stay in this job – even if he had to live in a poky, damp little flat and put up with the poltergeist – he would be closer to heaven that he ever thought a werewolf could get.

As soon as he got back, he and Barraclough closeted themselves in the very back of the office, as far away from the tempestuous Zarrubabel as possible. Joanna had already gone home for the day, and if it weren't for the jingle of the shop-bell they would never have realised that they had a customer over the noise of sulking ectoplasm.

Morton left him to his own devices for a few minutes as he went out to help. He heard the Professor laugh a few times, and came to the conclusion that he must know this customer reasonably well.

Christopher applied himself to the cataloguing system

once more, knowing that the quicker he got it established in his mind, the easier his life would be in the next few weeks. As he worked, a strange prickly feeling started in the back of his mind: it was insistent, prodding at the edge of his consciousness as if it really wanted his attention. He shook his head to clear it, reasoning that the books were misbehaving again.

Morton came in, after a few minutes, and started hunting through the books on the shelf by the door, muttering to himself and checking volumes against a short list.

"Be back with you in a minute lad, one of the regulars, you understand," he said, over his shoulder.

Christopher made a noise of assent, and continued to stare at the page in front of him.

Zarrubabel, however, was suddenly very interested.

"A regular?" he cried, scattering parchment everywhere. "Anyone interesting? Someone I know? Put my book by the door, old chap, so I can see!"

"After the way you've been behaving?" he asked. "I don't think so, you old devil."

"Oh, go on, Morton," he wheedled. "I get ever so bored on my own back here..."

"Oh, *fine*," huffed Barraclough, and lifted the book to a desk near to the door, before returning to his search.

Zarrubabel peered out into the shop. "Oh, it's little Ivy!" he cried, happily, clapping his translucent hands. "I always like to see her, Morton – it would warm my heart, if I had one!" he cackled, swinging his legs.

Professor Barraclough mumbled something unintelligible, but Zarrubabel carried on, ignoring him.

"What's she looking for, Morton?" he asked. "A new spell-book? Something for her friend, maybe, what's-her-name – you know the one, talks to Joanna about cooking all the time..."

"Mahri."

"That's her! Is she after some more of those mundane books, again? I could never understand why she'd read that rot – a fine, upstanding witch like her..."

He continued in this vein for quite some time as Barraclough hunted through the shelves and 'little Ivy' presumably entertained herself.

That peculiar feeling began to steal upon Christopher once more, as he memorised classifications, filtering through his consciousness and eventually thoroughly destroying his concentration.

He looked up: the Professors were still engaged in their strange, largely one-sided conversation, nothing new there. He couldn't hear the books making a fuss, and with a customer in (even a Practitioner) they were unlikely to play up too much.

He reached out with his mind, to see if the magical potential of the books had altered: it hadn't, or at least, no more than he was becoming accustomed to. Joanna had told him, earlier, that daily fluctuations were nothing to worry about – though she had also added that until he got used to it he might well develop the odd twitch.

This didn't feel like a magical change though, it was too intangible, too subtle.

Checking that his potential audience were sufficiently distracted, he took a diagnostic sniff – there *was* a new smell: curiously subtle, with hints of linen and honey, tea and something floral, and something spicy that he just couldn't place.

He inhaled again, careful not to be too conspicuous.

The combination of scents made him feel very odd indeed – alert, and awake, and safe, and at home – all at the same time. His skin prickled: he shivered involuntarily. It was curiously inscrutable, just beyond his reach – unsettling, but oddly pleasant.

Christopher gazed absently at the ledger in front of him, thoroughly distracted.

He was still trying to puzzle it out when Professor Barraclough clapped him on the shoulder some time later. He nearly jumped out of his skin.

"In your own little world?" Barraclough asked, cheerfully.

"Oh – yes – I'm sorry..."

"Not to worry, lad, I go a bit doollally staring at the paperwork all day," he said, cheerfully. "Go and have a walk around for a bit, clear your head."

Christopher nodded, rubbing at his face and ignoring Zarrubabel's derogatory comments as he passed him.

The scent was much stronger in the shop proper, and Christopher slowed down, trying to capture those notes of it that evaded him.

He stared around him, flustered and increasingly annoyed. It was frustratingly faint, despite the fact that it had apparently permeated every corner of the bookshop, and he had the urge to follow the scent to its source and take a big breath of it, certain that he'd be able to figure it out – if he could only smell it for longer. It was all he could do not to go around sniffing things.

Painfully aware that the iridescent Professor Zarrubabel could still see him from the back room, he made himself walk outside and take a large gulp of fresh air, knowing that he couldn't let a person's scent get to him like that, or he would never get any work done.

It must belong to 'little Ivy', he decided, as he calmed down. But how could the way someone smelled have that much of an effect on him? He'd never even met her.

With any luck, she wouldn't be back for a while. After all, he reasoned, with the amount of time Professor Barraclough had spent on her order, she must have requested quite a few books, and it would take her a while to read them all.

Collecting himself, and steeling his nerve against the onslaught of sensation that he knew would be waiting for him behind the door, he went back in.

000

By the end of the week the Professor had deemed Christopher sufficiently trustworthy for him to leave him in charge while he accompanied Joanna on a shopping trip around the town.

At the first opportunity, Christopher had firmly closed the door on the incandescent Zarrubabel, whom he was certain was now engaged in making as much of a mess of the office as he could, out of sheer spite. Since he did this regularly, and often without the slightest provocation, it didn't worry him too much, and at least this way he could get on with his afternoon without constantly being referred to as a 'Dratted shop-boy', or an 'Eel-faced whelp', or whatever new insult Zarrubabel had deigned to come up with this time. It was a bit like being abused by a thesaurus.

Christopher had quickly discovered that the only times he was ever pleasant was when there was a new delivery of books that he wanted to read, or when one of the regulars came in. He knew most of them by sight and nearly all of them by reputation, and his subsequent running commentary was sufficiently fascinating for Christopher to ignore the verbal abuse hurled in his direction.

After dealing with several mundane customers, tempted in by the second-hand books and maps, and providing the elderly gentleman who was researching lithography – and had taken up temporary residence at the work desk in the corner – with a few useful texts, he settled down on a chair behind the counter and closed his eyes.

He relaxed into the atmosphere of the bookshop, feeling the fluttering of several thousand living books. It was an extraordinary feeling, to be surrounded by so many partially sentient minds.

It is often said that books have a life of their own, and this, as it turns out, is a far more accurate saying than most people imagine. Consider the act of writing: it's not just the act of ordering words on a page, you have to choose *which* words and what you want them to mean – and words can be powerful things. No matter what kind of book they are writing, whether fact or high fantasy, an author pours their heart into those pages. It's a small wonder, really, if those pages carry a little of the author's personality with them, and small wonder if they start to develop a personality of their own. Particularly old books.

Old books have more than a little of their readers in them. Old books remember.

Anyone who has more than a few books in their home will know: they breed. You may start out with only a couple of them neatly lined up on a solitary bookshelf, but leave them unchecked and soon enough they will be sprouting up everywhere. There is always one book on every bookshelf that you don't remember buying.

The right book at the right time can start a revolution; end a war; inspire a scientist to make the next great leap; help someone to learn enough to stay alive...

Books can change the world.

And that's just mundane books. Add in a few magical books, and the whole lot of them start to quiver and rustle with life, flickering and buzzing like a colony of bees. They talk amongst themselves, whisper things; watch you. The next time you see a second-hand book shop, on a quiet day, go in and stand softly for a while.

You might even hear them breathe.

Fully engaged in listening to what he was beginning to think of as *his* unruly flock of paper, Christopher didn't notice the scent until it was almost upon him. His eyes flicked open, nostrils twitching at the now familiar smell.

It had been following him around all week, pouncing on his senses at the most unexpected moments – lurking behind books he was moving, jumping off the pages of the ledgers in the back room, even hiding in the clouds of steam billowing from the constantly boiling kettle.

Always the same symphony of smells, and always just beyond his grasp.

It was maddening.

Whoever this Ivy person was, she was beginning to get on Christopher's nerves.

Around the shop, book pages rustled at him, as if they were laughing.

He glanced at the elderly lithographer. He was fast

asleep, pen in hand, face resting against the pages of his notebook, snoring peacefully.

Now would be as good a time as any.

Quietly, Christopher stole across the room and pulled out *Culpepper's Herbarium*, letting it rest in his hand for a moment before allowing it to fall open at random. He glanced at the page. The brilliant blue of the Aconite flower stared back up at him. Closing the book, he checked the spine: it was in excellent condition, with no cracks or creases that might make it open to the same page.

He held it away from him and let it fall open again: Aconite. Frowning, he repeated the action several times, before closing the book again.

The atmosphere in the shop was suddenly tense, as if several thousand books were holding their collective breath, waiting to see what he would do.

"Alright," he said, softly, knowing that whatever he said would eventually reach even the highest pages. "You know what I am. I accept that, but I would appreciate it if you didn't fly open to Wolfsbane every time I brush past you." He smiled slightly as the paper equivalent of a snigger flowed around the room. "And in turn, I promise to keep you as well as I am able, and not sell you to people who intend to turn you into up-cycled, Bohemian furniture. Deal?"

There was an acute silence for a moment, then he felt the book in his hand wriggle a little; he let it open. This time it displayed a sprig of Geraniums, a flower associated with friendship.

"I'll take that as a yes," he said, and returned to the desk, intending to read through the Herbal while he had the chance.

As he placed it on the desk the scent came back to him, strong and insistent.

He exhaled in annoyance.

Culpepper's Herbarium flew open, pages turning themselves until they came to rest on a plate covered in tendrils of ivy.

"Oh, shut up," he grumbled.

ooo

"Christopher!" shouted Joanna, pulling him out of his thoughts. "Ah, there you are. Almost finished?"

He had been reorganising the slightly shambolic poetry section, and was only partly visible behind the stacks of dusty books.

"Nowhere near," he chuckled. "By the way, some of the scripts appear to be breeding back here…"

He passed her a series of folios, with titles like '*Much Ado About the Tempest*', and '*Love's Labours End Well*'.

"Good grief," she said, scanning through them. "These are terrible…"

"Yes," he agreed, dusting himself off as best he could. "I was reading one earlier where the heroine swoops in to rescue everyone on a trapeze – I think they're getting a bit muddled."

"Plays are like actors," said Joanna, absently, still flicking through the uppermost folio. "They're better not left to their own devices – particularly if there is a large group of them." She looked up at him in amusement. "Perhaps you ought to move onto the Drama section when you finish in Poetry."

He smiled at her.

"Morton and I need you to take an order out to one of our less mobile customers, if that's alright?" she asked.

"Oh, sure, no problem," he said, interested. He liked meeting the strange medley of people that made up the shop regulars, and after a morning spent swamped in clouds of dust, a walk across town sounded like an excellent idea.

"Can you ride a bicycle?" Joanna enquired, as she led him back to the main counter. "Ours is a little battered, but it should do the trick," she said, pointing to a slightly bent but perfectly sturdy bike, resting against the front window of the shop. "Morton brought it around earlier – we haven't used it in years, but it should be just fine for deliveries. Here's the address, and the list of books. Do you think you'll be able to find them alright?"

Christopher nodded. "It's up by Theatre," he said. "The street with the old Butter Cross..." he scanned the list of titles. "Bit of an eclectic list..."

"Master Post is a bit eccentric," she said. "Usually he comes out and works here, but he's broken his leg you see – had some sort of accident. Charming young fellow."

Christopher nodded, and started to collect the requested books. They were largely historic volumes, much to Christopher's growing curiosity, and mostly of local interest, but one or two were related to magical laws.

Soon he had the books stacked on the desk and wrapped in brown paper, ready for transport; he nearly dropped them, however, when a particularly loud crash rang through from the back office. Apparently Zarrubabel had woken up again.

Wanting to make as quick an exit as possible, lest he be drawn into whatever argument Joanna and Zarrubabel were having this afternoon, he picked up the towering stack of books and made for the door. They weren't particularly heavy – at least, they weren't particularly heavy for a reasonably healthy werewolf – but the stack was just tall enough to impede his vision.

He was glad that he was walking slowly when the shop-bell jingled, and he managed to stop just short of walking right into whoever it was that had opened the door.

"Sorry!" he said over his books. "Can't see a thing over these!"

The customer laughed.

"Not to worry," she said, and he could tell from her voice that she was smiling. "Here, I'll hold the door..."

"Thanks," he said, and walked out of the shop, wondering why his throat suddenly felt so tight.

Depositing the books in the wire basket of the rickety bike, he was assaulted once more by the tantalising smell of linen and honey – this time it was a little earthier, a little leafier somehow.

He spun around, but the woman had already vanished; he caught a glimpse of a flowery skirt disappearing behind the edge of one of the great bookcases.

He inhaled deeply, but her scent was already dissipating on the summer breeze. For a moment he was seized by the desire to go back into the shop, just to get closer to her; he shook his head, his brain feeling quite woolly and distracted.

Aware that he was staring at the window and mildly worried about his own state of mind, he cycled quickly away, hoping that the short ride across town would clear his head.

Feeling much less ruffled, he pulled his bike up against the wall of a beautiful Georgian town-house, about a hundred yards up the street from the old Butter Cross. He took a moment to simply stare at the building: it was beautiful, built from good, clean stone with a slightly pinkish hue, the cream-coloured quoins balancing the house perfectly. Virginia creeper had been artfully trained up one side of the building and onto the roof, softening the harsh, architectural lines. A meticulously cared-for garden was laid out in front of it, finished by a short, brick wall with metal railings.

It was magnificent, even if it did put Christopher slightly in mind of a large doll's house.

He carried the books up to the white, wooden front door and rang the bell; he didn't have to wait long.

The door was opened by a slightly flustered young woman, whose hair was escaping in all directions from what had been a neat bun. He glanced down at her nurse's uniform, which had been hastily and inaccurately buttoned up, and she blushed hotly.

"Yes?" she asked, a little breathlessly.

"Er – I have some books for Mr Post."

"Oh yes," she said, ushering him inside. "Just put

them there – I'll take them up later. He's resting, you see," she added, a little defensively.

"Of course," said Christopher, trying not to gawp at the magnificent décor, and stunned by the overpowering stench of furniture polish.

However eccentric Mr Post was, Christopher decided, as the front door slammed behind him, the man had taste.

Wheeling the bicycle into the shop and back into the office, Christopher immediately noticed the absence of the woman with the floral skirt. Her scent lingered, and he inhaled, surprised at how familiar and comforting it had become, where days before it had been annoying the hell out of him.

Secretly, and to his own acute embarrassment, he hoped that she would be back soon.

4
Temptation

Much to his own annoyance, Christopher had started to really look forward to Mondays. If he were asked about this, he would have said that it was because he enjoyed his work – which was certainly true – or he might make a self-deprecating reference to his lack of a social life. The truth (which he would only admit to himself late at night, when none of the books could see into his mind) was that he liked Mondays, because Monday afternoons were when Ivy came in.

He still hadn't seen her for more than a few moments at a time, and had only the impression of long, dark hair and a friendly smile to match to her voice, which he often heard filtering through into the back room. And her smell, of course, which was continuing to infuriate him – though more and more, now, the absence of it was much more irritating than its presence.

He would be working through the ledgers, trying to decipher Morton Barraclough's spidery handwriting and work out whether a book had been ordered, loaned out, or cannibalised by its neighbours and it would steal upon him: teasing him, comforting him. It was always the same basic scent of linen and honey, but with fascinating undertones that he longed to identify. She would smell of rose petals one week and chocolate another – or spices, or herbs, or (once, on a particularly damp day) enticingly of rain.

He had absolutely no idea why the scent of rain would be a turn-on, but mixed up in *her* perfume, it really was. He'd felt rather hot under the collar all week.

He would really start to miss it on Fridays, when it became fainter and less tangible, and it became a sort of game for him to hunt for it in the shop when there were no customers, finding the books that she had touched or read, and he would spend a few moments in each place where the scent was strongest. Aware that this was becoming something of an obsession, he did his best to ignore it, and put the mysterious Ivy and her scent out of his mind, but it was hard work, and more than once he found himself staring out of the window as time ticked nearer to Monday afternoon.

As usual, his ears pricked up as the shop-bell jingled that afternoon, and he heard Professor Barraclough greet his customer.

Shaking his head at himself, he concentrated on delicately repairing the end papers of the book in front of him: *'The Compton Book of Verse'*; at the back of his mind, he could feel it keening in panic and distress.

"Not long now," he said, soothingly, and stroked the marbled paper flat with the paste brush. "Now, try not to flap about too much, and you'll soon be dry, and I'll have you back on your shelf in no time..."

The shop-bell jingled a second time, and there was the sound of a panicked discussion; Christopher looked up, intrigued.

"Ah, Christopher," said Barraclough, sticking his head around the door, an oddly fierce expression on his face. "I need to pop out for a bit – something of an emergency up at Brightwell. Can you watch the shop?"

He nodded, leaving the traumatised book to recover.

"Good. Now, I've found the special orders for Mistress Burwell, they're all ready for her on the desk – she might want a few others, too. You know how to book things out?"

"Yes, Professor – Joanna showed me last week."

"Excellent!" He clapped him on the back, grabbed his extraordinary top hat from the hat-stand and strode up to Zarrubabel's book. He rapped on the cover. "Hector! We're going on a field trip – some young idiot has manifested a Dark Horde in the cafeteria up at Brightwell. Behave."

"I'll be as good as gold, Morton, don't you worry!" announced Zarrubabel's disembodied voice, clearly thrilled to be getting out of the bookshop.

"Hold the fort!" the Professor called, as he rushed out of the door, Zarrubabel's book tucked under his arm; the sound of the shop-bell jingling wildly told him that he and the mysterious messenger had exited at some speed.

Christopher looked at the space they had recently occupied with mild amusement. Not for the first time, he tried to imagine what Morton Barraclough would do without his petulant old friend haunting the place. Whatever they said to one another (and Christopher had witnessed more than a few disagreements over the past few weeks) both parties seemed to know implicitly that neither one really meant it. Really, the strength of their friendship, to last beyond one of their deaths, was admirable, and Christopher couldn't help but feel a little envious.

Pushing such maudlin thoughts away, he heaved a stack of returned books off the side and went through to the shop proper, where Ivy's enticing scent had infused the room with a strangely warm glow.

Refusing to look in the corner where he knew that she was sitting – and where that intoxicating scent was strongest (with just a hint of soap today, apparently) – he went about returning the books, as quietly as he could, trying not to disturb her reading.

Sliding the final one into place on the top shelf of one of the bookcases, he noticed an entirely out-of-place book: a slim volume on the mating habits of the Brownheaded Leafroller moth.

"What are you doing all the way up there?" he asked, softly. The book did its best to appear innocent, as if he had caught it misbehaving – loitering in the Engineering section. He chuckled at it and climbed back down the short step-ladder.

"Now, do you live in 'Fauna', or is there a special place for insects?" he enquired, but the book stayed stubbornly uncommunicative. Running his finger along the spines of the volumes in the 'Fauna' section, he found the 'Insect' collection. "There you go," he murmured, slotting the treatise back into its proper place.

Smiling to himself, he glanced up as a movement caught his eye: through the gap above the books, he could see her.

His mouth fell open.

A book of fungi was open on her lap, the warm glow of a Light Orb that was balanced on her shoulder bathing it in golden light, and she was completely engrossed. Leaning on one elbow, she chewed absently at the pendant around her neck, the chain wound around her fingers. Her hair (how had he not noticed it before now?) fell in dark, chocolate waves about her face and shoulders; unconsciously, she brushed a tendril of it away from her eyes.

He couldn't see her eyes, focussed on the page in front of her, but he thought that he could detect a flicker of blue. There were a few freckles scattered about her face, and a small, peaceful smile played about her lips as she turned a page with slender, creamy fingers.

Christopher bit his lip, aware that he oughtn't be staring, but couldn't look away: she looked so happy, so serene – quietly closeted with a book.

He was about to make himself turn away and find something useful to do when she looked up, suddenly aware of his scrutiny.

She smiled at him, still peering at her through the gap in the books.

"Oh, hello – you must be Christopher."

"Hi – er – I was just – I mean... yes," he stuttered, colouring up to his eyebrows.

"I was wondering when I'd finally get to meet you – it seems like every time I'm here Professor Barraclough has you off running some errand or another."

"Yes – well – I l-like to keep busy," he explained, the very picture of awkwardness.

"Me too," she smiled, and looked at her watch. "Crumbs – I was supposed to pick some things up at the market this afternoon!" she muttered.

Rising, she closed the book of fungi with a snap, and put it back on the shelf – in its proper place, he noted, with admiration. The Light Orb dissipated with a faint 'pop'.

She smiled at him again, a little shyly this time, and began to walk to the counter. Realising, abruptly, that she probably wanted to collect her order, he hurried to help her, tripping over a stack of books that he'd entirely forgotten about at the end of the bookcase.

He tumbled to his knees and did a sort of clumsy half-roll across the floor; he sprang up again, desperately trying to ignore Ivy's muffled giggles. Red-faced, he walked behind the counter, and refused to meet her eyes as he checked out her books.

She dropped two more in front of him. "And I'd like to buy these two, please," she said, quietly. She was clearly trying to make him feel better, and he risked a glance at her face. Their eyes met, and for a moment Ivy managed not to smile, before breaking off into peals of laughter, muffled by her hand.

He appreciated the effort, however short-lived it had been, and managed a weak smile as she entered her PIN. Mortified, he wrapped the books for transport.

"Sorry," she said, softly, and this time *she* couldn't meet *his* eyes.

"It's alright," he said, equally quietly. "It *was* pretty funny."

Her eyes flew to meet his and she smiled, gently. He had never seen eyes so blue. He smiled back, a little more strongly this time.

"Well..." she gathered up her books and was gone. He stared after her, aware of the tendrils of her tantalising scent following her, reaching out to him, leaving him behind.

Professor Barraclough was quite a sight when he returned from Brightwell: he had bits of stringy, purple slime attached to his hair and ears and they vibrated alarmingly when he moved or talked. When Christopher – who was working through an order for a tiny, young witch with a bit of a zombie obsession – eventually noticed his presence, he was unable to take his eyes off the bits of slime. They had a curiously corrosive smell to them, and he was strongly reminded of his high school chemistry laboratory.

"Er – you have – I mean, on your ear..." he managed, hypnotised by the swinging tendrils of gloop.

"What?" the Professor reached up to his ear. "Urgh. Excuse me."

He walked back to the tiny bathroom to remove the worst of it.

Christopher watched him go, wondering just what the Professors had done to the Dark Horde.

A series of bangs and muffled swearing made him turn around. Professor Barraclough had left Zarrubabel's book on the corner of one of the desks, and when he had tried to get out, in his usual exuberant way, it had fallen between two of the shelves and become wedged. The arrogant spectre was thoroughly stuck, and Christopher allowed himself to enjoy his fruitless struggles for a few moments before moving to pull the book free. He put it on one of the armchairs by the range, and watched as it snapped open; Zarrubabel didn't so much jump out of the book as fall out of it.

Somehow, Christopher managed not to laugh, and averted his gaze as the ghoul righted himself.

"You could at least have put me the right way up you imbecile!" he grumbled. "But at least I'm by the stove again..." He wriggled slightly, as if making himself comfortable. "This was *my* chair you know," he said, almost to himself. "Joanna is forever stealing it. Always did." He smiled slightly, and it was the most genuine smile Christopher had ever seen on his features; he turned his grey-green face to him, and the smile evaporated. "What are you gawping at, boy?" he demanded. "Get back to work!"

Rolling his eyes, Christopher went back into the shop proper, intending to tidy away some of the errant stacks of books. As he worked, his mind began to drift to Ivy, and the way she had looked as she read. Recalling his sudden and appalling clumsiness, he blushed again. He had always been quite good at talking to girls, in his youth, but his lycanthropy had made him somewhat shier. Apparently, he was out of practice.

Not that he should try to initiate anything. No self-respecting witch would ever want to be seen with a werewolf (except possibly as a dare), and he had no wish to damage her reputation (which he was certain would be flawless).

Putting the pang of intense disappointment away to think about later, he turned his attention to the Light Orb that he had seen her conjure. It had been elegant, he recalled, and quite pale, with some kind of flowing decoration around it there had been a white, metallic band around it too. He wondered what that signified.

Every Practitioner's Light Orb was unique, he knew, a reflection of themselves at the time of their conjuring. His had always been ringed with black when he was a child, because he had thought it was cool, and he and Rachel had often snuck out of bed and made their orbs dance around the ceiling of the living room, filling the room with every colour that they could imagine. Rachel's had always had an element of stained glass to it, whilst his was plainer, simpler. She had always teased him about that, saying that he didn't have any imagination. She was probably right.

These days, the frame of his orb looked like it was carved from wood, reflecting his having experienced a bit more of the world, he supposed. It was also duller, and he would rather not think about that. If he were honest, he was a little embarrassed for anyone else to see it.

He would like to get another look at Ivy's though – but how would you phrase a request like that?

'Good afternoon, Mistress Burwell, would you mind awfully showing me your Orbs, please?'

He snorted. *That* would go down well – he would probably get a smack for his trouble, if not worse. He was about to pick up a hefty-looking tome whose title was turned away from him, when his hand was smacked away.

"What in hell do you think you are doing?" Joanna

demanded.

"I-"

"Think, boy! Look at the book under your hand!"

He turned back to it, obedient under Joanna's ferocious gaze, and reached out with his mind: sensing the shape of the magic in his mind he pulled his hand back as if burned.

"If you had touched that cover, even for an instant, you would have been under its thrall – many fine witches and wizards have wasted away clinging to that curséd thing!" She smacked him on the back of his head, hard. "*Morton!*" she shouted. "*Why in hell's name is this thing out here?*"

Professor Barraclough stumbled out of the back office, a bit of purple goo still attached to one bushy eyebrow. He looked between the two of them: Christopher rubbing the back of his head, embarrassed, and Joanna's furious countenance.

"Er – oops?" he offered, hands still frozen in the act of trying to detach the slime.

"Oops?" she asked, advancing on him with her hands on her hips. "*Oops?*"

"Er – one of the customers wanted it, and I must have forgotten to put it away," he said, backing away.

"You *forgot*?" she demanded, enraged. "What would have happened if a customer had picked it up by accident? What if one of their children had? Do you *know* how hard it is to remove a thrall like that?"

"Well, yes, I –"

"*Then why the hell was it on the floor in the shop?*"

For the first time, Christopher could see the resemblance between Joanna and her brother; when they were enraged, it seemed they had the same vicious single-mindedness. He wouldn't want to meet her in a fight, that was for certain; he suspected that Joanna Barraclough was a formidable battle witch.

He hung back as she berated her husband, feeling guilty. He really should have spotted it – and would have, with that strength of enchantment on it, if he hadn't been so distracted.

He went to release his patient from the binding clamps in the back room; Professor Zarrubabel was watching the argument with unabashed interest.

"Which book was it, shop-boy?" he demanded, as Christopher passed him.

"I don't know," he replied, loosening one of the screws. "I didn't see the title. It was large, though, and old – with faded green bindings."

"*The Devil's Mirror*'," said Zarrubabel, eyebrows rising. "Who would want to read that tosh?"

Christopher ran his fingers along the freshly glued end-papers, checking that they were dry; he could feel the book relax in his hand, glad to be free of clamps. He stroked the cover, absently, and the book shivered in appreciation.

"What's it about?" he asked.

Zarrubabel peered at him over his pince-nez. For once he looked curious, rather than annoyed, and this was sufficiently unusual to give Christopher pause. He decided to tread carefully: keeping the ex-Professor in a talkative mood could prove to be useful.

"You've not heard of it?"

"No, sir."

"No education," he scoffed. "What use are you, really? It's a compendium of the ill-effects of dark spells," he continued. "Some of which are quite accurately illustrated."

"Sounds delightful," said Christopher, with feeling.

To his surprise, Zarrubabel nodded.

"It's usually checked out by those with a fascination with the macabre – a means to feed their sadistic side, I suppose. Although we all have a strange attraction to the grotesque," he rubbed his long, pointed nose, thoughtfully. "You do get the occasional madman who wants to see if he can work out the spells from the effects – wants to attempt to manifest something nasty, usually – but thankfully they don't come around too often."

"Why would they want to do that?" asked Christopher,

perplexed.

"Beats me," said the spectre. "The only benefit I've found about being dead is that you can't be killed when your neighbour's ill-advised spells go awry."

"And you can't get covered in purple goop."

Zarrubabel sniggered indulgently.

"He *does* look a fright, doesn't he..."

"Why is it called that, do you know? *'The Devil's Mirror'*?"

"Of course I know, you impudent brat!" Zarrubabel spat. "It refers to the properties of the book as a reflection of the author and his readers, as you should damn well know! Nobody knows its original title – or even the author's name, since he had it erased from every copy he could get his hands on, ashamed of his own foul creation and what it was being used for. These days everyone calls it *'The Devil's Mirror'*. Wholly unimaginative, if you ask me," he grumbled to himself. "Why not: *'The Compendium of Darkness'*, or something? Equally melodramatic, but at least you'd know it was a book." He continued to mutter to himself, apparently no longer aware of Christopher's presence.

Christopher took the opportunity to return to the shop proper, and snuck past the beleaguered Professor, who was continuing to get a tongue-lashing on the proper storage of dangerous books.

He had just returned the relieved *'Compton Book of Verse'* to its shelf when, calming down a little, Joanna remembered him.

"And *you* should have spotted it," she said, making him jump and very nearly sending him toppling down the tiny stepladder.

"I – yes, I'm sorry."

"No harm done," she said, taking a deep, steadying breath. "Morton, get that thing put away will you – and get those entrails off your face, you look ridiculous." She rubbed her neck in frustration. "I think we could all do with a cup of tea," she said, striding into the back room.

Christopher stared at his employer, aghast.

"Entrails?" he asked, as Barraclough pulled on a pair of sturdy leather gloves.

"You don't want to know," he said, with a grimace, and carried the book through; Christopher followed him, thinking that he was probably right.

Once three steaming mugs of tea were on the table, everyone appeared to have been forgiven, and they drank in reasonable quiet for a few moments (Zarrubabel's laments on a lack of taste buds notwithstanding).

"I'm surprised that you didn't spot it," said Morton, as if he had been puzzling it through for a while. "That amount of magic, that close to you – the books we tested you with were much subtler."

Christopher winced.

"I just wasn't thinking," he said, with a half-shrug. "I must have been distracted."

"Hell of a distraction," muttered Joanna, still a little upset by the potential accident.

"I know why," said Zarrubabel, delighted to be able to discomfit someone.

They turned to look at him, expectantly.

"Well, isn't it obvious?" he asked, with glee. "He gets all dopey on Monday afternoons – well dopier than usual, bloody fool," he cackled at Christopher, whose face was fast becoming a picture of horror. "He's sweet on little Ivy!"

The Barracloughs turned back to Christopher, who had frozen with his mug halfway to his mouth, mortified.

"I am not!" he refuted, glaring at the jubilant spectre.

"Are too!" he grinned, cackling.

"Am *not*!" he couldn't help but retort. "I – I've only just met her!" he managed, horribly aware of the blush that was starting somewhere around his neck. "I hadn't even *seen* her before today!"

Joanna and Morton exchanged a look, both of them apparently trying not to smile.

"Yes," cried Zarrubabel, happily. "But you've *smelled* her before!"

It was perhaps fortunate that Christopher's expression

was already one of shock and dismay, and couldn't therefore, betray anything further.

"Oh, be quiet you daft old thing," Joanna said, turning back to her brother, who was rocking back and forth with merriment.

He stopped and glared at her. "Oh, don't tell me you don't know?" he said angrily. "Really, you ought to thoroughly check potential employees so as not to let in vermin like that." He jerked his head in Christopher's direction.

Christopher, who was looking on in helpless dread, stared at him.

How could he know?

"Really, Hector," said Barraclough, quirking an eyebrow. "You aren't suggesting that Christopher goes around sniffing the customers, are you? What utter rot," he laughed, taking a lengthy swig from his mug.

"But he –" Zarrubabel began, infuriated at the flippant manner in which he was being treated.

"That's quite enough!" snapped Joanna, and closed his book with a snap.

For an instant, Zarrubabel hovered above it in astonished fury, before his internal universe righted itself and he vanished with a sort of wet popping noise.

Joanna put a crate of mending supplies on top of the book, and the three of them listened to the muffled noises of outrage for a few awkward moments.

Christopher played with the handle of his mug, refusing to meet his employers' eyes.

"He does talk some absolute rot sometimes," said Barraclough, kindly, trying to ease the tension. "Best to ignore him, probably."

Christopher risked a glance at them, they were both looking at him. He looked back at his tea.

They can't know, he thought. *They just can't...*

"He was just trying to get a rise out of you, dearie," said Joanna, sympathetically.

"We'll close up tonight," said Barraclough, with an air of finality. "You get on home, eh? Bright and early tomorrow – fresh start."

Christopher nodded, picked up his coat, mumbled a 'goodbye' and fled without looking at them.

Joanna watched him go with a frown.

"Poor boy," she said. "I do wish Hector hadn't brought it all up. It's made him very uncomfortable."

"Small wonder," said Barraclough, with a sigh. "It can't be easy, living with his condition. He's probably expecting us to throw him out at the slightest notice."

"The book couldn't be wrong, could it? Opening to aconite like that."

"I shouldn't think so," said her husband, rubbing his stubbly beard, thoughtfully. "We could be wrong about what he is, of course, but I for one would rather think of him as a werewolf than some deranged poisoner."

He looked at his watch.

"Come on, Jo. Let's get off home, old girl."

Joanna smiled at him.

"You're just eager to get back to Charlotte's Toad in the Hole," she said, with a smile.

"You see right through me, my dear," he grinned.

They spent a few minutes tidying the back room; Barraclough was just about to remove the packing crate from on top of Zarrubabel when Joanna stopped him.

"Leave him be, Morton, let him get the sulking out of his system."

"He won't be happy," said her husband, with a worried frown.

"He never is, so it won't make any difference," she said, pulling on her coat.

"Hmm," he said, then: "Do you think Christopher really *is* sweet on Mistress Burwell?"

Joanna smiled, despite herself.

"He *did* go rather pink when Hector brought it up," she allowed.

"He won't get very far," her husband observed. "Not with Ivy Burwell, she's still grieving."

"You never know," said Joanna, thoughtfully. "He's got a laughing way about him, and he's quiet. They might suit one another quite nicely."

"Now, Jo, you can't go around match-making again," he admonished, giving her shoulders a light squeeze.

"And why not?" she asked, amused. "I'm good at it – Charlotte and John are very happy, aren't they?"

"Yes, but we'd known both of them for years –"

"Oh, hush, man," she shushed him, good-naturedly. "I'm not going to meddle – I was simply making an observation."

"Of course you were, my dear," he said, voice admirably level.

They locked the door to the shop and pulled down the metal shutters. Arm in arm, the Barracloughs set off out of the plaza in companionable silence.

"I wonder if Christopher likes Toad in the Hole," said Joanna, thoughtfully.

Professor Barraclough shook his head in fond amusement.

5
The Crooked House

It was a very wary werewolf who returned to work the following morning, but the Barracloughs had apparently ignored the sizeable hints their spectral friend had dropped the previous evening, and Zarrubabel appeared to have given up. He was in an even fouler temper than usual, however, and Christopher spent most of the day dodging books, inkstands, boxes, and anything else within the ghoul's reach.

He seemed to have blamed him for his friends' disinterest, and hurled an equal amount of abuse as missiles, some of which – to Christopher's mild alarm – weren't too far off the mark.

He was a little disconcerted to find that Joanna Barraclough had left him a portion of Toad in the Hole in a dish on the range. Professor Barraclough informed him that she was worried that he was too skinny, and left him with the warning that if he didn't eat it she was likely to start standing over him at meal times. Christopher, who had been attempting to politely refuse the gift, kind as it was, had capitulated in the face of the inevitable.

It wasn't half bad.

Joanna had given him a small, satisfied nod in the afternoon, which he took as approval. Usually, he would have hated the gesture, interpreting it as pity, but the elderly witch had a way of making you believe that it was simply the result of friendship, and he was happy to go along with that.

As it turned out, the Toad in the Hole was only the beginning: every few days Joanna would leave a dish of something on the range, and give him increasingly pointed looks until it was eaten. Every time, he thanked her and told her that it was thoroughly unnecessary, and every time she simply tutted at him, and told him that it would continue to be necessary until he stopped looking so thin and pasty, inevitably making Professor

Barraclough snort into whatever book he happened to be poring over at the time.

He had avoided speaking to Ivy, since his spectacular performance on their first encounter, other than the most basic pleasantries. He didn't know what it was about her, but she appeared to bring out the shy, stuttering madman in him, and he would rather not be remembered as such.

Since Mistress Burwell appeared to be just as shy as he was, they spent Monday afternoons in companionable silence, as Christopher repaired or hunted for or moved books, and she became absorbed in whatever tome had caught her attention this week. It hadn't escaped his notice that since Zarrubabel's accusation, both Barracloughs had invariably found reasons to be absent on Monday afternoons.

He wasn't at all sure how to feel about that.

His deliveries to the old Georgian townhouse in the old town had continued, at erratic intervals, and he had met several young nurses now, each equally flustered at his arrival and equally keen to add to his pile of returns and have him gone. He was beginning to build up a very intriguing picture of the convalescing Mr Post.

Languishing behind the counter on an unreasonably hot summer's day, Christopher had looked up with mild interest to see an unfamiliar customer entering the shop, the bell above him jangling wildly.

He was quite a young man, only a few years older than himself, Christopher guessed, and effortlessly handsome. With pale green eyes, dark blond curls and an enviable tan, he looked as though he could easily sway any young woman in his path – and frequently did. His well-tailored clothes suggested the kind of wealth that didn't feel the need for ostentatious gestures, and he gave Christopher a warm smile as he approached, supporting himself on a curiously ornate ebony cane.

The stranger put several books on the counter and gave him an appraising look.

"So you would be the intriguing young man my nurses

keep telling me about," he said. His voice was calm, confident; it had a warm, rich tone to it that made Christopher feel completely at ease. "I would like to return these, if I may," he continued, tapping the uppermost book with a manicured finger.

Christopher glanced at its title, and looked up at the man in mild surprise.

"Certainly – Mr Post, is it?" he asked, already checking the books in.

"Indeed it is, young man, although it is polite to call an adult Practitioner 'Master' – or 'Mistress', as the case may be," he said, with tolerant amusement.

"Oh, I'm sorry – I didn't know," Christopher began, but Master Post cut him off.

"Not classically trained, then? I would have thought Barraclough would have hired one of the young bucks from Brightwell."

"Er – no, sir."

"But you *are* a Practitioner?" he asked, subjecting him to his steely gaze.

"Yes – er –"

"Excellent," he said, clapping his hands together. "Be a bit dangerous if you weren't." he grinned, by way of explanation; Christopher, who noticed such things, saw that his teeth were perfectly white and even. "So, do you think you can find these, old chap?" he handed him a list of books, written in beautiful cursive script. "Some of them are a little obscure – and some rather suspect," he smiled, affably. "You get the strangest looks when you research dark magic."

"I can imagine," said Christopher, with a smile of his own. "These shouldn't be too troublesome – I'll have to check the ledgers in the back for some of them – and *Grey's Necronomicon* is on loan to the Widow Jenkins – but I'll be able to put my hand on a few of these straight away, to get you started. Will you be working here?"

"For the moment," he said. "My lovely nurses will have my hide if they catch me out of doors, but I was losing my mind cooped up at home."

Christopher, who couldn't imagine ever feeling 'cooped up' in a house of that size and grandeur, smiled politely.

"Perhaps you ought to sit down, sir – I understand you injured your leg, and it wouldn't do to make it worse."

"You're probably right," said Master Post, and eased himself into the chair at the desk by the window. He grimaced and rubbed his leg. "Mountain climbing accident," he said, conversationally. "Out in America – wanted to see a different view of Yellowstone – it's so boring to see the same woodland paths all the time, wouldn't you agree?" He grinned, and ran a hand through his dark curls. "Lost my footing halfway up a cliff. If I hadn't been a wizard I'd have bought it."

Christopher nodded and went to find the first items on his list, marvelling that anyone could ever spend so much time in a park so vast that they got bored.

He put the kettle on in the back room as he worked, and came back out a few minutes later with a stack of arcane books.

"Ah, capital!" Post cried, and took out a fine leather notebook and pen. "You *do* know your way around books!"

Unused to compliments from customers, Christopher preened.

"Thank you, sir – would you like a cup of tea? I'm just making a pot."

"That would be very kind – what was your name again?"

"Christopher – Christopher Porter."

"Well, Christopher, you can call me Quentin if you like, none of this 'sir' nonsense," he smiled, holding out a hand for him to shake. "I can see that we're going to be fast friends."

By the time the Barracloughs – who had been at a lengthy, soul-destroying meeting at the Brightwell Academy – got back to the shop, it was already ten minutes past closing, and Christopher and Quentin were thoroughly engrossed in conversation.

With the exception of *Grey's Necronomicon*, all the items on Post's list had been tracked down and perused, and a small pile had been set aside to be booked out. On his second cup of tea, Post had invited Christopher to join him, and had told him all about his study of the misuse of magic, and about the book he was writing along those lines. Christopher, always fascinated by history, had been able to follow nearly all of his conversation, and had even suggested a few new avenues of research.

"The central question that I'm investigating is what makes people *decide* to use dark magic," Post was saying. "Is it a conscious decision, or are people forced into it – or even, are there instances where they don't have any idea that they're doing it at all?"

"Well, I suppose it depends on what kind of magic it is," said Christopher, fascinated. "I mean, if you end up using a book with a powerful Enticement Charm on it, you can't have much control. Although," he allowed, "I suppose you would still be able to decide which spell to follow – or even to make a deliberate mistake in the casting."

"Exactly!" cried Post, enthusiastically. "There are a few such cases listed in the *Leicester Codex* – one involving a particularly unpleasant malefactor, named Carstairs..."

"Is that the one where he made it rain fish heads in someone's bedroom because they'd cut down a hedge of his?" Christopher asked. "And every time they tried to stop it, it just made things worse, because Carstairs had put a Rebound Jinx on them?"

"Meaning that everything they cast failed spectacularly," nodded Post, impressed. "You know your history."

Christopher coloured slightly. He'd remembered the Carstairs story primarily because he had read about it in one of his father's books when he was ten, and rains of fish heads tend to stick in the minds of ten-year olds with the occasional taste for mayhem.

"I studied it for a while."

"An excellent discipline."

"Well, I enjoyed it," he said, smiling.

The two of them looked up as the shop-bell jingled, and the Barracloughs walked in, grumbling to one another about their fellow governors.

"Good Gods, is that the time?" asked Post. "I'll be for it when I get back home."

"I'll get everything booked out for you," said Christopher, jumping up. "I should have been keeping an eye on the time, I'm sorry."

"Nonsense, I've had a much more interesting afternoon discussing history here than I would have at home with my overzealous nurse, I assure you," he grinned, getting stiffly to his feet, and clicking a strange device that he took out of his pocket. Christopher had only ever seen one once before, when his parents had taken him and Rachel to see a play in Stratford; it was an expensive device that rerouted the nearest taxi, mundane or otherwise, to your present location. He had always imagined that there were a lot of very confused taxi-drivers in the general vicinity of rich wizards.

"Morton, Joanna," Post greeted the Barracloughs with easy charm. "I must congratulate you on your choice of assistant – a most intriguing young man."

Christopher tried not to blush as he prepared the books for transport, deliberately not eavesdropping on the conversation, which was turning to recent hitches in the running of Brightwell Academy, where Post had apparently studied.

After a bark of youthful laughter, Post turned and shook Christopher's hand.

"Until next time, Christopher – and remind me to tell you about that fabulous party I attended last year in the Parisian catacombs," he grinned. "Not entirely *legal*, but excellent fun – and fascinating for a history buff. I'll bring some of the photographs."

"Thanks, Master Post!" said Christopher, surprised.

"Quentin, my dear boy. Quentin," he insisted, before

gathering up his books and bidding them all a fond farewell.

"Such a nice young man," said Joanna, as she unhooked the till. "Shame about his leg, did he say how he'd done it?"

"Rock-climbing in Yosemite National Park," said Christopher, following her with the mugs.

"Well it's alright for some," said Barraclough, affably, as he checked through the day's ledger entries. "Whenever I get injured it's doing something unpleasant."

"You two back?" asked Zarrubabel, sleepily, not even bothering to get out of his book.

"Yes, Hector," said Joanna. "You'll be pleased to know you missed quite possibly the most boring meeting of the year."

"Excellent," mumbled the irascible spirit, and resumed snoring.

"He was up all night, reading the new stock," Christopher explained on their inquisitive looks. "Didn't even bother throwing anything at me this morning – just mumbled something about 'ungrateful runts' and rolled his book over."

Barraclough laughed. "He was always like that at school," he said.

"Did you go to Brightwell?" Christopher enquired, interested.

"Yes, we all did," Barraclough replied, screwing the lid back on a jar of ink. "It was bigger back then – a proper boarding and day school. These days it's mostly just evening classes and the odd day-student."

"Well, it's the fees," said Joanna, putting the day's takings in the safe. "These days it just isn't feasible to put your kids through a magical school – particularly since most of them will take mundane jobs to make ends meet."

Christopher nodded.

"I would really have struggled without my A-Levels," he said, leaning against the door frame.

"Well quite," agreed Joanna. "And somewhere like Brightwell just isn't equipped to teach mundane qualifications."

"We have fifty day students," said Barraclough. "Fifty... it just seems so sad, some days."

"But more in the evening classes?" Christopher asked.

"Yes – a lot of young students who attend mundane school, and the odd adult learner looking to branch out."

"We have to learn to move with the times," said Joanna, pointedly. "And some of the governors just don't see that."

Barraclough sighed, and polished his monocle. "They'll come around, Jo. They'll have to."

Joanna, her head still inside the safe, snorted.

Barraclough shook his head at her, wearily.

"How do you feel about lamb hot-pot, Christopher?"

Caught off guard, Christopher stammered. "Er – no strong feeling?"

"Well, you'll make your mind up tonight," said Barraclough. "Charlotte, our housekeeper, is an excellent cook, and I suspect she will be just as interested in feeding you up as Joanna is," he added, in a conspiratorial undertone.

"Sir?"

"You will join us for dinner, won't you?" asked Joanna, swinging the door of the safe shut with a loud clang. "We have some things we need to talk through with you – about the shop."

"Oh – I," he began, intending to turn them down, but Joanna clapped him on the back.

"Excellent."

"Alright. Just as long as you don't live in a gingerbread cottage," he added, in an undertone to Barraclough.

The Professor snorted, and covered it with a wholly unrealistic coughing fit.

It was definitely not a gingerbread cottage.

The Barraclough's house was a magnificent old rambling town-house, whose owners had apparently felt the need to update it in nearly every major architectural time-period. It was a spectacular hotchpotch of nearly every style and taste from the last eight centuries, and probably made passing architectural students burst into tears. There was cornicing, there were quoins, there were three different brick patterns and at least four different types of window on the front of the house alone – he could just make out a patch of white framed wattle and daub partly concealed by a section of red bricks in a herringbone pattern. It looked a lot like several different houses had somehow collided and that *this* house was the result.

Christopher couldn't even begin to imagine what the sides and back might look like.

The foundations of the house must have been laid a very long time ago – long before the strict lines of medieval plot division had taken over the town-planning mentality – and the house had quite a sizable plot of land surrounding it, largely taken up by a small orchard of all manner of fruit and nut trees, their branches tangled and interlocked with one another. What looked like a ragged tribe of stubborn sunflowers had grown up in between them, and the ground was covered with wildflowers. The effect was quite pleasant, in a *Grimm's Fairy Tales* sort of way. Large parts of it looked as if gravity had long since ceased trying to assert itself, and had simply looked the other way in the face of improbable architectural insanity. He had a shrewd suspicion that at least some of it was held together using magic.

Like their shop, the house looked fabulously out of place as a sort of central break in the long line of red-brick, up-market Victorian terraces. He wondered, vaguely, how irritated their middle-class neighbours must have been with the erratic and improbable building.

He liked it enormously.

The inside of this architectural nightmare was a delight: every room he peered into appeared to represent a different period in the house's history. On the brief tour that Professor Barraclough insisted upon giving, he noticed that this was not necessarily respected by the house's occupants, as evidenced by the small television he spotted in the seventeenth century parlour and the candlestick telephone in the modern kitchen. The dining room had apparently been designed during the Arts and Crafts movement, and was resplendent with violently colourful William Morris wallpaper and a magnificent tapestry of birds; beautiful as it was, it made Christopher's brain hurt.

The Professor's study (or rather, the parts of it that weren't covered in books) was panelled in fine eighteenth century style, and covered with fascinating maps and prints, cases with interesting artefacts – and one case that contained only butterflies.

"Take a closer look," said the Professor, waving him over.

Christopher, who had never quite got over the shock of seeing the creatures pinned to a board in his local museum when he was a boy, approached it warily.

There were several dozen of the things, like brightly coloured jewels, in a strange, scientific tribute to the macabre. The sort of thing that could be seen in any lepidopterist's study – except that these weren't butterflies.

As the tiny arms and legs came into view, horrible realisation began to dawn.

"They're *fairies*?" he asked, recoiling in shock.

Professor Barraclough nodded.

"One of my great-great uncles had a bit of a thing for the fey," he said, sadly. "Family legend proclaims that he fell in love with a fey – thought that if he could understand them properly, he could get her to stay with him. Became something of a grim obsession, sadly. I believe that they had a child, but no one would ever talk about her. He was a vicar, you see, and there was quite a scandal…"

"Why do you keep it?" asked Christopher, aghast.

"Can't get the damned thing off the wall," said the

Professor. "Some kind of impenetrable sticking spell. Crafty old devil, was Uncle Bertram... shall we go, only I suspect we'll be for it if we keep Joanna waiting."

Christopher fled the room, gladly leaving the scent of death behind him.

The kitchen, as it turned out, was largely modern, which – Christopher suspected – had rather a lot to do with the middle-aged woman presiding over the stove. Charlotte, the Barraclough's housekeeper, appeared to have a no-nonsense approach to life; as soon as he walked in, she took one look at him, sniffed in faint disapproval, and started buttering large chunks of bread.

It was warm in this room, and the whole world was beginning to smell mouth-watering.

Joanna, who had been setting the table, walked back in and nodded in his direction.

"You see, Charlotte, far too skinny."

Charlotte nodded emphatically, and handed Christopher a lump of bread.

"Nothing but skin and bones."

Somewhat nonplussed, he glanced at the Professor, who was trying very hard not to laugh.

They ate in the garden, given the weather, at a large, wooden table that would have been at home in a Norman castle, with tiny lanterns glittering in the trees.

The hot-pot was, as expected, scrumptious; so scrumptious, in fact, that they didn't speak very much during dinner, preferring to enjoy the magnificent food in peace. As he ate, he looked around their sprawling gardens. He guessed that this was more Joanna's realm: she appeared to have her study in the nineteenth-century glass orangery that was just off the kitchen; from what he could see through the glass, this room was also largely covered in books. He spotted an old wireless that was in danger of being buried by multiple volumes of the *Diaries of Samuel Pepys*.

The gardens were beautiful, and much more orderly than those at the front: they largely resembled one of those old kitchen gardens of crumbling brick and ordered beds, except that no one seemed to mind what was planted in each bed, so that there were nasturtiums under (and, in fact, in) the runner beans, and courgettes winding their merry way around a bed of roses.

The middle of the garden was taken up by a large, Tudor knot garden with a dovecote in the centre; the fat, well cared for birds were energetically waddling around the herbs, cooing at one another and generally making a lot of noise. At each corner of the knot garden was a fruit tree whose branches had been intertwined with its neighbours, forming a sort of living trellis, up which sweet peas trailed.

The myriad scents of the summer garden were heady and sweet, and not at all unpleasant, if not necessarily the best accompaniment to a savoury meal. Christopher imagined that the evening, when all the aromas began to fade and intermingle in the cooler air, was the best time of day to sit in the garden: drinking a cool glass of wine and reading a book in one of the arbours he had spotted in amongst the flowers.

More fruit trees had been trained up the southern wall of the garden, the end of which was taken up by what looked like a Norse longhouse, currently in service as a garden shed.

Their gardener, John, was sitting in the lee of it, eating with Charlotte, his wife. He had a ruddy complexion and a bright smile; he looked like a very genial man, and Christopher thought that he and Charlotte suited one another perfectly. Once he had finished eating, he extracted a long, curiously shaped pipe out of his waistcoat and began to smoke it, puffing out great rings of blue smoke into the evening air.

Charlotte gave him a small smile of approval as she cleared his empty bowl; Joanna had insisted on serving him extra helpings. Christopher couldn't remember the last time he'd been this full. Even with his greatly improved salary he was trying to save most of it, partly in order to move out of the flats he was living in, and partly because it was a good idea, given his condition. A full stomach made a pleasant change.

They sat for a few moments in companionable silence as Professor Barraclough fetched a bottle of wine, and Joanna and Christopher, left to their own thoughts, gazed in companionable silence at the twinkling lights above them.

"It really is beautiful here," said Joanna, happily. "I love it in the summer, when we can spend so much more time outside – it's just as beautiful the rest of the year, but in different ways."

Christopher nodded, in agreement.

"I'd hate to live somewhere where the seasons never changed," he remarked.

"It can be quite magical," Joanna laughed. "Although, around here, that goes without saying!"

"I can imagine," said Christopher, smiling. "The house is quite... odd. Beautiful," he added, not wanting to offend, "but very odd."

"Yes, it is rather," said Joanna, laughing. "One of Morton's ancestors built into the foundations the magical tenet that things could be added but not universally changed – hence the slight insanity indoors."

"How..." Christopher began, searching for an appropriate word.

"Batty?" asked Professor Barraclough, returning with a bottle and three glasses.

"Ridiculous?" asked Joanna.

"Bizarre," he finished, diplomatically, and they laughed.

"It is a bit," said the Professor, filling up his glass. "But then, what kind of arcane bookseller would I be if I *didn't* have a house that was a little bit mad?"

Christopher chuckled, and took a sip of his wine. It had been a long time since he'd had wine, too. It was extraordinary, really, how something that was essentially the juice of things that had gone off could be so tasty and relaxing.

He sat back on the bench, enjoying the peace of the

summer evening.

"So," began Joanna, with a pointed look at the Professor. "I imagine you're wondering why we asked you here."

Christopher looked at their faces and tiny notes of panic began to rocket around his consciousness. He licked his lips, which suddenly felt quite dry.

"I did have a bit of a theory about gingerbread houses..." he said, trying to lighten the sudden dip in the mood.

Professor Barraclough snorted into his drink, and Joanna elbowed him in the side.

"I'm not intending to cook you," she said, with a slight smile. "Although I *will* tell Charlotte that you said that. No, there's nothing sordid about our concern – we're just a little worried about how thin you are. You don't look as if you had had many square meals before we hired you, and I – *we* – wanted to remedy that."

Professor Barraclough gave her a fond smile, which told Christopher that although he supported her actions, he would have been equally happy not to interfere, whatever his feelings about his employee's diet.

"I suppose times have been a little hard," he admitted, quite embarrassed.

Joanna nodded, not with pity, he noted, but with acceptance. She glanced at her husband, who took the hint. He cleared his throat.

"We want you to know, Christopher, that whatever happens in your personal life – with the probable exception of arrest – your job with us is safe," he said.

Wondering where the hell this was going, and stunned beyond belief, Christopher managed to simply croak. He had intended to say 'thank you', but a croak was all that they were getting.

He looked from the one to the other of them, feeling that he couldn't be more astonished if he tried. Apparently, he was wrong.

"We also want you to know that we don't care a penny about your – er – condition," said Joanna.

His stomach had dropped so quickly Christopher felt as though he had fallen off the bench. His internal fight or flight mechanism was now making urgent demands on his brain. A rapid assessment of his situation told him that he hadn't, in fact, moved, and that he was probably required to say something at this point.

"I don't know – what – you mean –" he managed, fighting to stop his voice and hands from shaking. "I don't have a condition!"

The Barracloughs sat quietly in front of him, watching him.

He was breaking out into a cold sweat, he knew, and suddenly a full stomach didn't seem like such a good thing, after all.

One thought was taking over his mind, blocking everything else out.

They know!

It repeated, over and over, making his heart beat like a timpani drum.

He was about one second away from jumping up, thanking them for the meal and then running like hell, when Joanna decided to intervene.

"You aren't listening to us Christopher," she said, matter-of-factly. "It doesn't bother us that you're a werewolf."

Oh Gods, there it was, out in the open! He flinched, visibly, at the word.

"Come now," said the Professor, reasonably. "It's hardly the strangest thing either of us have ever seen – I mean, just look at Hector, for example. If we can cope with *that* on a daily basis, I'm sure we can cope with an employee getting a little, well, *hairier* once a month."

Christopher stared at them, as far back against the bench as he could get.

This couldn't be right – neither of them were attacking him, or throwing him off their property, and there were no drawn staffs or wafted shotguns.

He coughed, trying to calm down enough to let his brain catch up with the conversation.

"You've gone awfully pale, old chap," said the Professor, worriedly.

Christopher swallowed, experimentally. "I – uh –" he stammered.

They looked at him expectantly.

"U-usually this is the part where weapons are pointed at me – I'm a little confused..."

Joanna tutted, angry – he realised – on *his* behalf.

"Well, we have no intention of doing that," she said, firmly.

"You don't?" Christopher asked, gulping, and looked at their faces. "I mean – you don't, do you...?" he trailed off, wonderingly.

"We don't," said Joanna. She cleared her throat again, but Barraclough gave her a warning look.

"Give the man a chance to recover, Jo," he said. "We've given him a nasty shock."

They waited for Christopher to calm down for a few minutes, sipping their wine. He gripped the stem of his wine glass rather harder than was necessary, afraid that everything was going to come skidding to a terrible halt at any second. He drank a little wine, and some of the colour returned to his cheeks; he felt warmer, slightly more – well – *human*.

"Alright," he said. "I think I'm okay. That is, if you s-still are," he stuttered.

"We are," said Professor Barraclough. "We'll work out the days you'll need off in advance – I imagine you need a day afterwards to recover?"

Christopher nodded, swallowing hard. This *couldn't really be happening – could it?*

"Topper!" he said, smiling. "We'll sort it all out on Monday."

"Which brings us to the other thing we need to talk about," said Joanna.

Professor Barraclough's face fell, and Christopher's heart nearly stopped, wild, nightmarish scenarios chasing themselves around his mind.

"We found out this morning that the Council are

buying up the buildings around the Plaza," he said, clearly annoyed. "Which means that we're going to have to move."

"M-move?" asked Christopher, surprised. "When? Where are we going to – how are we going to transport the books?"

"One thing at a time, boy," said Joanna, pleased that he had already forgotten his fears.

"We have to be out by the end of the month, apparently," said the Professor, gritting his teeth. "Although they are willing to pay us for the inconvenience. We should be able to afford to set up the new place nicely, wherever it is."

"Have you any idea where?" Christopher asked, worriedly.

"No," said Joanna, simply. "We looked at a few locations in the estate agents this morning, but there wasn't really anything suitable."

"That warehouse in Rouse Abbey wasn't bad," Barraclough said, mildly.

"It would be fantastic for the mundane books," said Joanna. "But the magical ones would play havoc with the structure. Ideally we would need somewhere that has had magical tenants before – a place that already has some of the Insulation Charms in place. Plus, as picturesque as Rouse Abbey is, it's a little out of the way."

"Where is it?" asked Christopher, interested.

"About twenty minutes drive out of Brindleford, to the West," said Barraclough, with a dismissive wave of his hand. "Built around the site of an old monastery. Lovely place. But Joanna's right, it is a little far out."

"We'll just have to keep our eyes peeled," said Joanna, contemplatively. She sighed. "Oh it will be such a shame to move; that shop has become like a second home to us."

Barraclough nodded, sadly.

"You know what else we'll have to do," he said, ruefully.

"What?"
"Tell your brother."

6
Temper, Temper

As predicted, the late, lamented Professor Zarrubabel did not take the news of their impending move well, turning a peculiar shade of blue in shock before demonstrating his rage in no uncertain terms. He appeared to be inconsolable, and, Christopher discovered, spectres swell in their grief. Zarrubabel was soon bobbing around on the ceiling, wailing and hurling things about.

Barraclough had moved the ledgers to a shelf under the counter so that they could still continue serving people, and the three of them had to run a strange sort of distraction-come-counter-attack whenever they needed something from the back.

By the weekend he had begun to produce flurries of ghostly torn paper from the ether, which decayed after a while, covering everything in the office with a strange, cold mist. The smell reminded Christopher strongly of graveyards, with an eerie tang of mould and damp.

He spent as much time as possible in the shop proper, whilst the Barracloughs fruitlessly scoured the local area for suitable locations. Returning each day with a sad shake of their heads, spirits dampened to match Zarrubabel's.

Really, Christopher was astonished by how much energy he continued to have; he was getting increasingly angry as the week wore on.

By Monday morning, it was clear that something had to be done, and the Barracloughs stationed themselves in the back room after lunch, in an attempt to calm him down a little.

This meant that when Ivy Burwell arrived for her weekly perusal of the book shop, Christopher was already wincing at the raised voices and occasional crash from behind him.

"Hello..." she said, staring at the door to the office, which had just shuddered under the assault of a missile.

"Is everything alright?" she asked, in mild alarm.

"Yes," he lied, wincing slightly with every new bang. "Everything's fine."

They looked at one another for a few moments, Ivy carrying her returns, Christopher standing next to the counter, pen in hand.

A particularly loud crash, followed by quite a lot of cursing, made them both jump.

Christopher pointed at the door behind him.

"I'm just going to –"

"Yes..." she nodded, as he stuck his head around the door. He jumped back moments before a particularly large catalogue hit the door frame. There was a stream of muffled cursing. Barraclough had taken refuge behind an upturned desk; Joanna was nowhere in sight, but he could hear her hissing angrily at her brother.

"Best get out while you can, lad," said Barraclough, urgently. "He doesn't like you at the best of times."

As Zarrubabel picked up a fresh box of writing supplies to hurl at him, Christopher slammed the door.

He looked warily up at Ivy, who was watching him with wide eyes.

"I think it's safe to say that we *might* have a poltergeist," he said, as the box and its contents hit the other side of the wall. There was the sound of splintering wood.

"I think you're probably right, there," said Ivy, slowly. "Are they going to be alright, do you think?"

They both glanced at the office as something shattered; an acrid stench was beginning to seep out of the wood, like burning ink.

"DON'T OPEN THE DOOR!" Professor Barraclough bellowed. "EVERYTHING'S UNDER CONTROL!"

Christopher highly doubted this, but he shrugged helplessly at Ivy.

"It might be a little difficult to find anything obscure, this week," he offered, with the barest twitch of a smile. "I can book things back in, however. Professor Barraclough resc- er... brought the ledgers out last

Wednesday."

Ivy, who was torn between disobeying Professor Barraclough's last instruction and just carrying on as normal, stared at him. He sighed.

"I don't think he'd actually hurt them – or damage the books," he said, feeling wretched. "It's mostly just ink and stationery that gets thrown."

"It sounds like this happens regularly..."

"You could put it that way," he said, rubbing the back of his neck. "I really can't say..."

She nodded, slowly, apparently coming to a decision.

"Alright," she said. "I need –"

But he didn't find out what it was that she needed, because she gasped and pulled him around to the other side of the counter. The door had turned pitch black, and the blackness was beginning to spread out across the walls. It was moving slowly, ponderously – like hot pitch, sticking to everything in its path. Christopher was strongly reminded of the air filters in the clean room at the Records Office, sucking all the life out of the room when the doors were shut; the darkness on the wall smelled like that: cold, empty, of nothingness. If oblivion had a smell, that would be it.

More frightened than he had been in a long time, Christopher took a step back, nearly trampling on Ivy, who was still unconsciously holding onto his arm in a mixture of surprise and horror.

In the back of his mind, Christopher heard the books flinch and rustle in panic; cases started rattling as the volumes tried to get as far away from the encroaching darkness as they could. They started to fall to the floor with dull thuds, trying to pile themselves up against the far wall. He felt Ivy turn around.

"My Gods," breathed Ivy, pressed against his back. "They're *screaming*..."

She meant the books, he knew, because although he could still hear the Barracloughs roaring themselves hoarse in the office, the noise coming from the thousands of terrified books was almost a physical force now, and still building.

He came to a decision.

"Get the books away from the darkness," he instructed.

"But –" she began, before stopping herself. She gave him a curt nod.

He felt, rather than saw, the books begin to fly across the room, responding to whatever it was Ivy was doing. Taking a deep breath, he wrapped the sleeve of his shirt around his arm and he opened the door. The stench of oblivion hit him like a wave, making him shudder through waves of nausea. Billows of gelatinous nothingness were rolling silently around the room, like great black, slow moving clouds. The Barracloughs, too busy firing shield charms at the Special Collections and around one another to notice him coming in, were trapped in the corner by the range, their exit route entirely cut off.

Zarrubabel was barely recognisable in the centre of it all, bloated and frozen, as black as the clouds of despair around him, face contorted in a scream of rage. The only definition surrounding his distorted and congealing form were bright white flashes of deathly energy; he was, quite literally, coming apart at the seams. His rage had entirely taken him over now: he was as helpless as everyone else, locked in a maelstrom of his own creation.

Picking up one of the upturned desks as though it were made of cardboard, Christopher flung it across the room and dove after it, not even pausing to watch it begin to dissolve and disperse. As the desk slowly began its descent against the other bookcase, bursting into fragments of void at roughly the speed of glacial drift in the area of weird slowness surrounding the poltergeist, Christopher flung himself forwards, catching the edge of Zarrubabel's book with his fingers and snapping it shut.

With a sound like the motor of an infernal engine warming up, the world snapped back into focus.

After the cacophony of sound, the resulting roar of silence was deafening. Christopher picked himself up from the floor where he had landed and surveyed the wreckage: the black clouds were gone, now, leaving bright sunlight and four stunned mages behind them. The Barracloughs were helping one another up, wearily, and he could hear Ivy picking her way through the piles of fallen books in the shop proper.

He began righting desks and boxes, determinedly ignoring her approaching scent, and the accompanying urge to take hold of her and not let go.

She stuck her head around the door, cautiously, as Joanna slumped into the surviving chair by the range; Professor Barraclough sat down heavily on a large, wooden box. Christopher hovered uncertainly in the background.

"Are you all –" she began, looking around.

Christopher glanced up at her, and watched as her foot collided with the kettle, which had rolled across the floor. She picked it up with sudden resolve, and strode across to the range, relighting it with a flick of her fingers.

"I think we could all do with a cup of tea," she said, firmly, and started hunting for the mugs.

The Barracloughs, clearly drained following their ordeal, barely lifted their eyes, silent in their exhaustion.

Christopher helped her find the tea, sugar and milk (kept on top of the particularly energetic *Journal of Polar Exploration*), and set about mending the other armchair. After setting the tea to brew, Ivy joined him, pulling together papers that had floated wildly about the room and stacking them on the desks, and righting ink pots with barely a thought.

They worked in terse silence for a few minutes, until the aroma of the tea took over the room and Christopher poured it out, putting mugs with three sugars in the hands of the Professor and Joanna.

He and Ivy sat, side by side, on one of the desks to drink their tea, legs swinging through the papery dust, uncertain what to say or do. As the colour began to return to the Barracloughs' white faces, the Professor reached out to his wife, taking her hand either in comfort or in sheer relief. Feeling distinctly intrusive, Christopher got up and went into the shop proper, drinking his tea as he went; Ivy followed him.

The books were erratically stacked up at the far end of the room, and some of them were still flapping feebly towards the far wall.

"I knew that they had a sort of half-life," said Ivy, quietly. "In that way you develop a relationship with the book you're reading – but I didn't think they were *alive*."

"It depends on the book," said Christopher, picking up one that was flapping ineffectually against his shoe. "All books have a personality, which can develop and change over time, but when you have magical books around it gets a bit more pronounced." He stroked the spine of the book, absently, and it settled in his hands; he felt it shift, taking comfort from the contact. "Even the mundane books begin to respond."

Ivy was looking at him a little oddly.

"You have quite a way with them," she said.

"Just treat them like a cross between mischievous children and frightened animals and you can't go too far wrong," he said.

He handed her another frightened book. "Here, you try."

Looking rather dubious, she ran her fingers along the cover, and the book shivered happily; she nearly dropped it in surprise. A few of the nearer volumes changed direction and began to flap towards her.

"Oh," she said, as they started to bump against her feet and ankles. "Hello..."

"I think they like you," Christopher chuckled. He took her hand and helped her hop over the bouncing books. "You'd better sit on the counter for now."

"Thanks," she said, settling on the wooden top. "If I throw one of my sandals, do you think they'd chase it?" she asked, contemplatively.

"A book about dogs might," he said, and smiled slightly as she laughed. After a week of wailing and moaning, it was a very pleasant sound.

He knelt beside the anxious books and whispered comforting words to them, touching one or two of the more frightened ones to calm them down. Slowly, the 'all clear' seemed to filter through the piles, and books stilled, tired and relieved.

Movement from the back office caught his eye, and he turned to see Professor Barraclough emerge, looking pale and exhausted.

"Are you both alright?" he asked.

"I've been worse," said the Professor grimly. "And Joanna's more annoyed than anything else. And you, Christopher: that was very dangerous."

"I couldn't see another way," he said, shrugging slightly. "You and Joanna were trapped, and *he* couldn't stop it."

"Not by that point," Barraclough agreed, then spotted Ivy, who was still sitting on top of the counter, watching proceedings with interest. "Oh, Mistress Burwell, I'm so sorry about all this," he said, wretchedly. "You aren't hurt?"

"I'm fine," she said. "Thanks to Christopher, I think."

"Indeed."

There was a pause, where the two men tried to think of some plausible explanation for the chaos, and Ivy tried to work out how to phrase her question.

"So, who is it?" she asked. "The ghost, I mean."

She surveyed their faces as they looked at one another, unsure how to begin.

"Oh for hells' sakes, you two," grumbled Joanna, who appeared to have recovered on sheer force of will. "Do you remember my brother, dear?" she asked Ivy, resting against the door frame.

"Yes," she said, a little surprised. "He used to give me sweets when I came in with Mum. He died when I was still quite small." She paused. "Oh."

Joanna nodded.

"We got back from the funeral, and there he was, waiting for us. Sitting on an old accounts ledger, bewildered and very, very annoyed." She sighed. "He's much the same as he was in life: opinionated and difficult. Although these days he has more of a proclivity for throwing things – particularly at Christopher."

"He doesn't like me," he offered, as Ivy glanced in his direction.

"Usually, though, he takes the hint if we ignore him, or lock his book in the safe. This week has been something of an exception."

"He was having a bit of a tantrum," said the Professor, and again, Ivy glanced at Christopher, mostly to check that she was still sane.

"'A bit of a tantrum'," she repeated.

"More like a complete melt-down," said Christopher, quietly. "He'd worked himself up to the point where he was beginning to congeal."

Joanna nodded, sadly.

"I just hope he comes back in one piece," she said, and Christopher realised that she was still shaking very slightly, afraid that she might have lost her brother once and for all.

The Professor put an arm around her.

"What on Earth was he so upset about?" Ivy asked, still reeling slightly from the understatement of the century.

"We have to move," said Barraclough, sadly. "We don't want to, we've been here for years – but the Council is expanding the Town Hall, and buying up this building in the process."

"Can't you appeal?" asked Ivy, who clearly felt for them.

The Professor shook his head.

"We tried, but they didn't listen..."

"We've been trying to find somewhere new, but nowhere is really suitable – and they've only given us until the end of the month to work it all out."

"Seems a little harsh."

"Well, you know what bureaucrats are like these days," said the Professor. "They don't really think about anyone but themselves."

"I was hoping that thinking about a new shop would cheer Hector up," said Joanna, sadly. "But everywhere we looked was either too small, or too far away, or just not secure enough. I mean, you've seen what the books are like – they could get really out of hand without the proper controls in place."

Ivy nodded. "So you're looking for somewhere local, preferably magical, with sufficient space for the books..." she trailed off, frowning. Christopher looked at her: oddly, she seemed to be at war with herself, though he couldn't put his finger on why that might be. Outwardly, she was quite calm.

At last, she cleared her throat, having come to a decision.

"Well, you know that I live in the old arcade, down near North Walls?" she asked.

"Of course, dear. Everyone knows that," said Joanna.

Christopher hadn't known that, and he was puzzled as to why they thought he should.

"Do you remember the old dress shop that was in there?"

"Next to that craft shop?" the Professor asked.

"That went years ago, Morton," said Joanna, exasperated.

"Did it? Oh that's a shame, they had fabulous end-papers."

"Anyway, the dress shop," said Joanna. "Do go on, dear."

"Well the lady that ran it closed up shop a few months ago," said Ivy. "So half of the Arcade is empty these days – it's just me and Mahri in there now. You could rent one of the units, if you wanted."

It was as if a great cloud had been lifted from the room.

"Really?" asked Barraclough, astonished.

"Yes," said Ivy, simply. "Although, if Professor Zarrubabel acts like that in the Arcade he will meet a rather sticky end," she added, almost apologetically.

"There are all manner of protection spells on the place."

"I can imagine," said the Professor.

"You can come and look it over, if you'd like," she offered. "When you're feeling up to it, of course – and you could move in when you wanted, since it's empty."

The Barracloughs looked at one another, recovering a little of their usual vigour.

"Could we go now?" Joanna asked. "The faster we get the move over with, the better it will be," she glanced into the back office, "for all of us."

"Of course," said Ivy, and hopped off the counter, startling the books that had made a sort of ring around her. They scattered, rustling wildly.

"Christopher, hold the fort," the Professor ordered. "Don't bother tidying up too much – we might be on the move sooner than we thought. And if anyone comes in, warn them that there might be some disruption," he said, as they headed out of the door.

Ivy gave him a small wave as she left, and he stood for a moment, watching her.

Something collided with his ankle: the fickle books that had befriended Ivy Burwell were clamouring for attention around him now.

"Alright, alright," he chuckled. "Settle down."

It was nearly closing time before the first customer came in, staring around at the general chaos and stepping over the stacks of books (he had been unable to leave them in the pile, and had become a little tired of small lines of them trailing after him as he worked).

"Bloody hell!" she exclaimed, tottering over to the counter. "What on Earth?"

"Some of the books got a little excited," he said, having decided that omission was the best form of lying at this point. "How are you this afternoon, Mistress Jenkins?"

"Better looking than your shop at least, boy," she said, still peering around. "Are you open for business?"

"That rather depends on where the books you require are," he said, gesturing at the mess. "It might be tricky."

"Perhaps I had better come back next week," she said.

"Perhaps – oh, but we might be moving!" he exclaimed, and explained about the Council and the relocation.

"We don't have anywhere in particular just yet, but the Barracloughs are looking at somewhere right now – I think we have your address in our delivery ledger. Would you like me to send a note around with the details of the relocation?" he asked, and she smiled toothily at him.

"You're a good boy," she said, patting him on the arm. "That sounds excellent..." she shifted her basket of books. "Can I leave these with you?"

"I don't see why not," he said, pulling out the returns ledger. "I know where *this* is, at least."

She waited while he checked her items off, her beady eyes following the route of his pen, curiously.

"I might take one or two away, too," she said, thoughtfully, and looked around. "Let us see what fate has brought me," she said and clicked her fingers. Three of the nearest books flew to her grizzled hands. She peered at the titles. "Hmm: *Human Rights in Albania*, *Classical Myths and Legends*, and –" she snorted. "A Regency romance novel. Well, I'll book out these two, if I may," she said, putting the romance novel firmly back on the counter top.

Obediently, he booked the items out, and started work drafting a letter informing the shop's regulars about the move. He left the part with the new address and reopening date blank, and had just put down his pen when the Barracloughs returned.

They were both smiling, which he felt was a good start.

"It's perfect!" cried the Professor. "Just perfect – we'll take you over there first thing in the morning and start getting things shifted. I'll write to all our regulars –"

Christopher handed him the drafted letter.

"The Widow Jenkins was in earlier, I thought it might be a good idea," he said.

"Capital!" the Professor cried, beaming. "Excellent work, lad. Best get off – tomorrow will be a busy day!"

As he grabbed his coat, Christopher heard a weak voice coming from the back room.

"Joanna?" Zarrubabel called, in a thin, reedy voice. "Joanna, are you alright? Morton?"

Joanna rushed past him into the office.

"We're alright Hector – are you?" she said.

"And the boy?"

"Even him," he heard her say. "If he hadn't closed your book when he did, we wouldn't be."

"I thought I'd killed you," he said, and Christopher heard his voice break.

"There now, we're alright," Joanna said, whispering comforting things that Christopher couldn't quite catch.

He went to leave, but Barraclough stopped him, gently.

"Christopher? Could you come here?" Joanna called.

Warily, he stuck his head around the door to the office.

The ghost of Hector Zarrubabel was a very pale green, like the fur he had sometimes seen on middle aged sage leaves. He was wringing his hands, wretchedly.

"I'm sorry Morton, I –"

"Don't fret, old chap – as long as you don't intend a repeat performance."

"No – I – I *never* want that to happen again!" he cried, and turned to Christopher. "You saved my sister, boy, and my oldest friend. Thank you."

Christopher, aware of how bad he must be feeling, and rather embarrassed himself, simply nodded.

Zarrubabel nodded back.

There was one of those awkward silences that happen when no one quite knows how to proceed. Hector cleared his throat, but couldn't think of anything to follow it.

"We've found somewhere else," said Joanna, gently.

"You have?" he asked, hopefully, and Christopher wondered whether he had thought they might give up the shop entirely if they couldn't find new premises.

"At the old Arcade – *The Vineyard*," Professor Barraclough supplied.

"The Chambers' place?" he asked, surprised.

"That's the one, Ivy Burwell's running it these days – took over the place from her great aunts," the Professor continued. "Has a tea shop. Sells all manner of things over the counter, too, to the right customer – and wool. Apparently tea and wool go together," he went on, in the manner of one unconvinced.

"And you remember Mahri Glass," Joanna put in. "The one I used to go to choir with? She has a florist's in the same building."

"And we can go there?" Zarrubabel asked, wonderingly. "When?"

"Tomorrow," said Joanna. "Morton and I signed the papers just now."

The colour returned to Zarrubabel in a flood: it was as if someone had switched a light bulb on behind him. He did an excited sort of flip in mid-air and clapped his hands.

"Excellent!" he crowed.

"We'll start the move first thing – after we show Christopher where it is," said the Professor.

Some of Zarrubabel's earlier animosity returned as he glanced at him; Christopher had wondered how long that would last, but he had thought he might get a day's grace at the very least.

"Of course, you're from out of town," the disagreeable spectre said, as if this were intensely distasteful.

"Be nice, Hector," said Joanna, in a warning tone.

"Ivy took it over from her great aunts," Barraclough explained. "And they took it over from *their* mother. I think if you looked back as far as the Norman conquest there would be a Chambers woman living on that spot – though you might find that their name had changed. But for the last five centuries, they've all been a Chambers – not even changing their names when they married."

"Until Ivy," said Joanna.

"Until Ivy," Barraclough echoed.

"She always was a little strange as a girl," said Zarrubabel, as if grey-green ghosts throwing spectacular tantrums were a perfectly normal occurrence. "Got the impression, as she got older, that she didn't like being a Chambers very much."

"I don't blame her," said Barraclough. "After all that business with her parents."

"Some of the neighbours didn't like them very much," said Joanna, as tactfully as she could. "People stopped going to them – even when they really should have."

"They passed away when she was quite young," said Zarrubabel. "And then it was just her, her grandmother and her sisters. Then she went off and married that mundane Burwell chap she'd gone to school with, and *he* got himself killed in some damn' silly war."

"He was protecting a school full of children," Joanna admonished. "He died a hero."

"Yes, and left his wife – an exceptionally good witch, I might add – a widow at twenty-three."

"Hector," said Barraclough, with a warning in his voice.

"Well, I'm sorry. He just wasn't the right sort."

"You mean, he wasn't a Practitioner."

"He was a nice young man," said Joanna, in a tone that ended the conversation. "And he died trying to help people. Small wonder if she wants a quiet, stress-free life – and she wouldn't get that as a Chambers."

Joanna deftly steered the conversation to the impending move, and away from their new landlady.

Christopher walked home deep in thought, wondering what being a 'Chambers' had to do with anything. He felt for Mistress Burwell, waiting at home for that awful letter or phone call... Gods knew he missed his family like a hole in the world, and they were still alive. She was so very alone.

ooo

Mason McQueen locked his shop door, glad that the heat of the day was finally beginning to diminish, and set off towards his favourite café – a grubby, anglicised place that suited him down to the ground. It was run by an infamous ex-army type and largely catered for ex-pats; a poky little place, the café was crammed between run down clubs. The whole area smacked of decaying finery. It had two saving graces that kept its clientele coming back despite the neighbourhood: it served a decent cup of tea and there were never any tourists.

It had been a rather strange day, Mason reflected as he wound his way through the maze-like streets of the Merchant Quarter. There had been the usual stream of tourist types passing through the shop and crowing over the cheap tat he kept in the window. One or two of his more discerning clients had dropped in after lunch, and he'd led them to one of his back rooms to peruse his more unusual acquisitions.

He'd had to keep a close eye on them; as refined as his clientele liked to think they were, a bigger bunch of light-fingered cheats he had never met.

He'd actually had to close the shop when one of them had accused another of theft – accurately, as it turned out. Mason had had half a mind to turf the oily little bugger out, but he was a powerful man with a lot of friends, and he didn't fancy having to reapply for his trading license any time soon.

Still, the man had clearly been in the wrong, and had eventually returned the stolen book to its owner, turning a curious shade of puce before leaving the premises in a state of high dudgeon.

Daft bugger, Mason thought.

The first rule in antiquities – as far as Mason was concerned – was *'don't shit in your own street'*. You never knew when you would need a sneaky favour, or who you'd need it from.

That pompous little bastard was burning bridges in the trade left, right and centre.

Mason shook his head and put him from his mind. The darkness was coming in fast, now, as it always did in this part of the world, and he paused a moment to let his eyes get accustomed to the shadows.

As soon as he got to Café Pauvre there would be a hot beef sandwich and a steaming pot of Indian tea, and he would be able to forget all about irate antiquarians, sand and oily little rich boys for another day.

'Never mix business and pleasure' – that ought to be rule number two, he decided.

He turned the corner.

His foot hit something lying across the ground; he stumbled and swore, casting about him in the dusk for whatever it was he had fallen over.

Shock seized him, squeezing the breath from his lungs; for several seconds he couldn't really breathe.

Mason's mind was insisting that he had, in fact, fallen over a corpse, but the terrified, irrational part of him that was currently in control refused to believe it, until –

He leant closer to get a better look and immediately wished that he hadn't.

The empty eye-sockets of Ignatius Pond, a veteran antique dealer and one of his oldest customers, stared back at him.

Unwilling to abandon a man he might cagily have described as a friend, Mason reached out and gently closed what was left of Pond's eyelids. The skin hung limply across the empty sockets; his stomach turned.

"Such a pity," murmured a voice in the shadows behind him; Mason didn't even have time to turn around.

After a few moments of exquisite agony, he fell lifelessly beside the elderly antiquarian, his last expression of terror plastered on his eyeless face.

7
The Vineyard

The Vineyard was an old, Victorian arcade in a back street just outside the heart of Brindleford, and looked rather like it had been there forever – the neighbouring buildings appeared to be huddling under the protective wings of a giant, glossy mother hen. It was all iron and glass, resembling a stocky greenhouse, designed to emulate the Crystal Palace of the Great Exhibition; there was a half-domed protrusion to the apex of the frontage, which had the name above it, wrought in great white, iron letters. The metal stems of climbing plants wound their way around it, making it look strangely organic.

Despite having stood for a hundred and fifty years in the midst of the cacophony of English weather, it looked as if the decorators had finished with it only the day before: its white painted metal gleamed in the sun, and the great glass panes that made up the majority of its outer walls and roof were so clean that they sparkled.

Which was odd, because although it was blatantly an inherently magical place, it didn't really feel like it; it felt oddly mundane, as if it was trying really hard to look innocent. It made Christopher feel slightly on edge, as if it was somehow watching him, and – little as he wanted to admit it – he could almost understand why people had stopped visiting the businesses there.

It was three generous storeys high, although Christopher couldn't see anything room-like above the second storey; there were curtains against the glass walls on the first floor, and supposed that this was where Mistress Burwell lived.

The inside was bright and airy, sunlight spilling down from an enormous light well that stretched up to the half-dome at the top of the frontage. The central corridor had been expertly tiled at some point in the past, and it too was kept scrupulously clean; the tiles were still glossy and bright, clicking in a friendly fashion with every step. In keeping with what he was beginning to suspect was the original theme, someone had painted elegant vines around the doors and windows of the bays. It had a sort of homely feel to it, despite the strange and deliberate absence of any sign of magic, and Christopher began to relax a little as he acclimatised to the barrage of new smells.

Ivy's tea shop took up two bays on the right hand side, and seemed like a peaceful sort of place. The second of her bays, that looked out onto the street, was a little smaller, and couldn't be accessed from outside the teashop (someone had put rather a lot of potted shrubs around the door to stop people trying to use it) and was wall-to-ceiling full of wool, threads and fabric in every colour imaginable. It strongly reminded Christopher – who had very little interest in knitting or sewing, except in emergencies – of a fantastical sweet shop. Even though the shop had only just opened, there were already two women in there, fondling various balls of wool and talking in an animated fashion.

The bay furthest from the entrance on the right was taken up by a busy florist's, which had possibly the most vegetation in one place that he had ever seen outside of the woods; it smelled bright and fresh to Christopher, and he smiled at the middle-aged lady who was putting a bucket of irises out in front. She gave him a friendly sort of nod and continued shifting buckets of fresh flowers, giving Joanna a small wave as she caught up with him.

All three bays on the left of the Arcade were empty, and as he looked at them Christopher was struck by a strange feeling of sadness, as though the building was lamenting its emptiness. It felt distinctly wrong that these shops should be vacant, and he was suddenly very glad that they would be moving here.

He watched as Professor Barraclough unlocked the doors to the middle bay – opposite Ivy's tea shop.

The doors (which resembled church doors, and had pale glass panes in them to match the walls) had a satisfying creak to them, and – Christopher was surprised to see – an old mortise lock. He supposed that burglary wasn't that much of an issue here, with at least two respected witches on the premises.

Although there was the slight tang of a room that had been shut up for too long, the empty shop was surprisingly clean, and he wondered for a moment whether Ivy had aired it out for them, before deciding that there was probably some form of cleaning charm in place. The walls were papered in a rich red with gold trim, presumably selected by the previous tenant, and a wooden floor had been put down at some point, making the room seem larger and full of light.

Barraclough showed him the back office, which was a room that ran behind all three of the bays on that side of the Arcade; there was a spiral staircase behind a curtain, roughly in the middle of the space, which apparently led to the rooms above. There was definitely magic on the curtain: a warding spell designed to keep anyone who didn't belong upstairs firmly on the ground floor.

There was a muffled discussion occurring outside, and he rejoined his employers.

"I think we should move everything we can from the back room first," Barraclough was saying. "Get it packed away safely."

"That's all very well, Morton," said Joanna, looking mildly exasperated. "But how are we going to put it away if we don't move the furniture first?"

"Ah..." he said, somewhat nonplussed. "Well... Alright, how about this: Christopher and I start moving the heavier things across, while you and Hector continue packing up all the books and papers?"

"Continue?" asked Christopher, recalling the state the shop had been in when he had left the previous evening.

"Apparently Hector was so excited about the move that he actually made himself useful for once," said Joanna, amused. "He spent last night packing up the back room – most of it just needs moving."

"He'll be ratty as hell come lunchtime," Barraclough observed. "But with any luck he'll be too tired to do anything but sulk."

They worked through the morning, Christopher and the Professor getting progressively weaker as they magically transported the furniture from the old shop. Fortunately, Joanna had thought to put an illusion on the windows that made it look as though they were using slightly more mundane means of moving, so the customers leaving the florists and sitting in the tea shop were curious about the new shop, but not about the large pieces of furniture appearing out of thin air with two wizards hanging off the sides.

The magical transportation of an item (or a person) takes a certain amount of energy to fuel, as any Practitioner learns fairly early on. In order to move, say, four wooden bookcases that someone had bound together with an old rope (discovered, oddly enough, in the back of the mug cupboard) you would expend roughly the same amount of energy as if you had carried several very heavy bags of shopping up a couple of flights of stairs.

Imagine packing up all your things, then magically making them much smaller, so that they would all fit in the one suitcase, bag or even your coat pocket; they might be a good deal smaller, but because of the way the universe works, they would still be the same weight – and when you're carrying things, it's the weight that really gets to you.

It *is* a lot easier to move things by magic, and it takes longer to wear you out, but wear you out it really does. By lunchtime, Zarrubabel wasn't the only one of them that was flagging, Christopher and the Professor having made around fifty trips back and forth from the old shop.

Backs aching from lifting, and drained from all the transport spells, they collapsed gratefully into the two armchairs that were currently arranged around the counter in the shop proper, making a sort of impromptu table. Joanna, who had brought over the first of the documents for the back office, had perched on the edge of a packing case, Zarrubabel's book beside her.

His exertions the day before had apparently worn him out completely and the sounds of heavy snores were drifting up from between the pages. They were debating what to do for lunch, with various unhealthy options on the table (including, to Christopher's delight, the possibility of ordering a pizza), when Ivy nudged the door open, carrying a tray full of sandwiches and cakes; the genial lady from the florists followed her in, with a large pot of tea and a pile of precariously balanced cups.

"We thought you might be a little peckish," said the florist, deftly setting the cups down with a surprising lack of accident. Her voice was of the crisp, British variety, and it immediately put Christopher in mind of the formidable female sports teachers at his high school, who had all seemed very interested in making the girls play hockey in conditions that would make North Sea oil rigs shut down for the day. A few tendrils of her fading auburn hair were escaping from the no-nonsense bun perched atop her head and she brushed them out of her eyes with mild annoyance.

As she and Joanna chatted, happily, and Ivy passed around the sandwiches, he was aware of the florist's sharp brown eyes watching him; it was clear that this woman didn't miss much.

"Mahri Glass," she said, waving a plate of food in his general direction. "I don't think we've met, Mr...?"

"Porter – Christopher," he said, taking the sandwiches with gratitude.

"Nice to meet you Christopher," she said, briskly. "I own the flower shop across the way – if you need anything and these two rogues aren't here, come and find me." She turned back to Joanna, who was the last person Christopher would ever have chosen to describe as a 'rogue', and gave her a brief hug. "I'll have to get back to the shop," she said, apologetically. "Lunchtime is when it begins to pick up around here – I'm glad you're over here, Jo – we need to catch up."

She hurried off without a backwards glance, calling out to a customer as she went.

"One of my students, you know, when I taught at Brightwell," said Joanna, fondly. "Quite ferocious when she wants to be, but a lovely girl."

Ivy, who had lingered, met Christopher's eyes at this description, and both were forced to suppress a chuckle.

"Are you settling in alright?" she asked, still smiling.

"Oh, yes," said Joanna. "Morton and Christopher have worn themselves out moving most of it –" she glanced at her husband, who had fallen asleep in the armchair with his half-eaten plate of sandwiches balancing on his stomach. He was snoring faintly. "And there are only a few bits left now – I'll bring them over while they recover, and we'll move the safe and the range last thing."

"Range?" asked Ivy, interested in how they would move it. "The one at the old shop? I thought it was part of the building."

"Yes, it's an old cast iron thing my father found in a skip after the war," Joanna said, and looked up at Ivy. "He fixed it up and made a portal for the chimney – all the smoke and steam just disappears up the flue and comes out in the marshes over by Rouse Abbey. Probably frightens the life out of a few ramblers now and then, but they really shouldn't be wandering through the marshes to begin with."

"I *was* wondering about that," she said. "Especially as your old shop was under the council offices."

"It won't be a problem, will it?" asked Joanna. "To have it here?"

"Not at all," said Ivy, with a smile. She stood and went to the door. "I'd better get back, as well. Just bring the plates and things over when you're finished," she said, and then she was gone.

"Right," said Joanna, who had already finished. "I'll get back over to the old shop – no," she said, as Christopher made an effort to move. "You stay here and have a rest. We'll have a busy afternoon."

Since his mouth was full of sandwich, he nodded, and Joanna blinked out of existence. It was a sight that he had never got entirely used to, despite his own proficiency at it.

Now you see me, now you don't, he thought, reaching for a slab of chocolate cake.

He made quick work of his remaining food, and settled back into the armchair with his freshly poured cup of tea. To his surprise, it was probably the best cup of tea that he had ever tasted. It warmed you up from the inside out.

She must use some kind of charm on it, he thought, inhaling the delicious aroma. It made him feel comfortable; drowsy.

He glanced around the shop, briefly considering getting stuck in again, but decided instead to take Joanna's advice and rested his head against the back of the chair. Closing his eyes, he allowed the sounds and smells of the Arcade to seep into his consciousness. He yawned, deeply.

He could hear the snores of both professors, echoing slightly against the empty shelves, and the clicking of people's feet as they walked up and down the tiled corridor outside. He could tell each person apart by the sound of their footsteps: some shuffling along in leather soled shoes, some echoing with the distinctive clicking of high heels, the oddly broken rhythm of a child skipping along with their mother or father, the squeaking rattle of a pushchair.

Idly, he wondered whether he would learn to recognise each person's footsteps while he worked in the shop, knowing who was walking in even before he smelled them.

He could hear other sounds too, out in the teashop and florist's: people chattering to one another, the clink of china, a sudden burst of childish laughter, the slight hiss of a kettle, the slick-and-snap of Mahri's shears, the rustle of paper. They were good sounds, he decided; the sounds of people getting on with living.

He yawned again, settling back into his slump.

And the smells! What had been a morass of new scents

assaulting his nose in the morning were much more distinct now, and he could pick out the smell of each type of flower in Mahri's shop, if he wanted, or the fragrance of each variety of tea.

There was a warmer note, too, which he decided was the wool. It was fainter than the tea, being in the furthest bay away from him, but it was still powerful – and even *that* odour now had different layers to it. Curious, he concentrated on the warm sheepy smell, and was rewarded by several distinct flavours of scent. It would take more investigation, but he suspected that there were a wide variety of fibres in that back room, and not all of them from sheep.

Ivy's scent, that maddeningly elusive mixture of linen and honey, was all over the place, and he enjoyed its proximity, following it in his mind as it blended with the tea, and the wool, and the flowers, and the dark, spicy, leathery parchment smell that the bookshop was beginning to take on.

Intensely comfortable, he too began to drift off, and soon his snores had joined those of the professors, in a quiet chorus of slumber.

He awoke to find Joanna unpacking the miniaturised range in the back room; hearing the small noises she was making, he stirred and stretched, stifling a yawn.

Professor Barraclough was still fast asleep, and the snores emanating from Zarrubabel's book showed no signs of diminishing. Carefully, he removed the plate that was still balanced on his employer's stomach, and gathered the crockery together on the counter.

Sticking his head around the door, he startled Joanna.

"I thought you were all asleep," she said, clutching her chest.

"Sorry," he grinned. "Need a hand?"

"I'm alright back here," she said, and waved an arm at the restored cupboards and shelves. "I thought I might get things in order. You could make a start in the shop though. Quietly, if you can – I don't like to see Morton wear himself thin like that."

"I'll be as quiet as a mouse," he promised, and went to take the plates and cups back to Ivy, muttering a quick muffling spell to hide his footsteps.

Silently getting the bookshelves laid out around the armchairs and their sleeping occupants – he had moved Zarrubabel's book to the relative safety of the other chair – was no mean feat, and he was feeling rather pleased with himself when he opened the first crate of books.

He frowned down into it: it was immense on the inside, with stack after stack of miniaturised books rustling about in excitement. Getting them out would be a bit tricky without waking anyone up.

Luckily, Professor Barraclough took this opportunity to snort himself awake, and he stared around the room, befuddled with sleep.

"What? Oh..." he mumbled, and struggled to his feet. "Sorry, old chap."

"No worries," said Christopher. "I had a bit of a nap for a while there too, and Zarrubabel's still out of it."

The book gave a particularly loud snore, as if to confirm this.

"Joanna?"

"In the back," he said. "Could you take his book back there? I don't want to wake him up."

"You seem to have it all in hand..." said Barraclough, still befuddled with sleep. He nodded in bewildered approval and carefully carried the snoring tome into the back office, where the burble of his and Joanna's quiet conversation filtered through the door.

Christopher smiled after him, and muttered the reversal charm over the crate, before hastily standing back, casting a faint levitation net across the shop floor so that they wouldn't damage themselves when they landed.

The books quickly returned to their original size, fountaining out of the crate and floating to the floor like fat, enormous feathers.

He set about stacking and sorting them into roughly

the places that they had occupied in the old shop, humming happily to himself.

ooo

It had been a long time since anyone other than Mahri had been in the Arcade with her – the ever altering stream of customers notwithstanding. It had put her on edge all day, and she couldn't help glancing over at the newly occupied shop. It wasn't that she didn't want them there – on the contrary, the Arcade needed to be full of people. It felt distinctly lost and unhappy when it was empty, and the extra bit of money from their rent would undoubtedly come in handy. They certainly weren't loud, or offensive, or unpleasant – but she was very aware of their presence, all the same, taking up a part of a space that she had come to think of as wholly *hers*.

It was odd to have more people around, making decisions and moving around and just sort of *living* in the same space as her.

She would simply have to get used to it.

Clearing away the tea things from one of the small tables near the window, she glanced across at the shop. Joanna's illusion didn't have any effect on her, and it wouldn't have made a difference within the Arcade at any rate (it had a habit of showing Ivy everything that was going on, just as it was). They seemed to be getting on pretty well: the bookshelves were secured against the walls and arranged to form smaller, more intimate spaces where people could read or peruse. She had always liked that about their shop: that you were almost expected to lose yourself in a good book.

There were even a few books on the shelves now, though a lot of them still stood bare and empty. She looked across at them for a long moment and thought about the two unoccupied bays of the Arcade. The shelves looked similarly forlorn and bereft; as if they felt that they had failed in some way, unable to fulfil their intended purpose. Frowning, she turned away and piled the dishes into the small sink in the back room, where they immediately started washing and drying themselves, in a curiously elegant, mid-air dance.

It shouldn't matter that much, she told herself. The shelves would soon be shelves again, and she would find someone to occupy the other bays.

Knowing that she wasn't really thinking of either of those things, she made herself tidy the flowers in the windows. Flowers from Mahri's wildly disorganised shop always lasted longer than those bought at any other florist (and were generally available in the most unlikely seasons), but these had been there for a couple of weeks now, and they needed refreshing – some of the freesias looked particularly unhappy. Idly, she batted something away from the base of the vases, just poking up enough to graze the bottom of the window; apparently she wasn't the only one who was curious about the new shop. She should pop over and ask her old friend to choose some more flowers, really –

Somebody was humming.

The sound wound its way into her mind, and she turned, half expecting to see *him* – but it was just Christopher, happily working away in the bookshop across the way.

She sighed. It just wasn't healthy, she knew, to still be thinking of him – expecting him to come home, even – after all this time, but she couldn't stop herself. He had been such a large part of her life for so long.

With a sad smile, she watched Christopher open a new crate of books and make them zoom around the room like excited paper birds. Sam would have liked him. They had the same gentle optimism, that same inability to stop laughing when they shouldn't be.

Rearranging another vase full of flowers – roses and mimosa – she looked at him as he worked, stacking and organising the books, and thought how pleasant it was to have met someone so friendly, and so quiet.

He was laughing now, with a smile that lit up his whole face, trying to catch a particularly eager volume that was flapping around his head, thrilled to be flying about and covering him with dust.

Plucking it out of the air with a speed and grace that seemed unlikely in someone who spent so much time in a bookshop, he shook the dust out of his messy light brown hair, making motes of dust swirl and dance around him. He had such a pleasant, playful way about him when no one was looking; she wondered why he didn't let everyone see it. And he was very good with the books, letting them have just enough freedom that they behaved when he needed them to.

He would make a good father, she thought, and then wondered why she had thought it.

He looked so content amongst the flapping pages and towering shelves.

He reached into the crate, freeing a couple of books that had managed to get tangled up in the packing paper. She wondered idly how he had become so underfed – she had noted, with approval, that he was beginning to look healthier as his time with the Barracloughs progressed, but she still a little worried about him. She couldn't stop herself smiling as he stuck out a leg, almost all of his upper body inside the box now, just barely keeping his balance. He was surprisingly agile for such a thin man, and she suspected that under his baggy shirt and trousers, he was quite lithe.

Banishing such unhelpful thoughts from her mind, she checked on a few of the old ladies having a contented witter around the table in the wool room, and popped next door to ask Mahri for some more flowers.

They had a working arrangement where they would swap tea or wool for flowers, each surreptitiously advertising the other's business by having their products around their shop.

Ivy leaned against the smooth, metal counter as Mahri cut and wrapped bundles of zinnias, sunflowers, and acanthus leaves for her.

"You're chewing your lip again," she observed, as she passed her, pulling roses and lilies out of the aluminium buckets behind the desk.

"Am not," said Ivy, absently, continuing to bite and worry her chapped lips.

"Whatever you say," said Mahri, giving her a shrewd look. "It's going to be alright, you know. Sometimes you have to let people in."

"I know."

"And no matter how scary it is now, being on your own forever is a lot worse, believe me."

"Yes," she said, blatantly unconvinced. "I suppose it is."

Mahri gave her a long look as she gathered up the flowers. She sighed, apparently deciding to let her be.

"Do you want agapanthus and carnations, or gerberas?"

"Hmm? Oh, gerberas, please – and agapanthus."

Mahri shook her head at Ivy as she took her bundles of flowers away.

She had known Ivy since she was a baby, having been friends with her mother, great aunts, and grandmother, and felt a sort of proprietorial concern for her, particularly after she had moved into one of the old Coach Houses at the back of The Vineyard.

She had always been quite a bright and happy child: adventurous, confident – even precocious at times. She was always finding her way into scrapes, and out of them again, and had often been defiantly joyful, even in the worst of circumstances. Ivy was like a bright candle in dark times, helping her parents in their shops when they needed her, and begging to learn magic from her grandmother when Griselda had felt sad or lonely. She had always had a talent for it, and the old lady had been happy to encourage her, telling her the stories of the Chambers family through the ages, how they had been the Witches of the Manor, the people that everyone would turn to in times of need.

Ivy had lapped it all up with an extraordinary patience and thirst for knowledge; by the time she was thirteen she was an exceptionally accomplished witch, and could put many of the older students in her Brightwell Academy evening classes to shame.

It was hard to say when the light had gone out for Ivy, but it had begun soon after her thirteenth birthday, when her father had gone down to his carpentry shop one day and had collapsed, pale and shaking on the floor of the Arcade. The doctors couldn't find what was wrong with him, and he had just kept getting sicker. Ivy's mother, Frances, had taken time out of running the shop to tend him, along with her sisters, but nothing had worked. Ivy had snuck out of school early on the day that he had died, somehow knowing that she was needed. They found her holding his hand when they had closed the shops for the evening. She had been there in the gathering darkness for hours, long after he had squeezed her hand for the last time, completely alone.

After the funeral, there were whispers of malignancy amongst the neighbours. Customers stopped coming when he died, though none of them could ever say why, citing a sort of feeling of general discomfort in the premises. Ivy's mother had carried on in the sisters' haberdashery for a while, but she, too, had started to become ill – stress, everyone said.

They buried her beside Matthew in the winter, in the pouring rain; it had been as if the weather was grieving alongside them. At her mother's funeral, Ivy confided in Mahri that she thought her mother had died of a broken heart, and for a while it had looked very much like she might follow them. She had stopped smiling so fully, so openly, as if she feared that if someone noticed, then that happiness might be taken from her. There had been a time when Mahri had worried that her young friend would never be happy again.

And then she had met Sam Burwell.

A bright, cheerful boy, he had joined her school when his family had moved to the area, and for both of them it had been a case of love at first sight. Ivy began to smile again – proper smiles that reached right up to her eyes.

The pair of them had left school as quickly as they could, both equally eager to get away from Brindleford – Sam because it had never really been his home, and Ivy because she longed for a place where no one knew her name, and the expectations that went with it.

Mahri knew that she blamed those high expectations for her parents' deaths, and she loathed the way that the townspeople had turned their backs on them in disgust. Even the great aunts, who had seen their fair share of sickness over years of tending their neighbours, had been unable to persuade her to stay.

Eventually, her grandmother, Griselda – very much the matriarch of the Chambers family – had told them to let her be. She needed to make her own way in life, whatever that way was.

Ivy and Sam had married in the tiny church out at Rouse Abbey, and had moved away, as happy as two young people could possibly be. Ivy had got a job working in an office, and Sam had joined the army, wanting to 'do his bit', as he called it. Settling down in a cosy little house in a leafy suburb of a nearby city, they had led quiet lives, Sam volunteering at the local youth club, while Ivy put everything that she had into their tiny back garden. She had written to her aunts and grandmother often, asking for advice on plants and recipes, and sending photographs of her and Sam's smiling faces.

The letters had increased following Griselda's death, in response to how lonely Ivy felt that they must be. They had visited Sam and Ivy's house a couple of times, on birthdays and festival days, and Mahri had been pleased to see Ivy back to her old self, beaming happily as she tended her flowers and vegetables, covered in soil.

They had been planning to start a family, and Sam had begun to build a tree-house at the wooded end of the garden; he had said that he wanted to start early since he was notoriously bad at finishing things.

And then a couple of politicians had made mistakes in a country that had seemed so very far away, and Sam had gone off, leaving Ivy in the tiny house alone. She had worked hard at her job, and at the small garden in the back, and had waited patiently for him to come home, content to be alone as long as he was doing something that he believed in, something that he was proud of.

She was proud of him.

She had really believed that he was coming home, even on the day when she had opened the door to two very serious men in pristine uniforms and a vicar, and her world had entirely collapsed.

There had been a hostage situation in a school, the men had told her, as the pastor held her hand: the enemy had been threatening to shoot the children and Sam had volunteered to help 'resolve' it. He couldn't have been kept away, and Ivy knew in her heart that if he hadn't volunteered he wouldn't have been her Sam any longer. One of the hostage takers had shot him in the chest as he provided cover for one of his colleagues. The first bullet had killed him instantly, stopping his heart, but the man – just a boy really, half-mad with fear and anger – had just kept on firing.

They had buried Sam in the little church by Rouse Abbey where his mother still lived, and Ivy had gone home to a tiny house that now seemed cavernous. She had sat in their bright little kitchen, compulsively drinking tea and jumping at every small noise, convinced that it was Sam coming home to her. After a few days, she had walked out into the garden in the driving rain, and pulled down the wooden frame of the tree-house that never was, ripping out nails and clawing at the boards with her bare hands.

Afterwards, defeated and lost, with long splinters of wood lodged into her hands and arms, she had walked back into the house that was no longer her home, and set about dismantling it. She had had to stop, eventually, to treat her broken hands, but as soon as she could she had stoically packed their belongings – separating out everything that she thought Sam's mother might like.

The removals van was ordered even before she spoke to the estate agents, and arrived just as she was carefully digging up and packaging up the plants in her beloved garden.

Great aunt Ruth and great aunt Marion had made room for her in the Arcade, glad to be able to help her, and secretly glad that they had her back at home at last. For weeks, Mahri and her aunts had been unable to coax Ivy out of her room; it was as if she had simply given up on life. Mahri, who had lost her own husband years before, and understood the inability to conceive of a life without him, left her to it, knowing that she would come to them when she needed to. The aunts had begun to give up hope for her, until one morning they had come out to the kitchen for breakfast and there she had been, dressed, sitting at the table, drinking tea.

That morning Ivy asked for the keys to the haberdashery shop, empty through lack of business, and because the aunts were by now quite elderly. They gave them to her without complaint, feeling that it was her right to do with the place as she wished. She put everything she had into the shop, selling up the old haberdashery stock and putting up shelves of tea and small, homely tables in their place. Soon, the tea shop was a vibrant, bustling place, and she had saved up enough to open the wool shop, as a kind of afterthought, in the neighbouring bay. She didn't talk about Sam much, but Mahri knew that he was always in her thoughts, and that it was a horror of disappointing him that had eventually made her get out of bed. Although she smiled sometimes, her smiles were smaller, wearier, and they never seemed to reach her eyes.

Ivy seemed to have decided that she had had her quotient of happiness, and the best she could hope for was simply an absence of sadness. It broke Mahri's heart to see her like this, and she wanted nothing more than to see her smile – really smile – just one more time; to see the light put back in her eyes. These days, she had a habit of shutting people out so that they couldn't be lost

– she seemed to feel safest that way. Her open friendliness was still there, she couldn't have lost that in its entirety, but it was delicate now, fragile.

It had worried her aunts, who had charged Mahri, on their death-beds, with keeping an eye on her, and helping her to live again. So Mahri had stayed, content as she was with her home and business, and determined to see Ivy's face light up once more, however long it took.

8
Time for Tea

It had been a month since the move and the books were finally beginning to settle down after all the excitement, although Christopher did occasionally find the odd one or two playing an apparent game of musical chairs across the shelves, clearly of the opinion that they knew where they ought to be better than he did.

The Barracloughs had decided to spend less time in the shop, dropping by once a day to check on things and keep Zarrubabel company. He was rapidly regaining his usual, vibrant personality. Christopher was mostly left to his own devices, keeping the shop ticking over and working through the enormous stack of new acquisitions – the result of having more space and a juicy Council payout. He rather felt that the Professor had been a little over-enthusiastic when ordering the new books, but since he was fascinated by the majority of them and perfectly placed to read them in the quieter parts of the day, he didn't particularly mind the extra work.

Many of the regular customers had been delighted with the new premises, which allowed room for a couple more desks, and three squashy chairs that Joanna had received from a friend who was intending to throw them away. They had also been impressed by Ivy's teashop, and Christopher had seen more than one of them take their books in and start reading them immediately, over a hot drink and morsel of cake. One or two had visited Mahri's shop, too, leaving with enormous sprays of flowers. It was quite nice to know that their presence was having a positive effect on the already established businesses in the Arcade.

A few of the more curious mundane customers had wandered into the bookshop, had a look around and delightedly discovered a book that they had apparently been after for years; Christopher suspected that the books, happy in their new home, were trying just a little too hard to impress the new clientele.

Despite their new proximity, Mistress Burwell had not deviated from her Monday routine, closing the teashop at around two o'clock, and walking the short distance across the corridor.

Since her scent was now more or less omnipresent, it was beginning to bother him significantly less during the week, the exception being immediately after she left the shop on a Monday afternoon, when a large part of him wanted to follow her back through her shop and up the spiral staircase on that side of the building.

Infuriating as that was, he was glad that she was still coming to the shop; he liked being around her, as they were both quiet, and enjoyed working with someone else around. Sometimes she would read a passage out to him, or show him an illustration that she found particularly pleasing, and he would smile, and nod, and suggest a related book, or recall an anecdote from his extensive reading.

Professor Zarrubabel had been reasonably well behaved so far, possibly because he was so embarrassed at endangering Ivy during his tantrum, particularly as he still regarded her as a little girl – though he knew that she was an accomplished witch. A fact that he seemed determined to impress upon Christopher. Joanna had re-introduced them on the morning after they had moved in. The spectral Professor had been polite to a fault, complimenting her on her skills and successful business.

He often brought these up on Monday evenings as Christopher tidied the shop, making pointed comments about his background, or skills, or condition.

Christopher largely ignored him, though he knew that a lot of what the disagreeable old ghost insinuated was true. He didn't have a chance with Mistress Burwell – but that was okay, and it certainly wouldn't stop him from being her friend.

On the Friday after the move, he had ventured across to her tea shop at lunchtime, and taken up residence at a table in the corner. He had taken his book with him, and had spent a pleasant hour reading, sipping Ivy's delicious tea, and eating sandwiches. There were very few customers around on Friday afternoons – even more so now that a lot of the children were back in school after the long summer break – and Ivy had joined him for *her* lunch break, with *her* book, and that had been particularly pleasant.

This had quickly become a part of the weekly routine, and one which Christopher very much looked forward to. The Barracloughs, who were occasionally around on Friday afternoons – Joanna and Mahri would go out to a painting class at one of the town's churches on Friday evenings – were very carefully Not Mentioning It.

On this particular Friday, Christopher had spent the morning with the Widow Jenkins, going through some of the new acquisitions for references to necromancy. Although she was nice enough, he was mildly concerned about her proclivity for the undead. He wondered, briefly, whether he was feeding a dangerous obsession, but Professor Barraclough and Joanna both trusted her, and Zarrubabel had reasonably inoffensive things to say about her, so he put his concerns to the back of his mind.

Mistress Jenkins was greatly impressed by Mahri and her flowers, and by Ivy and her teashop – particularly when she discovered Ivy's over-the-counter 'herbal' concoctions. He didn't blame her. Somehow, Ivy had access to some of the rarest spell ingredients he had ever seen, and had developed a quiet reputation for excellently brewed potions and ready-made spell kits. Already, one of these had eased the pain of his transformation and he was intending to go back for more – just as soon as he could work out how to prevent her from wondering why he needed it.

Patiently, he waited for the final impromptu customer to wander back out of the shop before locking up, idly watching Widow Jenkins scurry out of the Arcade, clutching a shopping basket full of clinking potion vials.

A chattering family came out of the teashop as he put

up the 'Out for Lunch' sign and locked the door; he watched them go, a little sadly. The little boy seemed to be a bit of an escape artist, and his father scooped him up, squealing with delight, and put him on his shoulders. His little sister was skipping alongside her mother, singing her own little song to herself. To Christopher, it looked idyllic.

He smiled after them, but it was bittersweet: he remembered being part of a family like that, and he missed them like a constant ache at the back of his mind. Quietly, he packed the ache away inside himself, turning back towards the teashop and pushing the door open.

The shop was emptier than usual, and the young family appeared to have been the only people left before the Friday afternoon lull. Ivy was bent over her most popular jars of tea, which she kept on the counter behind the till. Not wanting to disturb her, he closed the door softly behind him, and waited patiently for a few moments, absently scanning the sandwich menu and wondering whether he might have a cake this afternoon.

After a couple of minutes, he glanced up at Ivy, who was still refilling the large glass jars of tea with her special mixed blends; Christopher frowned: she was working more slowly than usual, much more slowly. He watched as she pushed the lid back on to one of the jars, and stowed the larger storage barrel back under the counter; he couldn't be sure, but she seemed to be shaking slightly.

"Ivy?" he said, quietly, suddenly concerned.

She half-turned towards him, startled. He could see that she had been crying.

"Oh, I'm sorry!" she choked, furiously wiping at her face with her hand.

"Are you alright?"

"Yes – I'm fine – I'm sorry!" she said, between sniffs and sobs. "Were you waiting long?"

Christopher stared at her for a moment: she was struggling to control her tears.

"No," he said, slowly, fighting the overwhelming urge

to leap over the counter and wrap his arms around her. "Are you sure? I –"

"I'm fine, really," she assured him. He didn't believe it for a second, and the way she looked at him suggested that this had registered on his face. "Really," she said, more firmly. "What can I get you?"

Taken aback at her pragmatism, Christopher floundered. "I – er – I'm not –" he cleared his throat. "Surprise me."

She nodded, and shook her head, as if to clear it.

"I'm going to go and wash my face – could you help yourself to sandwiches today?"

"Sure..."

He walked slowly around the counter, listening to the sounds of Ivy hurrying up the spiral staircase in the back room; a few of the stairs creaked, and he heard her footsteps retreating across the floor above him.

Frustrated at his inability to help his friend feel better, Christopher rubbed a hand across his face and through his hair. Listening for movement from above, he made up two plates of sandwiches and two slices of cake. Whatever else was going on, Ivy clearly needed a break.

He set them down at the table that he was beginning to think of as his, and sat down to wait.

ooo

Ivy swore at herself in her bathroom mirror.

"You stupid, stupid girl," she hissed at herself. "Pull yourself together!"

Angrily, she washed away the tears still falling from her red-rimmed eyes and attempted to dry her face. She met her own eyes in the mirror.

There had just been something so *homely* about the family that had eaten in the teashop. There had been something about the young father's eyes when he smiled that had reminded her so strongly of Sam.

But she couldn't think about them now, not with a customer in the shop – even if it was only Christopher, who could be trusted on his own. It was rude of her to rush off like this, and she shouldn't keep him waiting.

Taking a deep breath to compose herself, she strode back across her rooms and down the spiral staircase, hoping that no one else had come in during her absence.

She risked a glance around the door, and the shop seemed empty enough. Christopher was sitting at his usual table by the window, gazing out of it as if he were watching something that only he could see. He had put out some food for her too, she noted, and was seized by a sudden wave of gratitude. Really, it was very good of him not to be offended by her sudden need to flee – it was strange how such small things still had the power to make such an emotional impact.

Quickly, she filled a pot with boiling water from the Perpetual Kettle in the back room, and took it out to her friend.

ooo

The feeling that all was not right had begun to creep over Christopher as he waited for Ivy to return. At first, he couldn't put his finger on it: everything seemed the same as it always had, the odd person walking to and from the flower shop.

But now their heads were bowed down, as if something about the Arcade was uncomfortable, oppressive, even. Their footsteps were hurried, as though they couldn't wait to get outside into the air and the light. Which was odd, because it was still brilliantly sunny outside, despite it being late September – the great chink of light from the light well was still illuminating the corridor, making the russet tiles sparkle just as brightly as they always did.

Except that they weren't quite as bright as he remembered: the light seemed duller, somehow, as if the sun had gone behind a cloud. But it couldn't have, since the light outside the Arcade was just as intense as ever.

He looked around, skin prickling with unease: it

wasn't just the light. Everything seemed duller somehow, from the shine of the tiles and the glass to the tones of the wooden table at which he was sitting. Even the pale mint paint in the teashop that was usually so warm and welcoming seemed to have faded, as if the colour had leached out of it.

He glanced at the flowers in the vases along the window – they seemed just as bright and vibrant as ever, though a couple of the blooms had faded over the week and needed to be changed.

"What on Earth?" he said to himself, softly.

He looked up as Ivy came out of the back office. He had been so engrossed by the sudden, strange atmosphere of weariness in the Arcade that he hadn't heard her come back down the stairs.

For a moment, he was worried that whatever was affecting the building was taking its toll on her, too: she looked so pale and washed out. But then she smiled, weakly, and things seemed to brighten slightly.

"Feeling better?" he asked, as she set the pot of boiling water down on the table. Ivy gave him a strange sort of half-shrug, and glanced at the plate of sandwiches that he had put out for her. "I thought you might like to join me," he explained, a little self-consciously. "If you want – I... I thought you might need a break."

"I think I do, thank you," she said, and gave him another fragile smile. "You said to surprise you with the tea – is there anything that you really don't like?" she continued, suddenly business-like.

Christopher smiled, glad to see some of the old Ivy back.

"I don't know, I've never tried anything other than English Breakfast tea," he admitted.

Ivy raised an eyebrow.

"Then you have come to the right place," she said, and retreated to the great jars of tea.

To his surprise, she closed her eyes, running her hand over the glass lids, as if waiting for something. She paused over the lid of the furthest jar and opened her eyes; she smiled, reaching behind the jar for a small scoop. With a practised hand, she scooped two small measures into one of her extraordinary teapots (they were all different shapes, sizes and colours – no two were the same) and loaded it onto a tray. Christopher caught a whiff of an odd, but pleasantly fruity fragrance as she collected a couple of teacups and carried them all over.

"Earl Grey," she said, adding hot water to a violently orange tea pot; this one had large, brightly coloured hearts on, and generally came out for families with small children. "It has a bit of a citrus-y kick to it," she told him. "Which is the flavour of the bergamot oil. You can have it with milk or lemon, but I prefer it plain."

"Then plain it is," he said, and was rewarded with a small smile.

"Good," she said firmly. "If you put milk in it, it tastes very strange – almost like liquid lemon cake – and while I accept that everyone has different tastes, doing *that* to a perfectly good cup of tea is akin to sacrilege."

Christopher chuckled.

"Remind me not to get on your bad side," he said, with enough of a smile to let her know that he was joking.

They ate in companionable silence for a few minutes, each busy with their own thoughts, waiting for the tea to steep.

Sandwiches devoured, Ivy poured a steaming cup of amber liquid for each of them, smiling as she inhaled the exotic steam.

Christopher followed her example somewhat warily. He remembered that his mother had enjoyed fruit teas, and he had always hated both the smell and the taste.

This tea, though, smelled sufficiently bitter and tealike. There was the bright, lemony note that Ivy had warned him about, and a peculiar, metallic tang, but it was definitely tea.

Eyes closed, he took an experimental sip. It tasted largely like it smelled: agreeably flavoursome and calming. He took a longer drink, feeling his muscles begin to relax.

"What do you think?" Ivy asked, curious.

"It's odd, but not unpleasant," he said, opening his eyes and searching for an appropriate description. "Like giving your brain a hot bath."

Ivy laughed then, properly, like she had stopped holding back.

"I've never heard it described like that," she said, amused. "But I do know what you mean – it's curiously refreshing."

"Yes," he said. They smiled at one another for a moment, happy in their agreement. Christopher pulled his piece of Victoria Sponge towards him and applied himself to it, eating it carefully, so as not to lose any crumbs. It was a habit born of years of not being able to afford decent food very often; Ivy was picking at her own cake, watching him contemplatively, smile fading.

"What?" he asked, pausing briefly, suddenly very aware of her eyes on him.

She shook her head slightly. "Nothing," she said quietly, staring at her barely touched slice of cake.

Christopher frowned, his concern for her intensifying once more. Ivy looked back up at him, as if she was about to say something, but stopped herself, retuning her gaze to her plate.

He was about to ask her what was wrong when she cleared her throat.

"About earlier," she said, staring at her hands. "I'm sorry about that – I... I was just... thinking," she finished, lamely.

"You've nothing to apologise for," he said, longing to reach over and pull her into his arms. "Everyone is entitled to a bad moment or two."

"Thanks," she said, softly, giving him an embarrassed, sideways glance. "But I shouldn't have gone to pieces like that. I just –"

She paused, startled: Christopher had reached out and placed his large hand over hers. It was warm, and for reasons that Ivy could not explain, it steadied her.

"It's okay," he said, trying to put everything that was comforting into his voice and the light pressure of his fingers. Mildly concerned that she would take the contact as an affront – and aware that the longer he maintained it the less he wanted to let go – he was about to pull away, but Ivy turned her hand palm upwards and squeezed his fingers in thanks.

"I was remembering my husband," she said, her piercing blue eyes on his. "I imagine that you've heard people describe me as 'Widow Burwell'."

"Not often," he admitted. "Most of them just call you 'Mistress'."

She nodded, thoughtfully.

"It's polite," she said, and then added, quietly: "I used to be 'Goody Burwell' instead, when Sam was alive."

"'Goody'?" Christopher asked, perplexed.

"As in Good-wife," Ivy explained. "It's almost as if you aren't any good anymore – as if all your usefulness has been used up. As if your relationship to your husband defines everything you are. On top of everything else you're dealing with, it's really quite distressing when your title changes."

"I can imagine," said Christopher, softly. Ivy was still holding his hand, lightly, reluctant to let go. With her other hand she was drawing invisible patterns on the table-top. "What was he like?" he asked her, and she looked at him oddly.

"I can't remember the last time anyone bothered to ask me that," she said, a little tensely. "Even Mahri won't talk about him anymore. It's like everyone wants me to forget him."

"I don't," said Christopher, giving her hand a light squeeze; Ivy leaned towards him, suddenly intense with candour, and relief, and something else that he couldn't quite describe.

"He was wonderful," she said, whispering. It was as if she were afraid that if she spoke too loud, she might be heard and be forbidden from mentioning him. "Kind, loving, good-natured... he had a way of making people smile – no one could help it around him, he had this sort of infectious happiness about him – and when *he* smiled, it was as if he was laughing along with you," she gave a strange little hiccup, and Christopher realised that she was holding back tears. "He made me so happy," she said, and put her other hand over her mouth, trying to hold back the emotion that was beginning to shatter her still-fragile demeanour. "I loved him so much," she said softly, voice cracking. "I really miss – I mean, there are so many things, but the thing I miss most is his face. It sounds so silly, but it was just so open and friendly."

She turned away, crying openly now; Christopher threw caution to the wind and pulled her into an awkward sideways hug, rubbing her back gently.

A strange shudder passed through her body, but she accepted the gesture readily, finally giving in to her grief and allowing herself to weep uncontrollably. He felt each sob as it wracked through her body, and wondered how on Earth she had managed to keep all of this bottled up inside her for so long.

Gradually, the sobbing diminished, and she rested her head against his chest.

"I'm sorry," she said, into his shirt.

"Shh," he instructed, and she gave a wet and muffled little giggle.

"Thanks," she said, pulling away from him, and running her hands across her tear-streaked face.

Christopher gave a shy little half-shrug. He was missing the contact intensely, and hoping fervently that the blush that was hovering just below his neck-line would stay firmly where it was.

"I must look a right state," she said, embarrassed.

"Yes," Christopher responded, with a small smile, and she laughed a little.

"You're an older brother, aren't you?" she said, giving him a mock-glare that didn't fool him for a moment.

"Guilty as charged," he said, holding his hands up, and she laughed more convincingly. "Why don't you give your face a wash, and I'll make up another pot of tea?" he suggested, and Ivy gratefully agreed.

By the time she had come back down the creaky spiral staircase, Christopher had figured out how to get the dishes to wash themselves, and was investigating the tea jars behind the counter.

"Getting a taste for unusual teas?" she asked, and he grinned, sheepishly, looking a bit like a child caught with his hand in the biscuit jar.

"Yes," he said, happy to see her smile widen, even if it was at his expense.

They sat back down at the table, feeling curiously shy around one another, after their earlier candour.

"Would it be okay," Ivy began, tucking an escapee strand of hair behind her ear, "if I told you more about Sam? It's such a relief to be able to talk about him."

"Of course," said Christopher, and her resulting smile was worth every ounce of embarrassment.

So she told him about their perfect little house, and Sam's volunteering, and the garden; about the office where she had worked, and watching Sam play football on the weekends; about the visit, and the tree-house, and the rain. Then she asked about Christopher's family, and he told her about the endless, marvellous puzzling, and the things his mum liked to cook, and the way he and Rachel loved to run around in the rain. Ivy guessed that he didn't see them very much anymore, but she didn't press him for details, and he was glad; they had already had more than enough unbridled emotion for the one afternoon. Instead, he told her about his father's books, and the way his study had always smelled slightly of toffee, because he had a bag of them locked in his top drawer, and about how much he enjoyed history, and the places that they had all visited together in the summer.

By the time their lunch break had ended, and Mahri had come in for a cup of tea, they were chatting like old friends, smiling and laughing with one another in the corner. For a few moments she openly stared at them, and Ivy's countenance began to close off, slightly.

Christopher picked up his unopened book and bent to

whisper in her ear.

"I don't think it's that she wants you to forget him, I think it's that she wants you to be happy again," he murmured, and Ivy pressed his hand, lightly, to show that she had understood.

ooo

The following Tuesday, Quentin Post, who had been away in Egypt, apparently to celebrate the full recovery of his leg, returned. He was astonished that the bookshop had been forced to move, and willing to speak to the Mayor – who was an old friend – on their behalf.

Reassured of their happiness in their new location and seeing that all was well, he set about telling all three of them about his trip. He talked excitedly, almost like a small child in his enthusiasm. He showed them photographs of the tourist areas, and told them stories about travelling through the desert with a group of Bedouin whom he had befriended.

It sounded wonderful, learning how to survive in such an extreme environment, sleeping under the stars. Christopher would have given anything just to have been able to visit even *one* of the sites on the Nile, and Post had been to them all.

He had brought things back with him, too, and in a curiously magnanimous gesture, presented Professor Barraclough with a book of tomb maps and Joanna with a beautiful Scarab pendant necklace. He had even bought a book for Christopher: it was a wonderful thing, made to reflect the colours of the most elaborate tombs, all gold and lapis lazuli. It was largely a compendium of Egyptian myths, with a section on the most up to date translation crib for hieroglyphs.

It was a very kind gift, but Christopher felt a pang of discomfort in accepting such a lavish present.

After the Barracloughs had left, he and Post spent a busy afternoon taking advantage of the new catalogue. He had had a brainwave in Egypt, spending so much time in the tombs and temples, and had decided to base a couple of chapters on dark magic in religious architecture. He had decided to concentrate on two periods: high medieval, and the seventeenth century, since he viewed those eras as the most eventful in terms of church construction and nefarious wizardry.

They were clearing away after an enjoyable few hours of research, putting their chairs away and stretching their aching backs, when a particularly loud man on a mobile phone left Mahri's flower shop and hurried past. As they looked up, so did Ivy, and she rolled her eyes at Christopher, who smiled.

"Wow," said Post staring through the panes of glass at Ivy. She noticed his gaze and blushed, turning away to clear a table. Christopher's eyes narrowed as he looked up at Post. He was watching her as she bent over to clear the tables, raking his eyes over her body appreciatively. Not that Christopher had any problem appreciating Ivy's body, but he definitely had a problem with someone else doing it – even if it was someone as affable as Quentin Post.

"Who is *that*?" Post asked, far too enthusiastically for Christopher's liking.

"That's Ivy," he said, coldly, but Post seemed to entirely miss his dangerous tone. "Mistress Burwell."

"Ivy, eh?" said Quentin, thoughtfully. "I think we've done enough for the day, don't you, Christopher?" he asked, not even looking at him. He gathered up his books, abandoning the pile that he was intending to take out, and flashed a blinding grin in Christopher's direction.

"You'll book those out for me, won't you? There's a good chap. This won't take long."

He rushed out of the shop and towards Mahri's shop; Christopher watched him go, dismayed. He came out a few seconds later, carrying a single red rose. He made a beeline for Ivy and Christopher glared at him across the corridor, gathering up Post's books and stamping across the room to the counter, aware that he was jealous and equally aware that he had absolutely no right to be. He processed the books quickly, stamping them with perhaps a little more force than usual, his eyes never leaving the two people conversing in the teashop.

A shiver of concern passed through the books on the shelves, metaphorically wincing with each abuse of their comrades' pages.

He looked around as a particularly violent shudder knocked a couple of books to the floor.

Christopher sighed, suddenly aware of his uncharacteristic violence.

"I'm sorry," he said, softly, picking up the fallen volumes and returning them to their places. Returning to the pile of nervous and abused books on the desk, he ran his hands down their spines, murmuring apologies and words of comfort to them. Gradually, they began to calm down, though forgiveness would take a while longer. One of the books, though, was entirely still and unresponsive. A little worriedly, Christopher checked it over, mildly concerned that he may have made it do the textual equivalent of fainting.

He needn't have worried, however: this book wasn't one of his.

It was a slim volume, clearly mundane, and looked as though it belonged in a private collection; it had no title. Curious, he ran his fingertip along the page edges, longing to open it up and see what was inside – but that would be akin to snooping, and very impolite.

He glanced up at the teashop, where Post was invading Ivy's personal space, exuding charm all over the place with his ornate, silver handled cane and fresh cut rose.

A vicious sound made Christopher jump and volumes all around the room flap madly on their shelves. He looked around him in alarm: something – a very large and angry sounding something – had growled; it took him nearly a full minute to realise that the noise had come from him.

Horrified at himself – and feeling fully justified – he

turned his attention back to Quentin Post's book.

The frontispiece identified it as a history of dangerous artefacts. Filled with curiosity, he flicked through the pages, taking in the beautifully inked pages of gruesome illustrations. He noted with some amusement that *The Devil's Mirror*, the compendium that had nearly caught him out, had been awarded pride of place near the front of the book, on a page covered with the direst of warnings.

He paused at one page, a graphic depiction of a miniature decorative birdcage that ate everyone that touched it, leaving them confined inside the tiny wires, various body parts oozing out between them.

Profoundly grateful that this particular artefact had been destroyed over fifty years ago, he turned to a page that Post had marked with a scrap of extremely expensive writing paper. His scent was all over the page, as if he turned to it often: all expensive aftershave and brushed silk.

He ran his finger over the illustration: a golden, ornately decorative medieval goblet. There were precious gems fixed around the rim of the cup: predominantly rubies but with the odd darker stone that Christopher didn't recognise; the artist had managed to give the impression of skulls hidden amongst the lines on body of the goblet. It was altogether a quite unsettling piece, and Christopher lingered over the description, fascinated.

'The Chalice of Knowledge' it said at the top of the page, in glorious indigo ink. There was a scant history of places where the *Chalice* had been, places which had generally been burned down quite shortly after it had arrived. There were a lot of gaps in the brief timeline, and the artefact appeared to have vanished from historical notice on several occasions, most recently in the mid-seventeenth century.

It was purported to provide anyone who drank from it with the knowledge of the ages, making it incredibly powerful and incredibly dangerous; it seemed to cause chaos and disruption everywhere it went. It also apparently sucked out the soul of anyone that drank from it whom it didn't consider 'worthy'. It seemed that rather a lot of people had been unworthy over the years.

Christopher closed the book, putting it gingerly on top of the pile he had booked out as if it was something distasteful.

He glanced over at the teashop. Post appeared to be leaning in close to Ivy now, smiling an altogether different smile than Christopher usually saw. He watched him present her with the rose, which she took – perhaps a little hesitantly. Christopher frowned: he couldn't see her expression.

Really, he should leave them to it.

He was picking up the books and heading into the teashop before he knew it himself, interrupting Post mid-flow.

"Perhaps you would join me –" he was saying, having taken one of her hands.

"I've booked them out for you, Master Post, but it's closing time now – I need to lock up the shop, so I brought them over," he said, smiling with helpful innocence. "You left one of your own, too, I put it right there on the top."

Just for a moment, he thought he glimpsed annoyance on Post's face, but it was quickly hidden.

"Ah, yes, thank you Christopher," he said, with effortless charm. "I'd best be getting on, too – let you close up, Ivy, dear." When he said it he turned to her and gave her his very best smile.

Ivy nodded, and he pressed his lips to her knuckles, gallantly.

"Christopher," he nodded, friendly as ever, and swept away, books tucked under his arm. Christopher however, could smell his frustration, and felt cheerfully superior for about thirty seconds, before remembering who he was with.

To his surprise, Ivy looked intensely relieved, though she was still blushing.

"Thank you," she said, fervently. "He was very nice,

but he just wouldn't take the hint. It's been a long time since anyone flirted with me so openly – and it was very flattering, he seems quite lovely, but... well, it made my teeth hurt a little bit, to tell you the truth."

Christopher gave her a genuinely happy smile as she put the rose in one of the vases in the window.

"Pleased to be of service," he said, and gave her a small bow.

She blew the air out of her cheeks and smiled back.

"It made quite a nice change to get a bit of attention though, particularly from someone so handsome," she said, almost ruefully, a faraway look on her face; Christopher clenched his fist by his side. "When everyone knows you as the grieving widow, most people avoid even looking up at you, let alone flirting. There's only really you and Mahri that speak to me as if I'm not some fragile, broken thing. I should thank you for that, too, by the way."

"You're welcome," he said, relaxing slightly. "And if you want any more unwelcome suitors chasing off -"

"I'll know where to come," she finished for him. "I suppose you had a lot of experience playing the protective older brother?"

He nodded. "None of them will ever be good enough for Rachel, as far as I'm concerned," he admitted. "But if she's happy, then I'll be happy."

Ivy smiled at him, and gave him a pat on the shoulder.

"My knight in shining armour!" she said, and he beamed. "Even if I have only borrowed you from your sister."

9
Storm Warning

Christopher ran through the driving rain, dodging people huddled under their umbrellas and splashing through puddles. It was mid-October, and the weather – which had hitherto been doing a very good impression of the middle of summer – had changed character overnight. Thursday evening had been cold and misty, which had been a bit of a shock to the system, given that people were still walking about the town in shorts, summer dresses, and flip-flops, and at some point during the early hours of Friday morning, it had begun to rain.

It must have been quite gentle at first, since the river outside Christopher's flat wasn't particularly high when he had woken up, but by the time he set off for work it was driving down hard, and the river was muddy and angry-looking. He decided to keep an eye on it as he hurried out of the main door, passing his grey-haired neighbour, who was returning from a short walk; his dog, a heavily pregnant Labrador, had not looked impressed at this turn of events.

By the time he reached the Arcade he was soaked to the skin and seriously considering spending some of his meagre savings on a waterproof coat. Mahri had given him a sympathetic look as she put out her buckets of flowers, clearly glad that her walk to work was short and predominantly indoors.

"Raining cats and dogs out there?" she asked, wiping her hands on her apron.

"More like bedposts," Christopher said, and shook some of the water out of his hair. "You can barely see four feet in front of you!"

"I imagine that the shops will be quiet today, then," she observed, thoughtfully. "I might pop over in a bit, get something to read."

Christopher managed a damp smile and unlocked the shop, not even bothering to put the ornate wooden sign outside the door. He headed straight for the back office, where he lit the range with a click of his fingers. The noise of ignition woke Professor Zarrubabel, who stuck his ghastly head out of his book to peer around.

"Oh it's you," he said, in the tone of someone who might have been hoping that Christopher had died since the last time he had seen him. He fumbled with his ghostly pince-nez, and climbed a little further out of the book, presumably in order to insult Christopher properly. However, once he saw him, dripping wet and completely dishevelled, he burst out into gales of cackling laughter, which echoed slightly, as if it was coming from a long way off.

Christopher gave him a withering look and put the kettle on. He muttered a brief warming spell. Usually, he would dry off and warm up the mundane way, but he was just a bit too wet today, and he didn't want to damage any of the books, so he could justify what he generally regarded as a frivolous use of energy. Using large amounts of magic is fine when you have a decent amount of fuel (i.e. food) to replace it. Ivy's teashop had smelled promisingly of scones as he walked past, and this would provide him with the excuse for a cream tea at lunch-time – something that he hadn't had since before he went to university.

Leaving the giggling spectre to his own devices, Christopher took his tea and the ledgers into the shop proper and shut the door on him. He carried the two wooden signs outside, leaving one by the door of the shop and taking the other to the entrance of the Arcade. Since the weather didn't seem to have improved, he set it up just on the inside of entrance. He listened to the rain pounding against the great glass windows for a moment, collecting and pooling on the pavement before rushing along down the street like a kind of impromptu urban stream.

Sighing at the knowledge that he would eventually have to walk home in it, Christopher turned and walked back to the shop, giving Ivy a wave as he passed the teashop.

It was the first time that the illumination from the great light-well at the front of the shop was dull enough to need alternative lights outside the back office, and it took Christopher a couple of minutes to find the light-switch, hidden – in his opinion – on entirely the wrong side of the wooden door frame. He was impressed by the lamps when they came on, and suspected that they were, at least in part, magical.

They looked like a combination of nineteenth century oil lamps and Light Orbs, giving them a homely and elegant feel; they gave the same clarity and glow as a Light Orb, too, and filled the bookshop with warm light. Immediately feeling better about the weather that he could still hear howling around the Arcade, Christopher set to work.

Mahri came in before long, and since she could see anyone going into her shop passing by the window, had a good, long peruse.

She seemed to be particularly interested in cooking and crafts, and Christopher imagined that there wasn't ever a great deal of time when Mahri's hands weren't occupied with something or other.

"Joanna not coming in today?" she asked, dropping a small stack of books on the counter.

"No – Professor Barraclough rang and said they were both staying in today," he said. "Borrowing or buying?"

"Borrowing for now," she gave a wry smile. "Very sensible of them – if only you could have done the same, eh?"

Christopher returned her smile.

"I don't mind too much," he admitted. "I like it much better here than sitting alone in my flat all day – and I get to read anything I want."

"It's a good way of looking at it," she said, gathering her books. "If you get too bored, though, and there's no one about, pop over for a chat."

"Will do," said Christopher, amused. Clearly, Mahri did not enjoy days when her shop was empty.

There were only a couple of bedraggled customers in all day, all uniformly cold and damp, and none of them stayed for long, even Mistress Jenkins, who stalked amongst them, smug and completely dry. She soon departed, however, having visited all three shops, as she needed to call at another arcane shop on the other side of Brindleford and was worried that he might close early because of the weather.

"It would be just like Ernie to let his customers down like that," she said, performing a strange balancing act with her bunch of flowers and bag of tea as she picked up her texts. "The shop's not a patch on the way it was when his father ran it, but there's nowhere else in Brindleford that does decent newt's eyes these days."

He watched her depart into the rain, a bubble of dry space around her and her shopping and shook his head. Really, it was astonishing what the average mundane person could ignore simply because it didn't fit in with their own personal set of universal rules.

Ivy greeted him warmly and waved him over to the table, where she had already put out their lunches. After their first candid conversation in September, they found that they had rather talked themselves out, and had agreed to spend their lunch-break working through a particularly tricky book of puzzles that Christopher had found living feral under one of the bookcases during the move. He was slowly beginning to tame the volume, and found that the more he copied out for their weekly puzzling sessions, the more social the book was becoming. Soon, he hoped, it could be rehabilitated with some of the tougher volumes in the collection, and eventually sold or loaned out. For the moment, however, it lived quite comfortably in the drawer in the counter, and ate elastic bands.

They settled down companionably and pulled out their notebooks and pencils, working through the first set of problems while nibbling, absently, at their lunch.

"You know," said Ivy, chewing the end of her pencil,

"you're the first person in the shop today that hasn't commented on the weather."

"What's there to say?" Christopher asked, frowning as he got to grips with a particularly gnarly code puzzle. "It's bloody awful out there."

Ivy chuckled.

"I think people feel the need to explain why they're walking into somewhere wet through," she said, contemplatively. "Which is really silly, because you can actually see the rain through the windows in the wool shop."

Christopher, who had had a gander outside before coming in for lunch, nodded.

"People are strange creatures," he said, and entirely missed Ivy smiling at him. She watched him work for a couple of moments, a frown of deep concentration on his face, before getting back to her own puzzle.

ooo

As the weather maintained its assault on the area, very few people arrived during the afternoon, most preferring – quite sensibly – to get home as quickly as possible and to stay there indefinitely.

Mahri had shut up shop early, deciding to curl up with the books she had borrowed, leaving Ivy to her own devices in the empty teashop. Eventually, she had given in and started knitting a child's jumper, intending to put it in the inspiration display by the window in the wool room. It kept her occupied for a few hours. She wove in her ends contemplatively, pretending to herself that she hadn't been watching Christopher as he worked.

She had found herself strangely drawn to her curious friend, and was putting it down to having had so few people to talk to for so long. She closed up the shop, singing lightly to herself, but paused before heading upstairs.

The lights in the bookshop were still on, and Christopher was hard at work with a couple of ledgers open in front of him. Deciding that it must be the monthly inventory – which in a bookshop where the texts had a tendency to breed was a regular and necessary task – she continued upstairs.

The spiral staircase on this side of the building led to Ivy's living quarters. Despite having been designed in the mid-nineteenth century, the main room was large, spacious and airy, with more large glass panels lining one side of it, making the expansive garden beyond look like an extension of the room. The ancestor who had built the Arcade had had a great love of space, bucking the Victorian trend for cramped, dark rooms. The main room ran the whole width of the Arcade, with a second wrought iron spiral staircase winding down to the back office of the bookshop on the far side.

Ivy's parents had had the tiled floor replaced with wood, giving the place a light and warm feel; Ivy herself had repainted the walls a warm cream, covering up the much loved but slightly overbearing orange and brown shell pattern that her parents had chosen. The layout hadn't changed for as long as Ivy could remember, but various generations of the Chambers family had had an impact on the furniture in the house, meaning that for the most part, no two adjacent items matched. The far wall was taken up by a ramshackle, open-plan library, which melded almost seamlessly into a spell preparation area. The centre of the room had several large sofas and armchairs in various stages of dilapidation, along with a large television – one of the few mundane things that Ivy's magically conservative aunts had allowed in the house.

While they had been firmly of the opinion that magical means of entertainment were far superior, when Ivy had brought it back with her from her and Sam's house she had often caught them sitting in front of the screen in the small hours of the morning, engrossed in re-runs of old television programmes.

There was a herbarium of sorts next, with a hefty oak table and several cupboards and shelves full of jars and boxes. A dining table that got very little use these days was off to one side, by the glass wall to the gardens, with a variety of chairs around it. The area around Ivy's spiral staircase was her kitchen, which also didn't see much use: she tended to cook large batches of food at once, since there was only the one of her, and freeze single portions of it. On the nights when she hadn't been kidnapped by Mahri to try out a new recipe or three, she tended to just eat the leftover sandwiches from the shop, or toast.

To Ivy, there was something inherently calming about making toast. She wasn't sure why, but it made her feel safe and at home, and had been one of the things that had helped to get her through the long, empty nights after Sam had died.

She put the television on as she buttered her toast, and curled up in her favourite armchair with a mug of tea, her back to the chaotic weather outside. Toast finished, she flicked around the channels for a while, getting steadily sleepier until her head was nodding against her chest.

She awoke in the dark, having neglected to turn the lights on, with what sounded like all the demons of hell pounding on the glass behind her. Something brushed against her shoulder and she patted it, absently.

"I'm alright," she murmured, and the something withdrew.

The television was still buzzing merrily at itself in the darkness, like so many bright, angry bees trapped in a box. The remote had fallen to the floor while she slept, and the channel had changed to one of those constant news programmes: the anchor, a young woman with an overly serious expression on her face, was nodding, clearly listening to whoever was outside in the rain. The picture cut to a windswept, rainy mess of a reporter, whose wholly inadequate designer raincoat appeared to be acting as a sail, buffeting the poor woman back and forth in front of the camera.

She stood up and stretched, glad that she wasn't

outside on a night like this. She bent to retrieve the remote to turn the television off, but paused when she read the caption that flashed up on the ribbon at the bottom of the screen: *'Widespread Flooding Across Britain – Brindleford, one of the worst hit areas'.*

Pictures of Brindleford high street – thankfully well above the flood plain, flashed across the screen; she turned the sound up.

'Some of the town is on higher ground, where refugees fleeing the rising waters hope to find shelter. Properties all along the bottom of the valley have been flooded, and there are concerns that some – particularly the elderly – will be trapped in their homes.'

They switched back to the woman in the studio, who gave details of local helplines; Ivy bit her lip. She hoped that Christopher was alright.

The Barracloughs, she knew, lived in one of the hillier parts of Brindleford, and would be well protected – as the Arcade would be, placed, as it was, in the middle of town.

She glanced at the spiral staircase: it was well past eight o'clock, surely he would have gone home by now?

It can't hurt to check, she decided, pulling her cardigan closer around her in the chill of the evening.

Sure enough, the lights were still on in the bookshop, and Christopher was still beavering away, sitting cross-legged in the middle of the floor, the ledgers spread out in front of him.

At the same time, he appeared to be trying to coax a couple of reluctant books out from under one of the shelves, where they were hiding (and possibly breeding).

"It's alright," he was murmuring. "You can go back under there as soon as I'm done, I promise..."

The books were rustling and wriggling on their shelves, chattering to one another in their secret, papery way. Ivy had never seen them so active. She suspected that they were a good deal more energetic when there was no one else around.

Zarrubabel was banging around noisily in the back room, muttering to himself and rearranging things that Christopher would have to put back in the morning.

He looked up as she came in, and a curious stillness rolled around the room, as if the books felt that they had been caught in the act, and were suddenly shy in her presence.

"It's alright," he said into the hush, smiling. "It's only Ivy, you know her."

"Hello," she said to the room in general, feeling self-conscious and foolish. "I need a word with your keeper."

Christopher got to his feet, wincing a little at his cramped muscles. He must have been sitting in that one attitude for a while, Ivy guessed. He looked at her expectantly.

"I was watching the news," she explained. "Most of the lower town is under water – did you say you lived by the river?"

"Yes," he said, suddenly concerned. "In the flats by Hot Lane."

"They were saying that anything below Trench Street has flooded – come upstairs and see."

He nodded briskly and picked up the ledgers, setting them down on the counter. He paused, looking around at the books, anxiously. They rustled restlessly, as though picking up on his concern.

"Will the waters reach up here?" he asked; the rustling increased a notch as his question was understood amongst the shelves.

"Not unless this flood reaches Biblical proportions," she assured them all.

"Good," he said, and turned out the lights, quickly locking the door behind him.

They hurried through the teashop and up the creaking iron stairs. Christopher stopped at the top of them, astonished at the sheer size of the dark room that had appeared, cavernous, in front of him.

Ivy clapped her hands as she hurried across the room, and half a dozen Light Orbs sprung into life and began to orbit her head like a gigantic, bizarre halo. Another clap sent them hurtling around the room, where they embedded themselves into lamps and lanterns.

"It's quicker than running for the light switch," she explained, noticing his expression. "There," she said, indicating the television.

They stood watching the broadcast for a few minutes: it was much of the same, with several miserable weather-worn presenters trying to shout down the storm from various villages and towns around the country.

As they waited for Brindleford to reappear, Ivy glanced out into the raging storm outside. The light in the room was illuminating the nearest plants in the rooftop garden; they were being mercilessly lashed and beaten by the wind and rain. Instinctively, Ivy wanted to go out and protect them, but she fought the urge. 'People first', her family used to say – and Christopher might well need her help.

She turned back to him as he swore.

"What?"

"That's my building!" he cried, as the camera zoomed in to show a family being helped out of their living room window and into a rescue boat. "That's my flat!" he pointed at the dark corner of a window, barely visible at the very top of the shot.

"Shit," Ivy observed, and he nodded, at a total loss.

"Do you think they've got everyone out?" she asked, as the camera followed the rescue boat away from the building, the young children huddled inside looking as if this was the adventure of their lives.

"I hope so," he said, fervently. "But I don't know how they'd be able to tell – it looks like the power's out."

They stared at the screen for a few moments in silence.

"What am I going to do?" Christopher asked himself softly. He had probably intended only to think it, Ivy decided, but she heard it nonetheless.

"You can stay here," she offered, surprising them both.

He gaped at her, stunned. "Really?"

"Yes," she said. "For as long as you need."

She frowned at the television, and turned it off with an electronic whoomph noise.

"There should still be time to collect your things, the water isn't rising *that* quickly – assuming your roof is sound."

Christopher snorted in a derisory fashion.

"I wouldn't count on it," he said. "Are you sure – I mean –"

"Yes," she insisted, as much to herself as anyone. "But if we don't go soon we'll lose our chance."

For a moment it looked as though Christopher was about to say something, but he stopped himself.

"You're right," he said, holding out his arm. "Here."

Ivy took a deep breath before taking his arm.

Transportation spells, more than any other kind of magic, felt different to each individual Practitioner, a disparity that became much more tangible when someone else did the 'leg work', so to speak.

Christopher's spell, which had had to fight the weather on the way over, felt like a blast of warm air; it was also more abrupt than most, the movement of the spell ending with a faint popping sound.

She let go of him as he started packing up his things. They were standing in a tiny, dilapidated flat that had most certainly seen better days. In the glow of Christopher's Light Orbs she could see that bits of paint were flaking off the ceiling in places and a forceful draft was blowing from the cracked windows, a feeble reflection of the ferocious weather outside.

He had done his best with it though, she noted, feeling suddenly nosy: the few things he had around the flat were neat and well cared-for, despite their age, and the rooms were scrupulously clean.

Ivy leaned backwards slightly as some of Christopher's possessions whizzed past her head. He was being very careful not to meet her eyes, and she guessed that he was quite embarrassed by the decomposing state of his living quarters. He needn't be, as far as Ivy was concerned, but people are strange and judgemental things at times.

"Could you do the kitchen?" he mumbled, waving an arm at the cupboard-sized room to her left.

She nodded and walked into the tiny kitchen; there was barely enough room to stand inside it. Pots and crockery were stacked erratically along the tiny window ledge, and what might be the world's thinnest fridge stood against the back wall.

"Is the fridge yours?" she called back, sticking her head around the door.

"No," he replied dully. "Only the food and the general kitchen stuff – all the storage came with the flat. There should be a box under the sink."

"Right," she said, as things from the bathroom flew across the room and packed themselves into a large bag on the sofa.

Opening the doors of the fridge and the tiny cupboards, and pulling out the cardboard box, she closed her eyes and concentrated. Christopher's things started to fly out of their places and towards the box; they hovered above it for a split second before shrinking themselves down to an appropriate size and storing themselves neatly inside. Ivy watched the last of them disappear beneath the cardboard walls of the box – which closed itself up and packed itself together – with an air of satisfaction. She had never used a packing spell before, preferring to enjoy the tactile nature of the task, as part of the moving process. Here, however, time was of the essence, and it had seemed less intrusive to use magic instead. She thought it had gone rather well.

She levitated the box into the living room, now depressingly bare. Christopher was looking sadly around. It might not have been much of a home, or even a home for long, but it had been his, and he had felt reasonably secure here.

"I could take the first load," said Ivy. "If you want a moment..."

"It's okay," he said, and then hesitated, glancing at the front door. "Actually, could you? I want to check on my neighbour – he's a little scatter-brained and I'm not sure he has any family. Can you find your way?"

"It shouldn't be too hard," said Ivy, wondering whether this neighbour might need to find shelter too. "I know where the Arcade is from here and I think I can find my way back again."

"Thanks," he said, and Ivy crouched down beside the kitchen box and a large bag; grateful that she didn't have to try to pick them up, she muttered the Transportation spell under her breath.

ooo

Christopher leaned over the banister of the concrete staircase; below him, he could see the river lapping against the walls on the ground floor. Apparently, the rising water had picked up a pace.

He hurried along the hall towards his neighbour's front door, carrying his Light Orb in his hand like a lantern. He was reasonably certain that Reggie was mundane, and there was no need to frighten the man any more than necessary.

"Reggie?" he called, knocking on the door. Inside the flat, someone barked.

"Get the door! Get the door!" someone squawked.

"I'm coming," Reggie called out to him. "It's just a bit dark in here –"

Christopher listened as he made his way across the room, navigating around various pieces of furniture. He sniffed at the door, and behind it, Reggie's dog growled; since his bite he had had trouble gaining the trust of canines, whose noses told them that he should be a totally different shape to the one that their eyes were providing. There was something else in there, though, something that his nose couldn't quite put a finger on.

Finally, Reggie got the door open, holding his dog back with one leg; there was a flapping sound coming from the ceiling above him.

"Get the door! Awk! Get the door!" an apparently disembodied voice cried out. Christopher held up the

Orb as Reggie turned.

"Shut up, Boscoe, you daft bugger," he said. "My parrot," he explained, squinting at Christopher in the glow of the Light Orb. "You're from next door, aren't you?"

"Yes, Reggie, we met about a month ago," he said, patiently. Reggie might not be particularly old, but his memory was a little sketchy.

"That's a funny kind of torch," said the older man, nodding at the Orb.

"The flats are flooding," said Christopher, who could hear the water on the stairs now. His nose told him that Ivy had returned, briefly, and left again, presumably with the rest of his stuff.

"I thought they might be," said Reggie, pulling the dog gently but firmly out of the way. "Come in, boy. We'll be safe up here."

"No, Reggie, I don't think we will," said Christopher, following him into the flat. It was a little bigger than his, and in a much better state of repair. He wondered how long Reggie had lived here.

Boscoe, the parrot, landed on the top of a tall shadow in the corner which turned out, under closer inspection, to be an old, brass cage, and was presumably where the bird slept.

The dog growled at him.

"There, there, Saffy," Reggie said, soothingly. "It's just the lad from down the hall. No, we'll be fine here," he continued. "We're much higher than the water – the only time it was ever nearly high enough to touch these flats was when I was ten, and I doubt that this is anywhere near as bad."

"Actually –" Christopher began, but he paused, hearing Ivy coming down the corridor. She stuck her head around the door, which was still ajar, Orb held in front of her.

"Hello," she said, coming fully into the room to give Saffy the dog a cuddle; she immediately stopped growling. Apparently Ivy had that sort of effect on people.

"Hullo Miss," said Reggie. "Are you here with –" he paused. "I'm sorry, I'm terrible with names."

"Christopher," said Christopher. "Look, we really need to leave Reggie – the water's already halfway up the building."

Reggie started.

"It is *not*," he said. "It can't be –"

Ivy took the opportunity to interrupt.

"I just had a look down the stairs," she said, almost apologetically. "And the hall below us is beginning to fill up."

Reggie stared at her.

"Just look out of the window, Reggie," urged Christopher, very worried about having to move a lot of people, pets and belongings in a very short amount of time.

Reggie moved across to the window, and Boscoe flapped across the room to peer out into the street. Sure enough, only a few metres below them a sizeable part of a tree floated past.

"Abandon ship! Abandon ship! Awk" cried Boscoe, whistling shrilly.

"We have to go, Reggie," Christopher insisted.

"But we can't *leave*!"

"We have to, sir, or we'll drown," said Ivy, matter-of-factly.

"But we *can't* leave," Reggie repeated, miserably. "Bessie will never find her way home."

"Bessie?" asked Christopher.

"My wife," said Reggie, indicating a laughing woman in a silver frame on the sideboard. "She died a few years ago – but she promised that she'd come back for me when it was my time. If we go," he continued, wringing his hands, "she'll get here and I'll be gone, and she'll be all on her own!"

He peered up at them, helplessly.

"She hated being left alone – I nursed her, you see, and she got so lonely when I wasn't here." His voice cracked.

Christopher looked away, completely at a loss for what to say.

"She'll be coming back to *you*, sir," said Ivy, taking his hand. "So she'll find you, wherever you are."

He looked at her. "Do you think so, Miss?" he sniffed.

"I know so," she insisted. "And there are things that we can do to make it easier for her to find you," she continued.

"Like what?" he asked, interested.

"There are things that you can plant in the garden to help her find her way," Ivy said.

"We *really* have to go," said Christopher, feeling wretched for interrupting.

"Yes," said Ivy. "Christopher's right – I can tell you all about it tomorrow, if you like."

Finally, to Christopher's relief, Reggie nodded. "Do you have a boat?" he asked. "I'm not very good in boats..."

"Something like that," said Christopher, quickly, feeling that it would take too long to explain.

Reggie looked around, helplessly.

"But what about my things?" he asked. "I'm not as young and energetic as you two, I can't just s-start again from the beginning –"

"We can take them with us," said Ivy, firmly.

"But it would t-take too long –"

"Not a problem," said Christopher. "Do you have a suitcase or some boxes or something?"

"There are a couple of s-suitcases in the top of the w-wardrobe, but –"

"Perfect," said Christopher, and went to fetch them.

"B-but where are we *going*?" asked Reggie, and this time it was nearly a wail. Christopher felt for him, but time really was running out now.

"To my place," said Ivy.

"Are you s-sure, Miss? That's so k-kind of you..." he stammered.

"Not a problem, sir," she said. "Can you get your

winged friend into his cage?"

"Oh, er – yes. Boscoe!" he commanded, in a much steadier voice. The parrot, who had been circling the ceiling anxiously, immediately responded to the tone of authority.

"I think, perhaps, we ought to stand back," said Ivy, gently pulling Reggie and Saffy back against the wall as Christopher began to pack the suitcases magically. It was an impressive sight, in the half-light, and took rather a lot of concentration on his part. His Light Orb, which he had hung in mid-air beside him, winked out.

It was replaced, after a few moments, by another; he half-turned to it, surprised. It was one of Ivy's.

"Thanks," he muttered, struggling to maintain the spell.

"No problem," she said, from somewhere behind him.

Reggie, who was having quite a difficult time with the mundane events of the evening to start with, stared in open astonishment as his furniture marched about of its own accord.

"Bloody hell," he said.

10
Deluge

They landed in Ivy's enormous living room with a soft thump. Ivy and Christopher had taken three shifts each to move Reggie's belongings and furniture, which was now miniaturised and stacked on the floor, near the spell preparation area.

They had returned one final time to find Reggie hanging halfway out of his bedroom window, trying to rescue a window-box full of red geraniums that Bessie had loved. Christopher had gently moved him out of the way and pulled them out of the storm and, for a moment, Ivy was convinced that he, too, was about to plunge into the roiling waters below. They had given Reggie a moment to say goodbye to his home – he clearly had a lot of memories of this place – while they had checked the rest of the doors that weren't already submerged. There seemed to be no more residents anywhere else in the building, which was a bit of a relief, but Ivy had tripped over on the stairs and subsequently had a very wet and muddy leg.

When they returned, Reggie had pulled his coat on, his hat firmly jammed down onto his head. Saffy's lead was wrapped tightly around his arm and his knuckles were white where he was gripping Boscoe's cage.

Christopher had gently taken the cage out of his grip and offered him his arm, while Ivy had taken the geraniums and Saffy, who was already much more comfortable around her, anyway.

Reggie had his eyes tight shut, as if afraid of what might happen on the way over; he was also holding his breath.

"There we are," said Ivy, giving Saffy a reassuring cuddle. She whined in confusion.

"Bloody hell," said Reggie. This was more or less all he had been saying for the last twenty minutes.

He stared around the Arcade in shock and surprise.

"Well, that wasn't so bad," he said, weakly. "Better

than the bus, anyway..."

Ivy looked him over, critically, and glanced at Christopher, who shrugged.

Reggie was looking around in a dazed and distracted fashion, and she guessed that the shock of leaving the home that he had shared with his wife, coupled with learning of the existence of magic in a fairly blunt fashion, was taking its toll.

She looked out into the gardens, still being savaged by the weather; the lights of Mahri's coach house twinkled through the rain-soaked windows. Deciding that Reggie might do a little better with some pragmatic company, she strode towards the doors.

"Come on," she said, pulling open the glass doors. The noise of the storm was incredible, taking on an almost physical force.

Christopher stared at her as if she had gone mad; Reggie, who was already beginning to question his own sanity, meekly followed her.

She glared out into the storm-swept garden, hands on her hips.

"Well, I think we've had quite enough of *that*," she said.

Christopher joined her in the hopes that he might see whatever it was that she was seeing.

"What?" he shouted, over the wind.

"Do you see that house over there?" Ivy asked, pointing at Mahri's front door.

"But we're on a roof!" said Christopher, astonished.

"So?" she asked, taking off her shoes and socks. "Get Reggie over there and knock on the door, will you – there's something that I need to do."

"What could you possibly need to do out *there*?" he demanded, eyes wide, as she strode out into the wild night. "Come on Reggie," he said, trying to sound like he knew what was going on. "I'll bring Boscoe."

They struggled along the path, hunched down against the wind and the rain. Boscoe was squawking in alarm and trying desperately to find a way out of his cage to where the sane people lived; Christopher stripped off his jumper and wrapped it around the parrot's cage, after which the volume of his protests diminished, somewhat. Saffy had stayed inside, peering after them through the glass with an expression that conveyed her absolute faith in their insanity.

Christopher reached the door and banged on it, trying to shake the rain out of his eyes. He propped Boscoe's cage under the lee of the door where Reggie was sheltering, and waited.

All of a sudden, the magical potential of the world around him shifted dizzyingly. He turned, trying to see Ivy amongst the rain-battered foliage: she was just visible, standing in the garden – presumably barefoot – her face turned to the sky and her eyes shut, arms stretched wide. She looked serenely and illogically peaceful in such a chaotic environment, and he stared at her in wonder.

She was – no, she couldn't be... he shook his head, trying to see clearly through the sheets of water falling across his face.

She was! He stared, astonished.

Ivy was glowing.

The light had a strange quality to it: it was pale and luminescent, with curious flashes and arcs of light – iridescent blues and greens that seemed to be there one moment and gone the next, as if they were taunting the eye.

The plants in the garden were reaching out to her, as the light spread, winding around her arms, and face, and hair – tangling around her as she worked her spell. He could practically taste the magic now, and despite her rather shocking appearance he didn't feel any concern: Ivy was clearly in control here, completely within her own element.

A great creak sounded above, and he looked up to see vines growing purposefully up the old brick walls and attaching to – no, becoming! *Becoming* the large white metal struts that formed the structure of the Arcade.

As he watched, enormous blue flowers bloomed between the growing metalwork and coalesced with their neighbours, solidifying to form plates of glass. He stared at them as they stretched and linked with one another, coming together as a strong and sturdy roof. It looked as though it had always been there. The noise of the storm ended, abruptly, and the rain stopped falling; the entire garden, protected by the new roof, seemed to breathe a sigh of relief.

His gaze fell back to Ivy, and he promptly forgot how to breathe; she seemed to be encased in a magnificent framework of leaves and light. She looked extraordinarily beautiful, sinking gently back to the ground, surrounded by the glorious radiance of her own, personal magic.

The vines flowed back into the foliage almost reluctantly, as if they had genuinely enjoyed their proximity to the witch. She walked towards them with a slight smile on her face, the odd vine still trailing after her, her dark hair swimming wildly behind her. To Christopher, she resembled some kind of ancient priestess, dressed incongruously in a cardigan and jeans. There was still an ethereal glow to her eyes and skin, and Christopher couldn't force his eyes away from her, mortifyingly aware of how rude he must seem.

Fortunately – for him, at least – Mahri opened her front door and he fell backwards at her feet, saved from damaging his friendship with Ivy any further.

He scrambled up, embarrassed, as the florist stared between their soaking wet faces.

"I think Reggie here could do with a good cup of tea," said Ivy, giving her a pointed look.

Mahri caught on and ushered them into her warm, dry living room.

"You poor things, you're soaked through!" she cried, somehow making the kettle in the adjacent kitchen boil by will power alone.

Ivy drew her to one side as they clattered around in the kitchen, pulling out cups and jars of tea; Christopher suspected that Ivy was explaining their impromptu rescue. Reggie was slumped in one of the chairs around the kitchen table, staring blankly around, so Christopher detached his jumper from the outside of the ruffled parrot's cage and let him out.

Boscoe was off like a shot, flapping around the roof of the Arcade as a flash of grey and green, clearly relieved to be out of the weather and eager to explore his new environment. He made several passes over-head, squawking and whistling merrily to himself.

Christopher looked down, detecting a warm presence beside his legs. Saffy had decided to join them now that the weather had been banished to the outside. She looked up at him suspiciously and he stepped out of the way to let her pass.

He turned back to the kitchen, gratefully accepting a mug of hot, sweet tea from Ivy, who had balanced her mug on the windowsill, and was trying to get her sodden shoes back on. They stood awkwardly on the edge of the boundary between the kitchen and the living room as Mahri set Reggie's drink down in front of him.

Automatically, he picked it up and took a sip – immediately, some of the colour returned to his pale face, and he seemed to come back to himself a bit more.

Reggie was a stocky gentleman in his mid-sixties with thinning grey hair and a penchant for woolly vests. He looked much older, however, something that had never really fitted him. He was clearly a hearty chap, seeing as he walked Saffy at least twice a day, and had never yet succumbed to the temptation of using the generally broken lifts in his building. Now that Christopher knew that Reggie had spent several years caring for his ailing wife, he made a lot more sense. Without Bessie, Reggie seemed to be at rather a loss. Christopher was beginning to think that his absent-mindedness stemmed from a combination of exhaustion and a keen but inaccurate sense of having let her down.

"Feeling better?" asked Mahri, with sympathy.

"Yes, thank you," he said, sounding much steadier.

"It's been a bit of an eventful evening."

"I can imagine," said Mahri, contemplatively. "You didn't know about magic, did you?"

"No, ma'am," he said, weakly. "I had an inkling that this sort of thing went on from time to time – you know, herbal remedies and spells and things – I just didn't expect to ever see it so *clearly*." He took another mouthful of tea and continued. "My nan used to tell me stories, of course, but I never thought it could be so *effective*."

"It can be quite spectacular," said Mahri, with an understanding smile.

She must have seen Ivy's magic before, Christopher reasoned. *I've never seen anything like it.*

"It's a little disconcerting to see at first," said Ivy, having had to explain magic to someone without it before. "But there's really no harm in it – assuming a person's intentions are honourable."

Reggie nodded, and stared into his tea for a moment.

"Thank you," he said, to the world at large; everyone made non-committal noises of welcome. "If you hadn't come and talked me out, and brought me away, I would probably be neck-deep in river by now – and you were right, lad," he added, turning to Christopher. "Bessie wouldn't want that for me."

"You can stay with me for the moment," said Mahri, and he looked up at her in stunned gratitude.

"I *can*?" he asked, and Christopher recognised that familiar note of disbelief; it was odd to hear it in someone else's voice for a change.

"Of course," she said, in that matter-of-fact way of hers. "I wouldn't have offered, otherwise."

"But I have nothing to give you in return," he said, wretchedly.

"Pish," said Mahri. "Your good company will serve well enough." She gave him an encouraging smile.

Reggie opened and closed his mouth a few times, looking like an overgrown, grey-haired goldfish.

"Well, I'm glad we've settled that," said Mahri,

satisfied. "I suppose you'll be staying with Ivy, will you?" she asked, and Christopher nodded, colouring up to his eyebrows.

"Excellent!" she cried, clapping her hands together. "Let's get a bed made up for you, my dear, and then see where we're at."

She and Reggie rose and started towards the stairs, where Mahri paused.

"Could you two find him out a clean set of clothes and his night things?" she asked. "I imagine you will have packed in something of a hurry," she continued, "and that things might be quite difficult to get to – oh! Hello!" she cried, shocked.

A wet nose had pressed into the back of her knee, in greeting.

"And who are you?" she asked, bending down to give Saffy a fuss.

"This is Saffy," said Reggie, feeling that he was on firmer ground here. "My dog – she's in pup, probably quite shaken up."

"I would imagine so," said Mahri, fondly. "Here…" she led Saffy to the sofa and patted it; after a glance at her master to make sure that this was alright, Saffy jumped up and made herself comfortable.

Mahri gave her another stroke and the Labrador settled down, clearly of the opinion that wherever she was, being petted by everyone and being allowed on the sofa made it all worthwhile.

"Where's Boscoe?" asked Reggie, with a frown at the empty cage.

Christopher nodded in the direction of the great glass ceiling outside.

"Exploring," he said, and Reggie chuckled.

"Good. It'll make a nice change for him to be able to stretch his wings a bit."

Ivy and Christopher finished their tea and prepared to head back across the roof garden, happy with their night's work and ready to get a few of their things sorted before retiring to bed, but Reggie stopped them.

"Do you think they got everyone else out, lad?" he asked, a hand on Christopher's arm.

"I hope so," Christopher said. "We had a look at the flats on the floor below and we couldn't find anyone."

"Good," said Reggie, thoughtfully. "That's good."

Something was clearly bothering him.

"Do you think they would have checked the roof?" he asked, finally.

"The roof?" asked Christopher, surprised. As far as he could remember – having checked it out for the purposes of an emergency transformation space – there wasn't much up there, save a couple of metal boxes that had something to do with the heating for the building. There was only one access point, a small metal door next to Reggie's flat; it was usually locked, but Christopher recalled with inexplicable dread that the locks had been broken for the past few weeks. He had assumed that it was a direct result of the unseasonable heat, but now he wasn't so certain.

"Yes," said Reggie. "I think there might be someone up there – I can hear footsteps at night sometimes – and I saw someone hiding behind the door the other week." He turned a worried face to Christopher. "I've been leaving food out – it's always gone by morning, and the dishes I get back are very clean."

They all exchanged a speaking look.

"Perhaps we ought to check," Ivy suggested. "Just to be sure."

Christopher nodded. "We'll sort your things out when we get back, Reggie," he said, and he and Ivy concentrated on the rooftop of the block of flats that he had very recently called home.

The storm had, against all reason, intensified, and Christopher stumbled as he landed, weakened by the continuous travelling and the extra force it took to fight against the battering wind.

After a couple of seconds the weather became his whole world, filling up his consciousness with sound and water and pain; the scouring wind was picking up the enormous raindrops and hurling them at the ground (and anything else that happened to be in the way), and every impact stung. There was no escaping it, and it ran in rivulets across his face and body, making his clothes cling and stick as he struggled to find his feet on the peeling tar roof. He could barely see, and his sense of smell was entirely useless in the raging torrent. He was exhausted, his limbs protesting as he slipped and slid.

Ivy pulled him to his feet; from what he could see through the driving rain, she didn't seem to be struggling at all, despite the extraordinary amount of magic it must have taken to roof over the Arcade.

She tried to shout, but her voice was lost to him, carried away on the howling wind. They clung to one another in the darkness, the merciless wind buffeting them from side to side as Ivy's hair whipped around them like dark, sodden streamers, getting in their eyes and slapping at their frozen skin.

There was a faint light ahead, in the lee of one of the mysterious metal heating boxes. They stumbled towards it through the driving rain, slipping and staggering across the rain-soaked roof.

Christopher tried to shout, but all that happened was his mouth filled up with water and he nearly choked. Deciding that they would need to sort out some form of visual communication, he huddled closer to Ivy, trying at the very least to shield her from the worst of the weather.

As they got closer to the flickering light, a ragged make-shift tent came into view, the ruined tarpaulin snapping in the wind. Christopher crouched by what might have been the opening before the climate had objected, Ivy close beside him. Two pairs of eyes stared out at them from within a massive bundle of blankets and clothes, frightened but defiant.

Ivy shouted something, but it would have been a miracle if either of them heard it; the wind had ripped right through their shelter, and everything inside was dripping wet, including the bundle.

One of the pairs of eyes turned out to belong to a young girl, probably no more than eight years old, with black hair and fierce, green eyes. She glared at them as she fought to stand up, shooing them away. They couldn't hear what she was saying, but Christopher got the message: this is *our* place – leave us alone!

Leaving Ivy to silently reason with them, he struggled across the tarmac to the edge of the roof and peered down into the swirling darkness. The river was much higher now, surging around the neighbouring buildings and carrying large chunks of debris with it. The bungalows further down the row were already entirely submerged, and Christopher watched – with an odd sense of panicked calm – as part of the heating system from another building drifted past, dragged by the current and trailing the bent and broken remains of its ladder.

Beneath him, the building creaked and groaned under the force of the torrent, and he stepped back from the edge, suddenly afraid. Not a moment too soon, as he was knocked off his feet by a fresh surge of wind.

ooo

Trying to convince someone that you weren't a threat in extremely inclement weather, without language, was difficult enough, Ivy decided, quite without having to communicate, at the same time, that you were trying to rescue them.

She stumbled out of her crouching position, buffeted by the intensity of the gale, and fell to the floor. For a moment she stayed where she was, waiting for any slight reduction in the wind to right herself. To her surprise, a pair of hands reached for her, helping her find her feet; she met the eyes of the girl, who was frowning in a sort of combination of annoyance and fear.

"Let me help you," Ivy mouthed, and this time the girl appeared to understand. She glanced at the other bundle behind her, who was watching them in genuine anguish.

He seemed younger than the girl, and she was definitely protective of him.

Ivy glanced along the roof to see where Christopher had gone to, and the children's eyes followed her gaze.

Her heart leapt into her mouth as he dropped out of sight, right on the edge of the roof. She staggered forward a few steps, battling against the wind, and he crawled back into view, still clinging to the roof in the insane wind.

Ivy fell to her knees, weak with relief that her new friend hadn't just fallen to his death. She reached out to him as he drew level, as if to check that he was still real, and he pulled her closer, shouting to her in the wind.

"The river's nearly at the upper windows," he yelled, and this time he was close enough for her to catch the words. "We *have* to go!"

She nodded, hating to let go of his arm, even for a moment.

Together, they struggled back to the children, who were watching from the midst of their wrecked shelter.

The girl, who was paying close attention to their faces, looked at the tiny boy beside her and bit her lip, before desperately trying to gather their things together. Sensing a move, the little boy – who was a few years younger – tried to help, but the wind was just too strong.

There was no way that they could get everything together in time. The boy – and he looked enough like her that he must have been her brother – was carrying a brightly coloured back-pack across to where the girl was hastily stuffing clothes and blankets into a larger, pink carry-all. He stumbled and fell. Despite the noise of the storm, they heard him cry out, clutching his knee; the girl looked around, wide-eyed.

Christopher, who was closest, crawled over to him, shielding him from some of the wind. Instinctively, the child turned his face into Christopher's chest, grasping at his sodden jumper and shaking with cold. Christopher wrapped an arm around him, and suddenly Ivy realised just how pale her friend was. There was no way he could safely make the jump back to the Arcade; she would have to take them all – and quickly. The roar of the wind was being superseded by a second, much more frightening sound. The rush of the waters around and through the block of flats was building, and it wouldn't be long until the whole rooftop was swept away.

She wasn't sure how far she trusted the strength of the building beneath their feet. There was a rumble below them as a window broke. It travelled up through Ivy's shoes.

Ivy caught the girl's arm as she frantically tried to pack their meagre belongings. For a moment, she tried to pull away, but stopped, recognising the look of outright fear on Ivy's face.

She clutched the bright pink bag to her chest, and Ivy made her decision; the contents of this tiny, ramshackle den were all these children had, so it would have to come too.

Crouching beside the girl, Ivy closed her eyes, trying to collect their possessions in her mind. She concentrated on the main room at the Arcade, trying to force the images of these children's belongings into it, along with four working bodies.

It was no mean feat, and for several moments nothing happened at all. Ivy frowned, pushing just a little harder as the water began to surge through the building below.

All at once, the noise and force of the storm ended abruptly, the absence of it all knocking the four of them flat. For a couple of minutes they lay amongst the rain-soaked blankets and clothes, marvelling at the power of the silence.

It was the little boy who broke the silence, still sniffling into Christopher's saturated jumper.

"Tha-that was magic!" he said, in a small, slightly hysterical voice. "Astrid! R-real magic!"

Astrid scrambled over to him and pulled him away from Christopher, hugging him protectively and glaring defiantly at the two adults trying to pick themselves up.

Christopher was still worryingly pale, Ivy noted, as she

clambered to her feet. He pulled himself up on the herb table.

Ivy shook some of the water out of her eyes.

"We aren't going to hurt you," she said, to the children. "The rooftop was flooding – you would have been pulled into the river."

Astrid didn't look wholly convinced, but she nodded. She appeared to be trying to take in everything about Ivy and Christopher at once, and was – for the moment – ignoring her surroundings.

"You can stay here tonight, if you want," Ivy paused, noting the look of panic that flashed across the small girl's features. "You don't have to," she continued, hurriedly. "But you're more than welcome – at least until the storm dies down."

For a moment, she thought that Astrid was going to turn them down, but her brother pulled her closer, apparently desperate not to lose the chance of a warm bed.

"P-please Astrid," he begged. "J-just until the rain s-stops – it's so w-wet and c-cold!"

The girl, clearly worried about becoming trapped with these strangers, looked at her brother in indecision.

He wiped his face and peered out from between her arms.

"He's the man that lives downstairs," he said, pointing a small finger in Christopher's direction. "He hums songs on the stairs."

"That's right," said Christopher, the exhaustion beginning to break through into his voice.

Ivy pointed at the further of the two corridors leading away from the main room.

"My room's down there," she said. "And the spare room where Christopher will be sleeping is down there, too. I can make up a bed for you on this side, and you can lock yourselves in if you want," she continued, indicating the other corridor. "Please, just stay until it's safer out there."

The two children shared a look that seemed to

communicate a great deal. Astrid nodded curtly at Ivy, who sagged in relief. She didn't like the idea of these two outside on a night like this – even if they did seem able to take care of themselves. They'd looked so small and vulnerable in the remains of their tent. She had a strong urge to hug them both.

Resisting, she jerked her head towards the second corridor.

"Come on then," she said. "I think you could both do with a hot bath." She led them to the second before last door in the corridor, which opened to a white and black tiled bathroom. Going in before them, she lifted down a tin of bandages, plasters and healing salves, putting it on the floor by the sink.

"For his knee," she said, with an encouraging smile. "All the jars have labels and instructions, and there should be enough towels. I'll have a dig through my old clothes – see if I can find something dry for you," she looked them over, critically. "Will you be alright?"

"Yes," said Astrid, firmly. As she shut the door behind her, she heard her add, in a small voice: "Thank you."

Christopher was still leaning against the table, his eyes closed tightly, as though he was trying to collect his energy. He didn't even hear her approaching, and jumped slightly when she laid a hand on his arm.

"I think you could do with a hot shower, too," she said, gently.

"I'm fine," he said, shivering violently. "I'll just change my clothes, and –"

Ivy rolled her eyes and pulled on his arm, reasonably gently; he nearly fell, and she gave him a pointed look.

"You're freezing, and you need to get warmed up," she tugged him firmly towards the other corridor and the other bathroom; he could barely walk straight. "And then you need to rest – we did a lot tonight."

"You seem okay," he mumbled, as she pushed him through the door.

"Shower first," she ordered, with quiet firmness.

"Thinking later. I'll grab some of your clothes and put them in your room – second door on your right when you come out."

"But –"

"No arguments."

She shut the door on him, smiling to herself at the harassed expression on his face as it clicked shut. Taking her own advice, she dried her clothes with a click of her fingers, and muttered a quick warming spell. She felt a trickle of icy water run down the nape of her neck and reached up: her hair was still dripping wet. Whatever Christopher might think, the evening's urgent activity had taken its toll on her energy, too.

She ducked back into her room to grab a towel and a brush, rubbing her hair dry as she walked across the rain-soaked garden to Mahri's coach house. She glanced at the empty house next door and frowned slightly. It would take a little while to clear up, but perhaps it wouldn't be empty for too much longer, since Reggie didn't seem to have anywhere else to go, either. She would have to see.

The door opened before she even had chance to knock; Mahri raised a worried eyebrow.

"They're fine," said Ivy, before the older woman had a chance to ask. "I made them have hot baths – Christopher too."

Mahri breathed a sigh of relief.

"Children?" she asked, and Ivy nodded.

"Very young," she said. "Very fierce – and very capable – but very young, too. I'm glad that Reggie knew they were up there."

Mahri nodded, and they shared a look that conveyed both how close a thing it had been and how relieved they both were that everyone they knew about was now in the warm and dry.

"Reggie's in the shower," said Mahri, hurrying into the kitchen. Ivy followed her, trying to get the worst of the wet out of her hair. "I thought I would heat up some stew – I had a few batches in the freezer."

Despite her weariness and her tension at the sudden proximity of so many people, Ivy smiled. Mahri was an excellent cook, and sometimes just made food for the fun of it, storing it for when it was needed in the enormous chest freezer in the corner of her kitchen.

A large pan was currently resting on the stove, a warm and delicious smell pouring forth.

Mahri looked at her expression. "What?" she asked, feigning innocence.

"Oh, nothing," said Ivy, with a cheeky grin. There was no way that Mahri could have defrosted that much stew in so little time using mundane means – physics had several rules to which it had to adhere, and the heating of frozen stew was no exception. Mahri had a bit of a thing about using magic in her cooking; she rather felt it was cheating.

"That's what I thought," the older witch muttered, stirring the stew. She gave Ivy a sideways look, as if she was unsure whether she ought to continue. "You're becoming yourself again," she said, and Ivy frowned.

Mahri sighed. "I mean it," she said, turning to her. "Helping people, tucking them into the Arcade – and don't give me that look, I know you're thinking about it, particularly for Reggie and the children."

Ivy tried to hide the annoyance on her face, but failed. Mahri had always been able to tell what she was thinking. Her expression softened.

"I was thinking about it, too," she said, gently. "It's just – it's nice to see you..." she trailed off, not wanting to finish the sentence with 'the way you were before Sam died'. "You're a Chambers again," she said, instead, and Ivy grimaced.

"I'll have a look through Reggie's things for some clothes," she said, ignoring her friend. "If your stew doesn't need watching could you have a look in the cellar for some of my old things for the children? Neither of my aunts ever threw anything away, there's bound to be something."

Mahri nodded, and watched her young friend walk

slowly back across the garden, unwelcome memories flooding her head. She sighed, sadly, and put down the wooden spoon.

She wished that Ivy hadn't had to grow up so quickly.

11
New Friends

Ivy found the things she thought that Reggie might need reasonably easily, bundling them up and carrying them back across the garden. Mahri had apparently gone in search of children's clothes, so she went upstairs and laid them on her spare bed.

She went back into the kitchen, conscious of how much Mahri cared about the quality of any food she produced, and stirred the stew until her friend returned. She peered into the large pot, inhaling the enticing smells of lamb, parsnip, and leek. Unusually hungry after all the moving about, it made her mouth water.

Mahri hurried back up from the basement, a pile of old clothes in her arms. She looked mildly relieved to see Ivy looking after the stew, and the younger witch had a hard time keeping the smile off her face.

"Here," said Mahri, handing her the bundle of clothes; she looked at her critically. "Your hair's a mess," she observed.

"One thing at a time," said Ivy, patting the hairbrush that was jammed into the back pocket of her jeans.

Mahri made a noise of approval.

"Good. I'll get Reggie to help me bring this over when it's ready."

Ivy nodded and left her to it, hoping that it would be ready sooner rather than later.

Her guests appeared to be being obedient for the moment, so she set the kettle on the hob and went along the corridor towards the bathroom where the children were getting warm and clean; she could hear them talking through the door. Not wanting to eavesdrop, she knocked lightly on it.

There appeared to be a brief and hurried discussion before she heard the latch being drawn back, and the door was opened by just a crack.

The little boy looked up at her, apprehensively.

"I thought you could do with some dry clothes," she

said. "Luckily no-one in my family ever throws anything away, so we still have some from when I was little."

He looked from her to the bundle of clothes in her hands, before opening the door slightly wider and taking them from her.

"Thank you," he said, shyly, and Ivy smiled.

"You're welcome. My friend Mahri is making some stew, if you'd like some, and some hot chocolate?"

At the mention of food his whole face lit up.

"Yes please!" he said, this time with much more confidence.

"Right, well I'll get a bed made up for you two and Christopher while you're getting changed... how about we meet in the kitchen in about quarter of an hour?"

The boy nodded, apparently ecstatic at the prospect of a hot meal, and disappeared back into the bathroom.

As she went into the room next door she heard the latch slide back into place, almost as an afterthought.

It took very little time indeed to make up the beds, and – after a mildly embarrassing episode where she encountered Christopher coming out to look for some of his clothes, wrapped only in a towel – Ivy was staying firmly in the living area of the Arcade.

She was torn between leaving the children's things alone and respecting their privacy, and trying to get some of them dry. Given that a couple of the things on the top of the pile were books and photographs, she decided on the latter, clearing a space on the herb table to prop their mementos up to dry off a little. Setting in motion a gentle drying spell that could begin to undo any water damage, she pulled out her old, wooden clothes-maids and set them up by the radiators along the children's corridor.

The lack of warm clothes amongst their scattered possessions made her a little sad, but she made her mind up not to ask them about it. It was their business, after all.

The little boy came out of the bathroom while she was

hanging some of their clothes up to dry. Wary, he paused a few feet away from her, watching her closely.

Ivy watched him back, out of the corner of her eyes: he was a tiny scarecrow of a child, and looked particularly ridiculous in an ancient t-shirt and pair of hideous yellow shorts that Ivy had entirely forgotten about. His jet black hair stuck out in all directions – possibly from where his sister had attempted to dry it – and startlingly blue eyes peered out from under his fringe.

Shy though he seemed, he was bolder than his sister, perhaps because he was younger and more innocent. Wordlessly, he scurried behind Ivy into the main living area, trying to keep as close to the wall (and as far away from her) as he could. He returned a couple of minutes later, carrying a pile of clothes that was bigger than him.

He started hanging them haphazardly on the next clothes-maid, occasionally glancing over at her and re-adjusting things that didn't look quite right. After a few minutes he came and sat down beside her, putting socks on the bottom rung of the clothes-maid.

The bathroom door opened again as Ivy hung the last blanket over the top of the one free radiator in the hallway. Astrid stared around, finally spotting her brother hanging the last of the socks on the bottom of the racks. As soon as she saw him, she visibly relaxed – although not by much. She turned to Ivy.

"Thank you for drying our clothes," she said, in a strangely tight voice that suggested she was wondering what she might need to give in return.

"Not a problem," said Ivy, lightly. "Although I had a bit of help," she added, smiling at the boy, who had gone to stand slightly behind his sister, holding her hand and sucking his thumb.

They made quite a pair, Ivy reflected.

Astrid was almost twice the height of her brother, with the same jet black hair – still damp from the bath – and oddly pale green eyes. She looked torn between defiance and gratitude, and Ivy liked her immensely.

"I have to ask," she said carefully, not wanting to upset

them, "and you don't have to tell me what you're running from if you don't want to, but is there anyone looking for you?"

"No," said Astrid, at once – almost petulantly.

"And your parents?"

"Don't have any anymore," said Jake.

"Foster parents?"

"No," said the girl again, and Ivy strongly suspected she was lying. She had answered just a little too quickly.

"I just have to make sure no one's missing you – or out in the storm, looking for you," she explained, gently.

"There's no one," said Astrid, firmly. "Just us."

"Alright," said Ivy, letting it go. "There's stew, from the smell of it and some more people to meet, if you want to."

The girl nodded and allowed Ivy to lead them both to the kitchen table. She saw the girl's eyes flicking around, trying to see everything all at once. Mahri was already doling out stew into Ivy's bowls, and had pressed both men into service as soon as they had appeared: Reggie was laying the table, ferrying bread and butter and crockery across the kitchen, while Christopher was wrestling with the kettle, making mugs of steaming hot chocolate.

He glanced up at her as she passed him and his cheeks went pink. Clearly he was just as embarrassed as she was about the towel incident. As the children climbed onto the kitchen chairs, keeping careful eyes on the adults around them, Ivy telephoned the Barracloughs to let them know that their books – and their young employee – were safe, for the moment.

Professor Barraclough sounded very relieved, and Ivy heard him shout the news to Joanna, who seemed to have been on the verge of venturing out, just to check. They agreed to call in the following day, when the weather would hopefully be less ludicrous.

She paused for a moment before joining them all at the table, struck for a moment by the sheer number of people in the midst of her usually empty home. She sat between Christopher and the little boy, who seemed to have rather taken to her. He was staring at the bowl of stew in front of him with wide, hungry eyes, and probably would have already been eating if it wasn't for his sister's hand, holding him back in his chair.

"Well, tuck in," instructed Mahri – no-one needed telling twice.

They ate in peace, the only sounds food related, interspersed with occasional requests for condiments. Several times, Ivy caught movement out of the corner of her eye, both out in the garden and at the top of the walls of the room; she grimaced inwardly. This was not going to be easy.

The first bowl having taken the edge off their hunger (and replaced some of Ivy and Christopher's depleted energy supplies), Mahri passed out seconds, even buttering more of her mouth-watering soda bread. She watched, satisfied, as it was wolfed down by five hungry mouths.

Ivy was the first to slow down, having already had toast, and took to dipping her bread into the remains of her stew to soak up the delicious juices, melting butter dripping off her fingers and into the bowl.

Wiping her hands, she cleared her plate and refilled the kettle, since everyone's hot chocolates appeared to have evaporated. Leaning on the counter, she rediscovered her hairbrush, still lodged in the back pocket of her jeans, and brushed her hair through, quickly braiding it so that it was out of the way. Noticing the way that Astrid was watching her, she offered to do hers too.

"Well," said Mahri, when everyone had finished, and was in that agreeably sleepy stage of digestion, "perhaps it's time we found out about one another."

Ivy gave her a warning look over the top of Astrid's head, but she needn't have worried.

"My name is Mahri Glass," said the older witch. "I have a florist's shop downstairs, and I live in the old coach-house, over there." She waved a hand at the lights twinkling across the garden, then looked mildly startled as Boscoe flew in, inquisitive as ever. He perched on the back of an empty chair and gave a shrill cry. Astrid shuffled away from him slightly, but her brother looked greatly interested. "I've known Ivy here since she was a little girl, and it's very nice to meet you all."

She looked expectantly at Christopher, who cleared his throat uncomfortably.

"Er – I'm Christopher, I work in the bookshop downstairs... and that's about it," he finished, lamely.

"Ivy Burwell," said Ivy, ignoring the flicker of sadness in Mahri's expression – she wasn't a Chambers, *not any more*. "I have a teashop and wool emporium downstairs, and I own the Arcade – this building... and you're all more than welcome here."

Gently, she wrapped a hair tie around the end of Astrid's plait and sat back down in her seat.

The boy beside her looked at his sister expectantly.

"I'm Astrid Healy," she said. "And this is Jake, my little brother," she looked around at them for a moment. "Thank you for coming to get us," she said, earnestly, to Ivy and Christopher. "And for letting us stay, and for drying our things."

"And for the food!" Jake added, happily. "It was yummy!"

"I'm glad you liked it," Mahri chuckled.

Everyone turned their attention to Reggie, who was watching, quietly, from the end of the table.

"Oh," he said, with a cough. "Reggie Long, at your service."

"Awk!" screeched Boscoe, feeling the need to introduce himself. "At your service!"

"This is Boscoe," said Reggie, mildly embarrassed. "My parrot – and this is Saffy."

Saffy, her muzzle in a particularly meaty dish of stew, looked up at the mention of her name, before enthusiastically licking the remnants of food off the bowl.

They talked for a while, about general, safe topics like

weather and stew, until everyone's heads were nodding and little Jake was completely asleep on the table.

Astrid shook him awake, gently, and led him off to the bedroom that Ivy had prepared for them; he was practically asleep on his feet, and the four adults smiled after them.

"It's good to see them safe and warm," said Reggie, pushing his seat back.

Ivy set the dishes washing themselves while Mahri picked up her massive pan and gave her a one-armed hug, balancing it on her other hip.

"You did some good tonight," she said, giving her shoulders a squeeze. Ivy rolled her eyes at her. Christopher, who had blatantly overheard, turned away, smirking.

Reggie, who was giving Saffy a well-deserved fuss, paused by the door before following Mahri across the garden.

"Is it alright if Boscoe just flies around a bit tonight?" he asked her. "It's been a long time since he's had so much space to roam around in."

"Of course," she said.

"You know," said Reggie, looking at her in a thoughtful sort of fashion. "You remind me of a lady that I used to know when I was a lad. Griselda Chambers, I think her name was. She was a good woman."

"She was my grandmother," Ivy told him, surprised. Usually people remembered her family with distaste.

"Was she, indeed?" he exclaimed, impressed. "She was a great lady," he said, regarding Ivy in what appeared to be an entirely new light. "Helped the women down my street when it was their time. There were a lot of kids my age who wouldn't have been around if it weren't for her and her daughters."

Ivy nodded, slowly. The birthing of children wasn't something that her mother had passed down to her, having died before she was – in her mother's opinion – old enough. Her aunts had tried, of course, but by that point Ivy had wanted as little to do with her family's skills as possible, only using the parts of her magic that had a reasonably low impact – or the parts that made Sam smile.

Reggie took her hand and shook it, firmly. "I am proud to know you, miss," he said, with a wide smile. "Very proud."

Ivy watched him go, bewildered.

She jumped slightly, as somewhere behind her Christopher yawned, loudly.

"Sorry," he said, trying – and failing – to stop.

She waved him off, sleepily.

"Don't worry about it," she said, wearily. "I'm just not used to there being so many people around, that's all."

He gave her a sheepish smile as she said goodnight, and he paused outside the door to his room, suddenly under the impression that something, somewhere, was watching him. Shaking his head as the Light Orbs in the main room winked out, he dismissed his concerns (what could possibly be in here that Ivy didn't know about, after all?) and went into the spare room, not even bothering to turn on the lights. He practically fell into bed, and was asleep before he hit the sheets.

ooo

Christopher awoke from a restful, dreamless sleep – in a magnificently comfortable bed – to a face full of foliage. The air was thick with deep green, glossy leaves. He closed his eyes and opened them again a couple of times to check that he wasn't dreaming. The vines were still there, in a strange sort of full-body halo around him; none of them were touching him, and he got the distinct impression that they were looking at him funny. He peered at them, the sensation that he was engaged in a thoroughly bizarre staring match creeping over him. The plants peered intently back.

As he watched, a red flower budded, bloomed and died, the large petals fading and falling onto the bedspread in a mildly sinister fashion. He picked one up;

it felt real enough, and the inquisitive foliage had a leafy, earthy smell to it that he recognised from somewhere.

He sat up, cautiously. The vines maintained a uniform distance from him, still not touching him, but flowing around him as he moved. He got out of bed, noting a slight increase in urgency in the twisting vines. Standing in the middle of the room, he realised with a horrible sinking feeling that whatever he chose to do, the vines could probably suffocate him with the greatest of ease if they felt threatened.

But why weren't they?

To Christopher's relief, a familiar scent worked its way through the stems, and he called out.

"Ivy?" he asked, in a slightly higher voice than usual.

He heard her pause on the other side of the door. "Yes?"

"Er – could you come in here for a moment, please?" he asked, fighting to keep the panic out of his voice.

He heard the door open, and a strange sort of ripple went through the foliage; for some reason that he couldn't quite place, they looked sort of sheepish now – as if they had been caught doing something that they shouldn't be.

"Ah," said Ivy, in a wholly unsettling way.

"Ah?" he repeated, remembering the behaviour of the plants in the garden and the familiar way they had flocked to her the previous evening.

"Hang on," she instructed him, and the stems rippled again. She emerged in the midst of them, walking towards him, the vines twisting gracefully around her. She paused a few feet away, finding her path blocked.

"I don't think so," she said, to the plants – they backed away from her reluctantly, cowed but still a little defiant. They were protecting her, he realised, from *him*. He swallowed, not wanting particular facts to emerge just yet – well, *ever*, really.

"Sorry about them," she said, quite embarrassed. "They have something of a mind of their own."

"Indeed," said Christopher, keeping his eyes on the

nearest vines.

"They don't normally swarm around people like this though," she continued, thoughtfully. "Usually they either like someone or they really don't... it's as if they can't work you out."

Christopher attempted to look confused and innocent all at the same time; Ivy smiled at him.

"Maybe they just don't like me."

"Believe me when I say that if they didn't like you, you would have woken up outside, or upside down, or something," she laughed, which was somehow more frightening than mutant, mischievous plants. "There was this chap who wouldn't leave my Aunt Ruth alone, and –" she paused, taking in his expression. "I'll tell you another time. It *was* funny though... for the rest of us."

He gave her a look that was torn between panicked desperation and manic hysteria and her smile became less pronounced.

"Alright," she said, to the vines. "That's enough, leave him alone."

They twisted and shifted madly around the room, becoming thicker and thicker. Christopher, now entirely unnerved, stood very still, trying to look small and non-threatening. Ivy was frowning at the vines.

"Well then, if you won't leave him alone, come and meet him," she told them, sternly. The vines rippled at her. "What can you possibly be afraid of?" she asked, exasperated. "Oh, come here," she ordered, holding out an arm to the indecisive foliage.

The leaves and stems curled around her hand and wrist, flowing across her skin almost hungrily. They came to a stop around her shoulder, and she leaned towards him. Just before she touched him, she paused.

"Do you mind?" she asked. "They might calm down a bit."

Wanting more than ever to back away, he nodded, trying to stay as still as possible as the agitated greenery recoiled away from him before her fingers touched his chest. As soon as the contact was made, however, they surged forwards, enveloping his body.

It was a curiously unsettling sensation, feeling these alien tendrils creeping along his skin, investigating him. The urge to bolt was fierce, but he knew that death by insane plant was a distinct possibility (and he didn't particularly want to look like a complete Jessie in front of Ivy). After a few moments of agonisingly gentle prodding and inspection, the movement of the vines altered – if it had been a conversation, he would have thought of it as a change in tone.

They became slightly rougher, but in a familiar sort of way, as if they were used to him now. It was a good deal less ticklish, which he was exceptionally grateful for.

"See," Ivy said to them, fondly. "I told you there was nothing to worry about. Daft old thing."

The foliage around them withdrew and abruptly burst into bloom, showering them both with petals of every size and shape and colour. Ivy and Christopher they shook them out of their hair.

"Well, they seem to like you," said Ivy, laughing. She took her hand back, smiling, and gave a little yelp of surprise as the vines pushed her – without warning – into Christopher. Determinedly, the plants wound their way about them both, wrapping them together.

"Alright, that's enough!" Ivy admonished them. The vines were ruffling his hair, playfully. "Yes, yes, we're friends – now lay *off*!"

The vines retreated, but in such a way that left Christopher in no doubt whatsoever that they wanted them to know that it was *their* idea, and not Ivy's. He stepped away from her, blushing so hotly that he was certain she would feel the heat from his skin.

She coughed awkwardly, and when he glanced up he noted that she was equally pink.

"They like to play tricks," she said, not meeting his eyes. "Anyway, I should check on Astrid and Jake."

She fled, leaving a bewildered and embarrassed werewolf behind her.

ooo

Jake was the first to wake up, since Astrid had stayed up late thinking. She did that from time to time: trying to think of a way out of a tricky situation, or work out a new way to get food, or to find a new place to pitch their tent. She would get a determined sort of look on her face and would sit, hunched up, for hours, looking at a situation from every angle until she decided how to deal with it.

Jake thought that she was marvellous.

He pulled the covers around him happily. He couldn't remember the last time he had woken up warm – even in the summer the mornings had been chilly, even when he did as Astrid told him and wore two pairs of everything. She tried so hard for him, he knew, but there was only so much that they could do. He glanced down: his sister looked so peaceful when she was sleeping. These days she usually had a frown on her face, so he liked to see her asleep. Sometimes, her dreams even made her smile.

Jake liked to save up those moments in his head, so that he could look at them later when he was sad or lonely.

He wriggled out from underneath her arm and looked around.

The bed was covered in blankets and cushions that he didn't remember being there the night before. Some of their things had been piled up around them, along with a few soft toys that he didn't recognise, like some kind of ramshackle magpie's nest.

It was a bit of a puzzle.

He looked around. He hadn't been paying that much attention the night before, when he had been sleepily led to bed, but he liked what he saw now. The walls were a pale yellow colour, and there were a few old pictures around, the people in them watching over the room like guardians. There were no windows, which he thought was a little odd, after living so long out of doors, but there was plenty of light streaming in through the coloured glass in the door. Careful not to wake his sister, he climbed out of bed and walked over to it: he put his hand against the glass, which was rippled and cool, and pleasant to touch. There were flowers in the glass, pale pink and white petals climbing up what must have been a frame of some kind. They looked vaguely familiar, but they had always lived in cities before they came to Brindleford, and he had never been particularly interested in flowers. There was what must be grass beneath the flowers, and bright blue skies above, which made Jake smile widely.

He turned back to the room, and looked over at Astrid, still sleeping. He wondered whether she would be very angry if he snuck out and had a look around.

Ivy and Christopher seemed friendly enough, and despite Astrid's stern warnings, nothing about them suggested that he would get into any trouble, and he might be able to see whether or not the rain had stopped.

He caught himself guiltily hoping that it hadn't, and that they might be able to stay a little longer, in this friendly place with its warm blankets, and hot food, and smiling faces. Although he had felt safe nestled into their tent with his sister – safer than when they had thought that they might lose one another, at least – this place felt friendly and comfortable.

It might be nice, if I could get everyone to agree, if we could stay for a while, he thought.

Astrid wouldn't mind too much, if he was still in the building. Yes – she would come and find him safe and happy, and be pleased with the place! Then she might – *there was something under the bed!*

Jake froze.

He stared at the dark space beneath the bed, unable to move, or make a sound. For a few minutes nothing happened, and then, just as he felt able to move an inch away from the door – and inch towards his sleeping sister – he saw it move again. Something dark, and shadowy, and sinuous.

Without thinking, he leapt onto the bed, silently shaking Astrid awake and burrowing into her surprised arms.

"Something u-under the bed!" he hissed, quivering uncontrollably. "I th-thought it was g-going to e-eat you!"

Astrid, who had had a younger brother long enough to know that this sort of scare happened from time to time, paused for a few moments, before remembering that they had, in fact, been taken in by someone who was quite blatantly a witch.

And witches might well have things lurking around that could hide under beds and eat children.

She stayed very still.

Astrid had hoped that not all witches were like the ones in the story books that cooked children, or stole people's voices, or had nasty things lurking in their houses ready to do those things on their behalf.

Ivy had seemed like a friendly and open person, she had even seemed to care about them. Astrid didn't like to think that she might have been so completely fooled.

And then there were the lights...

Astrid was almost certain that anyone who could make the lights dance for her little brother when he was scared or sad was a witch, and she didn't want to eat *anyone*.

The thing under the bed moved again, making a terrifying slithering noise against the floor. She heard Jake whimper, very quietly, and – for the second time in as many nights – couldn't think of a thing to do except hold onto him.

The thing slithered again; Astrid picked up the heavy book that had been on the bedside table, ready to fight back, when she heard soft padding footsteps outside in the hall. Both Astrid and the thing froze.

Someone knocked softly on the door.

"Are you two alright in there?" Ivy asked. "Mahri's cooking bacon, for some reason..."

Astrid wasn't yet ready to hope, but Jake was: he wriggled his head out of their tangled blankets.

"Help!" he squeaked, trying but failing to make himself any louder, as if the fear itself had squashed his voice out of his chest. "It's going to eat us!"

His cries hadn't been very loud, but Ivy had heard them, and she threw open the door, looking surprised – and to Astrid's horror, angry.

She *had* meant the thing to eat them after all!

But Ivy had dropped to the floor and was glaring at the space under the bed.

"Get out of there *this instant*!" she snapped, and there were some urgent slithery noises as whatever it was made a hasty retreat. "Of all the stupid –"

She got to her feet, quite beside herself.

"If you think that was funny, you've got another thing coming!" she shouted – apparently at the ceiling. "You will treat my guests with respect – not *scare them half to death!*"

There was the sound of running feet in the corridor, and Christopher skidded into view, half dressed. He'd been halfway through putting his t-shirt on, and still only had one arm in it.

"What?" he asked, looking around wildly. Then he caught sight of Ivy, who was bright red and still breathing hard.

It seemed to Astrid that Christopher had never seen Ivy so angry. He did quite an impressive double-take and stared at her for a few moments, before his eyes narrowed. He appeared to be looking at something on the wall of the corridor behind Ivy.

"Oh," he said. "Plants?" he asked Ivy, who gave him a terse nod. "Oh." He looked at the children. "Are you two okay?"

Astrid considered this for a moment, and lowered the book. She nodded dubiously.

"Can I come in?" he asked.

Another nod; Jake wriggled around so that he was sitting on her lap and he could peek out of the mess of pillows and blankets.

Christopher went and sat on the far end of the bed, pulling his t-shirt on properly as he passed Ivy, who had managed to control her breathing now, although her face was still quite blotchy.

"What happened?" Christopher asked, as Ivy perched across from him.

"I-I was looking at the flowers in the door," Jake said, in a small voice. "A-and there was a – a – a *thing* under the bed, and it was going to *eat* us!"

Astrid tightened her arms around him, silently letting him know that no one was going to eat *her* little brother.

Christopher crouched on the floor and had a good look. "Well there's nothing there now," he said, indistinctly.

"Ivy came and shouted at it," said Astrid, suspiciously. "And it did what she told it to."

"They don't always," said Ivy, who – Astrid realised with surprise – looked rather embarrassed. "But they would never have eaten you. I'm reasonably sure they're vegetarian, except for the odd slug."

Christopher and the children gaped at her, unanimously confused.

"And I *did* see them chewing on an old leather boot once, when I was little, but I think Dad had fed it to them as a joke – they weren't very well for a while after that."

"What are they?" asked Astrid, with more confidence than she felt.

"Er..."

"They look like plants," said Christopher, helpfully. "I woke up surrounded by them – but I think they were just trying to work out whether I was a threat or not."

"Are *we* a threat?" Jake asked, in a wondering voice.

"No," said Ivy, firmly. "They aren't very subtle. The fact that Christopher woke up with them all over the place meant that they couldn't decide about him –" Astrid saw that he looked mildly dismayed at this, "– and the fact that they were trying to keep out of your sight means that they like you."

"What do they do to people they don't like?" Astrid blurted out, before she could stop herself.

"Hang them up by the ankles, generally."

Ivy couldn't help smiling a little at the memory, and

Jake giggled a little, feeling much better about the whole affair.

"It's probably why you're covered in pillows and toys and things," she went on, indicating the mountain of blankets. "The irony is that they were probably doing their best *not* to scare you."

Astrid stared at her, incredulously, and Ivy felt compelled to continue.

"They haven't met a child since I grew up, so they're a bit out of practice."

There were a few moments of awkward silence.

Astrid's eyes flew to the wall beside Ivy: a tendril of green was working its way up it, looking for all the world like it was trying not to be seen. She suppressed the ridiculous urge to laugh.

"I'm sorry that they frightened you," Ivy said, unaware of the impish greenery behind her. Astrid thought that she was speaking as much to Christopher as she was to them. "Would you like some breakfast? Mahri's cooking sausages and eggs and bacon, and things – and there are crumpets, or cereal –"

"Yes please," said Astrid, quietly, as her brother shouted it.

Ivy smiled. "Good. I think Mahri's as excited about cooking as you are about eating," she said to Jake, which made him laugh, all his worries forgotten at the prospect of hot food.

She went away, then, to help in the kitchen, and Christopher wandered off muttering vaguely about the location of his socks. Jake climbed off the bed and raced after them, apparently completely reassured.

Astrid, however, had learned to be much more cautious.

She looked at the plant on the wall, which had burst into an enormous yellow flower as soon as Ivy had left the room, trumpeting its defiance behind her back.

It looked perfectly normal, apart from its size. She narrowed her eyes and touched one of the petals: it shivered under her fingers, as if it was ticklish.

"Thank you," she said, and the petals took on a slight peachy tinge.

Even if they weren't going to be eaten by things under the bed, she decided, she had better keep her eyes open.

By now, the kitchen was beginning to smell encouragingly of bacon, so she picked up a much-loved and oversized jumper that Ivy had lent her, and followed her brother down the hall.

12
Mistress Martha

It was odd seeing so many people in their pyjamas, Ivy reflected, sipping a cup of tea. Only Christopher had attempted to get dressed, and everyone else was wearing quite a variety of cotton and flannel. The children and Christopher were tucking into eggs and bacon around the under-used kitchen table, talking and laughing in that quiet, awkward fashion that occurs when people haven't known one another for very long.

She had had a quick peek across the garden when she got up, and Mahri's curtains were still drawn, suggesting that she and Reggie had stayed up late talking – though apparently not late enough to prevent her finding and cooking the largest plate of sausages that Ivy had ever seen. She also noted that Reggie's window-box of geraniums had apparently planted itself inconspicuously beneath the kitchen window of the empty coach-house. Apparently, she and Mahri weren't the only ones who wanted Reggie to stay. Boscoe was asleep in the plum tree against the wall of the garden, his grey feathers blending elegantly against the dusty green of the leaves.

It was still raining outside the great, glass windows, but with much less enthusiasm. A brief consultation of the news channel had informed them that the waters – while not receding – were also not getting any deeper any more. Seeing the images of the half of Brindleford that was underwater was quite disturbing, and they had all stood around, sipping from their mugs of tea, glad that they had escaped the worst of it. There had been a lot of damage to buildings – particularly along the river – and both Reggie and Christopher had been quite upset about seeing their former home entirely submerged. The camera had lingered on the building for quite some time, and they could see a pair of curtains that had escaped from a broken window still streaming out from their frame, rippling and snapping in the strong current.

Happily, most people had reached higher ground

safely, and were taking shelter with friends and family, or in a couple of village halls and churches that had opened their doors to the bedraggled remainder. There had been only one casualty: an extremely ill-advised canoeist.

Ivy shook her head, sadly. It seemed that wherever there was danger, some poor fool would shed their last modicum of common sense and fling themselves at it. Involuntarily, she glanced up at the picture of Sam, resting against a pile of books on one of the shelves on the far wall. With a pang of misery, she missed him intently for a few minutes, turning away and busying herself with the breakfast things until it passed, and she could face the room once more.

As tense as the proximity of so many new people made her, the house felt happier, more alive. If its antics this morning were anything to go by, it was ecstatic to have people inside of it again, and intended to do what it could to keep them safe and happy. She didn't blame it; many of the rooms of the Arcade had stood empty for the past few years, with the fewest inhabitants inside since it had been built. The house and the plants thrived on company, on being useful and needed. However awkward it might make her feel, Ivy was determined to extend the same kind of welcome to her guests as the house had extended to her upon her return.

She had needed a home, and it had grown around her; now, these people needed a home, and Ivy wasn't about to leave them out in the cold. The Arcade had made its opinion of their guests perfectly clear, with the exception of Christopher. She had never seen the vines act like that before, as if they were afraid to touch someone. Still, they seemed to like what they saw in him, so she left the thought in the back of her mind to mull over later.

She looked up from her musings as the toaster clicked and popped; she buttered her crumpets and carried them over, sneaking Saffy a lump of sausage under the table.

"Nice to have people around for breakfast," said Mahri, quietly, as she went to sit by Astrid, with a smile. Ivy returned the smile; she knew that – like the house – Mahri had found the loneliness of the last few years imposing.

They settled at the table with their choice of breakfasts, and joined in the conversations. Ivy stayed quiet. It had been a long time since she had felt comfortable in a group, and faced with the task of conversing with such a diverse mix of people, she felt that she didn't know quite where to start.

Christopher glanced at her a few times, perhaps out of curiosity at her silence or remembered embarrassment after the vines had tried to force them to 'make friends', but Ivy preferred to keep to herself. She was, despite herself, enjoying listening to the burble of conversation, so she sipped her tea in unaccustomed cosiness.

She had nearly finished when Christopher cleared his throat, uncomfortably. She looked up at him expectantly, trying to banish the creeping feeling of dread from the back of her mind.

"Um, about the vines..." he said, leaving the statement hanging in the air, like a cloud of uncertainty.

Ivy sighed, and put down her cup.

"First of all," she said, taking a deep breath. "I would like to assure you all that you are in no danger, whatsoever –" there was a general stiffening of bodies around the table at this ominous pronouncement, "– and that there is absolutely no need for anyone to panic."

She glanced at Mahri, who looked unhelpfully blank. Having spent her life amongst Practitioners, she had never needed to explain things to people who thought that flying kettles or plants that followed you about the house were unnatural.

"The house might be a tiny bit alive," she said, and winced, waiting for her new friends to run away, limbs flailing madly. No one moved, however, and she continued, more hopefully: "It mostly just manifests through the plants, since they're the most mobile, but you can sort of feel it everywhere inside the Arcade."

Christopher nodded, and she wondered when he had first noticed it.

"How do you mean 'alive'?" asked Reggie, with a frown.

"You know the feeling you get in old buildings?" Mahri asked. "That somehow they remember the things that have happened in them over the centuries?"

Reggie nodded, slowly.

"Well, they do," she explained. "Except that in the case of the Arcade, her occupants have always had magic – and fairly strong magic, too. It makes everything more pronounced," she went on, ignoring Ivy's wince. "And here, that means occasionally the Arcade will throw people out that it doesn't like, or try to help around the place. She definitely has character."

"Keeping it all hidden from the public is quite tricky," said Ivy. "But I think we've mostly secured the 'no vines downstairs until after dark' rule now."

There was a pause as everyone digested this.

"Hang on," said Christopher, abruptly. "You called the Arcade 'she' – how do you – well... how do you know it's a girl?"

"The Arcade was built by my great-great-great grandparents, Arthur and Lettie Chambers," Ivy began, fingering the handle of her teacup. "My great-great-grandmother was born on the day that the plans were drawn up, and she spent most of her early childhood scrambling around the building site, as far as I can tell. She and the Arcade sort of grew up together, and family legend suggests that they really understood one another – that they were a part of one another."

She glanced around the table, uncomfortably aware that they were all hanging on her every word.

"She lived for a very long time, long enough to see my grandmother, Griselda, born," she continued, more softly now. "Grandma told me once, about the day that she died: she was one-hundred and two, and still insisting on doing the gardening herself. She couldn't get up and down the stairs anymore, so she stayed up here and kept the house, preparing herbs and things for when they were needed. She had been out in the garden, Grandma said, and they found her out there, looking supremely satisfied with her work. There wasn't anything wrong with her as such, she just died of not being alive anymore," Ivy paused, before continuing. "I always thought it was such a lovely way to go. Anyway, it was the day after midsummer, and they had had a particularly good planting season, so the garden was full of flowers and fruit. When Martha died every single flower and leaf on every single plant in the garden fell.

"There were great drifts of leaves and petals, my grandmother said, and Martha among them. I think a part of the Arcade died with her... It took months for the garden to recover, and when it did, it had a little bit more *personality* than it had before, so we call her Martha," she finished, looking up at them.

There was another digestive pause. Movement along the top of the walls caught Ivy's eye. Martha liked having her story told, and tended to creep in to listen.

"I remember my nan telling me stories about Martha Chambers," said Reggie, slowly. "Quite an extraordinary woman, by all accounts."

"So we're told," said Mahri.

"So, the house is *possessed* by Martha?" Christopher asked, shaken.

"No," Ivy explained. "It's more like the house *is* Martha — with a large amount of its own personality mixed in."

"Oh," he said, like this didn't really explain anything at all. He lapsed into a frowning silence, resolving to work it out in his own time.

"She listens to Ivy though," said Mahri, almost proudly.

"Sometimes," Ivy qualified.

She looked around at them: no one appeared to be entirely floored by her unusual accommodation, although she imagined that it might take some getting used to. Everyone appeared to be lost in their own thoughts, except for Jake, whose eyes were fixed on the ceiling. She didn't even need to turn around to know what the boy was gazing at.

"Martha," she said, and five pairs of eyes flicked up towards her. "Stop freaking people out and introduce yourself properly."

Several people jumped as what had previously been empty space became dense foliage. Fronds of vines extended gracefully down from the ceiling around them, near enough to touch, but still allowing them room to move away if they wanted.

Saffy barked, wary and upset, but a few of the vines reached out and ruffled her fur, and she settled back down on the rug once more, content to tolerate their presence, and continue to be fed sausages.

Boscoe also appeared to be a little shy of the suddenly fidgety foliage, landing on the back of one of Ivy's mismatched kitchen chairs and giving the vines a very bemused look.

"Er, hello again," said Christopher, as Jake shrieked with laughter beside him, being enthusiastically tickled by the wandering stems.

"Glad to make your acquaintance, Mistress Chambers," said Reggie, in his careful way. "My nan spoke very highly of you."

A ripple of approval flowed around the nearest flora.

The only person who looked dubious was Astrid, possibly because the vines seemed particularly exuberant around her, flowing about her wrists and arms. She met Ivy's eyes over the table, and Ivy gave her an apologetic smile, muttering to the nearest stem: "Alright, you've made your point, now leave her alone."

The vines withdrew back to the ceiling, leaving their new friends staring up at them; Astrid rubbed at the skin of her arms, clearly astonished that the wandering plants hadn't left a mark; Ivy watched her for a few moments, thoughtfully.

"Well," said Mahri, clapping her hands together. "I'm glad we've got *that* out of the way. Would anyone like another cup of tea?"

She responded to the vague mutterings of assent as people shook themselves out of their plant-based contemplation. Ivy joined her by the kettle.

"I'm going to invite them to stay," she muttered. "If that's alright with you – they all need somewhere to be, and I think Martha would be happier having them around."

"I think it's a marvellous idea," Mahri whispered back. "As long as you're happy with it, too." She gave her a pointed look before continuing. "I know you, Ivy, you like it quiet and peaceful – with four other people around, two of whom are children – it is going to be anything but that. Not to even mention the dog and the parrot."

Ivy gave her a smile that was probably more like a grimace.

"I'll get used to it," she said. "It's what needs doing," she added, by way of an explanation.

And Sam would have convinced me to do it, too, if he were here, she thought, carrying cups of tea back to the table. *He'd want people to be looked after, and he wouldn't want me in here on my own – even if I do prefer it that way.*

"So," said Ivy, as they sat back down again. "Since you're all reasonably comfortable with the whole 'living house' thing, I was wondering if any of you would like to stay here."

Eyebrows were raised all around the table. Jake tugged urgently on Astrid's jumper, and there was a brief and hushed discussion.

"What, really?" asked Christopher, dumbfounded.

"Yes," Ivy assured him. "As you can see, there's plenty of room up here, and Martha clearly likes you." A wicked smile crossed her face, and for a moment Christopher understood what it was that Mahri missed in her old friend. "After all," she continued, loudly. "I wouldn't want the old girl to get lonely."

From the vine-covered ceiling there was a noise like ripping fabric, and Ivy was suddenly swamped in blue petals; she shook them out of her hair, laughing.

"Anyway, you're all more than welcome, is my point." She leaned on her elbows. "What about you, Reggie?"

"W- I –" he stammered, staring at her in surprise. "Really? You'd let me stay?"

"Of course she would, you daft thing," said Mahri. "Or she wouldn't have asked. I'd like you to stay, too – I've missed having company."

Reggie opened and closed his mouth a few times, astonished; he cleared his throat, pulling himself together.

"I would love to," he managed, somewhat overwhelmed. "I mean, if I'm not in the way –"

"Nonsense!" Mahri cried, brusquely.

"Well, I... I would very much like to stay, i-in that case," he told them, beginning to smile. "It reminds me of the stories my nan used to tell me... and the way things were when I grew up." He beamed at Ivy and Mahri. "My Bessie would have loved it here, too – I'm sure that she won't have any trouble finding me, it feels like the kind of place she would come to check. Thank you – both of you."

"Not at all," said Ivy, as Mahri rolled her eyes at him. "I was thinking that since there's the three of you, you might like to take up the other coach house. It's been empty for a while, and needs a little work, but there's plenty of room over there – it's a mirror image of Mahri's house."

Reggie turned around in his seat and looked across the garden to the two coach houses for a moment.

"All that space, just for me?" he squeaked. "It's – it's beautiful – I couldn't - I wouldn't want to be any trouble."

"Pish," said Mahri, who felt that the word wasn't used nearly often enough. "You've got to be somewhere, and it will be nice to have a next door neighbour again – Ivy excepted."

Reggie stared between the two of them for a few moments, before nodding, quite overcome.

"We'll get to work on it in a little while then," said Ivy, who could see the overgrown vines on the old coach house retreating and rearranging themselves neatly around the door and windows. She watched as they swung open, airing out the rooms, and smiled. Martha really *had* missed people being around. "And then we'll help you get your things moved in."

"Welcome home! Awk! Welcome home!" Boscoe screeched from the back of his chair. He took off abruptly, a flurry of grey and green feathers, to investigate his new home. Saffy, who was curled up at Reggie's feet, watched him go, looking tolerantly unimpressed.

"Good," said Ivy, amused by the familial exchange. "That's you sorted then. Christopher?"

He jumped slightly, surprised.

"Me?" he asked. "You want *me* to stay?"

"Yes."

"Here – *with you*?"

"Well, why wouldn't I?" she asked, looking perplexed.

"Well, I – er..." he trailed off, apparently consulting a long internal list of reasons why he would not be wanted. "I can't give you much in the way of rent, just yet, though once I've saved up, I –"

"You wouldn't need to," said Ivy. "Martha doesn't approve of charging rent except for in the shops. Besides, I wouldn't take it if you tried to give it to me."

He stared at her, dumbfounded.

"But-"

"All I'd ask is that you keep the main area reasonably tidy..."

As one person, everyone turned to look at the organised chaos adorning the two preparation tables.

"I don't mind what you do in your own room – aside from the usual taboos of murder and fencing stolen goods, and so on," she went on.

"I – there's not much chance of that, at least," he said, apparently quite flustered.

"You can have the two rooms at the end of the far corridor," she said.

"*Two* rooms!" he exclaimed, astonished.

"Well, yes," said Ivy. "I have two – a bedroom and a sort of study type area. It would be unfair to just give you one."

"Really, I couldn't accept –"

"Yes, you can," said Ivy, firmly.

"But – are you *sure*?"

Ivy narrowed her eyes, interrupting him. "Christopher Porter, if you ask me whether I'm sure about something that I have repeatedly offered you once more this week, I'll get Martha to string you up by the ankles."

The children giggled as Christopher struggled to come up with an answer that didn't make him feel like he was taking advantage of anyone and wouldn't mean he would spend the rest of the day dangling from the rafters. He glanced at Reggie and Mahri for help, but they were both sniggering into their hands.

He gave up.

"In that case, I would very much like to live here," he said – and a large part of him was genuinely delighted that he could. "Thank you, very much."

Mahri snorted, but managed to turn it into a highly suspicious coughing fit.

He gave Ivy a warm smile, determined that one day he would repay her kindness.

She smiled back, secretly pleased that he had accepted; telling herself that the feeling had everything to do with helping a friend in need, and nothing to do with how nice he looked with a smile on his face, she turned to the children. They were still giggling to themselves, and it took a few moments for them to notice her attention.

"How about you two?" she asked. "You said last night it was just you two, and if that's true you can stay here."

Astrid's face immediately became closed, as though

she didn't want any of them to see her reaction. Jake was staring between Ivy and his sister, an intently hopeful expression on his face.

"You don't have to – I won't pressure you into staying, and if you'd rather we can take you somewhere else where you can make a fresh start, but you are more than welcome here. In fact I think it would be safe to say that even though we've only known you for a very short time, we would all miss you both very much if you left."

The adults around the table nodded, and a vine curled up from under the table. Somewhat comically, it was clutching one of Ivy's old teddy-bears, as if to make it absolutely clear how Martha felt on the subject.

Astrid bit her lip, glancing around at the adults' faces; then she turned to Jake, and instigated a muffled conversation.

Ivy caught words like 'warm', and 'food' – and once, the word 'magic'. Eventually, Astrid turned back to her.

"We would very much like to stay, if that would be alright," she said in a tight voice. "On one condition."

Ivy nodded, interested.

"That we can stay here together, and neither one of us will have to leave unless we want to."

"Together," said Jake, fiercely, still clutching his sister's sleeve.

"Of course," said Ivy, as though the thought of separating them had never crossed her mind (which it hadn't).

A shy smile appeared on Astrid's face. "Then we want to stay, please," she said, almost timidly.

"Excellent!" said Ivy, surprised at how happy she was to hear their answer. "You can have a few of the rooms on this side of the Arcade if you'd like – a bedroom each with a playroom-study type thing in between. How does that sound?"

"It sounds lovely," said Astrid, properly smiling now. "Thank you!"

"Thanks!" said Jake, practically incandescent with happiness.

"Good," said Ivy, and really meant it.

Mahri stretched, and stood up.

"We should get on, then, if we're moving four people in," she said, briskly. "Divide and conquer?" she added, to Ivy.

"Sounds good to me," she replied. "I think we should get bedrooms sorted first – and Reggie's kitchen and bathroom."

"Oh, don't worry about me," Reggie put in.

"Shush, you," said Mahri, tolerantly.

"How about I help Reggie," said Christopher. "I used to be pretty good at decorating – painted sets for the drama club when I was in school."

"I'll get cleaning the bits that don't need a lick of paint," said Mahri. "You can start thinking through where you want your things moving to – I'm sure we have some stickers and a pen somewhere. Mark them all up and then when we get to that point we can help you move it all in."

Reggie saluted, he couldn't help it; everyone laughed, even Mahri.

"Yes ma'am!" he said, and hurried off to get changed.

"I'll get you two settled, then," said Ivy to the children. "I think we should get your rooms done first, and then raid the cellar to see if there are any old things of mine that you can use."

They raced off to the guest room, excited at the prospect of having their own rooms.

Ivy had barely pulled her old jeans and blouse on when Jake came skidding to a halt outside her door. She could tell that it was him through the glass, and that he was excited about something. She laughed to herself as he hovered outside the door, not wanting to disturb her, hopping from one foot to the other in excitement.

"Come in," she said, and he opened the door cautiously.

"The plants are moving things," he said, urgently.

Ivy tied back her hair and went to have a look. Jake

was quite right: there were great swathes of vines around Christopher's boxes. It looked rather like Martha had run into problems by not taking into account the combined weight of his miniaturised possessions, and was having to use quite a dense tangle of foliage to lift anything.

"I didn't think they were supposed to," the tiny boy said, watching them with extreme interest.

Ivy laughed.

"Don't rummage through them," she instructed, as they walked past the tangle of undergrowth. One of the vines snapped vertically and made a creditable impression of Reggie's salute. "And that one's for the kitchen," she continued, patting the vines surrounding the rather battered cardboard box, which immediately changed direction.

Jake was obviously fascinated by the vines, and he was still watching them slowly wriggle about when they turned into the corridor that was to have the children's rooms in it.

Astrid came out of the guest room as they did, a little uncertain as to how a witch might go about redecorating. Jake immediately ran to stand beside her. Ivy smiled. They were very much alike when you saw them together, and their mutual care for one another was obvious.

"I think we'll leave the guest room as it is," she said, contemplatively, stopping in front of the room next to the bathroom. "Shall we do Jake first?" she asked them both.

Astrid nodded, and Jake gave a small whoop of joy. He walked over to her, trembling with excitement.

"Do I get to do magic?" he asked, breathlessly.

"Yes," Ivy confirmed. She opened the door to his new room, which was full of dusty boxes. "Hmm... I think these would be better off in the basement," she said, and made a complicated looking sign with her hand. The boxes sort of faded, leaving the impression of themselves on the back of the eye for a few moments.

"Wow!" said Jake, as he and his sister peered into the now empty room.

"That only works in here, and only on things that have been here for a long time," said Ivy. "One of my ancestors thought that moving heavy objects sounded too much like hard work. I must say it's one of the saner decisions my family made about the building." She turned to Jake, who gave her his full, excited attention.

"Now," she said. "Try to think about what colours you would like on the walls and ceiling, and what you'd like the floor to feel like –"

"Blue!" he said, beaming.

"You don't have to tell me," Ivy said, her eyes crinkling into a smile. "But try to keep it in your head. "You'll also need somewhere for clothes and things, but the rest is up to you... Martha will get a sort of feel for you, and try to match the image in your head."

She put her hand on the stained glass of the door, pulling it shut. The coloured flowers that had been there before faded until the rippling panel was entirely clear.

Jake wasn't paying attention – he had his eyes squeezed shut in concentration – but Astrid watched, fascinated, as all the colours seemed to drain out of the glass and into Ivy's hand.

"Now," she said, gently steering him towards the door. "Put your hand on the glass and concentrate on how you'd like the room to be – that's it. Your hand might tingle a bit, but it's just Martha getting the measure of you."

The look of concentration on Jake's face was adorable, Ivy decided, and she gave Astrid a warm smile. There were the sounds of movement from within the room, and both children tried to see what was going on through the glass, Jake's hand still firmly pressed against it.

They gasped in surprise as the glass underneath his palm began to fill up with colour – slowly at first, and in very pale shades, but building in both strength and speed. Ivy watched, interested, as shoots grew up from the wooden frame at the base of the door and flowed upwards, budding and blooming as they went. It had been a long time since she had had the chance to watch a door take shape – not since her Grandmother had died. When the aunts eventually followed her she had simply kept the doors as they had been, friendly and lasting reminders of her family.

Great red and yellow peonies had burst into bloom near the bottom of the door, which became variegated gladioli, further up the pane. The whole thing was a riot of reds and yellows, except for the flowers at the very top (Jake and Astrid had to step backwards in order to see properly), which were like great white bulrushes.

"Interesting," said Ivy, and Astrid looked like she was longing to ask her why, but Jake got there first.

"Can I look inside, now?" Jake asked her, practically bobbing up and down.

Ivy nodded, and he reached up to turn the shiny brass handle.

He squealed with delight and ran inside.

The room had – not unexpectedly – turned out blue and green, and clashed horribly with the door; Ivy was sure that Jake wouldn't mind this at all.

Martha had done a very good job, growing a very comfortable-looking bed, shelves for books, cupboards and drawers for clothes and toys, and – in the very centre of the room – a big, blue rug with squashy beanbags on it. Jake was engaged in jumping onto one of them when Astrid gasped.

"Look at the ceiling!" she cried.

It was beautiful.

There was a full map of the solar system up there, complete with fist-sized planets orbiting a sun that was the size of a bowling ball. They were travelling along their celestial paths very slowly, a backdrop of twinkling constellations winking and sparkling all around them. Ivy had a shrewd suspicion that when the light went that evening, the whole thing would glow.

As she watched Jake charge delightedly about his new room, squealing happily in delight at every new thing he saw, she wondered briefly how they were ever going to convince him to sleep.

Astrid, she noted, was hanging back, enjoying her brother's happiness, running her hand along the top of his chest of drawers, as if trying to reassure herself that it was all real.

The girl had a look of deep concentration on her face, as if she expected reality to fail under her scrutiny.

She must have had to grow up extremely quickly, Ivy thought, sadly, watching Astrid's eyes follow Jake around the room. *And to find ways to protect and care for her little brother.*

That sort of responsibility was tough on anybody, let alone on a seven year old girl.

I wonder what they're running from, she mused, as Jake began to drag his sister around the room, showing her things and surprising laughter out of her as he went.

Whatever the reason, I'm glad they're here now, she thought, firmly, surprising herself.

Unwilling to examine her own motives, she moved towards the door.

"Shall we get you sorted?" she asked Astrid, who turned away from a close examination of her brother's bed with a shy smile.

"Yes, please," she said.

It sounded to Ivy as if she wasn't sure whether to be excited or cautious as she followed the witch to the door at the end of the hall, just behind the kitchen.

"This was my grandmother's room," Ivy murmured, more to herself than to the children. For some reason, putting Astrid in here seemed rather appropriate.

She stuck her head through the door and dismissed some more boxes to the nether regions of the Arcade, before closing it once more and cleaning the glass with her hand.

She watched Griselda's fronds of willow and asphodels disappear with an accompanying bite of sadness.

"Your turn," she said to Astrid as she stepped back, wondering why everything she did at the moment made her think of her family.

Astrid approached the door with the same deliberate

concentration that she applied to everything. She closed her eyes and unconsciously stuck her tongue between her teeth, a slight frown upon her young face.

This time a border around the edge of the panel formed first, building itself up out of vines and flowers. At the base of the border a bright cacophony of daisies burst into flower, giving way to a stand of deep purple dahlias; finally, dark branches reached out across a bright azure sky and burst into cherry blossom.

Ivy appeared to nod to herself, as if acknowledging Martha's assessment of her new young friend, before motioning for her to try the door.

The room was a lot like her brother's, but somehow Martha had managed to make it appear more elegant. The walls were a pale pink – something that Astrid appeared to be distinctly embarrassed about – and covered with painted plants. Every kind of flower that Mahri sold or herb that Ivy used in her shop was there, and each one was labelled in a graceful cursive script that Ivy associated with some of the older jars and boxes on her shelves. Martha clearly had plans for these children's education.

Jake was happily careening around his sister's room now, while she appeared to be trying to take it all in.

She turned to Ivy with a strange look on her face.

"You want us to have all this?" she asked, clearly quite concerned.

"Of course," said Ivy, a little taken aback. "Besides, if I happened to disagree and removed something, Martha would only put it back again. She's quite stubborn when she wants to be."

"Oh," said Astrid, thoughtful and a little nonplussed. "Thank you..." Then: "I don't *really* like pink you know," she said, defensively.

Ivy tried not to laugh.

"Fair enough," she said. "But there's nothing wrong with liking it – it's a perfectly good colour, you know."

The girl appeared to be considering this.

"And Martha prefers people to be themselves," Ivy

continued, a wicked glint in her eyes. "But if you'd rather change it –" she raised her hands as if to begin a spell.

"No – it's alright," said Astrid, hurriedly. "I can cope with a bit of pink!"

Her cheeks stained almost the same colour as the walls, she went to investigate her new room.

13
Full House

Christopher was perplexed.

He had been helping to decorate Reggie's new home for most of the morning, getting thoroughly covered in flecks of paint and really rather enjoying himself. The same vestiges of cleaning magic that clung to the rest of the Arcade had remained in place in the coach house, so it had only really needed freshening up, once Reggie had agreed that the paint colours they had found in the cellar were alright for him. He rather suspected that, at this point, Reggie would agree to anything.

He had all but finished by lunchtime and had ambled across the garden that he still couldn't think of as partly his, to find the pile of stuff that they had removed from his flat conspicuously absent. He had found one of the boxes on the kitchen table – this, upon investigation, had had kitchen things in it. Unable to find Ivy, and deciding to leave Reggie and Mahri to it for a little while, he had tried to get back into the spare room on Ivy's corridor – the one that he suspected was now his.

The door, however, was stuck fast.

The glass panel, which he was reasonably sure had been covered in roses that morning, now had ferns and bright flowers all over it. One of the flowers, he noticed, uncomfortably, was Aconite. Clearly, even if Martha had accepted his presence, she wasn't about to hide anything from Ivy.

He frowned at the small, blue flowers; they sat perfectly still on their stems, looking innocent. Although he knew that he would have to say something about his condition sooner or later, but he had been fervently hoping for 'later' since he'd first set eyes on his friend.

Deciding to worry about it another time, he tried the second door, which was also locked. This one had the same ferns as the other, but with flowers of slightly different hues. He stood back for a moment, realising that if he looked at them both together, the panels formed a sort of continuous meadow.

He shook his head.

Martha must have got a fairly good impression of him when she had 'made friends' that morning.

Seized by a sudden curiosity, he followed the corridor along to Ivy's doors, glancing over his shoulder as he did so.

The panels in Ivy's doors appeared together to form a whole, too: there was a border of ivy around them both, which became brambles as they reached the bottom of each door. He recognised a few of the flowers on her doors: there were bluebells and yellow roses, and he thought that the spiky-looking plant in the corner might be rosemary. A dark, small leaved plant had grown up to the top of the panes, and was swathed in bright yellow star-like flowers; he liked those, particularly.

For reasons that he couldn't quite fathom, he really *didn't* like the drifts of dead leaves that surrounded the bottom-most flowers, or the slightly malicious way that the brambles seemed to be crowding around the ivy, forcing it back up the sides of the glass.

He stood, trying to work out what it was that the Arcade was trying to tell him for a few minutes, before the sounds of Ivy and the children in the kitchen brought him back to himself. He followed the sounds of enthusiasm, hoping that perhaps they would be making lunch.

He was in luck.

Ivy and Astrid were making a vast pile of sandwiches, while Jake was playing with Saffy, completely oblivious to anything else. Christopher grinned. It was good to see the children so happy – and Ivy with a smile on her face.

She turned and saw him approaching, then, and he couldn't help but grin at her.

"You look cheerful," Ivy observed, absently filling sandwiches.

"I quite like painting," he said, wishing that he could think of something more interesting to say. "It's the kind of job that makes an immediate difference."

Ivy nodded. "You might want to change before eating lunch," she suggested. "You're a little bit painty."

"Er – I was trying to," he said, scratching his head. "But my stuff's all gone – and the doors don't seem to work."

"Ah," she said, wiping her hands on a tea towel. "Martha's being helpful again. Can you finish these, Astrid?"

"Yes," the girl said, abandoning her buttering and taking over the sandwich-filling. Jake immediately sprang up to help, and was immediately directed towards the sink, to wash his hands.

Christopher followed her back to his rooms, leaving the good-natured bickering that had blossomed in the kitchen behind them.

She tried the doors, which remained stubbornly closed.

"What *are* you up to?" she asked the room at large. "She's usually quicker than this," she said, somewhat apologetically. "Do you want to – oh."

The door had clicked open under her hand.

Christopher peered into his new bedroom, which appeared to be warm and bright: he had more furniture than he could ever remember having, all of it in a glorious honey-coloured wood. There were, he noted, to his growing delight, several bookcases; above one of them was a strangely organic-looking multiple picture frame, it looked almost as if it was growing out of the wall. Thinking back to the previous evening, he decided that it probably was. He felt a rush of intense gratitude to the Arcade: he finally had somewhere to put the pictures of his family that he had been keeping tucked safely inside books and carefully wrapped in boxes.

His boxes were in the middle of the floor, ready to be unpacked.

Ivy had remained by the door, not wanting to intrude, but he turned to her and beamed, wonderingly.

"This is excellent!" he said, with such enthusiasm that she chuckled.

"I'm glad you think so," she said, graciously. "Martha certainly seems to have made you a lovely room."

He nodded, happily.

"I'll let you get changed," Ivy said, and closed the door.

Christopher stared around his new room, happily breathing in the new, homely scents of wood and beeswax and linen. It was just the kind of room that he had always dreamed of – back when he had thought that dreams could actually happen. Since he had been bitten he hadn't allowed himself the luxury, preferring instead to dwell on more necessary things like food and shelter. Things that might, one day, actually be achievable.

He re-joined them in time for Jake to come skidding in from the garden, presumably having been sent to collect Reggie and Mahri. The boy looked insanely happy to be in an environment that involved regular meals. Christopher chuckled as he raced past him and clambered up onto a chair next to his sister.

"You've been playing with that dog again, have you washed your hands?" Astrid asked her brother sternly, and he nodded in a thoroughly unconvincing manner.

Deciding to provide a good example, Christopher made a show of washing his, much to Ivy's amusement. She was still trying not to laugh as she carried glasses of fruit juice over to the table, which made him smile widely. Christopher was just about to join them when the phone rang, and Ivy motioned for him to get it, since he was closer.

It was Professor Barraclough.

"The water's going down a bit," his voice said, tinnily, from the other end. "We were thinking of heading over and checking on the shop, if that's alright."

Christopher couldn't think of a reason why it wouldn't be, but he asked Ivy anyway.

"Not a problem – by magic?" she asked.

Professor Barraclough agreed that this would probably be quite sensible, and Christopher nodded.

"Tell them to give me five minutes to warn Martha,"

Ivy said. "And ask them if they want some lunch."

Lunch also seemed to be a popular idea, so Christopher climbed down the stairs into the teashop to meet them. Behind him, he could hear Ivy calling up to the rafters: "Martha, we've got incoming, and they're friendly, so be nice."

He unlocked the doors with the heavy key that Ivy kept on a hook in the kitchen and went to wait in the bookshop. The books were mostly still asleep, this being a Sunday. Zarrubabel's snores could be heard emanating from behind the office door.

Looking around, Christopher was glad that they had had to move premises: the old shop might well have been underwater, and he could only imagine what a panic the books would have been in if that had happened, let alone the damage.

He had always hated the thought of books being damaged or defaced, but now that he knew that they were at least partly sentient, the thought of their ink slowly washing away was downright unsettling.

The image of an irate Professor Zarrubabel, floating about atop his book was quite amusing however, and he was still chuckling at it when Joanna and the Professor popped into existence in front of him. For a few moments, the world felt odd – tighter, as if there was suddenly less air and a good deal more pressure – but it quickly snapped back to normal, as if the world had suddenly relaxed. Christopher swallowed, and his ears popped.

The nearest books did the paper equivalent of rolling over sleepily and slumbered on.

Joanna and the Professor were looking at him in surprise. He suspected that their journey over had been slightly more energetic than they had been expecting.

He put his fingers to his lips and cocked his head towards the door, hoping that they wouldn't disturb the slumbering spectre in the next room. They followed him into the corridor of the Arcade, and waited while he locked the bookshop, and then the teashop.

"What in blazes was *that*?" Professor Barraclough asked, as they followed him around the back of the counter.

"I'm not sure," said Christopher, over his shoulder, "but I think it has something to do with the Arcade's security. You'll have to ask Ivy... Ah," he said, as they reached the top of the spiral staircase.

Astrid and Jake, who were happily giggling about something, stopped abruptly at the sight of the newcomers, and became immediately quiet and shy. Reggie, who had had enough surprises in a short space of time to last a lifetime, gave them an amiable smile.

"Er –" said Christopher. "Reggie, Jake, Astrid, these are my employers: Professor Morton Barraclough and his wife, Joanna. This is Reggie, Astrid and Jake." He turned to them and gave an uncomfortable half-shrug, not wholly sure how to go on in a place that was sort of his and still sort of not.

Fortunately, Mahri came to the rescue by rushing in and giving Joanna a brisk hug.

"I'm so glad you're alright!" she said. "I had an awful moment this morning when I thought the waters might have reached you, but Christopher was saying that you're all the way up the other side of the valley."

"Oh, yes," said Joanna, who looked equally pleased on her friend's behalf. "We're well above the water line – and I'm glad you are, we were getting quite worried last night."

"It was quite a night," said Mahri, motioning for them to sit down, handing out sandwiches and drinks as if it was her kitchen and not Ivy's.

Ivy, who must have been used to Mahri taking over in social situations, simply gave Christopher a wry smile on his expression of mild surprise. Somewhat nonplussed, he sat down beside her.

Lunch was a friendly enough affair, everyone taking the opportunity to get to know one another a little better, and fill the Barracloughs in on the events of the previous evening. The children warmed to the Barracloughs very quickly, largely because Joanna seemed very taken with the both of them, and Professor Barraclough was soon reminiscing about the old town with Reggie. The only person who didn't seem to be joining in was, once again, Ivy.

He had noticed her reserve at breakfast, and it had bothered him a little, but he had assumed that it had more to do with having to explain the presence of lunatic man-eating vines than anything else. Now, however, he wasn't so certain.

She was sitting back in her chair, nursing her glass of juice and watching the others interact with an odd expression on her face: somewhere between concentration and discomfort.

He had never really thought of her as particularly shy, with her easy manner around the customers, but now he realised that she was used to there being a lot fewer people around. With the house filling up as it had over the past few hours, she probably felt quite crowded, particularly with the high level of energy the children were exhibiting.

He wondered suddenly whether she had really let anyone other than Mahri in since Sam's death, and felt incredibly intrusive and out of place.

She must have noticed his gaze, and she turned to him, a question in her eyes. He gave her a small smile, hoping that his attention wouldn't be interpreted as another imposition, and she returned it – though he noticed that it hadn't entirely reached her deep blue eyes.

The meal concluded, Professor Barraclough stripped off his jacket and offered to help Reggie get settled in, leaving Christopher to do some unpacking of his own. Mahri immediately leapt up to clear away the dishes and Jake was jumping up and down in excitement.

"Come and see our playroom, Joanna!" he cried happily, tugging on her sleeve. "It's got sunflowers on the door!"

"Sunflowers, eh?" the older witch asked, eyes crinkling

as the child pulled her along.

Jake's excitement was infectious, and Astrid was just behind him, talking more than she had all day, about how Ivy had pulled out some old boxes of toys for them to see if there was anything that they could use, and given them some of her old clothes.

"I should get some linen out for the children's beds," said Ivy, without relish. "And towels and things."

"I'll do that," said Mahri, swooping down on the kitchen table and taking away more of the dishes. "It'll give me a chance to get to know the kids a little better, and Reggie's got Morton helping him for the moment, so he'll be fine. You give Christopher a hand," she instructed, and bustled off, her arms full of plates.

Christopher watched her go, wondering why she didn't simply use magic.

"She thinks it's cheating," said Ivy, wearily, as if she'd read his mind. "Likes to do things the mundane way, most of the time – particularly housework. Although," she glanced at Mahri to check that she couldn't hear her, and added, "I happen to know that she's never dusted in all the time she's lived here."

Christopher smirked, and Ivy gave a light chuckle.

"Come on then, let's get you sorted – can't have you feeling left out." She rose from the table and stretched, tiredly.

"I'm alright," said Christopher, following her towards his rooms. "You look like you could use a rest."

"Probably," said Ivy, with what might have been a grimace. "But there are people."

"You're not used to there being a lot of people about, are you?" he asked, quietly.

She looked at him for a moment before answering. "No, I'm not. It feels so crowded today. It's quite wearing, after a while."

"I can manage if you want to creep off for a bit, have a bit of peace?" he offered.

To his very great surprise, Ivy smiled a little and put a gentle hand on his arm.

"That's very kind of you, Christopher, but I'd rather give you a hand for a bit." Her smile widened a fraction, and he had to work very hard to stop his heart from somersaulting out of his throat. "I don't feel so crowded around you."

"Good," he managed. "Er – look, I'll tell you what, I'll keep the children entertained after tea, and you can have some time to yourself then."

"Bless you," she said, almost fondly. "I just might take you up on that."

He endeavoured not to smile too brightly at her as he opened the nearest door, catching the same cacophony of smells that he had enjoyed in his bedroom, earlier on.

Martha had apparently decided that this room was to be his study: the walls were lined with great, oak bookcases, some reaching the ceiling, others stopping at waist height, leaving room for notice-boards or picture frames above them. There was a sturdy desk against the far wall, with a comfortable-looking chair tucked under it, and even a big, squashy sofa where he could read if he wanted to. This was definitely a place that he could get used to.

"Martha really seems to 'get' people," said Ivy, softly, as he stared around, dumbfounded; he turned his stare onto her. "Well, she gave Jake the sky, and Astrid the earth – I think she's up to something there. And she's noticed how much you like reading."

He frowned at her odd turn of phrase, but forgot it instantly when he spotted another of the great, organic photograph frames on the wall above the sofa. He immediately crossed the room and ran his fingers along the edges of it almost affectionately.

Ivy, following his gaze, wondered again when he had last seen his family.

"Ivy?" he asked, turning back to her, a pensive expression on his face. "How long – I mean..." he tried to collect his disarrayed thoughts into an order that didn't sound too rude, or too needy. "How long will I be able to stay here?"

Some of his concerns must have shown on his face, as Ivy moved towards him.

"As long as you like," she assured him.

"And... I won't be in the way, or taking any more of your peace and quiet? I don't want to –"

"You won't be," she said. "At least, no more than Mahri does – and with everyone else around it will be nice to have someone here that I can be quiet with – or that I know won't mind if I need to shut myself away for a bit." She sighed, and he had to fight the urge to comfort her. "Having people around is just something that I will have to get used to, but I'm looking forward to spending a bit more time with you. You're a good friend, Christopher."

Blushing hotly, he waved her praise away with his hand.

"And you're sure you don't want help with the rent?"

"Why is it that people can't take a little kindness?" Ivy asked him, exasperated. "I meant what I said – have people been so... Have you been let down so often that you can't trust me on that?"

Christopher floundered a little, shocked, and Ivy immediately looked like she regretted her question.

"I'm sorry," she said, hurriedly. "I didn't mean – I just meant I'm happy to have you here, no strings and no expectations – as long as you're safe and happy."

Aware that he looked like he didn't believe her, he mumbled, "Thanks," and turned away, trying to collect himself. "Well," he said, and she seemed glad to see he had the ghost of a smile on his face again. "If you won't take rent, I'll at least insist on helping out with the food, and whatever the children need. I remember my parents constantly complaining about how fast we grew out of things or how much we ate."

Possibly realising that this proposal was Christopher's way of trying not to take advantage of her kindness, she relented, pleased to have come to a compromise that suited them both.

"Alright," she said. "Thank you – that will be a help."

"We should probably make a start," he said, looking a little less uncomfortable.

Ivy nodded. "Where do you want me?"

They spent a companionable few hours investigating and moving boxes around. Christopher chose to unpack his bedroom, leaving Ivy to organise his books into piles on the shelves, knowing that he would prefer to order them himself later. He hoped against hope she hadn't spotted how his face had coloured when she'd asked him where he wanted her.

ooo

"This is a good thing you are doing," Professor Barraclough said to her, as they made cups of tea together, later that afternoon. "Taking in Reg, and the children, and Christopher."

Ivy, who was struggling with the constant interaction required by her larger household, merely shrugged.

"They needed somewhere to be," she said, pulling out two of her extraordinary teapots. "And it's not like I needed all those rooms."

"Still," he said. "Not many people would have done it, and you did." He smiled at her in a fatherly fashion. "You need to learn to accept praise, Mistress Burwell."

She looked at him, surprised. "Well," she said, uncertainly. "Thank you."

"Good."

"The water hasn't gone down very much," said Mahri, peeling off her coat. She and Reggie had taken Saffy for a walk and used the opportunity to go and have a look. "They've got most of the lower town cordoned off."

"We saw a couple of policemen in a boat," added Reggie. "They're taking people across the – well, the lake, I suppose you'd call it. Wanted to know if we were all alright up here. Nice lads, really."

Mahri chuckled. "I think they were relieved to see that someone was managing without their help," she said. "They think the water level will hold for another few days, so there won't be too many customers for a while – only our immediate neighbours and Practitioners that can make the hop."

"I'll halve my orders then," Ivy said, and Mahri – who did most of the baking for the teashop – nodded. Ivy frowned. "I hope the meat in the fridge will last, I'll have to check it over."

"Check what over?" asked Christopher, joining them.

"The stock for the teashop," Ivy explained. "Most of it is fresh from the garden, or baked by Mahri in the week, but the meat might go off if it's not eaten up. The water level isn't going to go down anytime soon," she added, on his questioning look.

"Which also begs the question of what to do for the evening meal," added Reggie. "I don't mean to sound greedy, but I haven't been shopping for a few days, and everything on this side of the water is closed."

Christopher nodded.

"We'll pool our resources," said Mahri, with all the confidence of someone that knows she has a chest freezer full of food that could finally be put to good use.

"Actually," said Ivy, suddenly sounding wistful. "I'd love to order a pizza from somewhere – it's something Sam and I did whenever we moved or decorated."

"That sounds excellent," said Christopher, hoping that no one else would notice Mahri's obvious surprise at Ivy's candour about Sam.

"I've never had pizza," said Jake, who had followed Joanna and his sister back into the Arcade.

"That settles it then," said Ivy, firmly, before Mahri could object.

"Someone will have to collect it," said Reggie. "I doubt anything on this side of the river will be open."

"I'll go," Christopher volunteered. "There's one that my colleagues used to go to from the Records' Office, it's just around the corner from the Rose and Crown – I should pop in and check on Charlie."

"I'm sure *he's* alright," scoffed Joanna. "I'd hate to see the weather that could put off an eight-foot half-Troll.

Even if he'd been right in the middle of the flood he would have had some sort of protection on the place that stopped the water getting in."

"Still," said Christopher, with a smile. "I need to drop something off for him."

"I think we should take the opportunity to introduce everyone to our... business partner, while you're out," said the Professor, thoughtfully.

Christopher grinned at his expression.

"I'll take my time at Charlie's then," he said, and Joanna chuckled. "Anyone know what they want?"

ooo

Charlie had greeted him at the door with his big-stick-with-nails-in, but had relented when he'd made out his young friend's face in the neon orange murk, and let him in. Being a traditionalist, Charlie refused to open after four o'clock on a Sunday, preferring instead to closet himself with his books in the tap-room. He seemed rather surprised that Christopher had found somewhere new to live so easily, but was pleased enough for him, and had very nearly squealed with joy at the small stack of romance novels Christopher had been saving him as a thank-you for letting him stay.

Christopher was still grinning at the image when he arrived back at the Arcade with a teetering pile of pizza boxes.

He was confused to find the main area bereft of life, with the exception of Boscoe, who started up at his sudden appearance and flew off with a disgruntled squawk towards the plum tree in the garden. Curious, he set the pile of boxes down on the kitchen table and sniffed the air: nothing seemed to be particularly out of place. The lights were on in both of the coach houses, and the Barracloughs' coats were still hanging from the hook beside the stairwell.

Distantly, he thought he could make out the sounds of shouts and bangs coming from downstairs.

"Everything alright, Martha?" he asked the room at large, interpreting the subsequent flash of flowers along the wall as a shrug. Whatever was happening didn't seem to bother her particularly, which meant that it was either nothing at all, or something to do with the noises downstairs.

Still, he thought, *it can't hurt to check...*

He padded towards the children's rooms: Astrid's room was empty, and after a few moments spent marvelling at the flowers on the walls he moved on, pushing the door to the play room open.

In the middle of the bright room, Jake was sitting on Joanna's knee, sniffling; Astrid and Joanna were saying soothing things to him while Ivy hovered nearby, looking at something of a loss. Jake looked like he had been crying for some time, and his face was red and blotchy.

"Hey, are you alright?" he asked, as they looked up.

Jake continued to sniffle, so Joanna answered for him.

"My ridiculous brother had one of his moments and frightened him," she explained, and he could tell from the tight way her lips had pressed together that things would shortly be going very badly for Hector Zarrubabel. "Morton and Mahri are giving him a good telling off."

He nodded, remembering the sounds of chaos emanating from the stairwell.

"Reggie had to have a bit of a sit-down – I think it's all been a bit much for him."

"I'm not surprised," said Ivy, quietly. "Finding out about magic, losing your home *and* meeting your brother all in one go would make anyone question their sanity."

Christopher snorted, making Jake giggle wetly, and Astrid look up at him gratefully. Looking at the girl, she was white and shaken, and he imagined that if she hadn't spent the last few months on the rooftops of the county she would be in a similar state to her brother.

He was strongly reminded of his own sister, and how quickly she seemed to bounce back from scrapes. With this in mind he sat on the floor in front of Jake and Joanna and smiled up at the boy.

"I shouldn't worry," he said, candidly. "He doesn't like me very much, either."

The little boy gave a small wet smile, and Joanna gave him an encouraging nod.

"The thing is, he can't get out of the back office of the shop downstairs, so there's no way he can bother either of us up here," Christopher continued. "Which I have to say – sorry Joanna, I know he's your brother – I am very glad about."

"Not at all, Christopher," said Joanna. "If I had to live with him I'd have locked him in a trunk years ago."

Astrid giggled, despite herself, and Christopher adopted a thoroughly mischievous expression, just for the children.

"You know, that sounds like a good idea..." he said, with a wink at Joanna, who smiled.

"None of us would ever hear the end of it," she said, and he contrived to look really disappointed.

Jake giggled, drying his eyes with his sleeve.

"That's more like it," Christopher said, with a sideways grin. "I'll tell you what," he said, poking Jake gently on the nose with his finger. "I bet you like ice-cream – I got some for after the pizza," he said.

The effect on Jake was instantaneous: the little boy's face lit up like the sun coming out from behind a cloud.

"Ice-cream?" he asked, suddenly looking much happier.

"Ice-cream," said Christopher, firmly. "Unless, of course, you don't like chocolate, or strawberry, or vanilla, or mint," he continued.

"I like ice-cream – every kind!" Jake assured him, and Christopher grinned.

"Me too – tell you what, if you finish your pizza, you can have a bit of each flavour, how does that sound?"

"Brilliant!" Jake cried, and Astrid laughed.

"Excellent," Joanna said. "Let's get our hands washed then," she added to Jake, lifting him to the floor and making her way to the kitchen.

Astrid made to follow them, pausing at the door.

"Thanks for cheering him up," she said to Christopher, and he shrugged.

"No worries."

He got to his feet as she left the room, her black hair whipping behind her as she went through the door.

"That was masterful," Ivy observed, giving him an appraising look.

"It was nothing," said Christopher, blushing and grinning all at the same time. "Worked on Rachel every time – still does, actually."

Ivy chuckled.

"I wouldn't know where to start – the only experience I have with children is that I was one, once," she said, leading him back to the kitchen. "If Joanna hadn't been here I don't know what I'd have done."

"You'd have managed," said Christopher. "The children already like you a lot, and if the books are anything to go by then I'd say you're a natural."

It was Ivy's turn to blush.

14
Bathroom Potions

It had been a long day, and Ivy was exhausted.

Despite a large part of the town being flooded, the teashop had been reasonably busy, what with Practitioners appearing sporadically, announcing happily that a 'little bit of rain' wasn't going to stop the likes of *them*, and having a good old natter with one another while the chance afforded itself. Quite a few of the residents of the old town – that part of Brindleford that had been made into an island by the flood – had been excited and relieved to discover that the Arcade was open. The majority of businesses were closed, and only those whose proprietors lived in the old town were even vaguely open.

A bedraggled stream of people who had expected to be able to go shopping or to work at some point in the week had begun to trickle in, particularly young people who had moved into the low-rent flats above the high-street shops. Several of them had remarked to Ivy that they had never really noticed the Arcade before, and had very happily closeted themselves in the teashop or bookshop for the day, discovering that, actually, reading or knitting wasn't that bad a way to spend a stolen afternoon.

Ivy had kept the shop open a couple of hours longer than normal, pleased that some good might come out of the floods, and had forgone her usual trip to the bookshop in order to restock her dwindling provisions and get some much needed supplies for the children in the big supermarket out at Rouse Abbey. They had spent the morning with Reggie, who seemed very happy indeed to have other people around, and had helped them to clean and repair a train set that they had found in the store rooms beneath the coach houses, that Ivy remembered from her childhood.

It was good to see things being used again, and she knew very well that her father would prefer his trains to be out and making people smile rather than packed away in a dusty store room.

It was the first time that Ivy had really appreciated her great aunts' urge to hoard: up until now the boxes of toys, clothes, books and ornaments had been rather annoying, if she thought about them at all. An irritating job that would, at some point, have to be done.

But now, having several cardboard boxes of clothes from various generations of Chambers' at various ages was something of a blessing. They had had a rummage together, Ivy and the children, and had managed to find most of what they needed in terms of clothing. Really, they had only needed underwear and bedding from the supermarket, and a few other things that the boxes hadn't provided, like towels and toothbrushes, but Ivy had made sure that they had good shoes and coats too, and let them choose a couple of new things each.

They had been a lot more help in the supermarket than she had thought they would, largely because the fact that Jake was sitting in the trolley (he wouldn't let go of his new wellies) meant that fewer people tried to ram it than usual. It seemed to Ivy that, although they were both struggling just as much as she was with the sheer volume of humanity, they were rather enjoying being back in the world after months of living on the very edge of it. They were also rather enjoying being spoiled, though Astrid was trying very hard not to show it, and Ivy was trying not to overdo it.

Despite herself, she had rather enjoyed the trip, and the children had been very excited about travelling by magic again.

When they had got back to the Arcade Ivy had found Christopher attempting to cook, and had rather gratefully slunk off for some quiet time in the bath.

Ivy liked the bath. It was one of the few places that she had never minded the fact that she was a witch. She had been experimenting with what her mother had called bath 'potions' since she was a small child, and still had something of a mad scientist thrill when she mixed one or two of her potions and produced violently colourful bubbles when she was bored, or a pleasant peachy sort of smell for the middle of summer. Today, she had decided that relaxing lavender scents were the way to go, and had settled down in a bath that was really more large purple bubbles than anything else. Periodically, one would pop, leaving a small cloud of bluish-purple floating above the bath.

She spent at least the first ten minutes being thoroughly childish: popping bubbles and making a sort of lavender fog in the bathroom, before settling down to relax.

As much as she had always wanted to, she had never quite mastered the trick of reading in the bath without getting the book sopping wet, so she soon found herself staring idly at the ceiling, considering her new household.

Reggie appeared to be settling in well, along with Boscoe and Saffy, who were beginning to think of every tree and sofa as their own, respectively. She may have been imagining it, but Ivy thought that since he now had people to talk to, Reggie seemed a little less confused. Not that she had much experience of the man to go on – but he certainly seemed happy, and that was something.

The children seemed to be happier, too – or at least, cleaner and louder. Quietly, and safely locked in the bathroom, Ivy admitted to herself that, actually, having the children around had been absolutely lovely. She knew, of course, that feeling attached to them was silly unless they were going to stay for a while, but she couldn't help it: their laughter, affection and stubbornness were infectious, and she was very tempted to offer them a permanent place in the Arcade – and in her family.

But that might frighten them off, she thought, and she definitely didn't want that.

It felt very odd indeed, thinking about taking on the responsibility of having children without Sam by her side – almost a kind of betrayal – but she dismissed the thought. In her position, Sam would have done anything he could for them, even tucking them into his life without a second thought if he had to, and Ivy wasn't about to let him down. It wasn't exactly the kind of family life she had envisaged – either as a child herself, rattling around the Arcade and dreaming of magic, or later as a married woman, living and working alongside the man she loved – but it would do.

It would have to.

They needed her, and that was that.

Ignoring the nagging voice at the back of her mind that was trying to add that she needed them just as much, she steered her thoughts to the Arcade itself. It had felt different from the moment that she had offered Christopher a place to stay, almost as if it was waking up.

She had been noticing it at odd moments all day, while serving teas and selling wools and wondering what the hell children were supposed to eat: the Arcade was brighter, happier – almost swelling with new purpose. She thought that Christopher might have noticed it too – he certainly seemed much happier than he had been, though she admitted to herself that his cheerfulness might be more to do with a happier home and some rather eccentric new housemates.

The weight of worrying about his rent seemed to have lifted off him like a lead balloon, though there was still something troubling him from time to time, like a shadow crossing his face at the oddest of moments.

And then there were his doors.

Privacy was something that she had had to teach Martha, who had largely had the run of the place after her grandmother's death, and she was getting a lot better at respecting boundaries, but she couldn't stop herself making the panels in the doors reflect their owners; it was part of who she was.

You could be anything you wanted in the Arcade, assuming it didn't hurt anyone, but the one person that you could never fool was Martha and if she felt that other people needed to know something, she'd let them know. The doors were a part of that. Ivy had walked past her own doors so many times that she had stopped taking them in. The last time she had really looked at them had been the morning that she had decided to engage with the world again, and she hadn't been wholly pleased with what she had seen in herself, all brambles and dead leaves.

Martha had grown up at a time when every flower had a meaning, and in a family for whom those meanings were at times deeper and more magical. A rose could mean true love, or friendship, or rejection, depending on its colour; honeysuckle could be a happy marriage or infidelity depending on its species; a hollyhock, ambition; a bluebell, solitude. It had seemed to Ivy when her aunts had taught her the language that a lot of it depended on semantics; one misplaced flower must have caused no end of confusion.

The magical uses of plants were more unusual, but no less ambiguous. Often, several things could mean the same thing, allowing Practitioners to substitute more exotic or out of season ingredients for things more readily to hand; problems tended to come when someone forgot that a plant might have *other* meanings, potentially sending a spell off in an entirely unexpected and unpleasant direction. She would have to start teaching Astrid about that, if she wanted to learn.

The flowers on the children's doors had been interesting, but not unexpected. She had already known that they were both very brave, and that Jake would probably grow up to be strong and good, and that Astrid would be intelligent and beautiful. Martha had already claimed her as a Chambers, which worried Ivy a little. She hated the idea of so much responsibility falling on someone else – but then, Astrid had already shouldered a fair amount of it by taking care of her brother.

You can't force someone to be something that they're not, she thought, frowning.

She would have to be careful that Martha didn't become too aggressive about it.

Still, their meanings would change a little as they grew

up – if they chose to stay – and they would grow into themselves.

Christopher's doors, however, were much more difficult to read. Some parts were reasonably easy to work out, like rose campion for gentleness and ferns for sincerity, but others were ambiguous, like aconite, which could be gallantry *or* misanthropy. She knew which interpretation she preferred, but Martha chose her meanings very carefully, and there were other plants that could have stood for chivalry.

Celandine ('joys to come') was fairly straightforward, but chamomile, which meant 'love in adversity' and dog-rose, which was 'pain and pleasure' made no sense at all. Ivy frowned to herself.

She had actually had to look dog-rose up, it not being a flower that she had much call to use in her teas or her spells, and it had continued to irritate her all day, as if it was a clue to some mystery that she hadn't even known she was unravelling.

There is another interpretation of aconite, she remembered, suddenly, one eyebrow rising of its own volition. *Surely not...*

She lay very still in the cooling bath water, as if the slightest ripple might disrupt her train of thought, the sounds of various people helping out in the kitchen drifting through the closed door.

'Pain and pleasure' and aconite. Well, well, well.

Ponderously, she stirred the lavender scented bubbles with her toes.

No wonder he has trouble trusting people, she thought. *He's probably been moved on from every home he's ever had.*

Idly, she popped another large bubble with her big toe: the resulting cloud floated gently up to the ceiling to join its friends.

I wonder if he'll tell me about it.

A soft knock at the door made Ivy jump, slopping cold water and large, purple bubbles onto the black and white tiles below.

"Er, Ivy?" Christopher asked, awkwardly, from behind the frosted glass. "Dinner's nearly ready."

"Oh – okay," she said, watching a water lily spontaneously burst into life in the puddle on the floor. "Thanks, I'll be out in a minute."

"Right."

She listened to his retreating footsteps for a moment as the water lily sucked up the purple liquid, its white petals stained indigo.

"You really shouldn't drink that," she said absently, heaving herself out of the bath.

The water lily gurgled thirstily and started to crawl its way into the bath, extending stems and leaves and using them to climb the cast iron sides, crab-like.

Ivy shook her head at it and wondered what it would be like to live in a normal house.

ooo

"Good bath?" Christopher asked, as they cleared away the plates.

Ivy nodded.

"I like baths," she said. "They're good places for thinking. Thanks for cooking, by the way."

He smiled toothily as he turned away, and Ivy wondered how on Earth she hadn't seen it before. It was with him when he moved, giving him that strange athletic grace that she'd seen in him when he wasn't concentrating.

He must make himself appear smaller than he really is, she thought, watching him as he wandered off towards where Jake was sitting on one of the sofas. *Trying to stop people from noticing how strong he is, or how skinny...*

She found herself watching him a lot that evening, trying to spot all the little tells that she hadn't noticed before, and wondering just what to make of him. He'd noticed her eyes on him a few times over dinner, and he shot her the occasional questioning look, but she had simply smiled, or asked him to pass her something, and he seemed to have brushed it off. Now that she was watching him more closely, however, she could tell that her scrutiny was making him really quite uncomfortable, but she couldn't help that. She needed time to think.

He didn't feel like a threat, and Martha liked him – but only after Ivy had introduced them. She must have felt that something was out of place that morning, the way her vines had swarmed all about him, never quite close enough to touch – afraid of being burned.

Should I be afraid of him? she wondered.

She knew that werewolves kept their mind when they transformed – to varying degrees – but how far could she trust Christopher to keep his? She frowned at him. Until he changed – or until he talked to her about it – she couldn't be sure, and she had a responsibility for the children now, and for Mahri and Reggie. She hoped that he would talk to her.

He was grinning at Jake now, in an almost predatory fashion.

And if he does *tell me, how far can I trust his word? I barely know the man.*

He noticed her stare again, and she turned away, picking at the edge of the sofa she was sitting on. She couldn't quite resign the image of the kind, gentle man that had become her friend with that of a vicious killer.

What if it turns out that I don't know him at all?

But then, he was so much like Sam, and Ivy didn't want to think that anyone like Sam would deceive her – or try to eat anyone, for that matter. Her eyes flicked back to him.

He's certainly playful, she thought, as he chased a squealing Jake around the room. *And good with the children – I wonder how much of that was in him before? Wolves are pack animals, after all.*

He caught up with Jake on the other side of the sofa and hoisted him into the air, triumphantly. The little boy shrieked happily and tried unsuccessfully to wriggle out of his captor's grasp.

Christopher bundled him under his arm as if he weighed nothing at all and strode off towards the bathroom, calling over his shoulder.

"Someone else needs a bath – you don't mind, do you?"

Astrid giggled as her brother tried his best to explain that this sort of thing really wasn't necessary; Christopher ignored him, whistling loudly.

Ivy watched them go, conflicted, and moved to help Astrid go through another old box of things at the kitchen table.

ooo

The box had turned out to be full of old toys, and after a quick clean they had carried several board games, an old chalk board and broken chalks, a set of plastic cars, a jar of very old glass marbles, four dolls, and a selection of probably very annoying children's musical instruments into the playroom. Astrid had looked around with that same expression of mild distrust, and had gone to help Christopher bundle a very reluctant little brother into his new pyjamas.

Ivy could hear them laughing quietly through the wall and suspected that the little boy was actually perfectly happy and only really making a fuss for the sake of form.

She had settled back down on the sofa, intending to read, but had quickly fallen asleep, more tired than she had been in a long time.

She awoke suddenly, in pitch darkness, surprised to find a blanket carefully tucked around her. Someone had put a bookmark in her book and laid it by the edge of the seat, out of the way. She squinted at the clock on the kitchen wall: its slightly luminous hands indicated that it was after two in the morning.

Groaning, Ivy stood and stretched, massaging the crick that was developing in her neck. She wondered what had woken her, and was about to go to her own bed when she heard someone whimper.

She paused.

It had been quite a small sound, but loud enough for her to have heard it from the main room. There definitely wasn't anyone suspicious about, or she would have been woken by a tangle of mildly hysterical vines. All of the fears that had had been playing about her head earlier in the afternoon came back in full force, and she glanced uncertainly along the corridor to where Christopher *should* be sleeping. Staying very still, she strained to hear anything out of order.

Nothing.

Perhaps she had imagined it.

But there it was again – it sounded like somewhere nearby, someone was very frightened indeed.

Ivy followed the sound to Jake's bedroom door; quietly, she conjured a pale Light Orb, and opened the door.

To her relief, the room was bereft of monsters of any kind, other than the ones that were in the little boy's head. She crept over to his bed, and he whimpered again – calling out, this time, for his daddy.

Shading the Light Orb slightly so as not to wake him, she could see the tracks of his tears, silvery in the half-light. Jake had been crying in his sleep for quite some time.

Perturbed, and being rather at a loss for what to do, she reached out and gently brushed his fringe away from his eyes. He frowned slightly at her touch, screwing his face up even more for a moment – Ivy flinched away from him, worried that she'd made it worse – but Jake quickly began to relax.

Realising that she might at least have disturbed the dream that was causing him such grief, she reached out once more and stroked the little boy's hair until he stopped crying entirely, snuggling deeper into the covers that he'd picked out earlier in the day.

She sat quietly with him for a few minutes, to make sure the nightmare didn't resurface before gently tucking him in. She watched him for a moment in the half-light, wondering what the hell she was doing looking after children. She turned to leave.

Astrid was standing in the doorway, an unreadable expression on her face.

"Is he okay?" the girl whispered.

Ivy nodded.

"Bad dream, I think," she murmured.

Astrid tiptoed across the room to check on her brother, and Ivy left her to it, feeling that she had intruded.

She padded into the kitchen, her glowing Light Orb bobbing behind her like a strange luminous balloon. She sighed, as she put the kettle on. She was completely awake now, and she decided that she might as well take advantage of it. She reached for the jar of 'special' hot chocolate that was tucked behind the large variety of teas on the top shelf. It was her mother's recipe: it had several of the more unusual herbs that Ivy grew in the garden mixed into it, and had the curious effect of tasting entirely different to whoever drank it.

She filled the kettle, her brow furrowed: her mind was racing with a cacophony of unpleasant thoughts, ranging from what it was the children had run away from, to being deeply sad that Sam wasn't here to meet them, to how foolish she was being in taking on responsibility for two children when she had absolutely no idea what she was doing.

There was also a nagging guilt at the back of her mind about suspecting Christopher of anything. He had been nothing other than a good friend thus far, and she had let her prejudice – and her imagination – run away with her. She glared at the kettle, furious with herself.

The skin on the back of her neck prickled, and she turned to see Astrid watching her, still with that carefully blank expression – though now she could see that there was a slight frown to it, as if she was trying to work something out.

Ivy glanced along the corridor: Jake's door was still open, which explained why she hadn't heard the girl coming. She must have left it ajar in case he needed something.

"Do you want a hot chocolate?" she asked softly, and the girl nodded, guardedly.

She's just so uncertain around people, Ivy thought. *It's sad in a seven year old girl. When I was seven I was still spinning in circles until I fell over and drawing chalk art on the paving stones.*

She smiled slightly at the memory as she stirred the hot chocolate.

They sat down across from one another at the kitchen table, both feeling distinctly uncomfortable in the presence of someone who was, essentially, a complete stranger.

It was a while before either of them broke the silence; Astrid cleared her throat.

"Thanks," she said, quietly. "For checking on him."

"That's okay," said Ivy.

Silence reigned again as Astrid fixed her with a searching look; Ivy gazed back, uncertainly. She took another sip of her hot chocolate, and felt the tension in her neck and shoulders diminish

"Why are you doing this?" she blurted out. It was as if the question had been bubbling up inside her and she could no longer keep it in. It had almost sounded like an accusation.

"Doing what?" asked Ivy, tired and perplexed. *Drinking hot chocolate in the dead of night?* she thought.

Astrid's frown deepened considerably.

"Helping us."

Ivy's eyebrows shot behind her dark hair. She stared at the girl, stunned. It was a few moments before she could answer.

"Because you need it," she said, slowly. "Why else would someone help you?"

Astrid looked mildly nonplussed.

"Your own reasons..." she said, surprised. Given that Ivy still looked baffled, she continued, "Like, our last foster mother did it because she missed her daughter – she'd grown up and moved away, or..."

Guessing where this might be going from the look on Astrid's face, Ivy interrupted.

"I don't want anything in return," she said, firmly.

"But –"

Ivy sighed, and tried not to think about what it was that had made this seven-year old girl so suspicious.

"Look, sometimes people just help you because they want to," she said. She assessed Astrid's dubious expression and made a decision. None of this was going to work if they didn't have trust. "You remember what I told you about Martha?"

Astrid nodded, puzzled.

"And Reggie said that he'd heard stories about her?"

Another nod.

"Well, my family have something of a – a *tradition* of helping people," she frowned. "Whether we like it or not."

Astrid was still staring at her, frowning. The child had a way of creating a silence that somehow needed filling up, compelling you to talk about things when you weren't sure you wanted to.

"It's got a lot to do with the role of a Witch in society," Ivy said, slowly. "It used to be that every village – or group of villages – would have a Witch, sort of like an itinerant Preacher."

"Itinerant?" Astrid asked, screwing up her face at the word.

"Travelling," Ivy explained. "They'd go from village to village ministering to their flock – as would the Witches. But where the Preacher would do christenings, or marriages, or read last rites over the dead, the Witches would sort out the actual birth or death. They'd watch over the sick and do their best for them, mediate in minor local disputes and keep whatever was going on in the local magical area from interfering too much with everyday life.

"The Preacher looked out for your soul, while the

Witch tended your body – and occasionally gave you a smack around the head when you needed it... and then there were the local Law-men." She was rambling, she knew, but Astrid was still watching her, apparently fascinated, making the silence roll out in front of her like a chasm.

"They were usually elected by the people – or chosen by the local lord. They handled any disputes that the Witch and the Preacher couldn't sort out, and helped to keep the peace in the name of their lord and monarch, whomever it happened to be at the time.

"So most old manors had three: a Preacher, a Witch and a Law-man. It was a reasonable system," she went on, thoughtfully. "Most of the time the three of them would get on reasonably well, and could intercede on one another's behalf if there was a falling out. Threes work, you see.

"It's not like that anymore – hasn't been for a long time, but my family seemed determined to cling to their traditions." She sounded bitter, she knew, and stopped herself. She took another sip of chocolate and closed her eyes.

Astrid probably didn't care about any of this anyway.

"So," Astrid began, and Ivy opened her eyes again. She was frowning at her mug, less suspicious now, as if this fresh puzzle had distracted her. "Your family were witches?"

"Yes," said Ivy heavily. "For our sins."

"But not all witches are Witches?"

Ivy smiled, she had actually heard her pronounce the capital letter. "That's right."

Astrid gave her one of her piercing looks. "You don't like being the Witch very much, do you?" she asked.

Ivy looked at her for a moment.

"I'm not the Witch – there isn't one anymore," she said, quietly. "My grandmother was the last."

"Oh. So, you aren't helping us because of your traditions?" Astrid looked quite confused now, and Ivy didn't blame her.

"Yes. Er, no..." Ivy said. "Sorry. It's more – growing up, there was always a sense of obligation to the community – one which I have to say I wasn't much interested in. You and your brother, Reggie and Christopher are the first people I've actually ever *wanted* to help. And I wanted to help you because you needed it – not for any sense of duty, or obligation."

No matter what Mahri thinks.

"Sometimes people just do things because they need to be done." She looked squarely at the girl in front of her. "And if I'm honest, I didn't like the thought of two young children out in the elements over the winter."

Astrid winced, and Ivy wondered if her words had stung slightly. She hadn't intended them to, but the girl had asked for the truth and there it was.

They were both quiet for a few minutes.

"Thank you, then," she said, apparently coming to a decision. "We do need your help, and it's very kind of you."

It was such a grown up statement that Ivy couldn't help but smile a little.

"Then you're welcome," she said.

"Ivy?" Astrid asked, after a few moments.

"Yes?"

"Why didn't you want to be the Witch?"

Ivy regarded her for a few moments, before setting her mug down on the table and leaning back.

"Sorry," said Astrid, looking worried.

"It's alright," said Ivy. "I was just thinking. Lots of reasons really."

She stood up and walked to the bookcases lining the walls, and came back with a couple of photograph frames.

"That's my mum and dad," Ivy said, pointing at the two people laughing on a picnic blanket. The woman looked a lot like Ivy, but her eyes and smile had definitely come from her father. Astrid took the picture almost reverently.

"They died when I was quite young," Ivy told her,

softly, her eyes on the glinting glass of the frame.

"You must miss them," said Astrid, softly, and Ivy knew that she wasn't just talking about the people in the picture.

"Every day," said Ivy, sadly.

"What happened?"

Ivy told her, and they both cried, and she told her about her great aunts and grandmother, and the things that they used to teach her. Then she told her about Sam, and how much she loved him, and how he had never come home.

By the time she was finished they had both cried themselves out, and were sitting side by side at the table, Ivy's pictures spread out in front of them.

"Right," said Ivy, wiping her sleeve across her face. "I think we could both do with another hot chocolate." She busied herself with the jar and the kettle, saying, "We'll need it after that," as she put Astrid's mug down in front of her again.

Astrid was fiddling with something under the table, and she brought it out as Ivy sat down.

"That's mummy and daddy," she said, in almost a whisper. The photograph was dog-eared and faded, but Ivy could make out two people in a garden swing-chair, two tiny, black-haired children on their knees. "That was the last time we were together," said Astrid, very softly.

"What happened?" Ivy asked, and immediately regretted it: the pain on Astrid's face told her everything she needed to know. "You don't have to tell me."

"I don't want to talk about it," she said, and Ivy nodded.

"That's fine, it's your business, not mine." She gave Astrid a hard look. "I do need to know, once and for all, whether there's anyone looking for you, however."

Astrid appeared to think about this.

"I think some people are. Our last family were nice enough," she said. "But they aren't very good at finding us."

Ivy nodded again. When a witch or wizard decided

that they didn't want to be found – even if they didn't necessarily know that that was what they were – it was nigh on impossible to hunt them out.

Astrid was frowning now.

"We're good at not being found – even Jake. I thought someone would have noticed us by now."

Ivy smiled. "I think there's more to the two of you than meets the eye," she said.

Astrid gave her a look that was almost furtive. "Can I show you something?" she asked, and Ivy could hear the excitement in her voice. Intrigued, she nodded.

Astrid held her hand out in front of her and concentrated, screwing her eyes up and sticking her tongue between her teeth.

Ivy leaned forward, feeling the magic gathering around the young girl: for a few, tense moments nothing happened at all. All of a sudden a small blue flame appeared in mid-air, settling down and dancing on the palm of her hand.

Ivy gasped – this was a spell that she'd never seen, probably one of Astrid's own invention. She clapped her hands in sheer enjoyment as another flame – pink this time – joined the first, then another, and another; soon, a whole host of dancing flames skittered across Astrid's skin.

"They burn cold," she said, looking up at Ivy. Ivy beamed at her. "I make them when Jake can't sleep."

"They're *brilliant*," said Ivy, and Astrid looked delighted. Concentrating again, she closed her palms around the flames and they winked out.

There was silence for a few minutes in the kitchen. Everything seemed strangely dark after the riot of light. Astrid's face was flushed and she was happier than Ivy had yet seen her, as if she were finally coming to accept the existence of kindness. Magic could be quite exhilarating at times.

"I always thought," said Astrid, and Ivy got the impression that if she wasn't currently so excited, this would never have been said, "that witches were evil. Like in the stories, with toads – and crooked noses – and green skin – and warts." She looked up at Ivy. "But *you're* not – so maybe *I'm* not, either."

"Thank you," said Ivy, with a chuckle. "I don't think I'd suit warts."

"Me either," said Astrid, and she giggled shyly. "Would you teach me the old ways?" she asked, and Ivy looked at her, thinking hard.

She'd even asked in the proper manner.

"There are conditions," she said, after a while. "It's not a thing that you can take on lightly – a little bit of learning can be a very dangerous thing. You would have to agree to stay for a while – perhaps even years."

She waited for this to sink in before continuing.

"If it's still what you want it would have to work like an old-fashioned apprenticeship," she said. "By teaching you I would be taking responsibility for you and your magic – if something were to go wrong, I would need to put it right. This being magic, that's pretty likely. You would have room and board here, and schooling in both magic and mundane things, and you would need to help make things for the shop – you have to learn about things like obligation and duty of care. It's not how they do it over at Brightwell – though for all their flash, they aren't bad sorts. I'm not them, and the only way I know how to teach is how I learned."

Astrid looked a little overwhelmed, but Ivy knew what she would be letting herself in for.

"It will be very hard work, but if it's what you want to do – sometimes you just can't help the magic inside you crashing out, no matter how hard you try, and it's worth knowing how to control it." She paused before continuing, "Basically, I'd need the assurance that you'd be here for a good few years, and you'd need the assurance that I'd keep my end of the bargain."

"What do you we do?" Astrid asked, in a small voice, awed by Ivy's words.

Ivy thought about it.

"Well, it used to be that a contract would be drawn up

between the business owner and the apprentice's parents for a certain number of years – I think seven was the usual number – and detailing the duties of the apprentice, and the treatment that they would receive in return. What meals and time off they were allowed, that sort of thing." She frowned. "I'm not sure that would entirely work these days, though if you still want to go ahead with it I'm more than happy to work out a contract out with you – we could have the professors draw it up.

"It might be best – in terms of a guarantee of us both sticking around – for me to adopt you. It would be entirely up to you, of course," she added, on Astrid's expression of shock.

Well, Ivy thought, *these things did have to be done properly, after all.*

"Could – would it be possible to do without contacting…"

"The people who may or may not be looking for you?" Ivy finished. "I don't know, but I think I remember a couple of the students I had classes at Brightwell with doing something similar – one of them had run away from the modern equivalent of an evil step-mother, and had arranged an adoption of sorts through Brightwell. It makes a difference that you're quite blatantly magical. I'm assuming that the people looking for you aren't?"

"I doubt it," she said. "They were completely ordinary." Ivy suspected that this had been something of a disappointment to Astrid, but didn't press the point. "They were very nice, though," the girl qualified, and Ivy wondered, if this were the case, why she'd felt the need to take Jake and leave.

Maybe it had something to do with their insistence on staying together; Ivy could well imagine them revolting at the idea of being split up, no matter how well-meaning their caregivers had been.

"Obviously, I don't expect you to have an answer for me right now," she said, and Astrid looked mildly relieved. "We both need to think about it… but it's a possibility, if that's what you want."

Astrid nodded, and asked, "Could Jake stay, too? I'm not going anywhere he isn't."

Ivy smiled. "Naturally. The offer would extend to both of you," she assured her. "Though of course Jake wouldn't be bound by your contract – if he wanted one he'd have to ask himself, and he's a bit too young, yet."

Astrid nodded.

"I think we should sleep on it," said Ivy, yawning.

They said goodnight, and Ivy trailed to her bedroom, the Light Orbs from the main room following behind her like her own personal fireflies, bobbing and bouncing in invisible eddies of magic. Christopher was snoring in his room and Ivy felt another pang of guilt for her earlier suspicion.

She would still have to speak with him about it, sooner or later, but she swore to herself that she'd at least listen to him before making up her mind.

She glanced at the clock as she climbed into bed and groaned.

Tomorrow was going to *hurt*.

15
Part-Time Monsters

It was a busy Wednesday in *'Zarrubabel & Barraclough, Purveyors of Fine Books'*, and Christopher hadn't even had time to take a lunch break. Since the move the Barracloughs had added two more study tables, and all three had been occupied for most of the day. The ancient lithographer was back, apparently having taken a very fruitful coach tour of the ancient churches of Kent, which had spurred him on in his research to the point where he was considering writing a book on the subject. Happy though he was for the man, he could have done without the new fervour. The Widow Jenkins had taken up residence in the back of the shop, surrounding herself with the usual array of obscure and dangerous books, periodically summoning him over and demanding new ones.

He didn't like to keep Widow Jenkins waiting: he wasn't entirely sure what she'd do to him if he did.

Quentin Post was back, too, and just as jovial as ever. After his performance with Ivy, Christopher was a good deal less impressed with the man than before, but he tried not to show it. It was difficult helping him find sources and discussing his adventures with relish, and he was oddly grateful for the constant trickle of visitors, both mundane and magical. They were keeping his mind occupied.

He'd never seen the shop so busy. It was as if the people of Brindleford had decided to make the most of the remaining week before the school term started and all of them wanted books.

Even Charlie had been over, looking exceptionally uncomfortable and out of place in the bookshop, looming over the bookshelves as he waited for Christopher to hunt out his order and pretending that he couldn't read.

It was hot and sticky, and the number of people in the shop made it hotter and stickier, their scents mingling in a hot morass of utter confusion. It was as if every customer had come in and started bellowing at the top of their lungs with everyone else. By three o'clock he had a headache that probably wouldn't shift for days; it felt like something was banging repeatedly on the back of his skull with a frying pan. Everything seemed to be intensifying in the heat, and he longed for five minutes of fresh air.

Joanna Barraclough had taken the children out for the day, with promises of a visit to a playground and a sweet shop, and the Professor had taken Zarrubabel out to a commotion at Brightwell. He had run out of the shop, his jacket trailing behind him, shouting that Christopher oughtn't worry.

Given that Christopher knew the pair now, and knew that Zarrubabel only went along in emergencies, he seriously doubted this. He took the opportunity, during a brief lull in business, to run across to the teashop and put in a pre-emptive order for restorative tea with Ivy. He'd been ready to dash back without another word but she'd grabbed his arm and pressed a plate of roast beef sandwiches into his hand.

He'd nodded gratefully at her and the stern look on her face had made him chuckle all the way back into the shop. He didn't have any time to enjoy lunch, however, since the tiny old man in the corner had a new list of sources for him to trace. He stashed them under the counter, trying not to salivate.

It was dangerously close to the full moon now, and temptations like food were tough to resist.

He looked up from the list as Ivy came in and left a pot of tea on the counter, giving him a pointed look as she left.

Christopher tore his eyes away from her, aware that food was currently the least of his temptations. He swallowed a growl as he saw Post's eyes follow her departing form just as hungrily as his had, and hurried back to the registry books, determined to concentrate on his work.

"Well, that's me done for the day," Post announced, dropping two piles of books on the counter. "I can't say I envy you boy, it's baking in here."

Christopher nodded, and turned to the elderly gentleman. "Do you mind if I check out Master Post's books first, Dr Fitzhearn?"

"Not at all, dear boy," he said, and scuttled back to his chair to wait.

"Thank you," said Post, turning to the man and making polite scholarly enquiries about his research as Christopher worked.

"There you are, sir," Christopher said eventually.

"How many times, Christopher?" sighed Post. "It's *Quentin*."

"Sorry," said Christopher, secretly pleased to be able to exasperate the man. "Quentin."

"That's better." He checked his watch. "I'll see you in a fortnight – have to head to the continent for an auction."

"Best of luck, Quentin," said Christopher, and turned back to the lithographer. "Dr Fitzhearn, I'm afraid a number of these are on loan, but I can probably find alternatives."

"Oh? Which ones?" He scurried forwards again and peered at the list. "I see – that will be fine, thank you."

He leaned on the counter as Christopher picked out a series of volumes for him.

"He seemed like a fascinating character," he said, thoughtfully. "Genuinely interested in lithography."

"Don't believe a minute of it," scoffed the Widow Jenkins, emerging from her pile of books and glowering at Dr Fitzhearn.

"What's that, my dear lady?" asked Dr Fitzhearn. He and Ms Jenkins had struck up an odd sort of friendship over the past few weeks, and Christopher had been wondering whether he ought to mention her more unusual hobbies to the gentle old man before it was too late.

"Why?" asked Christopher, interested.

"He's bad news, that's why," the ghastly old woman

announced. "Just like his father, always poking his nose in where it shouldn't be, leaving nothing but tangled messes and broken hearts."

"You seem to speak from experience, my dear," Fitzhearn said, gently.

"I do – my sister Flossie fell for the evil old warlock and it did her no good at all. Broke her heart."

"But he seems so pleasant – and you can hardly blame him for his father's conduct," said Fitzhearn, clearly troubled by the possibility that a fellow scholar could be so callous. He glanced out of the shop window and Christopher followed his gaze.

His fingers tightened around the book in his hands: Post was leaning casually on the cake counter in Ivy's shop, preening and fawning over her. He'd taken her another extravagant bunch of flowers – roses and lilies this time – and was practically exuding charm. Christopher thought he could almost *smell* it. He could see Ivy's blush from here.

"Christopher has the measure of him," said the Widow Jenkins, cackling. "Put that book down before you hurt it, boy."

Caught out under their scrutiny, Christopher put the book down on the counter, carefully, trying not to think about the way Post was looking at Ivy.

Dr Fitzhearn stared at him. "Good grief, Christopher, what's got into you?" he asked. "You look ready to eat the man!"

"He just might, at that," Ms Jenkins observed, and winked at Christopher; he paled. "Would do us all a turn of good. No, Vladimir, the boy's in love, and that jumped up little oik is all over young Ivy there."

"No I'm n-" Christopher began, annoyed, but his brain caught up with his ears and forced him to do a mental u-turn. "Vladimir?" he asked, staring at Dr Fitzhearn.

"Yes," said the man.

"Oh."

"My mother was Russian," the tiny man explained with a slight sigh; apparently this happened a lot. "An extraordinary woman – she danced with the Russian ballet, you know. My father met her in Europe and brought her home to Scotland."

He nodded, and looked back towards Ivy's shop. His fists clenched: she was laughing at something he'd said.

"Don't let him get to her," said the Widow Jenkins, softly. "He'll win her with his fancy words, all smiles and promises, then he'll butter her up and eat her heart. Leave her nothing but an empty shell."

Both Christopher and the Doctor stared at her, she glared back at the both of them; her knuckles were white where she gripped the desk in front of her.

"My Flossie used to sing," she said. "Every day, while she worked, every day. Even when she was sad – she had a soul of music, did that girl. Voice like a bell ringing out. And he took it from her. Stole it. Tricked her with pretty words and a handsome face, and when he was finished with her she never sang another note. Not one. He ate her heart, and that was the end."

Christopher looked at the ancient woman behind her pile of necromancy tomes and understood. In all of her dabbling, all of her reading, she was trying to find her sister's heart. He wondered whether she had ever admitted it before.

"She wasted away without her song," she said, and her voice was tense and gravelly. "Bastard didn't even come to her funeral."

Vladimir stood up and crossed the room, placing a withered hand on hers. "My dear lady..." he said, and fell silent. Neither of them really needed to say anything.

Quietly, Christopher returned to his book hunt, leaving the two friends in peace. They were talking quietly together, sharing some private grief, and Christopher didn't want to intrude. He wondered whether Dr Fitzhearn knew she'd been speaking literally about warlocks and the eating of hearts, or if he'd simply assumed she was being lyrical.

He looked up as the shop bell jangled; neither Vlad the Lithographer or the Widow Jenkins appeared to have noticed.

The two men who strode in were quite imposing, in their own ways: the first was tall, black and poised, his green eyes taking in the bookshop almost lazily. He had a natural air of authority that Christopher immediately found difficult to resist, even before he spoke. His companion was smaller, but no less striking. He was wiry, lithe, holding himself like a coil that was ready to spring. He glanced at the elderly friends in the corner, curiously, before he and his friend turned to Christopher.

The taller of the two spoke, with a deep, confident voice that reminded Christopher of summers spent cavorting across the countryside with his class, following the commands of his youth leaders. It was a voice in which you could place your trust, and Christopher was in no doubt whatsoever that the man in front of him knew this.

He decided, therefore, not to trust him at all.

"Good afternoon," the man said, smiling, his features shifting from commanding to friendly. It was quite an effect. "My colleague and I are researching ancient artefacts and were told that this bookshop would be a good place to start."

"I should think you've come to the right place," said Christopher, politely. "May I ask if you intend to work here or take books out?"

"Both, eventually," said the man. "Regrettably, we're otherwise engaged this afternoon, but we were in the area and thought we might – take a look around."

"Of course," said Christopher, smiling. He leaned forward slightly, aware that Dr Fitzhearn was still in the shop. If this pair weren't magical he'd eat his checking book. "May I enquire as to the nature of the artefacts you're interested in?"

The two men also glanced at the Doctor and the Widow.

"Unusual," said the first man, pointedly, and Christopher smiled.

"Then I think we can help you. If you have time, I

could organise a reader's card for you each – and if you give me some idea of the sort of area you'd like to start looking, I can work on a list of sources ready for your next visit?"

The men exchanged a glance, looking mildly impressed.

"That would be very kind of you, Master…?"

"Porter – but everyone around here calls me Christopher," he said, pulling out a couple of forms.

The man extended a hand, Christopher took it.

"William Hoxley," he said, shaking his hand with a surprisingly gentle grip. "And my colleague is Colin Morris."

Master Morris, who had apparently become engrossed in a stack of books about flower arranging, looked up at his name and gave Christopher a curt nod.

"I'll need addresses and some form of identification – for our records," he added, as Morris looked mildly puzzled. "Don't want anyone running off with the books," he said. "We can't be too careful, these days."

"Of course," said Master Hoxley, glancing at his friend. "Would it be alright if we brought our identification next time?" he asked.

"Naturally," said Christopher, handing him a pen. "Something with a photograph and something with a house address, please – like a utility bill." He lowered his voice slightly. "We also accept Insignia," he added, and Hoxley nodded.

"Excellent," he said, as he signed his form with a flourish and handed the pen to his friend. "Do you get much business up here?" he asked, conversationally.

"Quite a bit," Christopher nodded. "From all kinds of people…"

Hoxley nodded, he'd understood perfectly: Christopher had been warning him not to be overtly magical.

"Today's been particularly busy, actually," said Christopher, with a mild smile. "But I'm hoping it'll calm down a little when term starts again."

"Ah yes," Hoxley grinned. "My nephew is starting school next week, he can't wait – I think his mother would happily wait another year or so, though."

Christopher smiled. "I'm sure his eagerness will wear off over time," he said, and Hoxley chuckled.

"No doubt," he glanced over at the research desks. "Do you get many people in for those?" he asked, nodding in their direction.

"A few," Christopher told him. "It varies – if you're intending to spend a few hours here it might be wise to book."

"In the *usual* way?" Hoxley asked.

"Yes," agreed Christopher, grinning. "But we do have a phone, as well."

Hoxley nodded thoughtfully, and turned to look at the bookshelf behind him as his friend completed the form.

This pair must be from the old families, Christopher thought. *Not many Practitioners use Etching anymore.*

Etching had been in use for centuries, and was grudgingly considered to be effective, even now. A block of wood or stone – it didn't really matter which kind, as long as it was kept smooth, was maintained in a quiet part of the home or business, along with a very special kind of stylus. As with everything, there was a perceived hierarchy of style within the system that meant that most Practitioners preferred marble or ebony if they could afford it.

Christopher wasn't sure how they were made, but he knew that the number of people who had the skill was falling now that they were less popular. They kept their secrets to themselves. The stylus was made in a material that matched the Etching Block and it hummed slightly when picked up, as if it was alive. If you wanted to send a message to someone, you'd simply pick up the stylus, write '*For the attention of –*' whomever and scrawl your message beneath it. As long as they had an Etching Block of their own, the message would get through, and would wait for them to pick it up, spreading parchment or paper over the top and rubbing it over with charcoal or chalk to record it. It was a very good system, as long as the person you were writing to had a block and remembered to check it; it didn't even matter if they had a common name, the stylus took care of that: forming an image of the person for whom the message was intended from your mind.

His mother had never liked them, complaining that she'd rather use something that couldn't see into her head, and that it couldn't be good for her. More and more Practitioners had come to the same conclusion, though there was really no evidence that it was harmful in the slightest – or even that the stylus could retain your thoughts, another frequent misconception – and since the invention of the telephone Etching had gone out of fashion, somewhat.

"That's me done," said Morris, flashing him a brief grin.

"Thanks," said Christopher, scanning the information before filing it under the counter.

"We'll let you know when we're ready to start," Hoxley rumbled. "Thank you for your help."

"Any time," Christopher said, watching them leave.

He frowned.

"There's something very odd about those two," he murmured, and the books in front of him rustled as if in agreement.

He glanced at the Widow Jenkins and Dr Fitzhearn, still deep in conversation. He came to a decision, fetching three mugs from the back room. He carried the tea, mugs and sandwiches to the free desk.

"Tea?" he asked, interrupting them.

"Bless you, my boy," said Dr Fitzhearn. "That's just what we need."

"Thank you, dearie," said the Widow Jenkins, uncharacteristically shaky. "And sandwiches too, you're spoiling us."

Christopher shook his head and glanced at Ivy's shop. Happily, Post had departed, though his flowers were still on the counter top, waiting for a vase.

ooo

She'd put the flowers in her study. Christopher could smell their sickly sweetness them from his room, even with his bed covers over his head.

As soon as he'd closed up shop he'd headed upstairs, glad that Ivy had released the security charm on the spiral staircase in the back room. He'd grabbed a glass of water and climbed into bed, hoping that no one would bother him for a couple of hours. No one had, but the scent of those flowers had wound its way into his subconscious and was slowly driving him insane.

The pounding in his head hadn't diminished, despite the lack of light and sound in his room, and he was sprawled, bereft of sleep, in the cave of duvet that he'd created on his bed.

So he sulked.

He was aware that he was being childish and petulant – it was up to Ivy what she did with the flowers, after all – but he couldn't think about anything else, not so close to the full moon.

There were still three days to go, and already he could feel the need to change: his skin was tight and itchy, as if something was crawling around inside, prodding and probing, trying to find a way out. His muscles were beginning to tighten, and he knew that there would be a point where they would refuse to relax, and he would spend the day before he transformed in agony.

He rubbed at his arms in annoyance.

It didn't have to be this maddening, this agonising – if only he could learn to stop fighting it. He had heard that transformations needn't be painful at all, if you just let them happen, but he couldn't. He was too afraid.

Too afraid of the pain, and too afraid of what letting go might mean.

Not that he'd hurt anyone, while he was in his right mind, but he'd met too many werewolves who had become monsters, seeing their condition as an excuse to rape and murder and torture.

He never wanted that part of the wolf, the part that spoke to him, to take him over. The part that was – even now – whispering darkly about what they could do to Post if he hurt Ivy.

Letting go didn't mean that he would become a ferocious killer, but it might be one step nearer to it, and Christopher was unwilling to let that happen.

Even two transformations a month would be enough, the wolf wheedled. *Then it wouldn't hurt, then I'd sleep...*

He growled at himself. At this rate, this month would be particularly bad.

And he still hadn't spoken to Ivy about it.

ooo

Christopher hadn't made an appearance all evening, and it worried her. The children, exhausted from their day out, had fallen asleep in front of a film, and Ivy had had to carry little Jake to bed. She had been standing outside Christopher's door for several minutes, debating whether she should disturb him, hands on her hips.

He hadn't eaten until late, she knew, and he'd looked particularly worn when he was locking up. She bit her lip, it *was* getting close to full moon now; he could be feeling the effects of it already.

Still, she thought, coming to a decision. *He has to eat, and the worst he can do with Martha around is shout at me.*

And he still hasn't talked to me about it.

ooo

Christopher woke from a fitful doze to a knock on his door.

He made a noise that sounded a lot like "Mlargh."

"Are you alright?" a voice asked.

Ivy.

He intended to assure her that he was fine, thank you

very much, but all that came out this time was "Whrzl."

There was a pause, and Christopher could have sworn he heard Ivy mutter:

"You'd better not be naked."

The door opened and her marvellous smell filled the room, she took a few, uncertain steps towards him.

"Christopher?" she asked, tentatively. He struggled with the duvet and peered blearily at her.

He apparently looked about as good as he felt, as Ivy frowned and came closer. To his unreserved surprise, she perched on the bed next to him and held a hand to his forehead; it was cool and soft, and he closed his eyes for a moment in relief.

"Bad head?" she asked, and he nodded, making tiny explosions happen in the back of his skull. He blinked woozily. "Have you taken anything for it?"

He shook his head. This time, in place of explosions was dizziness. The room shifted uncertainly around him, as if the Arcade had suddenly developed the urge to go for a walk.

"Have you eaten?"

"Not since the sandwiches," he slurred. "I'm fine," he added, unconvincingly, and Ivy snorted.

"Lie down, I'll be back."

Christopher did as he was told, slipping reluctantly back onto the already tangled sheets – it wasn't as if he would be able to do much else, anyway. The smell of the flowers wafted through the open door like an unwelcome guest, mingling with Ivy's scent. It didn't bother him as much anymore: she might have brought the flowers upstairs, but Ivy wasn't sitting on Post's bed, or worried about him enough to check on him.

He heard her come back in and struggled to sit up.

"Here," she said, and shifted his pillows to make it easier for him. "Drink this." She handed him a glass of suspiciously thick liquid. "It's one of my aunt Muriel's concoctions," she explained as he gave it a suspicious sniff. "It'll get rid of your headache – but I'd try to get it all down in one go, if I were you. The lumps aren't fun."

He gave her a dubious look before swallowing the contents of the glass in one gulp. He grimaced and tried not to retch. Whatever Ivy's aunt Muriel had prescribed for headaches tasted *foul*.

"Now this," she pressed a glass of water into his hands and he drank it thirstily, anything to get rid of the taste. Whatever it was seemed to be doing the trick, however, and he relaxed as big pink clouds of pain-free oblivion burst into his brain.

"Better?" she asked, sitting next to him again as the world cooled to a much more sensible temperature; even his skin felt less taut, less itchy.

"Much," he said, and rubbed his head. "What was in that?"

"Oh, nothing much – willow extract, buttermilk, and a few other things." She patted his hand absently. "I've never really understood about the buttermilk, but it *is* good for you."

"Thanks," he said, and she gave him a mild smile.

"You looked like you needed it," she said. "Do you feel up to eating?" she asked, and he nodded in potion-induced contentment.

"I'll put something together then – the children are already asleep, so we shouldn't make too much noise."

To his surprise, he found that standing up wasn't all that bad. He padded unsteadily across the main room and flopped onto one of the big, comfortable sofas, watching the rain water the plants in the garden. Ivy had unroofed it for the moment, saying that she tended to keep it that way until the frosts hit – her plants needed to be robust to remain healthy, and a bit of weather didn't usually bother them.

The weather had apparently broken while he had been sleeping, and the world felt fresher now. It was easier to breathe, and think.

Whatever Ivy was cooking smelled amazing, and he sniffed the air hungrily, forgetting about the importance of remaining inconspicuous in his current daze.

"That smells fantastic," he said, watching his friend

cook.

"Macaroni cheese – my mother's recipe," she said, over her shoulder. "You should probably drink some more water, it'll help with your head."

"My head feels great," he said, looking down at his glass in mild amazement. He didn't remember finishing it. "Still..."

He went to get himself some more, running the tap for a minute so that the water was really cold.

"It tastes better," he said, on her look.

Ivy chuckled. "My dad always used to say that, too," she said, and he beamed at her.

Leaning against the counter, great aunt Muriel's headache cure working a slightly befuddling magic on him, Christopher felt content – at peace with the world.

"Bacon?" he asked, watching her hungrily.

"Family preference," she said. "And paprika." She licked the wooden spoon and pulled out a second bowl, putting it down next to his. "I haven't had this in *years*," she said, smiling. "I'll join you."

He grinned, toothily, and watched her stir and taste and adjust the sauce on the stove. He liked to watch her cook, even though she seemed out of practice with it, like she hadn't really bothered before he and the children had moved in. She knew what she was doing, however, and even if she didn't have the gift that Martha had, her food always tasted great to him. She tucked an errant strand of hair behind her ear, smearing cornflour on her cheek. Christopher laughed.

"You're all floury," he said, and brushed the flour away without thinking. He carried the two glasses of water back to the sofa, not noticing how Ivy had frozen at his careless touch.

"Here," she said, joining him. If she held herself more awkwardly than before, he didn't notice, intent on the warm bowl of food in front of him.

They ate in silence until there was nothing left, Ivy licking as much of the sauce as she could from the inside of her bowl, putting it down almost regretfully.

Christopher found this very funny indeed, and laughed like a child. She shushed him, lest they wake the children, but chuckled at herself.

"I take it you like that, then?" he asked, amused.

"It's my favourite," she admitted, tucking her legs underneath her comfortably.

"You were right about the bacon," he said. "And the paprika – it made the dish."

"Mmm," she said, and stared over at the calendar tacked to the wall by the spell preparation table thoughtfully. "I'll have to make it for the children when the weather turns colder…" she trailed off, her mind on other things.

"They'll love it," he said, enthusiastically.

Their legs were almost touching now, he realised, and if he shifted his foot slightly –

"Christopher," she said, hesitantly, and he looked up to see a face clouded with concern. What had he done wrong? "There's something I need to ask you."

He put his head on one side and nodded. Comfortable, relaxed and well-fed, he was entirely unprepared for what she said next.

"I know you're a lycanthrope," Ivy said, matter-of-factly. "I need to know if you're a threat to the children – or to me."

He blinked at her, stupidly. "What?"

"I know that you're a werewolf," Ivy repeated.

Very slowly, Christopher paled, inching himself away from her; given that he was sitting with his knees up to his chin it was rather like watching him collapse in on himself. Her eyes never left him as he crumpled up, hugging his knees tightly.

"Christopher?" she probed, and he tried to wriggle further away, refusing to meet her eyes. "I have to know."

His eyes were darting around the room. He looked like a man about to bolt, and she couldn't have that. He was her friend, after all. Gently, she laid a hand on his arm – he jumped at the contact as if he'd been burned, but she didn't let go.

"Please," she said.

He stared at her, shocked and miserable. "I'm – not a threat," he managed, haltingly.

"You keep your mind?"

"Y-yes."

Ivy nodded and looked away, thinking. He watched her, afraid of what his admission would mean for their friendship.

"I was going to tell you," he said, disconsolately. "I just didn't know how to start..."

"I hoped you would," she said, gently.

He glared despondently at his knees. She'd hoped that he would and he hadn't. He'd ruined everything.

"Where will you go?" she asked, quietly, and the yawning gulf of despair in his mind threatened to swallow him up.

"I don't know," he said, his voice surprisingly level. "I can go right now if you want – come back for my things when I've found somewhere –"

"No," said Ivy, and he forced himself to look up at her. "No, I meant where will you go to transform?"

He swallowed, watching her eyes in incomprehension.

"You – you want me to *stay*?" he asked, shock mingling with the tiniest shred of hope as she gave him the slightest of smiles.

"I wouldn't be a very good friend if I didn't, would I?" she said, and rubbed his arm. "As long as you swear to me you won't hurt any of us, on pain of Martha interceding, I don't have a problem with it."

"Really?" he asked, uncoiling a little bit. He caught the expression on her face and added, "I mean – usually people are a little more reluctant to share their home with a – with a monster."

"I'm not everyone else," she said, simply. "There was a time when the people around here were reluctant to share their *town* with my family. Besides, I live in a house full of plants that come to life and probably *could* eat someone if it wouldn't give her indigestion, you can't get much stranger than that."

"Remind me to tell you about the Barracloughs' house," he said, unwrapping his legs a little more.

"So if you promise me that you aren't dangerous, and keep that promise, then you can stay," Ivy continued.

"I swear to you I'm not a threat – I keep my mind when I'm a wolf and I would *never* hurt the children, or you, or *anyone*," he said, looking her dead in the eye.

Ivy nodded, accepting this. "Good," she said. "I'm glad we've got that sorted out – though you will have to talk to Mahri and Reggie about it."

"I'll talk to them tomorrow, after Mahri finishes work," he said, with more confidence than he felt. Even if Ivy had accepted him (and he was currently not willing to believe it in case it all turned out to be a dream), there was no guarantee that Mahri would, and Reggie wouldn't even know where to *start* thinking about it.

"I'll help you speak to the children," she said. "But I don't think they'll be put off too much, they're young and their minds are still flexible."

"Thank you," he said, with feeling. Tomorrow was not going to be a good day.

"Could you transform here?" Ivy asked, bringing him back to the present.

"Er – I could, but it's not pleasant. It would probably terrify the children..."

"Noisy, is it?"

"Well, it hurts quite a bit," he said, and Ivy's face softened. "I used to change on the roof of the flats – people just assumed it was someone being beaten up outside."

"Hmm," said Ivy. "If the children were at Mahri's, would they still be able to hear?"

"No," he said, after a moment's thought. "The Arcade seems to damp out a lot of sound."

Ivy looked mildly smug. "One of the perks," she acknowledged.

"So I could change in my room – if everyone was over at the Coach Houses. Saffy won't like it," he added, suddenly. "She'll be able to sense the change as it happens – most dogs can – it will probably panic her."

"Which isn't necessarily good if she's in pup," Ivy agreed. "Well, we'll take that hurdle when we reach it."

There was a companionable silence for a few minutes, each of them lost in their own thoughts. Christopher couldn't believe his luck.

"Christopher?" Ivy asked. "Your family – you haven't been home for a while, have you?"

"No," he replied, after a few moments. "I couldn't bring this on them. The shame alone. I mean, having a monster like me in the family would ruin any chance Rachel had for education or work, my parents would lose their jobs – maybe even their home. I couldn't do it."

Ivy nodded, though it looked to Christopher as if she didn't quite agree with him.

"You're not a monster," she said, and he scoffed. "Well," she continued, acknowledging this, "maybe only a part-time monster."

Christopher thought that his heart might burst from the strain of the evening. She had no idea what a few kind words could do for someone who had spent their life running from persecution. He managed a brave smile for her, uncurling his legs so they dangled off the sofa beside hers.

"How did it happen?" she asked, softly, scooting a little closer to him.

He took a deep breath; this was something he'd only ever told one person before, and since Rachel hadn't been there in person, he hadn't had to watch her reaction.

"I was nineteen…"

16
Harvest Moon

Christopher lay in the tangled sheets of his bed, beads of sweat forming on his naked skin. His flesh felt taut and hot, his muscles tense and aching as he resisted the change.

He ground his teeth together as the wolf, frustrated by his inactivity, made fresh attempts to take over; he fought it with every fibre of his being.

He didn't want it to begin, even though he knew that everything would feel better when it did.

It wasn't that he was afraid of hurting people, as such – though it always remained a dreadful possibility at the back of his mind. Everyone would be safe in the Arcade, Martha would see to that. In many ways, he was better placed this month than he ever had been, in terms of keeping others safe.

He writhed and bucked as a fresh wave of agony shuddered through him.

Let go, the wolf was whispering to him. *Let me out, we're safe here, no one will hurt us, and we won't hurt them.*

He took great gulps of air, his hands clenching fists of fabric as he struggled to keep the monster at bay.

Let me run, we need to run! the beast whined, shoving and heaving against the edges of Christopher's resolve.

"No," he said aloud, though it was really more of a growl.

He could smell Ivy moving around in the main room. He didn't want to change this near to her, didn't want her to hear his screams.

She'd promised to stay at Mahri's with the children. If he could just hold on for a few minutes longer, she would go and he could change in peace, safe in the knowledge that he wasn't traumatising anyone.

The torrent of sensation was building now, accompanied by the sick feeling of terror deep in his stomach, and he knew that he couldn't restrain the wolf in him much longer.

Just a little push, the wolf wheedled, *and it won't hurt anymore, just a little push...*

Christopher moaned as his insides twisted violently, he lurched over to his hands and knees as his skin boiled and prickled.

Just a few more moments –

Let – Me – OUT.

With what seemed like one last great heave, the wolf broke through the remnants of his control, rending a scream from his throat as his body twisted and contorted. He felt his spine begin to lengthen as the pain became too much for him. No longer able to contain his agony, his screams became one continuous, wrenching noise. His bones cracked, and broke, and reformed, altering the shape of his body as his ragged muscles snapped into unaccustomed places.

Great clumps of fur tore through his taut skin as his nails lengthened and hardened into cruel claws. His teeth were growing too, now, and his screams became indistinct as his humanity was stripped from him, becoming snarls and yelps as the sickness took hold.

When his flesh had finished crawling and the pain diminished he collapsed onto his bed, panting and exhausted.

ooo

Ivy sat outside Christopher's bedroom door, resisting the urge to open it, despite having promised to stay in Mahri's house with the children. Especially since Mahri had taken Saffy out for a long walk with Reggie. They were both worried about how she would react to Christopher's transformation.

Reggie had taken Christopher's halting admission rather philosophically, and since he had no previous experience of lycanthropy, had based his acceptance of his young friend's condition entirely on Ivy's lack of concern. Mahri, however, had been a different story.

She had grown up in a family of Practitioners and had been raised to view werewolves with terror and deep suspicion. She had refrained from saying much aloud, in deference to the fact that Christopher had hitherto appeared to be a good sort, but it had been painfully obvious that she no longer trusted him, particularly around the children. Christopher had hidden his distress at her reaction well, but Ivy could see how much it had hurt him.

Ivy hoped for his sake that Mahri would come to understand that none of it was Christopher's fault; she suspected that a full moon with no casualties would do much to allay her fears.

The children had needed to have lycanthropy explained to them before they could express an opinion on the matter, and Mahri's behaviour had left them wide-eyed and frightened. Ivy had stubbornly continued to interact with him normally, which served to reassure them a little, but they were still nervous.

She had been pacing around Mahri's living room when she had felt the change begin; he was fighting it so hard that for a few moments it had altered the magical atmosphere of the Arcade as Martha tried to compensate.

She'd stopped by the window, unable to tear her gaze away from the glass.

She was afraid for him.

"Will you two be alright on your own?" she asked the children, who were watching Mahri's battered television.

Astrid shot her a look of fear, so Ivy continued, "Martha will look after me, don't worry."

"We'll be okay," said Astrid, after a moment's consideration. She gave Ivy a desperate look, silently begging her to be careful, and Ivy nodded before crossing the quiet garden and letting herself in.

She resumed her pacing in the main room, glancing periodically across the garden to the coach houses. Astrid, she noted, had taken up her previous position by the window, equally worried.

Tensely, she forced herself to sit down. It wouldn't do the children any good to see how worried she was. That was when Christopher had begun to scream.

She'd shot to her feet, almost frantic with worry, and rushed to his door. She had been about to barge in when she'd remembered her promise about his privacy. Angry at herself, at Mahri's prejudice, at the moon, at the cruel man that had bitten him, she'd hovered in the corridor, wringing her hands as her friend screamed, and screamed, and screamed.

As his yells had turned to keening and snarling, she'd sunk against the far wall, uncertain how to help him and reluctant to leave.

Ivy hugged her knees.

It had been silent in the Arcade for some time, and it seemed that even Martha was afraid for him, keeping her distance. A couple of tendrils wound around Ivy, and she accepted them gladly, wishing that she could do the same for Christopher.

A scrabbling at the door startled the vines, and they withdrew, unnerved.

Ivy watched as a dark shape on the other side of the glass reached and groped for the handle, struggling to gain purchase on the polished metal. Eventually, the door opened a crack, and a hairy muzzle stuck through, sniffing the air. It retreated very quickly, as if its owner had found a scent that disturbed it, aware of her imposition.

Knowing that this was probably her fault, Ivy stayed as still as she could, knowing that nothing on Earth would move her from her present position until she knew that her friend was alright. She didn't want to make him even more skittish by shifting about.

She would have to allow him to come to her.

Minutes passed in silence, neither of them willing to move or leave.

Eventually, a careful paw curled around the wood of the door and pulled it open enough for the wolf to slink through, looking despondent.

His baleful stare was almost an accusation, and Ivy felt very keenly that her presence was, in itself, a betrayal.

"I'm sorry," she whispered, wanting desperately to comfort him, to let him know that none of this mattered to the people around him. "Are – are you alright?"

Christopher's pale blue eyes stared at her from his wolf's face for a few moments, before he nodded, slowly.

"Oh, good," she said softly. She brought her agitated hands to her mouth, unsure what to do with herself. "I – " she began, but found that she couldn't continue. She didn't know what to say. Abruptly, something within her snapped, and she flung her arms around Christopher's neck.

The wolf staggered slightly, astonished.

"It sounded horrible," Ivy mumbled into his fur. "I just wanted to make it stop – I couldn't stand the idea of you being here on your own."

She felt Christopher relax slightly, and he nuzzled his maw against her shoulder, letting her know that she was forgiven.

"I'm sorry I broke my promise," she said, letting him go and brushing away tears that she didn't know she had shed.

Christopher pawed her arm, gently, and she smiled slightly.

"You make a handsome wolf," she said, quietly, and he snorted. "Well, you do," she continued, laughing a little. "I expect you want to go off and run."

The wolf in front of her nodded, and Ivy climbed to her feet.

"Martha will let you in and out," she said, biting her lip. "I think it would be best for the children to see you like this – you're inherently non-threatening, for one thing." She ignored the flash of panic that crossed his lupine features and continued, "I'll keep them up until you come back. No, don't look at me like that," she admonished, suddenly firm. "Children's minds are flexible, and those two strike me as being very sensible about this sort of thing. I mean, they've been on the run for months without anyone finding them, clearly they think things through."

She reached down and ruffled his fur soothingly. "No, I don't think you'll have anything to worry about there."

Christopher met her eyes and she knew that they were both thinking about Mahri.

"She'll come around," said Ivy softly. "Given time."

Christopher looked away, full of doubt.

Ivy watched him as he padded away and listened as his wolfish footfalls crossed the kitchen, pausing for a moment at the top of the spiral staircase. She turned the corner in time to see his tail disappear, claws clicking on the cast iron.

As strong as her faith in Mahri and the children was, she hoped for his sake that she was right.

ooo

He heard the door shut behind him with a click and released the breath that he had been holding. The annoyance that he'd felt at Ivy's presence was fading to forgiveness now – after all, there were far worse reasons to break a promise – and the air outside was cool and damp. He shifted his feet on the wet paving stones outside the dark Arcade and sniffed the air.

Everything was so much sharper when he was a wolf, smells heightening, twisting, and merging into living patterns and shapes. He could almost *see* where Joanna and the Professor had walked out of the Arcade when they had left for the day; could smell where a young girl had been skipping ahead of her parents, pausing at the corner of the road to wait for them; taste the fumes of the delivery truck that had pulled up outside the greengrocer's earlier in the day. It was as if every moment had tattooed itself on the atmosphere of the street, all fading at different rates, all swarming around one another in a morass of sensation.

As a human, it all became too confused to pick out the individual strands, but as a wolf –

He lowered his snout to the paving stones to investigate the tones of a tabby cat that had passed by days before.

As a wolf, it felt like this was *his* world.

The power of the feeling frightened him, sometimes, made him wonder what he might do if he began to believe that that level of control was really his.

He glanced up and down the street, aware that the local Council occasionally ran initiatives to round up strays. They were easily evaded, since the officers thought that they were dealing with animals. It was the one time that the wolf would defer to his judgement during the change, seeing the advantage it gave him.

He looked up at the Arcade, one last time, catching the now-familiar scents of his home; just on the edge of his vision he spotted a few of Martha's vines coiling up in the empty bay at the front of the shop, watching him. He could never smell them coming, he realised, because their smell was so much a part of the fabric of the Arcade. He suspected that Martha was rather smug about that.

Certain in the knowledge that Ivy, at least, would be pleased to see him return, he padded off along the edge of the street, dodging puddles made lurid by the neon streetlights, following the scent of the little girl and her parents.

He paused as someone further up the road opened a window and leaned out. Shrinking into the shadows, he watched as the man lit a cigarette, staring off into the night. He wasn't looking down into the street, and didn't notice as Christopher slipped away along a side-street and across the main square, glad to be away from the acrid smoke.

He paused again under a tree by the bank, waiting patiently for two drunken friends to make their way past him, examining their aromas as psychedelic bursts of colour.

Early on, Christopher had come to the liberating realisation that the wolf had no interest in hurting anyone unless it became cornered, and he had rewarded this non-aggression by saving up for the best raw steak that he could afford so that the wolf could feast when he returned home.

The urge to hunt was still there, but in a more playful form; out near the edges of the town he could chase rabbits and cats, always letting them get away at the last moment.

The hunk of steak waiting at the end of the night was always enough to persuade the wolf to let them go. Besides, one taste of tabby cat could make *anything* else preferable.

The two men wove and stumbled their way down the street, singing something bawdy about a girl named Alice.

He continued along the high street, pausing to investigate the trails of the people of Brindleford. He picked out some of his regular customers, tracing Dr Fitzhearn to a used camera shop, following Widow Jenkins through a maze of back alleys to a non-descript shop front in a dingy corner of Brindleford. The cracked and faded sign above the door identified it as 'E-nie's Del-cate-sa-'. The shop, like the street, had seen better days; Christopher padded away from it, storing it in his mental mind map.

He padded down to the edge of town and crossed the bridge that led out of the main town and into the smaller villages. There was countryside out here, or at least an approximation of it, and he picked up his pace a little, the sweet scent of grass reaching out to him from the fields.

He ducked behind a wall as a late night delivery lorry rumbled past, turning his snout away from the cloud of exhaust fumes that momentarily blinded his senses. Emerging, he stretched languorously in the moonlight, the wolf in him revelling in the feeling. He tensed: a rabbit was making an unfortunate detour across one of the long, grassy fields in front of him. He crouched low, tracking its scent hundreds of metres away; he felt his

muscles coil deliciously, ready for the hunt.
He sprang.

ooo

The tension in the main room could have been cut with a knife. Reggie and Mahri had returned from their walk with Saffy. It had been universally agreed that it would be a good thing to leave her in the coach house until Christopher was human again.

Reggie was sitting at the kitchen table with a newspaper, allegedly completing a crossword puzzle. He had actually been doodling in the margins of the paper for the good part of an hour, uneasy at the tension, the situation and the argument that Mahri and Ivy had had upon their return.

He liked to think that he had good instincts when it came to people, and he had warmed to Christopher immediately. He didn't like to think that such a pleasant young man could be a vicious killer. But that was exactly what Mahri had been suggesting for the past few days – admittedly not in Christopher's presence, but to anyone that would listen. And Mahri was such a pragmatic woman, whose advice it might be foolish to ignore, particularly as Reggie himself had absolutely no experience with magic or magical creatures, and the florist had grown up with it all.

He glanced over at her, sitting straight-backed on one of Ivy's mismatched chairs, her arms crossed tightly in front of her, glaring out at the garden as if it had personally offended her. Ivy was silently putting together small bundles of spells at the work table, her back to the room. Her shoulders were tense as she worked, and Reggie wondered when the two women had last had an argument like this.

He didn't like to see his new friends so uncomfortable.

Jake was already asleep on one of the other sofas, and his sister was watching both women carefully, as he was. Astrid acted so much older than she really was, so much of the time, it was easy to forget that she was only seven. Tonight, though, she looked small and vulnerable, not knowing what side to take, or how to accept the fact that one member of her new household was currently an entirely different shape.

Reggie frowned. He was beginning to get used to the presence of their odd extended family, and he didn't want it to be broken up so soon.

Ivy glanced over her shoulder at the spiral staircase for a moment, and Reggie guessed that Martha had informed her of Christopher's return. That, he reflected, was another point in Christopher's favour. If a partially sentient and curiously sentimental being like the Arcade didn't have a problem with Christopher being around, then perhaps he shouldn't either.

He put down his newspaper expectantly as the clicking of claws on metal drifted up from below. Out of the corner of his eye, he saw Astrid sit up straighter, shaking her brother's shoulder gently.

Slowly, the wolf came into view (no mean feat for someone with four legs on a staircase), looking apprehensive.

"Hello," said Ivy, not turning around. She was acting as though none of this was out of the ordinary, for his sake. "I hope you had a good run."

Christopher nodded, though she couldn't see, and surveyed the room balefully.

His heart went out to his young friend. This couldn't be easy. Reggie cleared his throat. "Didn't get caught in the rain, then?" he asked, and the wolf shook his head, taking a couple of unconscious steps towards him – hopeful steps, he realised. "Well that's something," he said.

Somewhere behind him, Mahri huffed; Reggie ignored her. The horror stories she had been regaling him with on their walk all fell down in the face of the frightened creature in front of him.

He must be dreading their reactions, Reggie thought, and smiled encouragingly at the wolf, who had backed away a little at Mahri's continued resistance. He felt for the man. Even after so long being on his own with the memory of Bessie, he would have had to drag himself back into the Arcade if their places had been reversed.

Mahri tutted, and Reggie turned to look at her – she was clearly uncomfortable with him even being in the room.

"It's not his fault," he found himself saying aloud. Her eyes swivelled to meet his, and he was dismayed by the look of disappointment there. "Come on, old girl, it's *Christopher*. The man who only last week you were practically force-feeding chocolate cake because you thought he was too skinny."

"It doesn't matter how nice a person he is," Mahri said, tersely, deliberately not looking at the wolf across the room. "Right now he's a vicious, savage beast."

Reggie glanced at the cowering wolf by the kitchen stairs. Ivy had very carefully put down everything she had been working with, a tangible anger coming off her in waves.

"There's nothing that can change that," said Mahri, tersely. "And he lied to us about it."

"He didn't lie," said Ivy, in a quiet, heavily controlled voice.

"A lie of omission is still a lie," said Mahri, getting stiffly to her feet. "I'm sorry Christopher," she continued shortly, barely glancing at him. "But there it is."

She turned and stalked across the garden, shutting her front door firmly behind her. Reggie watched her go, sadly.

He glanced over at Christopher, who had the look of a wolf about to bolt, and tried to think of something comforting to say. "She'll come around," he managed, unconvinced.

Just for a moment, there was the sense that Christopher was going to leave and never come back – and perhaps he might have, had Jake not chosen this moment to conduct an experiment.

The children had been watching the exchange

carefully, wary of the large animal in their midst and enthralled by the largely silent argument that had been taking place around them for hours. It was difficult to resign the image of the skinny young man who had chased them around the Arcade with the powerful beast in front of them.

Carefully, Jake lowered himself to the floor and began to make his way over to the wolf, a look of utmost concentration on his face. It was as if he was convinced that this must be some kind of trick, and that if he looked hard enough, he'd figure it out and the real Christopher would jump out from behind one of the big squashy sofas and applaud.

The wolf baulked, backing away until there was nowhere to go except back down the staircase. He sat at the top of the stairs awkwardly, trying to make himself look as non-threatening as possible; Jake stopped nearly a foot away from him and gave him the kind of appraising look that only a four year old can manage.

For a minute or two, no one did anything, the occupants of the main room afraid even to breathe and break the atmosphere of ordinary, quiet magic that surrounded Jake.

He appeared to reach a decision and gingerly held out a hand to the wolf, letting him smell it, Reggie realised, so that he wouldn't be afraid. Then he petted Christopher's snout, still looking perplexed. The wolf sneezed, and Jake laughed, startled.

"You're not scary at all," he declared, happily, and flung his tiny arms around the werewolf's neck. "I missed you reading to us, Christopher!"

Astrid, emboldened by her brother's courage, came and knelt beside them, and rubbed the fur on Christopher's back and neck.

"It's alright," she said to him, as his great, baleful eyes turned in her direction. "We're not afraid."

Reggie beamed at them as Astrid joined her brother in giving their friend a many armed hug, glad that children were capable of such kindness.

ooo

"I've actually come into possession of a few new treasures," Post was telling Dr Fitzhearn, enthusiastically.

Christopher had no idea how he did it, but he always managed to sound disarmingly modest, like the acquisition of valuable magical artefacts was a perfectly ordinary occurrence. For him, he reflected, it probably was.

He picked up a fallen volume from the floor. '*101 Things to do with String,*' flapped at him disconsolately as he returned it to its proper place, like it could sense his mood.

Although it was a Monday, and Mondays meant that Ivy would spend the afternoon in the bookshop, and despite the challenging list of requests Dr Fitzhearn had presented him with earlier in the day, he couldn't shake his melancholy. Mahri was still avoiding him, after the early Blood Moon, and she and Ivy were being very stiff around one another. He hated that the animosity between the two old friends was because of him.

He hadn't heard the row they'd had, but Jake had filled him in almost breathlessly. He allowed himself a small smile. The children had been so desperate to prove that they weren't afraid of him that they had settled on the floor of his bedroom the day after full moon – Jake with his trains and Astrid with one of Ivy's old books – keeping him company as he healed. It had been a generous gesture, and Christopher had been greatly touched.

He fought a yawn as he ticked off the new acquisitions in the ledger under the desk, piling the books – still slumbering from their journey – on the side. He'd put them out later, when Post had gone; he didn't have the energy for him today, weary as he still was from the change.

He looked up at Post's bark of youthful laughter: Dr

Fitzhearn had been decidedly less open with the man since Widow Jenkins' confession, but Post always seemed to take that in his stride. He watched as Post clapped the tiny man on the back, nearly knocking him into the desk.

Another downside of it being Monday, Christopher thought, was that Post might still be here when Ivy locked up the teashop, and then he'd never get rid of him.

"Excellent notion! What do you think, Christopher?" Post declared, turning to him.

Christopher forced a smile. He still hadn't forgiven him for buying Ivy flowers. "I'm sorry, I was miles away."

"I must say, you are looking a little peaky," Post frowned in affectionate concern. "I hope they're not working you too hard."

"I've just been a little off colour of late," Christopher lied.

"Still," Post insisted. "You should get away for a while – take a break."

"Yes, Mr Post – sorry, *Quentin*," he corrected himself on Post's look.

"I tell you what, I'm heading down to London to an auction in a few weeks time, you should come with me."

Startled by Post's continuing generosity, Christopher tried to turn him down politely. A whole two days in his company would be a little too much to cope with, given his general ebullience. It would be like being in a train carriage with a large, excitable elephant.

"No, really, I could-"

But Post wasn't listening. "Capital!" he declared. "I'll sort it all out with the Professor – we'll have a smashing time!"

Christopher, too weary to argue, nodded glumly.

"Now, to the matter at hand," said Post, putting a conspiratorial arm about his shoulders. "Dr Fitzhearn has brought to my attention the proliferation of hiding places in church architecture," he announced. "It'll be just the ticket for my chapter on seventeenth century dark magic – I'd be willing to bet that some of those hiding places are still occupied, what do you think?"

Christopher made a non-committal grunt. At this rate, Post's book would never end.

They looked up as the bell above the door jangled cheerily.

The imposing figure of William Hoxley filled the doorframe.

"Ah, Mr Hoxley, good to see you again," said Christopher, glad of the interruption. "How can I help you?"

For a moment, Hoxley and Post eyed one another with interest, before Hoxley turned to Christopher, who was watching them with open curiosity.

"I've brought the documents you asked for – and for Mr Morris, too."

He handed Christopher a sheaf of papers, and leaned against the desk almost nonchalantly.

"I was hoping to have a browse today, if I may," he smiled, and Christopher fought the urge to grin back, wary of the man's easy authority. "I have a little time."

"Be my guest, sir," said Christopher. "I'll finish off your reader's tickets while you browse."

"Excellent," the man purred. Christopher followed him as he moved towards the back of the shop. He had a curiously graceful way of moving, and Christopher was strongly reminded of the large cats he'd seen at the zoo as a child.

"I think that's me done for the day," announced Post. "Nothing out today – got a minor expedition to the Alps this week – skiing. Pity you can't join me."

Christopher managed a smile.

"I've a new list for you to ferret out though, if you'd be so kind." He handed the page over, torn, it seemed, from his notebook. "Could you have them ready a week on Wednesday?"

"Absolutely," said Christopher, looking forward to a week and a half of peace. "Good luck in the Alps, Quentin."

"Thanks, old chap," he grinned, perfect teeth shining brightly. "Hope it's not as boring as last year – we got snowed in, would you believe?"

He'd turned away to collect his things as he'd said it, and Christopher was glad that he hadn't seen the look that had passed over his face when he'd described regular ski trips to the Alps as boring.

"See you in a week!" he grinned, shaking Christopher's hand. "Dr Fitzhearn," he nodded to the tiny lithographer, and departed.

Dr Fitzhearn gave Christopher a look that spoke volumes, and he snorted. Movement at the other end of the shop caught his eye, and he noticed Hoxley, poised between the shelves, his steely gaze following Post's departure.

ooo

"Hoxley?" Ivy asked, as she chopped up vegetables. "No, I've not heard the name."

"That's odd," said Christopher, scooting past her with a pan of water. "He struck me as someone that people would remember."

They were making dinner together, a regular occurrence now that there were hungry young mouths to feed. Christopher liked it. It felt stable, ordinary.

"And he asked about Etching," he went on, throwing potatoes into the pan. "From the way he spoke I'd have thought he was a local."

Ivy frowned at him. "And he was acting oddly?"

"He was watching Quentin Post like a hawk," he said, clicking the stove on. Vaguely, he wondered why he'd never thought of cooking on magic instead of gas before coming here. "He's sticking to his area of research though, and knows what he's talking about."

"What's he studying?"

"Magical artefacts," he said promptly, remembering the short stack of books that Hoxley had checked out that afternoon.

"Perhaps they're rivals," Ivy said, wiping her hands, "encroaching on one another's territory."

Christopher nodded.

"That would make sense," he said, then added: "he's working with a man named Morris, I don't suppose you've heard of him?"

Ivy shook her head as he raised a questioning eyebrow.

"Perhaps you should ask the Professor," she said, apologetically. "I've rather lost touch with the local families."

Christopher nodded, not wanting to press her on a subject that made her uncomfortable.

They worked in companionable silence for a while before something else occurred to Christopher, as he was lifting the plates out of the cupboard.

"You know, I've never seen him just ignore someone like that," he said, thoughtfully. "Post, I mean. Even if he's never met someone before he'll shake their hands and put them at their ease." He met Ivy's curious gaze across the table. "It was almost as if Hoxley scared him."

17
A Portable Poltergeist

Ivy was dreaming, which was unusual. She was wandering the rooms of the Arcade, searching for something – someone – but she didn't know who, or what. The rooms were bright and fresh, smelling of chamomile and lavender as they had when she was a child; like the sunshine had poured in through the great glass windows and didn't want to leave. She felt safe and happy, comfortable both in her surroundings and her own skin as she walked, barefoot, on the polished wooden boards of the hall.

Somewhere, her father was singing as he worked: a jaunty song that he was applying himself to with gusto, if not accuracy. The strong smell of bitter herbs greeted her, and she knew that her grandmother was working at the stove, concocting the potions that she would sell to her more unusual customers. Ivy walked across the main room, not needing to glance into the kitchen to know that her Nanny Griselda was there – always a comforting presence – and pressed her hands to the bright glass.

There must have been a fall of rain – the garden shone and sparkled with a thousand tiny droplets of water, like diamonds in the sunlight – and there, sure enough, were her mother and great aunts, younger than she remembered, laughing together under the canopy of a large pear tree. They were sitting around a table, working together to make a blanket. Each woman was knitting large coloured squares to be sewn together among the roses.

Somewhere below her, she heard something fall over, and the incongruity of the sound in the idyllic Arcade amplified the sound in her mind. She moved her hand from the glass to investigate, and as she did so she noticed a crack forming beneath her palm. It was small at first, growing and spreading as she watched in horrified fascination. It shot upwards with startling rapidity, expanding and splitting as it went, until it reached the edge of the pane. There it hung, as if uncertain whether to proceed; Ivy held her breath –

Then, with an almighty crash, the great windows of the Arcade shattered, raining white hot shards of glass down on Ivy's cowering body.

Somewhere nearby, somebody swore.

Abruptly, Ivy realised with some relief that she had been dreaming, and that she was now awake. Puzzlingly though, the crashing sounds had not diminished. She swung her legs out of bed, disoriented.

Distantly, she heard Christopher's door open; the crashing sounds had not been a part of her dream. Ivy shot out of her bed, ready for anything.

She found Christopher in the hall, looking sleepy and annoyed. He rolled his eyes at her in the darkness.

"Oh," she said, and went back for her cardigan, irritated.

He was waiting for her when she re-emerged, and together they set off across the main room, grimacing at the dreadful caterwauling emanating from below.

"Ivy?" asked a tremulous voice in the darkness. "Christopher?"

"It's alright, Jake," said Christopher, pausing to ruffle the small boy's hair comfortingly. "It's nothing, go back to bed."

Ivy spied Astrid some steps behind him, hovering silently and protectively, a large book of spells ready in her hand in case anything unpleasant got too near to her brother. If she had been less tired it might have been funny.

This had happened every other night for a week now, and each night the inhabitants of the Arcade had turned out of their beds, dishevelled and ready for trouble, only to find their resident poltergeist expressing his displeasure at their apparent need for sleep.

Ivy suspected that he felt left out now that he was in a place where people could, and would, avoid him for hours at a time.

Angry shouts echoed up the staircase as she and

Christopher trotted down, the crashing rising to a crescendo as they descended into the back of the bookshop.

"Professor –" she began. Beside her, Christopher ducked as a well-aimed inkwell rebounded off the wall.

"People are trying to sleep," Christopher said, through clenched teeth.

"What do *I* care, shop-boy?" Zarrubabel asked, voice dripping with venom. "*I* sleep in the day time, when you selfish flesh-bags bang around everywhere, without a thought about me!"

He knocked over a stack of acquisition papers.

Christopher winced. He'd have to tidy them up in the morning.

"Yes," said Ivy, unimpressed. "But we're getting on with things. You're just being vindictive."

"Of course, Ivy dear, I *am* sorry to have disturbed you," said the ghostly Professor, in a simpering tone.

"No you're not," said Christopher, surprising both of them. "You just want another chance to shout at me in front of a regular, and you know it." It took a lot to get the young werewolf angry, but a pattern of nights of broken sleep and dealing with an irascible spectre were taking their toll.

"Am not!" shouted the spectre, outraged, gesturing so wildly that his pince-nez flew off his nose and hung, bizarre and luminescent, from the edge of a tea mug.

"Are too," retorted Christopher, who was really not in the mood for this. "You were a petulant, whiny, spoiled, spiteful person, and now you're a petulant, whiny, spoiled, spiteful ghost, who can't stand the thought that we mere mortals can manage perfectly well without you!"

"YOU IMPUDENT WHELP!" cried Zarrubabel, stung. "You've got a nerve, speaking to me like that – my sweet, foolish sister gave you a job when no one else would, you foul creature!" He bobbed about angrily, apparently so enraged that he had forgotten to keep throwing things.

They carried on in this vein for some time, shouting all

kinds of horrible things at one another in the darkness, the books around them rustling uncomfortably. It was oddly mesmerising, watching the spectral Professor bobbing up and down a foot or so above the ground, pointy nose mere inches from Christopher's as they shouted themselves hoarse, the back room bathed in Zarrubabel's odd green light.

Ivy closed her eyes; she was too tired for this.

"That's enough!" she shouted. They both stared at her, looking like they'd forgotten their audience. "From both of you," she added, and Zarrubabel shot Christopher a smug look. "You know better than to rise to his bait, Christopher, he wants a fight – you *know* that," she continued, glaring at the sheepish young man. "And *you* need to learn to behave!" she hissed, rounding on the Professor. "You weren't a child when you died, and nothing gives you the right to act like one. You should be *ashamed* of yourself, spending your days winding up Morton and Joanna – who, I might add, have the patience of saints just for keeping you around – and spending your nights frightening children and disturbing people's sleep. It's sickening."

She took a deep breath and surveyed them both. The Professor was much paler now, surprised that his 'little Ivy' would speak to him like this. Christopher looked like a deer that had been caught in the beam of a fast moving lorry.

"Now, we'll have no more of this silliness," she declared. "*We* are going back to bed, and *you* are going to tidy up this mess. I'm going to speak to Joanna in the morning, so this had better all be cleaned up by the time she gets in, or you'll be in even more trouble." She turned to go back up the stairs and added: "And if you feel like misbehaving again then I will have Martha close your book and wrap her vines so tightly around it that you'll never get out without our goodwill – which, I might add, is running quite low at the minute. Goodnight."

She climbed the stairs impatiently, towing a chastened

Christopher behind her. She nodded at Astrid, who was watching her thoughtfully from the mouth of the other hallway and made her way back to her room.

"I'm sorry," said Christopher, quietly. "I shouldn't have let him get to me like that."

Ivy gave a light sigh. "It certainly didn't help," she said. "But it was only a matter of time before you snapped at him, he's so rude to you."

Christopher gave an awkward shrug.

"Night," Ivy said, and closed the door behind her with a click. She climbed back into bed, pulling her blanket with its bright, knitted squares around her, thinking hard.

What they needed was some way for Zarrubabel to feel less left out, less cooped up.

She smiled to herself in the darkness.

Ivy had a plan.

ooo

"What are you doing?" asked Astrid, peering at the strange contraption that was taking form on the work table.

It was the next day, and Ivy had spent the morning rummaging in various cupboards, pulling things out and putting them back, muttering to herself. She had attracted a curious trail of spectators, in the form of Boscoe, Saffy and Jake, until the latter had been tempted away by cake and a Frisbee, and Boscoe had followed him, deciding that the thing whizzing about the garden was much more interesting than the funny glass box inside.

Saffy had sent a sniff of derision in their direction, and settled down on a rug that Ivy dragged out for her. She was still watching Ivy with disconcerting curiosity.

Reggie had been playing with the children in the garden, and had retreated inside for a welcome sit down. He was helping Jake read the cartoons in the newspaper, but the two of them now paused and peered over the back of the sofa, curious.

"I'm trying to make Professor Zarrubabel less of a pain in the –" she glanced at Astrid. "Bottom."

Astrid frowned. Ivy was leaning over an old glass display case, with a panel in the back that could be opened and shut. It was made of thick, slightly green glass, and had a sturdy wooden base. Ivy had removed the base and was fitting four small, robust wheels to it.

Reggie and Jake joined them at the table.

"A moving box?" Reggie asked. "Won't that make him more of a nuisance?"

"Possibly," said Ivy, with a slight frown. "But if he feels he's being included he'll have fewer excuses to mope." She marked the edge of one of the wheels onto the wood with a pencil. "Besides, if he misbehaves up here I'll let Martha have at him."

Astrid giggled.

"Could you pass me a cross-head screwdriver, please Jake?"

There were the sounds of dedicated rummaging in the tool box beneath the table before Jake reappeared with a selection of screwdrivers, held carefully in his tiny hands.

"Which one?" he asked.

"This one," said Ivy, smiling. "See, at the bottom of the handle where it's painted red? Mum did that, so we'd know which ones were which at a glance."

Jake squinted down at the screwdrivers in his hand: sure enough, half of them had been painted red at the bottom, and the other half yellow.

"That's a good idea," said Reggie, approvingly.

"She had her moments," Ivy smiled, and started screwing the wheels onto the base.

"Can we help?" Astrid asked.

"Yes, actually," said Ivy, thinking for a moment. "Do you see that panel over there?" She pointed to a wooden panel set into the wall by the top of the spiral staircase. "It used to be a sort of dumb-waiter system. Grandmother used it to get batches of potions downstairs. She always complained that it was too low –

I've really no idea why my ancestors thought it should be at floor level," she paused. "Unless it was for sliding really heavy things into, I suppose. Still, it'll work well for Zarrubabel. It's been years since I've had one of the panels open, and it's probably stuck – do you think you could have a go at opening it? There's another one by the other spiral."

Reggie, Astrid and Jake went to look at the panel: it had been painted over several times in the last few decades. Astrid ran her fingers down its side.

"There's no handle," she said, puzzled.

"It's supposed to open when you press the top of it," said Ivy, indistinctly.

"Oh," said Astrid.

Reggie reached past her and pressed the top of the panel. Nothing happened.

"Hmm," he said, and pressed harder. Still nothing happened.

Jake stuck his fingers into the gap between the panel and the frame and wiggled them about, speculatively.

"There's no room," he said, pulling his fingers out.

"Hmm," said Reggie again. He retreated to the toolbox; Saffy eyed him, curiously. "Have you got a plasterer's knife?" he asked, pulling out a chisel and a hammer.

"Er..." said Ivy, peering into the box. "Probably not. Would a metal spatula do?"

"Perfect," said Reggie.

"Second drawer down on the right," she said, returning to her work.

Reggie knelt in front of the panel and slid the spatula along the top, feeling for a catch.

"Right," he said, when he'd found it. "Astrid, you hang onto this... that's right. I'm going to pull it open, Jake, you let us know when it starts to move."

For a few minutes, nothing happened, then, with a great crack the panel fell open in a shower of dust and paint flakes.

They poked their heads through and looked down the

shaft.

"Wow," said Jake.

"There should be a platform at the bottom," said Ivy, coming up behind them. Saffy pushed her nose between Jake and Astrid, and gave the contraption a once over.

"The pulley seems to be in good shape," said Reggie. "It'll just need some new rope and a bit of a clean –"

"I'll clean it!" Jake volunteered, thrilled at the thought of being lowered into the ancient mechanism.

ooo

"Morton! Morton! Look at me!" cried Zarrubabel.

Professor Barraclough had stopped in to have a chat with Christopher while Joanna met up with Mahri for their painting class. They had been discussing the repair of some skittish poetry books when Zarrubabel had come zooming round the corner of one of the bookshelves, whooping in delight.

"Good grief," said Morton, with feeling.

"He's been like this all afternoon," Christopher told him, moving out of the way as the apparition made another run at his shins.

Professor Zarrubabel was perched atop a glass box, his book safely contained within. The box careened erratically about the bookshop at high speed, only just missing furniture, stacks of worried books and the feet of Christopher and Professor Barraclough. He stopped in front of his old friend, grinning madly.

"Ivy made it for me!" he announced, happily. "And the brats and that daft old fellow upstairs repaired the dumb waiter system, so now I can go anywhere!"

He cackled, and sped around them a few times.

"You ought to be grateful to them, old boy, rather than insulting them," Morton, observed, unnerved. "And it's not like you can go zooming about outside willy-nilly."

"I can if you put a Glamour on me!" he cried, screeching to a halt by the door. "Just think how much help I'd be when things go off at Brightwell – you wouldn't even have to carry me!"

"I'll think about it," said Morton, exchanging a speaking glance with Christopher.

"Don't give me that look, ungrateful boy!" he screeched at Christopher, but Christopher wasn't looking at him.

"Customer," he said, kicking the back door open. "Hide."

"Bugger!" cried the spectre, and veered around the counter. Christopher closed the door behind him as the shop door jangled.

"I'm sorry, sir, but we're closed," he said, leaning on the counter.

"I thought you were," said Mr Morris, apologetically. "But I saw the two of you, and I wondered if I could just drop this off – Mr Hoxley finished with it this morning and I said I'd pop in. But then the day got rather busy, so..."

He trailed off, looking hopeful.

"Oh, alright," said Christopher, off the Professor's nod. "Did you want a replacement?"

"I would, actually, if you've got a couple of minutes – he wrote one down for me..."

The man dug in the pockets of his jacket and extracted a folded scrap of paper that had seen better days.

Christopher nodded, reading the title.

"Harding's *Encyclopedia of Dark Artefacts*," Morton observed, peering over his shoulder. "Not what I'd call a light read."

"No," agreed Mr Morris. "But Hoxley seems to be enjoying himself."

"I thought you were working on it together," Christopher said, scanning a bookcase for the *Encyclopedia* – one of the few dark magic texts that could be left on the shelves. Rowland Harding had had nothing other than a scientific interest in the artefacts, which made his *Encyclopedia* a bit of a dry read, considering the subject matter, but also rather less likely to do unspeakable things to your brain while you were reading it.

"We are. Well," Morris clarified. "We will be – I'm just finishing off another project."

"Nice to see people keeping busy," said Professor Barraclough, kindly.

Morris smiled, and paid the lending fee for the book.

"Oh," he said. "Just a minute –" he hurried over to the far wall and picked out a book on flower arranging. "Could I have this, too? I spotted it last time I was in here – my wife does the flowers for our church."

Christopher smiled. "Of course," he said, and noted it down in the ledger.

"Thanks again," said Mr Morris, with an easy grin.

They watched him go, the shop bell jangling in his wake.

"There's something odd about those two," said Christopher, speculatively. "I mean, they're polite enough, but there's just something..." he trailed off and shrugged. "They don't smell right," he explained. "Like they're hiding something."

The professor raised an eyebrow. "I know what you mean," he said. "Morris and Hoxley, did he say?"

"That's right," said Christopher, double checking the ledger. "Colin and William."

"I've not heard of them," said Barraclough, thoughtfully, cleaning his monocle. "Practitioners?"

"Definitely," said Christopher. "They asked about Etching – I thought they must be from the older families. Although," he said, remembering something, "neither of them had Insignia – at least, they both brought documents in instead of using them, if they had."

"Why would you choose mundane documents over Insignia?" Barraclough asked, surprised. "It's so much quicker the old way."

"Not if you don't want people to know who you are," said Christopher, suddenly uncomfortable.

Professor Barraclough looked at him and chuckled. "It's alright lad, you had good reason."

"Thanks," said Christopher, sheepishly.

"I'll wager they think they have good reason, too," said Barraclough. "I'll ask Joanna about them – if they're local, she'll know who they are." He glanced at the door to the back room. "And if she doesn't, *he* will," he nodded his head in the direction of Zarrubabel's excited cries. "But I think he's had quite enough excitement for one day, don't you?"

ooo

"Did you *have* to build him that?" Christopher asked, unhappily, as they watched Professor Zarrubabel careen happily around the garden, whooping with malevolent glee. Both Astrid and Jake were watching him warily from Mahri's bedroom window. They had quickly learned to avoid the cantankerous old spectre, and Mahri had already chased him out of her kitchen twice. She was standing guard at her kitchen door with a broom, periodically shifting her glare from Zarrubabel to Christopher.

"We're more likely to sleep," said Ivy, hoping fervently that this was true.

"Yes, but I'm not sure my shins are happy about it," Christopher grumbled, rubbing his bruised legs.

"Sorry," she said, smiling at him, and he laughed.

"I suppose I might be overreacting very slightly," he allowed.

"Just slightly," Ivy said, giving him a playful shove. She walked to the door of the main room. "Professor," she called. Zarrubabel burst through a flowerbed, the plants swarming away from him as he passed. "Given that you seem to be enjoying yourself so much, perhaps you'd give Jake and Astrid a ride?"

Zarrubabel looked like he had just eaten an ectoplasmic lemon. In the relative safety of the kitchen, Christopher sniggered.

"They did help to repair the lifts, after all."

"I suppose I must," Zarrubabel grumbled, looking very much like he'd rather not. "Oy! Brats! *Ivy* says you can come and have a ride."

The children warily appeared beside Mahri, who folded her arms menacingly.

"You be careful," she admonished the Professor, who blew a raspberry at her.

"Thank you," said Astrid, politely. "But I'd rather not."

Zarrubabel harrumphed at her as she darted past him, taking the opportunity to dash across the garden and join Christopher at the kitchen table.

"I'd like to, please," said Jake. The ghostly Professor gave him a derisive appraisal.

"Get on then!" he hissed, impatiently.

Jake looked like he was having second thoughts, but he screwed up his courage and clambered on top of the box, as if he were sitting between the old spectre's green, glowing legs, and held on to the metal rungs that ran around the top.

"Hang on tightly!" called Mahri, watching, hawk-like, from her door.

Jake did as he was told, and Zarrubabel set off across the garden like a giant, square rubber ball, narrowly avoiding trees and walls as he went. It wasn't long before he was whooping with excitement again, Jake along with him.

"I don't believe it," said Christopher, watching their erratic progress about the garden. "He's actually having so much fun he's forgotten to be horrible."

"Hopefully he'll be so worn out tonight he'll forget to throw things around," said Ivy.

Christopher laughed. "You are one cunning witch," he said, in admiration.

To their surprise, Ivy took a small bow. "I've been told it runs in the family," she said. "I just fancy some lemonade – anyone else?"

"Yes please," said Astrid as Christopher nodded, enjoying seeing Ivy relax a bit.

She brought the glasses to the table and sat down to watch the Professor and Jake; the three of them sat in companionable silence, greatly entertained.

"Ivy?" said Astrid, after a while.

"Yes?"

"I've been thinking about what you said," she said, tucking her dark hair behind her ear. "I'd like very much to become your apprentice, please."

Christopher looked at the girl, surprised. "What's this?"

"Astrid wants to learn the old ways – it's the only way I know to guarantee responsibilities on both sides," Ivy explained. "I'd be delighted to have you as an apprentice," she told Astrid, who blushed. "Have you spoken to your brother about it?"

"Not really," the girl admitted. "But he's really happy here, I don't think he'd mind staying."

"He'd be mad not to," said Christopher, happily. "It's wonderful here."

Ivy stared at him for a moment, surprised, before a slow smile lit up her face. "It is, rather, isn't it?" she said, as if only just discovering this for herself. "Still, you'd better ask him."

As if on cue, Jake stumbled in from the garden, reeling slightly from his high speed escort. Professor Zarrubabel shot past him, cackling, careened around the staircase and flew into the lift. The sounds of his laughter faded away slowly as he made his descent.

"Jake," said Astrid, when her brother had been supplied with lemonade and had climbed onto one of the mismatched kitchen chairs. "Do you like it here?"

"Yes," he said, beaming. "Very much." A thought appeared to strike him, and his face fell. "We don't have to go away, do we?" He looked between the three of them, hoping desperately to be proved wrong.

"Not at all," said Ivy, reassuringly, and his smile returned in full force.

"Would you like to stay here forever?" asked Astrid.

"Oh, yes!" the tiny boy cried. "Can we? It's *brilliant* here!"

"Good," said Astrid, happily. "Ivy's going to teach me to be a witch," she told him, importantly. "Which means we can stay here for good."

Jake's eyes were suddenly as wide as dinner-plates.

"Really?" he asked, awed. "Wow!" Then: "Can you teach me, too?"

Ivy laughed. "Yes, but not for a while – you've got years of playing to do first," her smile softened at the disappointment on his face. "Ask me again when you're Astrid's age, and we'll see."

"Anyway," said Christopher. "You'd probably be a wizard, not a witch – unless you wanted to."

"Oh," said Jake, thinking about it. "Okay."

"I'm glad that's settled," said Ivy. "Do you think the Professor would draw up an agreement for us?" she asked Christopher, who nodded.

"I'll give him a ring," he said, getting to his feet. "Are you two scamps going to help me make tea?" he asked, to general agreement. "Excellent – go and get cleaned up then. We want shepherd's pie, not mud pie." He winked at Jake, whose hands were stained brown and green from his adventures in the garden.

He watched the two children run off to the bathroom with a smile, before turning to look at Ivy.

"What?"

"At the risk of being strung up by my ankles," he said, "are you sure about this? Taking on an apprentice is a lot of responsibility – and from the sounds of it, you're offering to adopt the both of them, which is even more."

"I've given it a lot of thought," she said. "And I've realised that I like having them around. I didn't think I would, but I think I'd just got into the habit of being on my own." She looked around. "This place feels better with people in," she said. "And I think I'll enjoy passing on some knowledge. It just *feels* right."

She shrugged, unable to thoroughly explain herself. Christopher didn't mind, however.

"I think you'll be brilliant," he said, firmly. "And if you need any help, I'd be more than happy to pitch in – I know a fair amount of spells, and Jake will need help with reading and writing and stuff." He paused, "Are you going to send them to Brightwell?"

"Not for a long while," she said. "It's not really a day school anymore, and they'd get more out of mundane school – I did. I'll sign them up next year, give them a chance to catch up on anything they've missed before they start."

"You just can't stop yourself being kind, can you?" Christopher said, reaching for the phone.

Ivy looked at him, bewildered. "Astrid asked for my help," she said, and he shook his head.

"Yes, but not everyone would have said 'yes'."

ooo

"I think we're all happy with the terms, so if you'll just sign here, Astrid... that's right," said the Professor, passing her a pen. She held it in front of her delicately, and wrote her name carefully in purple ink that seemed to sparkle for a moment before it dried. "And Ivy, here... good."

He looked around at the group assembled at the kitchen table.

"We'll need four witnesses to make it binding – I can't do it, since I'm drawing it up."

"I'll do it," said Joanna, pulling the contract towards her.

"Er..." said Christopher uncomfortably, as the Professor looked at him.

"Ye-es," said Barraclough. "Perhaps it would be best if you *didn't* sign anything... Joanna, go and see if Mahri will come over, would you?"

Jake tugged on Christopher's sleeve.

"Why can't you sign things?" he whispered, awed by the solemnity of the occasion.

"In case someone that doesn't like what I am finds me," he whispered back, crouching down in front of the boy.

"Why wouldn't anyone like you?" said Jake, clearly finding the thought incomprehensible.

"Because there are all sorts of people out there," said Christopher, after a moment's thought. "And I don't want to be found."

"You ran away, like me?"

"Yes."

"I won't tell anyone where to find you," said Jake.

"Thanks," said Christopher, chuckling.

"Do I count?" asked Reggie, as Joanna went to find her friend. "Being non-magical, I mean."

"Of course," said Professor Barraclough, handing him the pen. He frowned. "We'll need one more... Ivy? May I enlist my old friend?"

"Does it still count even if he's dead?" asked Astrid, surprised.

"Anyone that argued would have to deal with him, so absolutely," said Joanna, striding back in.

Christopher suppressed a groan. He'd had more than enough of the spiteful spirit for one day, and was beginning to think that his shins might never recover.

Jake ran across the room and knocked on the wooden panel concealing the lift.

"Mr Zarrubabel! Can we talk to you, please?" he shouted.

The pulleys began to creak, and Jake immediately went to hide behind Christopher. Zarrubabel kicked the panel open, grumbling as he came. The smell of mouldering books flowed out of the lift shaft and sloped into the room like Zarrubabel's own, personal atmosphere.

"Never get a moment's peace," he grumbled, rolling across the floor towards them. "No one thinks of me, do they? Oh no, it's Hector *this* – Professor *that*."

He came to a rest next to Professor Barraclough.

"What is it, Morton?" he asked, arms folded. "I was in the middle of a really good book."

"We need a witness for Astrid's apprenticeship contract," Barraclough explained. He gave Christopher a sly wink. "We couldn't do it without you, old chum."

Zarrubabel looked momentarily flattered. "Of course

you couldn't," he said, and turned to peer at Astrid through his ghostly pince-nez. "This is a big step, young Miss," he said, sternly. "I hope you're not taking it lightly."

"No, sir," said Astrid, standing her ground – though she looked like she'd rather like to join her brother, who was still peeking out from behind Christopher's legs.

"Good," he said, with a perfunctory nod. "A decent education will take you a long way, as *some people* –" here he glared at Christopher – "should have learned a long time ago."

Christopher rolled his eyes, unfazed.

The spectre leaned forward and read through the contract carefully, mumbling to himself and nodding sagely at each of the terms of the agreement. He reached into his jacket and drew out an ink pen. It left an ethereal trail of green on the paper when he signed his name, and he snapped the lid back on with a satisfying click.

Christopher suspected that for all his moaning, he was pleased to be included.

"Hello Morton," said Mahri, smartly. "Joanna tells me I need to witness an apprenticeship."

"Ivy didn't tell her?" Joanna murmured to Christopher, surprised.

"Er, no," he said. "They've had a bit of a falling out..."

"Good grief," exclaimed Joanna. "Over what? They've been friends for years!"

"Er," said Christopher, going a bit pink around the ears. "Over me."

Joanna looked at him in astonishment for a few moments before understanding dawned. She patted him on the shoulder.

"Don't you worry, dear, I'll speak to her," she said, determinedly following Mahri back across the garden.

"Well, everything seems to be in order," said Professor Barraclough, straightening up. "I hereby declare this contract right and binding."

He made a complicated sign above the paper with his hand, and it split in two, leaving a jagged edge. The room tasted abruptly of magic and, for some reason, plums.

He handed one half of the contract to Ivy and the other to Astrid.

"Keep those somewhere safe," he advised, putting his writing things back into his satchel.

"Would you take care of them for us, Professor Zarrubabel?" Ivy asked, politely.

The apparition swelled with importance.

"Of course, my dear girl!" he cried, and swept both halves of the contract away, intending to secret them somewhere in the back room of the bookshop. "If you ever need them back you have but to ask," he announced, pompously, and disappeared down the lift shaft with a puff of green smoke.

"Show off," muttered Professor Barraclough, good-naturedly.

"Well, I think this is an occasion that warrants cake," said Ivy, clapping her hands together.

A large, decadent chocolate cake appeared on the table, making Christopher's mouth water. Someone had inexpertly written 'Welcome Home Astrid and Jake' on the top in white icing.

He caught Ivy's eye and raised his eyebrow, amused.

She gave him a look that said, distinctly: 'What?', and he chuckled.

"May we join you?" asked Joanna, practically dragging a stony-faced Mahri back through the door. "Oh, excellent. Cake!"

18
Lessons Learned

The weather was turning cooler now, and Ivy's garden had been covered for a few weeks, allowing the plants a little more time to grow before the coming winter.

Astrid was sitting at the kitchen table, poring over a book that Ivy had found for her, copying out the basic forms of plants into an exercise book and annotating her drawings.

Christopher watched her from the big squashy sofa by the window, waiting for Jake to find a picture that he'd drawn that he wanted to show to him. Astrid stuck her tongue between her teeth when she concentrated on the sketches, making unfamiliar strokes with her pencils, her sheet of jet black hair tucked behind her ears. She had thrown herself into any work Ivy set for her with a strange and determined passion, eating up knowledge like she was starving.

The day after Ivy's apprenticeship had been officially agreed, Ivy had sat down with the other adults and arranged a programme of work that was intended to take them up to Christmas. Christopher was beginning to doubt that this would be the case, the way that Astrid was applying herself.

Ivy had her helping her mix teas two evenings in the week, and learning about all the plants she used in the shop, mundane and magical. She set her projects to complete – like homework, but with no set deadline; Ivy had explained that it didn't matter so much how long things took as long as they were done well. Astrid had surprised her by finishing some of them much faster than Ivy had anticipated, and the older witch had had to think of longer and more challenging tasks to keep her young charge occupied. They'd spent a good deal of time in the past few weeks making copious amounts of jam from the various fruits the Arcade garden produced.

When she wasn't working with Ivy, Mahri was teaching her to cook, chattering away to her about ingredients and plants and the chemistry involved in both food and potions. Reggie had quietly volunteered his services and took both children for a couple of hours a week, teaching them to play music on his old piano – though Jake was much more interested in making as much noise as possible with the collection of old tins that Reggie had found out for him. He had even ventured to a nearby hardware shop and fashioned Jake a rainmaker from some plumbing supplies and a bag of rice. The sound it made enthralled and mystified the boy, and he had sat for hours on the day he'd got it, convinced that every time he tipped the copper pipe over in Reggie's kitchen he was really making it rain outside.

It might have been his imagination, but Christopher thought that Reggie seemed a lot sharper than he had been when they had met, cooped up in the flat that he and Bessie had shared, waiting patiently for the end. Here, where there was so much to do and so many people to talk to and work with, he seemed constantly surprised to be of use. Christopher suspected that he was thoroughly enjoying himself.

He would often take the children out when he walked Saffy, pointing out the everyday landmarks of the town and telling them stories of its history. Few people knew it like Reggie, it seemed, since he had spent his childhood escaping from his family for hours at a time and roaming the streets of Brindleford or borrowing his older brother's bicycle and cycling out to the neighbouring villages of Rouse Abbey, Winthorpe or Netherdale. By the time they were of age, Christopher suspected that they'd know the town better than most of the natives.

Astrid spent a miserable hour every other day in the stuffy back office of the bookshop, taking tuition in arithmetic and mathematics from Professor Zarrubabel, who would float about dictating notes or cackling cruelly whenever she got something wrong. Even he had to admit (grudgingly, and only to Professor Barraclough) that she was picking things up quickly.

Ivy and Joanna had had to put a stop to the large

volume of homework he had wanted to set her, though, and had managed to limit him to only a couple of pages every week. He had been most put out by this, and had been extra horrible to Christopher all week, which suggested that he quite liked his young pupil, despite his protestations. Astrid had not found this observation particularly encouraging when it had been put to her by Joanna Barraclough one morning.

Joanna would collect the children on Tuesday mornings and take them back to Crooked House where she would teach Astrid the basic concepts of magic while Charlotte and John would spoil Jake rotten in the kitchen and garden. Here Astrid learned about balance and intention, and about the proper order of spells – she would arrive back at the Arcade on Tuesday evenings feeling that she understood it all and Ivy would gently inform her that sometimes the 'proper' form of things could be ignored, and Astrid would go off for her bath confused and mildly frustrated. Professor Barraclough would take her into his study on Tuesday afternoons and teach her Astronomy and Astrology, and the impact the planets had on the mundane and magic worlds. He spoke to her about the way that physics and chemistry interacted with magic, about the movement and alteration of matter – about all manner of fascinating things until Astrid felt that her brain was so full of knowledge that it couldn't possibly hold any more. At this point, Charlotte would call them all into the kitchen and serve up one of her filling and delicious meals, and Astrid would attempt to digest what she'd learned at the same time as her dinner, and Professor Barraclough would remark that there were many different kinds of magic, and that Charlotte's cooking was proof of this.

On Thursday mornings, the Professor would sit with Astrid at the kitchen table in the Arcade and take her through the history of the magical and mundane worlds, with Christopher's help. Although Astrid had a desk in the playroom, they had quickly decided that it would be simpler for all concerned if they let Jake make as much noise as he wanted on Thursday mornings while they worked elsewhere in peace. Every so often, though, Jake would install himself under the kitchen table with a colouring book and listen intently to the lesson taking place above his head, fascinated by the Professor's stories.

Christopher had agreed to help both children with their reading and writing to bring them up to an appropriate school level in time for next September. Jake seemed delighted to have stories read with him, and had taken to spending lunchtimes in Ivy's teashop with a growing stack of children's books, asking Ivy or her customers for help when he got stuck. A couple of the customers had remarked to Ivy that she had an adorable son, and she'd felt a curious flush of pride each time.

The regulars – many of whom had known Ivy since she was Jake's age – were bursting with curiosity about the boy and were stunned to learn that Ivy had adopted him and the quiet, dark haired girl that they saw reading in the bookshop from time to time. Astrid seemed to be channelling all of her reading energy into study, and Christopher had instituted an hour of storytelling before bed-time so that she didn't miss out on the tales that he had enjoyed when he was a child – and so she didn't wear herself out.

He wasn't the only one who was worried about Astrid's work ethic. Ivy, noticing dark circles forming under her young charge's eyes had decreed that no work was to be done after six o'clock during the week, or at all on weekends – unless something practical needed doing for the shop, when she'd let her watch or help out. This appeared to have helped, though Astrid had still looked like she felt guilty for not studying her craft in every waking minute until Ivy had told her that balance was one of the most important parts of magic.

"It's always a good idea to do a bit of living," she had added, on the girl's dubious expression. "My grandmother told me that you had to, really, if you want to help people – and that's a big part of the Duty."

The 'Duty' was something that Ivy took very seriously, though Christopher had only heard of it in his older history books. It didn't seem to have been written about much, a tradition that quietly continued among ordinary witches and wizards as Kings and Queens came and went.

It was an understanding, largely unspoken, that since you had the power to do so, you ought to help people out when they needed you to. The general consensus in the modern magical community seemed to be that it wasn't necessary anymore, that people could work things out for themselves in this wondrous age of street lights and all-night shopping centres and reasonable health care. Christopher, who had seen first-hand the impact one mistake could cause, wasn't so sure. Neither was Ivy, and although she didn't practice it any more, she was determined to instil in Astrid the knowledge and understanding that the Chambers women had tried to instil in her.

She had been startled to discover that perhaps they had done a more thorough job with her than she remembered.

So she had Astrid read about and write up the process of laying someone out following a death, and the things you needed to remember to do with the living at the same time, like making cups of tea, and who you needed to ring. She pulled out her mother's books on common illnesses and compared them to her grandmother's handwritten books on their cures, unsurprised at how little she remembered and determined to learn enough to help Astrid. She had briefly considered talking to her about birth when they dealt with death, but she had balked at the thought of the questions that the girl (and probably her brother, if he was eavesdropping) would have. That could wait until they were both a bit older. In any case, Ivy rather felt that in many ways she was the wrong person to ask.

Where Astrid seemed committed to increasing her knowledge as fast and as thoroughly as possible, Jake seemed equally committed to enjoying himself, and Christopher was glad. The last remnants of sadness and caution from his months on the run were leaving him now, and he was becoming a happy and vibrant child, as was his sister, when she allowed herself to bo.

Christopher turned his attention back to Jake, who was by now curled up on the sofa beside him, trying to choose which story he most wanted to read from his *Treasury of Children's Stories*. It seemed to be a complicated decision.

He settled on a story about a frog that had lost his hat and the two of them began to read, each taking alternate pages.

In the back of his mind, Christopher registered the opening of Reggie's front door. Astrid looked up from her work, surprised.

They hadn't seen Reggie all afternoon, which was unusual since he came over at least twice a day to check on the children or chat with Christopher or Ivy, choosing to spend his evenings with them or Mahri.

Both Ivy and Mahri were out this evening, attending a talk at Brightwell with the Barracloughs, and Christopher had been trying to ignore how much he missed Ivy's presence, even for a few hours.

Reggie hurried over to the Arcade side of the garden and knocked urgently on the glass. Jake ran to open the door, abandoning his book on the floor; Christopher bent to retrieve it, pausing as a curious smell followed Reggie into the room.

It was an incredibly faint scent, with odd notes that made him feel curiously protective. His eyes flicked to Reggie's front door. He'd closed it behind him, and Christopher was seized by the sudden urge to rush over there and make sure that everything was alright.

"Saffy's having her puppies," Reggie explained, continuing over the excited whoops of the children. "I need another couple of old towels, if you have any."

Astrid leapt into action, scraping her chair against the floor as she hurried towards the bathroom.

"Use my old red ones," said Christopher. "They're mankier than Ivy's and it's about time I replaced them." He looked Reggie up and down. "How's she doing?"

"Really well," said Reggie, glancing over his shoulder. "She's had five puppies so far. It's her first litter – I shouldn't leave her for long."

"Can we go look?" Jake begged, and Reggie nodded.

"It's quite a thing to see," he said. "But you'll have to promise to be quiet, and do exactly as I tell you."

The children nodded. Ivy handed Reggie the towels almost reverently.

"No offence, Christopher, but if she objects to your presence –" he said, as they made their way across the garden.

"I'll make myself scarce," he said. "Don't worry."

The smell was stronger the nearer they got to Reggie's coach house. He pushed open the door, the children almost falling over themselves in their eagerness to see.

Saffy was curled up in a box full of old bedding and towels in the corner of Reggie's kitchen, five tiny puppies – in every imaginable colour – already suckling and mewling. She gave Christopher a hostile look and then proceeded to ignore him; she had more important things to worry about.

Even so, he hovered by the door, watching Jake and Astrid kneel by the box, utterly fascinated.

"They're so wriggly," said Jake, in hushed tones.

"Look," said Astrid, pointing excitedly. "There's another one!"

They watched in rapt silence as Saffy licked at the newborn puppy, cleaning it up and chewing away its umbilical cord. The tiny creature squeaked and squealed, helpless and confused. Reggie looked incredibly proud of his dog.

"She's doing everything herself, clever girl," he said, happily. "I'm really only here if she needs help, and she's just fine."

Reggie bent down and gently moved the new puppy – now making as much noise as it possibly could – over to its siblings, where it began to suckle.

"It's incredible how they know exactly what to do," Christopher observed.

Reggie nodded. "Instinct," he said, and rubbed Saffy's head affectionately.

"There's another!" whispered Jake. "Only that one's already clean!"

Christopher saw Reggie's face fall, and recognised this as A Bad Sign.

"Astrid, Jake, come over here for a minute," he said, frowning.

Reluctantly, the two children stood beside him, standing on their tiptoes to see as Reggie blocked their view, cooing at Saffy soothingly.

After a few minutes, Saffy began to keen and cry, and Reggie straightened up, sadly.

"This little poppet didn't make it," he said quietly. All three of the onlookers stared at the miniscule bundle of towel in his hand as Saffy mourned her final pup.

"It happens," said Reggie to the children, who looked stunned and heartbroken. "But she has six healthy puppies and we need to concentrate on those."

Carefully, he placed the small, desolate thing in a shoebox that Christopher suspected he'd had ready just in case.

Saffy keened pitifully and Astrid went over to her, stroking her head to comfort her as her six remaining puppies clamoured for milk.

Without realising what he was doing, Christopher responded to the keening cry and crossed to the shoebox, delicately picking up the bundle. Saffy growled, but he ignored her, knowing that she would stay close to her living pups.

Carefully, he arranged the towel around the pup in his hand so that it wouldn't tangle about it, and began to rub it. The puppy was so small that she fit entirely in the palm of his large hands. He was aware that he had the attention of every human in the room, Saffy alternately licking her other puppies and growling at him, but he ignored them, concentrating everything he could on the small animal in his hands.

"Come on, little one," he said, quietly.

"It's no good," said Reggie sadly, after a few minutes, but Christopher persisted, swapping the puppy to his other hand when he got tired and gently nudging its mouth open with his little finger. It was full of fluid.

Frowning, he held the puppy securely and swung her – slowly and gently – downwards, before bringing her back up and checking her mouth a second time; he cleared what was there with his finger before resuming the rubbing.

Reggie had turned to Saffy and her other pups, and was checking them over, while Astrid and Jake stared at Christopher. They both gasped when he swung the puppy down, and Reggie turned back, surprised.

"Come on now, fight," said Christopher, firmly. "You can do it."

There were a few moments of agonising silence, before Christopher laughed, feeling the creature in his hands begin to wriggle and squirm and squeal.

A tiny black nose snuck out from the edge of the towel, sniffing at the air. Christopher stroked her, gently, and she squeaked at him, waterlogged and tender.

"Wow!" said Astrid, at a loss for words.

"You've done it!" cried Reggie, stunned. "Saffy, look!"

Christopher held the tiny thing out to Jake, who was tottering on the tips of his toes, and the little boy clapped for joy.

"You saved her!"

Saffy barked, uncertainly, and Christopher approached her.

He put the fox-red puppy in front of her gently.

"She'll be alright," he said softly. "She's a fighter."

Saffy sniffed the pup and licked her happily, nudging her towards her siblings.

Christopher smiled, settling back on his haunches as Reggie clapped him on the back.

"Bloody good show!" he said, forgetting that the

children were present and making Astrid giggle. "Thank you!"

Christopher shrugged. He couldn't have left the puppy be, not with Saffy keening like that. The wolf in him had stirred at her cries and demanded action.

"I'm just glad it worked," he said. "I really had no idea what I was doing."

"Instinct," said Reggie again, knowingly.

Saffy barked again, suddenly and Christopher lost his balance, falling on all fours. Saffy licked his face, enthusiastically.

"Argh," he said. "You're welcome."

ooo

"Where is everyone?" asked Mahri, looking around at Astrid's work things and Jake's abandoned book.

Ivy, who was following her friend up the spiral staircase, paused at the top and called out.

"Astrid? Jake?" She frowned, and took a step forward. "Christopher?"

No one responded and the women exchanged a worried look. Wordlessly, they checked the bedrooms on each corridor, meeting back in the main room, faces clouded with concern.

"If he's hurt either one of them –" said Mahri, angrily.

"He would do no such thing," Ivy snapped. "And I'd thank you to remember that."

"You have no idea what he could do," Mahri retorted. "You're too trusting – just because a young man takes an interest in you –"

"Because he *what*?" demanded Ivy, surprised and affronted. "Now look here –"

"He's a savage beast, Ivy, and you'd best accept it!"

Ivy gasped, stung on Christopher's behalf. "That's enough!" she snapped. "Christopher is –" But Mahri never found out what Ivy thought about Christopher, since Jake ran full tilt into the room and flung himself at her, panting.

"Saffy – puppies –" he managed, between gasps, too excited to breathe and too out of breath to speak.

"Saffy had her puppies?" asked Ivy, fears forgotten.

"Seven!" Jake cried, bounding out of Mahri's arms and jumping up and down in front of them, looking a lot like a puppy himself.

"Seven, good grief," said Mahri. "And she's fine?"

"Yes!" cried Jake. "We thought the seventh one was dead," he continued in hushed tones, "it was all still and couldn't breathe." He looked up at them joyfully. "But then Christopher saved her – come and see!"

Ivy gave her friend a pointed look as they were dragged along in the wake of the small boy. Mahri looked away, abashed.

"Mahri! Ivy!" Reggie called. "The puppies are here, look! Four boys and three girls!"

Obediently, they peered into Saffy's nesting box. Seven tiny chocolate, black and yellow furry bodies were wriggling and squealing, falling over one another to share their mother's milk. One of the puppies had a deep auburn fur and was gamely vying for position with her siblings.

"Well done, girl," Mahri congratulated Saffy, rubbing her neck.

One of the yellow puppies was dislodged by his siblings, and Ivy picked him up, giving him a brief cuddle before returning him to his mother. He was soft and warm, and smelled oddly sweet.

"They're sort of irresistible, aren't they?" said Christopher, trotting down the stairs. Ivy turned to him, beaming.

"They're adorable," she agreed. "Why's your hair wet?"

Christopher ran a hand through his damp hair, resisting the urge to tell her how beautiful she looked when she smiled.

"Saffy was rather enthusiastic – I needed a wash."

"He saved her puppy," said Astrid, reverently.

Saffy barked her approval.

"Hero of the hour, this one!" Reggie grinned, clapping

him on the back once more.

Christopher blushed, embarrassed by the attention.

"I think this calls for a celebration," said Mahri, straightening up. "I have a batch of scones in the kitchen I could warm up," she suggested.

"Excellent plan!" cried Reggie. "I'll put on the kettle."

"I'll bring over a pot of that raspberry jam," said Ivy, making for the door.

"Excellent," said Mahri, making for the door. "Christopher? Would you give me a hand?"

"Er, yes," he said, surprised, following her next door.

The older witch dropped her notebook and bag on the kitchen table before stripping off her coat and lifting a tin of scones out of a cupboard.

Christopher hovered by the door, uncertain, as she turned her oven on and transferred the scones to a plate.

"It appears I may have misjudged you," Mahri said, keeping her back to him.

Christopher said nothing, watching the back of Mahri's head. She bent and put the scones in the oven to warm.

"I'm sorry for that," she continued, straightening up and moving imaginary crumbs about the worktop with a cloth. "There is an exception to every rule, and as far as werewolves go, you are it."

She turned to him then, and met his eyes hesitantly.

Christopher cleared his throat, awkwardly.

"Thank you," he said, amazed at this new development.

They shared a brief nod, acknowledging an end to any hostility, and Mahri turned back to her scones, feeling that she had made amends.

ooo

Reggie settled in for a quiet afternoon – well, as quiet an afternoon as you can have with seven mewling puppies in a box in the corner of your living room. It was a Wednesday, and Ivy had taken the children shopping with her; Christopher and Mahri were hard at work in the shops below. Mahri would be going out to her yoga class with Joanna Barraclough once she closed up her shop in a couple of hours and he suspected that Christopher would also be enjoying a rare hour of quiet before Jake and Astrid got home.

He'd probably drop in to see Saffy and the puppies at some point. His act of kindness appeared to have won him Saffy's undying loyalty, and on the one night he hadn't visited, she had trotted over to the far side of the garden, taking her puppies one by one and making a pile of them outside the door until Ivy had spotted them and let them in. She and Christopher had helped carry them back to their impromptu nest after giving both Saffy and the puppies a big cuddle.

Mahri had found the image of Saffy scratching on Christopher's door for a fuss hilarious when Reggie had told her that evening.

Reggie was glad that Mahri had forgiven their young friend – after all, being a werewolf was hardly *his* fault, it was just the way things were – and that Christopher had the magnanimity to not take offence. Particularly as Mahri had about as much control over what she'd been brought up to believe as Christopher did over the lunar cycle.

It gave Reggie great comfort to know that he was living with a group of people that could adapt in the face of new information and accept someone who was inherently non-threatening despite their beliefs.

"You would have liked it here, Bess," he said, to the black and white photograph of his wife that rested on the mantelpiece. He sighed. Some days were easier than others, but he missed her every day.

He filled a small watering can and opened his door. He'd never been much of a gardener, preferring to be charging about the countryside in his youth or inside playing at the piano as he got a little older. Bessie had loved her garden, though.

It was how they had met.

Reggie had been riding his bicycle out past Rouse Abbey and had stopped at the crest of a hill, resting his bike against a dry stone wall that was overflowing with sweet-smelling flowers. He had been about to sit down in the lee of the wall to eat his lunch when a head had popped up from the other side, framed by the flowers like some kind of garden nymph, her red curls shining like burnished copper in the sunlight. They had stared at one another for a few moments, startled, before bursting out laughing.

Bessie had invited him in and they'd had an impromptu picnic under the branches of her father's birch tree.

Reggie smiled at the memory as he dead-headed the enormous geraniums in his window boxes – something about the Arcade had made the flowers grow to an extraordinary size, and he suspected that Bessie would have loved that too.

They had been married in Netherdale Chapel in the autumn, Bessie resplendent in the flowers from her garden and her mother's white dress. They had lived contentedly in her parents' house – with them at first, but later alone – and Reggie had made a living riding his bicycle around the villages teaching music to the children of vicars and doctors while Bessie had tended her garden and sold honey from her bees to the village shop.

They had never had very much money, and had been very lucky to inherit the house on the hill, but as long as they had been together they had wanted for nothing.

The only sadness that crept into their lives – and even then, it was only a prickle – was that they had never had any children. Bessie had accepted this reality with her usual grace and found other ways to be around kids – helping at the Sunday School, taking her gardening skills to local Junior Schools to get their pupils interested in growing things. Reggie had had his music, and while he would have liked to have children, the fact that he had Bessie more than made up for it.

When she had told him that she had cancer, the bottom had fallen out of his world. He'd watched her fight it, tooth and nail, and the fight had taken its toll. He realised, one day, that she couldn't take care of her garden the way that she once had, so he looked after it with her for as long as she could manage and took over its care when she couldn't.

It had broken both their hearts when they'd had to move out of the house on the hill. It had steadily been becoming too much for them, and they had moved to their tiny flat in Brindleford when Reggie retired from teaching. He had planted red geraniums in the window boxes where Bessie could still care for them – and later, see them from her bed as he cared for her.

He walked upstairs to water the higher window boxes sadly, remembering her sweet smile. Even as the illness had sapped her strength her smile could light up a room, and every day she would light up at the geraniums, and at him.

She had died on a Tuesday, in the rain, and Reggie's life had ground to a halt.

Feeling useless and used-up, he'd stuck to his routine: caring for the geraniums, doing his shopping at the market twice a week, talking to Bessie's photograph – watching the world go by.

It was on one of his lonely shopping trips that he had come across Saffy. It was a warm day and he had decided to take a detour through the park, intending to see what flowers the council had planted this year – Bessie would have wanted to know – and to eat his lunch. A teenage boy had been sitting under the trees by the edge of the river with a basket of puppies, hoping to sell them to passers-by.

Reggie had watched him from the bench where he had decided to eat his lunch. The boy was kind to the people that passed him, calling out greetings and making children laugh. He had even got up to help a tiny old lady who had dropped her shopping, briefly abandoning his precious basket.

Reggie had been impressed.

As the boy returned to his spot under the tree, the basket had fallen over from the sheer pressure of squirming puppies, and he had had to chase them all over the park, passers by helping him out as he collected his mischievous charges.

One of them, not wanting to go back in the basket, had jumped out of the boy's arms in a second bid for freedom, and had charged towards Reggie's bench.

Reggie had picked her up, intending to return her, and fallen in love. He had brought Saffy home that evening and watched her explore her new home. In taking her out for walks he had rediscovered his town, and had begun to enjoy the unexpected detours that Saffy occasionally took him on.

That was how they had met Boscoe, in a pet shop in Rouse Abbey that Saffy had been determined to investigate and pulled him into. The man behind the counter had been engaged in what appeared to be a fight with a large grey bird, the flashes of green beneath his wings identifying him as a parrot.

Once Reggie had helped the man get him into a cage he had explained that 'Boscoe' had an attitude problem, meaning that no one would take him. He was in the process of trying to get him put down, since he couldn't find him a home and couldn't afford to keep him.

Reggie, appalled, had shared a long and understanding look with the parrot and had offered to take him at once. The pet shop owner had been so grateful that he'd given him the cage free of charge, telling Reggie that if he wasn't already mad, that Boscoe would drive him insane within a week.

The drive home in the taxi had been a fraught one, with Boscoe flapping about inside his cage, squawking like some sort of demented, feathery kettle, and Reggie had begun to worry that the chap in the pet shop had been right.

Boscoe, however, had other ideas. As soon as the taxi had stopped moving and the driver had helped Reggie to get the cage into the lift in his block of flats, the parrot had quietened down, appraising Saffy and his new owner.

"Are you going to behave, Boscoe?" Reggie had asked, before opening his cage for the first time and letting him out into the flat.

Boscoe had looked right at him, head on one side, his onyx eyes gleaming in the electric light, and squawked: "Behave!"

Saffy had barked at him, excited to have a new roommate, and he had subjected her to the same fixed stare before barking back.

Reggie had given him a long look, wondering whether there might be more to this bird than met the eye – certainly not for the last time; Boscoe had flown around his new home a few times before settling on the back of chair and crying: "Welcome home! Welcome home!"

The three of them had swiftly settled into their own routine, watching the world go by together, and little had changed in the three years since Boscoe had first flapped into their lives until the night of the storm.

Reggie closed his bedroom window and took the watering can back downstairs, pausing to check on the slumbering puppies.

Things are changing now, though, he thought as he watched Boscoe cleaning his beak in the branches of Ivy's peach tree.

The feeling had been stealing up on Reggie for some time that perhaps he wasn't quite as useless as he had come to believe. In a matter of months he'd moved house, made friends with his neighbours, discovered magic, met ghosts and werewolves, repaired a dumbwaiter, rediscovered the joys of trifle (courtesy of Mahri), and started teaching again.

He hadn't realised how much he'd missed it.

He sat at his piano, playing idly with the sheet music that Astrid had been learning. It was a piece that Bessie had loved to hear him playing, and he tapped out the first few bars as he sat and pondered.

He knew music tuition inside and out, but he was in no shape to go cycling about the countryside in all weathers these days, even if he could get clients, and he had no wish to own a car.

Idly, he played a few more bars, thinking. Saffy began to howl along with his playing and he chuckled.

"Do you fancy some singing lessons, old girl?" he asked, and she padded over to him and licked his hand before returning to her litter, already missing their warmth.

Perhaps tutoring wasn't the only thing he could do.

Reggie looked up at Bessie's photograph and came to a decision. He'd speak to Ivy in the morning; right now, he had plans to make.

ooo

Jane McGarrigle sighed and put the shopping down outside Cypress Cottage. It wasn't the first time her employer has forgotten to unlock the door for her. He was always engrossed in his Research (even in her head, the word deserved a capital letter).

She dug around in her handbag for a few minutes, vowing to clean the thing out properly when she got home and knowing that once she got there she would instantly forget. Finally, her fingers closed around the spare key to the cottage.

She chuckled to herself. 'Cottage', indeed.

She let herself in as quietly as she could.

Austen Peters was an Important Person, and Important People didn't like to be disturbed.

She had kept house for Mr Peters for nearly ten years, since he had moved to Barnes, and she was used to his little ways now.

Careful not to spill anything, she carried Mr Peters' shopping through to the kitchen, and quietly set about putting it all away.

She tutted to herself. The man never gave a thought to

the cleanliness of his fruit bowl. With a long-suffering sigh, she padded across to the sink to clean the thing out.

That's strange, she thought, glancing at the nearly full bottle of wine on the usually spotless worktop. *It's not like him to leave an open bottle out like that...*

Mr Peters always took meticulous care of his wine, she knew, as many collectors did. To find a bottle uncorked and abandoned like that was downright odd.

Thoughtfully, she pulled out one of his wine corks and stoppered the bottle.

It wasn't the only thing out of place that morning, she reflected, as she slowly filled the fruit bowl. There were lots of things that were ever-so-slightly off, she realised. She hadn't given them a thought on her way in, but now –

Perturbed, she walked back out into the hall, still carrying the bag of oranges. The feeling of 'not-quite-right' was stronger out here. Lots of little things were very slightly out of place: the vase on the sideboard was the wrong way around. She walked over to it, frowning. The flowers she had arranged in it only two days before were wilted and stubby. She reached out and touched the papery petals, fascinated: they turned to dust beneath her fingers.

She glanced up at the watercolour on the wall behind the vase: it was very slightly askew. She looked at the next one, and the next – they were all wonky, like something had rocked them on their pegs.

The coats on their pegs in the sunlit porch were rumpled. It was as if some great force had rushed through the house, buffeting everything in its path.

"Mr Peters?" Mrs McGarrigle called, and she was ashamed to discover that her voice had turned into a whisper.

Clutching the half-empty bag of oranges to her like a shield, she started down the hall to Mr Peters' study, a sick feeling gathering in her stomach.

She would say later that she'd had no idea, no premonition of what awaited her behind that polished wooden door.

But here and now, with her hand resting on its bright brass handle, she knew.

She knew so strongly that it made her dizzy.

Still, she thought, *can't leave him there forever.*

It took a lot for her to turn the handle, but she did it, and stood for a moment in the doorway to the study, surveying the mortal remains of her former employer.

She was mildly impressed that she hadn't screamed, but the truth was that the sound had been frightened out of her.

Jane McGarrigle turned and ran, oranges scattering behind her, leaving wild, rambling tracks in the viscous pools of blood.

19
Prospero Bone

Christopher grimaced into the bookshelf, catching the familiar scent before the shop bell had finished jangling.

"Christopher, old chap!" cried a dishevelled Quentin Post, striding in. "Just the man I needed!"

It was a Saturday afternoon, and since Post usually spent the weekends in the company of fellow artefact enthusiasts, fellow adventurers or various nubile young women, he hadn't expected the energetic wizard to come in.

"Hello, Master Post," said Christopher, turning around with a smile that he didn't feel like smiling on his face.

Excitement was coming off the man in waves and Christopher's eyes flicked to Ivy's teashop, hoping that she wasn't the source of the Practitioner's unusual exuberance. Happily, though, Post cut him off before his startled imagination could get the better of him.

"I've had a breakthrough!" he exclaimed, thumping down a pile of books on the counter; Christopher heard their pages flutter in distress. "Remember when Dr Fitzhearn and I were discussing seventeenth century churches as hiding places for dark artefacts?"

Christopher nodded, mildly amused; Post was so excited that he'd abandoned caution. Both Master Hoxley and Master Morris were paying very careful attention to their conversation. Christopher took care not to glance in their direction: although their eyes were firmly directed towards the books in front of them he suspected that any movement would be noticed. He was aware of Jake and Astrid, who had been sitting on the floor behind one of the large stacks, peering at them through the bookcase.

Post's clothes were crumpled, like he'd worn them for too long, and he looked as if he hadn't slept. Christopher was willing to bet that he'd been up reading all night.

"Well, I did some reading on that trip down to London – such a shame you couldn't make it – and I found a candidate for suspicious activities!"

He looked like a child that had discovered that the sweet shop he had inadvertently wandered into was giving away free samples. For all his dislike of the man, Christopher couldn't bring himself to burst his academic bubble. Besides, he was interested.

"Who?" he asked, nonchalantly running his fingers down the spines of the shocked books on the counter to quiet them.

"His name's 'Mortimer Bone'," he said, flicking through the pages of the top book and turning it so Christopher could see, grinning his electric grin. "Sometimes referred to as 'Prospero Bone' – I think it might be a middle name – not sure yet. Anyway, that's him!"

Christopher looked down at the proffered page with interest.

It was a book of famous British architects, and Post was gesturing at an entry between Inigo Jones and Christopher Wren.

There was a portrait of a serious-looking man of about sixty, wearing a dark velvet coat and shirt of high quality; unusually for the time he was wigless, with a full head of long, auburn hair that probably drove the women in his life wild with envy. There was something about his dark eyes that drew you towards him. He looked like a man who had had to learn to be cautious and reserved – to whom it had not come naturally.

He was leaning against a desk covered in the tools of his trade: plans, instruments, cut stone, stained glass. His arm rested on the dressed stone with a proprietary air and, curiously, his left foot rested atop a pile of books of natural science.

He couldn't put his finger on why, exactly, but Christopher got the impression that there was more to this man than he let others see.

He studied the brief description with interest.

'Mortimer Bone (1641 – 1717)

Mortimer 'Prospero' Bone was the third son of a successful stone mason in the small town of Paddock Wood in Kent. Although his parents, Milo and Iola Bone, had seven children, only three survived: Mortimer and his two younger sisters, Tabitha and Mathilda, who were five and seven years his junior. After his father's death in the Great Fire of London in 1666, Mortimer took financial responsibility for his sisters and their ailing mother.

After attending the local church school until he was seven, Mortimer was apprenticed to his uncle, Dominic Bone, a carpenter with whom his father shared a workshop and yard. Thus, by the time he became a journeyman at the age of seventeen he had a solid grounding in both trades, gaining experience that he would put to use in the design and construction of the churches for which he was famous.

It has often been said that his primary influence was Inigo Jones, famous for his development of the Renaissance style in British architecture, and often used the now-familiar symmetry, proportion and geometry of that style in his designs. In much of Bone's work it is his love of well-executed masonry that comes to the fore; he was often heard to remark that one could give him 'good, clean stone over great, futtery columns any day'.

While his contemporary, Christopher Wren, is famous for rebuilding London churches following the Great Fire of London, the majority of Bone's work was undertaken outside the capital, repairing and rebuilding parish churches at the request of the English Gentry. One notable exception was a later work which the Bone family paid for themselves: the rebuilding of the parish church in their home town, Paddock Wood. Unfortunately, little of this personal project remains as the building was destroyed by enemy action during the Second World War and replaced by the extant church, though the family tomb – including a monument to Iola Bone – survives in the graveyard.

Like many of his contemporaries, Mortimer Bone was fascinated by the world around him and took an active interest in what historians have termed the Scientific Revolution. He was a member of the Royal Society of London for the Improvement of Natural Knowledge (better known today as the Royal Society) and regularly attended lectures there while he lived in the capital. Later in life it was rumoured that Bone had dabbled in the magical arts, though this is probably a reaction to the widespread atmosphere of paranoia throughout the western world at this time, typified by the Salem Witch Trials in Massachusetts. Many individuals who took part in the Scientific Revolution were divided over the questions of magic and heresy, and Bone was no exception.

Neither Bone nor his sisters married, and all three died quietly in their substantial home at Paddock Wood, leaving generous bequests to the Royal Society, a Charitable School in London, and their beloved church.

(Note: Iola Bone, nee Babcock, was the elder sister of the Reverend Babcock, famous for his treatise on science and modern thought in the earlier part of the Seventeenth Century.)

See Also: Inigo Jones; Christopher Wren; Renaissance Architecture; the Scientific Revolution; Seventeenth Century Architecture; Churches.

Christopher looked again at the portrait of Bone, completed later in his life. There was a wisdom and weariness in his eyes that the artist had somehow managed to capture. He could well believe that he had weathered accusations of witchcraft – a dangerous practice at the time; many of this man's contemporaries had been tried and murdered for it. The fervour of the witch-hunters had been renowned, even kings and noblemen had fallen under their charm, condemning countless innocent people – both mundane and magical

– to excruciating deaths.

The man in the portrait had the look of a man who knew what it was like to be hunted.

Christopher suppressed a shudder. He hoped that he would never have to see whatever Mortimer Bone had seen.

"What do you think?" Post asked as he looked up. "Likely candidate?"

"It looks like it," Christopher admitted, though in the spirit of annoying the man, he felt compelled to continue. "Although it has to be said, an accusation of sorcery at the time doesn't mean that he had any connection to magic – and if he did, it seems unlikely that he'd come into contact with anything particularly dark."

Post's face fell slightly, but he wasn't to be deflected so easily.

"That's true," he allowed, "but several of his churches are around here, and anything unusual would probably be recorded."

"Anything unusual?" Christopher asked, before he could stop himself.

"Oh, you know," said Post, dismissively. "Dark artefacts have a habit of making themselves known – they have been known to give rise to stories of hauntings, possessions, that sort of thing."

Unbidden, the image of Professor Zarrubabel lurking behind an altar and jumping out at unsuspecting parishioners rose into Christopher's mind.

He suppressed a snort of laughter and turned his attention back to Post, who was still talking excitedly about the unconscious effects of dark artefacts.

"Even the non-magical can sense them," he was saying, as if this was a great achievement on their part. Fleetingly, Christopher wondered what Reggie would make of it. "That's what makes them so fascinating," Post continued, caught up in zeal for his own subject. "They're powerful things – deadly, in most cases – but powerful."

Post appeared to have run out of breath for the

moment, and stopped, staring in wild excitement at Christopher.

Ignoring the slightly manic look in the man's eyes – having seen it before in many others who were passionate about their research – Christopher smiled at him.

Post cleared his throat, collecting himself. "Er, yes," he said, looking unexpectedly bashful. "Have you got anything on him?"

"I'll check," Christopher promised him. "And I'll see if there's anything on his churches in the area."

"Thank you, Christopher," said Post, with more of his usual control. "Excellent. It would be just the thing to include a little local flavour to the volume – if there is anything in his churches, that is."

As Christopher went to look at his ledgers, Post shook himself slightly, as if admonishing himself for losing his cool. He straightened up, tucking in his shirt and buttoning up his waistcoat; feeling more presentable, he relaxed for a moment before noticing eyes on him.

He turned to the bookcase, spotting Jake and Astrid peering at him over the tomes.

"Hello there," he said, glancing around – and entirely failing to notice the two men industriously Not Watching Him in the corner. "Didn't see you there."

He walked around the bookcase and took the children in.

In the entirely unthreatening environment that the Arcade was, neither Astrid nor Jake felt the need to creep closer together under the scrutiny of such a charming stranger, but simply peered up at him in silence.

"I must say," said Post, with a bright smile, "you're a bit younger than the usual clientele." He sat cross legged on the floor next to them. "May I join you? Excellent. I'm Quentin."

He held out a hand to Astrid, who shook it.

"Astrid," she said, in quiet but clear voice. "And this is my brother, Jake."

"Hi," said Jake, shyly.

"What are you reading?" he asked, pulling Jake's book closer so that he could have a look. "*Forty Tales for Four Year Olds*?," he smiled, returning the book. "Does it have the one about the porridge pot in there?"

Jake shook his head.

"A pity, that was my favourite when I was a boy – they couldn't stop it filling up with porridge, do you see? And then they had to eat it all!" He laughed in a strangely child-like way. "It's one of the reasons I started looking into magical artefacts, actually, and it was written by a mundane author, would you believe? I spent a lot of my childhood sneaking out and reading in bookshops and libraries," he told them, conspiratorially.

The children smiled, charmed.

"We didn't sneak out," Astrid assured him.

"Oh, really?" he leaned back and called out to Christopher, who had climbed his short step ladder to reach one of the top shelves. "Christopher, you devil, they're not *yours* are they?"

"No," said Christopher, an odd tone in his voice. "They're Ivy's."

"Ivy's?" Post exclaimed. "Good Gods."

He looked more closely at the two children.

"You don't look alike," he said. "Though you are certainly just as beautiful," he added, and Astrid blushed.

"Ivy 'dopted us," said Jake, happily.

"Is that so?" said Post, apparently pondering this. He fixed Astrid with a disarming smile. "A bright thing like you, reading on a Saturday, reading – ah yes," he glanced at the title of Astrid's book. "*Cunningham's Herbal* of all things – you wouldn't be an apprentice, now would you?"

Astrid flushed, flattered, but glanced at Christopher before answering. Christopher, who couldn't think of a reason why Post shouldn't know, nodded.

"Yes sir," she said. "I haven't been here long, though," she added, hurriedly, as though this amiable new friend might feel the need to test her.

"How exciting!" Post exclaimed. "Congratulations," he said warmly, "it's an exciting time, when you just start out – so much to learn, so much to experience. And Ivy's an extraordinary witch," he went on, "quite extraordinary. Sticks in one's head."

Somewhere behind them, Christopher made a noise that might have been classified as a cough.

"I say," said Post, suddenly. "Would either of you like a toffee?" He dug in the pockets of his well-tailored jacket. "I've usually got some somewhere."

Yes, for luring unsuspecting children into your house, no doubt, thought Christopher, uncharitably, and immediately felt very silly for thinking it.

"Yes please," said Jake, brightly.

Astrid paused, and looked at Christopher again. "Can we?" she asked, and the werewolf nodded.

"Not too many," he said. "We're having bacon potatoes tonight."

"Oh, do you live here, too?" Post asked, surprised, as the children enthusiastically tried to bite through their toffees.

"Yes – Ivy rents me a couple of rooms," Christopher answered, shortly, not wanting to talk about her – or his living arrangements – with Post.

"Stunning, smart *and* kind," said Post, approvingly. "What a witch."

This time he might have caught the dark cloud that passed over Christopher's face at his words, but if he had, he didn't show it. Deftly, he changed the subject.

"Still, must be convenient for work," he joked, getting to his feet. "Is that my book list?"

"Yes," said Christopher, forcing his jealous mind back to the task at hand. "There's quite a few on architecture, although I'm not sure if Bone's in all of them."

"I'll take the first six, if I may," said Post, pulling out his reader's ticket. "Would you keep your eyes peeled for him in the meantime?"

"Of course."

"Excellent!" Post exclaimed, again. He nodded his

head towards Christopher: "You two will be Practitioners in no time with this one and Ivy to learn from."

Astrid and Jake grinned around their toffees; Christopher was unimpressed, but he smiled, anyway.

"Thanks, Master – er, Quentin," he said, and went to exchange his books.

"I'll see you two another time," said Post, on his way out of the door, "Best of luck with your studies!"

"He seems nice," said Astrid, when she'd finished chewing her toffee.

"Ye-es," said Christopher, reluctantly.

Astrid frowned at him, unaccustomed to Christopher disliking anyone. "You don't like him very much, do you?" she asked.

"Not really," Christopher admitted, after a moment. "But not because of anything sensible. I wouldn't worry about it."

The young girl nodded, and went back to her brother, who was by now lying on his stomach, reading his stories.

The bell jangled again, and Joanna Barraclough bustled in.

"Morton's been held up at the Town Hall," she said, stowing her shopping in the back office. "Says he's sorry – can't be helped, I'm afraid, business permits."

Christopher nodded, unfazed.

"Could you hold the fort for the rest of the day?" Joanna asked, pushing her greying hair away from her face. "I promised to take Jake shoe shopping."

"Sure," he said, pulling out the accounts ledger. "Could you sign last night's accounts for me?"

Jake, whose ears had pricked up at his name, raced past them to collect his coat. Christopher effortlessly plucked him out of mid-air beside him and the young boy squealed and laughed.

"Not so fast, you," he said, amicably. "Put your books away first, and *walk* up the spiral staircase, please, or I'll get Ivy to make Martha eat you."

Jake roared with laughter at this and ran back across

the shop proper to tidy up his books. Within seconds he had reappeared at Christopher's elbow.

"Could I take this book out, please?" he asked, as Joanna signed the ledger, trying not to chuckle too much.

"Certainly," said Christopher, enjoying winding him up. "Reader's ticket please, young man," he held out his hand.

Jake stuck his tongue out at Christopher and held out the ticket as his sister sniggered at him from behind the bookcase.

"There you are," said Christopher, carefully writing Jake's name in the Lending Ledger. "Careful on the stairs!" he called after him as the boy raced away. "I hope you're feeling energetic," he said to Joanna, as she laughed.

"I think Jake's energetic enough for the both of us, today."

Christopher nodded, smiling.

The chaos that one small child could create around himself was extraordinary to Christopher, and for the first time in his life he could understand the exasperation that his parents had once expressed at his own indomitable energy. Thinking about his parents hurt, though, and he forced his mind away from them with a pang.

He liked having the children about, it made him feel needed, wanted – like he wasn't all that different from the people around him.

"Ready!" Jake cried, stumbling back into the room with one arm in his coat. "The Professor was saying horrible things about Christopher again," he added, in a stage whisper.

"Oh, was he now?" asked Joanna. "Well, we'll see about him later. Are you sure you don't want to come, Astrid?"

"No thank you," she said, turning a page in her book.

"Alright," said Joanna. "You keep out of Christopher's way, though."

"She couldn't be in my way if she tried," he laughed, closing his ledger. "Ah, hello there," he said to a young couple, who had just come in. "Can I help you?"

Joanna and Jake slipped out of the door as he spoke with the customers – before tranquillity descended once more upon the bookshop, Jake's delighted voice could still be heard retreating down the corridor.

"He gave me a toffee!"

Christopher winked at Astrid as her brother's voice echoed about the Arcade.

As his customers got down to the serious business of browsing, Christopher felt his nose being pulled to the desk in the back corner of the shop, to two scents that shouldn't have been there.

To his surprise, he saw Masters Hoxley and Morris there, still diligently working away at the back of the shop, forgotten in all the chaos.

Christopher stared at them, nonplussed. How could he have overlooked them? It was as if they had simply melted away into the background of the shop while Quentin Post had been excitedly retelling his good fortune. Which was particularly interesting, given Post's earlier discomfort at Hoxley's presence.

He frowned.

Those two were definitely up to something, and if there was one thing he could count on, it was that Professor Zarrubabel liked people being up to something in his shop even less than he liked Christopher.

"I'll just be in the back room, if you need me," he said, to the shop at large, and ducked behind the door, narrowly avoiding a flying inkstand.

"Professor, could I have a word?

ooo

Astrid lay on her stomach, idly turning the pages of the *Herbarium* and kicking her heels in the air. The book was beautifully penned, and she loved the way the colours the artist had chosen made each flower or plant seem to come alive on the page.

She was learning a lot here, she knew, and she could afford to indulge in the odd day-dream – particularly since Ivy had outlawed working too hard on Saturdays. She closed the book and leaned it gently on its spine, the way Christopher had taught her, letting go suddenly so that it would fall open on a random page. The book stayed where it was for a moment, shivering slightly – hanging improbably shut before gently falling back to the floor.

'Lemongrass,' she read. *'Repels snakes; also used in infusions to develop psychic powers.'*

Gently, she ran her finger over the illustration, committing it's shape and colour to memory.

Snakes...

Abruptly, something made her look up: there were two men at the desk in the corner. She remembered them coming in earlier, she realised, but had forgotten them, assuming that they'd left while she and Jake had been reading together. She frowned at them.

It was odd that she'd forgotten them so completely when they'd been there all along. It was almost as if they'd *wanted* to be forgotten.

As nonchalantly as she could, she closed the *Herbarium* and walked to the other side of the bookcase, where she pretended to be studying titles. Confident that she looked like nothing more than a studious child selecting her next book, she examined the men.

The one closest to the wall was large and black, with hands like a bear. When he had first come in, Astrid had thought that he had kindly eyes, twinkling as he'd smiled down at her and Jake, but now she wasn't so sure. Kind people oughtn't have reasons to want to be forgotten.

Now, with Christopher busy in the back office, he seemed more powerful than he had before, like a great, fierce animal making himself seem smaller. He was daintily turning the pages in front of him, camouflaged in this forest of books.

She looked at the other man: he was smaller than his

bear-like friend, and didn't look at all out of place behind a desk – though he seemed more athletic than many of the Professors' customers, like Christopher. There was a strange energy to him that Astrid couldn't place, and it unsettled her.

In one of her lessons at the Crooked House, Joanna had told her how difficult it was to become invisible, and this had surprised Astrid, given her and Jake's ability to remain hidden for so long. Mrs Barraclough had explained that this was because there was a big difference in intending to become invisible and simply not wanting to be noticed. Becoming invisible meant fiddling with the laws of physics, which – while by no means impossible – was a lot of rather pointless hard work when all you really had to do was to be forgotten by the people around you. Astrid had done it herself, sliding into the background of a crowd in the market when she'd had to steal food for her and Jake.

Joanna Barraclough had also told her that other Practitioners were much harder to hide from, largely because seeing things that shouldn't be there was second nature to them.

Astrid frowned, deeply.

The pair of them must have been very powerful wizards indeed to hide from Christopher, Joanna and Master Post.

The two men quietly began to pack their things up, slipping pens back into notebooks and sliding their books into their messenger bags. Astrid shrank back as they passed the counter, confident that they had been forgotten. Curiously, the door opened without its customary jangle, the bell jiggling about silently on its fixing. Astrid stared at their retreating backs, astonished at their brazen deception.

A strange outrage was growing inside her chest: they had betrayed Christopher's trust, and the Barracloughs – they wouldn't have let them become readers if they'd suspected them of anything nefarious. The anger on behalf of her new friends burned inside her, bubbling up until it forced her forward.

Without thinking, she hurried after them, flitting out of the door seconds before it closed. She saw them turning out of the Arcade and ran after them, turning the same corner in time to see them disappearing down the street.

Ignoring a very small voice inside her head that was whispering about how this was probably a bad idea, she pressed on, her face set. She wouldn't be gone for long – Ivy and Christopher probably wouldn't even notice – so she didn't need to worry about getting in trouble. It was just a walk through Brindleford on a sunny autumn day. After all, she reasoned, she'd kept both her and Jake hidden for months, what were the odds that these two scoundrels would spot her?

The children in the stories that Christopher read to her were always following suspicious people and solving mysteries. They never got caught, and they always saved the day.

She sped up, not wanting to lose them as they crossed the town square, busy with market traders loudly calling to passers-by, shoppers, lounging teenagers and young families navigating the crush.

Knowing that she'd easily be lost in the crowd, she latched onto the tail end of a large family, who were happily chattering about lunch and school and where they should go next. Astrid smiled to herself, pleased at her own cunning. If they looked back now, all the men would see was a happy family – and who would suspect a child dawdling behind? Yes, even if they noticed her – and she was confident that they wouldn't – she could simply pretend to be lost! Ha!

A few feet in front of her, the children's father bent and lifted his small daughter onto his shoulders and Astrid forced back the pang of sadness she felt, intent of her quarry. The crowd was thicker here, and for a moment she was afraid that she had lost them and would have to turn back, but she spotted them taking an alley between two shops. The young family carried on down the street, unknowing accessories to Astrid's espionage.

The alley looked dark and dank from the street: creepy and singularly uninviting. Undeterred, she followed them, surprised to find herself in a pleasantly leafy walkway that the council had clearly decided needed brightening up. Facing the banks of flowers, there was a toy shop and a shop that sold more sweets than she had ever seen in one place.

Momentarily distracted by the vibrant windows and mouth-watering displays, Astrid lost sight of the men. Annoyed at herself, she used a word that she'd heard Professor Zarrubabel say and blushed, glad that no one had heard her. She ran down the alley, looking down the tiny, ancient roads that branched off it, but there was no sign of the men.

Irritated, she sat down on the steps of a small war memorial and looked around. The alley widened out into a small square, here, with the monument at its centre. Around the square were squat, old cottages that had been kept brightly painted by their inhabitants; hairy doormats were set at the front of each door and pots full of bright flowers clustered under the windows. From the windowsill of the nearest cottage a fat orange tabby cat was staring at her, aloof. Astrid stared back and the cat began to wash itself, indifferently.

One side of the square was taken up by a little chapel that looked like it might have been in Brindleford for as long as Brindleford had been. Astrid peered over the low wall into the graveyard, joyously overgrown with long grass and daisies, liberally strewn amongst the higgledy-piggledy tombstones. Climbing over the wall, she brushed dirt and lichen off the nearest one, struggling to make out a name. She stared at it for a few moments before it resolved into the shape of a skull, and she snatched her hand away, with a startled cry.

Astrid looked at the skull for a long, wary moment, worried that its owner might not approve of her presence. She listened hard for the sound of stone scraping on stone, or the moaning of anything less dead than it should be, but all she could hear were birds chirping merrily at one another from the trees and the gutters of the church. She glanced back at the skull, finding it distinctly less frightening now that she knew what to expect.

It was inexpertly drawn, appearing almost friendly.

"Hello," she said, quietly. "I hope you don't mind me being here."

She looked around, hurriedly, feeling a little bit silly for talking to the picture of a skull (however friendly it might appear to be), but there was no one around except for the cat, which had given up its washing and was perched on the wall of the graveyard, watching her intently.

Unnerved, Astrid frowned at it. "Go away," she said.

The cat didn't move, staring implacably at her with its great, golden eyes.

"Hmpf," said Astrid, and waded through the long grass towards the chapel, determined not to be frightened away by cats or skulls.

She glanced behind her – it was still there, watching her as she made her way between the tombstones.

Some of the stones looked familiar, with fragments of names or dates showing through the moss, but others were just simple lumps of rock, worn down through the ages until they were nothing more than anonymous markers in the grass.

Astrid bent down next to a squat stone that stood in the lee of the church; tangles of ivy surrounded it, but she thought she saw faint shadows of carving on the stone. She passed her fingers over the rough stone, wondering what might once have been carved on it.

Perhaps she would ask Christopher when she got back to the Arcade.

Frowning, she wondered why Reggie had never told her about this place on one of their walks. It had clearly been here forever. Perhaps she'd show it to him when the puppies were old enough to go outside.

She straightened up and glared at the cat, which was

still watching her – this time from atop the gravestone with the skull. Huffing at it, she walked to the end of the chapel and had a look around the back, where fallen stones had been stacked. It was mossy and dank behind the ancient church, but not unpleasant; it smelled green and oddly fresh, like the oldest of Ivy's five compost stacks. There had been a garden back here at some point, though the flowers had long since escaped any attempt at a formal bed and now angelica, sweet woodruff and poppies were clambering all over the mossy ground, honeysuckle tangling over the walls and fallen gravestones.

She inhaled the sweet vanilla scent of the woodruff happily. Perhaps she would pick some flowers for Ivy before she left.

Astrid looked around – there didn't appear to be anyone about that might object, and the chapel seemed to have been long since abandoned. A movement caught her eye, and she turned, surprised to see the cat slinking around the corner of the chapel. Catching sight of her, it sat down, continuing its vigil.

"You are a very odd cat," said Astrid, and to her surprise, it meowed at her.

Still, she thought, *it wouldn't be right to take them without leaving something in return.*

She thrust her hands into the pockets of her trousers, hoping for inspiration; her fingers closed around a stone, which she pulled out, remembering. She'd been helping Ivy in the Arcade garden that morning, and the stone had caught her eye. It was smooth and round and white, and she had intended to put it on her bookshelf after lunch, where she could take it down and look at it every so often.

She must have forgotten.

It was cool and smooth in her palm, and she weighed it thoughtfully.

One stone wouldn't be enough, though, she reasoned, since the little graveyard had been so lovely to explore, so she searched her pockets, coming upon a handful of seeds she'd pulled from plants in the garden. Ivy had collected enough for next year's planting, and had let Astrid keep some to paste into her notebook.

Astrid smiled. Seeds for flowers sounded like a fair exchange to her, and she scattered the seeds around before picking some of the flowers, careful to leave enough that the plants could reseed themselves. Satisfied, she turned, intending to add some daisies to the posy before she left.

The cat was standing at her feet. Astrid frowned at it, and it began to rub itself against her legs, purring.

"There's more to you than meets the eye, isn't there?" she said, softly, tickling the cat under its chin. It purred loudly.

Shaking her head, Astrid made her way to the front of the chapel, stooping to pick some daisies as she went.

She left the white stone in front of the grave with the friendly skull and climbed back over the low wall, tying the posy with some long strands of grass to stop the flowers from escaping.

Setting off towards the bright, flowery alley, she hoped that no one at the Arcade would worry about her little excursion, and that she wouldn't get into too much trouble. Saturdays were busy days, and the shops were always full of people. Hopefully, they would simply assume that she was in one of the other shops until she got back, and then she could tell them about her walk.

Even if she did get in trouble, she reasoned, she had found the chapel, and its secret garden, which more than made up for losing the two strange men.

Abruptly, Astrid stopped, confused.

There was a door on the wall to her left that she would have sworn wasn't there before.

Jammed in between the back of an inn and the back wall of the graveyard was a low, white cottage with lumpy walls. Its door was also white, and freshly painted, with long black hinges that made it hang slightly askew.

Astrid pressed her fingers against it – it was stuck fast.

Must have just missed it before, she thought. *Nothing*

unusual about that.

Still, a feeling of uneasiness crept over Astrid, and she backed away, almost tripping over the cat, which had followed her from the graveyard.

"Shoo," she said, wanting nothing more than to go home, and angry at herself for her unaccustomed skittishness.

But the cat ignored her, and instead approached the door, which swung open.

Astrid stared at it, and at the cat, which was waiting for her at the top of a flight of stone stairs that looked like it had been cut straight through what used to be someone's living room.

She bit her lip, frightened. She craned her neck inside the door, trying to see the bottom of the staircase: it didn't go too far down.

Astrid looked at the cat, which stared implacably back.

"Well," she said to herself. "I've come this far. I'll go to the bottom of the staircase and come straight back up. What harm could that do?"

She nodded to herself, trying to quiet the fear that was fluttering in her stomach. The cat set off down the stairs, flicking its tail, and she followed it, feeling that this was probably not the best idea that she'd ever had. It was dark and cool inside the passage, and there was a pleasantly fresh smell in the air that she couldn't identify.

She stopped at what she had thought was the bottom of the staircase and stared. There were more steps leading down into the gloom, lit by dim light orbs set into the wall. What she had thought was the end of the passage was simply a bend.

She shouldn't go on. No – she'd go back to the Arcade and tell Christopher and Ivy what she had found, no matter how angry they were with her for wandering off. She would walk back to the Arcade now, yes – walk, and not run, no matter how much she wanted to.

Decision made, she turned back up the stairs and stopped, full of dread.

The door had closed behind her, silently, shutting the daylight out and Astrid in.

She rushed up to it, trying to pull it open, but to no avail.

Her heart pounding, she leaned against the door and stared down the passage in the gloom, wondering what horrors were waiting for her at the end of it. She looked down the passageway, not wanting to move, and sank to the floor, hugging her knees.

At least Jake wasn't here, and couldn't be hurt.

Jake.

Astrid felt hot tears begin to fall down her cheeks and she scrubbed at her face angrily. No. She had to get out of here. Jake needed her. She'd have to find another way out.

Swallowing her fear, she set off down the stairs, determined and more afraid than she'd like to admit.

The passage seemed to go on forever, winding downwards through the gloom; the walls of the passage were sandy and rough, like they'd been carved out of the earth itself. As she walked down the interminable stone steps, Astrid wondered if they really had been.

As she descended deeper she realised that she could hear voices – not just one or two, but lots and lots of voices, all talking over one another. Astrid felt her heart constrict. Just how many people were down there? Periodically, the voices were eclipsed by distant brief explosions. In amongst the audible chaos were strange zips and whistles that Astrid couldn't identify – and, if she were honest, didn't particularly want to.

The cat was waiting for her at the bottom of the stairs, patiently washing its paws. Astrid crept to the edge of the wall and risked a look around the corner. She gasped, staring at the vast, low cave in front of her.

Screwing up her courage, she crept into the brightly lit cavern, hiding behind a large rock that the builders of this extraordinary place had apparently been unable to move.

The room was full of desks of all shapes and sizes, and

people were striding around them purposefully, doing inscrutable things with folders and stacks of papers. There was a distinct air of barely controlled chaos. A man at the desk closest to her was trying to force a giant purple chicken into a shoebox. As she watched, it squawked in distress, spitting bright flames at the luckless man and singeing his eyebrows.

Next to him, an exceptionally hairy man was eating something red and slimy out of a large dog bowl, slurping noisily.

"Keep it down, Everett!" said a crisply dressed woman in a pencil skirt as she hurried past him. "Some of us have appetites we want to keep a hold of."

"Sorry Mary," the man grunted, before returning to his lunch. Astrid shuddered. Whatever it was he was eating, it had clearly never seen an oven.

Further on a witch was crying noisily into a large silver handkerchief and talking to a sympathetic gentleman with the biggest beard that Astrid had ever seen. He seemed to be filling in some kind of form, and kept glancing up at the woman as she struggled to keep her composure.

"And that's when you noticed it was missing?" he asked, triggering a fresh bout of sobbing.

Astrid stared around, alert and fascinated.

Several large tunnels led off the main cavern, and she wondered whether any of them led to exits.

In front of her, the large purple chicken squawked loudly in astonishment before exploding wetly, covering the man with the shoebox in sticky blue goop. Astrid grimaced, watching as the man sank into his chair, looking despondent. Nobody seemed to be paying the exploding chicken much notice, and Astrid decided that if she kept low, she might be able to reach the next tunnel without being seen.

Crouching, she turned around and froze, her heart turning to ice in her chest.

There were a pair of boots in front of her, and attached to the boots were a pair of legs, and a body, and right at the top, staring down at her, was the unsmiling face of the fierce man she had followed from the bookshop.

20
Wizards Underground

Professor Zarrubabel glared malevolently at Christopher over the top of his pince-nez. Christopher stared back, determined.

"Oh, *fine!*" cried the spectre.

"Thank you," said Christopher, as graciously as he could.

"What do you want, you foul wastrel?" Zarrubabel spat. Christopher closed his eyes briefly as tiny droplets of ectoplasmic spittle scattered around the ghostly Professor, orbiting him like thin, green cloud. It had not been easy to engage the irritable spirit in conversation, and Christopher had received more than a few bruises for his trouble. He wasn't about to give up now.

"There are a couple of customers that I want to know more about," he said, when he deemed it safe to open his mouth again.

Zarrubabel gave him a scathing look that suggested that any lack of knowledge was a major failing on Christopher's part, but Christopher ignored him.

"I don't trust them."

"Anyone *you* suspect *must* be trustworthy," sneered Zarrubabel, but Christopher could tell that he was interested.

"They're clearly wizards," he continued, "and seem like they come from one of the older families, but neither Ivy nor Professor Barraclough have heard of them."

"Curious," said Zarrubabel, stroking his goatee thoughtfully. "I suppose you didn't think to ask my sister about them," he continued, adding 'Oaf', under his breath, along with a good few other words that Christopher chose not to hear.

"Professor Barraclough said that he'd ask her, but neither of them have said anything, so I'd imagine she didn't know them."

"Hmm," said Zarrubabel, curious despite himself. "What are their names, shop boy?"

"William Hoxley and Collin Morris," said Christopher, calmly. "Neither of them are using Insignia, but they did ask about Etching."

"That *is* odd," rumbled the spectre, raising an eyebrow. "I can't say I've come across them, either."

He floated over to the large stack of ancient ledgers in the corner.

"Perhaps they're from out of town," he muttered to himself, pulling ledgers out apparently at random and carrying them over to the desk. "Well, clear a space boy!"

Christopher did as he was told, making an island of free desk in the midst of the chaos of paperwork that was Morton Barraclough's idea of filing.

The ledgers landed on the table with a thump, narrowly missing his fingers.

Biting his tongue, he stood back and let the ghost in front of him work. Zarrubabel scanned through the ledgers quickly, muttering to himself.

"Hawkes, Higson, Hoft, Honniton, Hooch... Ingleson. Hmm. Milton, Moseley, Moss, Mossley, Morrison..."

He discarded the ledger and opened another, continuing in this manner for some time.

"No," he declared, eventually. "No Hoxleys or Morrises here – and these records go back to the sixties, when we opened the shop."

He frowned, perplexed, as Christopher tried to imagine his employers in their younger days.

"They might have some records at Brightwell," he suggested. "Not everyone has the good taste to use our service." He sniffed, and Christopher could practically hear him think: '*Fools*'.

Christopher nodded, wondering whether the Professor might look them up for him the next time he attended a meeting.

"Are they in the shop?" Zarrubabel asked, sharply.

"Yes," Christopher nodded. "Or rather they were – they came in after lunch, but –"

"But *what*, boy?"

"But as soon as Quentin Post came in they..." he

searched for an adequate description. "Faded."

Professor Zarrubabel blinked at him. "Faded?" he repeated. "You mean they were Glamoured, idiot boy!"

"No," Christopher insisted. "I would have noticed that. It was as if we simply forgot that they were there."

"Well, I'm not surprised *you* forgot," said the spectre. "But young Quentin is a fine wizard."

Christopher bridled.

"Perhaps he simply didn't wish to speak to them."

"No," said Christopher, firmly. "Because if he *had* seen them today he'd have been much quieter. The last time they were in the shop at the same time he practically ran out of it."

"Did he, indeed?" exclaimed the Professor, animosity forgotten in the face of this new information.

"I thought they might be rivals in the artefacts trade," Christopher continued. "I know Master Post is a collector."

Zarrubabel nodded. "He takes after his father," he said, knowledgeably. "Bit of a rogue, but very well-to-do. If he's uncomfortable around these two newcomers we'd best keep an eye on them. They're still in the shop, you say?"

"I think so – I've not heard the bell go."

"Tell me if I've got a decent eye-line and I'll have a look at them," he instructed.

Christopher went back into the shop proper, which was bereft of mysterious men.

"No, they're gone," he said. "Sorry."

"Imbecile," said the spectre, but without too much venom. "If they come back, shop boy, you let me know. We can't be leaving you in charge with people like that around – who knows what could happen."

With that he somersaulted backwards through the air and landed in his book, which closed with a snap.

Christopher shook his head, closing the door to the back office behind him, relieved that the encounter had been relatively painless.

He rubbed his shoulder, where Joanna's old tin mug

had rebounded off it.
Relatively.

ooo

Ivy cleaned down the last table and set the teapots washing in the back room, pausing for a moment to watch them bob cheerily through the air. It had been a very busy day, and she was glad that she had reached the end of it.

She turned and started putting the unsold sandwiches and cakes in the large refrigerator behind the door, looking up when she heard the teashop door open.

"Sorry, we're closed," she called.

"It's me," said Christopher, who sounded worried. Ivy stuck her head out of the back room.

"Everything alright?" she asked, with a frown. He looked worried, too.

"I can't find Astrid," he said, wringing his hands. "She was with me in the shop earlier, and now she's just gone."

"Didn't she go out with Joanna and Jake?" Ivy asked. Out of the corner of her eye she noticed vines beginning to coil down the walls. Martha had sensed her concern.

"No," Christopher said, sounding like he was forcing himself to stay calm. "She wanted to stay and read. I went in the back office to talk to Zarrubabel and when I came out she'd gone – I thought she was upstairs or with you."

"No," said Ivy, worriedly. "I haven't seen her."

They shared a look, neither wanting to admit that Astrid being missing was a distinct possibility.

"I'm sure it's nothing," said Christopher, sounding unconvinced.

"She might have snuck past one of us," Ivy said, slowly. "We should check upstairs."

Christopher nodded and they hurried up the stairs, Ivy stripping off her apron as she went, the vines surging up the walls after them.

"I'll check the bedrooms," said Ivy, heading for the nearest corridor.

"I'll see if she's with Mahri or Reggie," called Christopher over his shoulder as he bounded away.

Ivy hurried along the corridor, opening doors and calling Astrid's name. Her fear grew with every empty room – where could she be? It was unlike Astrid to just wander off – particularly without Jake.

She checked her and Christopher's rooms to no avail, and rushed back into the main room. The walls were thick with vines, filled with a nervous energy; leafy tendrils were everywhere, opening cupboards and lifting up cushions, swarming out from under the furniture, searching all over the Arcade for their young friend.

"Any luck?" she asked Christopher as she hurried into the garden, but his face was grim.

"No," he said. "Reggie and Saffy are checking in the basement, but –" he raised miserable eyes to her face. "I can't smell her up here," he said. "I mean, I can tell that she's *been* up here, but she's not *still* here."

"No sign of her?" asked Mahri, hurrying out to them.

"Nothing," said Christopher, wretchedly.

Ivy stayed quiet, gripped by a dizzying fear, as her friends desperately tried to think of anywhere they hadn't looked.

What if something happened to her? Astrid was *her* responsibility.

More than that, she realised. She'd grown quite attached to the children since they'd lived at the Arcade, and the thought of something happening to either of them made it difficult to breathe.

For the first time in months, she wished that Sam was here beside her. He would know what to do.

She turned and looked at his photograph through the glass, resting in its familiar place on the bookshelf, in between her aunts and her parents' wedding portrait.

Sam isn't here, she thought. *And nor are my parents. I'm here. I have to do something.*

She turned back as Mahri hurried past her into the

Arcade.

"I'll check my shop and the empty bays," she called, moving faster than Ivy thought she could.

Ivy was intensely grateful that there were other people around.

"No luck!" shouted Reggie, emerging from his kitchen door with Saffy and a trail of squealing puppies.

Around Ivy the vegetation shuddered restlessly, responding to panic that she was struggling to keep a lid on. She swallowed the tears that were threatening to start and frowned.

She needed to be able to think.

"What are we going to do?" Christopher asked, despondently.

"It's not like we can go to the police," said Reggie, worriedly; Boscoe was flying around his head like a strange, feathery meteorite. "Where can she have gone?"

"Find girl! Find girl! What to do!" screeched Boscoe.

Saffy whined and stared up at her, a mobile pile of puppies heaping up at her feet like rocks around a pier.

They were all staring at her like somehow *she* would have their answers – like she could simply wave her hand and Astrid would appear. Abruptly, Ivy felt some of the pressure that her parents must have felt, tending the needs of their community. She didn't like it one bit.

"I..." she swallowed, forcing herself to be calm.

What *could* they do? Reggie was right, it wasn't as if they could go to the police – as far as they were concerned, Astrid and her brother were vulnerable children that had run away from home, however binding the magical contract was. Even if they could find Astrid (and Ivy wasn't sure they'd be able to, given the girl's ability to stay hidden) they'd take her and Jake away from them and place them with a foster family, and Ivy wasn't willing to risk that.

But if Christopher couldn't smell her anymore...

"That's it!" she cried, struck by sudden inspiration. "Christopher, can you track her scent?"

Christopher smacked himself in the forehead. "Of

course! Why didn't I think of that?" he nodded. "I'd know her smell anywhere – although..."

"Although?" Reggie prompted.

"It depends where she went – if there was a lot going on it might be harder." He gave a humourless snort. "For the first time in my life I wish it was full moon. It would be easier to follow her then."

"Right," said Ivy. "Reggie, you and Mahri stay here in case she comes back – and so there's someone here to look after Jake, who won't take this well." Reggie saluted and Saffy barked.

"Take Boscoe with you," said Reggie. "He can get up high, see if he can spot her."

Ivy nodded. "Alright – Martha, keep a look out," she ordered. She looked up at Christopher. "Let's go."

ooo

Astrid walked briskly through the maze of desks and filing cabinets that encrusted the floor of the cavern, trying not to let her fear show on her face.

The fearsome man from the Arcade had one of his great, powerful hands on her shoulder and with it he guided her through the chaos, maintaining a firm grip to keep her in front of him.

Refusing to be intimidated, Astrid stared around her at the barely controlled bedlam. The ceiling of the cavern was fairly high above their heads, but the size of the place made it seem long and low. It was lit, at intervals, by the same, dim Light Orbs that Astrid had seen in the passage below the white door. They had an odd, greenish glow to them and Astrid was beginning to suspect that they weren't really Light Orbs at all, but things made to resemble them.

At every occupied desk personal Light Orbs hung above their owners in a cacophony of multi-coloured light, illuminating paperwork and folders – ordinary things rendered sinister by their surroundings.

The hand on her shoulder her pulled her to a halt in

the centre of the maze of desks, and she stopped just in time. A series of shopping trolleys hurtled past them, tied together with rope. They were filled with the oddest collection of objects that Astrid had ever seen, old radios and picture frames, coat-hangers and kettles. Astrid stared after them, the rush of air in their wake tugging at her cardigan and hair.

Nearby, two wizards were arguing over what looked like an old, glass water dispenser. One of them, who looked even older than Professor Zarrubabel, was standing his ground, arms crossed, while the younger man huffed in frustration.

"Seriously Garth, you can't keep your newts in there, people drink from it!" he cried, waving his arms around.

"Newts are a sign that the water's good for drinking," the old wizard rumbled, steadfastly.

Astrid watched the younger wizard burst into frustrated tears as the hand on her shoulder indicated that they should move on.

Astrid stumbled forwards, the powerful hand steadying her; she risked a sideways glance, but all she could see were the man's dark clothes. She couldn't bring herself to look up at that grim countenance that had surprised her by the entrance.

Instead, she peered along the tunnels that branched off the walls of the chamber. Most of them were fairly short, coming abruptly to doors that could just be seen at their ends. These tunnels were bright and well used, with people scurrying between the doors on mysterious errands. As they passed it, the door at the end of one of the tunnels bounced open, belching clouds of turquoise smoke out into the tunnel, followed by a number of distressed wizards. They piled up against the walls, hacking and coughing, as one of their colleagues pushed the door shut with his foot.

"That was definitely too much salt," he said, slumping down against the tunnel wall.

Two of the tunnels looked more promising, from Astrid's point of view. They seemed to slope temptingly upwards, hinting that they might lead to an exit and freedom. She tried not to stare too hard at these, but it was very difficult – her eyes flicked back to them as they curved tantalisingly away.

If only she could figure out a way to elude the bear-like man, she could make a dash for them – but which one should she pick? They might not both lead to the outside... in fact, there was no reason to suppose either of them did. She might break free only to be recaptured. Or even find something worse than the fearsome man and wizards with newt obsessions at the end of the tunnels. Something that might even *eat* her.

She swallowed. She had to get back to Jake.

While the chance remained, she would just have to risk it. If only her captor wasn't gripping her shoulder so tightly.

They came to a halt, and Astrid stumbled, surprised. She'd been so intent on planning her escape that she'd failed to notice that they, too, had passed into a tunnel. In front of her was a great, black wooden door covered in locks and bolts.

She stared up at it in terror.

As the locks on the door slid back one by one, Astrid hoped that the man couldn't feel how hard she was shaking.

The treacherous cat was nowhere in sight.

ooo

They hurried out into the darkening streets, Boscoe soaring above their heads.

"Keep a look out!" he screeched, distantly. "Find girl! Awk!"

"Down here," said Christopher, running along the road; the hunter in him was taking over and he was no longer hiding his athleticism.

Ivy dashed after him, struggling to keep up.

They followed the curve of the street, rushing past the closing shops and opening pubs, Ivy's eyes flicking to every child that they passed. She was resisting calling Astrid's name, but only just – they couldn't let anybody know that a child was missing, or some conscientious person might call the police, and then Astrid would be in even more trouble.

Christopher stopped abruptly at the junction of three streets. Ivy crashed into his back, surprised.

"Oof, sorry," she said, but Christopher wasn't listening, concentrating everything he had onto the scent of his young friend.

Ivy looked up at the council building they'd stopped beneath. The windows were dark now, their occupants having long since made their way home for the evening. She wondered whether any of them had seen Astrid pass as they looked up from their work – whether any of them would remember if she'd been with someone, or if she'd walked out alone.

Ignoring the tightening she felt in her chest, she ran after Christopher, who had hurtled off along the right hand road. Ivy felt dismayed as they passed right by the great library building with its classical columns, looking out of place amongst the red brick shops on either side. If she could have guessed where Astrid might have run off to, the library would have been it. She half expected the girl to come out of the door as she ran past, blinking up at her over a towering pile of books, innocent and confused at all the fuss.

But no such child emerged and Ivy kept on after her friend, puffing and gasping for air as she tried to match his sudden bursts of speed.

He stopped again in the town square, and this time Ivy had enough time to avoid another collision. She put her hands on her thighs, trying to catch her breath from all the unaccustomed exercise.

The square was fairly empty now, though the traces of a busy Saturday market were still visible; some of the stall holders were still packing their wares into their vans and brushing the litter away from their plots. Last-minute shoppers walked across the square, passing early restaurant goers. Everyone seemed to know where they were going, and none of them paying any attention to Christopher or Ivy.

Ivy looked around, frantic, but there was no sign of Astrid. She straightened up, out of breath and afraid. Christopher was turning this way and that desperately, his eyes tightly shut.

Ivy watched him, miserably, her hope failing.

She put a hand on his shoulder and he jumped, opening his eyes with something like despair etched in them.

Ivy didn't need to ask why. The market, with its morass of people, goods and odours was too much information for him to process. He slumped down onto a nearby bench, his head in his hands.

Ivy looked around. There were too many routes off the town square, they'd never be able to follow them all, and Astrid could be anywhere. Ivy sighed. This would be a lot easier if they could figure out why Astrid had felt the need to disappear. She'd thought that the girl was happy, that she was doing a good job with her, but perhaps she'd been wrong.

This was all her fault.

Frustrated, Ivy ran a hand over her face.

This wasn't getting them anywhere.

"We should head back," she said, quietly. Christopher didn't respond. "Christopher?"

He mumbled something that she couldn't hear and she wondered whether the cacophony of scent that a Saturday Market could produce had been too loud for him.

"Does your head hurt?" she guessed, and he nodded.

"I'm so sorry, Ivy," he said, looking up at her. "This is all my fault – if I'd only kept a better eye on her –"

He let the sentence hang in the air, wretchedly, and looked away.

Ivy knelt in front of him. "This is not your fault," she said, softly.

"If I hadn't gone in the back room to talk to

Zarrubabel –"

"Astrid's a clever girl," she said. "If she wanted to get out of the shop she would have found a way, whether you were watching her or not."

Christopher gave a damp sort of snort that suggested he didn't believe a word of it.

"Besides," said Ivy, miserably, "Astrid is my responsibility. It's me that should have been watching her."

"Ivy –" he began, disconsolately, but she took his hand.

"No," she said, firmly. "We'll have no more talk of whose fault it is, because we'll never agree and it doesn't matter. Finding Astrid and bringing her home safely is what matters."

Christopher subsided, unhappily. "What do we do next?" he asked, taking a deep breath.

"I don't know," she admitted.

"We could go back to the Arcade," Christopher suggested. "Maybe she'll have come back home."

He didn't look like he believed it any more than Ivy did, but she nodded anyway.

"Perhaps Boscoe will have had more luck," she said, straightening up.

Together, they looked up at the empty sky. Whatever Boscoe had seen, he was nowhere near them.

Slowly, they made their way back home, dejected at their lack of success, too despondent to notice that they were still holding hands.

ooo

Boscoe soared high above the shops and houses of Brindleford, looking for any sign of the human child that lived in the next-door nest.

From up here, even great big humans looked tiny amongst their nests of brick and stone, and Boscoe was worried that he might miss the little girl. He swooped lower, following the network of roads through the town.

He saw the dark haired human and the werewolf running along one of them, chasing a trail that Boscoe couldn't follow. He flew on.

He knew that there had been some kind of ruckus in the great glass nest over the presence of the werewolf, but it had been confusing and hard to follow. Still, his pet, Reggie, seemed to like the creature and that was good enough for Boscoe. Reggie was very useful when it came to understanding other humans.

He saw a flash of blue running along the street below him and dove; the little human girl had been wearing blue plumage today, hadn't she? He soared past the startled child, who pointed and stared at him.

Wrong human.

Boscoe flew off, leaving the child and its approaching mother staring after him in wonder.

It was extraordinary really, how frequently humans felt the need to change their plumage. Why couldn't they be happy with one set of feathers? Boscoe was. He was of the opinion that he was the handsomest bird in all of Brindleford.

It wasn't even as if they could use their feathers to fly – in many ways, humans were strange, foolish creatures, but Boscoe had a soft spot for his pet Reggie and his friends. They brought back delicious fruits and nuts for him, and fed him morsels of their own food – which he had to admit, was mighty tasty – when they thought the others weren't looking.

He chuckled to himself as he flew.

Silly humans, all trying so hard to be his favourite.

He settled on the flag pole on the Town Hall, ignoring a flock of silly pigeons that were cooing at one another and fighting. Feeling rightfully superior, he scanned the streets below him.

Most of the humans had gone back to their nests, now, though a few – mostly adults – were still roaming the streets. None that matched his little human girl though.

Boscoe was annoyed about that; he didn't like being wrong, and not being able to find the girl was like not being able to crack open a promising-looking walnut. He looked up at the gathering dusk. Soon it would be too dark for him to see, and the little girl might pass by him unnoticed. She might have to spend the whole night out there in the dark, unless someone had stolen her...

Yes – that might be why they couldn't find her! Some black-hearted poacher might have plucked her away from her branch and bundled her into a sack to be sold as a pet!

Unaccustomed worry gripped Boscoe's feathery heart and he took off, squawking unhappily.

Perhaps he'd make one more round of the streets, just to be sure...

ooo

The great dark door shuddered open, as though it didn't really want to, and Astrid swallowed. She really didn't want to know what was in the darkness behind it, but she didn't want her captor to see that, so she stayed as still as she could, bravely peering into the dark.

The bear-like man pushed her forward again and guided her into the room. Astrid shuddered as the darkness enveloped her, wondering whether she was going to be fed to some subterranean beast.

The man clicked his fingers and to her intense relief, half a dozen Light Orbs began to glow on the walls. Another rested on his outstretched hand, and he hung it on a hook suspended above a desk in the middle of the room.

She looked around. The walls of the room were covered in deep, wide shelving, every inch of which was covered with an extraordinary assortment of bric-a-brac, the like of which she'd seen whizzing past in the trolleys in the cavern. Things were beginning to spill out from the shelves, and everywhere small piles of random stuff were forming like flotsam on a beach.

Astrid nearly tripped over an old radio that was hissing to itself in a language that she didn't recognise;

next to it was a pair of gardening shears that had a large metal clamp around them. Someone had written on them in red ink: *'Do not remove clamp under ANY circumstances'*. They had underlined this several times.

A stack of teacups tottered unsteadily on the edge of the desk, moving of their own volition, occasionally dripping hot water into a bucket that had been placed beneath them.

On closer inspection, everything had a label tied onto it with string, and tiny writing was printed onto the cards. Most of them had red warnings written on them.

Astrid peered into a sealed glass case on one wall, which had a camera and a teddy bear in it.

Both were covered in something that she strongly suspected was blood.

The teddy bear appeared to be staring at her. Unnerved, she took a step backwards and, to her horror, bumped into her captor.

Before she could move, Astrid felt strong arms around her waist, and the fearsome man lifted her onto the large wooden desk. She was so stunned that she forgot to struggle and simply stared at him.

"Who are you?" he asked, in a deep, authoritative voice. There was something about that voice, Astrid realised, that made you want to comply; she was surprised to find that her mouth was already open – apparently of its own accord. She shut it with a snap and folded her arms.

The bear-like man laughed, and for a moment Astrid forgot to be frightened. It was a good laugh: deep, and rich, and warm, and it reminded her of a day – years ago now – when her father had taken her and Jake to a forest at Christmas. They had gone to buy a Christmas tree, and while they were there they had queued up in the snow to meet that god of tiny children, Santa Claus. Astrid had sat on his knee in the warm and toasty grotto, excited and awed, too afraid to speak in case she broke whatever spell it was that was keeping Santa there. The grotto had had a real log fire, and Santa had told her to warm herself by it; her clothes steaming, he'd asked her if she had been a good little girl, and she'd had to think very hard before answering, which had made him laugh a deep, happy laugh.

Astrid stared at him, outraged. This great, terrifying man shouldn't have the same laugh as Santa Claus. It wasn't supposed to work like that.

"Well, if you won't tell me who you are, will you at least tell me how you found your way in?"

Astrid glared at him.

"No?" he asked, raising a stern eyebrow. "And I suppose you're unlikely to want to explain *why* you're here?"

Astrid stared ahead, sullenly.

The large man sighed. "I thought not." He looked at her for a few moments. "Your parents are probably missing you, you know."

Astrid focused on the buttons of his shirt, refusing to make eye contact.

There was a stony silence for a few minutes as he glared down at her. Astrid stared at his chest, refusing to flinch.

"You're a tough little thing, aren't you?" he said, eventually, chuckling. "Oh well, perhaps Otto will know what to do with you."

Astrid continued to stare straight ahead, wondering fearfully who this 'Otto' might be. Perhaps he was employed to torture people who refused to talk. She gritted her teeth.

Her captor turned to leave, pausing at the door. "Don't touch anything," he added, as an afterthought. "Most things in here can kill you."

Astrid sagged as the door closed and locked behind him, and drew her knees up to her chin. She didn't want to show him how vulnerable she felt, but she couldn't help it now, when she was alone. She hugged the slightly battered wildflowers to her chest and cried.

21
The Court of Miracles

Astrid stared through the glass of the display case. There was just something about that teddy bear that wasn't right.

It had been about half an hour since the fearsome man had left her alone in the room – though it seemed much longer to Astrid. She had very quickly got fed up of crying and had decided to explore instead, in case there was a hidden exit or something that she could use to her advantage. She was mindful not to touch anything, though, as her captor had instructed, but she carefully read each of the neatly penned labels (some neater than others).

Each of these had a name, a brief description, a date, a reason why it had been collected and, usually, a dire warning. If this room was anything to go by, the people of Brindleford had been plagued by some appalling injuries over the years.

Who on earth would collect dreadful things like these? she wondered.

Astrid turned away from the display case, feeling the bear's orange, resin eyes follow her across the room. She sat back down on the desk, the muscles in her legs tense from all the stair climbing she'd done earlier.

Idly, she wondered whether Master Quentin had ever seen any of these things. They seemed just the sort of thing he'd like to know about for his book.

She kicked her legs, hoping that even if this Otto person was as scary as her captor, they'd at least hurry up and arrive. She hated waiting. She'd done a lot of it over the last few years – waiting for chances to get food; waiting for Jake to catch up; waiting for people to make decisions about the two of them. Waiting for their father to come home.

Astrid sighed.

At least if she never got out of here, she knew that Jake would be alright with Ivy and the others at the

Arcade.

Unbidden, fresh tears sprung to her eyes. She scrubbed at them with the sleeve of her cardigan, angry with herself. She hadn't realised how much she'd loved being at the Arcade until it was about to be taken away from her. Ivy and Christopher had become like a surrogate aunt and uncle, and she missed them terribly – and Reggie's music lessons, and Mahri's cooking – Boscoe flying about squawking at people, Saffy and her puppies...

She hugged her knees again, concentrating on not crying. The Barracloughs had become a part of her family, too, treating her and Jake like favourite grandchildren. She knew that they had been lucky to be rescued by such friendly, caring people, and longed to get back to her new family – because that was what they had become, almost without her noticing it.

Trapped in the room of dangerous artefacts, she thought she'd even miss Professor Zarrubabel and his terrible temper. Sort of.

Astrid looked up at the sound of the locks scraping back from the great wooden door. Quickly, she brushed the remnants of her tears away from her cheeks, determined to put on a brave face.

The door swung open to reveal her captor, who almost filled the entire door frame. Astrid gave him the stoniest look that could muster, and he chuckled at her with his stolen laugh. Behind him was the other wizard from the bookshop; Astrid felt his strange energy reaching out and filling the room. He appeared to be trying not to laugh, which made her even angrier. She glared at him, too.

"Come on, Otto, we're losing daylight," he called over his shoulder. Astrid braced herself for the worst, fervently hoping that he wasn't the really hairy man she'd seen eating at his desk earlier. For the first time that day, she was in luck.

The least frightening man that Astrid had ever seen followed them into the room, kicking the door to behind him. Distracted, she gaped at him.

He was tall and slim, with arms and legs that appeared to have been fitted to him at slightly the wrong angles; tufts of wet red hair stuck up in every direction from his head – left there, Astrid thought, by the towel that he was rubbing furiously over his face and arms. There were patches of turquoise powder all over him, and it looked very much like he might quite recently have dunked his head into a barrel of water.

There was a spaceship on his t-shirt.

He stared around blearily for a few moments until the second wizard handed him a pair of spectacles. He put them on happily and peered at Astrid, wiping his hands on his shorts.

Aware that her mouth was hanging open, she quickly closed it, unable to take her eyes off his spectacles. There was a piece of brightly coloured tape hanging them by sheer will power alone, and it fluttered every time he moved like a captive butterfly.

"Hello again," said the bear-like man. His tone was gentle, but Astrid wasn't about to be fooled by *that*; she turned her glare back on him. He ignored it. "We weren't properly introduced before. My name is Ogden Rake, and this is my colleague, Alexander Hardwick. The scarecrow is Otto Finch."

Astrid risked a glance at the bespectacled apparition. He didn't appear to mind his description one bit, and was studying her with interest.

"Now," said Rake. "We've told you our names, it's only polite that you tell us yours."

He sounded so reasonable that she was halfway through her name before she noticed.

"Astrid," she said, and huffed, furious with him.

Rake laughed again. "Well Astrid, it's nice to meet you," he grinned. "Welcome to the Court of Miracles."

The what? Astrid thought, but wasn't sure that she wanted to know. She folded her arms and pursed her lips, refusing to meet any of their eyes.

"I see what you mean," said Hardwick, arousing

Astrid's curiosity. She stayed very still, hoping that he'd elaborate.

"What did I say?" grinned Rake. His teeth glinted in the pale aura of the Light Orbs. "Toughest nine year old I've ever met."

"Seven," said Astrid, feeling smug.

"I beg your pardon?"

"I'm seven, not nine," she insisted, haughtily.

Rake raised an eyebrow, apparently impressed. "My mistake," he said, graciously. "Toughest seven year old I've ever met."

His eyes twinkled, and Astrid looked away, glancing instead at the mysterious Otto, who had thus far remained silent. She got the impression that he didn't quite know what to make of her, and it was a little unnerving. What was he trying to figure out about her? And – worse – what was he going to do to her when he did?

She looked at him out of the corner of her eyes. He still had a large smear of turquoise powder on his face, clashing horribly with his hair.

Despite the unpleasant possibilities, it was difficult to be afraid of him.

"Now Astrid," said Hardwick, gently. "We do need to know a few things – and then you can go home, alright?"

Her eyes flicked to him in surprise. "I can go home?" she asked.

"Of course," Hardwick assured her.

Hope blossomed in Astrid's chest like a cherry tree in spring; she looked between the three men towering over her, cautiously. What if he was lying? She glanced at the door to the room, which Otto hadn't bothered to close. Perhaps she wasn't in quite as much trouble as she'd thought. She surveyed her captors once more. Now that the door was open they looked a lot less threatening.

"Really?"

"You have my word of honour," said Hardwick.

"And mine, little one," Rake rumbled.

There was a moment's silence as the two men looked

expectantly at Otto, who was still staring at Astrid, apparently in a world of his own. Hardwick nudged him in ribs.

"What?" he blinked at them. "Oh, yes, of course you can go home – why would we want to keep you here?"

He looked genuinely bewildered, but Astrid wasn't fully convinced. She looked up at them dubiously.

"I don't know about you," said Hardwick, guessing her mind. "But when we give our word, we mean it."

"So do I," Astrid insisted, hotly.

"Excellent," said Hardwick, clapping his hands. "Then you know you can trust us to take you home. Will you answer our questions?"

Astrid nodded slowly, then paused. "Wait – you'll let me go home alive, unharmed and uncursed?" she asked.

Three pairs of eyebrows shot skywards.

"Little one, we're not going to hurt you," said Rake, who sounded stunned.

Astrid watched their faces for a few moments. They all seemed equally taken aback at the thought of hurting her, so she relented.

"I have your word," she said, uncrossing her arms. "Ask."

Hardwick coughed, and Astrid thought that he looked exactly the way Christopher did when he was trying not to laugh.

"You're a tricky little one," said Rake, and Astrid realised to her surprise that this was meant as a compliment. "I'd have thought you'd be from one of the old families – what's your family's name?"

"You mean my last name?" she asked, and he nodded. "Healy. We're not from around here," she added, as he considered this.

"Your family has magic?"

"Yes, sir," she said. If they were going to be polite then she could be too. "At least, I do – but I'm not sure about my brother."

"What about your parents?" Hardwick asked her.

"My mother died when I was little," she said, sadly.

"And I don't know where my father is. I – I think he might be dead, too," she added quietly. It was odd how easy talking to these strangers was. She would never have admitted it to Jake – or even to Ivy – but in the privacy of her own mind she had often wondered about her father's fate. She couldn't think of another reason why he'd never come home – he had always promised to be there, and she refused to believe that he would willingly break that promise.

"Is that why Mistress Burwell took you in?" Rake asked, gently.

The twinkle was gone from the big man's eyes, which held nothing but compassion. Astrid wondered how she could ever have been afraid of him.

"Yes," she said. "You heard us talking in the bookshop."

"We did," Rake admitted.

"I didn't think you'd noticed me," said Astrid, turning very pink.

"You did a good job of staying out of sight," said Master Hardwick, encouragingly. "We honestly thought we'd lost you in the square."

"I hid behind a big family," Astrid told him.

"Clever," he said.

"If I hadn't seen you sneaking around the entrance, you'd have got away clean," Rake teased.

Astrid tried not to feel too smug. She'd very nearly fooled two adult wizards; Jake would be impressed – she couldn't wait to tell him.

"How did you get in?" asked Otto, sounding curious. "We have all manner of Glamours and charms on the doors."

So there are *other ways out,* Astrid thought.

"The door just opened," she said. The three wizards exchanged glances, taken aback.

"Just like that?" Otto prompted. "You didn't use a spell or an amulet?"

Astrid shook her head. "I was following the cat."

"What cat?" asked Hardwick, frowning.

"Large? Orange? Unusually watchful?" asked Rake, suspiciously.

Astrid nodded.

Rake rolled his eyes.

"Otto," said Hardwick, exasperated. "You can't just let that thing wander the streets."

"It's a *cat*," said Otto, mildly abashed. "Wandering the streets is what they *do*."

"Yes, but what's the point of having security measures in place if the mangy furball just lets anybody in – no offence, Miss."

"He is *not* mangy," said Otto, with a face like thunder.

Rake leaned over to Astrid as the two of them argued.

"Xander doesn't like cats," he told her. "Thinks they know too much."

"I think he's right about that," Astrid told him. "It followed me all over the graveyard – I just wanted to have a look," she added hastily. "And then he led me straight to the door, as if he knew I'd been looking for you."

Rake nodded, thoughtfully. "I'm impressed," he rumbled. "Usually Cat doesn't like anyone."

"Cat?"

Rake gave her a warm smile. "Otto's a genius when it comes to inventing – spells, potions, alchemy, clockwork, you name it – but he's complete pants when it comes to naming things."

Astrid giggled.

"And he wouldn't have let anyone in if you two hadn't let her follow you!" Otto was saying, hotly.

As one man, he and Hardwick turned to her.

"Why *were* you following us, out of interest?" Hardwick asked.

Astrid frowned, thinking about their behaviour at the Arcade.

They seem trustworthy, she thought. *And no bad guy in any story I've ever heard used the word 'pants', or had a cat called 'Cat'. He'd have called it something with a lot of zeds in it.*

"You faded," she said. "When Master Post came in, you just sort of... slipped out of our minds. I thought you were up to something. Why are you staring at me?"

"Generally, seven year olds can't tell that someone's 'faded', as you put it," Otto explained, sharing a look with the others.

Astrid stayed silent. She was reasonably sure that Christopher had noticed, too, once Post had left, but she wasn't about to tell them that, friendly wizards or not.

"So you thought we were up to something?" Rake prompted.

"You were lying to my friend Christopher, and the Professor and his wife," she said, forthrightly. "I didn't like it."

"So you decided to follow two suspicious adult Practitioners across town to God knows where?" asked Otto.

Suddenly, and not for the first time that day, Astrid felt very stupid indeed. "I didn't expect to get caught," she said, shortly.

To her surprise, Rake laughed. "I *like* her," he said, and Hardwick gave him a Look.

"Well, you can't keep her," he teased his friend. "I'm not cleaning up after her, and she probably needs some kind of special food. Cat's bad enough."

Astrid stuck her tongue out at him, and he awarded her a small smile.

They seem much friendlier now, Astrid thought, and decided to risk it. "Master Rake?" she asked, tentatively.

"Ogden, please, little one."

"Ogden, why *were* you hiding from Christopher and Master Post?"

He looked at her for a few moments, as if he was weighing his options.

"Astrid," he said, eventually. "How much do you know about Master Post?"

"Not much," she admitted. "I know he's a regular customer at the bookshop – Professor Barraclough has mentioned him... And," she added, although she wasn't sure why, "Christopher doesn't like him very much."

"This Christopher is a very sensible bloke, by the sounds of it," said Otto.

"He's lovely," Astrid admitted, and he smiled.

ooo

"I just don't know what else we can do," said Joanna, sadly.

The occupants of the Arcade were ranged around the kitchen table, all trying very hard not to look at the conspicuously empty seat in their midst. Professor Barraclough had hurried over to the Arcade when Joanna telephoned him with the news, Charlotte and John – their housekeepers – with him.

"Isn't there any magic you can do?" asked John, worry furrowing his brow.

"Not really," said the Professor. "It would be different, perhaps, with another child, but Astrid has perfected the art of not being found – any spell we sent after her would just ignore her."

"Unless," began Jake, miserably, "unless she wants to be found, and somebody nasty has her."

The adults shared an uncomfortable look; the tiny boy had voiced the fear that none of them had wanted to share in front of him.

It hadn't taken Jake long to figure out that something was wrong when he and Joanna Barraclough had returned in the early evening. He had immediately sought out his sister, to ask her what the matter was, and had been unable to find her. Reggie had sat him down and told him about how she'd vanished that afternoon, and that everyone was out looking for her.

He'd accepted this quite calmly, certain that she'd come back with one of his friends. After all, she'd never ever leave him. They'd been through too much together.

The sick, frightened feeling in his stomach had grown a little more insistent with every person that returned without her. Christopher and Ivy had come back late, after the darkness had fallen, and Jake had known from the way that Christopher wouldn't look at him that the news was bad.

Ivy had given him a hug, and then gone to sit and think at the kitchen table where – one by one – the others had joined her. There had been an unanimous decision not to involve Professor Zarrubabel, who was unlikely to do anything other than hurl abuse at Christopher, and he was worried sick as it was.

After a while, a despondent parrot had flown in above their heads and settled silently on the back of a chair.

Jake had refused to be separated from them then, wanting to help his sister in any way he could.

"Perhaps we could do worse than to set up a few Locator spells," said Joanna, thoughtfully. She and her husband went to the preparation table and began to rummage about.

"I'll help you," said Mahri, looking hard at Ivy, who was still staring at the table.

Jake watched her, silently. Ivy had the look of someone who had run out of options and really didn't want to admit it. He glanced upwards.

The vines, always a good indicator of Ivy's mood, were coiling and bunching restlessly along the walls, like snakes.

Christopher was slumped in the chair beside her, looking dejected.

"It's okay, Christopher," Jake heard himself say. "We'll find her and she'll be okay. Astrid's brilliant."

Christopher gave him a painful look. "Come here, you," he said.

Jake clambered down from his chair and ran round the table to Christopher's waiting arms; he sat him on his knee, holding him tightly.

"Astrid'll be back," he said, into the older wizard's jumper. "You'll see."

He hugged him, trying to pretend that Christopher wasn't crying, because that would have been too scary to think about.

The House of Vines

Out of nowhere there was a crash. Jake stuck his head under Christopher's arm to see that Ivy's chair had fallen to the kitchen floor. She was standing next to it, ramrod straight and as white as a sheet.

"Ivy?" Mahri asked, hands frozen halfway to a jar of herbs.

Ivy bolted down the spiral staircase, the vines swarming after her; Christopher followed, hanging tightly onto Jake.

"Who are you?" Ivy demanded – but it didn't sound like Ivy. She sounded steelier, furious – terrifying. Jake – who had been handed to Reggie as soon as the older man reached the bottom of the stairs – craned to see. The huge metal lock on the door of the teashop had fallen open on her approach, and she strode out into the corridor between the two shops, a strange blue light shining from her skin. The vines were crowding around her jealously, protective and fierce as she faced the doors.

"The girl's place is here," she said, in that same, strange, un-Ivy-like voice. "You had no right to take her."

Christopher, Mahri and the Barracloughs were beside her now, ready to fight the strange, shadowy figures at the end of the corridor. In the bookshop opposite, Jake saw the eerie greenish glow of Professor Zarrubabel spill out of the door to the back office as he came out to see what the fuss was about.

There was a startled shout from the end of the corridor. It sounded like something unexpected and rather unpleasant was happening. Someone certainly wasn't enjoying it, from the sounds echoing along the corridor. Jake squirmed in Reggie's arms, straining to see.

"Reggie, what's happening?" he demanded. "I can't see! Is Astrid there?"

"I don't know," the older man replied, stepping closer to the windows of the teashop so they could see better.

"Blimey!" cried John, appearing at his side.

Two shadowy men were just visible at the end of the

Arcade, struggling to hold off Martha's vines with largely ineffectual spells that fizzed and crackled. Christopher was creeping forward through gaps in the vines, trying to get close to the intruders. He had a terrifying expression on his face and Jake was glad that he'd only glimpsed it for a moment: his teeth were bared, seeming somehow sharper than usual. The werewolf was growling, threateningly. Mahri and the Barracloughs stood, straight-backed and fierce beside their friend, magic crackling from their fingertips.

"Where is she?" Ivy demanded. "What have you done with her?"

The vines twisted and contorted urgently around the men, whose magic was beginning to fail them. Jake watched, wide-eyed, as they were lifted from the ground, their arms and legs caught in the furious vegetation, their cries muffled by the suffocating leaves.

"Give – me – back – my – little – girl!" Ivy cried, punctuating every word with a distinct tug on the vines.

A hole formed in the thick foliage below the stricken men, and an Astrid-shaped shadow crawled through on her hands and knees.

"ASTRID!" Jake squealed, and squirmed out of Reggie's grasp. Reggie and John shouted, making a grab for him, but he evaded their well-meaning hands.

Fearlessly, Jake ran out of the teashop, leaping through the twisting vines and hitting his sister square in the chest. She fell backwards, hugging him.

"You're okay!" he shouted happily, crying and laughing all at the same time.

"I'm okay," she said, holding him tightly. "Ivy! I'm okay!" she shouted, through the vines.

Abruptly, the enraged vegetation changed direction, reaching out to Astrid and swarming around her instead. The two men hung motionless in the air, still surrounded by vines, only their eyes visible through the tangle of stems.

Astrid petted the vines that were thronging around her. "I'm okay, Martha," she told them. She stood up,

Jake still clinging to her middle. "Don't hurt them."

"Astrid!" Christopher caught her and Jake in a hug. "I was so worried – I'm so sorry!"

Astrid hugged him back, happy to be home. "You didn't do anything –"

"I wasn't watching you properly," he mumbled into her hair, voice thick with emotion. "If anything had happened to you –"

"I should have told you where I was going," she insisted, but got no further, as she was mobbed by the rest of the occupants of the Arcade, who all wanted to hold her, and stroke her hair, and see that she was alright.

She squirmed out of the middle of them and ran up to Ivy, who was standing a little way away, a strange expression on her face.

"I'm sorry, Ivy," she said, suddenly afraid that she was angry with her. "I shouldn't have gone out alone – I won't do it again." Ivy stared down at her, silently – unable to speak. "I brought you these," Astrid added, holding out the bunch of battered wildflowers. "I swapped them for some seeds at the churchyard – oh," she said, dropping the flowers.

Ivy had sunk to her knees and pulled Astrid into her arms; she was trembling, and Astrid didn't know what to do about that so she hugged Ivy back, hoping it would help.

"I thought I'd never see you again," Ivy whispered, into her hair.

Astrid was shocked to hear the hitch in the witch's voice, and she pulled back to see tears on Ivy's cheeks.

"I'm so glad you're home," she said, stroking her arm listlessly. "I was so scared..."

Astrid nodded, overwhelmed by the rush of emotion she felt for her new family.

"Me too," she said, guiltily. "I'm sorry."

Ivy shook her head, laughing through her tears. "We'll talk about it tomorrow," she said. "But I'm really happy that you're safe. The flowers are lovely, thank you," she said, picking them up.

Astrid watched her gaze travel to the two captive men at the end of the Arcade; Ivy's eyes narrowed.

"It wasn't their fault," said Astrid quickly. "They brought me home again – they'll explain if you let them down."

"Hmph," said Ivy, and strode along the corridor, everyone parting as she went. "Astrid has vouched for you, gentlemen," she announced, to the helpless men. "So I'm going to let you down, but not here – the vines will escort you upstairs. If you try anything funny I'll let them do what they want with you, and believe me when I tell you that currently they're quite angry."

She turned and added, almost sweetly. "Oh yes, and they have been known to eat people."

ooo

Martha, while obeying Ivy in as much as she 'escorted' the two intruders upstairs, had other ideas about letting them go. She was currently dangling them upside-down by their ankles, still swathed in vegetation.

Ivy let it pass, pointedly ignoring them while everyone made a fuss of Astrid and her brother, who promised – at last – to go and put his pyjamas on now that his sister was safe. Astrid went to change too, after Ivy promised her in a whisper that Martha wouldn't really eat the two men.

A considerable amount of time was spent reassuring Charlotte and John that they were at no risk from Martha's wrath, being not only invited guests but also friends of the family. They were understandably rather nervous, and were standing as far away from the tangle of vines on the ceiling as they could politely get. Professor Zarrubabel, who had emerged from his hatch declaring that he didn't want to miss any of the fun, had scoffed at that – but Charlotte had glared at him until he shut up, one of the few people who could. Ivy was impressed.

When Mahri had supplied everyone with tea and the children had rushed back out of their rooms, not wanting to miss anything, Ivy asked Martha to let the men down.

There were a few minutes of silent argument between witch and Arcade, but eventually Martha relented, depositing the two rumpled wizards on the floor with the air of spitting something out.

The inhabitants of the Arcade stared at them.

"Hoxley and Collins," said Professor Barraclough, with a low whistle.

"I *knew* they were up to something," Christopher growled.

"That's not their names," said Astrid, surprised. "That's Ogden Rake," she said, pointing at the bear-like man who was warily getting to his feet, "and he's Alexander Hardwick. Xander." The other man blinked at her, trying to regain some kind of focus.

"Hello," Hardwick managed, from the floor.

"Awk! You're in trouble! Awk!" Boscoe squawked, making a feint at them. He soared away as Rake ducked, and landed on a bookshelf on the far wall, clicking his beak menacingly.

"You *lied* on your application?" demanded Professor Zarrubabel, outraged. "How could you?! The tomes of Zarrubabel and Barraclough have never been so polluted!"

"Oh dry up, Hector," said Joanna, automatically. "They've done worse than that."

"And *you* boy – you spotted them!" Zarrubabel rounded on Christopher, who got ready to duck. "Perhaps I was wrong about you," the spectre mused. "I'll give you one more chance – but if you mess this one up," he threatened, waggling his translucent finger under Christopher's astonished nose, "you'll be out on the street, d'you hear?"

He hurtled across the floor, narrowly avoiding a collision with the (current) source of his ire. "You wicked, pox-ridden, illiterate *fiends!*" he hissed. "You foul, putrescent haters of books!"

"Hector, steady on," said Professor Barraclough wearily. "They didn't actually *do* anything to the books."

But Professor Zarrubabel ignored him, caught up in his own righteous fury. "You dog-breathed, addle-brained, cowardly bibliophobes!"

"Hector –" Joanna interrupted, but to no avail.

"Malignant toads!" he shouted. "Wretched half-wit milksops! How dare you mistreat our books? You filthy cod-eaters!" He took a deep breath and drew himself up to his full height – which was quite impressive, given that he was already floating a foot or so above his box – and pointed a grey-tinged finger. "Long may you wake in torment!" he spat.

There was a ringing silence.

"Are you finished?" Ivy asked, brusquely.

"What?" he asked, twisting around like a demented spinning top. "Er, yes..." he deflated, unnerved by Ivy's fearsome countenance.

"Good," she said, striding forwards. "Why did you take Astrid?" she asked, her voice clipped and steely.

"Begging your pardon, Miss," said Rake, almost timidly, "but we didn't take her. She followed us."

Ivy looked at Astrid, who was wearing a very sheepish expression indeed, and raised an expectant eyebrow.

"I'm sorry," she said, quietly. "They were behaving suspiciously. I know it was stupid," she added, taking in the expressions on the assembled adults' faces. "I won't ever do it again, I promise."

"What were they doing?" Mahri asked, intrigued.

"They sort of *faded* when Master Post came in," she said. "And I didn't like it."

"Why?" asked Christopher, sharply.

Rake looked at him, head slightly to one side. "Yes, she said you didn't like him very much," he said.

Christopher blushed as everyone looked at him curiously.

"What's wrong with Quentin?" asked Professor Barraclough, bemused. "He's a charming fellow."

"I just don't like him, that's all," said Christopher,

looking at the floor. "And I've heard some awful things about his father."

"You shouldn't listen to rumour, idiot boy," spat Professor Zarrubabel.

Christopher gave him a withering look. "I don't, normally," he retorted. "And I'm hardly likely to get the opportunity with you making a racket all the time. Anyway, it was the Widow Jenkins who told me, and I believe her."

"Arabella Jenkins?" asked Joanna, diving further off-topic. "You know, now you mention it I *do* remember something about her and Old Post – something about her sister, perhaps... Oh, what was her name, Morton?"

"Florence," Morton replied.

"Yes, that's right," she said. "Florence. Folks used to say that he jilted her and she died of a broken heart."

"Widow Jenkins is of the opinion that he did considerably more than that," said Christopher, taking a perverse pleasure in how interested Post's apparent enemies were looking at this new development. "She thinks he ate her heart."

There was a stunned silence.

"You mean *literally*?" asked Reggie, agog. "He *actually* ate her *actual* heart?"

Christopher shrugged and Reggie paled; behind him, Charlotte put her hand to her throat, appalled.

"Right," said Reggie, in a small voice. "I just wanted to make sure."

"Well," said Joanna, shocked.

"It's not like old Arabella to just make things up," said Professor Zarrubabel, slowly, and Christopher wondered whether he, too, was equally appalled.

"Even so, old chap," said Morton Barraclough, "we have absolutely no proof – and neither party is still alive, so we'll never find any."

"And there's no reason to hold it against his son," said Ivy, in an uneasy tone. "Even if he is a bit, well..." she faltered under their gaze. "Smooth."

"Come on now girl, you can't take against someone

just because they're *smooth*," John chuckled. The mood in the Arcade relaxed a little.

"You can," said Christopher, sounding oddly like he was defending her.

"Oho," said John, chuckling again. He gave Christopher a knowing look and he went very pink.

"Actually," said Rake, interrupting, "we have very good reasons for disliking Quentin Post."

The two wizards had been listening to the conversation with interest, relaxing slightly now that the threat of being crushed alive by angry vegetation had passed.

"Oh?" said Professor Zarrubabel, coldly. "He always was devilishly clever when it came to finance. I suppose you're business rivals, out to occupy his niche."

"No, actually," said Hardwick, shortly.

"He's wanted in connection with several deaths," Rake explained, in his oddly musical voice. "And we suspect he might have been behind the theft of several – ah – *artefacts* over the last few years."

"Much like his father," said Hardwick, nodding. "He's a very dangerous man."

"Who *are* you?" asked Ivy, staring between the two of them, all anger forgotten.

Rake coughed and pulled a battered, copper medallion out of his pocket, which he held out for them to see.

Ivy leaned forward; engraved on the medallion was a twisting triquetra bound in a circle around an ornate 'CM'. She looked up at Rake, eyebrows raised.

"We're Special Constables with the Court of Miracles."

22
The Vesicae Piscis

Christopher wondered for a few seconds whether his ears had failed him; he shook his head just in case.

"I beg your pardon?" said Mahri, after a full minute of staring at them.

"The – er – Court of Miracles," Rake repeated, uncertainly.

"Good God, man," exclaimed Morton Barraclough, abruptly. "I thought you were a myth!"

Hardwick smiled and nudged Rake in the ribs. "How many times have we heard that?" he said.

"I thought they were shut down at the end of the nineteenth century," said Mahri, frowning.

Christopher nodded. "Something to do with the consolidation of the mundane police force," he said.

"Don't be stupid," Professor Zarrubabel sneered. "They were heavily involved with the war effort – both wars, as I recall."

Christopher rolled his eyes.

"*Rumoured* to be," Professor Barraclough corrected his friend. "Rumoured to be involved. No-one actually knew for certain."

"Oh come *on*, Morton," cried Zarrubabel, exasperated. "We weren't just fighting a mundane war – how in hell do you think we dealt with the magical factions?"

"You always did love a conspiracy," Joanna interjected. "And besides, a lot of witches and wizards shored up their local defences themselves. I know Mother did. Every time I came home from the Land Army there was a small coven of women in the parlour, knitting socks for soldiers and casting shield spells over them."

Ivy smiled slightly, despite herself, and Christopher wondered whether she was remembering doing the same for Sam. The trouble was that shield spells didn't last forever – and the recipient had to be wearing the charmed item in order for them to work.

"Yes, and my father was in the Home Guard with Great Uncle Bertram," said Professor Barraclough. "They were always sneaking up magical defences around the town."

"Well," said Mahri. "That's what it was about, doing your bit."

There was a rumble of agreement amongst the older members of the group. Christopher smiled quietly to himself, wishing that his father could have been amongst them; he would have enjoyed the discussion.

Reggie cleared his throat, feeling that they had become distracted.

"Er – I hate to interrupt, but – for the uninitiated – what *is* the Court of Miracles?"

"It used to be the sort of magical equivalent of the police force," Christopher explained, with a glance at Rake, who nodded. "Before there really was a police force."

"It's part of the old system of Triquetra," Professor Barraclough explained. "The 'Duties'."

"There were always three," said Rake, in his deep, melodic voice. "A Preacher, a Witch and a Law-man. We're the Law-men."

Astrid smiled; she knew this part. "Together, all three of them looked after the Manor – the area that they lived in and had responsibility for. The Preacher looked after the soul – sins and prayers," she said, and Ivy smiled at her with a hint of pride. "The Witch looked after the body – sickness and health –"

"Not to mention deflecting the odd curse," Mahri added. The corners of Christopher's mouth twitched upwards: his history books had been full of them.

"– and the Law-men looked after the community – crimes and disputes."

"That's right," Joanna agreed. "It was a good system, and it lasted for centuries – there was a fair bit of overlap between the three Duties, too, so you might find a Witch interceding in a dispute or a Preacher purifying someone plagued by demons, or suchlike."

"I think the earliest I've seen it called 'Triquetra' is in the late 7th century AD," mused Professor Zarrubabel, somewhat pompously. "Which is about the same time that the symbol –" he waved a spectral hand at the medallion that Rake was fingering, "the three *vesicae piscis* – was first beginning to be used. The circle twining around them was a later development of course."

"It wouldn't surprise me if the system wasn't in place earlier," Morton Barraclough mused. "Not a lot got written down after the Romans left."

"You can always tell a church that had a Triquetra Preacher because it had a habit of creeping into the architecture," said Professor Zarrubabel, knowledgeably. "It pops up on roof bosses and on fonts, that sort of thing. Sometimes it's the symbol of the three hares instead."

"Three hares?" asked Reggie. "You mean the Tinner's Hares?"

As one, twelve pairs of eyes turned to him. He blinked.

"Three hares, dancing in a circle, only have one ear a-piece when you look closely," he gave a half-shrug, a little embarrassed at the attention. "My Bess had a sister who lived in Devon and they're all over the place. The tin-miners were supposed to favour them as good luck."

"That's it exactly," said Professor Zarrubabel, giving him a distasteful look. "Though I'm surprised you'd know that."

"Behave, Hector, or I'll close up your book," said Joanna, automatically.

"Hmph," he grunted, and Morton picked up the thread of the story.

"It's said to be a puzzle of sorts," he explained. "What with the ears – an optical illusion. I think after a while it became a sort of mark of skill to get the motif right."

"Didn't it start off as a Buddhist symbol?" asked Christopher, remembering something from his dim and distant past.

"Yes, that's right," said Professor Barraclough. "Came over the Silk Road at the same time as the story of the

Silk Princess and the Moon Rabbit."

"What's a Moon Rabbit?" asked Jake, who had been absorbing all this with wide-eyed fascination, and had seized on the one thing that he at least knew the shape of. "I like rabbits. They couldn't go to the moon, though, could they? It's too far away."

"That's another story entirely," said Christopher, with a grin. "I'll tell you about it another time."

Jake nodded, mildly disappointed. He turned to Rake and Hardwick, unafraid. "Do you make miracles?"

"No, little man," said Rake, gently.

"Not for lack of trying," chuckled Hardwick. "We picked up the name in the seventeenth century – before that we had different names depending on what part of Britain you were from. I think most people knew us as 'The Sheriff's Men'."

He glanced at Rake, who continued the explanation.

"Have you heard of Robin Hood and Sheriff John, little man?" he asked, and Jake nodded. "Well, imagine that Robin Hood had been the Sheriff in John's place, and had been a good man, who treated his people fairly and tried to keep them out of trouble. He would have been worked off his feet if he'd had to do it all himself, so he appointed a Deputy Sheriff and Special Constables who did most of the legwork. He'd oversee the judgements and disputes, and keep them all in order. It's much the same today."

Jake's eyes had gone very wide indeed. "But Robin Hood stole – stealing's bad," he said, almost as a whisper. Rake laughed his great, deep laugh.

"That part we don't do," grinned Hardwick. "We try to catch people who do."

"But," said Jake, and this appeared to be troubling him, "if you don't do miracles…"

"Then why are we called the Court of Miracles?" Hardwick finished, amused at this small child with a thirst for knowledge. Jake nodded. "You're very much like your sister, you know," he said, and Jake beamed. Astrid, sitting on one of the mismatched chairs at the table, looked immensely proud of him. "It's all to do with the way people started to look at the world after the Great Purge."

"It was a time of rationalisation," said Barraclough, before the little boy could ask. "People were asking questions about their world on a scale that had never really happened before. The old ways began to get left behind, what with all the progress happening all over the place, and when things like magic or gods get left behind, people start worrying about what they might do, left to their own devices."

"Like Hades," said Christopher, chiming in. "In most of the early myths, he was the Greek god of the Underworld, caring for the souls of the dead – when other gods became more popular, he was vilified – made evil and feared."

"So when people started to understand more of the world around them during the Scientific Revolution," Professor Barraclough continued, "they started to become very afraid of the things that they couldn't explain – and magic was one of those things."

"A lot of people were punished for being Practitioners," said Joanna sadly. "Townspeople all over Europe dragged witches and wizards from their beds, tore open their store-rooms, burnt their books – they were dark times."

"Most of the time no one actually got hurt – with the exception of a couple of really bad years when the so-called Witch-Finder General was at work," Professor Barraclough allowed, grimly. "But a lot of people were fined, ostracised, that sort of thing."

"Most people hid what they were," said Christopher. "They went underground to an extent. It was much, much worse in continental Europe – people did awful things." He looked at the children and fell silent.

Joanna nodded. "When everyone had calmed down a little bit some communities came back around to the idea – they realised that there was still a place for magic in their lives," she said. "Things were passed down in families. That's what happened in Brindleford."

For reasons that Christopher couldn't quite fathom, Mahri, the Barracloughs and Professor Zarrubabel all looked at Ivy at this point. She ignored them.

"Anyway," said Barraclough. "At the time, a lot of Practitioners were forced out of their work and homes – less so here, as Joanna explained – but it was worse on the continent. Particularly in France, where there was already a vast division between the landed classes and the poor. The dispossessed started turning up in the cities – Practitioners and mundane alike – and they eventually ended up in the slums of Paris. And that's where the traditional story changes a little," he smiled.

"There was a large area of slums that became particularly famous for beggars and criminals," he continued. "Called the 'Court of Miracles'. Most of the beggars feigned injuries or handicaps of some kind in order to bring in a few more pennies, you see, and when they returned to the slums these injuries would 'miraculously' disappear. That's how the slums got their name."

"Of course, that's not the *whole* story," Zarrubabel broke in. "A good many Practitioners found themselves in the midst of this, and decided to ply their trade amongst the more unsavoury element of Paris society." He cackled. "Many of them became expert criminals, and when they revitalised the British Sheriff's Men, shortly after the clearance of the Paris slums they took on a lot of them."

"I think the theory was that they'd know all the tricks of the trade," said Hardwick. "So they'd be able to spot someone else doing it a mile off."

"And very effective it was too," said Professor Barraclough. He gave them a rather pointed look. "Until they were shut down."

"Not every unit was closed down," Rake chuckled. "There were a couple of Specials in every major town up until after the war –"

Professor Zarrubabel harrumphed.

"That all changed in the sixties, though – since no one thought we were still in operation, people thought they could get away with cursing their mundane neighbours or using charmed money when paying their Council Tax or what-have-you," said Hardwick with a wry smile. "A couple of the old Specials got together and reformed a few local units, away from the centres of mundane policing – we more or less went from there."

"At least that explains why you're in Brindleford, of all places," remarked Mahri, amused.

"Quite," said the Professor.

"It's one of the places in Britain with an unusually high proportion of Practitioners," Hardwick explained. "It made sense."

"So, you're a sort of underground magical police force?" Reggie asked, slowly.

"That's right," Hardwick confirmed.

"And you're after this Quentin Post chap, whose father is supposed to have *eaten* someone's heart?"

"Yes," said Rake, his smile evaporating.

"You mentioned deaths," said Ivy, speaking up for the first time. "I do think he's a bit too smooth, and I might be persuaded to think of him as some kind of gentleman thief, but I honestly can't imagine him killing anyone."

Christopher frowned to himself. If he was honest, nor could he, but he didn't feel like being honest just now.

"We've been monitoring Post for some time now," Rake began, and it struck Christopher that he was choosing his words very carefully. "His trips abroad have often coincided with the disappearance of particular magical artefacts," he said, slowly. "And occasionally he has left a city immediately before the discovery of a body."

"That doesn't make someone guilty," said Mahri, frowning. "Just because he was *there*. Do you want a cup of tea, by the way?"

"Er – yes, thank you –" said Rake, momentarily distracted.

"Thank you," Hardwick nodded.

"We know that he met with several of the victims, shortly before their deaths," said Rake, as Mahri busied herself with Ivy's kettle. "But up until recently it's been very difficult to make any other kind of connection."

"What changed?" asked Christopher, curious.

"We're not sure," Hardwick admitted. "But for some reason he's been getting sloppy. He was in Cairo earlier this year," he continued. Christopher and the Barracloughs sat up a little straighter, interested. "And he met with the owners of several small but exclusive antique businesses – most of them bent, as far as I can tell."

"Well," scoffed Professor Zarrubabel. "The trade in black market artefacts is as rife amongst the mundane as it is amongst Practitioners."

"Quite," said Rake. "But all of these proprietors held in their possession suspect magical artefacts."

"Like what?" asked Reggie, fascinated.

"Oh, well, you get the usual sort of thing," said Hardwick, accepting his tea from Mahri gratefully. "Kettles that attack people, books that try to read *you* –"

The Barracloughs both chuckled at this.

"– a huge variety of objects with potent love charms on. Then there are the more traditional things like Come-Again-Coins, Seven-League Boots, that sort of stuff."

"They're not necessarily evil, per se," Rake added, stirring his tea. "But they can cause one hell of a nuisance in the wrong hands."

"And then there are things that have taken on a life of their own, they're usually pretty nasty," Hardwick continued. "We had a bit of trouble a few months ago with one of those photo-booth things that was eating people..."

"The worst ones are things that are *intended* to be evil," said Rake, soberly. "They're difficult to spot until it's too late, usually, and the things they do to people are far from pleasant."

Christopher nodded, thinking back to some of the

gruesome illustrations that he had seen in Post's book.

"Anyway," said Hardwick. "The shops he targeted stocked all sorts of black market goods – a couple of them specialising in the most dangerous kind. That got our interest, as you can imagine."

"The day after he left Cairo, three out of the five shop-owners were found dead, their store-rooms ransacked," said Rake as his friend took a slurp of tea. "We found his name in the appointment books of all three – which is new, he'd taken care to erase that before – but the clincher was a scrap of paper found in the last victim's hand."

Christopher found himself leaning forward slightly, entirely drawn in; they all were – even Martha's restless vines were poised along the walls, waiting for revelation.

Hardwick took a plain, brown envelope out of his jacket pocket, and slid out a crumpled scrap of paper. There were splashes of blood on the clean, white surface, and Christopher recoiled, forcing down a retch at the smell.

Hardwick delicately handed it to Professor Barraclough, who gave a shout of surprise and thrust it under Joanna and Christopher's noses. On the back of the paper was the neat silver stamp of *Zarrubabel and Barraclough, Purveyors of Fine Books*.

Christopher felt himself growl. How could he have let this happen *and not report it?* Forgetting, for a moment, the far more heinous crime of murder that had doubtless led to the tearing of the book's pages, Christopher felt a hot wave of outrage wash over him.

Post had hurt one of *his* books! A helpless, flapping thing with a life and mind of its own.

Professor Zarrubabel, rendered silent with incandescent rage, hurtled off to the dumb-waiter; a series of distant crashes suggested that he was searching for their injured book.

Livid, and shaking slightly because of it, Christopher stood and walked to the sink, using movement to fend off his rage. Carefully, he poured himself a glass of water, glaring at the cupboards in front of him.

The Barracloughs were interrogating Hardwick and Rake about the shop-keeper, and about the kind of things that he sold – wondering, perhaps, if he'd had a part in the illicit book trade.

Christopher felt a hand graze his arm as Ivy settled against the kitchen counter next to him, offering silent comfort. Her delicious, homely scent took over his mind and he relaxed slightly. He shot her a sideways glance and a quick, grateful smile that probably looked more like a grimace.

He leant back against the cupboards next to her, enjoying her proximity and letting it calm him down.

"How did he die, exactly?" Joanna was asking, eyes narrowed. Christopher reflected that he really wouldn't like to be Post when Joanna got hold of him.

"Their deaths were all very similar – that's how we linked them to the earlier murders, in the end," said Rake. "They were burned from the inside out – organs scorched up like someone had filled up their bodies with fire."

Hardwick nodded, soberly. "The doctor we spoke to said he was a hell of a mess on the inside – like nothing he'd ever seen." He grimaced. "They were also all missing their eyeballs."

"That sort of magic isn't easy," Professor Barraclough said, while everyone else recovered from the image. "He'd need some pretty powerful modifiers to inflict that kind of damage – their skin was undamaged, you said?"

Rake nodded. "Barely a blemish: skin, lips, nothing," he said. "Though we did find a slight bruise on his upper arm, as if he'd been held roughly." He looked up at them, and Christopher caught the haunted look in his eyes before it was replaced once more by his usual amiable expression. "It was eerie – that level of internal destruction when it just looked like he'd gone to sleep."

"That's pure fury, that is," said Mahri, appalled.

"It was such a specific method of killing that we could link the man with two other deaths in Cairo, both merchants with ties to the black market."

"That got us thinking, and we had a hunt through our old international records," said Hardwick, and Christopher could hear the note of excitement in the wizard's voice – the satisfaction at a job well done. "We found a further four murders with the same cause of death – and Post was in town for every one." He counted each one off on his fingers: "Two in Prague – one four years ago, one last year, one in Paris last winter – and one in America in April."

"That's when he had his climbing accident," said Joanna Barraclough, hollowly. "He told us he'd broken his leg, rock climbing in Yellowstone National Park."

"It wasn't a climbing accident," Hardwick confided. "Miss Crawley fought back."

"Then he hopped on the nearest private jet and headed home, telling everyone he could about his misadventure in Yellowstone," Rake added.

"As if none of it meant anything," said Ivy, hollowly.

The two Specials nodded grimly.

Christopher thought about all the business trips that Post had described to him – and how jealous he had been. For a sickening moment, he wondered what would have happened to him had he accompanied Post to London – would he ever have come back?

"He went to London the week before last," he said out loud. "Something about an auction – rare books I think."

"Did he?" asked Hardwick, interested. "We had a bit of a bother that week – a couple of goblins causing mayhem in the Town Hall... Did he say where in London?"

"No," said Christopher. "But I can give you the dates – he wanted me to go with him. Said that I needed to get out more."

"Well, I'm glad you didn't," said Joanna Barraclough, with feeling.

Beside him, he thought he felt Ivy shift nearer to him, but it must have been his imagination.

"Did he say what he was after?" she asked, interested.

"No – but I'd guess that he came across Prospero Bone

in whatever he picked up."

"Prospero Bone?" asked Professor Barraclough, and Christopher filled the others in on Post's state of high excitement that morning.

"I wonder what he's after," said the Professor, when he'd finished.

"Something dangerous, I'll wager," said Hardwick, grimly. "And we can't let him get it, whatever it is."

"He seems to have decided that this 'Bone' fellow had it last..." mused Joanna, rubbing her chin thoughtfully. "Christopher," she said, suddenly looking up at him. "You've been working closely with him, do you think you have a reasonable handle on the ins and outs of his research?"

"Yes, I suppose so," he nodded, having an inkling of where this was going.

"Could you take these chaps through it, dear?"

The two Specials looked at him, intently excited.

"Easily – I could have a booklist and notes prepared by Tuesday, probably, if there aren't any deliveries."

"I'll take them," Reggie volunteered. "This is more important."

"I'll take you through the deliveries," said Joanna, as Rake gave Christopher an appraising look.

"By Tuesday, you say?" he grinned, amicably. "You really *don't* like Post, do you?"

"Apparently with good reason," Christopher said, not even noticing the slight tremor of a growl in his voice. "He tends to come in Monday mornings, Wednesday afternoons and Thursday mornings. This morning was something of a departure from normality."

Rake nodded. "We'd best avoid him for the moment," he said. "Wouldn't want him getting suspicious. You'll keep an eye on him?"

"Of course," said Christopher, uncharitably happy to be able to discomfit Post in any socially acceptable way he could think of.

He glanced at Ivy, profoundly grateful that she hadn't been taken in by Post's perfect smile and easy charm. If he had hurt her...

A crash from below interrupted his thoughts.

"I'VE GOT IT!" thundered Professor Zarrubabel, rocketing up the dumb-waiter so fast that he made the bookshelves rattle. Boscoe took off, startled, and perched on Reggie's shoulder, where he deemed it to be much safer. The ghastly spectre waved a book at them in enraged triumph. "The slimy, pox-ridden fiend repaired it – but the stamp's too perfect."

He thrust it at Barraclough; Joanna and Christopher immediately sprung to his side, peering at the book, which was flustered at all the sudden interest and vibrating very slightly.

"I wouldn't have spotted it if I hadn't known to look," said Zarrubabel, with a kind of grudging respect. "And I wouldn't have found it at all if the ledgers hadn't been kept as well as they are," he muttered.

Christopher looked up from the book, surprised. Zarrubabel refused to meet his eyes, instead hovering beside Astrid like some kind of grotesque, luminous balloon. Christopher kept his mouth shut, deciding to take compliments where he could.

"How are we going to get him?" the spectre demanded of the two Specials, who shared a look.

"We can't *officially* ask you to help," said Rake, carefully. "But –"

"Honestly," interrupted Ivy, in that same, quiet, reasonable voice. "I don't think you're going to be able to stop any of us." She looked around. "He's harmed the books, so there's no way either of the Professors, Joanna or Christopher will back down –"

"And where they stand, so do we," said John, firmly. He and Charlotte had stayed quiet through the discussion, but now they went and stood beside their old friends, resolute.

"Quite," said Ivy. "I can't see Mahri or Reggie letting anything nefarious go on in their own home," she continued, and they both nodded; Boscoe squawked his approval. "And nor, apparently, will Boscoe," she added, without missing a beat. "As you said, we can't let him have whatever it is he's after. If what you've told us is true, he's dangerous enough as it is."

"Don't forget us," Jake exclaimed, tugging urgently on the sleeve of her cardigan. "We can help!"

Astrid joined her brother, sticking her chin out in defiance. Christopher started - he had quite forgotten they were there in all the excitement. After the Constables' description of the bodies he suspected there would be a few nightmares to soothe.

"We won't let him get away with anything," she said, in a tone that brooked no argument. Ivy, however, gave her a Look.

"We'll stay out of trouble," the girl promised. "I wouldn't put Jake at risk – but we can help from here, with reading and taking notes and things."

"Yes!" said Jake, excited. "I like reading!"

Ivy relented, though she didn't look happy about it. "We'll talk about it tomorrow," she said.

Rake and Hardwick surveyed the assembled volunteers staring defiantly at them, and laughed, approvingly.

"Thank you," Rake said, in his deep, cheery voice. "As we said, we couldn't ask, but since you volunteered." He glanced at Hardwick, who grinned.

"I'll speak to the Sheriff," he said. "And see if Otto has got the odd thing lying around that could help you out."

"That's all very good," said Mahri. "But where do we start?"

"Well," said Rake, thoughtfully. "If Christopher could give us a brief summary of what he's after..."

"Something very powerful and very dangerous, I'd say," he responded, resisting the urge to calm the flustered book in the Professor's hands. "He thinks it disappeared in the seventeenth century – hidden by Mortimer Bone, who was an architect. He built a few of the churches around here, and Post was really excited about that. Oh –" he said, thinking back to the book of horrors that Post had forgotten, all those weeks ago. "He had a book – one of his own, it got mixed up in the returns."

"I remember," said Ivy. "He'd just introduced himself and wouldn't take the hint that I wasn't interested – flattering though his compliments were. Christopher came in and rescued me." She gave him a small smile that made him blush, hotly.

"Er – yes," he said, hoping that no one had noticed. "Anyway, it was full of the most awful dark artefacts I'd ever seen – even worse than the ones in *The Devil's Mirror*. There were bird cages that ate people and clocks that aged you uncontrollably – but he'd marked a particular page."

"Do you remember what it was?" asked Hardwick, urgently.

"Yes," said Christopher, the whole room hanging on his every word. "It was something called 'The Chalice of Knowledge'."

Professor Zarrubabel sucked in a deep, ghostly breath and they turned to look at him.

"Heard of it, old chap?" asked Barraclough.

"Ye-es," he said, apparently thinking hard. "My grandfather told me a story about it once – do you remember, Joanna?"

"No," she said, after a moment's thought. "But then he had a bit of a thing against girls learning anything that wasn't kitchen related, if you recall. It was a very different time," she assured Astrid, whose mouth had fallen open in horror.

"He was a bit of a *traditionalist*," said Professor Barraclough, carefully.

Christopher tried not to laugh, despite the seriousness of the situation, enjoying this rare glimpse of family politics.

Professor Zarrubabel coughed, awkwardly, and Christopher suspected that this had been something of a sore point in their youth.

"Nevertheless," he continued, huffily, "he told me that the Chalice of Knowledge was a very dark, very dangerous artefact, created by a well-meaning wizard that had no idea of the destructive power he was unleashing. It was said that if you drank from the Chalice you would receive all the knowledge of the ages – at a price. The Chalice would, in return, take a little part of you with it, increasing its knowledge and power. Grandfather said that over the centuries it became more than a little alive."

Christopher shuddered, putting a comforting hand on Jake's head and ruffling his hair. The tiny boy was silently shivering with fear – and doing his utmost not to show it. Jake wrapped an arm around Christopher's leg.

"It was a potent lure for many wizards of every age and nation, and much good it did them," he continued, grimly. "Death and war followed the Chalice as different individuals and factions sought control over it."

"You know what they say," said Mahri, quietly. "Knowledge is power."

"Quite," Zarrubabel agreed. "He told me that ultimately, it destroyed every place it came to, with rulers stopping at nothing to possess it, only to have it possess them in the end. Then, of course, it would be passed on to some unsuspecting nobody, who would transport it to a new location – but never without succumbing to its siren call.

"Grandfather told me that it had the power to speak. To whisper things," he trailed off, lost in his own narrative. "I remember as a boy thinking that giving something a small copy of my mind wouldn't be that high a price for ultimate knowledge..."

"Good job you never came across it, then," said Joanna, firmly. "As a general rule, you shouldn't trust anything that whispers to you in the dark."

"Hmm," said the ghostly Professor, unconvinced. "Anyway, he told me it was last heard of at the time of the Great Purge, down in London."

"Could it have been lost in the fire?" asked Christopher, suddenly. Everyone looked at him, surprised. "Well, we all know – pardon me Reggie, almost all – that the great fire that ripped through London in 1666 had less to do with an unattended candle in Pudding Lane and more to do with the baker who lived there being quite blatantly cursed." He looked around: Reggie and the children still looked bemused, so he went on, "He'd annoyed a witch who had been passing through – short-changed her, possibly – and she'd cursed him. His God-fearing neighbours had taken the effects of the curse as evidence of his being a wizard and dragged him out of his bed to teach him a lesson. They hunted through the house and bakery for any evidence of witchcraft – which of course they never found, since he wasn't actually a Practitioner – but they burnt it down anyway, because the lack of any actual evidence just made him more 'cunning'."

He paused. It was such a cruel and stupid thing to have done.

"Over the next three days a large portion of London burned down, which spurred more violence and even lynchings in the street – Practitioners weren't the only victims, either. The mob also tried their luck with the French and Dutch immigrants that lived in the burning slums, assuming that this was some kind of early terrorist attack. Surprisingly few people died, though, and most of *them* perished in the impromptu refugee camps that the survivors were forced to live in after the fire had been put out." He frowned. "A lot of magical books and artefacts were lost in that fire, as people took advantage of the flames and confusion to get rid of anything they feared or didn't understand – or anything that could have been used against them. They were afraid."

"Nothing much changes, does it, lad?" Professor Barraclough said sadly.

"Anyway," said Christopher, heavily. "There's always the chance that the Chalice was destroyed in the fire – given its rather violent history I'd have thought we'd have heard more about it over the last few centuries."

"Unless its name has changed," Joanna Barraclough

pointed out. "That happens all the time with rare books. People forget, or spell it wrong and no one can find the damn thing, even when it's right there in front of them. Maybe it's the same with artefacts?"

"Let's hope so," said Hardwick, diplomatically. "But we can't take the chance that it's still in existence."

"No," said Ivy. "He trusts you, doesn't he, Christopher? Post, I mean."

"Er – I think so," he said. "In a patronising sort of way."

"Perfect," she smiled, and his heart did that funny flip thing that it always did in her presence. He ignored it. "If he thinks he's cleverer than you he won't expect you to be up to anything," she continued. "Can you delay his research in any way? Lost books, people borrowing them, that sort of thing?"

"I can," he said. "But not by much – he's got used to me being pretty quick with requests."

"Yes," said Joanna, smiling craftily. "But he's after information on an obscure historic architect; it *will* take longer to look for things. Just make it take slightly longer than you should – we'll make a show of constantly piling work on you."

"Oh, good idea, Jo," agreed the Professor. "We can say we want you to do a full inventory or something – some kind of made up probationary exercise."

"Alright," said Christopher, even though he did a full inventory every four weeks. "But that will only hold him back for so long, eventually he'll get suspicious."

"While you're keeping him down we'll be reading up on this Prospero Bone, find out if there's anything to the church theory," said Professor Barraclough. "Then, if we find anything, we can have a nose about some of the churches. That is –" he looked at the Specials, aware that he was getting away from himself slightly, "if that's alright with you gentlemen."

"As long as you let us know what you find and don't do anything stupid, I can't see a reason to object," said Rake, with a sly smile. "Just last week, the Sheriff was saying we could do with a bit more community involvement."

"Excellent!" said Mahri, rubbing her hands together. "We can get started right now."

"We can get started first thing in the morning," said Ivy, sternly. "It's a day off for most of us, anyway. And –" she raised a hand to the many and varied objections being voiced – mostly by the children; "*And* it's well past Jake and Astrid's bedtimes."

Astrid looked very much like she wanted to argue with this, but she shut her mouth firmly, wisely deciding not to push her luck too many times in one day.

"Okay," she said. "Come on Jake, we should brush our teeth." She took his hand and led him – still protesting – away to the bathroom.

Behind her, as she had suspected that they would, the adults settled back around the kitchen table, planning the way forward.

The hunt was on.

23
The Font of Folly

Hector Zarrubabel was indulging in one of his favourite pass-times. It was up there with 'irritating Christopher' and 'making a mess that someone else will have to clean up'.

He turned a page, breathing in the memory of the smell of paper, content. He loved research. Particularly late at night, when there were no impudent shop-boys, chattering children or disapproving sisters to get in the way.

And what a fascinating topic!

He closed the book he was reading and reached for the next, making brief notes on a piece of parchment on the desk. It was dark and cool in the back office of the bookshop, which suited him fine. Everyone else had long since gone to bed, preferring to be up and around during the day, but Zarrubabel had decided to get a head start.

He hadn't even bothered to light a lamp while he worked; his own, ectoplasmic glow was sufficient to read by. He chuckled to himself. It wasn't as if he had to worry about damaging his eyesight these days, anyway.

He scanned the chapters of the book in front of him, searching for any reference to the Chalice of Knowledge. He had decided to start with the magical aspect of the research on the reasonable assumption that it would be easier for him to find information on the Chalice than on obscure mundane architects. The shop-boy would be better suited to hunting that sort of thing out during the day.

He might peruse the relevant material later, when he needed a break – if only to show the silly young whelp up.

History student.

Humph.

Zarrubabel sneered to himself in the eerie graveyard light of his own body.

He really was a worthless lump, that boy. He honestly

couldn't understand what his sister or Morton saw in him – let alone Mistress Burwell, who was far too well brought up to be mixing with *his* sort.

He snorted angrily to himself and moved onto the next book.

Perhaps he'd sneak upstairs later and wake him up, just for the sheer –

Aha, he thought. *This is more like it.*

He quickly examined the page: the story here didn't give him much more than the rambling tale his grandfather had told him, all those years ago. Really, it was more of a cautionary entry, verging on a dire warning, but it *did* have a list of the more famous possible owners of the Chalice through history. All of them appeared to have met sticky and unpleasant ends, as history attested. It read like a who's who of the powerful, evil or misled.

Emperor Qin Shi Huang... Attila the Hun... Mareschal de Retz... Vlad the Impaler... Isabella of Castille... Countess Elizabeth Bathory of Hungary... Ivan the Terrible...

They were all there, from vague references to Nero and Caligula, all the way to Queen Mary I of England. Zarrubabel grimaced at the last entry on the page.

'*The Chalice of Knowledge is thought to have last been in the possession of an Englishman named Matthew Hopkins (c. 1620 AD – 1647 AD). It has not been seen or heard of since.*'

He knew *that* name. Every Practitioner did.

Unconsciously, Zarrubabel picked up the cast iron poker from the stove, and spat into the grate. He pulled his notebook towards him and made a few, luminescent notes, poker still tightly gripped in his translucent hand, before settling back down to his reading.

ooo

It was very early, Christopher knew, but he was completely awake. He'd had too much information rattling around his head to sleep properly, and had been woken up at five o'clock by the dawn chorus.

He rolled over, putting off the inevitable. It was warm and comfortable in his bed, and as soon as he got up the chill of autumn would begin to steal over him. The hushed conversation they'd had the previous evening once the children had gone to bed came to his mind and he groaned into his pillow, knowing that he should get up and make a start on the hunt for Prospero Bone.

Blindly, he fumbled about on the bedside table until he found the switch for the bedside lamp. He screwed up his eyes at the light – it was far too early to do *anything* on a Sunday. He knew, though, that there would be little point in remaining in bed. There was no way he would get back to sleep while his head filled up with the gruesome possibilities the Chalice of Knowledge represented.

What would a man like Quentin Post do with ultimate power?

Christopher shuddered to think, remembering all of his nubile young nurses and his lust for dark artefacts.

Shivering, he pulled on his clothes and headed out into the main room of the Arcade still pulling his jumper over his head, feeling that he'd need a very strong cup of tea before he faced the day.

Ivy was already sitting at the kitchen table, a mug of peppermint tea in her hand. She was staring, as if for inspiration, at the photograph of her late husband, dressed in his battle-fatigues in some foreign land.

Not wanting to disturb her, he made his way to the sink as quietly as he could, using a muffling charm on the tap and the kettle. The smell of Ivy's peppermint reached out to him, clearing the remaining fug of sleep from his mind, and he changed his mind about the tea, reaching for the jar of dried mint instead.

By the time he had made some toast, allowing the crushed green leaves to steep for a couple of minutes, Ivy had noticed his presence and returned the picture of Sam to its usual place on the bookshelf.

"Toast looks like a good idea," she said, as he sat down, and set about making herself some.

They ate in silence, each lost in their own dark thoughts.

"Do you think we'll find it?" Ivy asked, eventually. "The Chalice, I mean."

Christopher shrugged, and continued munching his toast.

Then:

"Even if we *do* find it," Ivy said, slowly, continuing her own train of thought, "if Post is as powerful as we're being led to believe, it's going to take some strong magic to keep him away from it." She looked up at him, and he could already see the worry in her eyes. "He strikes me as someone who can be rather determined when he wants something."

Christopher grunted his agreement, thinking of Post's continued pursuit of Ivy.

"Christopher," she said, softly. "What happens if we have to fight him?"

She sounded frightened, but more than that – there was a strange calm about her, as if she had accepted that stopping Post's acquisition of the Chalice was something that had to be done. Something that *she* had to do.

"It may not come to that," said Christopher, hoping that this would prove to be true. "If we can find it before Post does – or convince him that it was destroyed in antiquity then it won't matter."

Ivy gave him a look that made him feel like his primary school teacher had caught him trying to be clever.

"There are plenty of other dark things he could go after if he wants to increase his magical power," she said, in a slightly withering tone that did absolutely nothing for his self-confidence. "If we stop him getting this one, he'll just try to find another, and another."

Christopher sighed; she had a point.

"Let the Court of Miracles worry about that," he said. "We're not part of the Triquetra – there isn't one, these days. It's up to them to figure out what to do with him."

Ivy looked out into the garden, and Christopher had the sudden impression that she was avoiding his gaze.

"What is it?" he asked, softly, reaching out for her hand. "Ivy?"

She looked up at him, surprised to find his hand on hers. She smiled slightly and bit her lip.

"Do you remember yesterday, when the Barracloughs were talking about the aftermath of the Great Purge?" she asked.

Christopher nodded, wondering why she looked so uncomfortable.

"And Joanna said that things were passed down in families in Brindleford?"

Another nod.

"Well, mine was the family that things were passed down in," she said, heavily. "Around here, the Witch of the Triquetra was always a Chambers – sometimes, of course, it would be a Wizard instead, but he'd still either be a Chambers by birth or by marriage."

Christopher was aware that his mouth was hanging open, and quickly shut it.

"Oh," he said, unable to think of anything more intelligent. He had a sip of his cooling tea, trying to fit this new information into his head.

He remembered Professor Zarrubabel and the Barracloughs talking, months ago, about Ivy's family, and how there had always been a Chambers in Brindleford, in one form or another. He remembered too, to their cryptic allusions to the stress of being a Chambers, and understood.

"Oh," he said again, and wondered how to phrase the next question. "Was your mother...?"

"No," said Ivy, with a sigh. "She and my father died when I was quite young. My grandmother was, and theoretically it then fell to my aunts, but they felt that they were too old when she died." She sighed again. "Everyone expected me to come home and take over, but I – I didn't want to."

"It does seem like a demanding thing to take on," Christopher said, carefully. "The care of an entire community."

"It wasn't that I didn't want the responsibility," she assured him, sounding very much like she wanted to convince herself.

"Of course not," he murmured, encouragingly.

"But after what they did when my father died..." she looked at him, and he saw the pain reflected in her striking blue eyes. "The people here more or less abandoned this place – said it was cursed, that my mother had brought it on him, somehow. And then she got sick, too, and it was just the aunts and my grandmother, and they couldn't keep their shops open alone. The businesses moved away because people were too afraid to come here."

Her words were tumbling out of her in a rush, like she'd kept them inside for so long that they'd never thought they'd see the light of day, and seeing the opportunity they were all falling over one another to escape. She held onto his hand tightly, as if the contact was grounding her, allowing her to let it all out for probably the first time.

More than ever, Christopher longed to pull her into his arms and make everything better – or at least, make it seem like it was for a little while, until things seemed smaller and more manageable once more.

"My mother tried *so hard*," she said, with an anger that had festered inside her for nearly two decades. "And when it suited them, they just walked away. Do you know, for all that she did for people, when my grandmother died there was only me and Sam, and Mahri and my aunts at her funeral. She probably delivered half of Brindleford, and tended them when they were sick, and helped lay their relatives out when they died – and not a single one had the decency to pay their respects to her!"

She pushed her dark hair out of her face with unaccustomed venom.

"It was like they'd just forgotten – like she wasn't worth the effort, and I just thought, why should I make the effort for *them?*" she thundered, brushing away hot, angry tears, "– when they couldn't be *bothered* to make the effort for my family? And now this whole Post thing has come up, and it's got everyone thinking about how nice it would be if the Triquetra was working again – and you know they're thinking that, it's in the way everyone keeps looking at me – but I'm happy as I am. I don't want to be the person that stands up for everyone. I don't want to work myself to death for people who are so ungrateful that they don't even turn up for my funeral. I don't want to be the Witch – *I don't want it*! It's not *fair*!"

She burst into tears, and Christopher moved to the chair beside her, wrapping his arms around her as she cried.

Social conventions be damned, he thought, as he rubbed her back and mumbled comforting nonsense in her ear. There was just no way that he would ever be able to stand by and do nothing when his friend was in this much pain.

"And the worst part of it is," Ivy said, thickly, when she'd calmed down a bit, "however much I don't want it, I know it's something that has to be done. There's only me left," she said, hoarsely, but with a good deal more control. "So I'll just have to get on with it. As much for you and Astrid and Jake as for anyone else."

She looked up at Christopher and gave him a wry, teary smile. "Thank you for just letting me get that out," she said, almost shyly. "I needed it."

He gave a half shrug, squeezing her shoulders.

"I just wish it didn't have to be this way," she said, sadly. "I don't know the first thing about fighting, or detecting."

"That's why you're the Witch, and Ogden Rake and Xander Hardwick are the Law-men," he said. "You're supposed to be taking care of bodies and curses."

"Yes," she allowed, "but I've got a feeling that any

'body' that gets in Post's way is going to need my help. I'm just scared that I'm going to have to stop him, and I have no idea how to do it. I don't want my inability to think to be the reason that other people die."

"Well," said Christopher, gently, patting her hand. "If it comes to it, we could always feed him to Martha."

ooo

Christopher crept down the spiral staircase into the back office of *Zarrubabel and Barracloughs'*. He could hear Professor Zarrubabel snoring noisily, and he didn't want to wake the irritable spirit.

The ghastly professor was curled up on top of one of the desks, clutching his accounts ledger and – for reasons best known to himself – the iron poker from the stove tightly to his chest. Christopher smiled, slightly. When he was asleep, Zarrubabel was almost likeable.

Almost.

Delicately, he peered over the slumbering ghost and read the notes he'd made the night before, raising an eyebrow as he noted the name 'Matthew Hopkins', which had been circled several times.

Well, at least that explains the poker, he thought, feeling an uncomfortable shiver crawl down his back. The Witch-Finder General would be enough to make anyone feel the need to take arms.

Using all the stealth he had, he extricated the inventory ledger from under Zarrubabel's nose and silently looked up everything they had on seventeenth century architects. Noiselessly, he slipped into the shop proper, collecting every book he could find into a large, tottering pile.

Balancing these, along with another couple of tomes that he thought might have references to the Chalice in and that Zarrubabel had ignored, he made his way back up into the main room of the Arcade. He nearly lost his balance at the top of the spiral staircase, knocking the wobbling stack of books against the metal rail with an audible clang.

He tensed, ready for the inevitable tirade and hail of portable items, but the poltergeist merely grunted in his sleep, and turned over.

Relieved, Christopher piloted the stack of books over to the sofas where Ivy was waiting for him, and dropped them carefully on the floor.

"I'm impressed," she said, handing him another mug of tea. "I would definitely have dropped them."

Christopher grinned, pleased that she was feeling more cheerful. "Being a werewolf does have its perks, I suppose," he said. "Weird feats of agility being one of them."

They spread the books out on the large, fraying rug between the sofas and started reading, making themselves comfortable on the floor. Periodically, one of them would tear off a sheet of paper from a pad that Ivy had found somewhere and make sporadic notes, or snort at something an author had written.

They worked steadily through the books as their Light Orbs faded and the late September sun rose behind them.

After a while, Jake wandered groggily into the room, and Ivy got up to get him his breakfast. He sat on the sofa next to them, eating his cereal and watching them with obvious curiosity while they worked.

Next to emerge was Astrid, who Christopher suspected had been up late, reading through any book she had in her room for mention of the Chalice or Prospero Bone. She made herself some toast before joining her brother.

"Have you found anything?" she asked, through a mouthful of toast.

"Some bits," said Ivy, cracking her neck. "You can give us a hand after you've got dressed, if you want."

Christopher glanced up at Astrid, who looked delighted at this, and began to wolf down her toast accordingly. He chuckled.

"You'll give yourself hiccups," he said, and a pair of emerald green eyes turned to him innocently.

Once Astrid and her brother were dressed and enthusiastically thumbing through assorted contents pages for references to their architect, it wasn't long before Mahri came over from her coach house and joined them. She picked up an armful of books and took them to one of the sofas to peruse through them.

They were so absorbed in their work that it was lunch time before anyone noticed. Reggie provided distraction in the form of bringing over Saffy and her puppies. The books were quickly whisked away to the kitchen table while the five of them stretched their aching limbs and got to their feet.

"I'll get some dinner on," said Mahri, wandering back to her Coach House. "Is cheese on toast alright for everyone? I'll stick a roast on tonight for when Joanna and Morton come back."

"The Barracloughs are coming over again?" asked Astrid, momentarily tearing her attention away from the seven delightfully squirmy puppies that were clambering all over her and her brother.

"They're doing a bit of research of their own at home," Ivy explained. "Then we're meeting up to talk through what we've found out – you and Jake can stay up, just this once," she added, pre-empting the question.

"Yes," said Reggie. "And I don't mind if you sleep in tomorrow and miss our music session. I've a little project of my own to work on." He winked at Ivy and she laughed.

"What project?" Christopher asked, lounging on the sofa with Saffy, who seemed to have adopted him as a sort of shape-shifting elder brother.

"You'll see, soon enough," said Ivy, over her shoulder.

"I want to see if it's feasible, first," said Reggie, mysteriously.

"Well, if you need any help," Christopher offered, amiably.

Reggie grinned. "I might have to ask you to puppy-sit at some point," the older man teased.

"That's not really a hardship," Christopher admitted.

He reached under the sofa and pulled out an enterprising puppy that had made a bid for freedom. "Ah, you again," he said, depositing her in Jake's waiting arms.

"You were right about that one," said Reggie, fondly. "She is a fighter – and mischievous. Like her mother was as a pup."

He ruffled Saffy's fur affectionately. She barked, possibly in reference to her alleged mischief making.

"We'll have to start thinking about finding homes for them all at some point," said Reggie, with a touch of sadness.

"You're sending them away?" gasped Jake, scandalised.

"There's just not enough room to keep them all," Reggie explained. "But we can make sure that whoever takes them will look after them well."

"I don't want any of them to go away," said Jake, fiercely, cuddling the puppy in his arms. She licked his face, affectionately.

"Sometimes that's just how things are," said Christopher, tactfully. "But Saffy will still be around, and Boscoe."

They glanced out of the window at the parrot, slumbering in the branches of the cherry tree.

"Maybe," said Ivy, as if she were thinking out loud, "Reggie would let you keep one of them."

"Really?" he stared between Ivy and Reggie with eyes the size of saucers.

Ivy looked at Reggie and raised an eyebrow – he nodded slightly, amused.

"If you promise to take very good care of her," he said. "I don't see why not."

Jake, who looked like he might be about to explode with excitement, stared at Reggie, then turned his eyes to Astrid, who was grinning.

"You'll have to ask Ivy very nicely," she said.

Jake walked up to Ivy, still clutching the young puppy in his small arms.

"Please could I keep her, Ivy?" he asked, breathlessly. "Please?"

"Do you promise to take care of feeding her, walking her, training her and cleaning up after her?" she asked, and he beamed.

"Yes," he said, nodding furiously.

"And you understand that that promise is binding, since you are making it with a witch?"

"Yes," he said, in a quiet, awed voice. "I promise to take very good care of her."

"Alright then," said Ivy. "When she's old enough, you can keep her."

Jake did a funny excited jump thing; the puppy in his arms yipped, startled by the sudden movement.

Christopher grinned and sidled up to Ivy as Reggie and the children talked happily about thinking of names for the litter.

"Your family just keeps getting bigger," he said, nonchalantly.

She gave him a playful shove. "I know – I don't know what's wrong with me," she said, smiling lightly. "First I take in you and Reggie, then the children – now a puppy..." she chuckled at herself. "I don't know what's wrong with me," she said again.

Christopher laughed.

ooo

"There's not much on him," Christopher was saying, as Mahri and Ivy cleared away the remains of a spectacular roast dinner. "He was brought up in Kent, was apprenticed to his uncle, became an architect charged with building things up and down the country – generally schools and churches," he reviewed his notes. "Substantially rebuilt the church in his home town as a sort of retirement project and died an unremarkable death in his family home."

"Not a bad life, all tolled," said Professor Barraclough cheerfully.

"There was some mention of occult involvement in his youth," Christopher added. "He was apparently fined a small amount of money in his early twenties in response, but no-one seems to know what it was for, and there's no later mention of anything."

"Also, he and his sisters seem to have lived steady and uneventful lives thereafter," said Ivy, settling back down. "Whatever people thought he'd done wasn't serious enough to warrant a full witch-hunt."

"He could have been associated with someone who was later found out to be a Practitioner," Joanna suggested. "That sort of thing happened a lot – it was supposed to discourage what was seen to be 'unhealthy' friendships." She rolled her eyes.

"What people manage to do to one another never fails to astonish me," said Mahri, refilling everyone's glasses with wine or fruit juice.

"There was one entry in the architectural dictionary that suggested his 'youthful indiscretions', as they put it, were the reason he had never married," mused Christopher. "Altogether, not particularly helpful."

"We *did* find one reference of note," said Mahri, leaning forward. "His father, Milo, died as a result of the Great Fire of London, and poor old Mortimer Bone witnessed it. He was one of the very few casualties of the fire itself. Apparently a burning beam fell in the street they were escaping along and killed him instantly. Bone was unable to save him, and his uncle – Dominic Bone, the carpenter – had to drag him away from his father's body. They returned the next day to pull him out of the rubble and took him home to Kent."

"That's rough," said Professor Barraclough, with a low whistle.

There were a series of sober nods around the kitchen; under the table, Astrid took her brother's hand.

"He seems to have gone off the rails a bit," said Mahri. "Locked himself away in his study for months on end, right in the middle of several well-paying projects that were underway up here."

"I'd bet that had something to do with the Chalice," said Joanna, eagerly.

Mahri nodded, enthusiastically. "His father had been the mason for one of our local aristocrats, the Duke of Morley, who was keen on rebuilding things that didn't really need rebuilding," she went on. "You know the one – redid that big house out Winthorpe way, moved the whole village out of the way of his view. Although," she added, fairly, "he did rebuild the village with all the finest amenities of the day, so no one minded all that much. Anyway, *he* commissioned the young Bone to rebuild rather a lot of the churches on his lands – a commission that set Bone up for life, I might add." Mahri paused for effect, clearly enjoying herself.

"Well?" asked Morton, impatiently.

"*Six* of those churches are within an hour of Brindleford," said Mahri, triumphantly. "And all six were under construction when Bone's father died and he had that funny turn."

"Excellent!" cried Morton. "Where are they?"

"That's just it," said Ivy, with a touch of scholarly annoyance. "It didn't say. It just listed major towns."

"Ah, well maybe that's where we can help," said Joanna. She pulled out a neat, brightly coloured book from her handbag. "I remembered I had a church spotter's handbook – a present from one of the ladies at choir from a few Christmases ago."

She opened the book to a pretty church in a well-kept graveyard.

"St Giles parish church," she said, pointing at the picture. "It's over in Scarcastle."

"Oh," said Mahri. "I know that church – I'm supposed to be over there on Friday morning to set up the flowers for a wedding."

"Perfect," said Morton Barraclough, with a rather roguish grin. "You can have a poke around while you're there."

He rubbed his hands together in anticipation, and Christopher laughed. In the space of one sentence, the whole atmosphere around the table had changed from one of mild worry to intense excitement: it would be good to be able to actually *do* something about Post instead of just wondering what he was up to.

ooo

"Hallo there!" said a cheery voice.

Reggie looked up, surprised. He was in the back bay of the Arcade, in a shop that was still mostly empty – he hadn't expected anyone to try to come in.

"Sorry," said the voice, from behind a large cardboard box. "I know you're not open, but everyone else seems to be occupied, hang on..."

The man set the box down on the floor and dusted his hands off.

The shock of orange hair took Reggie by surprise, and he stared at the pale, gangly man who was shaking his hand enthusiastically.

"I'm Otto," said the apparition, pushing his spectacles back up his nose. "Otto Finch. Our *mutual friends* sent me."

Reggie nodded warily as Otto waggled his eyebrows conspiratorially. He suspected that Otto wasn't often sent on undercover work.

"You're from the Court," he said, staring at the man's khaki shorts and brightly coloured t-shirt. He looked about the least likely candidate for secretly being a wizard that Reggie had ever seen. He wouldn't have been out of place at a science-fiction convention.

"That's right!" he beamed, brightly, and waved his medallion under Reggie's nose.

"Er – good," said Reggie. "I'm Reggie Long. Er – how can I help you?"

But Otto was already distracted. "Are you opening up a new shop?" he asked, interested. He peered around at all the open packing crates and empty furniture.

"Yes," said Reggie, a little nervously. "It's going to be a music shop – I used to teach it, you see, when I was younger, but life sort of got on top of me for a while, and I stopped."

"Life's like that," said Otto, cheerily. "I'm glad you're opening up – my mum's in a wheelchair now," he continued, happily, and Reggie wondered whether very much ever got Otto down. "She plays the piano, and she's always after me to find new sheet music. I'm beginning to think she's already learnt it all!"

He laughed, and Reggie grinned – he couldn't help it: Otto's impossible enthusiasm was infectious.

"I say," he said, suddenly. "You wouldn't be able to get hold of some new harp strings, would you? Mine had a bit of an accident last year."

"I reckon I could," said Reggie, surprised. "But it'll be a few weeks before I open properly. You play the harp?" he asked, trying to imagine this man staying still for even two minutes.

"Yes," said Otto. "And the trumpet – drives Mum round the bend."

"I can imagine."

Otto laughed again, and Reggie wondered whether this might be his magic – laughter and enthusiasm, and the ability to instil them into others.

"I'm part Elf," said Otto, helpfully, giving Reggie a shrewd look. "Everyone wonders – it's just quicker to tell people, in the long run."

"Oh, yes?" said Reggie, stunned.

So there are Elves, too, are there? he thought.

"Yep – on my dad's side. His gran, I think. Never met him, but Mum says I'm a lot like him – can't sit still," he laughed. "I love making things, too – and I can play music without even thinking. It has its downsides, though," he grinned. "I got all of the height of an Elf and absolutely none of the grace!"

He looked at Reggie blankly for a few moments.

"What did I come here for again?" he asked. Reggie wondered privately whether having the attention-span of a small dog was also an Elf thing. "Oh yes!" he cried, and opened the box at his feet. "Xander asked if I had anything that you lot could use to go snooping with – I say, it's all very exciting, isn't it?"

"Could be," said Reggie, carefully.

"And I found these knocking about at the back – they're very useful." Carefully, he took something out of the box. It was covered in brown paper which crackled as he unwrapped it, revealing a beautiful, white satin masquerade mask.

"What do you think?" Otto asked, critically.

"What does it do?" asked Reggie, a little taken aback at his new friend's enthusiasm.

"Oh! Well, you put it on, just like any normal mask," he said, happy to share. "It makes you sort of fade into the background. People will know you're there still – sort of – but the mask convinces their brain that you're unimportant and they overlook you. It's pretty cool," he beamed. "They're called 'Fades'. They take on the aspect of the person wearing them."

"What does that mean?" asked Reggie, eyeing the mask suspiciously. It looked so innocent and normal.

"It changes to suit its owner," Otto explained. "I have one at home – as soon as I put it on it went lime green – my favourite colour," he said, almost proudly. "Here, you try."

He passed Reggie the Fade and stood back, waiting.

Nervously, Reggie pressed the delicate thing to his face.

At once, he felt a strange warmth passing through his features as the mask changed shape to fit him perfectly; he looked up at Otto, whose eyes had crossed. Apparently the Fade was already having an effect.

He took it off and looked at it.

"Oh," said Otto. "There you are – effective, isn't it?"

Reggie nodded, staring at the thing in his hand. The mask had changed colour: now it was covered in black and white diamonds, like a harlequin's costume, with a solid black edging.

"Nice," said Otto, admiring it. He dove back into the box. "I found enough for all of you – even the children. I didn't want them to feel left out," he added, on Reggie's look of mild surprise.

"No," he said, amused. "I suppose you wouldn't."

"I also had a dig in the back of our cupboards and found a couple of amulets – they're old, but none of you should really be getting yourselves into too much trouble, so that won't matter."

Reggie smiled, and thanked the extraordinary man.

"Glad to be of service!" Otto exclaimed, taking a theatrical bow. "I should get back," he said, suddenly. "I left an experiment running. My apprentices should be fine, but just in case –"

"Actually," said Reggie, "before you go…"

He filled him in about the church in Scarcastle. Otto practically vibrated with excitement.

"I'll let Ogden and Xander know," he said. "Brilliant! And you found it so quickly – I'm impressed," he grinned. "You'll be putting the Constables out of a job at this rate! I'll come back in when you're open, have a chat with you about those harp strings! Cheerio!"

He hurried out of the shop, a bubble of sunny enthusiasm trailing after him like a train.

Reggie chuckled, and looked again at the mask in his hand. They were never going to get Astrid and Jake to stay put ever again.

ooo

Mahri hummed to herself as she put the finishing touches to the flowers either side of the altar. The bride had ordered russet coloured roses, variegated chrysanthemums, crimson daisies and brilliant red berries, wrapped in ferns. It was a riot of reds and oranges – perfect for an autumn wedding. She rearranged one of the fern stems and stood back, admiring her work.

"Oh, that's lovely," said the vicar, wandering past on one of his many and mysterious errands. "Emma will be so pleased."

"Thank you," said Mahri, justifiably proud of her skills. "I do like to do weddings – there's such joy to be had."

"Oh, absolutely," the vicar agreed. "Everyone's so happy, a young couple just starting out – or an older one, as the case may be. It's like doing the Easter services, talking about new beginnings. Always cheers me up."

Mahri beamed at him. Reverend Child had always been a kindly, if rather vague sort of man, and she needed to pick his brain.

"Reverend," she began, gathering up her scissors and ribbons. "I was wondering if I might have a moment of your time."

"Oh, yes?" he turned and peered at her. "Having a moment of spiritual indecision?" he asked, chuckling at his joke. He had known Mahri for a long time.

"No, nothing like that," she laughed. "I was given a rather interesting book by an old friend," she said, remembering Joanna's story. "It's about church architecture – I read about St Giles in it."

"Did you indeed!" exclaimed the vicar. "It certainly does have an interesting history – did you read about the plague pit at the North end of the cemetery?"

"Yes," said Mahri, who hadn't.

"And the Stations of the Cross?" he went on, happily. "They were a gift from one of the Dukes of Morley – he remodelled the whole church in the seventeenth century."

"Yes," said Mahri, again, flannelling wildly. "I was particularly interested in that – it was done by the same chap who rebuilt a church I visited in Kent. Mortimer something. He was very good."

"Bone, I think his name was," said the vicar. "Mortimer Bone."

"Yes, that's right," said Mahri, with a winning smile.

"He did a pretty good job," said Reverend Child, proudly. "Rather a sympathetic chap, left in a lot of the old details, restored them to their former glory – that sort of thing. He installed our marvellous font cover –

did you know?"

"No, I didn't," said Mahri, surprised.

The font cover was the first thing that anyone coming to St Giles noticed, and something that she'd often wondered about, during her many visits to the church over the years. It seemed entirely out of place in the small, friendly parish church in Scarcastle – which was a very pretty village in the middle of nowhere.

"He based it on some fifteenth century types – wanted it to be in-keeping with the rest of the church. It was church law then to keep the font locked, stopped people making off with the blessed water for nefarious purposes," he winked at Mahri. "Or not so nefarious, depending on the person." She grinned; when his daughter had been born she had provided a second, less heavenly blessing for the family. "We're having it restored, bit by bit. Well, I must get on," said the vicar. "Got some errands to run before the service – you can have a look around if you want," he offered. "Just lock up and drop the key off at the vicarage when you're done. My wife will be in."

"Thanks," said Mahri, as he wandered away.

Clearing up the rest of her things into her work bag, she turned and peered up at the font cover.

It was a hell of a thing.

Standing at least sixteen feet tall, the font cover was a spindly, winding triumph of carving that was raised above the font by a complicated series of pulleys somewhere in the eaves of the church. It nearly grazed the spectacular hammerbeam roof, and seemed to be guarded by a carved, gilded angel resting on the end of one of the beams.

Five tiers of crocketed pinnacles rose towards the roof, creating the impression of a completely over-the-top wedding cake. Four of the great tiers could recede into one another, giving access to the font during baptisms. For a fleeting moment, Mahri wondered what it must look like to the baby, being held between the vicar and its parents, being bewildered with cold water and looking up into that extraordinary structure, hanging high above its wetted forehead.

It looked like the tiers had once had statues fixed between the pinnacles, now long gone. There were faint traces of paintwork suggesting fantastic scenes on the few flat panels that the craftsmen had left un-pinnacled.

The bottom tier was the first and only portion to be restored – though there were a few, discrete pencil marks on the second tier, as though plans were already underway for its conservation – and it had been renovated in fine fashion. This tier was hollow – as if the craftsmen had wanted to give the impression of tall church windows opening onto a great, circular hall.

The tall, elegant arches were painted in a rich, dark blue and gilded, while the extraordinary pinnacles in front of them highlighted in crimson. All around the bottom of the tier were a series of brightly coloured shields, trumpeting the heraldry of the local families, affixed to a latticework of bright gold.

Inside the arches, which formed a strange sort of internal, decorative gazebo, the tier was painted a marvellous duck-egg blue with bright, gilded vaulting. The centre of this vaulting, like the centre of a chapter house roof, had a single, large roof boss in the form of a medallion. Wrought upon it in white and lilac enamel was a splendid columbine, a symbol of the Holy Spirit.

Mahri frowned at it.

If you wanted to give the impression of a sky – which seemed to be the intention with the gilded internal ceiling – surely a dove would be a much more appropriate symbol?

She walked around the font, wracking her brain for any other meaning of columbine.

The medallion was set almost flush with the top of the first tier – if only she could get a closer look. Mahri glanced around. The church was empty now and peaceful; great pools of autumn light were pouring in through the tall windows, creating a riot of light and colour where it touched the stained glass, putting her flowers to shame. She smiled: if the sun stayed out this afternoon, the service would be unforgettable.

She had another glance around.

Since there's no one here... she thought, hurrying to the back of the church where the cleaning supplies were kept. Reverend Child kept a small stepladder in the cupboard for cleaning above the pulpit and changing light bulbs. Mahri carried it over to the font cover, trying to ignore the flicker of excitement she felt. She was only going to *look* at the thing, after all.

Balancing on the ladder, she squinted at the medallion: it really was a beautiful piece of work. Whoever had made it had got the colours exactly right – it was almost as if you could reach up and pluck the bloom from its rather fancy place.

Folly, thought Mahri, suddenly. *Columbine means folly.*

She looked up at it.

Now, does that mean it marks a place of folly? she thought, *Or would it be a folly to have a closer look?*

She hesitated, precariously perched atop the ladder. There was really no reason to suspect that anything had been hidden here – for all she knew, Mortimer Bone and his churches could be a wild goose chase – and she really shouldn't attempt to deface something so old, and so beautiful. It wasn't hers, after all, it belonged to the community of Scarcastle and the parishioners of St Giles.

And yet...

And yet, it called to her.

If the Chalice of Knowledge is up there, and I don't look, she thought, *everything will have been for nothing.*

Without thinking, she reached up to the disc, running her fingers around its gilded edge. It felt fairly solid.

And anyway, she thought, *if there was anything there, they would have found it during the restoration. There's no room for a chalice up there.*

Reluctant to give up, particularly since she'd come so far, she pressed it again. This time, with a dreadful creak, it shifted slightly, turning in its place.

Mahri froze, her heart hammering in her chest. Terrified that she'd broken the thing, she supported it with both hands.

She looked around the church, afraid she'd be caught, but no one was in sight. Carefully, and with all the determination of a treasure hunter, she twisted the disc; it felt suddenly heavier, as if the weight of something was pushing it down from above.

All at once, the columbine disc came loose. She caught the leather bag that was concealed above just in time. A cloud of dust enveloped her and she climbed down the step ladder, coughing.

Her eyes and lungs clearing, she looked at the thing in her hands. The leather was old, but not worn – as if someone had bought it for the purpose of hiding something: something that jangled and clinked inside it. Mahri took another look above her head. The chamber it had been kept in must have been airtight to keep the leather in such good condition for all this time.

She opened the pouch, her heart thudding with excitement, and pulled out a few of the glittering things. Thin slices of pressed metal glinted in the light.

Coins.

Silver and gold coins.

Lots of them.

Mahri turned one of the coins over in her hand, stunned: on it was the face of a King that she didn't recognise; she squinted at the words around the edge, struggling to make them out.

Slowly, she dropped them back into the pouch, thrilled to have found them. She looked around the deserted church, thoughtfully.

Whoever had put the coins in the font cover – and that person was probably Mortimer Bone – had done that for a reason. It wasn't just a puzzle for future generations, but a kind of anonymous donation. A penance.

Folly, thought Mahri.

Carefully, she tied the straps of the pouch together and

climbed the step ladder. Slotting the disc back in place was easier than she had thought – though she left enough of the disc out that you would notice it from below.

Finally, she put the stepladders away and hurried out of the church to fetch the vicar's wife.

24
Atlantes in Buckridge

"Listen to this: 'The hoard – which was found by Mary Child, the wife of the Reverend at St Giles parish church, Scarcastle – was discovered when Mrs Child noticed that part of the font cover was coming away from its frame,'" Reggie read aloud. "'*One of our visitors noticed the damage, which I assume must have taken place during the recent restoration of the bottom tier of the cover, and I hurried in to have a look*,' said Mrs Child, 53, on Sunday. '*I got up on my stepladder and turned the disc – it just sort of came out in my hand*'. With it came a leather pouch full of gold and silver coins.'

"'Mrs Child showed the hoard to her husband, and together they took it to the local museum,'" Reggie continued. "'The coins are thought to date to the mid-seventeenth century and represent one of the only hoards of that date found in Britain that is not believed to be related to the English Civil War. One of the latest coins to be dated was a half-crown bearing the likeness of King Charles the Second, dated to 1663.'

"'The British Museum have expressed an interest in buying the hoard. Because the hoard was discovered within the church at St Giles, under British law a percentage of the sale will go to the church fund. Reverend Child and his wife said that they're hoping to use some of the money to keep their volunteer-run Friendship Club open, while the rest will go towards the restoration of the font cover,'" said Reggie, folding up the newspaper. "Well, that seems appropriate."

They had been perusing the local newspapers for the last few days, waiting for the story of Mahri's hoard to break. Everyone was ranged around Ivy's kitchen, being tripped over by puppies and trying to keep their tea out of the dogs' reach.

"They didn't print Mahri's name," said Astrid, peering over Reggie's shoulder. "That's not fair."

"I asked Mrs Child not to mention me," Mahri

explained. "I didn't want Post getting wind of it and cottoning on to our schemes."

"Oh, well, that's alright then," said the girl, satisfied.

Ivy shared an amused expression with Christopher, and they looked away, chuckling at the girl's concern.

"I suppose there's a chance it wasn't Bone that hid the coins," said Christopher, who had taken up what was now his usual place, leaning against the worktop. "It could have been any one of the craftsmen – or builders, if the font cover was installed when they were still at the church. They'd just need a quiet moment and a bit of skill."

"True," said Mahri, considering this. "But you said yourself that there wasn't a lot of external pressure at the time – not like twenty years earlier, at the height of the Civil War."

"Maybe he just liked hiding stuff," said Jake, from under the kitchen table. He had taken his solemn promise to take care of the young puppy very seriously indeed and was spending as much time with her as was physically possible. Saffy had even begun treating him like an eighth member of her litter.

"That's certainly a possibility," said Christopher. "Plenty of craftsmen put little jokes or puzzles into their work – even just for their own entertainment."

"Or their friends," nodded Reggie. "You get a bit of that in music too – little in-jokes between composers or performers, that sort of thing."

"I don't know," said Ivy, dubiously. "It was a lot of money back then – I mean if all it was meant for was some kind of practical in-joke. It's the kind of money you wouldn't part with lightly, external pressure or no."

"So: either it was someone who wanted the money kept safe and something happened to prevent them collecting it," said Reggie, thoughtfully, "or someone who put it there for a reason, and never intended to collect it."

"Which brings us back to Prospero Bone," said Christopher, with an edge of weariness in his voice.

"We could keep going round like this for hours," said Ivy. "But it's not getting us anywhere. Unless we check out all of the churches that we can, we can't be sure the Chalice isn't hidden in one of them, just waiting for someone like Post to find it." She sighed. "We'll just have to keep looking."

"What if we don't find it?" asked Astrid. "Or if he kept it with him, and hid it somewhere else entirely?"

"Then that's up to the Court of Miracles to look into," said Ivy, firmly. "If it's out of this Manor then I don't have the right to meddle with it."

"Then we just have to wait until he brings it home, and –" Mahri began, but Ivy interrupted, frustrated.

"And what, exactly? Wrest a dangerous and powerful artefact from the clutches of a dangerous and powerful wizard?" Mahri fell silent, abashed. "No," said Ivy. "We *have* to find it before him, and it has to be here. Somewhere."

"Then the real question is: where next?" said Reggie, delicately.

Christopher cleared his throat. "I've been speaking to a couple of my old friends from the Records Office – Harry and Joe," he said. "And they're running an enquiry down for me – hang on."

They watched him go into his study for a moment. Ivy wondered when she'd forgotten that he'd had a life before moving to the Arcade. These days it felt like he'd always been there.

He came back holding a sheet of paper, covered in scribbled notes.

"Joe remembered the name of one of Bone's churches," he said. "His brother got married there last year – St Mary's, in Buckridge."

"Oh, I know Buckridge," said Reggie. "It's quite a way out past Crestcaster – is St Mary's the church with the annual bell-ringing competition?"

"I don't know," said Christopher, intrigued.

"They used to hold it every spring," said Reggie, reminiscing. "Bess used to like to go to hear the bells. It's a lovely church, if that's the one I'm thinking of."

"It's a pity that contest is in the spring," said Mahri, ruefully. "It would have been a brilliant excuse to have a nose around."

"Ah," said Christopher, cheerfully. "But the bell-ringing competition isn't all that they do." He waved the paper at them. "Joe looked it up for me, since none of us have a computer. It said on their website that they're having a fete next weekend – they're raising money for an orphanage one or two villages over, that's in danger of closing down. They're looking for stalls."

"I could do a food stall," said Ivy. "It's this Saturday, you said?"

Christopher nodded.

Ivy bit her lip. "I could do with staying open this weekend," she frowned. "Business has been a bit slow these past few weeks."

"And you don't want to raise anyone's suspicions by disappearing all day," Reggie put in.

"Christopher could cover for you," Mahri suggested. Christopher nodded his assent.

Ivy stared at him, reluctant to leave the business she'd worked so hard to build up in the hands of someone else – even someone she trusted – for a whole day of trading.

"But what about the bookshop?" she asked.

"I'll ask Professor Barraclough to come in on Saturday," he said. "I'm sure he won't mind."

"And you'll be alright mixing up the teas?" she asked, still dubious. "And the different kinds of wools?"

Christopher and Mahri laughed.

"He's a bright boy," said Mahri. "I'm sure between the three of us we can make sure that you have a teashop to come back to."

Ivy blushed, embarrassed. "I wasn't suggesting that –"

"I know," said Christopher, amicably.

"Well, alright then," said Ivy. "But I'll need extra cake for the weekend Mahri, don't think you're getting out of this one."

Mahri smiled. "I'll whip up some of the classics, don't

you worry."

"Are you sure Professor Barraclough won't mind?" she asked, turning again to Christopher. He chuckled and patted her shoulder.

"Of course not," he grinned. "After all, it's for a good cause."

ooo

"Thank you so much for stepping in, Mrs Burwell," the vicar said, helping her carry another tray of cakes from the van Mahri had borrowed for her. Her fellow artists at the evening class had been happy to help out for charity. Ivy had seen one or two of them setting up a bit further along the path, hoping to sell their paintings for the orphanage.

"Oh, it's no trouble, really," she said, navigating around a table piled high with bric-a-brac.

The village green was already full of people, all of them trying to set things up, lay things out, and make a good impression. There were toy stalls, craft stalls, clothes stalls, sweet stalls and fairground games; tables piled high with old jumpers, second hand board games, homemade jam, truly dreadful pottery; Ivy had even spotted that stalwart of British fairs, the coconut shy. There was a splat-the-rat nearby. She noted with some amusement that all the other stall holders had given that particular game a wide berth.

Everyone appeared to be coming together to help the nearby orphanage, and there was a definite feeling of community amongst the local stall-holders. Ivy had been watching them carefully as she emptied the van and got her tables set up: this many people in one place made her a little nervous, and despite the spirit of cooperation that the good people of Buckridge were displaying, she could feel old rivalries and grudges bubbling away beneath the surface.

Her grandmother had explained that feeling to her when she was small. It was part of being the Witch – a sort of early warning system for low-level calamities. She hadn't felt it for a long time, having avoided this sort of event for the better part of a decade, but it was a talent that seemed to have matured rather than faded.

It made her edgy.

Technically, Buckridge was still within the bounds of her Manor – if she'd had a manor anymore – and the thought that it would be her duty to intervene if something kicked off was making her feel a little queasy.

"I was worried that we weren't going to have any food at all," the vicar was saying, as he deposited another crate of supplies down beside her. "I forgot to order any, and everyone seems to want to charge you so much more if you book them last-minute."

Ivy smiled, and started unpacking teacups, glad that she'd thought to put an unbreakable charm on them the previous evening.

"Happy to help," she said. "It's for a good cause, after all."

"Absolutely!" the vicar cried, clapping his hands. "'Happy Times' is such a good place for the children, and they've missed out on a lot of government funding this year. You remember the floods, a couple of months ago?"

"Vividly," said Ivy, with a small smile.

"Well their roof very nearly came off that night – the water damage was awful. We put the children up in the Village Hall until they made it safe again – and to be honest, I think they all thought it was some kind of summer camp and enjoyed themselves tremendously – but really it needs a complete overhaul." He shook his head, sadly. "You'd think that children's safety would be a priority, but every appeal we've made..." He glanced around, as if remembering himself. "Still, everyone has pulled out all the stops this morning, and that's a good sign – oh, excuse me."

He stepped back to let Astrid past – she was carrying a box full of paper napkins that was almost the same size as she was.

"This is Astrid," said Ivy, as Jake ran up behind his

sister. "And Jake."

"Are they yours, dear lady?"

"Yes," she said, and felt an unfamiliar touch of pride as she did so. "I adopted them a few weeks ago."

"Oh, how wonderful!" the vicar cried. "Just the sort of thing you like to hear – are you two settling alright with Mrs Burwell?"

"Yes, thank you," said Astrid. Jake was hiding behind Ivy's legs, uncharacteristically shy amongst the crowds.

"Excellent!" he beamed at Ivy, apparently thrilled to find someone who was doing what he saw as God's work. "Well, if you need anything, Mrs Burwell, just give me a shout."

Ivy watched him go, contemplatively. He was quickly absorbed by a group of women huddled around a craft stall. She could hear his laughter even over the chatter of the stall-holders around her. She smiled lightly, and turned back to her own table.

"I think that's everything from the van, Ivy," said Astrid, who had also been watching the vicar.

"Great," said the older witch, handing her the keys. "Could you lock it up for me? And come straight back!" she called after the two children, as they took off across the field, dodging between tables and people's legs.

It hadn't surprised Ivy when Astrid and Jake had offered to help out at the fete. She knew that they were as eager to find the Chalice as any of the others, and this seemed to be a safe enough way for them to get involved. The fact that they had become extremely helpful as soon as they had heard about the orphanage hadn't escaped her notice, either.

There were all kinds of duty, she knew, and this was probably what they felt to be theirs.

She had finished setting out her wares and was fiddling with the tea urn when they returned. The vicar had loaned it to her for the day, and it was a temperamental behemoth of a thing, alternately refusing to heat up and spitting steam out of the top like a demented chimney.

"Is anyone looking?" she asked Astrid, as she gave her back the keys.

The little girl peered around and shook her head.

"Good," said Ivy, and made a sign with her hand above the tea urn. Within seconds, the clunking, hissing noises emanating from within had stopped, and turned to a well behaved rumble.

Astrid grinned, impressed.

"That's better," said Ivy, checking the temperature of the water. "A little cheeky, perhaps, but I really couldn't have made it worse. Now," she turned to the children, who were watching her with something akin to awe, "do you two want to have a bit of an explore this morning?" she asked, and they both made noises of excitement.

"You can win a big purple dragon on the coconut shy," said Jake, almost breathless with excitement.

"Can you?" asked Ivy, eyes twinkling. "Excellent." She pulled out a little money. "This is for the both of you – stay together, have some fun, and don't eat too many sweets," she said. Astrid stared at the money in her hand.

"But we're supposed to be helping…"

"You are," Ivy assured her. "You're supporting the fete by going to the stalls and playing the games. Come back here for lunch, and then in the afternoon you can look after the stall while I have a bit of an explore."

"Okay," said Astrid, after a moment's thought. Ivy wondered whether the large purple dragon was having any bearing on her decision.

"Keep safe," she said, as they ran off, hand in hand, wellies flashing.

ooo

The children had been true to their word and had run back to the stall at half-past twelve, each of them clutching bags of sweets. Jake was almost hidden behind an enormous purple dragon, and was wearing an expression of unalloyed delight.

Astrid gave Ivy her very best innocent look, but Ivy

wasn't fooled for a moment. She raised her eyebrows at her young charge, and Astrid took Jake to wash his hands, looking very slightly sheepish.

"What did you win?" she asked her, while they munched their sandwiches.

"Nothing," said Astrid. "Only the dragon for Jake. I bought an owl, though." She reached into her bag and produced a stuffed owl with a slightly suspicious expression. "I was going to call her Artemis."

"Good name," said Ivy, amused.

"Has it been really busy?" Astrid asked, eyeing the diminishing stacks of cake and sandwiches.

"It has," Ivy smiled. "We'll be cleaned out by the end of the day, if the weather holds."

All three of them looked up at the sky, simultaneously, worried that Ivy's words might have been tempting fate. A clear autumnal sky smiled back down upon them, and they relaxed again.

"I'm going to have a wander," said Ivy, with a glance at the church. "Can you keep an eye on the stall?"

Astrid gave her a knowing smile and nodded. "I hope there's something interesting inside," she said.

"Me too," Ivy muttered. "I won't be long – send Jake for me if you need anything."

"We'll be okay, Ivy," Astrid insisted, and Ivy hid her smile.

She knew they'd be alright, and really she was just giving her young friend the opportunity to ask for help if she needed it, but her open defiance was quite endearing.

Ignoring the stalls, Ivy made a bee-line for the church. There would be time to peruse later: business first.

The air was cool inside the church – the warmth of the October sunshine barely penetrating the ancient stones of the building. The church was large and full of light; great swathes of coloured beams were falling across the pews from the stained glass windows above the altar.

Some diligent person had arranged autumn blooms around the nave, bringing the joys of the season inside.

The church was peaceful and serene, a place of contemplation, but to Ivy it felt stuffy and cramped.

The last time she had been in a church had been her grandmother's funeral.

Feeling oddly claustrophobic, she pulled her scarf and coat more tightly around herself and slipped along one of the aisles, avoiding the gaze of the few parishioners who had sought refuge from the crowds outside.

She ran her eyes over the memorials on the walls: Buckley, Hart, Kastor... *Dearly Beloved... Here lies... Beloved son... Eternal rest...*

The church at Buckridge had been serving its community for a long time – some of the memorials were so old that time and obsolescence had rendered them illegible. She traced the lines of one of the carvings: the name had long since disappeared, but the year (1673) and the decoration remained. Someone had felt it necessary to depict a skull with wings at the very top of the memorial. It looked slightly unreal, as though the artist had wanted to reduce the ghoulish impact of his work by making it a little more likeable.

She paused by the altar, staring up at the coloured glass suspended above it. Someone had done a good job of portraying the saints, looking serenely down on the congregation. Near the top of the windows, a choir of angels swarmed around Jesus, in a riot of white and gold. Beneath them was a reconstructed tapestry, completing the tableau. The window was fine work, and Ivy wondered how long it had been there – was it part of Prospero Bone's reconstruction? Had he left some hidden clue in the image?

It seemed unlikely that no one would have noticed something like that in over three hundred years.

But then, she thought, *perhaps you wouldn't see significance in something, if you weren't looking for it – particularly if you saw it every day, or every week.*

The familiar had that strange ability to fade into the background at times.

"It's beautiful, isn't it?" said the vicar.

Ivy jumped; she'd been so intent on the riot of colour above him she hadn't heard him approach.

"Er – yes," she said, startled.

"Sorry," he said. "My sister tells me I have cat-like stealth."

Ivy smiled. "She's not wrong," she said. "Is it alright if I have a look around? I wanted to get a bit of peace and quiet away from the bustle of the stalls."

"Understandable," he smiled indulgently at her. "Of course you may – have you left your young ones in charge of the stall?"

Ivy nodded. "They'll come and find me if I'm needed," she said, confident in their ability to win the crowd over.

"What wonderful children – they seem determined to show the rest of us up with all that hard work."

"Yes," Ivy laughed. "But I gave them the morning off – I'm not a complete slave-driver."

The vicar chuckled. "As long as you take the time to enjoy the fair, too, my dear," he said. "Feel free to look around – the tower's Norman, you know."

Ivy didn't, and thanked him.

He wandered off humming something by Gilbert and Sullivan under his breath.

The Lady Chapel, on the other side of the altar, was beautiful. It had been swathed in white and blue, and was illuminated by so many candles that Ivy was mildly worried that it might one day catch fire. A plaque by the curtained entrance told the world that it had been built in the nineteenth century for one of the pious wives of the local gentry. Ivy passed it by, contemplatively.

She stopped halfway along the aisle and peered up into the stern, marble face of a statue, upon whose shoulders rested one of the great beams of the roof. She glanced across the nave; where another statue should have stood was a pillar, covered in memorials.

Looking back at the figure above her, she wondered whether it had ever had a pair, or been liberated from some far flung corner of the empire in the days before that sort of thing was frowned upon. Except for the great spreading wings that arched above him, denoting (she supposed) his heavenly situation, he looked monumentally out of place in a quiet English church in Buckridge.

He was quite a striking figure: just a little larger than life, the sculptor had managed to convey a man patiently carrying an extraordinary burden and was focused entirely upon it. There was no pain in his white, stony eyes, nor compassion. His muscles were straining against the great pillar on his shoulders, his head bent forward from the weight of it – but it didn't look like he was struggling.

Perhaps, thought Ivy, *his faith is keeping him strong.*

She studied his austere face for a few more moments, wondering why she should be so drawn to him. He stared down at her, silent and watchful. She let her gaze travel down the folds of his tunic, marvelling at how something so hard as stone could be made to seem as delicate and flowing as fabric. There was a sword at his belt, hinting at the punishment for miscreants among the parishioners. The great, stone man held an open book in his hand, the pages curved open invitingly.

Ivy stood on her tiptoes and peered at it; there were subtle lines in the stone, as if the sculptor had wished to emulate writing.

Ivy stood back once more, impressed with the level of detail, and that was when she saw it. She let out a gasp.

There, between the great figure's bare feet, was a small, ornate goblet.

It was exquisitely carved – so paper-thin that when Ivy bent down to look more closely, the light from the windows shone through it. If she hadn't known better, she would have thought it was made of bone instead of marble. It rose up from the folds of his flowing tunic effortlessly, as though the angel and his charge had simply risen up out of the marble.

The goblet had been engraved. Elegant lines formed a simple design of intertwining lines around its rim. Ivy frowned at it, unsettled: the pattern reminded her of a line of eyes, staring out at her.

She looked up once more at his stony countenance.

"I wonder..." she breathed, and turned her attention to the base of the pillar on which he was resting. Centuries of scuff marks and scratches had accumulated on the very bottom of the stone. She ran her hands around it: it seemed solid enough.

"It slides out," said the vicar, who was standing over her.

Ivy nearly jumped out of her skin. She stood up dizzyingly fast and caught her head on the book the statue was holding.

She swore, and clutched her head.

"Sorry – oh, my dear, come and sit down," he said, brimming with concern. "I'm most dreadfully sorry – oh dear..."

"I'm alright," said Ivy, once the room had stopped spinning.

"Are you sure?" he asked, with friendly anxiety. "There's a St John's Ambulance stall outside, I could go and get one of them if you'd like –"

"No, really," she assured him. "I didn't hit it that hard – it was more of a shock, really."

"I should announce myself better," he said, apologetically. "I'm always catching people unawares."

"I probably shouldn't have been fondling the architecture," Ivy said, rubbing the back of her head.

"Well," the vicar chuckled, "I won't tell anyone if you won't."

Ivy gave him a slightly dazed smile and he looked away, embarrassed. His gaze fell on the angel.

"He's quite magnificent, isn't he?" he said, trying to make conversation.

"Yes," said Ivy, with feeling. "I like him."

"He seems to draw people to him," the vicar nodded. "As though they feel safer around him – although..." he scratched his head, and Ivy watched his expression closely.

If there was something dark and magical hidden here,

there would have been traces – regular visitors would have noticed it, and who better to notice something in the midst of a church than its vicar?

"Although?" she prompted.

"Oh, it's probably nothing," he said. "But my predecessor didn't like him all that much, to tell you the truth. He thought he was watching him – and I have to admit he's a lifelike figure. His eyes do rather follow you around the room."

"The way old paintings do," Ivy supplied, and the vicar nodded enthusiastically.

"Exactly – that's just what I said. Simon told me to keep an eye on him, all the same," he continued, quietly. "And I must say this place feels a little odd at night – as though I'm not the only one here."

He trailed off, and Ivy relaxed. Churches and graveyards were notorious for hauntings, and any building that had the Chalice in would have more going on than a statue whose eyes followed you across the room and the odd unsettling evening. In all probability it would be the kind of place that no one would ever want to go into.

"Are you suggesting that your church is haunted?" she asked, gently.

"No – well, not exactly," he smiled benignly at her. "That sort of thing is impossible, of course, but on occasion you do have to wonder. There have been noises, sometimes, from the tower – it's Norman, you know. Oh –" he chuckled. "I already told you that, didn't I? Well – I often have a glance in here to see that all is well of an evening, and sometimes there's a light under the door – not a strong light, more like someone had a candle burning – but when I open the door the room is empty, except for the bell pulls and the register."

"It must be quite unsettling," she said, sympathetically, thinking of their own nocturnal spectre.

"It is," he agreed. "But these days it's sort of familiar – comforting, even. I often think that I'd miss it, if it stopped happening."

Ivy smiled. Familiarity. The one thing humans couldn't survive without.

"Some nights I wonder what happened to the candle lighter," he mused.

"Probably nothing violent," said Ivy, contemplatively. "Or you'd feel threatened. I once went to a building in Kent with my parents – a National Trust property, I think. There was an eerie feeling in one room – it was awful, it made my skin crawl. When we'd all left the room – some of the women had even burst into tears for no good reason – and the tour guide saw how shaken up we were, he told us that someone had been murdered there. The way he told the story, I'm surprised anyone ever went back in the room." She frowned. "He was a ghastly little man, actually. Really seemed to enjoy frightening people. Anyway, I think if there had been any unpleasantness then whoever lights that candle would probably find a way to let you know."

"That's a nice way of thinking about it," the vicar said, comforted. "Perhaps he was even a vicar, working late into the night."

"I think you're probably right there," she said.

"You're a very unusual young woman, Mrs Burwell," he said, subjecting her to an appraising look.

Ivy smiled slightly.

"So I'm told."

There were a few moments' silence as the two watched one another, carefully.

"If I didn't know better, I would have said that you were a vicar," the man said, quietly. "With the exception of the ghost story."

"No spiritual aspirations, I'm afraid," said Ivy, apologetically. "Just tea and knitting."

The vicar chuckled.

"Er – you said that the base of the statue opened?" Ivy asked, taking the opportunity to pry while she still could.

"Yes!" the vicar cried, happily. "It's rather exciting, don't you think?"

He knelt in front of the statue and released a catch

concealed behind the pillar. The front of the pillar came away, revealing a large semi-circular draw.

Could this be it? Ivy thought, wildly. *Could the vicar have unwittingly found Prospero Bone's greatest secret?*

She and the vicar peered into it, curiously.

"I always expect it to be full of treasures," the man said, wistfully, and Ivy held her tongue, trying not to voice her disappointment. "But there never is. Simon used to keep his hymnbooks in it."

He closed the compartment with a sigh.

"I *did* find a nest of mice in there once," he admitted, candidly. "They were eating the hymnbooks."

Ivy laughed, despite her dissatisfaction.

"Still," he said, getting to his feet. "It's nice to have one or two mysteries about the place. Makes a building feel more lived-in."

Ivy smiled, and they walked together to the door, where the vicar paused for a moment.

"Sometimes I think there are more things in heaven and earth than we will ever really know about," he said, thoughtfully.

The corners of Ivy's mouth twitched upwards, gently.

"I think you're probably right about that, Reverend."

25
Heavenly Music

"I'm sorry, Mast- Quentin, I'm afraid that one's out at the moment," said Christopher, trying not to look pleased at the crestfallen expression on Quentin Post's handsome face.

He had guessed – and guessed correctly – that the rich young man hadn't often encountered disappointment. To give him credit, however, he hid it well.

"That one too?" he asked. "That is a pity... How about a guide to the local churches?"

He was clutching at straws now, and they both knew it. Christopher had managed to lose every second book on the architects of the reformation and Seventeenth century construction for the last week. He'd managed to give several of the most detailed to Dr Fitzhearn before he departed on a month-long trip to visit his niece in Northern Scotland. It was lucky, really, that the old man's research overlapped with Post's on several levels.

Dr Fitzhearn had been quite bemused at being allowed so many texts, but had departed happily enough with both Christopher and Professor Barraclough's blessings, determined to get the first draft of his book sketched out.

Widow Jenkins had sidled up to them both after he'd gone and offered to look after some of the others. She might not have known what was going on – and Christopher wasn't entirely sure that she cared – but she *did* know that Quentin Post was interested in seventeenth century churches, and there was no love lost there.

She had scurried away that afternoon, her basket weighed down with books, cackling happily and promising to keep them safe. The old hag had been delighted to find a new and subtle way of vexing him, and Christopher was happy enough to leave the books in her care: he knew she would look after them, and as powerful as Post appeared to be, he suspected that anyone breaking into Widow Jenkins' house would probably never be seen again.

Some of the others had been secreted away upstairs, on the basis that Martha might eat any intruders, and only the ones with the least useful information had been left in the shop. Joanna had even altered the entries in the lending ledger, in case Post demanded to see it.

"Well," said Christopher, in what he hoped was a thoughtful manner. "I'll see what there is – exploring churches is always a popular pass-time."

He ducked into the back room, trying not to snigger at the huff of frustration that Post had allowed to escape.

Professor Zarrubabel scowled at him, and went back to his reading, muttering something unpleasant. Christopher ignored him, and fetched the most recent copy of the inventory. Joanna had marked all the books that she and her husband thought would be the least dangerous in terms of increasing Post's chances of finding the Chalice. He nodded to himself, memorising the first three or four titles.

Post was just putting the lending ledger back underneath the counter when Christopher opened the door. Both men pretended that it hadn't happened.

"I think we have a couple in," he said, making for the bank of shelves on architecture. "They're either over here or in *Ecclesiastical Studies*," he muttered to himself.

Post's eyes followed him almost hungrily.

"Ah, yes –" he pulled down two very thick books and carried them back to the counter. "*One Thousand Outstanding British Churches* and *Betjemen's Best British Churches*," he said, handing them over. "There's probably something in those."

"Hopefully," said Post, almost gruffly. Christopher raised an eyebrow at the older wizard, and he shook himself. "Sorry, old chap," he said, suddenly all smiles again. "Just getting a little frustrated by other people's borrowing habits."

Christopher managed an empathetic chuckle. "It's quite inconsiderate of them," he joked, and Post grinned.

"Indeed," he said. "Could you put a few titles on hold

for me when they come back in?"

"Absolutely," said Christopher, and made a note of the request and tucked it into the front of the returns ledger.

He had expected Post to take the books away and start reading, but he was still there when Christopher looked up, studying him carefully.

Christopher looked back with a puzzled half-smile. "Are you alright, old chap?" he asked, and Christopher tried not to show his momentary panic – had he guessed what they were about? "You're not your usual efficient self."

"Er –" said Christopher, thinking fast. "I think so."

Post fixed him with a curious stare that made him wonder whether the wizard might be able to read minds. He was considering feigning illness when the shop bell jangled. They both looked up as Ivy came in, carrying a plate of sandwiches and a pot of tea.

"Oh," she said, closing the door with her foot. "Sorry to interrupt. Hello, Master Post."

"Mistress Burwell," he nodded, oozing charm.

She hovered by the door for a moment, before making her mind up and scooting past them both into the back room. She re-emerged a few moments later, giving them a hesitant smile and hurried off.

"Lunchtime rush," she said, over her shoulder by way of explanation. "Let me know if you need a refill."

Post turned back to him, understanding breaking over his face.

"A*ha*," he said, in a triumph of realisation.

Christopher stared at him. "Aha?"

"You poor fool," said Post, with what might have been genuine pity. "You've fallen in love."

Christopher felt himself blanch. Post laughed out loud, and Christopher sensed a ripple of laughter run through the books too, just on the edge of perception. He started to blush, desperately hoping that Professor Zarrubabel hadn't overheard. The last thing he needed was another tirade about how unsuitable he was.

To his surprise, Post patted him on the shoulder in a

brotherly fashion.

"It happens to the best of us, so I'm told," he said, cheerfully. "Not to *me*, of course. Well, well. Christopher and Ivy!" He gave him a lecherous wink. "I'd best back off then, give you a clear field."

He had intended to deny it, of course, to tell him that of course it wasn't necessary – not least because Post having any kind of advantage over them couldn't be construed as a good thing. He tried, he really did – even though he wanted nothing more than for Post to leave her alone and stop oozing charm all over the place – but every time he opened his mouth to refute it, no sound would come out.

Horribly aware that he looked like an overgrown goldfish, he shut his mouth and buried his glowing face in a pile of returns.

Post took the books away to the reading desk, still chuckling.

ooo

Reverend Arthur Starling lit the candles contentedly, enjoying the sporadic bursts of music emanating from the great organ that dominated the North wall of the church. It had been too long since they'd had a decent organist in the congregation. Their previous appointment had died several years before, and no one seemed to be interested in learning these days. For the past few years a young lady had been travelling in from a neighbouring parish and accompanying them on the electric keyboard. As much as he appreciated her help, it just wasn't the same.

It had been serendipity itself when a young family from London had moved to the parish (the father having studied Music at Cambridge) in the same week that the nice chap from the new music shop had offered his services. He had been wondering who they could get in to retune the thing.

He stood back and watched the man at work for a few,

proud moments. It was a magnificent beast, by all accounts: first put together when the church was renovated in the late seventeenth century. Their first organ had been torn down when Parliamentary troops had occupied the church during the English Civil War, and the local lord had drummed up the money for the new one as a gesture of goodwill to the new King after the Reformation. It was based on a German model of the time, he recalled, and fondly remembered by his mildly eccentric predecessor as '*Great Gertie*'. With its painted pipes and fine oak case it was far too grand, he supposed, for a small parish church, but the parishioners loved her.

It would be good to hear her played in services again.

Mr Long was doing an impressive job, bringing Gertie's voice back from the grave after years of neglect. Every few minutes he would fiddle with the apertures inside the organ chamber, almost climbing inside her in order to reach, then duck back out and resume his position at the organ stool and play a few bars of music. Reverend Starling was impressed: he liked to see people using their skills and doing a good job.

Cheerfully, he locked up the candles and matches – though the necessity always irked him – and went to check on Mr Long's progress.

He gave a small cough to announce his presence, since the man was halfway inside the great instrument once more. Mr Long wriggled backwards and gave the vicar a slightly bleary smile. There was a long smear of dirt on his face.

"How are you getting on?" the Reverend asked.

"Not bad," said Mr Long, wiping his hands on a dirty rag that was protruding from his work-bag. "She's being a little stubborn, but we'll get her there."

"Excellent!" the Reverend cried, pleased. "I was afraid she'd never get back to her former glory – it's been years since we've had anyone who could play, you see."

"I can tell," Mr Long chuckled, and the vicar smiled.

"Is it mucky back there?" he asked, nodding to the mark on the man's face.

"Centuries of grime," Reggie nodded, rubbing the cloth over his face; it didn't so much get rid of the dirt as much as smear it around a bit. "It's the same with most organs. I'm giving her a bit of a rub down as I go."

"Excellent," said the Reverend, again. "Would you like a cup of tea?"

"I wouldn't say no, Reverend, if you're making one," said Mr Long, breaking into a grin.

"Milk?"

"And one sugar, please."

"Coming right up." Reverend Starling smiled and went to wash up a couple of mugs.

He could hear Mr Long playing the odd phrase of music while he waited for the kettle to boil. Was it his imagination, or were the gaps between the music getting longer?

Must have found a particularly grubby part of the workings, he mused, warming the pot.

Sure enough, the music resumed – this time, the same few bars, over and over as Mr Long tweaked the mysterious apparatus behind the organ pipes. The note came through more clearly and sweetly with each repetition.

Reverend Starling smiled into the fridge. It was good to hear old Gertie starting to sing again.

ooo

Reggie stowed his work-bag in the back office thoughtfully.

The organ in St Chad's had been old and proud, and particularly stubborn, and as such he had rather enjoyed getting to know her. Her workings had been in reasonably good condition, given her age and the recent decade of neglect. He had always enjoyed crawling about in the innards of organs, where possible, and the Reverend had been very happy to have someone who knew what they were doing.

It was good to be working again.

He glanced at the black and white picture of Bessie he had hung next to the door of the back room and smiled. She could survey the whole of the music shop from there, and he was sure that she would be proud of him. She smiled back at him, serene and beautiful. It had been taken around their tenth wedding anniversary – he had its partner in a drawer upstairs, but he had never really liked having photographs of himself around, unless she was in them with him.

He made himself a fresh cup of tea, resisting the temptation to open the grubby bundle he had secreted out of the church. He didn't like stealing from a church, but in this instance he had felt it was necessary. The vicar at St Chad's wouldn't know what to do with it anyway, and it might yield some clue to the location of the Chalice – it wasn't as if he could have left it there.

If Joanna hadn't told him what to look for, he never would have seen it. She had found it one of the old woodblock prints of the church: a rose window that was there on an early sketch that had simply vanished during the restoration. Reggie had had a look at the wall on his way into the church, and had been greatly impressed. The filling in of the window had been done with such precision that only the barest shadow of its former shape was visible. Prospero Bone and his craftsmen had known what they were doing.

There had been a slight gap in the panelling at the back of the organ chamber – a result of age and slight subsidence – and Reggie had managed to slide the panel out of the way while Reverend Starling was making his tea. He had spotted the remains of the rose window when he shone his torch in the narrow shaft between the wooden panels and the wall; they had left the lead and glass in place, simply blocking the apertures up on the outside to keep moisture out of the organ chamber. At the base of the shaft he had found the bundle, and he'd lifted it carefully out, terrified of dropping it and alerting the kindly Reverend – or destroying its contents, whatever they were.

The whole thing smelled strongly of age and mould, and he had wrapped it tightly in one of his work cloths before hiding it in his bag. He'd had just enough time to replace the panel before Reverend Starling had come back out of the kitchen.

They had spent a pleasant few minutes chatting about the church, and about Reggie's shop before the vicar had departed to get on with the never-ending paperwork involved in running a church. He had more or less promised Reggie an on-going contract to keep the organ tuned, and had mentioned the possibility of ordering sheet music from him.

All in all, it had been a worthy afternoon's work.

He crossed back into the shop proper and started to unpack a delivery of music grade books, pulling off the reams of cellophane the supplier felt it necessary to wrap them in and stacking them on the shelves.

The shop was doing better than he'd expected, largely – he thought – given its proximity to Ivy's tea-shop. People always seemed to drift out of there and into one of the other shops in the Arcade, as if the atmosphere of the place made them want to stay.

Otto had been in, as promised, and had run around with the air of an excited puppy, moving suddenly from one thing to another as each book, instrument and gadget caught his attention. He had even tested out some of the instruments, drawing passing customers into the shop; even Mahri and Ivy had drifted in, completely enthralled by his music. Every instrument he touched was transformed in his hands, enchanting the ear and befuddling the brain. Reggie reckoned that he and the shoppers had lost nearly an hour listening to his odd young friend.

He was beginning to understand why, according to the reading he had been surreptitiously doing since Otto's first visit, people were a little edgy around elves. Reggie was aware that, like the Pied Piper from the nursery rhyme, he would have happily followed Otto and his music anywhere, oblivious to any outside influence or danger.

When he had noticed his impromptu audience, Otto had been very embarrassed indeed, and more than a little sheepish. He had apparently promised his mother that he wouldn't cast a thrall over people – except when the Court required it – but when he had seen the range of instruments in the shop he just couldn't help it. He confessed that when it came to music, he could never resist.

Apparently, it had got him into trouble before.

Reggie could well believe it – and was of the firm opinion that Otto's obvious exuberance probably got him into trouble with whatever it was he did for the Court, too.

Still, Otto's lack of self-control had come in handy, drawing more people into the shop to browse; he had made quite a few sales that afternoon, to some significantly dazed customers. A few of the local schools had enquired about sheet music and instruments for their students in the following weeks, and his diary was beginning to fill up with tuning jobs and repairs.

Slowly but surely, he was making a mark.

He looked up when the door opened, and was surprised to see Ogden Rake looking about him with approval. Constable Hardwick had visited Mahri's shop – under the cover of buying his wife flowers – only yesterday, and had been briefed on their progress. He wouldn't have expected any of the Court to be around today – particularly as Post had been studying in the bookshop all day.

"He's long gone," said Ogden, guessing the direction of his thoughts. "Constable Hardwick's following him, in case he makes a detour on his way home. He wasn't in the best of moods when he left," he chuckled. "Christopher appears to be running rings around him."

"I think he's enjoying it," said Reggie, getting to his feet with a smile. "What can I do for you?"

"I'd actually come in about this," he said, offering Reggie a piece of paper.

He took it in mild surprise: it was one of the posters that he and Jake had stuck up around the arcade about Saffy's puppies. Other than Jake's puppy, one had been promised to Joanna, and there had been a little interest from a couple of Mahri's fellow choristers, but they still needed to find homes for the other five.

"You want to adopt a pup?" he asked, surprised.

"Not for me," the big man laughed. "It's my nephew's birthday next month, and I thought a bit of responsibility would do him good."

"How old is he?" asked Reggie, curiously.

"Four," said Rake, with a grin. "He started school this year."

"Bit of a handful?" Reggie wondered aloud. Constable Rake was clearly very fond of the boy.

"No more than I was," he said cheerfully. "His mum keeps him in line, at any rate."

"Reliable?"

"As any four-year-old," Rake chuckled. "I'd see to it that the dog was cared for, if that's what you're asking."

"It was," admitted Reggie, with a grin. "I don't see why we can't let him have one. Would you like to come up and meet them? It'll be a few weeks before they're old enough for us to let them go."

"Certainly," Rake grinned. "If you have time."

"I was just about to shut up for the day, anyway," said Reggie, and went to lock the door.

Constable Rake looked around the shop with the air of one impressed.

"You've made some headway in here," he remarked.

"Cheers," said Reggie. "It's not what I'd imagined I'd be doing at my age," he chuckled. "It sort of took me by surprise, all this."

"Ah," said Rake, clapping him on the back. "You're still pretty spry – enjoy it!"

"I have been," Reggie chuckled. "That surprised me too."

Rake laughed, and he led him through the back of the shop, stooping to pick up his work-bag as he went.

"Evening Astrid," he said, as they made their way through the main room of the Arcade. The girl was lying on her front surrounded by books of magic. She gave them both a little wave, which they returned.

"She seems dedicated," said Rake, as they crossed Ivy's garden.

"Driven," Reggie agreed. "Honestly, I don't know where she gets the energy some days – she and her brother wipe me out after a few hours. And the pace at which she reads – it's hard to believe that she's only seven!"

ooo

Delicately, Professor Barraclough peeled away the wrappings from the bundle that Reggie had found behind the organ chamber at St Chad's. They were ragged and thin with age, blackened by the grime of four centuries.

The others were standing around Ivy's kitchen, tense with anticipation. They were ranged around the room at what each had decided was a safe distance – in case Reggie had discovered something particularly unpleasant. Unsurprisingly, this meant that Joanna was at one side of the Professor, and her ghastly brother on the other, neither of them willing to let him face peril on his own. Constable Rake stood a little way away, concentrating on containment and diffusion spells in case this turned nasty; Ivy leaned against the counter at roughly the same distance but on the other side of the table, vines coiling behind her like her own personal jungle.

Unusually, Christopher had drawn away from the group, finding the mouldering smell of the bundle tenacious and overpowering for his strong sense of smell. He was presently alternating between trying not to gag at the odour and growling very quietly. Whatever it was that Reggie had found was making him distinctly uncomfortable. The children, who had been allowed to watch, were huddled on the sofa between Mahri and Reggie, each adult ready to grab them and flee if it became necessary.

Ignoring his nerves, Professor Barraclough adjusted his grip on the iron forceps they kept for handling the more difficult tomes and peeled away another layer of cloth. The thick leather gloves he was wearing were unwieldy, which made controlling the forceps no easy task.

Everyone held a collective breath as he gently pulled away the last scrap of wrappings.

Christopher recoiled, retreating as far as he could as the stench of rotting blood poured forth from the decaying fabric.

The whole room, Practitioner and non-Practitioner alike, shared a collective shudder. Waves of dark energy washed over the room – on the sofa, Jake's nerve failed him and he wisely took refuge in Reggie's jumper.

Christopher didn't blame him. He felt a powerful urge to run into his room and barricade the door, taking the children with him. It was almost overwhelming.

The air had become palpably hotter, spreading the dreadful stench to every corner. Behind Ivy, the swarming vines rippled uneasily, only her calming influence keeping them in check.

"Hmm," said Professor Barraclough, peering down at the fetid thing through his monocle, a look of intense concentration across his features. The shadows cast by the dying sun briefly rendered the Barracloughs as macabre as their grave friend.

There was a feeling of great anticipation in the Arcade as every inhabitant – and even the building herself – waited to see what would happen next.

Professor Barraclough turned it over: within the tattered wrappings lay the degraded remains of an old, battered book.

"It's a book," Rake observed, in his rich, deep voice. It seemed very out of place in the tense atmosphere.

"It's not a very friendly book," said Astrid, in a small

voice. The girl's knuckles were white from gripping the back of the sofa. Mahri patted her back reassuringly.

It had clearly seen better days – great chunks of the pages were missing, but those that had remained were blackened with age and dirt, some of their edges charred by some ancient misadventure. It looked very much like something had tried to chew it at some point. There were deep gouges in what was left of the bindings and they oozed with a black, sticky, pitch-like substance that reeked of rotting flesh.

The ghastly tome radiated hatred and anger and white, cold fear.

Apart from its awful reek of carrion and evil, it appeared to be dormant, as if it were blind to the people peering down at it. Christopher got the impression that it was watching them all the same, reaching out from some deep, wretched place to take them all in, trying to find a way in, a means of control.

The thing on the table seemed to be sucking the very sound from their voices.

"No," said Joanna Barraclough, thoughtfully. "But it's also not a very well book."

"Powerful though," said Zarrubabel, with something akin to lust in his reedy voice. "Very powerful..."

"It's dying," Christopher growled, through clenched teeth.

Professor Barraclough nodded, one bushy eyebrow raised.

"I doubt it was ever very pleasant," he said, speculatively. He looked up at Christopher sharply. "What do you make of it?"

"I don't like it one bit," said Christopher, with distaste.

"That's hardly a reason to discount a thing," Zarrubabel scoffed.

Christopher grunted, unable to open his mouth long enough to retort.

"That's not what I meant," said Barraclough, rather shortly. "What does it smell like?"

Christopher swallowed hard before answering, afraid

that this time he really might be sick. "Like an overripe corpse," he managed, and the rest of the room grimaced.

"It's just musty from here," Ivy observed. "With a hint of iron. Can any of you hear it?" she added, and there was a hint of reluctance in her voice, as though she would rather not have her suspicions confirmed.

Christopher glanced at his friend: there was a hunted look about her. Returning his gaze to the repulsive book on the table, he wondered what awful things it might be whispering.

"I can hear it," said Mahri, softly, and Christopher was surprised to see the silvery tracks of tears on her cheeks. He looked back at the table, embarrassed.

Out of the corner of his eye he saw Astrid and Reggie move closer to the older witch.

"I'm picking up low-level stuff," rumbled Rake, slowly. "Not words, as such – just grumbling." An odd shiver passed across his face. "The tone, however, is quite clear."

"Can you make out the title?" Professor Barraclough asked, still frowning deeply.

Both Joanna and Zarrubabel leaned forward, squinting at the ravaged cover.

"That could be a 'D'," said Joanna. "What do you think, Hector?"

"These could be a 'C' and an 'H'," Zarrubabel mused, poking a spectral finger at the cover.

Christopher tensed: as Zarrubabel's ectoplasmic appendage had passed across the front of the ghastly book he could have sworn that the thing had stirred in his mind. He wished that Joanna and the professors would move away from it.

He clenched and unclenched his hands, restlessly.

"- and that wiggly one could be an 'S'," Professor Barraclough was saying. "'Dis' something, perhaps?"

"Could it be 'Discord'?" Ivy asked, still holding back a morass of unhappy vegetation.

"Aptly named," said Reggie, from the sofa.

"It could be *'Dischordia'*," said Joanna, looking up at

her, surprised. "But that hasn't been seen since…" she trailed off, her eyes falling back to the book on the table.

"Since the early seventeenth century," Christopher finished, catching on.

Professor Barraclough gave a low whistle. "It was a compendium of demons," he said, without looking up. "Rather famous and incredibly dangerous. Fatal, even, on occasion."

"Oh, let me read it, Morton!" Zarrubabel cried, and everyone turned to look at him in shock. There was a distinct note of desperate greed in his voice as he pleaded with his old friend. "Oh, go on, Morton! Please?"

The little man was bobbing up and down in barely contained excitement, his sage green eyes were wide with zeal, like great, green lanterns in his pale, translucent face.

Christopher had never seen the poltergeist so animated, even when he was engaged in one of his bouts of aerial bombardment.

"You'll do nothing of the sort!" cried Professor Barraclough, shortly.

Christopher frowned, unaccustomed to his employer's sharp tone. He guessed that the two professors had been having this kind of argument for as long as they had been friends.

Zarrubabel's temper began to flare, and Christopher privately wondered at the depth of the spectre's lust for knowledge.

"It's not like it'll kill me, Morton!"

"We can't take that risk – there are far worse things than death, as you well know," Professor Barraclough snapped. "And besides, you aren't the only one in here. If the stories about *Dischordia* are true, it won't just keep its wrath to you if it can help it."

But Zarrubabel wasn't listening. Like a child who has been forbidden the thing it most desires, he reached mould-green hands past the Professor and snatched the book from the table, clutching it tightly to his chest.

Professor Barraclough gave a shout of dismay –

everyone in the room lunged forward at once, intending to wrest it from his arms – but it was too late.

The sudden movement had startled the spectre and he rushed backwards, tipping his glass box over as it caught on a chair leg – the dreadful book fell from his arms.

It hit the wooden floor of the kitchen with a wet sort of thud.

It had turned as it fell, wrenching some of their pages free of their bindings: they scattered across the floor like ashes.

"My book!" Zarrubabel cried, scrambling to collect the wayward pages.

The wave of fury hit him smack in the ghostly chest and carried him backward several feet.

Christopher clutched his head as wave upon wave of pain and fear gripped his body. All around the room his friends were staggering and stumbling, unable to avoid the awesome power of the *Dischordia*.

It was as if it was singing to them, with a voice like thousands of nails being dragged down a blackboard, full of anger and terror and bitter, biting hatred.

Even Martha's stalwart vines had retreated, trying with all their might to put as much distance between them and the cursed thing as possible.

It sang of betrayal, and envy, and death, winding its hideous melody around their minds like bindweed, stifling any resistance.

Driven to his knees and supporting himself on his hands, Christopher fought the urge to change with every fibre of his being. The wolf in him was being driven mad with fear. It wanted nothing more than to bolt – to put as much distance between itself and the terrible, shrieking thing on the floor as it could. It felt trapped, and Christopher knew that if the tome didn't relinquish its hold in the very near future, it would burst out of him and lash out at every person in the room. It was almost beyond reason.

Christopher forced it back with all the will he had.

He couldn't let him escape – he knew exactly what

would happen if he did.

Images of bloodied corpses flashed through his mind as a fresh wave of terror possessed him. He cried out, desperate to escape the broken bodies of his new family, the stench of their blood filling his consciousness. These images were replaced with the faces of Rachel and his parents, faces frozen in screams of terror as he tore them apart.

He could taste their blood in his mouth, warm and ferrous, and horribly seductive.

He bit back a growl, trying to right himself amongst the torrent of sensation. It wasn't real, he realised, with dull, thudding hope. With fresh determination, he pushed the wolf back down, willing himself to be calm and whispering soothing words to his inner self.

Piece by piece he came back to himself, controlling his rebellious body, concentrating fully on every halting breath.

The storm of sound and light was subsiding now, crashing against them with less intensity as the power of the book faded.

Shaking with the effort, his skin slick with sweat, Christopher rested his forehead against his arm and waited for the room to stop spinning.

As the distant screams lost their intensity, other sounds began to seep into his consciousness: around him, people were sobbing, whimpering.

Weakly, he raised his head.

He couldn't see Astrid or Jake, but from the sounds emanating from the sofa they weren't alone. He could smell Mahri and Reggie cowering there, protecting the children.

The Barracloughs were slumped against the glass of the Arcade, Ogden Rake beside them. He was clutching Zarrubabel's book in his great, powerful arms.

Ivy, bereft of her vines, was huddled against the kitchen counters; she was extremely white and was making no sound at all.

Christopher crawled over to her, not wanting to

speculate on what the foul *Dischordia* had shown her.

She rested her head against his shoulder, trembling violently.

Gradually, the sounds of distress subsided as the fearsome tome lost its hold over them.

One by one they looked up, gazing blearily around at one another, pale with exhaustion and fear.

There was a very quiet sound, like the breathy crunch of new-fallen snow, and the *Dischordia* crumbled in on itself, reduced to empty flakes of paper, its final breath spent.

None of them spoke for a very long time, feeling the need of the soothing silence.

Eventually, Professor Barraclough spoke. "Hector?" he asked, quietly.

Professor Zarrubabel didn't even look up, still too shell-shocked to move.

"Don't *ever* do that again."

26
The Eye-Eater

"I wouldn't want to be our spectral friend right now," said Xander, his shoes crunching on the gravel path.

"Nor I, neither," Ogden agreed. "I'm hoping he learned his lesson, though – with or without his sister's remonstrations."

Xander looked at his friend out of the corner of his eyes. It had been a week since Reggie had found *'Dischordia'* rotting in the back of the organ at St Bartholomew's, and his partner hadn't been his jocular self since.

The two friends had been working together for nearly twelve years – ever since they had finished their training. Xander had joined the Court in London and moved north so that he and Rhosyn could be closer to her family.

He'd felt lost and completely out of place in the quiet Midlands town – until, that is, he had met Ogden Rake.

Ogden, who at the time had been scrawny and slight, had invited him back to his gran's house after their first double shift. His grandmother, a formidable woman who thought they both needed to put on some weight, had fed them so much of a fiery concoction she referred to as 'swamp gumbo' that Xander could barely walk by the time he left. He and Ogden had staggered back to the Court, discussing family recipes and swapping stories. By the time they got back on shift they were very tired, several pounds heavier, and best friends.

He was aware that most of the local Constables called them the Odd Couple behind their backs but, Xander didn't mind. He and Ogden might come from very different places, but they had the same drive, the same dogged determination, the same basic requirement for there to be justice in the world.

As dissimilar as they were, the partnership worked.

They nodded to the verger as they made their way up to the church doors.

The approach was impressive: the great doors were made out of iron and black oak – they made an imposing impression on the visitor, standing out as they did from the creamy local sandstone.

The inside of the church was no less impressive. Almost every inch of the small building was covered with memorials of every conceivable type. It was as if the wealthy and pious of the village had been successfully competing with one another for centuries in the austere business of death.

Ogden and Xander shared a speaking look: this was going to take a while.

Rake took the South transept while Xander set off along the North. There was a lot to take in: everywhere there were plaques and hangings, statues and busts. His shoes clicked on the polished marble memorials beneath his feet.

It was like treading on history.

He shuddered slightly and pulled his jacket closer around him. He'd never liked walking on graves, even when he was a kid. He and his classmates had made a game of it, hanging around their local graveyard at dusk and daring one another to stalk across the patches of gravel or grass – or, worst of all – to stand there, alone on the grave for a timed five minutes. He still remembered the thrill of fear he had felt, leaping through the air.

It had been a rite of passage in their minds, and anyone that failed their five minute sojourn would forever be branded a wuss.

Xander smiled inwardly at their naivety.

He had always been the best at it, despite his fear, until the day that one of the occupants of the graves they were trampling on woke up and rose, pale, terrifying and quite annoyed, through the turf beneath his feet. All of them had turned and run to their homes, too frightened even to scream, and vowed never to speak of it.

None of his friends had wanted to go back to the graveyard, but Xander had. He had taken the old lady they had disturbed a bunch of flowers bought with his pocket money, along with a heartfelt apology. He had spent several very interesting evenings chatting to her and her neighbours.

It had been his first inkling that he might not be quite as 'normal' as his peers expected him to be. His parents had been quite bemused by the thought of a wizard in the family, but had agreed to let him attend one of the more unusual evening classes at the local college and given him loving if bemused smiles when he had announced his intention to apply to the Court.

Sometimes he even imagined that they might be proud of him.

The names of Upper Fleet's long dead parishioners looked down on him across the ages, carved deeply in stone.

Annie Lodge, Everett Colby, Michael de Flowers, Hannah Procter...

He wondered about their lives, wondered if their days had been idle or well-spent.

Had Everett gambled the family fortunes? Had Hannah married the man she loved?

The church was full of half-whispered stories, dust and stone the only remains of lives lived so long ago. Xander peered at the nearest panel, dedicated to a Thomas Langley: '*2 Years & 3 Days*'.

He lowered his eyes and moved on, feeling something of the sadness the child's family must have known.

Xander walked to the rack beside the altar and lit a candle for the distant Thomas (those three days!). He raised his eyes to the icon of Mary above the votaries, smiling at the playful young Messiah in her lap. He wondered whether the young Thomas's parents had found comfort in knowing that he was with the highly favoured lady.

Tearing his eyes from the candles and his thoughts from the forlorn memorial, he ventured into a little chapel off the North transept.

Here too, the centuries of memorials had

accumulated, though these were all far more elaborate. Clearly the chapel had been reserved for the wealthiest patrons of the church.

The room was littered with disturbingly lifelike carvings of men and women in states of repose – though one fellow was striking what could only be described as a noble pose, shading his eyes and staring off into the distance.

Someone – possibly the artist – had positioned him so that he was looking out to the window, as though even in death he was dreaming of far off places.

Xander read the plaque at the gentleman's feet.

Captain Daniel Hollis
1769-1832
At home on the waves

He smiled: the sculptor had captured the Captain's wistfulness. Xander wondered whether he would have preferred to die at sea instead of in a quiet English Village.

He turned away and stopped, a glint of polished marble catching his eye.

She was tucked in behind the Captain, the silken folds of her dress catching the gentle sunlight, lending her an ethereal glow.

She laid upon the marble dais, peaceful and serene, her arms folded lightly across her chest.

Like the old seaman, her features were distinct, as though the sculptor had known her in life. She looked almost as though she were sleeping and might wake up at any moment; he half expected her to open her eyes and wink, a wry smile on her face. He shook his head to dislodge the image, not wishing to disturb her. It was always a risk, with skills like his.

He moved closer, squeezing between two other monuments: her canopy, which he had taken at first for yet more marble, turned out to be carved from a dense white wood, almost the same hue as the lady below.

Leaves and flowers had been carved into the canopy, interlocking so completely that for a moment Xander wondered whether they had simply grown there of their own accord.

There was a slight smile on the lady's face, as though she were dreaming of something pleasant.

No – thought Xander suddenly, unable to suppress his internal Copper's instinct – not like she's dreaming, like she knows something that we don't and is enjoying that fact.

He bent down to read the inscription and noted with mild dismay that parts of the plaque had been broken – shattered, perhaps, by unscrupulous persons trying to pry the lid off.

It now read:

16--
Her- -ie- the –dy of Ca-hryn Pe----n
Bubbl-s broken
But
Death's th- G-te t- Life

"Bubbles broken," he mouthed, conscious of every sound in the enclosing silence of the chapel.

It was a strange thing to write on a tombstone, particularly one so grand.

He laid his palm against the cool stone and closed his eyes, hoping that Cathryn was in a receptive mood.

For a few, long, quiet moments there was nothing at all, just the sound of his heart beat in the calm of the chapel.

Xander measured his breathing, waiting for the rush of sensation he was hoping would follow.

Suddenly there was the feeling of being out of doors in a warm breeze – the smell of pine resin – the feel of parchment under the hand – a flash of red hair – a woman's laughter – the taste of spiced pears...

As abruptly as the sensations had appeared, they were gone. Xander smiled slightly to himself.

Wherever Cathryn was, she was at peace.

He was glad for her, as unhelpful to his case this might prove.

He opened his eyes and took in the intricate decoration on the main trunk of the tomb once more. He was still gazing at it when he became aware of a presence behind him.

"Find anything?" Ogden rumbled from above him.

"Maybe," Xander replied, speculatively. "But it looks like someone has beaten us to it." He nodded at the damage on the tomb.

There was a rustle of paper above him as Xander squinted through the thin crack beneath the lid: it was too dark to see anything within.

Glumly contemplating Cathryn Pe----n's rest, he straightened up, wincing slightly at the familiar tightening in his back – an old football injury.

"Says here that the tomb of Cathryn Penrhyn was raided at some point in the early nineteenth century," said Ogden, waving an unexpectedly pink pamphlet under his friend's nose.

"Where did you get that?"

"There's a whole table of them by the old font – looked more like a boulder to me, but the label was quite clear. I left a donation," he grinned, on his friend's expression.

"I never doubted it for a second," said Xander, fighting a smile of his own. "Does it say what they made off with?"

"There's a lot of bluster about vandalism," said Ogden, in his measured voice. "As you'd expect..." he scanned the pamphlet for a few moments and Xander waited with mild impatience, feeling sure that they must – finally – be on to something.

"Sounds like they were treasure hunters – the thieves. There's something about rumours that Cathryn was buried with gold and jewels," Ogden continued. "It says that the circumstances of her death and burial were quite unusual."

"Unusual how?" Xander asked, glancing down at the

serene, knowing face below him.

"She died suddenly in what the vicar describes as 'Mysterious Circumstances'." Ogden snorted. "With extra capital letters – and she was buried at night, with – capitals again – 'Much Secrecy'." He looked over the top of his pamphlet at Cathryn's strange sepulchre. "Magic?" he wondered aloud.

"Wouldn't surprise me," said Xander. "Sudden mysterious deaths tend that way. Does it say when she died? That bit's come off."

"1671," Ogden read aloud. "That fits with old Prospero..." he trailed off as he read on.

"What?"

"Says here she wasn't the only one to have met an unexpected end," said Ogden, slowly. "They found the would-be thieves slumped against the tomb in the morning." He met his friend's gaze. "Their eyes had been burnt out."

"Like Cairo," said Xander, shocked.

"Like Cairo..." Ogden waved the pamphlet again. "It gets a bit confused after that," he said. "Apparently Cathryn's skeleton was pointing up out of the tomb accusingly, as if she had cursed them somehow – *and* the men's bodies were removed from their graves some weeks after burial."

"Body snatching?" exclaimed Xander, astonished.

"Maybe," Ogden nodded. "Local legend has it that they're still out there somewhere, Stalking the Night."

"Capitals again?"

Ogden nodded, smiling.

"Quite an odd fellow, this Reverend," he observed, with a light smile.

"Might not blame him, in a parish like this," Xander reasoned. "Grave robbing, curses, possible zombies – it'd be enough to shake anyone's faith. Or to confirm it. Do you think that was us, by the way?"

"Probably," said Ogden, carefully refolding the pamphlet and tucking it inside his coat. "Victor will know," he added, and this time there was the barest hint of reluctance in his voice.

ooo

"St Andrew's at Upper Fleet," Victor mused, scratching his stubbly chin. "Early nineteenth century, you said?"

There were two mumbled 'yeses' from the uncomfortable constables behind him.

Visiting Victor was often an unnerving experience, given his speciality and experience. It was rather like being called into the Headmaster's office – even if you knew you hadn't done anything wrong, he had the ability to make you feel as though you were six years old and had forgotten your PE kit.

There was a general suspicion among the serving constables of the Court that this was exactly what he had been, before circumstances had forced him down a very different path.

Still, he didn't do it on purpose and he was usually quite cheerful when someone visited his lonely record room. He had a formidable memory and besides, if you needed local information from the last few centuries there was no one better informed.

After all, he'd been there for most of it.

"Upper Fleet, Upper Fleet," he mused, running long grey fingers over the index cards behind his desk. "Bit of a rough one, I recall. Springtime. Some of the new recruits had a job coping with that business with the eyeballs."

"Did they ever find them?" Xander asked, interested.

"What? Oh, no – completely burnt out, nothing left to find."

Behind him, Ogden and Xander exchanged a speaking look.

"Aha!" Victor cried in triumph. "Here we are: April 1823 – Constables were McKay and Bickley – good coppers, as I recall."

He coughed and a great cloud of dust flew up about

him; Xander couldn't tell if it was from the box of records or from the man himself.

He tried not to dwell on it.

"Yes," Victor was rasping. "Nasty way to go – burned from the inside out. They exhumed the bodies a few weeks later."

"They didn't do a very good job of cleaning up after themselves," Ogden observed, dryly. "The resident vicar is still talking about it."

He showed Victor the pamphlet from the church and the zombie nodded.

"They were different times," he said, almost wistfully. "People were less sceptical – more prepared to believe in magic. If there was a rumour of curses then that would be enough to keep people away for decades. These days any whiff of a conspiracy and there's half a dozen journalists breathing down your necks."

"People are more inquisitive," said Xander.

Victor fixed him with a glassy stare.

"No, I don't think so," he said, quietly. "People were just as curious then as now – perhaps even more so. It's more that today everyone's more cynical. Everyone appears to be clamouring to prove that there's hardly anything we no longer know, and it's simply not true."

There was a stony silence for a few minutes as Victor located the correct file.

"Hmm," he said, as he drew it out. He carried it to the table, a frown creasing his decrepit brow. "Hmm..." he said again.

The constables watched him carefully. They knew better than to disturb him when he was thinking, however tempting it might be.

"Someone has read this file recently, without my permission." There was an air of wounded pride in his voice.

Victor seldom left his archive these days, particularly since someone had given him a second hand games console a few Christmases ago. When he wasn't dusting his precious records he spent most of his time playing games in the rooms at the back of the archive, where he slept.

"Recently?" Ogden asked.

There was no point asking whether Victor was sure. Somehow, he always knew.

Victor nodded, affronted by this discovered intrusion into his realm.

"Anything missing?" Xander asked, carefully.

They waited while Victor examined each typewritten page.

"Not that I can see," he said, at last. "What's here reflects the case as I recall it, but I can't be certain." He scratched his long nose speculatively. "I'll have to report this to the Sheriff."

"Can we take the file?" Xander asked, not wanting to be cheated out of any possible links to the Chalice.

"Not yet," said Victor, with understanding. "I'll need to catalogue its contents first. I'll bring it up to you."

ooo

"Any word from –" Otto lowered his voice "- our friends on the outside?" He waggled his eyebrows. They were tinted turquoise again. Xander tried not to laugh.

"Nothing," he said. "Listen, you haven't told anyone about them, have you?"

"No," said Otto surprised. "I've been too busy working on the Retrograde Engine. Why shouldn't I?"

"No reason," said Xander, and then – because whatever their differences over the peculiar Cat, Xander trusted him – he added: "At least, nothing I'm sure about."

Otto gave him an appraising look and his unaccustomed stillness surprised Xander.

"You will let me know when you *are* sure, won't you?"

"Naturally."

Otto continued his scrutiny for a few more moments before nodding, and Xander wondered whether he might have spotted some unusual goings-on in his own part of the Court. In an instant, his carefree demeanour had returned. Xander was relieved. A solemn Otto was an unnerving thing.

The Technomancer grinned lopsidedly and turned to go, very nearly crashing into Victor, who had materialised silently behind him. He managed to conceal his squeal of surprise quite well and backed up a few paces.

"I need a word," Victor said, ignoring Otto. "Get Rake – Sheriff's office." Finally, he glanced at Otto. "Stringbean too. Ten minutes."

He turned and shambled off, ignoring the stares of various colleagues in the great cavern. Victor spent so much time in his archives that any time he came up was a bit of an event.

Xander nodded to Otto, was raised turquoise eyebrows skywards.

"Rake's upstairs," he said, and Otto hurried off in the direction of the only above-ground section of the Court – the canteen.

Xander checked his watch and sighed. He'd never hear the end of this. He ducked his head into one of the administrative cells off the wing that tended to think of itself as the heart of the organisation. It was more or less an accurate assumption.

"Claire?" he called, and a cloud of violet hair emerged from under a desk.

Xander raised an eyebrow.

"Lost my bloody contact lens," she explained, squinting up at him. "What can I do you for?"

"Rosie?"

He glanced around, not overly surprised at the absence of his wife. Every Court in the country was understaffed and overworked. They kept their staff busy.

"Bank run – she swapped with me," Claire added on his questioning look. "Lunch date."

Xander grinned.

"Good looking?"

"Sublime," Claire agreed, and he laughed.

"If you're still here when she gets back can you tell her I can't make *our* lunch date?"

"No problem. Anything interesting?"

"Don't know yet, but I'm betting I'll be in the doghouse for this."

Claire grimaced in understanding. "Third time this month?" she asked.

Rhosyn and Xander had long ago adopted a system of strikes that kept their relationship running along at a cheerful consistency. This had rather a lot to do with Xander's unpredictable timetable and Rhosyn's fiery temper – it was one of the things that had first attracted him to her. Three strikes and you were in trouble.

"Fourth," he admitted, and Claire sucked air over her teeth in sympathy. "Criminals don't respect lunch dates, I'm afraid."

Claire snorted. "They don't respect weekends or public holidays either. I'll let her know."

"Thanks Claire – have fun with Mr Sublime."

"I intend to," she grinned and he left her searching for her elusive contact lens.

He hurried along a well-lit tunnel towards the Sheriff's office. Whatever Victor had found wouldn't be good. If someone had been down there without him noticing...

Fleetingly he thought of Astrid Healy, brave and fierce at seven years old, but quickly dismissed the thought. She and her friends would have no need for clandestine access to the Court archives – he didn't think that Ivy Burwell would countenance covert trespassing when simply asking a question would work just as well.

Besides, Otto's ridiculous cat had developed a bit of an affinity for the girl and would probably have followed her. That would have been the end of it, too; Victor had something of a sixth sense for cats – he hated the creatures.

If Cat had been within fifty feet of the archive door, the cantankerous old zombie would have got him with the plant mister he kept under his desk for just such a purpose, and Cat would have shot straight up to Otto's chaotic laboratory and taken refuge on his master's head.

Since he hadn't seen any turquoise felines recently, Xander discounted the possibility.

The caverns of the Brindleford Court were well guarded with charms and traps – even witnesses and complainants were carefully watched and searched on both entry and exit. Inventive children notwithstanding, the caverns were largely secure.

That left but one possibility, and he didn't like it one bit.

The only people who were never searched at the gates were the members of the Court themselves.

ooo

They left the Sheriff's office several hours later, grim faced and silent – though in Victor's case this wasn't much different than usual.

"Well," said Otto, restively. There appeared to be rather a lot that he couldn't fully articulate, because he said it again, letting it hang in front of them like a great cloud of distrust. "Well..."

"Are we sure there isn't more missing?" Ogden asked, in a low voice.

They had spent the last few hours going through their most recent records and had found a disturbing number of discrepancies – and not just amongst the documents.

Someone had made a concerted effort to leave no trace of themselves, and if it hadn't been for Victor's eye for detail and the occasional missing file, they might never have known that they had a spy in their midst.

"I'll keep looking," Victor assured them.

"Me too," said Otto, quietly. "I'll tell the lads it's research –" he cracked an uncertain smile. "I'll say it's a rethink – a look at where we might be going wrong. I think it's fair to say we need to do that anyway." He gave an unhappy little chuckle. "Maybe some good will come of all this, after all."

He rubbed at his turquoise-stained face unhappily.

There was little of his usual exuberance in him now. Like the other three, the Court was a large part of Otto's life, and like the other three, he had taken this flagrant betrayal of trust rather personally. He just wasn't as good at hiding it.

"There's really no way we could have missed it?" he asked again, hopefully. He took in their faces and nodded. "No, I suppose not..."

The file on the deaths at St Andrew's at Upper Fleet had led Victor into the evidence room, to the locked glass case at the very back of the room that could only be opened with a particular key. A key that had been charmed to respond only to members of the Court. It had been signed out, in the past year, over five hundred times.

More worrying still had been the space in the cabinet where one of the more dangerous items that the Court had seized should have been. Whoever had removed it had left behind the meticulously inscribed warning not to handle the object without the proper protection – in this case heavy duty welder's gloves were recommended.

Cathryn Penrhyn had died after the experiment that she and her older brother had been conducting all those years ago – as a direct result of the unassuming crystal orb that should have been in the locked cupboard.

They had listened with growing unease as Victor described the events leading up to the young woman's death. She and her brother Marcus had been searching for a means to communicate with their mother, who had died when they were small. The idea had been – Otto had worked out from the case notes – to attract their mother's spirit using some of her worldly possessions and catch her in a crystal globe for a short while.

To their credit, they hadn't intended to keep her. Their dearest wish was to speak with her one last time, and to say their goodbyes as they had been unable to when they were children. Then they would smash the globe and free her spirit once more, and be at peace in themselves.

They had been young and naïve – barely out of the

childhood that they longed to leave behind – too caught up in the thrill of their own brilliance to consider the possibility that it might not be their mother who came to them.

The two of them had watched, enthralled, as the orb had filled with a swirling pearlescent light, the beauty of which Marcus had later found impossible to describe. He had tried, in his suicide note.

He had allowed Cathryn to go first, out of simple filial love, and had watched as his beloved sister reached out a hand to the globe, hoping to find her mother.

What she had found instead was a particularly malevolent creature that had been lurking at the edge of the light for centuries, waiting for its chance to feed – and feed it had. Marcus had been paralysed with fear as he watched his sister scream and writhe in agony before dropping to her knees, stone dead.

The globe had rolled, unbroken despite its fall, to rest at his feet even as Cathryn slumped back, staring up at him through the empty sockets that once held her kind, brown eyes.

It had not been a pleasant death – and nor had Marcus's. His unfortunate father had found his son hanging from the post of his bed, the morning after Cathryn's night burial. His last confession had been found on his writing desk, along with a crystal globe emitting 'an unholy light'.

His poor father, faced with the task of burying both his children in the same week, had closed himself off from the world, commissioning memorials for them both. Marcus had been interred on the grounds of the Penrhyn estate, since by church law the manner of his death precluded burial in consecrated ground, and their father had sealed the orb in his daughter's tomb, hoping to leave her as its protector through the ages.

The grave robbers a century later had prised the carefully wrapped globe from Cathryn's skeletal hands and sealed their own fates.

When the Constables had concluded their

investigation they had locked the dreadful thing away in their evidence room, christening it the 'Eye-Eater' and hoping never to see it again.

And now someone had taken it.

One of the members of that same Court – the very people sworn to protect their community. They had gone behind their colleagues' backs and given the awful thing to the one man that could do the Brindleford Court the most damage.

Quentin Post.

The four men in the tunnel shared a grim look.

There was unpleasant work to be done.

27
Home Sweet Home

Christopher stared glumly out at the neon orange night, his arms crossed tightly across his chest.

It had been nearly two months since Rake and Hardwick had discovered that the Court had a spy in its midst and the hunt for the Chalice had ground to an infuriating and total halt.

The Court were reluctant to make a move until they had identified their traitor, and equally reluctant to let anyone else do any investigating in the meantime, just in case.

They had been lucky so far, in that Rake, Hardwick and Otto had been too busy to really mention the Arcade to anyone at the Court other than the Sheriff.

He huffed, a great cloud of steam forming in the chilly air.

It was terribly frustrating.

With every week that crept by, Post was edging his way nearer to the Chalice, if it still existed, and there was nothing they could do to stop him. They had all but run out of impositions: books that had been 'lost' had had to be recovered, those that had been secreted away by the Widow Jenkins and Dr Fitzhearn had to be returned, albeit reluctantly. The fine balance of being just unhelpful enough to keep the nefarious Post off-track without him noticing was getting increasingly difficult to maintain.

Christopher really didn't want to think about what might happen if he got his hands on the thing.

Post's manner towards him hadn't really altered over the past few weeks, though he did seem a good deal terser of late, particularly when he was informed that every other book he was looking for had been lost, taken out, or been cannibalised by its neighbours. So far, he appeared to be chalking it all up to a combination of bad luck and Christopher's infatuation with Ivy. For the moment – however uncomfortable Post's attempts at brotherly advice made him – Christopher hoped it would stay that way.

He didn't like to imagine what the son of a man who had voluntarily eaten another person's heart would do to an interfering werewolf.

He sighed and brought the shop sign back inside.

Quite apart from the dangers of a greed-driven psychopath getting their hands on a powerful magical artefact, Christopher *really* didn't want the slimy bastard to win.

He gave Jake a wave as he passed the window of the teashop – he had his face pressed up to the glass and was industriously pulling faces at passers-by. He grinned and blew a raspberry at his friend.

Christopher deposited the large metal sign behind the door, and switched off the lights, wincing slightly as his back twinged. It had only been two days since the last full moon, and he was still feeling it. The constant ache that followed every transformation was just beginning to fade, and its nagging presence wasn't doing anything for his mood.

Locking up, he ducked Zarrubabel's hurled missiles with barely a thought, the poltergeist's shrieks following him up the spiral staircase. Ivy was still downstairs with Jake, and Astrid was with Mahri this evening, so the main room of the Arcade seemed large and empty.

Briefly, he toyed with the idea of a quick nap while everything was quiet, but that seemed awfully self-indulgent while everyone else was still busy, so he went into his study instead, intending to read. Sleep took him almost as soon as he'd settled on the sofa, his book resting open on his chest.

He awoke an hour or so later with a crick in his neck, feeling refreshed. He stretched and returned his fallen book back to the shelf, wondering at how oddly quiet the Arcade had remained.

He padded into the main room, his thick woollen socks (a much-loved present from Ivy) making no sound at all on the wooden floor, and sniffed the air. A mixture of vanilla and soap told him that Ivy was indulging in a bath while the children were away. He glanced across at the coach houses where, sure enough, he could see Jake and Astrid 'helping' Mahri bake cakes for Ivy's teashop.

He padded to the table, where a covered dish of something that smelled strongly of chilli had been inexpertly labelled 'Cristafer'. Recognising Jake's exuberant handwriting he smiled, pleased to have been remembered. He heated it up in the underused microwave – both Ivy and Mahri had a healthy mistrust for it, but Christopher, who had lived for a long time with no cooking facilities at all, couldn't get out of the habit. For the moment, his one concession to luxury from his years on the run was being tolerated, but every time he came upstairs he half expected Mahri to have removed it.

Happy in the knowledge that his odd little family was safe and well, Christopher took his food and settled down on one of the long, squashy sofas. Idly, he flicked through the channels on the television, eventually deciding on a passable documentary on steam railways.

Ivy appeared after a while and joined him on the couch, her wet hair smelling distractingly of vanilla.

The program on railways turned almost seamlessly into a documentary on the Roman invasion, and Ivy made them both some tea. Christopher suspected that she, too, was enjoying the opportunity to think about nothing in particular. They had all done far too much worrying over the past few months, and whatever Ivy might say about there no longer being a Witch, he knew that she felt her family's burden keenly.

It seemed to Christopher that they had just reached a state where their brains were pleasantly empty when a clip advertising a program on late medieval religious architecture flashed up and shattered their careful cultivated indifference. They both made noises of acute annoyance, and Christopher muted the television, hoping that their thoughtless peace could be restored after the endless round of car insurance adverts.

"I had a message from Ogden Rake today," said Ivy, tucking her legs up beneath her.

Christopher looked up, surprised. "Have they found the spy?" he asked, hopefully.

"No."

"The Chalice?"

Ivy smiled at his optimism. "No, sadly," she said, and he slumped back into the sofa cushions, disappointed. "They've checked out the last few churches," she continued, and Christopher heard a matching tinge of frustration in her voice.

"Nothing?" he asked, sadly.

"Nothing useful. One was gutted in the fifties – bad bomb damage during the war, apparently –"

"Up here?" Christopher interrupted, surprised.

"There was a munitions factory on the other side of Buckridge," Ivy explained. "The Luftwaffe used to drop their spare bombs on it on the way back from Liverpool."

Christopher nodded, interested. He resolved to read up on it when things had calmed down a little.

"Another had the interior ripped out in the seventies – the diocese sold it when the congregation dwindled. Apparently it's a carpet shop now, nothing left to find."

Christopher snorted.

"And the last?" he asked, feeling the return of his earlier despondency.

"Largely intact," Ivy said, and he brightened up a little. "But the renovators beat us to it. Rake said there was quite an unusual porch above the main door of the church – fitted quite nicely with the church as a whole, but not quite the right style for when it was built."

"That's Prospero Bone all over," said Christopher, the corners of his mouth twitching upward.

"Well, quite," said Ivy, with an answering smile. "Anyway, they've been doing some work on the roof over the last few years, and when they opened up the porch they found four strong lock boxes."

Christopher sat up, hanging on Ivy's every word.

"The boxes were set over the four load-bearing beams

of the porch and each one contained a particularly fine copy of the King James Bible."

Christopher whistled appreciatively. "Anything unusual about the Bibles?" he asked, his professional interest piqued.

"Not as far as the Court could tell – they want the Barracloughs to go and take a look at them. They're in the museum at Rouse Abbey..." she broke off then and laughed at his expression.

"I'm sure they'd take you with you if you're very good," she teased, and Christopher was hard-pressed to keep the smile off his own face. He couldn't remember the last time he'd heard her laugh.

"Give over," he said, amiably, and gave her a playful nudge with his elbow.

Their smiles faded a little as they lapsed back into thoughtful silence.

"So that's all of Bone's churches," said Christopher, almost wistfully. Despite the worry and frustration of the past few months it felt rather as though a great adventure had been snatched from under him.

"Within the Manor, at any rate," Ivy was saying, and Christopher was surprised to hear the same wistful tone in his friend's voice. She rested her head against the back of the sofa and stared up at the ceiling. "Which means that the Chalice – if it still exists – is no longer our responsibility."

"Yes..." said Christopher, and they looked at one another for a moment.

"Could we have missed it, do you think?" Ivy asked, slowly.

"Can we take that chance?" Christopher countered.

As one, they rose and hurried to their respective studies. The television clicked off behind them, as if it knew it was no longer being watched.

Christopher pulled together all his notes and spread them out across his desk. Ivy came in a few minutes later, clutching a sheaf of papers and her notebook. He made a space for her and she joined him at the writing desk, reading through every note, every reference they had ever found to Mortimer Bone, his suspected involvement with magic and his passion for ecclesiastical architecture.

ooo

An hour later and Ivy had fallen asleep on her portion of the notes; noticing this, Christopher had draped his jumper over her shoulders and kept reading.

If they were to accept that the Chalice was no longer their responsibility they needed to be absolutely sure that it wasn't anywhere in the Manor. He knew that none of them would be easy until it had been found and safely contained by the Court, and the feeling was growing in him that he would follow the traces of the Chalice even if it *was* outside the Manor.

Ivy might be bound by her family's fealty to the Manor, but he wasn't.

Post was a menace – a murderer, even, if the Court were to be believed – and the Chalice would be a tool of immense might and corruption in his greedy hands.

As he read, he thought of his parents, his sister, his friends from school; none of them would be prepared for the havoc that cursed thing might cause, nor (he suspected) would they simply stand aside and let whatever Post was plotting happen to the people around them.

His mind followed this train of thought to its logical conclusion, and he frowned deeply.

No: it would be better for everyone for the Chalice to be found and destroyed.

Unbidden, his eyes strayed to the slumbering woman beside him.

Better for everyone.

He hoped that – if it came to it – she wouldn't mind his continuing the hunt alone. He couldn't imagine Ivy leaving Brindleford. However much she denied it, he knew that she was beginning to think of it as hers. He would never ask her to leave it behind, and now she had Astrid and Jake to think of.

He ignored the part of him that felt that he ought to think of them too. It wasn't that he didn't know that – and if they ever needed him he would be back here in an instant – but they would be safe here, whatever happened to him.

Swallowing the slight tightening in his throat, Christopher tried to convince himself that he hadn't already made his decision. More than ever, his friends felt like the family he had given up hope of ever having. He half smiled, though it hurt him to do so: he'd have to leave when everyone was asleep, he mused, or Astrid would probably follow him.

Jake's happy voice in the main room took him by surprise and he rubbed urgently at his face before going out to meet them both.

"We made fairy cakes!" Jake announced, traces of icing still sticking to his cheeks. He grinned up at Christopher as he was lifted into a bear hug. "But they don't have real fairies in."

"I should hope not," he said, giving the wriggling boy an extra squeeze. "Shall we get you ready for bed?" he asked.

"That's not really a question, is it?" Astrid said, giving him an innocent smile. He grinned at her.

"Not really."

Jake, however, really appeared to be thinking the prospect over.

"Can I have a story?" he asked.

"Yes, if you wash your face, and brush your teeth and hair, and get into your pyjamas."

"Okay," said Jake, and wriggled out of Christopher's arms. "Come on Astrid, and we'll get a story!"

"Oh, alright then," she said, doing a good impression of being a long-suffering sibling.

She knew perfectly well that if she was ready for bed, no one would mind if she wanted to stay up longer to read.

Christopher gave Mahri a wave as he closed the great, glass doors; she nodded and headed back inside her own kitchen. Even though there was nowhere they could go and nothing that could hurt them with Martha watching over them, she always stood at her door and watched the children back across Ivy's garden, just in case.

He watched as her kitchen light winked out and the lights upstairs came on. A glance at Reggie's blue-tinged windows told him that he and his canine friends were watching television. Somewhere in the plum tree under Reggie's bedroom window, Boscoe was sleeping peacefully.

Yes, they would be well looked after if he went after the Chalice, but that didn't mean he wouldn't miss them.

The Vineyard had felt more like a home to him that anywhere else for the better part of a decade and he was loathe to leave it.

He ran his eyes over the mischievous vegetation beyond the glass, roofed over now against the winter frosts. Behind him, the sounds of Jake and Astrid splashing around in the bathroom seemed muffled and distant, as though he had already begun to leave them.

Would he still be welcome, he wondered, if he went away for a time?

As if in answer, a single tendril of vine uncoiled itself from the apple tree above him and pressed itself to the outside of the glass, almost expectantly. Christopher laid his palm against the cool glass; the vines split and matched the shape of it.

"Thank you," he said, quietly, and the vine disappeared back into the tangled garden.

Minutes passed and still Christopher stood there, hand pressed against the glass wall of the Arcade, trying to put into order the great rush of warmth he had felt for Martha for letting him know, in her own, rather odd way, that she wanted him to stay.

That he was part of the family now.

"Christopher?" Ivy asked from behind him.

He jumped, snatching his hand away from the glass.

"Sorry," she apologised, sleepily.

"I didn't even hear you come in," he said, surprised at himself. Usually, Ivy's presence was enough to distract him from *anything*. "You made me jump."

"Sorry," she said again; she frowned. "Are you crying?" she asked, laying a gentle hand on his arm.

"No," said Christopher, who hadn't realised he had been. He turned away, scrubbing at his face. "I'm just tired, that's all."

To his surprise, he felt Ivy rest her hand on his back. "Yes," she said softly. "I know."

She gave him a half smile that told him both that she understood and that she was there if he needed her. He felt his face soften a little, glad that he had such good friends.

In the bathroom, Jake started singing a song about a fish very loudly indeed, accompanied by his sister's helpless giggles. Ivy turned towards the sound, her hand slipping from his back. He missed the contact immediately.

"I see the little terrors are back from their cake baking expedition," she remarked, and Christopher chuckled.

"I wouldn't let them hear you say that, or they'll try to live up to the title."

"No," said Ivy, smiling lightly. "We wouldn't want that. Are you reading to them tonight?"

"Yes," said Christopher. "Jake's already chosen the book from the sounds of it."

He watched, pleased, as Ivy's smile grew a little wider.

"You know," she said, almost to herself, "after Sam died I never thought I'd have a family again – and yet here you all are." She looked up at him and he was surprised to see real affection in her eyes; he stared back at her, nonplussed. Ivy blushed slightly. "I'll tidy up the notes in your study," she said, her cheeks tinged with pink, and left him standing in the main room, speechless.

Christopher shook himself, sure than he must have imagined her fond expression.

He had been about to hurry Jake out of the bath and into his pyjamas when Ivy came back out of his study, a pronounced frown on her face. She had several papers bundled together in front of her, and was reading them with such intensity that she nearly walked into the preparation table. Christopher reached out and gently steered her around it. She barely seemed to notice.

"Penny for your thoughts?" he asked, mildly.

"What if we've been thinking about this wrong?" she asked, the frown still twisting her gentle features.

"What do you mean?" he asked, trying to read the notes in her hands upside down. They were the ones she had made when she'd returned from the fete at St Mary's in Buckridge.

"We said that there would be activity at any place with the Chalice in it," she said, and Christopher nodded.

"Anything that powerful would have a pretty hefty impact on its environment – just look at the *Dischordia*. When that thing still had a bit of clout it was dividing the congregation every which way – and inciting the occasional riot."

They had looked more closely at the troubled history of St Chad's following their encounter with the compendium of demons: it had not come as much of a surprise to learn that it had caused centuries of trouble amongst the parishioners before its vigour had begun to fade. The church had really only begun to recover in the early twentieth century.

"The Eye-Eater didn't," Ivy pointed out, an edge of excitement creeping into her voice.

Christopher thought carefully for a few moments.

"Well, no," he said, eventually. "But that seems to be a sort of demon-trap – it can't do anything at all unless you're stupid enough to touch it." Ivy looked doubtful, so he continued: "And most of the fallout of that – in terms of zombies and body-snatching – was down to the Court of Miracles."

"True," she conceded, looking mildly annoyed at having her theory questioned. "But historical reports of the Chalice mention its ability to whisper 'dark thoughts' – I'd think someone would notice *that*."

"That could be artistic license on the part of the author," said Christopher, speculatively. "Or the product of an over-active imagination –" he took in her expression of exasperation. "Or, they could be right," he finished.

"Maybe they wouldn't hear it," said Ivy triumphantly.

Christopher looked at her, baffled.

"No, I'm sorry, you've lost me," he said.

"We're pretty sure that Mortimer Bone was a Practitioner, yes?" Ivy prompted.

"Most likely," Christopher agreed. "He knew exactly what the Chalice and the *Dischordia* were, and how dangerous they could be. The way he hid them wasn't particularly magical, but that was about the time he was fined for practicing, maybe it scared him off."

"Or the Chalice did," Ivy suggested. "If he came across it unprepared, or hoping to do some good with it –"

"Like bringing his father back to life," Christopher said, suddenly remembering how devastated Bone was said to have been following the Great Fire.

Ivy's frown deepened, as if she hadn't even considered the possibility.

"No," she said, slowly, thinking hard. "I don't think that's it. You'd need real desperation for that – like – what were they called? The Penrhyns?"

Christopher nodded.

"I mean, *I* thought about it often enough when I was growing up," she admitted, and Christopher's eyes widened in shock. She was speaking as if she had forgotten his presence now, quietly and urgently. "And after Sam... but it wouldn't have been him, however it might have looked or acted like him – and it wouldn't have been fair, trapping him in a body that couldn't function any longer. Just a means of prolonging a death, really, instead of reversing it. Utterly selfish."

She stood for a moment, lost in her own thoughts.

"Anyway," she said, bringing herself back to the

present. "Bone's actions are not those of a desperate man – they're thought through, calculated. All the things he concealed were done for the good of his community – whether he was protecting them or providing for their futures."

"Almost like a penance," Christopher added, realising where Ivy was heading with this.

"Exactly," she said, flicking through the notes on Prospero Bone. "What if he used the Chalice and it hurt someone that he cared about."

"Like his father…"

"Like his father," she echoed. The light of excitement was back in her eyes, but she'd lost him again. Christopher backtracked a little, trying to catch up.

"But he died in the fire."

She nodded, and he boggled at her.

"Are you suggesting that the Great Fire of London was started by the Chalice of Knowledge?"

"Why not?" she challenged. "Every other city it ever found itself in was razed to the ground, or swallowed by an earthquake, or flooded – the thing practically feeds on catastrophe. Why not London?"

"But, but… but that was started when they went after that baker in Pudding Lane," he protested.

"Christopher, you of all people should know, history is made up of a series of stories – sometimes the stories that get remembered, that get written down, are the stories that people *want* to believe, for whatever reason. That doesn't make them true."

Christopher gaped at her for a few moments as his internal universe rearranged itself.

"He never went back to London," he said, slowly. He met Ivy's excited eyes. "Okay," he said, after a moment, and she smiled in triumph. "So Bone had the Chalice, tried to use it and caused –" he sought for a suitable description, "– possibly the worst conflagration in modern Western Europe until the bombing of Guernica, and accidentally killed his father?"

"And spent the rest of his life trying to make amends,"

Ivy finished. She thrust the sheaf of papers towards him. "Look at all the things he did – the money, the churches, the Bibles –"

"The monument he built for his family..."

"Exactly!"

Christopher nodded slowly. On the face of it, it sounded insane – but who was he, a werewolf living in a house that was more than a little bit alive, to question it? Ivy might just be onto something.

"Alright," he said. "Supposing you're right – where does that leave us?"

Ivy spread the papers out on the preparation table, pushing untidy pots of herbs out of the way.

"With a very kind, very clever man," she said. "Wracked with guilt over his father's death, who has seen first-hand the kind of damage magic can do if it's used improperly."

"I can see how that might put a man off magic for life," Christopher remarked, but Ivy ignored him.

"A man who rebuilds churches as a penance, but who can't resist leaving puzzles behind because he knows that there will always be scholars like him, willing to chase a thing to the end, no matter the cost –"

"And foolish enough to think that they can control something like the Chalice," Christopher added, feeling Ivy's contagious enthusiasm. The wolfish part of his human mind could feel the first prickles of thrill at the possible hunt ahead.

"Exactly – so he'd need to be sure that no one could get at it – particularly someone without magic, unable to defend themselves."

Christopher nodded, flicking through Ivy's handwritten pages.

"One last piece of magic, guarding the Chalice."

"The statue?"

"No," Ivy shook her head, promptly. "But that's probably what he wanted us to think. No – the vicar of St Chad's told me about a ghost that haunts the bell tower – he says it's like a candle burning through the night."

"Like someone keeping watch."

"His last spell – Bone left a little piece of himself behind to watch over the Chalice through the ages. But he also left clues to its hiding place –"

"Because he couldn't resist –" he grinned at Ivy. "I wouldn't be able to."

Ivy grinned back, and Christopher caught himself longing to kiss her, caught up in the loveliness of her flushed cheeks and flashing eyes.

Luckily, she turned away before he had the chance and tapped her inexpert sketch of the statue with her finger.

"*That's* the first church to be built after the fire, *that's* where he worked his final spell, *that's* where we'll find the Chalice!"

A small noise made them turn.

Astrid and Jake were standing some feet behind them, wearing identical expressions of nervous excitement and both looking very small indeed in their colourful pyjamas. Jake was clutching a book of fairy tales to his chest, and Astrid had a small stuffed sheep that she usually kept hidden under her pillow tucked under her arm.

Christopher was struck, suddenly, by how very young they were.

"I'll read to him," said Astrid, with a voice that seemed to belong to someone much older than she was. "You go and get it."

"We'll be alright," Jake assured them, and he, too, sounded more collected than usual.

"Mahri will read to you both," said Ivy, firmly.

"And you'll both be alright," Christopher added.

A heavy silence hung over the four of them for a moment, as they all wondered what they would find at St Chad's.

Abruptly, Jake ran forwards and flung his arms around Christopher's legs.

"Be careful," he demanded, before running back to his sister's side. He watched them uncertainly, as though he was afraid that he would never see them again.

"We'll be back in no time," Ivy said, reassuringly, but the children's expressions didn't change.

They both remembered the power of the *Dischordia* – Jake was still having nightmares.

"I promise," said Ivy, and Astrid nodded, taking her brother's hand.

Christopher hurried towards Mahri's front door, trying not to dwell on the deep doubt in the little girl's eyes.

They would be back by morning.

They had to be.

28
Wizard Abroad

He was getting closer.

He could feel it.

Sometimes he even dreamed of it, calling to him as he raised it to his lips – he could almost taste it!

These past months of frustrated research had dampened his spirits, but he knew he was on the right track now, assuming that the lovesick fool at the bookshop could find the last few texts he needed.

He grinned to himself, carefully slipping slim silver instruments into a black velvet case. He had never had that trouble. He had what his father had described as a 'way with the ladies' that never failed to disappoint, but he had never felt the need to keep to just one of them.

The silly young fool had got carried away – but then, he didn't have the advantage of being a Post.

He laughed to himself. What a fuss.

Still, soon it wouldn't matter. Everything that had seemed so important to them would be insignificant when he had the Chalice. Brindleford, England – the *World* would be his!

Perhaps he would take Christopher with him – he wasn't a bad bookworm by any standards, and he could be useful. He would need someone who could handle magical books – not that he'd need to read any more, with the Chalice in his grasp, but his students would need them.

The Barracloughs would have to go, of course. They were powerful enough and stupid enough to stand in his way, and he couldn't have that. Same for the other governors at Brightwell; they had held the young Practitioners of Brindleford back for too long.

No, they'd all have to go.

He scratched absently at his chest, feeling the dual heartbeat that his father had given him.

Ivy Burwell might also be persuaded to stay – he could give her to Christopher to seal his allegiance, perhaps.

After all, she did have those beautiful young children with her now, she wouldn't want to see them hurt.

And when they were old enough they could join him. He had sensed their power – a power the young boy didn't even know he had yet – that day in the bookshop when he'd had his revelation about Mortimer Bone. They would make mighty captains for his Vanguard – with the proper encouragement.

Quentin slipped a gauntlet on his hand, delicately closing its clasps around his wrist. He disliked weapons, generally. They were clumsy things, designed for people whose innate magical abilities were insufficient to provide protection, and Quentin Post was not a man with insufficient magical abilities. They were useful in instances of sudden attack, however.

He frowned down at the garnets set into the metal, giving them a swift polish with the cloth the gauntlet was usually wrapped in.

The feeling had been stealing over him lately that someone else was on the trail of the Chalice. He couldn't think who – there were very few that he would credit even with the knowledge of its existence. Certainly not those imbeciles at the Court of Miracles.

Involuntarily, he pulled a face of disgust. It had been an unwelcome surprise to see them in Zarrubabel and Barracloughs', but since they hadn't made an appearance since, he was reasonably certain that they had been there on an unrelated matter.

He'd had a couple of run-ins with the Constables over the years, though they'd never been able to make anything stick. He would give anything to flush out their little rat's nest, but it would be too risky. He would be too visible.

It would be different when he had the Chalice.

He would annihilate them.

Quentin smoothed his immaculately trimmed beard, catching his own eye in the ornate mirror that hung in his study. He gave a cat-like smile, enjoying his own reflection.

Just think – all the knowledge of the most powerful Practitioners throughout all the ages...

With his gifts and the power of the Chalice he would be unstoppable.

He selected his walking cane from the umbrella stand by his front door, savouring the feel of the carved wooden handle under his fingers.

He had grown used to it after his injury, and it was becoming a decent staff. For a moment, his smirk faded. It had been a shame about Candace. He had been reluctant to damage something so exquisitely beautiful – it was the collector in him, he knew. She would have made an excellent prize; he would have enjoyed showing her off. He even felt a mild pang of respect for the woman who had fought so dearly for her life. Very few of the others had had time to try.

Still, her particular obstinacy had been her downfall.

Chasing such uncommon thoughts from his mind, he uttered his transport spell, coming to rest in the portico of a darkened church.

He had begun to narrow down the places that Bone could have hidden the Chalice now – he had visited a few already, but to no avail.

The crafty old bugger had gone to great lengths to conceal his quest for that ancient and powerful artefact, and he hadn't expected it to be easy. However, it was beginning to grate on Quentin, a little more with each fresh disappointment.

He glanced around him as he made his way up to the porch, careful to avoid the path with its noisy gravel – one footstep might give him away should anyone be passing. Distantly, he could hear the sounds of a raucous evening in the pub across the street; he waited in the shadows as a couple out walking their dog skirted around the edge of the graveyard.

It wouldn't do to be seen – not that he couldn't talk his way out of most things. Generally he found that people saw the money and the easy grace and didn't bother to look any further.

Swiftly, he picked the lock, sliding the black velvet pouch back into his coat. In an instant he was inside the church; he locked the door behind him in case the verger should appear on his evening rounds.

Churches were strange buildings in the dark, and Quentin paused in the nave, listening closely to the strange pings of the ancient heating system running the length of the walls.

He could have sworn he'd heard someone breathing...

He chuckled to himself, shaking the feeling.

Whatever else was in here he was undoubtedly scarier than it.

He set to work.

29
The Bells of St Mary's

Ivy and Christopher presently arrived in Buckridge. They had become so accustomed to travelling together now that the difference in their transport spells barely registered. If anyone had been watching the shadowy alcove behind the cricket pavilion, they would have assumed that these two watchful people had simply always been there.

Hearts hammering in their chests, they strolled towards the churchyard, trying not to look like they were hurrying.

The nature of the potential discovery in front of them had them both on edge and a sudden burst of laughter from the pub across the road took Ivy by surprise. She veered into Christopher, who took her arm.

Ivy squeezed his hand. "Good idea," she whispered in his ear. "This way we'll look like a couple out for a stroll."

Christopher nodded, trying to ignore the way his heart had jumped about in his chest when she leaned into him.

They smiled at a young family making their way home, the younger child fast asleep in his father's arms, reminding them of their two young friends, tucked up in bed in the Arcade. Was Christopher's his imagination, or had Ivy's grip on his arm tightened for a moment?

They slipped into the graveyard and hurried up to the door of the church, feet crunching on the gravel path. To Christopher it sounded monstrously loud; he glanced at the vicarage across the street, but all the lights were out. Hoping fervently that the vicar was out on call, he ducked under the slight porch, wishing that this side of the church was less open to the street.

"Damn!" Ivy muttered. "It's locked."

"Well, it would be," said Christopher. "People up to no good and all that – keep watch."

"What are you...?"

Christopher pressed his hand to the old, iron lock. He closed his eyes, reaching out with his mind for the proper alignment of barrels and tumblers. There were a tense few moments as he stood, trying to concentrate on the task in front of him, painfully aware of how exposed they were, standing in the violent orange streetlight that pooled around the door of the church.

He calmed his breathing, focusing on the intricate puzzle housed within the ancient wood of the door.

Abruptly, the lock clicked into place and the door swung open. Beaming, he pulled an astonished Ivy into the church and closed the door firmly behind them.

"My dad taught me," he explained, on his friend's baffled expression. "He was forever losing his keys."

Ivy stifled a laugh and together they hurried into the nave. The light from the acid orange streetlights outside was doing odd things to the stained glass, making faint pools of amber flow across the floor of the church. They conjured Light Orbs, deepening the shadows around them.

"There he is," she said, pointing out the statue of Atlas.

They cut across a line of pews to the great, marble demi-god, stoically holding up the roof of the church.

"Well," said Christopher, after a moment. "If that's not the expression of someone who has come into contact with the Chalice of Knowledge, I don't know what is."

"Exactly," said Ivy. "It's like Bone was carrying a great burden and he laid it down here. Not so that he could find peace, but for safe-keeping."

Christopher made a noise of agreement, still staring up at the patient eyes of the alabaster guardian.

"And there's this," Ivy continued, kneeling down beside the fine, nearly luminous cup at the statue's feet. Christopher followed her gaze.

"Gosh," he said, and joined her. He ran a finger along the rim of the paper-thin stone. "You'd have thought by now that something like this would have shattered."

"And yet it's still perfect," Ivy finished. They looked at one another. "It's definitely here, then."

"But where?" asked Christopher. "There must be a million hiding places in a church – particularly for an architect. You said yourself that the compartment at the base of the statue was empty. You don't suppose the vicar has it?" he added, with a sudden flash of inspiration.

Ivy shook her head, slowly. "No, I don't think so. He seems such a gentle soul – I don't think there's any harm in him, and there would be if the Chalice had got a hold on him. No," she said, getting back to her feet. "If anyone had found it, it would be one of Reverend Shaw's predecessors. He said that the vicar before him kept the hymnbooks in it."

Christopher's mouth slid up to one side at the image.

"If someone else had found it there would have been something in the records," Ivy speculated, smile fading. "Given the nature of the Chalice, if someone *had* had it there probably wouldn't be a Brindleford left for me to protect."

She turned away then, a pinched expression on her face. Christopher guessed that she was annoyed at herself for claiming her Manor aloud. While Ivy might well be coming to terms with her inherited Duty, it was very different to know a thing than to admit it to someone else. Somehow, the act of speaking made it more real.

He looked away, gazing across the darkened, empty church. At first glance there didn't seem to be anything unusual about the building, apart from their taciturn friend.

"Did you look in the bell tower?" he asked, finally, and Ivy nodded.

"Yes, as soon as Reverend Shaw went back outside." She pushed her dark hair back and tied it with a band she'd had at her wrist, suddenly business-like. "There was a cupboard with some old coats inside and some chairs that I'm assuming they move when they're ringing. Let's split up – have a better look around."

Christopher nodded and cut back through banks of the pews to the opposite wall of the church.

The neatly-dressed stone walls were adorned – here

and there – with an assortment of monuments and plaques. Christopher held his Light Orb up to them, looking for scratches in the wood or metal, shadows that shouldn't be there – anything that might denote concealment.

He ran his fingers along the edge of a large bronze memorial to a former patron of the church. It was fitted tightly to the wall, with barely a crack between the metal and the stone.

Christopher stood back and looked up at the date: 1668; close enough to Prospero Bone to warrant further investigation.

Allowing his Light Orb to float above him, he pulled out his penknife and carefully slid it between the plaque and the wall. Slowly, he ran it along the length of the memorial, holding his breath. Just when he was about to give it up as a lost cause the blade stuck fast in something softer, nearly at the far corner of the plaque. He twisted around, trying to see what his knife had caught on, shocked by the electrifying thought that this might be Prospero Bone's hiding place.

Carefully, he wiggled the knife back half an inch and drew it out into the pale, white light.

There were flakes of something chalky on the edge of the blade, and at the bottom – where misadventure had left a nick in the metal – was a thick, rough thread, stuck fast in the metal. He pulled it away and sniffed it: sacking, he decided. Old and very musty, and covered in plaster dust.

Packing, perhaps, for something someone wanted to keep hidden.

Christopher allowed the thread to fall to the floor and turned his attention back to the innocent-looking monument above him. He subjected it to a long, thoughtful stare, wondering to himself how the heavy sheet of metal had been attached to the wall so securely, and whether he could now dislodge it without doing too much damage.

He weighed his pocket knife in his hand for a few

moments before sliding it between the side of the plaque and the wall, testing his weight against it like a lever: it moved a tiny amount, sending a thin layer of plaster dust to the floor.

Christopher sneezed, the sound dwarfing him in the cavernous space. Dust billowed around him in the pale light of his Light Orb, still obediently orbiting his head.

He glanced up at it and smiled.

"Bless you," said Ivy, from the shadows.

When Christopher's breathing had returned to normal and Ivy had apologised for creeping up on him twice in one night, he handed her the knife, explaining as he worked.

"There's no real reason for the plaster," he clarified, as Ivy slid the knife back behind the side of the memorial. "All the walls here are dressed stone... That's right, hold it steady there –"

Christopher pressed his hand to the opposite corner of the plaque and muttered an incantation.

A dull light began to glow behind the metal, glimmering around the edges of it and shining through the tiny faults in the metal where the engraver had cut too deep. Christopher's Light Orb winked out beside him and the light behind the memorial began to build in intensity.

Christopher concentrated all his power into slowing the spell down, holding it back – his grip tightened on the cool metal and sweat broke out on his forehead and lower back.

Ivy put her weight behind the knife, wiggling and shifting it to pry the memorial loose from the wall. Slowly, painfully, the heavy sheet of bronze began to move, bright light spilling out from the bottom half of the plaque.

With one last great tug, the plaque came loose and Ivy dropped the knife. It made a deafening sound as it hit the floor and Christopher retrieved it swiftly, as if stung by the sudden noise.

Ivy laughed quietly, impressed.

"Nice," she observed, nodding at the Light Orb that had manifested between the wall and the memorial – and was even now holding the large sheet of metal perpendicular to the wall. "Unconventional – we would never have been taught that at Brightwell."

Christopher grinned, buoyed up by her smile.

"Sometimes it's not what you know," he said, "but how you use it."

He felt himself colour slightly under her continued gaze. In an effort to stop her noticing, Christopher turned his attention to the sizeable hole in the church wall. He felt the disappointment hit him like a slap in the face.

Wordlessly, he and Ivy pulled the hessian and plaster packing out of the cavity. As they did so, great clouds of plaster dust rose up around them and it was Ivy's turn to sneeze.

When she had regained her composure she searched through the mouldy material, not wanting to miss even the slightest clue.

Christopher screwed up his face against the harsh stench of rot and stuck his arm inside the wall, feeling the furthest edges of the broken stone with the tips of his fingers. He could almost reach the outer edge. He groped for it, determined to find something – anything – within the gap. Finally, his questing fingers closed on an edge, but what at first appeared to hold all the potential of being a box of some kind quickly turned out to be the edge of a loose stone block.

He pulled his arm back slightly, feeling himself get annoyed.

Suddenly, something small and warm and furry scuttled across his arm – he yelped, stumbling backwards and falling heavily to the ground, making billows in the plaster dust.

"Ahh! What?" cried Ivy, equally tense.

"Mice," he said, pulling a face and rubbing at the skin of his arm, where he could still feel tiny footprints running up and down.

"Oh," she said, looking relieved. "I thought –" Christopher looked up at her as she paused. She appeared to be trying quite hard not to laugh. "That was a really manly scream, by the way," she said, when she had regained control of her face.

"Be quiet, you," said Christopher, trying to glare at her.

He got to his feet, brushing the plaster dust from his jeans, ignoring her muffled sniggering. He conjured a second, smaller Light Orb and sent it into the hole in the wall, trying not to smile.

There was the brief and urgent sound of several mice getting away from the great, shining ball of light that had just invaded their home. Christopher muttered an apology to them as he peered into the hole. He sighed.

"Nothing?"

"Nothing," he replied, heavily. "Just a bloody big hole."

He glanced down at Ivy without much hope, and she shook her head.

"Just manky bits of old sacking and a lot of plaster dust."

"So it's nothing more than a really bad repair job?" Christopher remarked, irritated. "Brilliant."

He stood back and peered at the inscriptions on the other memorials on the wall. "The rest of them are too recent," he muttered, annoyed.

"Let's keep looking," Ivy suggested, getting to her feet. "It was never going to be easy to find."

Christopher nodded, a grudging acknowledgement. "It doesn't mean I didn't want it to be," he muttered, and Ivy chuckled.

"That goes for the both of us," she said, more lightly than Christopher felt was appropriate, given the circumstances.

Together, they packed the sacking back into the hole and stood back to admire their handy work.

"That really is one hell of a hole," said Ivy, head to one side. "They must have ripped something hefty out of there."

"You'd have thought they'd try to do a better job at repairing it," Christopher observed, still unreasonably irritated at this flaw in the architecture.

"Maybe they didn't have the money."

"Well, at least we can leave it in better repair than we found it," he huffed, and reached out to the packing.

He closed his eyes, forming a picture of a panel in his mind; beside him, Ivy raised her arm in a perfect mirror of his.

For a moment, the trace of her magic unnerved him, mingling with his own, but he quickly recovered his concentration. Together, they closed the gap in the wall, allowing wooden panels to form in front of the packing.

"That should do it," said Ivy, appreciatively, as Christopher allowed the great, bronze plaque to swing back into place.

Ivy made a sign in the air above the snowy dust on the floor; Christopher watched it vanish, impressed.

"You may have to teach me that," he said, and she laughed.

They walked the length of the aisle, watching the light from his Orb flash and dance over the stone.

"Old Prospero wouldn't have used so obvious a hiding place," Christopher observed, thinking out loud. "After all, he was a master puzzler – and the Chalice was the one thing he never wanted found."

"There must be some powerful dampening charms on that thing," Ivy remarked. "You'd think it would have tried to get out by now."

"It might be weakening like the *Dischordia*," said Christopher. "Or dormant – after all, it must be getting on a bit now. What?"

Ivy had screwed her face up, as if she had swallowed something disgusting. "My hands are all mouldy from that sacking. Come on – I think I saw a sink in the bell tower..."

Obediently, Christopher followed her to the other end of the church and into the bell tower, which seemed to serve as a bit of a dumping ground for everything that might at one point have been considered useful to the congregation of St Mary's. Unlike most bell towers it had a very wide base, creating a space large enough for the bell ringers along with a sink, a cupboard and several stacks of collapsible chairs. There was also an ancient battered desk covered in all manner of abandoned stationery.

The room smelled of damp parishioners and boot polish, and for some reason the sheer normality of it unnerved him a little. Like the Arcade, it felt like the bell tower was trying very hard to look ordinary.

"You can feel that too?" Ivy asked, watching him thoughtfully. He nodded, and she finished drying her hands on the pink flowery towel by the sink. "I think that's old Prospero, keeping an eye on things," she said, glancing at the overloaded desk.

Christopher had been about to agree when he caught the faintest trace of an approaching scent.

"What?" Ivy asked, noticing the change in his expression.

"Someone's coming," he whispered. He watched her eyes widen in shock as they both strained to hear the sounds of approaching footsteps.

Who would be coming to a church *this* late in the evening?

"Front door," he said, as the gravel crunched outside. "We should try to get to the –"

"There's no time," Ivy hissed urgently. "The door's still unlocked!"

Christopher swore under his breath, cursing himself for forgetting to lock it behind them.

"Can you tell who it is?"

"No," Christopher frowned after a moment. "They're too far away..."

He sent a silent prayer to whoever might be listening that they wouldn't be caught as Ivy heaved the door to the bell tower shut. It wasn't like they could just leave, either, in case whomever it was found the Chalice while they were gone.

"Did you bring one of the masks?" Ivy mouthed. It was her turn to swear as he shook his head.

"Light Orb," he reminded her as the footsteps stopped at the main door of the church. Both globes winked out, leaving them in sudden darkness. He could hear Ivy's panicked breathing several feet away as whoever it was outside paused in front of the ancient oak doors

"What if it's Post?" Ivy breathed, and Christopher could hear the tremor in her voice. If what the Court had told them was true, an all-out fight would probably kill them both and take the church with them too. He dreaded to think what revenge the man might take on the Barracloughs, or the children.

They couldn't take that chance.

He heard Ivy gasp as he took her arm, moving silently across the stone floor.

"Cupboard," he hissed, and they hurried across to it, climbing inside.

There wasn't much room. He heard the door click behind Ivy as she pressed herself against him.

Christopher swallowed, his heart in his mouth – listening hard for signs that the unknown person outside had come in.

"If he finds us –" Ivy breathed.

"He won't."

"But if he does?"

"Then it's to the death," he responded grimly, giving her hand a brief squeeze.

He felt her nod in the pitch black of the cupboard. They were too cramped, now, to use a transport spell – it might take part of the cupboard with them, or leave part of them behind, and that would be unhelpful.

"Just as long as we both agree," she murmured, and Christopher was reminded of the time they thought the Court had taken Astrid, and the icy fury that had coursed through his friend then.

With a certain amount of grim satisfaction he reflected that Post wouldn't know what had hit him.

She was readying a spell – he could feel it building within her, the tang of magic beginning to mix with the coarse mustiness in their cramped hiding place.

It seemed like they had been standing there for hours, poised for discovery, ready for a fight, desperate not to be found.

In a moment of pure relief, Christopher heard the sound of a key turning in the old iron lock. He sagged, fear diminishing, and closed his hand around Ivy's.

"It's the vicar," he breathed, beside her ear. "Or someone else with a key."

"Are you sure?" she murmured, tense and alert. Christopher gave her hand another squeeze.

"Yes – he's baffled by the fact it's unlocked. Keeps muttering to himself about his memory."

"You can hear that?"

"Yes."

"Oh..." Ivy let out a quiet breath of relief and Christopher felt the magical potential inside the cupboard dissipate as she undid whatever preparations she had made.

They listened as the vicar's footsteps passed the door to the bell tower and walked briskly into the church proper, echoing slightly as he entered the larger space.

"He must be doing his rounds," Ivy said.

There were a few minutes of silence in which Christopher became horribly aware of exactly how small a hiding place they had chosen, and exactly how close Ivy was. Her befuddling scent was beginning to drive him insane, trapped as he was.

"Oh, I hope he isn't long," Ivy huffed, abruptly. "There's something sharp digging into my side."

Christopher reached out to see if he could dislodge it. His fingers brushed her hip as he groped for the offending object and he felt her start.

"I think it's a hook or something," he mumbled, blushing so hard that he was sure she would be able to feel it. "I'm afraid it doesn't seem to want to move."

"That's okay," Ivy whispered, in a curiously small

voice. "Thank you for trying."

Christopher shifted uncomfortably, mentally repeating Ivy's wish that the vicar would be quick about whatever he was doing. It was bad enough being stuck in a very confined space with the utterly unattainable woman of his dreams, but Ivy's rather immediate presence was waking up the wolf in him – a wolf that was rapidly realising that it didn't much like being stuck in a small, dark space.

He gritted his teeth.

Time seemed to stretch out as they huddled silently together in the cupboard; what was probably only ten minutes felt like an age.

Christopher shifted slightly, trying to ignore how warm and soft Ivy felt, pressed up against him; trying to put her intoxicating smell out of his mind; trying with increasing difficulty to pretend that the insistent tightening in his right calf wasn't happening.

"Are you alright?" Ivy breathed, at his sudden movement.

"Cramp," he hissed back, trying to reach down to rub his aching leg.

"Oh."

There were more minutes of silence, in which Christopher tried to jiggle his tensing leg muscles into submission. When he finally straightened up – no mean feat in a small cupboard with another person in it – Ivy was shaking with silent laughter.

"What?" he asked, nonplussed.

"This is just so *weird*," she managed, and he chuckled in agreement. "Where is he?"

"Other end of the church, I think," said Christopher, after a moment. "His footsteps are kind of muffled, and that's the only part of the church I can remember carpet in."

"Oh," said Ivy, sounding annoyed. "Damn. I'd hoped he'd gone."

"No," Christopher whispered. "Still pottering about – he's probably making sure everything's ready for tomorrow's service."

Ivy snorted. "I suppose we should be thankful that they don't have a late service on Saturday nights."

"I didn't even think of that," Christopher admitted, sheepishly.

"Me either," Ivy murmured. "No, I'm sorry," she said, after a moment. "I'm going to have to move – I can't stand that bloody hook any longer."

"Wh-"

"Hold still, I'm going to try to turn around."

"Ivy, this is a *really* small cupboard," he managed, in a slightly higher voice than usual.

"Sorry," Ivy whispered, and Christopher was surprised to discover that he could feel *her* blushing.

"Just try not to be so... squirmy, ok?"

Ivy stifled a laugh and managed to wriggle around so that she was facing him. She huffed in relief and rubbed her side.

"That's better," she murmured, steadying herself against his chest.

Christopher, who wasn't altogether sure that it was, pointed out that the hook would be sticking in her other side now.

"Yes, but it isn't as sore yet," she whispered, leaning both arms against his chest. "Sorry, I'm not as stable this way round."

"S'okay," Christopher managed, desperately trying not to do what his entire body was suggesting would be an excellent idea.

She was just so *close*.

He could feel her warm breath on his neck as she listened for distant footsteps, hear her heart beating steadily in her chest.

Her delicious scent surrounded him, making it increasingly difficult to think. Despite the part of his mind that was telling him that any action on his part would end badly, he breathed her in, revelling in the delicate mix of flavours that was uniquely Ivy. He could smell her teas on her – that exquisite mixture of tannins and flowers, soil and cotton – softened, tonight, by the heady sweetness of the vanilla stuff she'd used in the bath.

He let it wind around his senses like one of her vines, the way it had when he'd first smelled it.

Ivy let out a sigh, her breath tickling his skin.

She has to be able to feel how tense I am, he thought, shivering slightly as her hand inadvertently grazed across his chest.

She must have had some clue, because the pattern of her breathing changed very slightly, as though something had just occurred to her and – yes, he wasn't imagining it – her heart was beating faster now, almost matching his own agitated rhythm.

Christopher closed his eyes in the darkness, willing himself to be still.

I'm locked in a very small cupboard with a woman whose very presence makes my heart do loops – who is also my best friend and therefore off-limits if I want to keep her friendship – which I really, really do.

In a church.

With the vicar wandering around, potentially within earshot.

He glared at the wooden roof of the cupboard, fighting his desire.

Seriously, he thought to himself, *if this is a test, I am going to fail it.*

A tiny delicate sound – which might have been Ivy moistening her lips – made him look back down to where he assumed his friend's face was.

"Christopher?" she whispered, and her breath chased across his face.

He gave in, closing the narrow gap between them and pressing his lips to her mouth, blood pounding in his ears. He kissed her tenderly for a few moments before pulling back, horrified at what he'd just done.

Before he could sputter an apology, however, Ivy returned the kiss, gently and sweetly. Stunned, he allowed himself to kiss her back, noticing with that tiny part of him still capable of thought that her soft, delicious lips were curved into a smile.

They broke apart after a few delighted minutes, primarily because Ivy had started laughing again.

"Er..." said Christopher, disconcerted.

"We – we're snogging in a cupboard in a ch-ch-*church*," Ivy whispered, between giggles. Christopher snorted into her neck and she went on: "I feel like a naughty teenager – I k-keep thinking what the expression on M-Mahri's face would be if she c-caught us in here!"

Christopher snorted again at the image, louder this time – and Ivy shushed him, still giggling as quietly as possible.

"Shh – he'll hear us," he managed, and with a little effort they calmed down slightly.

Contentedly, they settled against one another and Christopher reflected that actually, the cupboard wasn't that small or uncomfortable after all.

Happily, he listened to Ivy's breathing as she rested against his chest, and he smiled into her dark hair.

"What's in here with us?" Ivy asked, after a couple of minutes of companionable silence.

"Choir robes, I think," he whispered. "There are some rather pointy coat-hangers behind my head – and the whole thing smells of soap powder and muffled teenage boy."

"Urgh," Ivy muttered, with sympathy, and he nodded. "Muffled teenage boy?"

"Muffled by the soap powder."

"Urgh," she said again, and Christopher could almost feel her pulling a face. Then: "What do I smell of?"

There was a pause as Christopher decided how best to describe it.

"Of you," he concluded, simply.

"*Thanks*," Ivy admonished gently, and he could hear the smile in her voice.

"Well... like cotton, and tea, and gardens," he expanded, briefly. "And whatever you've been doing recently – today that means the soap from washing your hands and that vanilla stuff you put in the bath."

"You can smell all that?"

She sounded surprised.

"Most of the time," he murmured.

"Your view of the world must be quite different from mine."

"Like suddenly switching from black and white to full colour," he agreed. "After the bite it was as if a whole new dimension had opened up to me."

"One of the perks, then."

"About the only one."

He rested his chin against the top of her head, enjoying her proximity while it lasted.

"I think he's heading back," he whispered, after a few moments.

Ivy shifted her head slightly so that she could hear more easily.

"Did you hear that?" she whispered suddenly.

Christopher had – the distinctive sound of quill on parchment was filtering through the door of their sanctuary. Through the cracks at the hinges and keyhole, the warm yellow glow of candlelight trickled in, momentarily blinding them both.

Christopher was willing to bet that the atmosphere of the entire bell tower had just shifted slightly. Inside the cupboard it had grown warmer, as though the chill of November had been forgotten.

Where before he could detect that usual mix of damp coffee, weak tea and suspect plumbing peculiar to village halls and volunteer coffee stalls, now there were notes of charring wood and warm beeswax in the air, tempered by the stronger scents of woollen cloth and bookbinding glue. Pervading the morass of aromas was the unmistakeable tang of plain, uncomplicated worry.

He could just make out the shape of Ivy's face in the gloom.

"The ghost?" he mouthed, and she nodded, almost imperceptibly.

The vicar, who seemed to have paused by the door to the room, gave a happy little chuckle, as if the general oddness of his church had become comfortable over the years.

Christopher listened hard as the man left the building, locking the door firmly behind him.

"Ready?" he breathed.

"Ready."

As quietly as he could, Christopher pushed the cupboard door open. The man at the desk didn't appear to have noticed them.

Silently, they climbed out of the cupboard and closed it behind them. There was a certain amount of stretching out of unhappy limbs and rearranging of clothing. Now that he was out of the cupboard, Christopher was reluctant to disturb the young man, bathed in candlelight, working diligently away at his drawings. He glanced at Ivy, who seemed equally reticent.

Hesitantly, Christopher cleared his throat.

The man at the desk paused, carefully laying down his quill before he turned.

There – several years younger than his imposing portrait in the book of architects and subjecting them to a rather puzzled stare – was Prospero Bone.

30
An Elegant Solution

Mortimer Bone stood up, pushing an impossible chair out of his way, bathed in the warm yellow glow of candlelight.

Light eyes peered out at them from striking features, studying them as they studied him. He was a little taller than Ivy and slightly on the stocky side. His handsome features still held the traces of his youth, yet he looked like a man who had only recently become haggard and worn. The easy confidence that Christopher had seen in his portrait was yet to develop, though there was a certain self-assurance even now – despite their unexpected appearance, he didn't seem flustered, just curious.

His long hair was tied behind his head in a business-like sort of way. There was an ink stain on his left cheek.

It wasn't that he was bathed in candlelight at all, Christopher realised – it was as if he was *made* of it.

All those patient nights of watching...

Christopher wondered how much of it he remembered – did he start afresh every night or long for a time when he might sleep?

"Hello," said Christopher, awkwardly. The questing gaze of their long-dead opponent turned on him, making him distinctly uncomfortable.

"We've come for the Chalice," Ivy said, simply. The unearthly gaze turned to look at her and she continued: "There is a very cruel man who wants it, and we want to make sure he doesn't get it. Is there a way to destroy it?"

Bone shook his head, gravely. "Not that I could find," he said – it was a very strange sound, like an old record, playing in some distant room. "Flame, flood, the burning of acid, nothing I tried made a mark. I failed."

The pain of it came through his tinny voice, drifting along the air like an improbable echo. Christopher felt for him.

"We have to try," he said, watching Bone, closely.

"He's already guessed that it was you that hid it – it's only a matter of time before he comes here."

He was surprised to see the ghost of a smile flit across Mortimer Bone's face. "He will not discover it."

Despite the gravity of the situation, Christopher smiled at his confidence.

"We can't take the chance that he might," said Ivy, and Bone frowned.

"You are in earnest, Mistress," he observed, reedily.

"I am."

"And you would not hesitate to destroy it?" he pressed, and Christopher understood the temptation.

"Not for a second."

"And you would not be tempted to use it?"

"We would be tempted," Christopher admitted, almost lightly. Ivy shot him a look that told him she thought he had temporarily gone insane. "But we wouldn't open it."

The corners of Bone's mouth twitched upward. "Why?" he asked.

"Because we know what happened last time someone did," said Christopher, quietly.

For a moment, the guardian's face was a mask of agony; he looked long and hard at both of them.

"The man who is searching for the Chalice has killed – I have no doubt that he will kill again," said Ivy, firmly. "With the Chalice he would destroy everyone in his path."

Prospero studied her for a moment, apparently thinking hard.

"You hold this Manor?" he asked, and Ivy hesitated. "But you don't want to," he guessed; Ivy looked uncomfortable. "I find that those who long for responsibility are often the least suited to it," he said, gently. He sighed, steepling his ink-stained fingers. "Alright," he said. "We shall make an accord."

Ivy, who had been studying the stone floor of the church, looked up, interested. Christopher stiffened: magic was gathering around the architect in invisible coils. He braced himself, just in case.

"You may take the Chalice from this place – if you can discover its hiding place – on one condition," he said, in a voice that seemed to have strengthened somehow.

Christopher relaxed slightly, recognising a contract when he heard one.

"You must swear to destroy it, by any means – and if you cannot, you must take it far from here, and bury it deeply," Bone commanded. "It must remain outside the world."

"I swear it," said Ivy solemnly.

"I swear it," Christopher repeated, aware of the importance of the words.

He closed his eyes as the Oath settled upon him. His wrists felt suddenly heavy, as though they had been bound in iron. He could almost feel the edges of the shackles against his skin. As quickly as it had appeared, the sensation was gone.

"You are bound," said Bone, voice diminishing once more.

Christopher opened his eyes, blinking at the brightness of the architect.

"Now you may try for the prize," he informed them, folding his arms across his chest expectantly and putting a lot of emphasis on the word 'try'.

Christopher laughed, feeling keenly the ages between them. He felt that had they known one another in life, they might have been friends.

"Well then," he said to Ivy, who was looking at him a little oddly. "Ladies first."

He followed Ivy back out into the church proper, Bone walking a few steps behind them, glowing so brightly that they no longer needed their Light Orbs, his peculiar light spilling over the walls of the church and reaching nearly to the roof.

Ivy set off towards the altar, probably with the intention of seeing whether the vicar had moved anything in his preparations for the service the next morning. Christopher let his eyes follow her across the stone floor for a few moments, still half disbelieving their unexpected adventure in the cupboard. With difficulty, he turned his attention back to the puzzle in front of him. He looked about him thoughtfully for a moment and sat down in the pews, taking the building in and mentally collecting all the possible hiding places.

No point checking the bell tower. It wouldn't be anywhere obvious – even a double bluff would have been too risky for the penitent architect. He could safely discount the Lady Chapel, too, which was a relatively recent addition to the church, and the entrance area, which looked like it had undergone some significant remodelling in the last few decades.

That left the church proper.

He glanced up as Ivy passed him. She was heading to the back of the church now, examining the walls and occasionally throwing glances back at Bone, trying to gauge his reaction.

Christopher hid a smile. The old fox had been concealing the Chalice for centuries, he wasn't about to let his face or body betray it now.

Instead, he returned to his study of the ceiling: it was a fairly basic construction compared to the great hammerbeam ceilings of the larger churches. There were no angels hanging from the rafters, no ornate bosses picking out joints in the carpentry. The lack of them did nothing to detract from the grace of it, however. It had its own elegance, the dark wood contrasting with the cool grey stone at its heights, softening the colour and giving the building warmth.

Bone had liked things simple.

He frowned.

"What date did you say this church was, again?"

"Norman, I think," Ivy called, from behind one of the great columns that supported the roof. "They – *he* –" she nodded towards the watchful architect "– re-designed it in the seventeenth century."

"So it went from Norman to Restoration in one fell swoop," he mused.

"I suppose so," said Ivy, emerging from behind the

masonry. "Why?"

"Oh, nothing really," he said, rising from his pew and wandering towards the front of the church. "I was just thinking about the shape of the church and how it might have changed."

"You mean, how Bone changed it," Ivy observed, following him.

"Exactly," said Christopher, still peering up at the ceiling. "The roof was probably raised during the renovations – and they would have added the transepts then." He gestured towards the North transept: "The older churches wouldn't have had them, they were much simpler."

Ivy joined him at the steps of the chancel. "What am I looking for?" she asked, quietly.

"No idea," Christopher chuckled, and she gave him a light punch on the arm. "Although."

He walked to the nearest column and ran his hands along the cool stone.

"Although, I *was* wondering why these four columns are so hefty," he pondered. "There's no tower here now, but there could have been in the Norman building – and yet –" He looked up at Ivy, who had followed him; she, too, was studying the pattern of beams above them. "The tower would have been built on the walls for support – they wouldn't necessarily have had columns at all."

"Are they supporting the transept walls?" Ivy suggested, after a moment.

"Possibly," Christopher allowed. "But they still wouldn't need to be this wide – it's as if they'd planned for a tower and then changed their minds for some reason."

"I can think of a reason," Ivy said, grimly.

Christopher nodded, slowly, looking at the base of the column. "It all looks perfectly normal – except that there's no need for it."

"And Old Prospero didn't appreciate waste," Ivy finished. "Christopher, there are no graves under the floor here."

He looked at his feet, surprised. They had spent so long looking at the ceiling and walls that they just hadn't thought of the possibilities beneath their feet. He cast around at the bases of the other columns – there were none there either.

"Maybe they were worried about stability," Christopher said, slowly.

"Aren't the floors of churches usually packed with the pious?"

"Not all of them," Christopher said, moving to examine the second North transept column. "Depends on the church, its age, the religious landscape, the actual landscape. Some have vaults, some just have heating systems and organ pipes."

"How do you know so much about churches, anyway?" she asked, following his gaze up and down the stonework of the column.

"My dad had a bit of a thing for religious architecture – we used to spend the summers roaming the country churches. We went to Paris once, almost entirely to look at the rose window in Notre Dame, and he always talked about taking us to Istanbul to see the Hagia Sofia." He smiled ruefully in recollection. "He said that religious buildings were an expression of faith in stone, a means of reaching to the heavens with human hands."

He fell silent, throat constricting slightly at the memory. It had been a long time since he had talked about his parents, largely because it hurt too much. Ivy let him be, moving away to examine the other columns. He was grateful. It had been an altogether too emotional evening as it was.

When he had collected himself a little more, he joined her in the South transept.

"I can't find anything unusual," Ivy said, annoyed.

"Well, as you said, it was never going to be easy," he offered, smiling slightly at her mock glare. "Perhaps we're getting ahead of ourselves."

"How so?"

"Well, if this puzzle has a few layers to it we'll have no

hope of solving it if we skip ahead," he reasoned. "There must be a map or a legend, or something."

Ivy looked dubious. "What if that was what was in the base of the statue?"

"That would be a bit of a bugger," said Christopher, slowly. "But I don't think it was – Bone wouldn't have needed to make a contract with us if he didn't think it was still possible to find the Chalice."

"Unless he enjoys watching people going purple trying to achieve the impossible," Ivy muttered, with enough of a glint in her eye to tell Christopher that she was joking.

"Let's start at the beginning," Christopher said, moving on.

Together, they made their way back to the statue, trying to ignore Bone's smug expression.

"The goblet thing doesn't move, does it?" Christopher asked, eyeing it.

"I – I don't know," said Ivy, surprised. "I didn't try – I was afraid to break it."

She took hold of the stem of the cup and tried to lift, turn, push and pull it, all to no avail.

"It's no use," she huffed, straightening back up.

"What else would people avoid doing for fear of breaking that cup?" Christopher wondered aloud, peering up into the pupil-less eyes of the statue.

With a moment's consideration, Christopher climbed onto the atlantid's pedestal, testing his weight on the titan's pointing arm.

"What on Earth –"

He sent a grin back down at Ivy.

"There's a good view from up here," he said, looking about the church. "I wonder if that's the point."

He had wondered whether the statue's vantage would show him something new, but the church seemed just the same as it had before: shadowy and uncommunicative. He sighed.

"Ah well," he said, about to drop back down. "Worth a try..." he trailed off. He wasn't sure what had drawn his eye to the great book in Atlas's arms – a combination of the low light and a stray glint from Bone's intrinsic light, perhaps. There was something there – something you would never see if you remained on the floor, it would probably have been obscured in daylight, even for someone up a ladder, cleaning the statue –

Christopher stared at it, afraid to break eye-contact in case it disappeared.

He shifted position and ran his fingers down the delicately crafted page. What appeared to be smooth and finely finished felt rough under his skin, as though there were slender flaws across the stone.

He felt his pulse quicken.

"Ivy," he said, quietly. "Could you bring me a sheet of paper and a pencil from the bell tower, please?"

Perhaps recognising the urgency in his voice, Ivy immediately hurried away. She was back in under a minute, passing them up to him.

"What is it?" she asked, as he balanced precariously under the alabaster titan.

"I'm not sure," he said, rubbing the pencil diligently across the page. "Carvings I think – let me see what I can get."

It took a few minutes, and by the time he was finished his legs were aching from holding him steady in an unusual position.

He eased himself down and showed the paper to Ivy, his heart racing.

The graphite was darker where fine lines had been scored in the marble – someone had cut a perfect spiral across the two pages, along with a warning:

Take this tainted treasure if you may
Take it somewhere dark and deep
Never make it yours to keep
Bring it to its end before it becomes your own

"He might have been a genius when it came to puzzles, but he wasn't much of a poet," Ivy muttered.

Christopher nodded absently. "I think these are

instructions," he said, pointing to the rubbing from the opposing page. "Not that that helps a great deal."

First: My words in stone
Second: A golden thread
Third: A helping hand
Fourth: A leap of faith
Fifth: A gilded cage
Sixth: Decide your fate

Christopher shot an inquisitive glance at Bone's echo, who looked mildly impressed.

"Well, first thing's first," said Ivy. "We've got his 'words in stone', but a golden thread?"

"It could be a map of some kind," Christopher suggested, thinking hard. "Like Ariadne giving Theseus a ball of twine to escape the labyrinth of the Minotaur, in ancient Minoan legend."

Ivy thought for a moment, absently chewing on her necklace. "What if it's more literal?" she said, slowly. "Perhaps Bone had a tapestry made for the church."

"Would it have survived this long?" Christopher asked, a little incredulous.

"I don't see why not," Ivy said. "With the proper care – come on."

She took his hand and led him behind the altar, where a bright, luscious tapestry was hanging.

"There," she said.

"That can't be an original," Christopher said, doubtfully. "Surely the colours would have faded after three centuries –"

"It's a reproduction," Ivy said, with a touch of impatience. "The original's being restored in a museum. Look, there's a sign on the wall at that end." She pointed to a small plaque of white cardboard that quietly proclaimed that this fine piece of needlework had been produced by the local WI. "They based it on a seventeenth century original – copied it *exactly*."

"Ah," said Christopher, catching her drift.

They stood back to examine the work: it was richly colourful, depicting several saints venerating Jesus. A choir of angels shone brightly in the billowing clouds above them, watching as the saints and a group of penitent mortals crowded around their Lord.

Glints of gold thread shone in the warm glow of Bone's echo, picking out the rich clothes of the saints, the halos of the angels and Christ. There were touches of it on the edges of the fine book that one of the saints carried, and highlighting the edges of a goblet and a staff in the hands of two of the others. In short, it was a beautiful tapestry that seemed as reluctant to give up its secrets as the architect who had commissioned it.

"Are you sure it's an accurate representation?" Christopher asked, after a while.

"I hope so," said Ivy, glumly. "Otherwise we've no chance at all."

Christopher didn't respond. Instead, he retreated to the pews, where Prospero Bone had settled down to watch. "You needn't look so smug," he grumbled, as he sat down beside him.

"I didn't expect you to get *this* far," the echo told him, tinnily. "Why don't you just leave it here?"

"Because Quentin Post is a self-absorbed bastard who likes burning peoples' eyes out."

Bone stared at him.

"No, really," Christopher assured him. "Generally, but not exclusively, in pursuit of the Chalice. He recently picked up a demon trap in the shape of a crystal ball. It's quite unpleasant."

They both sat back and watched Ivy trying to solve the riddle of the tapestry for a few moments.

"And you think you can stop him?" Bone asked, after a while.

"Probably not," Christopher admitted, quietly. "But I have to try."

Bone nodded soberly and Christopher continued to search the tapestry for any hidden meaning. The glimmers of gold were less obvious from his new position in the pews so he ignored them, reasoning that since church art was intended to be seen from the back, as it were, then Bone would have continued this tradition of design. The image as a whole didn't strike him as particularly unusual, though he'd be the first to admit that he wasn't an expert. He wished his father was here.

He slumped back against the pew, scanning his rubbing once more, in case the words had somehow rearranged themselves while he wasn't paying attention.

He frowned.

"Ivy!" he shouted, jumping to his feet; his friend gave a little yelp of surprise, startled out of her close examination of the tapestry.

He held the page up against the outline of the work and laughed.

"It's not *in* the tapestry," he said, waving the paper triumphantly. "It *is* the tapestry! Look –"

He held it up again for her to see – now he'd noticed it, it was impossible to miss.

"That was a *good* one," he said to the echo, who shrugged serenely, giving nothing away.

"I'm sorry," said Ivy, still peering between the paper and his hand and the tapestry behind the altar. "You're going to have to make a bit more sense than that."

"It's the spiral," he said, buoyed up by his success. "The golden ratio – it's the limit of the ratio of consecutive Fibonacci numbers." Ivy still looked blank, so he went on: "Okay, in nature," he said, casting around for something she might recognise. "Some things grow in a particular pattern that can be associated with a sequence of whole numbers that a man named Fibonacci described in the thirteenth century." He paused. "He made up a bizarre and quite improbable scenario involving the mating habits of rabbits... never mind," he said, on her expression. "Anyway, they form a spiral – like the bumps on a pineapple, or the particular position of leaves on a stem, or the petals on a lupin.

"They hadn't worked out that they conformed to the golden ratio in the seventeenth century – or, if they had, no one had written it down – but they *did* know about the golden ratio and aesthetics," he took a breath, aware that he was rambling. "Painters and architects would organise their paintings in terms of the ratio – it's really important in proportional aesthetics. You know the Vitruvian Man?"

"The drawing of the man by Leonardo Da Vinci where his limbs conform to the arc of a circle?"

"Yes!" Christopher cried, happily. "That's sort of the precursor to it, in terms of proportions – anyway, great works of art were made to conform to the Fibonacci spiral, which expresses –"

"The limit of the thing of consecutive Fibonacci things, yes," said Ivy, hurrying him on.

"Because it looks better," he finished. "More or less, anyway."

"So this is a Fibonacci spiral?" Ivy asked, taking the rubbing from his unresisting hands.

"Yes – if you imagine it being made up of blocks of space, increasing in size –"

"It matches the way things have been organised in the tapestry," Ivy said, cottoning on.

"It's so clever," Christopher told her, ecstatically. "You could see the tapestry every Sunday for your entire life and never recognise it –"

"Unless you had the pattern from Atlas's atlas," Ivy finished, catching some of his excitement. "Alright then, smarty pants, what's the tapestry trying to tell us?"

He scanned the tapestry with his eyes for a moment.

"There," he pointed to the goblet in the hands of one of the saints. "That's the centre of the spiral – that's got to be the Chalice."

"And the other end?"

"Bottom left corner," Christopher said. Ivy followed his gaze.

"It's a book," said Ivy, thoughtfully. "Ok, if the Chalice is at one end and a book's at the other, then we need to find the –" She broke off suddenly, and laughed. "Atlas's book."

They hurried over to the statue and searched fruitlessly for a few minutes.

"Well, that's annoying," said Christopher, climbing back down from the pedestal a second time.

"Don't get disheartened," said Ivy, her voice muffled, from behind the base of the statue. "We'll get it."

"Eventually."

"Hopefully sooner rather than later," she replied, crawling back out. "It's getting late."

Christopher nodded, thinking of the children. Astrid was probably sitting up worrying about them, refusing to go to sleep.

"It could be anything," he said, glaring at the uncommunicative stone. "A number, a proportional block, another spiral – *anything*."

"Maybe we're getting ahead of ourselves again," Ivy muttered, pulling out the rubbing once more. "'A helping hand'," she read aloud, and sat back on her haunches.

"Oh," she said, suddenly. "Well, that's a bit obvious."

Christopher followed her gaze, confused, and burst out laughing when he worked out what she was looking at.

"Of course," he said, chuckling, and climbed back up the pedestal.

"What's he pointing at?" Ivy asked, getting to her feet.

Christopher lined his eyes up with the graceful arm of the marble titan, balancing on one leg on the edge of the pedestal.

"Hah!" he exclaimed. "The first column in the North transept – I *knew* there was something off about those columns!" He jumped down and raced after Ivy, vaulting over the last bank of pews out of sheer exuberance.

"'A leap of faith,'" read Ivy. "I would have thought that involved the possibility of falling from a great height, but unless there's a hidden pit here somewhere I'm stumped."

"Maybe there is," Christopher suggested. "Maybe that's why there aren't any graves... and you'd make sure there weren't any around the other columns too, so they looked less suspicious."

"You're probably right," Ivy nodded, examining the base of the column. "There doesn't seem to be anything obvious, though."

"No," Christopher agreed. "But he didn't really go for 'obvious'." He gestured over his shoulder at Bone, who was watching them from his pew, arms folded speculatively.

"Is he *still* watching us?" Ivy muttered, bending down beside him under the pretence of re-examining a join between the flagstones on the floor.

"Yes," said Christopher. "I think he's rather enjoying himself!"

"He'd be bloody good at poker," Ivy grumbled, straightening back up.

Christopher fought a laugh.

They were so *close* now, he could feel it.

He ran his hands over the finely dressed stone, wondering why Bone had made it so large –

"Could it be hollow?" he mused, aloud.

"Did that happen often?"

"Oh, all the time," he said, absently, inspecting joints in the masonry. "Cheaper option – you'd fill the inside with rubble to give it stability. Like those big, posh houses on the other side of Brindleford that have beautifully dressed sandstone on the front and rough brick on the sides."

"My dad used to say they were 'all arse and no trousers'," Ivy observed. "When Mum wasn't listening."

"Maybe we're not looking for a pit at all," Christopher mused, looking upwards. With a click of his fingers he lit a Light Orb and sent it spinning up to the rafters.

"Can you see anything?" Ivy asked, suddenly beside him again.

"No," said Christopher. "Enhanced sight *isn't* one of the perks of being a werewolf."

He ignored the strangled coughing sound that indicated Bone had heard him and walked slowly around the column, keeping his eyes focused on the very top of it.

"It would have to be somewhere *really* hard to reach."

"Wait!" said Ivy, suddenly. "There, right at the top –"

"Where?"

"There," said Ivy, stepping close to him and pointing upwards. He closed his eyes briefly as the smell of her hair hit him, struggling to focus. "That shadow."

"I see it," he said. He manoeuvred his Light Orb slightly, the light casting a longer shadow across the lines in the stone. "It looks like a mason's mark. Looks unusual."

"Could it be a snail shell?" Ivy asked, and Christopher craned to look.

"Could be," he said slowly, beginning to smirk. "Appropriate."

"Fibonacci again?"

"Yes. Now, what are we supposed to do with it?"

"Well, if it's a 'leap of faith' I suppose we need to make contact with it in some way..."

Christopher paused. "If we press it, do you think some kind of secret compartment will open?" he joked.

"Yes," said Ivy, quite seriously.

"I suppose that wouldn't be the strangest thing that's ever happened to me," he admitted, after a moment. "Though it does feel a bit like we're reliving a chapter of an Enid Blyton novel," he added, quietly.

"I wonder if the vicar keeps a set of ladders anywhere." She looked about her, speculatively.

"It'll be in the bell tower if he does," said Christopher.

"I'll go and check."

Christopher looked upwards, dubiously. The column was easily three times his height, and dressed so neatly that its surface was practically sheer. Even standing on the back of one of the pews he wouldn't have a chance of reaching it – at least, not as a human.

He rubbed the back of his neck, uncomfortably.

With a bit of a boost he might be able to scrabble up it as a wolf, but he found the thought of letting the wolf break through – even for a short while – utterly loathsome.

But, if it was the only way...

He looked up as Ivy came back, carrying a folding table under her arms.

"No ladder," she said, and Christopher sagged a little in disappointment. "But this is a lot higher than the pews."

Christopher eyed it uncertainly. "I'm not sure that's going to hold my weight," he said.

"Oh come off it," Ivy scoffed. "You look like you're made out of toast."

Christopher looked at her, uncertainly, trying to work out whether or not this was a good thing.

"See if you can reach."

Gingerly, he climbed onto the table, testing his weight. It seemed to be holding, so he leaned against the wall, stretching up as far as he could.

"Not even close," he said, allowing himself to relax.

"Can you lift me up?"

"Easily."

"Show off," she teased, climbing up beside him. The table beneath them creaked unhappily.

"Don't worry, I'm a bit of a lightweight," she joked, moving between him and the column.

Christopher cleared his throat. "Where shall I put my – uh –"

Ivy rolled her eyes, and put his hands on her hips.

"Only if I'm not too heavy," she said, bracing herself against the column.

"I seriously doubt that," said Christopher.

"Oof!" she exclaimed, as he lifted her up, as easily as if she were a doll. The table protested loudly, and Christopher felt it dip slightly beneath his feet.

"A little higher," said Ivy, in a muffled voice. "I'm nearly there – got it!"

For a long moment, there was utter silence in the empty church – distantly, Christopher could hear the pinking of the church's heating system. He had been about to lower Ivy back down when several things happened at once: an enormous grinding, grating sound started up, making both of them jump and sway dangerously – at the same time, one of the large paving slabs set into the floor began to slide away beneath the column. Unfortunately, as this was what two of the tables' legs were resting on, it lurched downwards suddenly, folding itself up and flinging them both to the ground in a heap.

Christopher groaned, loudly, rolling onto his side and clutching his hip.

"Are you okay?" Ivy asked, flexing her back.

"More or less, you?"

"Cuts and bruises, mostly..."

They both turned towards the hole in the floor as the quality of the noises it was making changed from grinding to scraping.

Christopher peered into it, watching, fascinated as a bundle of cloth emerged from beneath the column, pushed by some unseen mechanical device.

Carefully, they lifted it out, surprised to feel the edges of a box under the cloth; they pulled it away, caught up in the thrill of discovery. It emerged, layer by layer, hardly tarnished by age: a fine box made from a warm, honey coloured wood, inlaid with a bright, shining metal.

It smelled strongly of beeswax and good, strong wood. Christopher met Ivy's eyes, his heart jumping with anticipation. They had it!

"That's a hell of a lock," Ivy remarked, tipping it backwards slightly to get a better look. "Think you can get it open?"

"I'll give it a go," he said, reaching out to take it from her.

As soon as his flesh touched the surface of the box a searing pain ripped through him and he cried out, agonised, snatching his left hand back and cradling it against his chest.

He stumbled backwards a few steps, eyes watering from the pain in his hand.

"Christopher!" Ivy cried, abandoning the box.

"Silver," he hissed, teeth gritted. His hand was beginning to throb and he was beginning to shake. "Ahh – no, don't touch it!" He tried to move out of her way, but Ivy was too quick, taking hold of his arm.

"Let me see," she instructed, sternly.

Reluctantly, he unfolded his arm, and Ivy gently turned his hand over. Both of them grimaced. A deep welt had formed across his palm in the shape of the inlaid metal. The skin of his hand had bubbled and given way, leaving a painful, open wound. Ivy sucked air over her teeth.

"Can you move your fingers?"

"Yes, but I don't want to."

"We should get that cleaned," she said, gravely.

"At home," he insisted. "We can worry about it after we've got the Chalice."

"It'll only get worse –"

"This is more important."

"Christopher –"

"It'll heal," he assured her.

Ivy looked dubious, but she relented, nonetheless.

"At least let me bind it," she said, pulling off her scarf.

"You'll ruin it –" he protested, but Ivy swatted his other hand away.

"You're more important."

He winced as she wrapped the fabric tightly around his palm.

"Thank you," he said, as she worked. It had been a long time since anyone had cared for him when he had been injured.

"You're welcome," she said, tying a swift knot. "How's that?" He grimaced at her and she smiled slightly. "Good. At least it'll stop the bleeding." She paused as his expression changed. "What?"

But Christopher didn't have time to tell her about the shape he'd glimpsed moving through the shadows at the back of the church – he pushed her to the floor as a blast of magic bounced off the wall where they had been standing, sparks flying in all directions.

Ivy grabbed the box and hugged it to her chest as they scrambled to the edge of the pews, trying to find somewhere with enough cover to transport themselves away. Another blast of magic sent them flying backwards; Christopher put himself in front of her, ready to change – when from out of the shadows came a deep, commanding voice.

"I'll be taking that, I think."

31
Promises, Promises

"Not on your life!" Christopher roared, leaping straight for the man at the end of the row of pews. They fell to the floor, crashing into the stand of unlit votive candles that stood a little way behind the column.

He could hear Ivy hurling curses at their second assailant somewhere behind him, but he concentrated on wrestling the first man to the ground. Christopher was rapidly discovering that his opponent was quite a large man and unexpectedly strong. He jarred his injured hand on one of the pews as they scuffled on the floor and he yelped in pain.

His attacker seized the opportunity and flipped him on his back, pinning him to the floor; Christopher felt his head crack against the stone – his vision blurred alarmingly. He had been about to push the man off him again and try to get back to Ivy when his assailant suddenly stopped.

"Hey!" he shouted. "Stop – Christopher – it's me!"

Bewildered at being addressed by a half crazed madman that he didn't recognise, Christopher paused long enough for the man to reach up and remove the mask that was covering his face.

As the influence of the Fade left his features, Ogden Rake swam into view.

"Bloody hell," Christopher exclaimed.

"Xander! Stop – it's okay!" the Constable shouted.

Across the room, someone shouted something inaudible as they were hit by a sizeable blast of magic.

"Rake?" Ivy called, apparently having taken cover behind another of the columns.

The Constable hauled Christopher to his feet as Ivy emerged from the South transept; Hardwick was doubled up in pain behind the first row of pews. He straightened up in relief as Ivy released him from her grip. In the centre of the church, the echo of Prospero Bone was looking on in something akin to baffled shock.

"What the *hell* are you doing here?" Hardwick demanded, still clutching his stomach.

"Sorry," said Ivy, wincing. "I thought you were Post..."

"We could have killed you!" Hardwick gasped, but Rake chuckled.

"I think perhaps we might have been worse off than them," he said, clapping his friend on the back; Hardwick staggered forwards a few paces and glared at him. "You're stronger than you look, my friend," said Rake, glancing at Christopher.

"Er," said Christopher, who still hadn't fully recovered from the knock to the back of his head, "thanks."

He didn't like the way Rake's eyes had narrowed very slightly, but he swiftly turned back to Ivy.

"May I have a look at that box?"

"That rather depends," said Ivy, still clutching it tightly. "On him." She nodded towards the bewildered architect standing agog amongst the pews.

"Ah yes," said Hardwick, straightening up. "Mortimer Bone, I presume?"

Bone looked from one newcomer to the next, unimpressed; after a few moments of scrutiny he addressed Ivy. "Are they with you or against you?"

Ivy smiled slightly. "Definitely with us, Master Bone. They are Law-men of this parish."

"Then I will defer to your judgement," the echo announced, in his distant voice.

Ivy inclined her head and passed the box to Ogden Rake. Everyone craned forwards to look.

"It's heavier than I expected," he observed, weighing it in his hands. "Bound in silver – to ward against evil, I assume?"

His question was directed towards Bone, but the glowing remnant of the young architect kept his face entirely blank, staring impassively forward.

It was the only kind of response Christopher had seen from him, and he made an educated guess.

"To keep the Chalice from getting out," he surmised, and Bone glanced in his direction.

"I had to keep it safe, even from myself," Bone murmured, darkly. "It would whisper things... It wanted so badly to be used, but I couldn't let myself, not after the fire." The echo's eyes were wide with fear and pain, and for a moment Christopher could well believe that people thought he had briefly gone insane in his youth. He looked up at the four of them, huddled as they were around the box that contained the Chalice. "*Do not let it out*," he begged them. "For your own sakes – for the sakes of all you care for – leave it sealed inside! All there is within is madness and death."

"Perhaps we ought to leave it in its box for the time being," said Rake, in the silence that followed.

"Just a moment," said Ivy, and there was an unfamiliar note of command in her voice. "Master Bone, I have no reason to doubt you – we have an accord – but before we leave here with an unopened box, I have to be certain that the Chalice is inside." She paused, watching his face.

The echo stared at each of them in turn for a few long moments. Finally, he lowered his gaze: "It is within," he admitted. "And you may take it from this place, as agreed." His eyes opened again and he made to take Ivy's arm, but stopped himself. "You *must* ensure that it remains lost," he said, almost pleading with her. "You must not use it."

"Upon my honour," said Ivy, earnestly.

"And upon mine," said Christopher, joining her before the plaintive echo. It felt oddly like he was saying goodbye to an old friend.

When they took the Chalice out of the church would Prospero's echo remain? Would he fade away, finally able to rest?

Would that part of him that had guarded his charge so faithfully through the centuries *die*?

He fought the lump in his throat and kept his gaze on the young architect. If this was to be his last night then Christopher wanted to keep him safe in his memory – wanted him to know that he wouldn't be forgotten.

"And will the Law-Men of the parish also swear?" Mortimer Bone swept his gaze across to the two Constables.

"Far more than my wife likes," Hardwick joked, but Rake elbowed him in the ribs.

"On my station as Constable," the larger man rumbled, and his friend echoed the sentiment, rubbing his side.

"Then I am content," said the echo, though he didn't look it.

"Right then," said Rake, authoritatively. "We can't take this back to the Court with a spy loose – Mistress Burwell, could you hold onto it for the time being?"

"I wouldn't have let you take it anyway," Ivy admitted, with a half-smile. "You'd better come along with us for tonight – it's very late. What do you say?"

Constable looked at his watch and swore, raising a chuckle from Rake and Christopher.

"Rosie's going to *kill* me – I was supposed to be back *hours* ago."

"If the offer is there, Mistress, we will gladly accept it," Rake answered, graciously.

"We'd best get things put back to normal," said Christopher, reluctantly taking his eyes from Bone's glowing echo. "Can't have the Reverend opening the doors to a messy church in the morning."

"Where did this come from?" asked Rake, nudging the fold up table with his foot.

"Bell tower," said Ivy, taking the fine wooden box from him. "Right hand side, behind the chairs."

The Constable nodded and carried the table out. Behind him, Hardwick set about repairing the damage the brief and misguided fire-fight had done to the walls while Christopher and Ivy righted the votive candle rack.

He was aware that Bone was watching them while they worked, and he wondered if he, too, was dwelling on his future.

Absently, he lit one of the candles, leaving it burning as Rake returned from the bell-tower.

Christopher glanced at the gaping hole in the floor. "Er – how do we...?"

Bone's echo followed his gaze and gave a wave of his hand: at once, the wooden and leather apparatus retreated back beneath the column. With a sound like the closing of a tomb the great slab of stone ground back into place.

"Good as new," Christopher muttered, looking about the church for anything out of place.

Ivy was wrapping the box back in its protective layers of cloth while the two Constables checked the walls and windows for any damage they might have missed.

"Mistress," said the echo, quietly; Ivy looked up from her work, politely. "If he is the man you think he is, he will not stop until he has it. When he finds my hiding place empty, he will renew his efforts."

Was it Christopher's imagination, or was the candle-bright glow of the plaintive young man beginning to fade?

"He will have to come through us," said Ivy, firmly, getting to her feet.

"That is what I am afraid of," said the echo.

His voice is getting fainter too, Christopher realised.

"We won't let him take it," said Christopher, with more confidence than he felt. He put his arm around Ivy's shoulders, needing to feel someone solid beside him.

The glow was diminishing rapidly now, and Bone tried to speak, but no sound came out.

Christopher felt Ivy stiffen beside him as she realised what was happening. The remnant of Prospero Bone stared at them, worried and sad, as the rest of him faded from view. His eyes were the last to go, hanging in mid-air – bright and gold, like the gateway to another world – until finally the echo closed his eyes, leaving them with nothing but the tiny votive candle, flickering in the dark.

ooo

Quentin Post closed the church doors behind him with a snap, travelling home with an impatient click of his fingers.

He stalked through the darkened rooms to his study, frustrated. He had been so *sure* it would be at St Andrew's. His contact at the Court had mentioned some activity up there, and it was definitely one of Bone's old conquests.

Carelessly, he flung his coat and cane on the chaise longue under the window and kicked off his boots. He'd have them cleaned in the morning – they were dusty from the gravel path in the churchyard, blotted in places with a dark red liquid.

He had searched the church twice before giving up – and even opened some of the tombs of the era in the graveyard, but to no avail. The Chalice remained stubbornly just beyond his grasp.

Post scowled at his image in the mirror, he was flushed with frustration and it had brought an ugly look to his face. Carefully, he controlled his breathing, bringing his colour back to the hue to which he was accustomed.

He really shouldn't let things get to him like this, he knew. It was a waste of energy.

Delicately, he dabbed at the splatter of blood on his cheek with his silk handkerchief.

No: he would allow himself an evening of quiet indulgence and re-join the chase in the morning, with a fresh mind.

He undid his waterfall cravat and it too landed on the chaise longue, coiling at the end of it like a snake.

After all, if it wasn't at St Andrew's, that only left three more churches to search. The others had either been gutted or destroyed in the centuries since the sanctimonious fool had completed his restorations.

He slipped the gauntlet off and placed it back in its silk lined box.

Quentin patted the lid absently, as if acknowledging a pet. Despite his misgivings it *had* come in handy. He just wished it didn't insist on being so *untidy*. The Eye-Eater was far more reliable in that respect, but only a complete idiot would use an artefact purloined from the vaults of a local Court on their own turf.

His contact at the Court had gone to great lengths to secure it from him, and had been unexpectedly useful in terms of the gathering of information. He could afford a little caution if it kept that particular line of communication open.

Post peered at his stained hands with mild curiosity. It never failed to amaze him just how much blood the human body contained. It had long since dried, crusting at the edges and flaking away as he flexed his fingers.

It was odd how the colour of blood could change – it seemed to fade over time, as if it was no longer important.

He shrugged his waistcoat off, stretching his shoulders.

It had been a pity to have to kill in such fine clothes. Blood was very tricky to get out of silk – his tailor would know a way, he always did.

He poured himself a glass of excellent whiskey and arranged himself in the stately chair behind his desk.

Leaving a fresh corpse in so obvious a place was inconvenient, but not overly troubling. After all, who would think to connect a thing like that to a fine upstanding member of the community like himself?

000

It was well past midnight by the time they slipped through the doors of the Arcade. Martha had been waiting for them – doors opened and closed seamlessly before and after them as they walked, bruised and weary, up to the living quarters.

Mahri had apparently been crocheting furiously to soften her worries – she set it to one side as they came in and silently engulfed Ivy in a tight hug.

The children were sleeping fitfully on the sofas, the

space around them littered with books and brightly coloured granny squares. Christopher tiptoed over to Jake and stealthily removed the picture book he had clasped in his hands. The tiny boy opened his eyes and threw his small arms around Christopher's neck.

"Hi," he said, softly. "We're okay…"

Jake didn't seem to notice, he just buried his face into Christopher's neck and held onto him, as if he were afraid his friend was a figment of his imagination.

He was dimly aware of Mahri leading Constable Hardwick towards her Coach House and Rake standing in the background, looking mildly uncomfortable. Ivy had handed him the box containing the Chalice and was gently shaking Astrid's shoulder. It didn't take her long to wake up: she stared up at Ivy with a look of bewildered joy before she, too, hugged her friend.

As soon as her initial surprise had worn off she was all questions: "Did you find it? What does it look like? Was he there?"

Ivy laughed, somehow managing to sit down on the sofa with the girl on her knee.

"Yes, we found it, no, Post wasn't there – and I don't know what it looks like yet, it's still in its box."

Astrid looked like she was about to continue her interrogation, but Ivy interrupted her.

"Tomorrow," she said, firmly. "The important thing is that everyone is home safely. Off to bed, now."

"But –" Astrid's protest was cut off abruptly as she gave a particularly big yawn. "Okay…" she relented, almost sliding off the sofa.

"Come on, then," said Christopher, taking the little girl's hand.

"Where are you going to put it?" she asked, rubbing at her eyes.

"Martha's going to look after it," Ivy assured her. "Don't worry about it, there's not a lot that can get past the old girl."

Christopher smiled as a familiar writhing sound in the region of the ceiling indicated Martha's displeasure at that unflattering description.

Leaving her to make up the guest bed for Rake, he put Jake to bed, having a little trouble dislodging the little boy's arms from his neck. Although he was almost completely asleep he didn't seem to want to let him go.

"We didn't know if you'd come back," said Astrid, quietly, as they left her sleeping brother in his room. She continued in a barely audible whisper, "I was afraid we'd lost you."

Christopher knelt down beside her. "You won't get rid of me that easily," he said, gently. "Nor Ivy, neither."

Astrid briefly met his eyes and looked away, still dubious.

"Astrid," he put a hand on her shoulder. "As long as it is in our power we will always come back to you – we're a family now. An odd one, I'll grant you," he said, as she looked up at him, frowning. "But it's what we are, nonetheless."

To his surprise the little girl put her arms around him, hugging him tightly for a moment.

"Good," she said, very quietly. He picked her up, startling her, and carried her to her room.

"Try to get some sleep," he advised. "We'll be busy tomorrow."

"With the Chalice?"

"Yes."

He patted her head gently once she'd wriggled down inside her covers.

"What happened to your hand?"

"I burned it," he said. "It's alright, it barely hurts at all."

"You need to dress it with an oil of thyme and tea tree," she mumbled, sleepily. "To keep out infection."

"I'll make sure I do," he said softly, as she finally drifted off to sleep.

He left the door open by a crack so that Ivy could look in when Rake was settled.

A thick mass of vines were forming around the cloth-bound box on the kitchen table; they coiled more tightly as he approached, possessively.

"I don't want it," he said, and smiled slightly as the vines relaxed. "Keep it safe, eh?"

He jumped slightly as something brushed against the back of Ivy's scarf, still wrapped tightly around his injured hand.

"Everybody's worried about me all of a sudden," he chuckled, tickling the vine. "I'm alright."

"I don't believe you," said Ivy, behind him.

She was leaning against the wall just outside Jake's room.

He contrived to look confused. "I'm fine."

Ivy sighed and picked several jars and vials from the shelves beside her preparation table. She started down the corridor towards their rooms, beckoning him with a jerk of her head.

He expected her to go into the bathroom or one of their studies, but she walked straight past the doors, right to the end of the hallway and into her own room. He followed her to the threshold, feeling awkward.

Ivy placed the jars and vials down on a chest of drawers one by one, as if the action was helping her to think.

"Are you coming in, or are you just going to hover around the door?" she asked, examining one of her own labels with great care.

He took a few hesitant steps forward – he glanced behind him, wondering whether to shut the door and found that it had already closed.

"Sit," she ordered, without turning.

He perched on the very end of her bed, feeling distinctly uncomfortable.

"Take your jacket off."

"Ivy..."

"*Off.*"

He shrugged it off, trying to ignore the throbbing pain in his hand. "Really Ivy, I'm fine –"

She turned then, and he was astonished to see her face clouded with angry tears.

"Christopher, I don't care what you are, or what you turn into – and if you eventually decide to leave I won't try to stop you – but please, don't you *ever* lie to me."

He stared at her dumbly for a moment.

"I don't for one second believe that you didn't research your condition the moment you were bitten – and the least you can do is give me the credit to have done the same when I found out about it."

He sagged a little, and she joined him on the bed. It didn't really surprise him that she'd read up on his condition – it had been one of the first things he'd done, all those years ago – but he had hoped to keep it from her, at least for a little while. The last thing he wanted to do was to cause her any unnecessary pain.

"I'm sorry," he said, meaning a good number of things besides his deception.

Gently, she took his hands in hers. "Let me look at it," she said, quietly.

He allowed her to unwrap her bloodied scarf, fighting a wave of nausea as she teased the fabric – stiff and unyielding – from the welt on his hand.

It had already begun to discolour, a smoky grey colour tingeing the edges of the wound, just visible beneath the thick blood. He was surprised at how far it had already spread.

"I need to clean it," she said, reaching for her distilling alcohol. "It's a bit stronger than the stuff I'd normally use, but then there isn't much about this that is 'normal'. This is really going to hurt."

Christopher gritted his teeth and nodded.

He let out a tense growl as the alcohol met his open flesh, trying to control the agony that seemed to be running up his arm. As Ivy dabbed at it, the pain dulled a little, receding from his consciousness as his body acclimatised to the burning.

"There," she said, after what felt like an eternity of monotonous throbbing pain. They both peered at the wound, Christopher's eyes still watering from the effects of the disinfectant.

The greying around the welt seemed to have deepened, even in the last few minutes. Christopher eyed it uncomfortably, disheartened. Ivy bound it up again with gauze and bandages, pinning it closed with a neat series of folds.

"You're good at that," Christopher ventured, gently.

"My grandmother taught me," she murmured, apparently reluctant to relinquish his hand. "How long do you have?" she asked, fixing him with a hard look.

"I don't know," he said, taken aback at the pain he could see in her eyes. "I don't think anyone's paid attention to that part – either you're happy to see a werewolf suffering or you are the werewolf, and unlikely to be in a position to record your thoughts."

"*I'm* not happy to see you suffer."

"I know, I'm sorry for that."

"It's not your fault – any of it," she said, hotly. "It's just so *unfair*!"

Christopher wriggled uncomfortably, feeling helpless. "Well, it can't be helped now."

"I have access to some very unusual potions," she told him stubbornly. "We'll have you back up on your feet in no time –"

"Ivy, the rules are different for me, I'm not fully human."

Ivy slowly sat back down, frowning deeply. It seemed to Christopher that she was refusing to give up just yet.

"There must be something we can do – with all the books downstairs –"

Christopher sighed. "There is *one* thing," he said, miserably.

"What?"

Christopher paused. It was a long shot at best, he knew, and came with its own risks.

"Aconite."

He watched her face, guessing that she was mentally listing all of the properties of the plant. "Aconite..."

He nodded unhappily.

"Christopher, that's highly poisonous – it's – I mean,

if you get it on your skin it – it'll *kill* a man!" she stared at him, stunned. "It's even called 'wolfsbane' – I mean, '*bane*' –"

"I'm not fully human," he reminded her, unhappily. "I read somewhere that it can be used as a purgative in – in people like me. Particularly for silver. They used to use it to poison wolves out in the fields, and they even thought it was a cure for lycanthropy. I suppose it sort of makes sense that it would help something that's neither one thing nor the other."

"Are you *sure*?"

"No," he gave a hollow chuckle. "And from what I read the experience is far from pleasant, but it's a chance."

"Then we'll mix up a tincture right away – I've got plenty of aconite – it's not something people have much call for..." She caught his expression and faltered. "What?"

"I don't quite know what it'll do," he said, slowly, not meeting her eyes. "It could put me out of action for weeks, or put me in a coma, or even just kill me. Until we figure out what to do with Post and the Chalice, I can't take that risk."

He could feel Ivy's eyes on him, but he carried on, committed to this course of action.

"So I'm not going to take it – not yet."

He risked a glance at Ivy, who had gone very still. She was looking at him with a mix of horror and disbelief.

"Christopher, the longer we leave this the worse it'll get," she said, slowly, and he wondered if she thought he'd gone insane.

"I know," he said. "I know, but we said we'd carry this through to the end and that's what I intend to do."

"Even if it kills you?" Ivy demanded.

"Even if."

"And what about Astrid?" she asked, hotly. "You made her a promise – I heard you!"

He forced himself to meet her gaze. "Believe me, I don't want to die – but if Post comes after you, you'll need all the help you can get, and I'll be no use to you if I take the aconite now."

She looked away.

"Ivy, if he hurts you or the kids..."

"I can't lose you –" she mumbled. Christopher was startled to find that she was crying. "I can't lose you as well," she repeated, in a stronger voice. "I can't. I've only just *met* you. It's not *fair*." She scrubbed at the tears on her face. "But you're right about Post, and about our promise to Prospero."

She took his hand, coming to a decision. "Three weeks," she said. "We'll wait three weeks and no more, or until – or until you can't carry on any more. Then you take the aconite. Alright?"

For a moment Christopher wanted to assure her that he'd been suffering from temporary insanity and that he'd do whatever it took to get better, but he thought of Astrid and Jake, and what might happen if Post got his hands on them.

"Three weeks," he agreed.

"We won't tell the others, not yet," Ivy said. "We don't want them to worry."

"No."

"Why must I always meet brave men?" she sighed, ruefully.

ooo

Christopher struggled sluggishly to wakefulness. Although his hand and wrist still burned dully, he was warm and comfortable and he was willing to ignore it for the time being. Ivy's scent was all around him and he nuzzled into her neck, not wanting to open his eyes or admit that he was awake. He felt her arm snake further around his back, pulling him closer.

After running around the church for most of the evening and spending much of the night debating the merits of aconite, they had eventually fallen asleep on Ivy's bed, too exhausted even to get undressed. He was reasonably sure that Ivy was still asleep, and he was reluctant to move in case he woke her.

He hadn't wanted to hurt her, and once he'd had time to think about what the silver working its way into his body would do to him, he had resolved not to tell her. She had enough to worry about already.

He had been a little shocked at the strength of her reaction. Although he'd felt that they were becoming closer of late, he honestly hadn't expected her to care as much as she obviously did. He shifted guiltily, thinking about his friend. This was the last thing she needed.

Ivy sighed, and he raised his head to find her watching him. She smiled slightly – wryly.

"We should get up," she observed.

"Hmm," he said, in agreement.

Neither of them made a move and Ivy's smile grew a little. "I don't want today to start," she admitted, quietly, smile subsiding. "That way I can pretend that Post and the Chalice and your hand were all bad dreams."

Christopher didn't say anything, resting his head against her shoulder.

"How is your hand, by the way?"

"It itches like buggery," he said, heavily.

"Right," she said, shifting determinedly. "The sooner we open the box the sooner we can work out how to destroy it, and the sooner we destroy it the sooner we can get you sorted out."

Christopher sat up and immediately wished he hadn't. "Ugh," he said, his head swimming.

He felt Ivy's hands close around his shoulders.

"Just dizzy," he said, teeth gritted. "It'll pass."

He waited for the buzzing in his brain to subside and opened his eyes. Ivy was looking up at him, an anxious frown on her face.

"I'm alright," he assured her. "It just feels like I'm fighting off a cold or something."

Ivy watched him for another couple of moments before getting back to her feet.

"Let me know if it gets worse," she said, moving away.

Christopher understood this to be a dismissal, so he

left her to change, slipping into his own room for a couple of minutes.

He stripped off yesterday's jumper and shirt, wincing at the stiffness in his arm. He flexed it experimentally: it wasn't too bad yet, though he didn't much like the slight discolouration at the edge of the bandages.

He ran his other hand through his tousled hair in frustration. He'd finally found somewhere he wanted to be and it looked like it would be snatched away from him in a lamentably permanent way.

He sat heavily on his bed.

What was he going to tell Rachel?

32
The Chalice of Knowledge

"I'm sorry, love, it turned into a really late one – yeah, I know. I stayed over at Ogden's. Oh, really? Okay, that's great. Okay – I'll see you later, Rosie."

Hardwick hung up his phone and sat back down at the kitchen table where the denizens of the Arcade were watching Professor Barraclough tinker with the lock on the gilded box.

"Back in the doghouse?" Rake asked, shooting his partner a knowing grin.

"Less than I'd thought – she had Claire over last night, and she's at the church all today," he said, rubbing the back of his neck sheepishly. "My wife," he explained to Reggie, who grinned.

"I remember that look," he said, cheerfully. "My Bessie never liked me to miss a meal, either. Used to catch merry hell if I did."

"Quite right," said Mahri, tolerantly.

"How's it going?" Hardwick asked, in a flagrant attempt to change the subject.

"Tricky," muttered Professor Barraclough, a minute screwdriver clenched between his teeth.

"It's equal parts magical and mundane," Joanna said, closely watching her husband's work.

"Very fine work," the Professor said, around the screwdriver.

The room fell silent once more, everyone waiting with various levels of impatience for the box to be opened.

Jake, who had very quickly lost interest in the whole affair, had started work on a page of his colouring book, huddled with his sister behind the makeshift barricade they had all insisted on at the other end of the room. Astrid looked very much like she'd prefer to fetch a book of her own, but she was suffering from another bout of grown-up-ness and was resisting.

Zarrubabel was, as usual, sulking, disappointed that he hadn't identified the Chalice's hiding place – and more than a little irked that Christopher had had a hand in it. He had had a flaming row with Joanne earlier in the morning about not being allowed to help Professor Barraclough open the box. It had been audible upstairs in the Arcade and had ended only when Ivy had gone downstairs and shouted at him. Marginally chastened, he was hunched up on top of his box, periodically glowering at his sister. Joanna was ignoring him, fully absorbed in the task at hand.

The tense atmosphere into which they had all awakened had shifted directly into boredom as they waited, impatiently, for something to happen.

After a while, Reggie got up to check on Saffy and her puppies, banished for the moment to the relative safety of the Coach House.

Everyone stirred at his sudden movement, stretching lightly and shifting in their seats.

Ivy went and made a third round of tea and pulled a packet of fig rolls out of the cupboard, unwilling to start thinking about lunch just yet.

Christopher flexed his injured hand uncomfortably, feeling the wound pull as his skin stretched under the bandage. He bit into a fig roll, contemplatively, wondering how long he would be able to hold out before they had to try the aconite. It wasn't an experience he was looking forward to.

Kill or cure.

He huffed into his tea and took another fig roll from the plate on the table.

Really, if the damn' stuff killed him it would be just his luck.

"A-ha!" Professor Barraclough exclaimed, spitting out the screwdriver as the box on the table gave a loud click.

The whole room jumped, and for a moment Christopher was engaged in a silent but urgent struggle as he tried not to choke on the fig roll. Everyone rose out of their seats as they craned to see.

Professor Barraclough shared a look with his wife, who pulled a large pair of forceps out of the carpet bag by her feet. Both of them put on the heavy duty gloves they wore when dealing with particularly ferocious volumes.

Gently, Joanna lifted the lid of the box using the poker from the back room of the bookshop.

"Is it there? What does it look like?" Jake asked, breathless with curiosity, practically crawling across the table at the other end of the room to see. Astrid pulled him back by his jumper, though she looked equally agog.

"Just cloth so far," said Professor Barraclough, tensely. "Jo..."

"Here," said Joanna, handing him the forceps.

He let the lid fall open on the table so that they could all see.

They adults stood, tense and watchful, around the kitchen table. Fingers twitched through signs and symbols and lips mumbled incantations as each Practitioner prepared their own peculiar variety of shield. Christopher could feel the magic build around him as their spells solidified. Reggie's fingers closed on the hammer he had brought over from his tool box; he shifted his weight ever-so-slightly so that he and the hammer were between the Chalice and Mahri and the children.

Above them, the usually restless vines were still and silent, poised to protect them if necessary.

Christopher held his breath.

With unusual delicacy, Professor Barraclough peeled back the first layer of cloth.

"Anyone getting any containment charms?" Joanna asked, flicking her gaze around the room.

There was a chorus of negatives as nearly everyone shook their heads.

"Hang on," said Christopher, suddenly. "It doesn't smell right."

Professor Barraclough paused, wary of the unexpected.

"How so?" he asked.

"Non-metallic," said Christopher, sniffing the air.

"More like... leather and –" he frowned. "Something else – something... I don't know. I can't place it."

"Another layer of protection, perhaps?" Zarrubabel suggested, too caught up in the excitement to remember to be horrible to Christopher.

"Or another box or bag," Mahri added.

Professor Barraclough nodded and painstakingly pulled away another fold of fabric.

Christopher sniffed again, trying to identify the unknown scent. It was musty and just a little spicy – familiar and strange all at once, like something out of a dream.

"Parchment," he realised, as Professor Barraclough prepared to peel back the final layer of cloth. "But there's no way it could be that fresh..."

"I have to say," Professor Barraclough remarked. "The preservation here is quite remarkable – I'd have expected this fabric to be in tatters but it's survived incredibly well. Look," he poked at a bit of the cloth with the forceps. "Even the colour has stayed strong."

"It's not even musty," Joanna observed, leaning over her husband's shoulder.

"Part of the Chalice's power?" Rake proposed, intrigued.

"More likely the box it was sealed in," Barraclough replied, looking up. "With that lock it was more or less airtight."

"Good old Prospero," Mahri breathed, appreciatively.

Squarish edges were emerging from the swathes of dark cloth.

"It *is* in a box," Ivy said, watching the Professor's gloved hands. "It must be."

Christopher wasn't so sure, but he kept his mouth shut, mindful of the presence of the Constables. He hoped they had missed his earlier slip in all the excitement, and he wasn't about to give them another chance to figure out who and what he was. There was too much at stake.

The room held its breath as Professor Barraclough

moved the final strip of cloth away. From beneath it, deep red leather emerged. It was almost black, with darker spirals cut into it; in the bright November sunlight the surface shone blood red, as fresh as the day it had been constructed.

"It's –" Ivy began, shocked.

"It's a book!" Professor Zarrubabel cried, making them all start.

There was a ringing silence as everyone's mouths fell open in surprise. The silence was shattered, rather abruptly, by Professor Zarrubabel rising up towards the ceiling at terrifying speed. Several protective charms sprung into being in response to the sudden movement, and chairs fell over in the general chaos.

Among the startled and angry shouts in the kitchen, Ivy's voice rose, stern and unimpressed.

"*Martha!*"

Christopher, muscles tight and ready to pounce on the thing on the table at the first sign of trouble, followed her gaze and relaxed a little, biting back a laugh. Martha had apparently decided that Zarrubabel couldn't be trusted around dangerous books and had snatched the irate poltergeist's box up to the rafters. Zarrubabel was screaming bloody murder, flailing ineffectually at the vines that snapped and batted the air around him as he swung to and fro through the air.

"Well, while he's occupied," said Professor Barraclough, as everyone reassembled around the protective wall of magic that had formed around the kitchen table. There were so many interlocking charms there that the air looked a little glassy.

Together, the Barracloughs lifted the book out of its wrappings and gently placed it on the work-cloth they had spread over the table.

They stared at it as they moved the box out of the way. It looked perfectly innocent, despite its rather odd decoration. Felt perfectly innocent, too, Christopher realised with a frown. He found himself wondering whether Old Prospero had pulled a bit of a fast one the night before.

"Should we open it?" Joanna asked, running gloved hands speculatively over its glossy, embossed surface.

"Of course," said Constable Hardwick, at once. "We have to know what Post wanted it for."

"We promised Bone that we wouldn't," Ivy reminded them, hands on hips.

"That was when we thought it really was a chalice," Hardwick argued. "And even then we would have had to study it in great detail."

He looked as though he was preparing to remind her that the Court of Miracles had jurisdiction in Brindleford and could simply remove the book from the Arcade, but he stopped himself.

Christopher was mildly relieved. Apart from not wanting to see either of the constables hoisted up to join Professor Zarrubabel, who was still battling noisily with the recalcitrant vines, he wasn't sure that they *did* have jurisdiction within the Arcade. He didn't think Ivy would be comfortable exerting her not inconsiderable influence as Witch of the Manor, and rather hoped that she could avoid it, at least for now.

"Its contents might give us an idea of how to destroy it," Ogden observed, gently.

"It's far too dangerous," Mahri scoffed.

"It's just a book," said Hardwick, a little too dismissively.

"May I remind you that the last time someone read that book half of London burned down," Ivy argued, a note of real impatience creeping into her voice.

"Ivy is right, of course," said Professor Barraclough, slowly. "But I don't think we can avoid it. Particularly if we fail and it falls into the hands of Post or someone like him."

"Like my brother," said Joanna, glancing upwards.

"Like her brother," Professor Barraclough echoed, not missing a beat. "We would at least have an idea of what was coming at us."

"What could it do to us?" Reggie asked, tersely, after a

pregnant pause.

"We can't be sure," said Professor Barraclough, regarding the music teacher thoughtfully. "It might be something as simple as containing dangerously powerful spells – though given its history I'd say it would have to have something that compels you to use them as soon as you read them, too. Or, it could have been created for or evolved into a specific purpose – much like the Eye-Eater."

"There's an atlas downstairs that opens portals to other realities and dumps unsuspecting victims there," said Joanna; the constables' ears pricked up at this. "Safely under lock and key, chaps, don't you worry," Joanna assured them.

"The other possibility is that it has its own power," Barraclough continued, ignoring the aside.

"Like the Dischordia?" Reggie asked, clearly unhappy about the possibility.

"Yes," said Professor Barraclough, sharing his friend's perturbance. "Well, quite."

There was a pensive silence as they considered their next move.

"I think we'll have to do it," Joanna said, eventually. "Apart from anything else, it would almost be a shame *not* to have a look at it."

"Which is precisely why we oughtn't," Mahri interrupted. "To the bookish mind it's too tempting to resist – knowledge as bait."

"Bait for what?" Reggie wondered aloud.

"Exactly," said Mahri, almost triumphantly. "We won't know until someone does it, and I for one don't want to find out."

"Mahri's right," said Ivy, who looked relieved to find someone on her side at last. "And remember what Bone told us – once he'd read it the once he couldn't stop himself. It must have some way of getting under your skin."

She looked to Christopher to back her up.

He nodded slowly as his friends began to argue again.

Getting under your skin was probably precisely the point...

Christopher reached out with his mind to the innocuous-looking tome on the kitchen table.

It had power, and a lot of it – the condition of its pages, still crisp and smooth even after countless centuries, could attest to that – but there didn't seem to be anything too malevolent in its character. He felt a powerful urge to reach out and touch it, though, and he guessed that this was more than his usual book-lust.

Unlike the Dischordia, it wasn't drawing them in or calling out in their minds; it was more patient, preferring for its victims to go to it.

That must have been why we couldn't sense it in the church, Christopher realised. It wasn't being shielded by Bone's magic, it simply wasn't trying to catch anyone.

He wondered who had created the first part of it. It was clear enough, even from here, that it had at one time been a collection of papers that had been bound together. Not unusual, for a text of that age, but rare in terms of survival.

The life's work of a scholarly Practitioner, perhaps.

By now it would be the work of many authors – the people it had fed upon through the ages. To anyone interested in magic – whether for power or as some means of personal enlightenment – the combined knowledge of all those minds would be all but impossible to resist. Christopher felt another wave of longing to take the book away into his study and pore over it. He brushed it aside. You grew used to resisting powerful urges as a reluctant werewolf.

If it wanted contact then that was how it climbed inside the mind, Christopher reasoned. Anyone that was foolish enough to touch those pages would very quickly be under its thrall, gripped by a consuming madness that would kill them and everyone around them.

For a terrible moment that scholarly longing flared up again and he frowned, concentrating on staying where he was until it subsided.

Well, he thought. *Apparently I have its attention.*

He glared at it. It remained impassive on the cloth-covered table, continuing to be argued over. He wouldn't be fooled. There were too many lives at stake.

"I think we can read it safely," he said, aloud. Ivy's mouth fell open in shock. "Sorry Ivy, I know we promised, but the constables are right – we need to know how to beat it. It feels like it's contact driven – Joanna, Professor, is it influencing you?"

"No," said Joanna, slowly, as the Professor shook his head. "But we are wearing significantly thick gloves."

"There's probably more strength in the parchment itself than the cover," Professor Barraclough said, and ran his gloved finger along the page ends. "Nothing in particular," he said, but he shuddered suddenly, adding, "but it really does want me to open it."

"Well, I'm glad that's not just me," said Mahri, as everyone acknowledged the pull they could feel, but – at least for the moment – could ignore. "I thought I was going batty."

"It feels a lot like the contract of indenture you showed me when we first met," Christopher suggested. "But a good deal more powerful."

"As if it has a consciousness," said Ivy, quietly.

"Is that possible?" Reggie asked.

"You remember the *Dischordia*," Ogden rumbled, contemplatively. "No-one's going to convince me that *that* thing didn't know what it was doing."

Christopher nodded.

"So it gets a-hold of you when you touch it?" Reggie clarified.

"Yes," said Mahri, darkly. "And then it climbs inside your head and goes to town on it –"

"I wonder if it started life as a note-taking device," Joanna said, suddenly, thinking aloud. "Like a kind of magical dictaphone – we used to do something similar at Brightwell."

"I don't remember any of our old textbooks trying to eat our minds," Mahri scoffed.

Joanna looked at her with mild amusement.

"We weren't all that good at it," she pointed out. "If a really powerful Practitioner pushed it far enough, and asked the book to record thoughts instead of voices..."

"It might very quickly gather enough to evolve a mind of its own," Professor Barraclough finished.

There was an uncomfortable silence, broken only by Zarrubabel's lofty screeching.

"So it didn't start out evil?" Astrid asked, from the back of the room. Everyone jumped. They had almost forgotten the children, half concealed as they were behind the makeshift barricade.

"If whoever reads it wears gloves and isn't left on their own with it," Christopher began, putting thoughts of Post and what he could use this volume of knowledge for firmly out of his head, "then we should be okay."

"Should be?" Ivy demanded, staring at him. "Unless we're completely sure, then none of us can take that risk!"

"Actually, he might be right," said Professor Barraclough, thoughtfully. "The *Chalice* is ancient, by all accounts, and we know that tactile charms were one of the most common forms of enchantment back then. Not everyone could write, and those who could would rely on the methods they had learned as children." He glanced at Ivy, who was staring around as if they had all gone mad. "I'm willing to bet that only some really powerful magic would destroy it – like a ley point, or dragon's breath," he mused. "Not that there are many of those left. No, I think Christopher has the measure of it – and we *do* need to find a way to destroy it."

Christopher frowned. No matter how unpleasant the *Chalice* might be, it still pained him to think about killing it. He only hoped that when it came to it he wouldn't have to hear it beg.

ooo

They had reconvened at the kitchen table, the weak

November sunlight – diluted now, as the day wore on – casting faint shadows across their grim faces.

By mutual agreement the children had been banished to Reggie's Coach House. It was a mark of how frightened they were that neither of them had argued about it. Christopher could see them peering out of the window, the end of Saffy's nose poking out between their legs.

With Martha's help, Professor Zarrubabel had been locked in the vault in the bookshop for the duration. Joanna Barraclough had the key about her person and had said that she wouldn't let him out until the *Chalice* had been destroyed, as much for his safety as for anyone else's. Even so, Christopher didn't want to be around when they finally opened it.

Although they had ruled out many of the more immediate dangers associated with the *Chalice,* it was still a tense moment when Professor Barraclough – heavily gloved and wearing safety glasses, just to be sure – teased open the clasp on the side of the book with his pincers and lifted the ancient and beautiful leather cover.

Everyone craned forward, trying to make out the faint, spidery writing on the pristine parchment.

"It smells brand new," Joanna remarked, once more occupying her customary position and peering over her husband's shoulder.

"Has the ink faded?" Christopher asked, fighting the urge to climb over the table and look for himself.

"No," said Professor Barraclough, after a moment. "Rather, it looks like it was always pale."

"The colour of a man's thoughts," Constable Rake murmured, and the Professor nodded.

"Getting anything so far?" Hardwick asked. He and Rake were poised to intercede, should the *Chalice* make a move.

"Not really," said Professor Barraclough. "It's as if it's content to be read."

"It's practically purring," Joanna agreed.

"It thinks it has me," said Professor Barraclough,

thoughtfully. "We'll have to be careful when it works out that it's wrong."

Ivy shifted restlessly beside Christopher. Still of the opinion that this course of action was too risky, she had kept her mouth shut when it had become clear that the book was going to be read despite her, Mahri's and Prospero Bone's misgivings. Christopher had a shrewd suspicion that she was quite angry with him for not backing her up, but there was nothing he could do about that for the moment.

"It's made up of different sheaths of parchment," the Professor observed, leafing through the book with his pincers. "Look here, you can see where someone has cut the edge off this paragraph. At some point someone bound it together as a single volume – not particularly accurately, in places."

Christopher smiled slightly. It was nice to be proved right occasionally.

"The stitching is exquisite, though," Joanna said, running a gloved hand along the inner binding of the book. "A real work of art."

"Making it even more attractive to the scholarly inclined," Mahri observed, darkly. "Drawing you in and then –" she mimed smacking someone in the head.

"My dear lady," said Ogden, with a deep chuckle at her suspicious nature. "You ought to have joined the Court."

Mahri coloured lightly at the compliment, though she pretended to ignore him.

"There are several different scripts here," said Professor Barraclough, with a frown. "Aramaic, Persian, Latin, Greek, Hebrew, Arabic, Old English, Medieval French, Chinese – even Sumerian Cuneiform and Egyptian Hieroglyphs." He scratched his nose contemplatively with the handle of the pincers. "It got around a bit, didn't it?"

"Can you decipher it?" Hardwick asked, with a grimace.

"Of course," said Professor Barraclough, with a touch of professional pride. "Given several months and dedicated study."

"We don't have that kind of time," Ogden reminded him. "It's only a matter of time before Post realises that you're in the thick of this, and then we're all in trouble."

"Or our *friend* finds out and tells him," Hardwick added, darkly.

"I think we're all aware of that," said Ivy, rather coldly.

"Indeed," said the Professor. "I have some experience with some of these languages – but the real expert on ancient scripts is Hector."

"We are not letting my brother anywhere near this book," said Joanna, in a tone that was not to be argued with.

"Quite..." Professor Barraclough nodded, slowly. "I imagine, if I actually touched it, it would self-translate – which is, of course, out of the question. Christopher, which of those can you read?"

"Er –" said Christopher, as everyone turned to look at him. "Not many," he admitted. "Latin, Old English, Medieval French... there wasn't call for much else at the Records Office. Oh – and some forms of Norse runes."

"Between the three of us we ought to be able to translate a good portion," said Joanna, thoughtfully. "But there's always the chance that none of it will have anything to do with destroying the *Chalice*."

"Well," said Mahri, fairly. "If *I* was a devious, thought-stealing book I'd edit out anything that endangered my future – particularly if I had a habit of sending my readers potty."

There was a murmur of agreement.

"I think the best thing to do is come at it from several fronts," said Constable Rake. "You try to work out if it has anything useful in it and we'll have Victor dig through his records for anything on destroying powerful, sentient magical artefacts."

"And what do we do in the meantime?" Mahri demanded. "Just keep the *Chalice* on ice until Post works out it's here and comes to take it from us?"

"Yes," said Ivy, quietly. Mahri stared at her.

"But the children –" she began, but Ivy interrupted her.

"I know," she said. "The Court can't hide it, not without knowing who Post's spy is, and quite frankly I'd like to see the wizard who tries to get past Martha." She sighed at her friend's expression. "I'd rather we weren't in this, either, Mahri, but we are. We can't just sit back and let Post take the *Chalice*. We've know what he did to those poor people in Cairo and New York." She paused, frowning deeply. "He wants this book badly, and I'd rather not find out why."

She blushed slightly, suddenly aware that everyone was staring at her, but she stood her ground, voice steady.

"Sam used to say: you can't help everybody, you can only do the best you can for the people in front of you. Well, *you're* the people in front of me," she said, raising her chin. "And I will not see you fall."

Christopher swallowed, fighting the urge to applaud. Constable Hardwick coughed uncomfortably; Ogden Rake was watching Ivy with his head to one side, as though he hadn't seen her properly before. Mahri looked rather as if she had seen a ghost.

"We'd better get to it, then," said Professor Barraclough, with a glance at his wife.

ooo

Christopher lurked around the door to his study, trying not to be too obvious. He had seen Constable Rake take Ivy aside before he left, and seen how subdued she had been ever since. She had been avoiding eye contact with him all afternoon, as they worked out a rota for searching the Professors' books, and he suspected that she was still quite annoyed at him for breaking his promise to the architect. Any other day, he would have left her to her own devices, content to let her come to him if she needed to or to give her space if she needed that instead, but it wasn't any other day. Yesterday, maybe – but yesterday he hadn't kissed her yet, and his days hadn't been numbered.

"Are you alright?" he asked, as she came back from the children's rooms.

She looked up, tired and frustrated.

As much as the children wanted to help, there wasn't much they could do anymore. It had passed very quickly from being a bit of a scholarly adventure to being much too dangerous. He couldn't imagine they were taking being shut out very well.

"No," she said, heaving a sigh.

"Do you want to talk about it?"

"No."

"Cup of tea?"

"No."

"Sandwich?"

Ivy looked up at him, surprised. "You're persistent, all of a sudden," she remarked. He gave her an uneasy smile and she seemed to relent slightly. "I wouldn't mind a cup of tea, to be honest."

She followed him into the dark room and settled in her usual place on the big, squashy sofa beneath the main window. He could feel her watching him as he made the tea in the near-darkness and carried it over to her.

They sat in silence for a time, sipping their tea and listening to the rain drumming against the glass behind them. Christopher wondered vaguely whether he ought to get up and turn the lights on, but decided that he couldn't be bothered. The glow from his office was just enough to take the edge off the darkness, and he didn't feel like conjuring a Light Orb any time soon. He wasn't sure how his magic would react to the silver that was creeping insidiously through his system, but given his current run of luck he was reluctant to find out. He didn't mind the darkness so much, anyway.

It was restful.

Ivy shifted beside him and his thoughts turned to her. Had it really only been a day since they had sat here, watching documentaries and debating the internal politics of the Court of Miracles?

So much had happened in the last twenty-four hours that it felt more like a month.

"I'm sorry about earlier," he said, quietly.

"I know you are," said Ivy, with another sigh. "And I know we had to do it, but it just felt so dishonest."

Christopher squirmed in his seat. What must she think of him?

"Do you –" Ivy began, but stopped herself.

"What?"

"Nothing," she said, quickly, but Christopher didn't believe her.

"No, really," he said.

"It was nothing," she assured him. "I was just – it was rude, and stupid, and it doesn't matter."

She got to her feet and Christopher caught her arm, gently enough that she could pull away if she wanted to.

"It seems to matter to you," he said, and Ivy appeared to lose her temper.

"Fine. Do you always break your promises so easily?" she snapped, acidly. "Happy?"

Christopher's mouth fell open as she stalked away in the direction of the kitchen.

"No," he said, in a very small voice.

He doubted that she'd heard him. She was banging the kettle and the dinner plates around the kitchen, trying to reign in some of her frustration.

Hurt, and shocked by how little she obviously thought of him, Christopher stared after her, rooted to the sofa. He had hoped that their growing friendship had meant that she knew him better than that.

But then, he thought miserably, *perhaps she was right.*

He thought back to the previous evening, unhappily: he had promised Prospero Bone that they wouldn't open the *Chalice*, and that was exactly what he'd spent the morning convincing people to do – and he'd promised Astrid that he would always come back for her.

He had even lied to both of them about his hand. He'd

spent so much of the last few years lying to people that it had become a habit. It was easier, less painful.

His shoulders slumped.

She had every right to distrust him.

Quietly, he slipped down the spiral staircase that led into the bookshop, leaving Ivy to her own devices.

ooo

"Christopher?"

He raised his head from the little reading table in the corner of the dark bookshop, wincing as the feeling returned to his arm. He'd eventually fallen asleep on a book of terrible nineteenth century poetry, having had enough of feeling sorry for himself. He'd been reluctant to face Ivy, though, so he'd settled in for an evening of reading by the faint glow of a candle he had found in the back room, comforted by the presence of the books, chattering and rustling around him on their shelves, like the wind in the trees.

Ivy's head appeared around the nearest bookshelf and he sighed, running his undamaged hand through his tousled hair.

"Here," he said, a little sadly, and stretched.

"I thought you might have gone out," she said, awkwardly.

"No," he said, avoiding her eyes.

"I can see."

Christopher forced a smile and rose, carrying the little book back to the poetry section and putting it back in its proper place. It shivered in contentment, just as happy to be back amongst its fellows as it had been being read.

He turned to find her watching him, her face in the shadows cast by the candle.

"I'm sorry," she said, awkwardly. "For what I said."

"It's fine," said Christopher, though they both knew that it wasn't.

"I was angry and I didn't mean it," she continued, "I shouldn't have said it."

"Yes you should," he said, voice a little pained. "You were right."

"No, I wasn't," she said, firmly, stepping towards him and into the faint candlelight. She took his hand. "Christopher, there is no one that I trust more than you –"

"I lied to you."

"To protect me."

"And I keep making promises I can't keep."

"That's hardly your fault," she insisted, giving his fingers a squeeze. "You didn't intend to burn your hand, and neither of us knew that the *Chalice* was a book."

"But –"

"Christopher, shut up," she said, and kissed him.

He was so surprised that it was a few seconds before he remembered that he should be doing something too, and kissed her back.

"Are we friends again?" she asked, breaking the kiss after – in his opinion – far too short a time.

"Always," he said, a real smile beginning to creep across his features.

"Good."

She rested her head against his shoulder; surprised, he wrapped his arms around her, enjoying her closeness. He could hear the books sniggering around them, but he ignored them.

They stood there quietly for a few minutes, before Ivy huffed into his shoulder and he pulled away.

"Something else is bothering you," he observed, gently.

Ivy sighed and nodded, and sat down in the corner of two bookcases, resting her head against one of the shelves. Christopher joined her. It felt oddly like they were two teenagers, seeking refuge in a school library.

"Constable Rake had a talk with me before he left," she said, drawing invisible patterns on the fabric of her jeans. "He said I'd make a good Witch."

He heard her pronounce the capital letter with a certain amount of distaste.

"At the risk of being suspended from the rafters by my ankles," Christopher began, cautiously, "he's right."

He'd half-expected Ivy to argue with him, or even storm off upstairs, but she didn't. She raised sad, tired eyes to his face and smiled slightly.

"Even if I don't want it?"

"It's been my experience that what someone wants doesn't really come into it," said Christopher, softly.

Ivy nodded, sadly.

"It isn't as if you have to decide right now," said Christopher.

"Isn't it? I'd say with the *Chalice* upstairs and Post sniffing around, Brindleford could do with a Witch." She frowned. "Oh, I *wish* I knew what he was up to."

"Nothing good," Christopher remarked, quietly.

"No."

Gently, he interlaced his fingers with hers. "Whatever it is, we'll face it together," he said. "And that's a promise I intend to keep."

33
Pipped to the Post

"Police would like to speak to anyone who was out in Upper Fleet last Saturday night, between eleven o'clock and one the following morning. You can get in touch with them via email, or call the number at the bottom of the screen. The victim's wife, Alison May has made a public appeal for any information regarding the murder of her husband, who served as the verger at St Andrews for the last seven years."

Christopher flicked the television off, uncomfortably.

"That was where they found the Eye-Eater, wasn't it?" Astrid asked.

Christopher nodded unhappily.

They had been having a quiet afternoon – so quiet, in fact, that Christopher had closed the shop early and taken the children to the park. They'd arrived back, pink cheeked and cheerful, to a grim-faced Ivy, who had had the radio on in the tea-shop. Apparently, people had been talking about the murder all day.

"He's catching up," Ivy said. "I need to get a message to the Court – with any luck they'll already be on to this, but if they're not..."

"Astrid, go and help your brother get ready for bed," said Christopher.

The girl looked quite annoyed at being left out, but she did what she was told. Christopher had a shrewd suspicion that she was spending much of her time trying to eavesdrop on them, anyway.

He shared a worried look with Ivy. "They need to get a move on with that replica," he said, as soon as he heard Jake's door close.

"I'll have to risk it," said Ivy, pinching the bridge of her nose. "Drat that spy!" She sighed and picked up the phone.

Christopher left her to it and went to read Jake a bedtime story. He passed Astrid in the hall – she looked a little sheepish at being caught, but he didn't say anything. If he was being shut out, he'd be sneaking around, too. She glanced at the bandage around his hand.

"Your hand's still not healed?" she asked, in a small voice.

"No," he said, flexing his fingers slightly. He could still feel the poison creeping through him, the burn on his hand aching dully.

"You should get Ivy to look at it."

"Yes, I should," he said.

Astrid gave him a searching look. "What aren't you telling us?"

The tone was almost accusatory, though Christopher knew that she was just worried about him – about them both. She had good reason.

"Many things, little one," he said, breaking into the broad grin that had always disarmed his sister.

She gave him the kind of withering look that only a seven year old can produce, but let the subject drop.

"Do you want to listen to the story?" he asked, and her eyes flicked behind him to where Ivy was speaking quietly into the phone.

"I suppose," she said, grudgingly.

It was one thing to be caught, but another thing entirely to give up all pretence.

ooo

The dawn broke slowly in Buckridge, filtering gently through the winter mist.

He had checked ahead this time: there would be no members of the clergy or congregation to leave untidily behind him tonight. He still wore the gauntlet, though, just in case.

He had been at the church almost the whole night, following the ridiculous clues that Bone had set three centuries earlier. It had taken him a while to work out where to start, and that irritated him. It was like something out of a boys' adventure book, and the act of running after the architect's convoluted plan was seriously beginning to piss him off.

Still, he was certain he almost had it now.

With the confidence of a man who has been practicing slightly illegal magic since he was a child, he tapped his staff on the stone floor of the church. Slowly, and with extraordinary grace, he began to rise off the ground.

The Chalice of Knowledge has to be here, he thought, ascending to the very top of the column.

No one would go to this much trouble to hide something benign.

He huffed in annoyance as his eyes picked out the snail shell incised into the very top of the stone.

How droll.

He tapped it with his staff and looked down in surprise as a cavity began to open beneath his floating feet; one of the great, stone slabs was simply sliding away, grinding against its fellows.

Descending with more force than was strictly necessary, boots rapping impressively on the stone floor, he flung himself towards the dark space at the base of the column, greedily. He discarded his staff, letting it roll under one of the pews.

He had found it!

The Chalice would finally be his!

His screams of rage rent the peace of the dawn. Wildlife scattered in all directions in blind terror. They knew what that sound meant.

Somebody was going to pay for this.

ooo

Otto scrambled through the tunnels of the Court of Miracles, scattering Practitioners in every direction as they ducked out of the way of his flailing limbs.

He was going so fast that when he reached his destination he simply kept running for a few seconds and nearly crashed into the wall at the end of the corridor.

He dashed through the door to the archives and leaned against one of the spotless filing cabinets to catch his breath.

Victor stared up at him, one thin, indeterminate eyebrow raised. With a patience borne of being unable to die, he put the report he had been reading back on the desk, smoothed the paper, and neatly closed the file. He steepled his long, grey fingers and leaned on his desk, waiting for the young half-elf to speak.

Otto was mildly grateful, knowing how little respect the zombie had for him in the first place.

"I've – I've been going through my re-records," he managed, beginning to get his breath back. "Some of the plans are missing."

Victor nodded, soberly. They had suspected as much when the Eye-Eater had been missed.

"Which ones?"

"Experimental weaponry, mostly," said Otto, his usually open expression matching Victor's grim expression.

"Ah."

"I checked three times," said Otto. "Told the lads that spotted it that the Sheriff was looking through them."

There was a pause as they considered one another.

"How experimental?"

"We hadn't tried building all of it," Otto admitted, in a slightly pained voice. He was proud of his work and his staff, but there were some parts of being a Technomancer that weren't much fun. "Some of it was too risky, even for us."

"I see," said Victor, scratching his chin. "And that was all you could find?"

Otto winced, and Victor's eyes narrowed.

"What did you do?"

ooo

"Put her down," said Rake, affably, as he walked into the almost deserted canteen.

Xander glared at his friend, but the woman in his lap laughed.

"He's right, Xander, I should have been back at my desk ten minutes ago."

"Claire won't mind," Hardwick protested, playfully pulling his wife back on to his lap. "Ogden's just a workaholic, that's all."

Rhosyn playfully batted his hands away and picked up her stack of files; whatever she'd been intending to work on through lunch had clearly been interrupted.

"I'd say that goes with the job," she said, pointedly, and Xander managed to look sheepish.

"I'll make it up to you, Rosie, I promise," he said, making a cross sign above his heart.

Rhosyn laughed again.

"Sure you will," she said, giving his shoulder a light shove. Her tone softened a little as she continued, "Although dinner last night was a good start," she told him, giving him a perfunctory kiss on the lips.

She turned to Rake, who was watching them, amused at the couple's good-natured antics.

"You keep him out of trouble," she instructed him, and he saluted, making her laugh again.

"I'll see you later," Hardwick called after her.

"You'd better!" she shouted over her shoulder as she left the canteen.

"Jealous?" Hardwick asked, and Rake shook his head.

"My gran says I'm too foot-loose and fancy free – that and the job."

Hardwick sighed, and started picking at his lunch. Rake swung into the seat opposite him, grinning.

"I'm still in the dog-house," he complained, and his partner laughed.

"Could've fooled me," he observed. "You have lipstick on your cheek."

"There are bright spots," Hardwick agreed, matching his friend's grin as he rubbed at his face, "but if I miss dinner again this month, I'm for it. Thanks for covering for me last night."

"No problem," said Rake, stealing a couple of Hardwick's cooling chips.

"Did Ivy's tip come to anything?" he asked, lowering his voice.

Rake nodded slowly, contemplating the slightly rubbery chip he'd just stolen.

"The poor bastard was torn apart," he said, heavily.

"Post?"

"Not his usual MO, but if he was angry enough..."

"He must have walked in on him."

Rake nodded, waving to Claire, who had come up the stairs with Victor and looked like she rather wished she hadn't.

"Canoodling in the canteen again, were we?" she grumbled at Hardwick, as she passed their table. "There better be a bacon sandwich left, matey, or the criminals of Brindleford will have one less Constable to worry about."

"I take it the date with Mr Sublime didn't go so well, then?" he quipped, and then ducked as the stack of files Claire was carrying swished through the empty space where his head had just been.

"You have such a way with the ladies," Rake observed, drily, watching Victor make his way along the line, constructing one of his legendary tomato sandwiches. One of the interchangeable servers was following him closely, disinfecting the counter behind him.

She must be new, he thought.

"I spoke to the Sheriff this morning," he said, aloud. "We're no closer to working out who the spy is."

Rake made a noise of frustration into his cold, canteen tea as Claire hurried past again, muttering about love-struck constables.

"I don't like this," he said. "You ought to be able to trust the people around you. We all took the bloody oath, after all."

Rake nodded. He could understand how Xander felt; his partner solved puzzles by talking things through, not being able to would be driving him slightly insane.

"Come on," he said, as Victor threatened the terrified canteen technician with the heavy box-file his tomato sandwich was resting on. "We should call in at the Arcade, see how they're doing."

"Good plan," said Hardwick, abandoning the remains of his lunch. "I can get Rosie a bunch of flowers while I'm there."

They turned to leave the canteen, but were nearly bowled over by Otto, who had apparently been looking for them all morning.

"The plans for the replica are gone," he hissed, and Rake's heart fell. "I was only out of the lab for twenty bloody minutes, and when I got back they were gone. Out of a *locked desk*!"

"One of your lads?" Hardwick asked, careless of Otto's already wounded pride.

"Not a bloody chance!" he snapped, loud enough for the canteen witch, already rattled by a zombie eating tomato sandwiches, to jump at the other side of the room.

"All right, all right," said Xander, hurriedly. "Keep your voice down."

"They're all out on training today," he said, tartly. "That's why I was working on the replica."

"How many people knew you were out of your lab?" Rake asked, in a soothing voice.

"Rather a lot," said Victor, who was suddenly at Hardwick's elbow. The Constable swore, loudly.

"*I'm going to make you wear a fucking bell*," he muttered.

Victor ignored him. "He appeared in my office so out of breath he must have run all the way," he said, and Otto nodded, awkwardly.

"I must have been quite a sight," he admitted, unhappily. "Sorry guys, sometimes I just don't think."

Ogden patted him reassuringly on the shoulder, but Hardwick was watching him with narrowed eyes.

"Why were you running?" he asked, but Otto span around, making frantic shushing noises.

"What?" Hardwick muttered.

"I thought I heard –" Otto whispered. The four men shared a look; as one, they rounded the corner.

The staircase outside the canteen was empty. Hardwick shot down the stairs, in case there was someone just out of sight, but he quickly returned, shaking his head.

"Whoever it is, they're bloody fast," Victor grumbled.

"Or just bloody clever," Otto remarked, stooping. "But they left something behind."

He handed Rake a single sheet of paper; an excerpt from a recent report.

The big man swore.

"Half the cavern has access to these," Hardwick said, peering at the paper in his friend's hands.

"But half of them don't," Victor pointed out. "You can rule them out."

"We can, you mean," said Otto, giving the zombie an odd look.

"No," said Victor, "that would be bad form." He surveyed them, sternly. "I have access to those files, too."

ooo

Quentin Post flung himself angrily into his office chair, not even bothering to take off his heavy coat.

Someone had beaten him to it.

He fumed, lashing out at a passing fly, incinerating it in mid-air.

He had stormed back from St Mary's, exploding bins and cutting down telegraph-poles in the usually quiet countryside.

Someone had beaten *him*.

He didn't cope well with failure, as the churchyard at St Mary's could attest to.

He snarled, kicking the chair backwards and throwing off his coat. The fireplace burst into life with unusual ferocity, singeing the edge of the Turkish carpet. Post didn't notice.

He was livid.

When he caught up with them, he'd –

Fortunately for his office furniture, his phone jangled into life. He let it ring a few times, taking the time to compose his voice and breathing.

"Quentin Post," he said, voice remarkably steady.

There was a pause as the person at the other end of the line spoke.

"I see," he said, calmly. "Are you certain?"

Another pause; his fingers closed around the crystal whiskey glass on his desk.

"Excellent work," he purred. "Yes, absolutely. I'll meet you tomorrow morning. Indeed."

With great care, he dropped the fused remains of the glass back onto the teak refreshments tray.

"I look forward to it."

He replaced the phone receiver and sat quietly for a few moments.

"Ivy Burwell," he murmured, staring at the phone.

With one fluid motion, he seized the telephone, crossed his office floor and hurled it through the window, the ripped cable trailing after it. He bellowed obscenities, watching with some satisfaction as it crashed against his garden fence in a shower of glass, scattering wood pigeons.

Ivy Burwell.

ooo

Christopher perched on the edge of the tiny shop ladder, carefully cleaning the top row of botany books and pretending that he wasn't exhausted. He leaned heavily against the bookcase and started to replace the excitable volumes. They were unsettled today, worried about him. In the two weeks since he'd burned his hand, the grey tinge around the wound had spread up his arm, sapping his strength and making his whole body ache. He huffed, sadly. It would only be a matter of time before it reached his heart.

He heard the shop bell jangle behind him and frowned. It was a horrible rainy day outside, and getting on for closing time. He hadn't expected any more customers.

"Good afternoon," he called, not bothering to turn around. "I'll be with you in a moment."

He slid the last book back into place and paused: something wasn't right.

All around him books were falling silent; he ran his finger down the spine of a nearby volume of wildflowers. It stayed obstinately still in his mind. He repeated the action with the whole row, with the same effect. For some reason the books were hiding their true nature.

For some reason, they were afraid.

As unobtrusively as he could, Christopher sniffed the air: nothing. Just the usual combination of parchment, leather, glue, furniture polish and strong tea, along with distant notes from Ivy's teas, Mahri's flowers and the resin Reggie sold in his music shop.

If he hadn't heard the bell he would have assumed that he was alone.

Unnerved and preparing himself for whatever was waiting for him, Christopher turned.

There was a man behind him, standing stock still in the middle of the floor, hands in the pockets of his slightly crumpled suit. Pale blue eyes stared out from under a greying fringe; Christopher felt his heart stop.

"Hello, son," said the man, running a hand, distractedly through his hair.

Christopher fell off the ladder.

34
The Hollow Men

"Woah there, steady!" cried the man, and offered Christopher his hand.

Christopher stared at it, then at its owner, then back at it again.

He took the hand rather stiffly and the man pulled him to his feet.

They looked at one another for a long moment.

"Thanks," said Christopher, gruffly, and retreated behind the counter. He curled his fingers slightly. The man's hand had been warm and reassuring, just how he had remembered it. He felt sick. "How can I help you?"

"Christopher..."

"I'm sorry, I don't think we've met," he said slowly.

"Christopher, it's me – it's Dad," he laughed awkwardly, a pained smile on his face. "There's no use pretending you don't know me."

"I think you must be mistaken, sir," said Christopher tightly. "I'm sorry."

"I'm not," said the man. He reached into his coat pocket and pulled out a crumpled envelope. "Your sister gave me your address," he said, waving the envelope. Christopher felt himself go numb. He recognised it immediately; it belonged to the letter he had written to her only the week before, explaining his injury. "She's worried about you. So am I, actually – and your mother. She sends her love, by the way." Christopher didn't move, so the man continued, "You mustn't blame Rachel."

Christopher gripped the counter with both hands, rather harder than was necessary. He was dimly aware that he was breathing heavily – through shock or anger he wasn't sure. His hand throbbed painfully.

"We want you to come home, Christopher."

Somehow, he managed to control his breathing. The man must have taken this as a positive sign, because he tried again.

"Wouldn't you like that?"

"Yes, I would," said Christopher, and his voice came out as a croak. "More than anything else in the world."

The man's face broke into a wide, happy grin. "That's wonderful – really wonderful!" he exclaimed. "Your mother will be so happy! We've all missed you so much! You can't imagine what it's been like – when they found that note you left, we thought – But then Rachel told us you were alright, and –" He stopped abruptly and beamed. "Never mind all that now. I've found you and you can come home, that's what matters."

Christopher found himself nodding tersely. He felt his teeth lengthen very slightly and shut his mouth, hard.

"Obviously we're not going to tear you away from the life you've created for yourself here," the man continued, when Christopher didn't say anything, "and a bookshop – you must be in seventh heaven!"

"I'm not going with you," Christopher said suddenly.

The man looked confused, and a little hurt. "I'm sorry?"

"I'm not going with you," Christopher repeated.

"But your sister –"

"Rachel would never have given my parents this address," he said.

"But –"

"She might have marched in here and given me a piece of her mind, but she would never have given me away. She gave me her word."

"She was worried ab-"

"I trust my sister, sir," he said, interrupting the man in mid-sentence. "I do not trust you."

The man looked at him for a moment, expression full of hurt and concern. If it had really had been his father looking at him that way, it would have broken Christopher's heart.

"I would like you to leave now," Christopher growled, making the books on the counter jump; they shuddered almost imperceptibly.

"I don't know what you mean. Christopher –"

"You are not my father," he said, "I'm not even entirely sure that you're human. I don't know how you came to have that envelope, or how you can know so much about my family, but I will tell you this –" There was a dangerous growl in his voice now. "If you ever come near me or my family again, things will go very badly for you."

"Christopher –"

"You will leave now, sir, before I do something we both regret."

"But –"

"*Now!*" Christopher snarled.

Around him the books rippled suddenly, as if they had all come awake at once.

The man's expression had frozen, and Christopher wondered whether some of his lupine fury had leaked out in his features. He ran a hand over his face self-consciously. Finding only day-old stubble he let his hand drop back to his side, puzzled; the man was perfectly still. There was something missing from his eyes, Christopher realised: that glint of mischief that he had thought was unmistakably his father's had gone. It was as if someone had simply turned him off. He waved a hand in front of the man's face; nothing.

Christopher stared at him. A perfect replica in every way.

All at once, the books began to shudder and bounce on their shelves as the man's eyes rolled back in his head with a sickening snap, so that only the whites were showing. To Christopher's horror, the man's face began to twist and writhe, as though it was trying to escape from his skull. There was a dreadful tearing noise.

Christopher didn't wait to find out what it was: he cast the strongest shield charm he could muster around the thing that wasn't his father and dove under the counter.

There was a sound like a clap of thunder and the floor of the shop rattled – several books fell off their shelves with dull thuds. Christopher could hear them screaming in his mind, his ears ringing from the sound of the explosion.

He risked a look over the top of the desk and recoiled.

Where the replica had been standing was what looked like a broken statue, as though the man had simultaneously melted and baked hard. Parts of him were still the right sort of shape: his right hand, still holding the envelope, half of his face... the remainder had bubbled away, leaving a hollow where the inside of his head ought to have been. What was left of his face was contorted in pain or horror – Christopher wasn't sure which – and every part of him, from his clothes to the paper clutched in his hand, was the colour of baked clay.

There were shards of it around him, Christopher noted as he climbed out of his makeshift shelter, forming a perfect circle of lethal pottery fragments where his charm had held fast. The wooden floor inside the circle was blackened and scorched.

Christopher swallowed.

"It's alright now," he said aloud, still staring at the awful thing. Some of the books seemed to quieten. He picked up a book of nursery rhymes and absently stroked its cover until it calmed down. "It's over. Whatever he was, he can't hurt you now."

The book in his hands keened.

"Shhh, it's alright..."

He looked around at the fallen books, feeling that it could have been a lot worse.

"At least there weren't any customers in," he murmured, and instinctively glanced across to Ivy's teashop.

She *did* have a customer. An earnest young man was talking to her across the cake display. He was wearing battle fatigues.

One look at Ivy's face told him all he needed to know. He dropped the volume and hurried across the corridor, a trail of frightened and unhappy books following him like lost sheep.

"Hello Christopher," said Ivy, as he opened the door. She was very white. The young man turned to him and smiled: he was handsome and tanned, with an open, friendly face; he looked like he laughed a lot.

Christopher did his best to smile, but the panic that had seized him was making it difficult to control his face.

"Hullo Ivy," he managed.

Ivy was far too close to the man – if this one went the way his had she'd be right in the middle of it. He couldn't guarantee the shield would hold a second time. He wasn't sure he had the strength.

"Are you going to introduce your friend?" the soldier asked, cheerfully.

"Er, of course," said Ivy, weakly. "This is Christopher." She gave him a rather desperate look as he shook hands with the man. "And this is Sam – my husband... He's come home."

They had to keep him talking, Christopher realised.

"Very nice to meet you," said Christopher, as cheerfully as he could. "Ivy's told me all about you."

"I'm glad she's got such good friends to look after her," the soldier said, grinning. "There was a terrible mix up at the base. She must have told you – they told Ivy I'd *died*. It must have been awful for her!"

His face had clouded as he spoke. It looked wrong somehow, as though it was unused to displaying unhappiness. It quickly disappeared behind his grin once more.

"But I'm back now, that's what matters."

"Can you believe it?" Ivy asked, in a small voice. "After all this time..."

"Fantastic!" Christopher breathed, as the man turned back to her.

"We can pick off where we left off," he said and took her hand, stroking it tenderly.

Christopher moved behind him, silently.

"That would be lovely," said Ivy, clearly struggling not to cry. A single tear had escaped and trickled down her cheek; the soldier reached up and brushed it away.

"It's alright, love," he said.

Ivy met Christopher's eyes over the soldier's shoulder.

He raised his undamaged hand and made a sign over the back of the man's head. The soldier froze.

As though Christopher had pressed some hidden switch, the top of the soldier's skull lifted up. On the other side of the counter, Ivy closed her eyes.

Carefully, Christopher reached into the empty cavity of the soldier's skull and lifted out a small roll of parchment. As he did it, the soldier seemed to melt away. In his place was a simple clay figure, about the size and shape of a human, but with no distinguishing features. The very top of its head remained open, hinged at roughly the point the soldier's eyebrows had been.

Christopher stuffed the parchment into his pocket and rounded the corner of the counter. Ivy was very white and shaking, her eyes still tightly shut. She flinched when he touched her.

"He's gone," he said softly, and she let him pull her into his arms. After a moment she wrapped her arms around his chest, mutely.

The trail of frightened books that had followed him from the shop collected themselves around Ivy's feet in solidarity.

Christopher glanced down as something wrapped itself around his leg. Several of Martha's vines were coiled at their feet.

"You're a bit late," he said softly, and scrubbed at his face with his sleeve.

Ivy took a breath and wiped her own eyes. "I don't think she could see it," she croaked. "Like it wasn't really there."

"It isn't, really," Christopher mumbled. He rubbed her back. "That was..."

"Horrible."

"Yes."

Above them, a floorboard creaked; Ivy met Christopher's eyes. They raced up the spiral staircase, two steps at a time, and stared around wildly: Astrid's notes and Jake's colouring books were scattered across the floor in front of the television. Jake's favourite cartoon characters chattered away to themselves on the screen, rendered oddly sinister in Christopher's panic.

Ivy gasped and grabbed a handful of Christopher's jumper, pointing out into the garden, uncovered for once to catch the morning sunshine. A late autumn shower was catching what was left of the afternoon light, making the fading leaves glossy and bright.

Astrid and Jake were a few feet outside the doors, ignoring the rain. They couldn't quite see their faces, but Astrid was clearly tense, torn between approaching the man who was coaxing them nearer and pulling her brother – who was a few steps beyond her – back by the scruff of his shirt. He could practically smell her indecision.

Ivy swore and hurried to the Arcade doors. Christopher followed, trying to keep himself calm enough to think properly. The man under the roses looked enough like the children for Christopher to guess his identity. No one else could have tempted them both outside so effortlessly. Fleetingly, he wondered what had happened to the real Mr Healy. They moved forward slowly, hoping that the creature in the garden wouldn't see them as an immediate threat.

There is no way either of us can get behind this one, he thought. *And if we can get the children away safely we might be able to contain the shrapnel better up here...*

If only Jake would stop moving closer to it.

Christopher was suddenly aware of movement in the undergrowth: Martha was onto this one. Heartened, he glanced up at the Coach Houses. The windows of both were dark – Mahri was out at a choral evening with Joanna Barraclough, but Reggie might still be in his shop. Christopher frowned. As soon as the children were safe he'd check – it seemed unlikely that Reggie would be left out of this. Post was nothing if not thorough.

He squinted at the man in the undergrowth, shaking rain out of his eyes. He couldn't hear what he was saying over the rain but he could see that Astrid's resolve was wavering. Christopher watched with his heart in his mouth as Jake moved further away from them. This time his sister took a hesitant step after him.

"Come back to the house," Ivy said quietly, laying a hand softly on Astrid's shoulder. She looked up at the older witch, a pained expression on her young face. "Do you trust me, Astrid?" Ivy asked her, just as quietly.

Astrid bit her lip and nodded; at the same time, Jake hurled himself forwards and leapt into the man's waiting arms, right at the other end of the garden. He swung the tiny boy around and Jake squealed happily, calling for his sister.

"Astrid?" Ivy asked again, as the girl's attention began to waver.

"I trust you," she responded, nodding abruptly.

"Go and stand with Christopher," said Ivy, with an air of command that they didn't often hear.

Astrid glanced towards her brother and the man under the roses, but Ivy pushed her away firmly.

Vines were gathering around the man's feet and swarming through the gnarly, ancient rose bushes on the wall behind him. His attention on the children, he hadn't seen them yet, but it was only a matter of time.

"He'll be fine," said Ivy, turning back to face the creature.

Astrid backed away until her ankles hit Christopher's shoes. He grasped the tops of her arms loosely, wanting to make sure she couldn't run out in front of Ivy when she made her move.

"Jake..." she breathed, a tremor in her voice.

"Let Ivy handle this," Christopher said softly, giving her shoulders a reassuring squeeze.

Jake had stopped squealing now, and had seen the expression on Astrid's face. Unnerved, he peered up into the face of the man who held him. Christopher could see the uncertainty growing in the child's open, friendly face.

Whatever you're going to do, Ivy, do it soon, he thought, tightening his grip on Astrid's shoulders. Ivy was only a few feet from the man now. She looked relaxed, but Christopher knew better – she was watching the man carefully, waiting to see what he would do. He appeared to be speaking to her, but Christopher couldn't make out the words.

Jake stared at Ivy imploringly. He wriggled in the man's arms, which tightened around him without any noticeable change in the man's expression. Christopher felt Astrid stir. He felt for her – he felt so helpless hanging back here, but he'd seen Ivy work magic in her own garden before, and he suspected that any interference would be worse for Jake in the long run.

"He's safe as long as you're with me," said Christopher, hoping that this was true. "He can't leave without both of you – he can't disobey his instructions."

"Why?" Astrid demanded, squirming. He rubbed the top of her arms.

"Trust me," he whispered.

"You will return Jake and leave this place," said Ivy loudly, in that voice that was not quite her own. Somehow, it sounded more like her this time, as though she was growing into it.

The man replied, looking hurt and confused, but Christopher couldn't catch the words. He took a step forwards and so did Ivy. The creature stopped, uncertain.

"It's alright, Jake," said Ivy, loud enough for Christopher and Astrid to hear. "Close your eyes and I promise, everything will be okay."

"Astrid, turn away," said Christopher urgently.

"No –"

"Astrid –" he had a strong suspicion that she had worked out what was coming.

"Jake needs me!"

"Please." He dropped to his knees beside her. "Turn away – trust us."

He could practically feel her warring with herself. After what seemed like an age, she called out into the rain: "Jake, *close your eyes*!" before turning and burying her head in Christopher's sodden jumper.

The light started to build almost immediately, radiating from within Ivy like she was some kind of living storm lantern, cold and pale as ice. Tiny arcs of light spat out around her in her fury, making the drops of rain around her fizz and steam. He couldn't take his eyes away from her.

He watched as she rose on the tips of her toes, magic crackling through the arcade with that hot metal smell. Just in front of him Astrid's hair began to lift with static, responding to the vast magical energy Ivy was calling to her. If it had been a wizard facing her she wouldn't have had time – Christopher's head was reeling with the power of it – but the man under the roses had no capacity for abstract thought.

Urgent slithery noises were emanating from every part of the garden now – everything seemed to be coming to life, from the fruit trees that lined the walls to the geraniums in Reggie's window boxes. Everything seemed brighter. Christopher could taste Martha's anger permeating the air. It twisted his mouth, as though he had unwittingly bitten into a juniper seed. Amongst it, the man stood stock still, holding Jake firmly out of Ivy's reach; the rose vines behind him – dormant in the chill of the autumn – were writhing like thick black snakes, thorns glinting maliciously in the light from their Witch.

There was a feeling like the world was taking a great breath, ready to leap...

Arcs of blue and white light span around Ivy for a moment before both they and the vines shot about the man, swarming around him like angry vipers. The two forms were briefly connected, glowing brightly like orbs of molten glass, before they were engulfed by the crushing foliage.

Somewhere in the midst of the ball of light Jake started to scream – Christopher held Astrid fast in his arms, his own heart pounding with fear – and kept on screaming. There was a moment when the small boy's scream seemed to be coming from everywhere at once, then – with a slight change in pitch – it resolved and sharpened. Suddenly, Jake was hurtling towards them, propelled by the branches of the fruit trees, which were extending like great spindly limbs between them and the mass of twisting light and vines, sheltering them.

Christopher caught Jake with one arm and pulled him to him. Astrid shifted, wrapping her arms around her sobbing brother. Christopher held them both tightly, unwilling to risk moving them until the garden was calm once more.

He couldn't see anything beyond the protective branches, blinded as he was from Ivy's light, and their silhouettes danced with every iridescent arc, making his head ache.

A great hissing burst forth from the centre of the mass of vines as the creature at their centre cracked and buckled.

As abruptly as it had begun, all movement in the garden ceased apart from the continuing drizzle. Light and vines surged upwards, forming the great, glass ceiling once more, putting an end to the falling rain. Around them, plants were shuffling and slithering back to their posts with surprising grace. Amongst it all, Ivy strode towards them, looking wild. Her hair had fallen loose and was streaming around her like her beloved vines. fury still shone in her eyes and Christopher was put in mind of a young Medusa, unblemished by Athena's rage.

He looked past her: where the creature had been standing was a formless lump of clay, almost like a termite mound. He glanced up to find Ivy standing over them, eyes still shining and skin a-glow. For one horrible moment Christopher was truly afraid of her, and what she might do to them if she ever forgot who she was.

Something of it must have shown on his face because she took a step back, startled, and suddenly she was Ivy again: worried and very upset.

Somehow, Christopher found his voice. It sounded small and quiet in the large garden.

"It's alright," he croaked, rubbing Jake's back. "It's

over..."

ooo

It took a long time, but they managed to persuade the children to let go of one another and be led inside. Reggie had met them in the main room, blood running from a wound in his shoulder and a haunted expression on his face. Christopher didn't even have to ask what had happened. He'd stuck his head around the door of the music shop while Ivy patched Reggie up and Jake and Astrid clung to one another on the sofa, and found a fourth shattered effigy in the middle of the shop.

It looked like Reggie had sheltered behind the counter; there were fragments of pottery embedded into the wood. A larger sherd by Christopher's feet had borne the features of Reggie's late wife, hideously contorted as the clay deformed. Christopher crushed it with his shoe before going back upstairs, shaking with anger.

If Quentin Post ever darkened the Arcade's doors again, he would rip him apart.

He telephoned the Court while Reggie checked on Boscoe and his dogs and Ivy made everyone cups of tea. Then he telephoned the Barracloughs.

They sat around the Arcade in tense silence, waiting for everyone to arrive, unable to look at one another and unwilling to move. The Arcade felt suddenly cavernous, or as though they were all suddenly much smaller. Even the animals were subdued, the puppies piling themselves protectively about the children. It was also strangely bereft of Martha's influence. Christopher had a shrewd suspicion that she was guarding the doors.

Mahri was the first to arrive. She rushed up the spiral staircase with a curse at her fingertips.

"My God, are you alright?" she cried, when she saw them. "I saw those things downstairs, and I thought –"

Her brisk manner served to break the spell they seemed to be under. Suddenly everyone was able to move again and shuffled about restlessly. Mahri bustled the children off to get their pyjamas on (largely to calm them down, Christopher thought), then bustled back to fuss over Reggie's arm.

Christopher slunk downstairs as she questioned Ivy, knowing that they'd be alright without him. He didn't particularly feel like talking right now.

The evening's events had taken their toll on him, and he felt drained and rather numb; every inch of his arm ached where the poison had seeped through.

Automatically, he picked up a few of the fallen books, carefully avoiding the lump of twisted clay in the middle of the room.

After a while, its presence really began to bother him and he went to retrieve the books that had followed him into the teashop, still piled up around the staircase in the back room. One or two of them had made it a few steps up, but they couldn't get any further. It was quite endearing.

They vibrated with relief when they saw him, falling over themselves to get closer. He sat on the floor of the back room with them until they calmed down. Not for the first time, he was struck by how closely they resembled Saffy's puppies sometimes. In many ways they were uncomplicated creatures and it didn't take too long to get most of them to a state where they could happily be shelved once more, though one or two of them were still worryingly jittery.

He carried the lot back across to the bookshop, where he found Ivy quietly replacing more of the fallen books. He set his stack down on the counter and watched her for a moment, glad that – physically at least – they were all mostly alright. She finished putting away the last few books in her arms and stood for a minute, staring at nothing.

Christopher knew how she felt: it was as if someone else was piloting his body, letting him retreat, recover. He laid a hand on her back and she gave him a thoroughly unconvincing smile. She nodded towards a small pile of books on the nearest reading table.

"They were damaged when they fell," she said, and Christopher checked them over. There were a few torn covers and dented spines – nothing he couldn't fix in the morning.

He looked up to find Ivy gazing at the mutilated remains of the clay figure. He couldn't quite bring himself to look at it.

"Who was he?"

"My dad," said Christopher, an unexpected crack in his voice.

"I'm sorry, Christopher," Ivy sighed. "This is all my fault."

"No it's not," he said, taking her hand. "We knew that Post would come after us if he knew we had the *Chalice*. We all went into this with our eyes open."

Ivy moved restlessly and he knew that she didn't believe him.

"Don't do that," he said softly. "Don't try to shoulder all the blame – it's not yours to take."

She gave him a long look that told him he was definitely operating in an alternate universe, and changed the subject.

"How could he know so much about us?" she asked, frown deepening. "I mean, lots of people in Brindleford knew about Sam, but Post never met him – he hadn't even met *me* until this year – how could he make such a convincing replica? And there's no way he could have known about your dad, or Reggie's wife, or the children's father..."

"I might be able to answer that," said a rather sheepish voice from the doorway.

Both of them jumped. Around them, books rustled unhappily on their shelves.

"Sorry," he said. A scrawny, long-limbed man stepped into the room. His glasses were slightly wonky on his earnest, freckled face and his hair stuck up in ways that defied the laws of physics. Christopher, who had heard Reggie's rather unflattering description of the half-elf, decided that this must be Otto Finch.

"Is everyone alright?" Rake asked, following Otto into the shop. Christopher caught movement in the teashop beyond: he looked over to see Constable Hardwick inspecting Ivy's creature.

"No," said Christopher, at about the same time as Ivy said: "Mostly."

She shot him a mildly impatient look and continued, "Minor injuries."

"And long-term emotional scarring," Christopher added, in no mood to talk. Ivy nudged him in the ribs.

Otto, who had been peering at the twisted clay in the centre of the room, grimaced at him.

"I'm sorry – they weren't supposed to be used like this."

"*You* did this?" Ivy demanded, shocked.

"Er, n-no!"

"Otto had some plans stolen from the workshop," said Constable Rake.

"The spy?" Ivy asked, subsiding.

Rake nodded.

"They were highly experimental," said Otto, wretchedly. "Still in development – adaptive Golems, creatures that could emulate people, infiltrate criminal gangs, that sort of thing. They take the form of the people you most want to see – or are most likely to be able to persuade someone..."

"It knew things about me that I've never told anyone," said Christopher.

Otto nodded slowly. "I'd intended to teach them to retain information – surveillance mostly – but I did speculate about developing a telepathic component."

"Otto," said Ivy, with an edge to her voice, "don't develop them any further."

"No, Mistress," he said. Christopher felt for him – he was clearly unhappy about the use they'd been put to. "I don't think anyone will be working on these, ever again."

"Can I speak with the others?" Rake asked, and Ivy led him upstairs.

Christopher shared an eloquent look with Otto.

"It appeared as her husband," he explained. "He was killed in action several years ago."

Otto looked appalled. "I never meant for –"

"Of course you didn't," said Joanna Barraclough, who had been eavesdropping outside the shop – it was Otto's turn to jump. "But you always were a bit of an accident waiting to happen, Finch. I taught him at Brightwell," she explained, on Christopher's baffled expression.

Otto gave her a sort of half-grimace, as if his face couldn't work out if it was still supposed to be upset about the Golems or happy to see his old teacher.

"What's the damage?" Professor Barraclough asked, pulling off his hat and coat.

"Reggie's shoulder's pretty bad," said Christopher. "Everyone else is more or less okay – and there's these," he patted the small pile of damaged books. "Easy enough to fix."

"Never mind the books just now," Joanna told him. "The children?"

"Terrified," he said. "Mahri's with them."

"Good."

She hurried into the back room; they could hear her clanking up the iron staircase.

An uneasy silence descended over the three men. Professor Barraclough looked the shop over speculatively.

"You contained it pretty well – what happened?"

Christopher told them about the Golem's reaction when he refused to believe its identity.

"Accelerated meltdown," said Otto, thoughtfully. "Mine never did that – but then they were never intended for harm. Do you reckon they were after the you-know-what?"

Despite everything that had happened, Christopher's mouth twitched up at the corners.

"Probably," he said. "I can't think of anyone else who would be this annoyed at us…"

"Thankfully," said Professor Barraclough. Christopher nodded emphatically.

"It's a pity it exploded before anyone could get to its *Ajna*."

"Its what, sorry?"

"*Ajna*," Otto repeated, and sort of mentally shook himself. "Sorry. Um…Golems are Jewish in origin, right? And the old way of activating one was with a *Shem*, or a holy word, like 'Adam', for example, inserted in the mouth or forehead. Modern Golems – and by 'modern' I mean post-medieval, such as they are – have a set of instructions instead of a word of power."

"Which you access by opening the head, yes."

"Exactly!" Otto exclaimed, happy to have a knowledgeable audience. "Today the instructions are loosely referred to as the '*Ajna*', after the sixth Chakra in the Hindu tradition."

"It represents the third eye," said Professor Barraclough, cutting across Otto before he could babble any longer. "Spiritualism, intuition, sleeping and waking, that sort of thing."

"Er, yes," said Otto. "Specifically because of the sleeping and waking aspects… Um, were they all like this?" he asked, motioning unhappily to the wreckage.

"No," said Christopher, feeling in his pocket for the parchment he had pulled out of Samuel Burwell's head. "Reggie's exploded as well, and Ivy melted the one upstairs."

"*Melted?*"

"Good God!"

"But I managed to shut Ivy's down with an opening charm – here."

He passed Otto the Golem's *Ajna*.

"Oh, well…" said Otto, after a moment. "Short and sweet, I suppose."

He passed it to Professor Barraclough, who read aloud "*Bring me Ivy Burwell. If identified, self-immolate.*"

There was a rather pregnant silence.

"What other plans did he take?"

"The ones for the replica."

Christopher closed his eyes. There would be no

avoiding him, now.
    Quentin Post would be coming for them – and soon.

35
To Catch a Thief

Ivy cradled the cup to her chest, grateful for the warmth.

The last days of November had brought with them sharp frosts and harsh winds, and even with the great roof of the garden covered over, the Arcade was cold.

One solitary Light Orb hovered above her head, rotating in a slow orbit. She hadn't felt the need for more: too much light might disturb Saffy and her puppies across the garden, and Reggie had had enough reason to be losing sleep tonight. She glanced across at the Coach Houses, automatically. There was a dim light in Reggie's bedroom window.

Besides, after the worst fright she could remember having in a long time the darkness felt restful, restoring the place she had come to think of as a safe-haven to its familiar cosiness. It had seemed so vulnerable in the light.

Normally Ivy would have enjoyed the seclusion – especially as she seemed to be collecting family these days. The small hours of the morning were usually fairly peaceful in the Arcade, particularly since Professor Zarrubabel had been locked in the vault. Martha was making her presence known, winding a vine around the leg of her chair and onto her lap like a pet. Ivy patted it absently.

Her head was too full to enjoy the solitude, tonight.

The Golem of Sam had been a little too much to take. That first glimpse of him had convinced her that he really was home – that everything was going to be the way it was before – until reality had reasserted itself with all the subtlety of a sledgehammer.

It had knocked the breath from her body.

Even now she marvelled at its accuracy. Every tiny movement, every nuance of his manner and speech had been perfectly reproduced. If Sam had been alive and on deployment she would have been completely taken in.

Christopher had said that his hadn't smelled right. His expression had been one of deep and unexamined pain, and she hadn't known what to say.

Seeing Sam had transformed the delightfully straightforward feelings she was beginning to develop for her friend into something utterly complicated. It felt almost like a betrayal, though she wasn't sure, even now, whether Sam would have seen it that way. They had never really discussed the possibility that he might not come home – though of course they had both been aware of it. She knew he'd probably have preferred her to be happy, but that didn't make her feel any less guilty.

It really didn't help matters, particularly given Christopher's current condition. She didn't need the added confusion just when she had been coming to terms with the very real possibility that she might lose another person on whom she had come to rely. Two weeks of silver poisoning were beginning to take their toll. The poison was already sapping his energy, though he was trying quite hard to hide it. It didn't fool her, and she suspected that it wouldn't fool the others for very much longer.

He looked even more ill asleep than he did awake, and that frightened her more than she would ever admit.

Ivy turned the lightly crumpled envelope over in her hands.

The letter had taken her by surprise. Although she knew that Christopher often wrote to his sister, she'd never expected to hear from her herself. Clearly of the opinion that talking to Christopher wouldn't change his mind, Rachel had written an impassioned letter, pleading with Ivy to 'knock some sense' into her brother and make him take the antidote. She'd even included possible recipes. That same ferocity that she admired in Christopher had come through in the letter. The siblings' similarity had made her smile even as the letter had filled her with guilt.

Rachel was afraid for her brother, and Ivy was the reason he was delaying his possible cure.

Aconite might be a slim chance, but at least it was something. She didn't think she could bear it if he died, and right now the only way he could be persuaded to take it would be if he knew there was no longer a danger to her and the children. She had left him sleeping in her bed, the children curled up beside him. None of them had really wanted to face the dark alone tonight.

They had been so lucky, this time. She couldn't take the chance that their luck would run out.

She rose, determined, and slipped down the spiral staircase into *Zarrubabel and Barracloughs'*.

She had to find a way to end this.

ooo

Ogden Rake stretched and popped his back.

He had been reading administrative lists for hours, trying to isolate anyone that had access to internal reports and might have a grudge against the Court. Since this theoretically included the majority of the administrative staff in the County, it was taking some time.

He padded across the empty canteen and helped himself to a mug of bitter coffee. At this time of night there were few people around, but he didn't want anyone seeing what he was up to in case the spy got wind of it – in case they *were* they spy – so he'd dragged several boxes of files up to the canteen. The gastronomic heart of the Court of Miracles was locked up at midnight (much to the annoyance of the few members of staff who ran the graveyard shift) and the kitchen staff wouldn't return until at least six the next morning, which made it perfect for clandestine file sorting. The lock hadn't given him much trouble, and he wondered whether he ought to mention it to someone, given the nature of his investigation.

He'd sent Xander home hours earlier, aware that he'd be in real trouble with Rhosyn if he kept him too late, and ploughed into the boxes of paperwork, comparing the lists with the people whose whereabouts he could confirm during the times of the thefts. So far he'd got it narrowed down to the core administrative staff, Victor, the Deputy Sheriff (who was an unlikely candidate, but in possession of an unpleasant temperament) and the small team that worked in the mail-room.

Forty-seven people who might have sold information to a man who liked cutting people into small pieces, burning out their eyeballs, and setting Golems on small children.

Rake sighed, slumping in one of the uniquely uncomfortable plastic canteen chairs.

He hated investigating his colleagues.

He massaged the crick in his neck and pulled the files towards him once more. Now he'd done the groundwork, cross-checking alibis and whereabouts ought to take a good deal less time for the final forty-seven.

He managed to clear the Deputy Sheriff almost immediately, to his mild disappointment, and the few members of Otto's team who received the internal reports. The typing pool was next, and the members of the mail-room. By half-past five the list was beginning to dwindle.

He ticked off the majority of the people on the front desk, frowning. A feeling of foreboding began to creep over him with every name he removed.

These were the people he spoke to every day – girls he flirted with, mates he played football with on the weekend, people's brothers, people's wives – people he'd worked with for years.

Soon he had only seven names left to check. He scanned through the list, feeling morose: Walter Greenwood, who worked as a public liaison; Olivia Bennett, the Sheriff's personal secretary; Martin Googe, a junior clerk in the mail-room; Nigel Fortinbras, a County representative from one of their satellite offices; Claire Danning and Rhosyn Hardwick – both in general administration; Victor (illegible smudge), their indispensable Archivist.

He did Victor first, feeling that he'd rather be totally sure of the old zombie as quickly as he could. After twenty minutes of cross-checking – and a moment of surprise at discovering his last name (Percival) – he was satisfied that Victor could safely be ruled out.

He turned to the next file, scribbling industriously.

ooo

Christopher had woken up to two small children who were pretending to be asleep so they didn't have to leave the comforting warmth of the bed, and no sign of his friend.

He left the children eating their breakfast, both far too quiet for his liking, and went in search of Ivy. He followed his nose down the spiral staircase into the bookshop, mildly surprised that she hadn't sought refuge with her wool, and found Ivy sleeping peacefully at one of the desks. She had fallen asleep with her head propped on a stack of books, writing hand splayed out across the pages of an old magical text.

He watched her for a moment. Yesterday morning he had felt so close to Ivy, but now he didn't know where either of them stood. It was as if the Golems that the Court had taken away the night before had opened a chasm between them, and Christopher wasn't sure if he could cross it – or even if he ought to try.

Quietly, he moved a few of the more adventurous books away from where they had collected around her during the night, and shook her gently awake. She stared up at him blearily for a few moments before attempting to straighten up and discovering that her shoulder had seized in place.

"I'm making toast, if you want some," he said, on her grimace.

Feeling awkward, he left her to untangle herself, wondering what she'd been looking for in the old magical grimoires.

ooo

As the first, bleak streaks of dawn were painting themselves across the sky, Rake sat back in his chair, grim-faced and resigned.

There was only one name left on his notebook, everyone else either had cast iron alibis or wouldn't have access to Otto's lab.

He'd checked it four times – there could be no doubt at all.

He picked up his phone for the fifth time in ten minutes and put it down again.

This wasn't a conversation he wanted to have over the phone. It wasn't a conversation he wanted to have at all.

What was he going to *do*?

ooo

Christopher tensed as the shop-bell jangled, still uneasy, but nodded to Constable Rake in greeting as he shut the door behind him, making a couple of the other patrons – absorbed in their books – jump.

"What can I do f..." Christopher faltered, catching sight of his friend's expression.

The Constable's unshaven face looked haggard and worn; Christopher was willing to bet that he hadn't slept. He had the beginnings of a spectacular black eye and a deep cut on his lip that suggested his morning had been much more eventful that Christopher's.

"Is Ivy about?" he asked, wearily.

"Upstairs," said Christopher. "Are you alright?"

"I've been better." He gave Christopher the ghost of a smile as he ushered him through the back room.

Sounds of discontent were emanating from the vault at the end of the room.

"Still not let him out?" Rake asked, pausing at the bottom of the stairs.

"No," said Christopher, wincing slightly. "I don't want to be around when they do, either."

"No…" Rake sighed, ascending the spiral staircase.

Christopher went back into the shop proper, wondering glumly what new disaster was at hand.

He spent an uncomfortable hour working with a fairly hapless art history student who was looking for books on the development of stained glass, trying to ignore the pain in his arm.

It was burning today, all along the inside of the muscles. He wasn't sure if he'd ever been able to feel his bones before, but he *was* sure that they shouldn't feel the way the ones in his left arm were, right now: hot and fluid, and sort of gravelly. He'd woken up that morning with the first prickles of discomfort in his neck, too.

He flexed his fingers unhappily as Rake and Ivy emerged from the back room of the shop, wearing identical pensive expressions.

"What's going on?" Christopher asked, as Constable Rake headed out into the Arcade proper.

Ivy sighed and shook her head: there were still a couple of serial browsers in. Explanations would have to wait.

ooo

Claire pushed her food idly around her plate. It was a slow day in the Court, allowing her to get caught up with her paperwork. She had been so engrossed that she'd missed lunch – Rhosyn had hustled her out of the office when she got back from her own break in town. Consequently, by the time she'd got to the canteen it was almost empty and there were only a couple of portions of tepid cottage pie left.

In truth, she quite liked the canteen when it was quiet. It gave her time to think, which as an administrator in the depths of the Court of Miracles was something of a luxury.

She looked up as Xander Hardwick approached her table; she gave him a quick once-over.

He seemed restless today, and angry. He kept balling

his hands into fists.

"I need a favour," he said, sitting across from her.

"You want me to cover for Rhosyn tonight?" she asked, wondering what could have put the normally cheerful Constable in such a foul mood.

"No." For a moment he looked like he was about to say something more, but he changed his mind. Instead, he leaned back in his seat slightly and frowned at Claire. "Where was she at lunch?"

"She said she needed something from town – I think she grabbed a sandwich from that deli above the camera shop."

"Hmm," he said, nodding slowly.

"Why?"

Hardwick gave her a long look. "Do you trust my wife?" he asked, eventually.

"Of course I do," Claire responded, stunned.

He nodded again, this time with more confidence. "So do I," he said. He met her eyes, and Claire was surprised to see ferocity there. "I'm going to let you in on a secret, Claire, and you can't share it with anyone – even Rosie. Do you understand?"

"Not really, but go on," she said, wondering where this was going.

"You have to swear it," he said.

Claire rolled her eyes. She held her hand palm up above the table.

"I will not reveal what you are about to tell me to anyone – unless you tell me I can or the Sheriff orders me to," she said, with a sigh.

She pulled a face as Hardwick placed his hand above hers as witness and the skin of her palm tingled for a second. She watched the dark lines of the encircled triquetra fade into her skin.

"That's going to itch for hours, you know," she grumbled, scratching at her hand.

"There's a spy in the Court."

Claire swore, immediately forgetting about her hand. "No way!"

"Papers have gone missing, artefacts – and they've ended up in the possession of a very dangerous wizard we've been tracking."

"How do you know it's not just him getting in?" Claire asked, and then wished she hadn't. The thought of someone that Alexander Hardwick considered dangerous being able to get in and out of the Court without being caught was somehow worse than there being someone on the inside, helping him out.

"The charms on the doors: strip Glamours and concealment charms," said Xander, brusquely. "Even Fades don't work down here. No – there's definitely a spy, and one with access to some very specific documentation."

An unpleasant thought struck Claire. "Like me and Rhosyn."

He nodded again, an ugly expression on his face. "Rake cleared you."

But not Rhosyn...

She glanced at his clenched hands. The knuckles on his right hand were a little bloodied.

Claire swallowed. "Have you asked her about it?"

"No," he said shortly, avoiding her eyes.

Claire put her hand to her mouth and shook her head.

"I tried to," he said, in a low voice. "But when it came to it I couldn't do it. She'd never forgive me," he told her, glancing in her direction.

"She'd never do something like this," said Claire, but already a modicum of doubt had crept into her mind. She glanced at Hardwick, guiltily, and understood.

He hadn't been able to ask her because he wasn't certain that he could believe her.

"There's no way she would betray the Court," he said, with a certainty that she wasn't sure he felt. "But I need to prove it."

Claire nodded. Rhosyn was her best friend: she needed him to prove her innocence, too.

"What do you want me to do?"

ooo

Claire pushed the door to the laboratory open warily. As a rule, she and her fellow administrators avoided the Technomancers – things at this end of the Court were liable to explode, and many of the staff were a little odd. Well, even more odd, if you considered that the majority of people that worked in the caverns below Brindleford were magical in some way or another.

She knew Otto, of course, in a vague sort of way. He stood out.

Unusually for the time of day, the lab appeared to be empty. Distantly, Claire remembered something about field training.

"Excuse me?" she called, shutting the door behind her. There was the sound of someone hitting their head, and Otto's shock of red hair emerged from underneath one of the cluttered workbenches.

She stared at him for a moment, and jumped when a large ginger cat leapt onto the bench and started toward her, expertly weaving between the piles of glassware, cogs, paint pots and sheaves of paper that seemed to have colonised every surface.

"Oh, hello…"

"That's Cat," said Otto, rubbing his head. "My – er – my cat."

"I've seen him around," said Claire, as the tom-cat wound around her legs. She bent down to stroke his head and he purred in approval.

"He doesn't normally like adults," Otto said, coming around the edge of the bench. "Prefers children – and me," he grinned. "Which says a lot about my mental age, I suppose."

Claire chuckled, straightening up.

"And something about mine," she held out her hand. "I'm Claire."

"Otto," said Otto, and frowned. "You work in…" His open face scrunched up in concentration, and Claire guessed that his mind spent so much time flitting between inventions that there was little room left for unimportant things like names. "Admin?" he hazarded, and she nodded.

"Constable Hardwick sent me," she said and glanced around, lowering her voice. "About the spy."

She watched as his eyebrows shot skyward.

"What spy?" he asked. He turned away and nonchalantly began fiddling with a clockwork heart on the bench top.

Claire resisted rolling her eyes. He really wasn't very good at subterfuge, and for a moment she wondered why Xander would have asked for his help.

"He made me swear on it," she said, holding her hand under his nose. "See for yourself."

Otto glanced at her before making a sign above her outstretched palm. For a second the triquetra appeared on her skin like ink, a circle flowing around it to signify her promise.

"That doesn't prove anything," he said, watching her out of the corner of his eye.

"Check with him, then," she said, frustrated. "Here, you can borrow my phone and everything."

"Er, no thanks – I've got my own…"

He pulled out an ancient mobile phone that looked suspiciously like he might have made some unauthorised upgrades to it and moved off across the laboratory, putting some distance between them.

She sat down on a wooden stool to wait and Cat immediately leapt onto her lap.

"I bet you already know who the spy is," she said, softly. "You spend all your time in and out of this place."

The cat looked up at her inscrutably, then bumped its head against her chin.

"Yes, yes, alright," she chuckled. "I'll give you a fuss…"

She stroked Cat's head sadly. Going behind Rhosyn's back was bad enough, but ever since Hardwick had first put the idea in her head she couldn't shake the horrible possibility that Rake might be right about her best friend.

"Right, sorry about that," said Otto, pulling up a second stool. "Had to be sure."

Claire nodded unhappily.

"We shouldn't have to check up on people in the Court," said Otto quietly, guessing the direction of her thoughts. "We're a family – we ought to be able to trust each other."

"Rhosyn wouldn't do something like this," said Claire, firmly.

"I don't know her," said Otto, after a moment's scrutiny, "but both you and Xander have vouched for her…"

"Now we just have to convince Ogden Rake," said Claire. "Did Xander say what he wants us to do?"

"Yes," said Otto, scratching his long nose contemplatively. "It'll need to be something irresistible… And we'll need to watch through the night, probably." He looked at her. "I don't suppose you want to help with that, do you?"

"Rhosyn's my friend, I'll do anything that I can to prove her innocence."

He smiled at her.

"Oh good – otherwise I'd have to ask Victor, and he scares the pants off me."

Despite herself, Claire laughed. "He's not so bad," she said. "Although I don't think I'd like sneaking around in the dark with him either."

"We may need him anyway," said Otto, already lost in thought. "The East Boardroom would be the perfect place for it, and there's two entrances. Two people on each door." He leaped from his stool and immediately began rummaging in the drawers at the edge of the room.

"What are we going to use as bait?" Claire asked, interested. She followed him to his own desk where he spread out a complicated-looking blueprint.

Silver ink described the lines of an ornate goblet, covered in gems. Claire recoiled slightly: there were twisting faces hidden in the fabric of the cup.

"Something they're really going to want."

ooo

"Well at least we know who it is, now," said Christopher, a forgotten cheese sandwich halfway to his mouth.

Ivy nodded, a troubled expression on her face.

He had joined her for lunch in the upper quarters when the Barracloughs had come in to take the afternoon shift. Christopher had originally been planning to stay downstairs and help, but Joanna had taken one look at his increasingly gaunt face and chased him up the staircase, muttering darkly about poor diet.

"Ogden said that there wasn't anyone else it *could* be," she said, fiddling with her own sandwich. "He checked several times."

"I'm going to go out on a limb and guess that Hardwick didn't take it well."

"No, he didn't," said Ivy, heavily. "I wouldn't be surprised if he never speaks to Rake ever again."

Christopher put the sandwich down and rubbed his face, unhappily.

"He seems to have a hand in everything around here," he said, annoyed. "Post, I mean… Professor Barraclough was telling me yesterday that the sneaky bastard has been trying to force him and Joanna off the council at Brightwell over the last few days."

"I wish we knew what he was up to," Ivy huffed, frustrated.

"World domination?" Christopher joked, through a mouthful of cheese.

"I wish that wasn't so likely," Ivy said and they both grimaced.

They were quiet for the rest of the meal, lost in their own thoughts. Christopher left her and Astrid working at the preparation table and slipped into the back room of the bookshop to check on the books under repair. He muttered soothing nothings to them as he set about restoring the end-papers of an early astronomy book, happy to have his mind on a solvable problem for a change.

ooo

Claire couldn't concentrate.

It had been hours since she and Otto had laid their trap, enlisting a reluctant Victor for surveillance duty. Otto had put together a reasonable replica of the grotesque thing in the blueprints in the time it had taken her to get down to the archives and back. She had to admit, as horrible as the thing was, Otto had done an incredible job. She had left his lab with a much higher opinion of the flamboyant young department head than she had had before – and a thin file of requisition papers tucked under her arm.

She had slipped them into Rhosyn's in-tray when her friend had nipped to the bathroom – at a level that Claire was confident her friend would reach by the end of the day – and set to work.

The afternoon wore on interminably. Claire worked steadily through her own in-tray, trying not to glance at Rhosyn's desk every thirty seconds. Trying to appear normal.

She was immensely grateful for each distraction, even if it meant more work – though she tried to remember to moan about it. She hadn't realised that she grumbled so much, always having thought of herself as a fairly happy soul despite the challenges of the Court. She decided to work on that once Rhosyn was in the clear.

"I'm going for a coffee – want one?" Rhosyn asked cheerily, standing over her desk.

Claire jumped; she hadn't even noticed her stand up.

"Er – yeah..." She forced a laugh. "Sorry, got a transcript from the Community Witch meeting – the scribe's handwriting leaves a bit to be desired."

"You'll give yourself a migraine," Rhosyn said, peering over Claire's shoulder at the barely decipherable scrawl.

"Nah – I'm nearly done anyway," said Claire, wafting her hand at the typewriter in front of her, desperately hoping that Rhosyn wouldn't guess that something was wrong. As her best friend, she could usually read Claire like a book.

Rhosyn patted her on the shoulder. "Sugar?" she asked as she picked up her handbag.

"Er…"

"You look like you need it," she smiled. Claire felt perfectly wretched.

"Go on then."

"Be right back!"

The door closed behind her with a click and Claire stared at it for a few seconds before letting her head drop to her desk. She let out a breath she'd been holding in all afternoon. A fresh wave of guilt washed over her.

What was she doing?

There was no way Rhosyn would ever betray the Court – let alone her own husband. It was preposterous.

Rhosyn was completely innocent and right now Claire was the one doing the betraying. She and Rhosyn had had each others' backs for years – ever since the Hardwicks had moved to Brindleford. She had no right to question that trust now.

She lifted her head a fraction and stared at her friend's in-tray: the plans for the replica were only a few papers from the top of the pile. Rhosyn would reach them in no time at all.

Claire stared at them, sorely tempted to grab them and stuff them in her desk drawer – end this whole silly charade. She got to her feet, intending to do just that. Something indefinable made her pause, hovering uncertainly beside her own desk.

What if this was the only chance they had of clearing Rhosyn?

If she removed the file now, the whole operation would be ruined…

She huffed, frustrated, reflecting that while it was all very well feeling sorry for herself, it wouldn't change the fact that at the moment things looked very bad for her friend. If Ogden Rake suspected her – and was sure enough of that suspicion that he would share it with Xander, potentially ruining their friendship – then others would come to the same conclusion. At the very least Rhosyn would be suspended.

No, Claire decided. *I owe it to her to go through with this. Then we can work on figuring out who it* really *is.*

She sat down again, determined to get back to work, but her eyes slid inexorably back to that slim, grey file.

It seemed to Claire to be staring back at her implacably.

She bit her lip.

She couldn't go through with this. If Rhosyn ever found out it would break her heart.

She stood up at exactly the same time as her friend elbowed the office door open. Claire changed direction on the breath of a moment, astonishing herself.

"Here, let me help," she said, hurrying over to her friend.

"Thanks," said Rhosyn, gratefully. "It's bedlam out there –"

Claire stuck her head around the door – mostly to avoid meeting Rhosyn's eyes. The main cavern was full of large, fluorescent green bats. People were scattering everywhere, knocking files and furniture flying. Several of the younger wizards were running around with nets, trying ineffectually to round them up. Claire spotted Otto in the middle of the crowd, waving his arms and shouting orders that almost everyone was ignoring. He met her eyes across the cavern and gave a sort of helpless half-shrug.

Claire shut the door firmly behind her.

"Sometimes," she said, speculatively, "I'm very glad that we're locked away in here."

Rhosyn laughed. "Oh, I don't know," she said, grinning widely. "I thought it looked like tremendous fun!"

"You would," Claire grumbled lightly. She dropped

back into her seat with a sigh, reflecting that helping round up fifty magically enlarged bats would probably be better than this.

36
Reality Bites

Claire hurried through the maze of tunnels, keeping her head down in case they'd missed one of the bats.

The afternoon had been utterly horrible. She'd made up her mind to remove the files three times, only to change her mind again at the last second. Her insides felt like a knot of snakes had taken up residence and were arguing about real-estate; her head felt leaden and tight.

If she survived this week without losing a friend or going insane she was going to take a long, lazy week off.

She turned a corner at high speed, letting herself in to the room at the end of the corridor with the key Otto had given her earlier. He and Victor looked up as she closed it behind her.

"You're late," Victor observed, in his gravelly voice. "Hardwick is already in position."

"Had to finish the requisitions for tomorrow," she snapped, irritably. "Which would have been done hours ago if there hadn't been an invasion of angry green bats."

"Don't look at me," said Otto, holding his hands up in self-defence. "My lads just helped round them up – it was some kind of non-violent protest from the Rouse Abbey Wranglers."

"Their funding has been cut," said Victor. "Shall we begin?"

He shuffled off to the far door without waiting for an answer.

"How did they get that many bloody green bats?" Claire muttered as she and Otto moved into position.

"Beats me," said Otto. "They're supposed to release them. Er –" He gave her a sideways glance. "It's going to be okay, you know," he said. "I don't think any of us really believe it's her."

"Remind me of that when she decides she's never going to speak to me again, will you?" she grumbled, squeezing behind the stationery cupboard in the corner.

Otto stared after her for a couple of moments before

apparently remembering where he was and what they were supposed to be doing.

He slipped out into the corridor, locking the door behind him. Claire watched him melt into the shadows through the glass.

She shifted uncomfortably behind the cupboard.

Their plan was a simple one: there were two entrances to the board room – she and Otto were watching the main one, Xander and Victor had the other. They had made sure that she and Victor could see all of the room from their hiding places, too, in case someone transported themselves in from the outside.

It was enormously unlikely that anyone could, given the sheer volume of protection spells on the place, but they couldn't take that chance.

The replica itself was locked in one of the secondary safes that had been installed in each of the five board rooms. They had originally been intended to furnish the members of the Court with weapons and shield amulets in an emergency, but these were calmer times. These days they acted as a good hiding place for the office stash of decent coffee, and the place where staplers went to die. There was a fairly complicated lock on the safe door, as well as several protection charms. Anyone who went after the replica would be hard pressed to get out without triggering something loud or permanent.

It was another reason to doubt that Rhosyn could be the spy, Claire reflected, trying to stop her legs going to sleep. Like Claire, Rhosyn wasn't a Practitioner. They'd picked up a few charms here and there as part of their work, but the vast majority of magic was beyond them.

It had been a bit of a disappointment for Claire, when she had first joined the Court. Who wouldn't like to be able to cast enchantments like a witch from a storybook? It never seemed to have bothered Rhosyn. Her friend's response had taught Claire to take it in her stride, along with the myriad other bizarre and sometimes frightening things that had happened over the years... On the scale of the weird and the wonderful under Brindleford, a horde of green bats barely even registered.

Claire huffed, deciding that when she got out from behind the cupboard she'd make it up to her friend.

She stiffened as the sound of hurried footsteps echoed down the corridor towards the board-room. Her heart sank. Claire peered through the glass, desperate to see the owner of those familiar clicks. At the last second, she realised that she didn't want to know, either way. A sudden, blinding flash of light forced her to squeeze her eyes shut – someone had smashed a portable Light Orb.

She cracked an eyelid, head reeling from the spots in front of her eyes, and waited for her vision to clear. Claire glared around the room, trying to make out the indistinct shape of the person standing by the safe. Whoever it was, they were going to pay for making her headache worse.

A loud series of popping sounds indicated that they had removed the protection charms around the safe. Claire held her breath, hope rising in her: their spy was a Practitioner – they had to be! Rhosyn was in the clear!

She heard the creak of the safe door as it swung open. She pressed herself further back into the space behind the cupboard, suddenly aware that the owner of the shadow by the safe would be facing her if they made for the main door.

Otto had assured her earlier that he couldn't see her, but she didn't entirely trust his judgement.

The silhouette by the safe was becoming clearer as the effects of the Light Orb wore off. Claire frowned: it was an unsettling familiar shape, though she still couldn't see the face.

She watched them close the thick metal door of the safe before carefully wrapping the replica and – almost lovingly – putting it into their bag.

Claire sagged against the wall as the intruder hurried towards her, the sudden knowledge knocking the breath from her body.

She knew that bag. She knew those clicking heels.

She watched, numb with shock, as Rhosyn Hardwick strode out of the room, pressing the strange metal device in her hand. In the back of her mind, Claire registered the protection wards slipping back into place. If someone checked on the defences no one would be the wiser – until they opened the safe and found the replica gone...

The woman she had thought of as her friend locked the door behind her, radiating smugness, and hurried away along the corridor.

Claire wasn't sure she could move. Across the tunnel, Otto slipped out of his hiding place, his face a mask of horror – mirroring her own.

Claire closed her eyes, wishing she was anywhere else.

She opened them again, feeling a sudden pressure on her arm. Otto was peering worriedly down at her. She allowed herself to be pulled out from behind the cupboard. On the far side of the room, Victor silently emerged from wherever it was he had secreted himself. Her distracted mind marvelled at the old zombie: the moment before there had only been a chair and a flipchart where he was now standing.

Otto patted her awkwardly on her shoulder.

"I'm sorry," he said. "I know she's your friend..."

Movement at the far side of the room caught his eye and he glanced up.

Involuntarily, Claire's gaze shifted to Alexander Hardwick, standing just beyond the far door, staring glassily at the place where his wife had been.

ooo

Ogden Rake rolled out of bed, clutching his pounding head.

Lack of sleep from the night before and a fist fight with his best friend had caught up with him, despite the small bottle of pain-relief potion Ivy Burwell had pressed into his hands. The woman seemed simultaneously unwilling to acknowledge and unable to avoid her heritage. On another day, at another time, Ogden would have found it amusing.

He glared at the alarm clock his nephew had given him for his birthday. Nothing was particularly funny at half-past two in the morning.

The knocking that had dragged him out of his bed resumed.

With a heartfelt groan, Ogden padded through his living room, collecting the cricket bat he kept under the coat rack as he went. A wizard he may be, but he'd found that very few things kept attacking you after two foot of hardened wood smacked them in the face.

The knocking was insistent but not heavy, as though the person outside wanted to come in but didn't want to wake the neighbourhood. He waited for a moment before opening the door a crack.

Xander Hardwick stood in the little pool of light the one remaining bulb provided, holding a large packet of fish and chips and looking very sorry for himself. Ogden opened the door a little more and leant on the cricket bat.

"Alright?" he asked, gruffly. He felt he probably ought to be more sympathetic, but the movement had made his face hurt again, reminding him precisely why he had the headache in the first place.

"Alright..." Xander croaked. "You want some chips?" he asked after a moment, waving them under his friend's nose.

Ogden looked at them, and then back up at Xander; he knew a peace offering when he saw one.

"Go on then," he said, letting him in. He padded into the kitchen and found two clean plates – a rarity after a week of late nights. Xander was hovering just inside the door. Ogden took the greasy package from his friend's unresisting fingers – it was stone cold. Ogden frowned, muttering a quick warming spell. He must have been wandering out there for hours.

"Sit down," he said, more gently. "Beer?"

Xander nodded mutely and sank into the large leather sofa.

They ate in silence, the way old friends can – saying more with that silence than they could out loud. They would talk properly when all this was over – but not tonight. Tonight, things were too raw.

When they'd finished, Ogden wiped his hands clean and patted Xander on the shoulder.

"You can stay as long as you like," he said, and got to his feet.

Xander rubbed his hands over his face. "I trusted her – I love her," he said unhappily, stumbling over the words.

"I know you do, mate," said Ogden sadly.

"I thought she loved me."

"You can look for reason all you want, but some things can't be explained," said Ogden heavily. "Some things just are."

Xander nodded slowly. Unable to offer further comfort, Ogden went to fetch his friend a pillow and some blankets, reflecting that perhaps his bachelor existence was something of an advantage after all.

ooo

"Christopher?"

Christopher groaned, pulling the duvet further over his head, hoping that Ivy would give up and go away

The sound of the door opening and closing, along with the subsequent dip in his mattress, suggested that he was out of luck on that score.

He squinted morosely up at her as she peeled back the cover.

"You look awful," she said, in a matter of fact tone. "I'll fetch you something." Ivy lingered for a moment and through his fever, Christopher could tell she was worried about him, despite her outward pragmatism. She hurried away to the kitchen. He watched her go, feeling helpless. Whatever her remedy was he doubted he would be able to keep it down.

He had spent the last twelve hours vomiting and

retching. The pain in his arm, shoulder and neck was nearly unbearable. He had hoped that he'd be able to sleep the fever off, but it looked as though the poison was finally beginning to win. It was only two weeks to the next full moon, and he was under no illusion: in this condition he wouldn't survive a transformation.

He'd expected a little more time to get his affairs in order.

He started as Ivy rubbed something cool on his forehead. It smelled a lot like menthol.

Ivy pulled him upright, despite his protests. "Yes, I know," she said. "Drink this..."

She pushed a small flask of golden, syrupy liquid into his hand and pushed a pillow behind him so that he could sit up more easily. Christopher sniffed it experimentally; his stomach turned unpleasantly and he swallowed hard.

"It'll help with the nausea," Ivy said gently, sitting beside him. "Trust me."

Christopher did as he was told. The potion was sweet and cool, and after a few moments of intense discomfort in his stomach everything seemed to settle down.

"Thanks," he croaked, as Ivy took the flask away and handed him another.

"That's for the pain – no, don't pretend it doesn't hurt, just take the potion."

She ruffled his hair. "You should have told me," she said softly.

"You've got enough to worry about."

"That's as maybe, but if you don't tell me I can't help – and that's worse," she told him shortly. "Looking after people is what my family is for."

"Not all the time," said Christopher, looking at her. "Sometimes you have to look after yourself instead." There was something different about Ivy today. She seemed more centred somehow, like her world had shifted into focus.

"We're there when we're needed." She bit her lip. "Your sister wrote to me."

Christopher's head snapped up in shock, sending shooting pains down his neck and arm.

"She's worried about you."

He nodded stiffly, astonished. He and Rachel had communicated for years without involving anyone else and the sudden change was unnerving. Two parts of his life had abruptly collided and he wasn't sure what to do about it.

"Have you written back?" he asked, worried that Ivy would have told Rachel exactly how ill he was getting – he had passed over most of the details in his own letters.

"Not yet," she admitted. "I wanted to wait until I could give her good news."

"Oh," said Christopher, and looked down at his blankets, privately of the opinion that Ivy would be waiting a long time. Another thought struck him. "Has she told my parents?"

"She didn't say," said Ivy. "I think she's more concerned with trying to help – she seems to have read up on every case of silver poisoning she could find."

"She wants me to take the aconite," Christopher guessed.

"Yes, and I agree with her," said Ivy, a touch of ferocity creeping into her voice. "We can't leave it much longer."

"No," said Christopher, bluntly. "Post's still after the *Chalice*, if he gets in here –"

"Yes, and what would you be able to do about it if he did?" Ivy demanded. "This is ridiculous. You're dying, Christopher, and I'm not about to stand here and watch it happen."

Christopher stared at her, unable to think of anything to say. Any words of comfort would have sounded hollow. She was right, after all. He *was* dying.

After a moment she looked away and sighed. "Try to get some sleep," she said, getting to her feet. "I'll call the Barracloughs and tell them you're ill – no, stay put," she added, as he struggled to get out of bed. "You can barely sit up, I'm not trusting you near those stairs. The Barracloughs can watch the shop today. The children are out with Reggie this morning, and they can help downstairs later – I'll check on you at lunchtime."

"Ivy..."

She sighed again. "Just – don't give up, Christopher," she said, patting his hand. "I haven't, and nor has Rachel. I'll see you at lunch."

He watched her go, closing the door behind her.

The bright winter sunshine shone through the stained glass, illuminating his bedroom. Was it his imagination, or were the colours in the glass paler? Christopher turned away from them, trying to get comfortable. He watched patiently as one of Martha's vines crept down the wall towards him.

"Keeping an eye on me, are you?" he croaked, and reached up to pet it. It coiled around his arm and slithered along the bed, pulling the blankets up so they covered his shoulders. "Thanks, Martha," he yawned, beginning to feel the numbing effect of Ivy's concoctions. "You just worry about Ivy, okay?" he mumbled, no longer able to keep his eyes open. "She needs you more than I do."

ooo

Ivy took one tea caddy off the shelf at a time and shook it, making the odd note on her pad of paper. She would need to restock soon; the Christmas period was almost upon them, half-forgotten in the excitement of the last few weeks, and her customers would expect some themed beverages. Perhaps she would enlist Astrid and Jake's help in choosing a new syrupy confection as a cold alternative.

She added 'hot chocolate' and 'gingerbread syrup' to her list and sighed.

It was all very well keeping busy, she reflected, but sooner or later her mind would return to the very sick young man upstairs.

He didn't deserve any of this.

She'd checked on him after the lunchtime lull, and

he'd managed to keep some food down – which was heartening in itself. The silver was moving quickly now, robbing him of his energy and appetite. Where weeks ago Christopher had been a happy, healthy werewolf, cheerily tending his books and playing with the children, the poison had left in his place a pale, haggard man. The dark shadows under his eyes were looking every day more skull-like, and it frightened her.

Watching him struggle upright in his bed that afternoon had made her chest hurt.

She'd had to retreat to her bathroom and have a quiet cry before she faced the teashop again.

Luckily it had been quiet all afternoon, the cold, windy weather keeping most people indoors, and Ivy had been able to take her frustration out on the imaginary dirt in the shop. She had cleaned every last millimetre of it – which now smelled of honey and lemons – changed the flowers, and fixed the dodgy hinge on the display counter. Once she'd finished the inventory she had plans for the wool shop, where she was relatively sure the resident spiders had retreated to during her onslaught.

She reached for the next tea caddy and promptly dropped it on the counter. It landed – mercifully upright – with a thunk, giving out a great puff of tea-scented air.

Vines were creeping unobtrusively into the corners of the room. That part of her that was also a part of Martha told her that something wicked was within her bounds.

The part of her that was entirely Ivy straightened her back and took a deep breath. By the time the door to the teashop jingled open she was calmly putting the tea caddy back on its shelf with one hand, making notes with the other. She didn't even look up as the door closed again.

"Mistress Burwell."

"Master Post," Ivy acknowledged calmly, reaching for the next tea caddy.

"You have something of mine, I think."

Ivy shook the tin of chamomile tea, replaced it and made another note.

"On that, Master Post, I'm afraid I must disagree," she said, turning. Post was standing just inside the doorway, leaning nonchalantly on his cane. He was hiding his fury well, but Ivy could see it, hidden behind his carefully constructed mask.

"Must you, indeed?"

"Would you care for a pot of tea?" Ivy offered. She could see Joanna Barraclough glaring across the Arcade at him, while her husband ushered the children into the back room. As long as Martha was aware of him and the Barracloughs were watching there wasn't a great deal he could do – and she needed to buy them all some time.

"Thank you," he accepted, cordially.

Forgoing the usual caution she executed in the shop – Post wouldn't have wanted people around to make his move, and was probably behind the lack of customers – she made a sign in the air above the counter. An austere white china tea set span through the teashop to a table in the centre of the room. It was joined – after a brief clatter in the kitchen – by a matching teapot full of hot, steeping tea.

Post, with all of his usual swagger, pulled out a chair for her, and she took it, gracefully avoiding the plate of dainty cakes that landed softly on the sparkling table top.

"How very kind," Post remarked, taking the seat across from her.

"Not at all." Ivy waved her hand and the teapot poured two cups of tea; a white porcelain milk jug pressed forward to oblige. There were standards to maintain, after all.

"I'm glad we can be civil to one another, Mistress Burwell."

Doubting this very much indeed, Ivy smiled, raising her cup to her lips.

She watched as Post sipped his tea, savouring the taste.

"What an excellent flavour," he remarked. "You have the Chalice of Knowledge in your possession."

Ivy nodded, there didn't seem any point in denying

what he already knew. He wouldn't have sent the Golems until he was sure.

"I must warn you that it is a singularly dangerous artefact, known to have killed many who have handled it," he paused.

Ivy inclined her head, taking another sip of her tea before responding. "I am aware of its history."

"Then you are aware of the threat it poses to the other members of your household."

"I am," she said. "Though – if you'll permit me – it seems to me that the threat lies less with the *Chalice* and more with those who seek to obtain it."

Post's eyes narrowed. "My dear lady, I couldn't agree more," he said, in a voice laced with sugar. "That is why I want it – to protect those who would put it to inappropriate use. You see – we have a golden opportunity here, to keep the Chalice safe."

Ivy worked very hard to keep her features unmoved. "Naturally," she said, impressed at how level her voice was.

He gave her a winning smile; it struck Ivy as rather ghastly. She wondered how she had ever thought Post was handsome.

"Then we are of the same mind?" he asked.

Ivy licked her lips, deciding how best to word her response. "May I ask you a question, Master Post?"

"Quentin, *please*, dear lady. Anything." He seemed reasonable enough, Ivy thought, but his impatience was almost palpable. Out of the corner of her eye, Ivy saw a thin vine creeping nonchalantly towards them.

"What *did* your father do with Flossie Dawson's heart?"

Post covered it quickly, but she caught the frown and the distracted way his hand moved to his chest. More than anything, he looked confused.

"I don't believe we can ever be of one mind, Master Post," said Ivy quietly.

Post's nostrils flared slightly. This conversation wasn't going the way he had planned. "May I ask why I must be so summarily dismissed?" he asked, with flawless politeness.

"Because you didn't even know her name," said Ivy softly.

Post's green eyes momentarily narrowed once more. "What does it matter?"

Ivy rested her hands together on the table. "As long as it is in my power to prevent it, you will not hold the *Chalice*," she said. The flowers along the window stirred slightly, as if there had been a breeze.

Post sat back in his chair, regarding her with barely concealed distaste. "I do not wish to appear vulgar," the wizard said silkily, carefully stirring his tea, "but if we cannot come to some arrangement I shall be forced to kill your children."

Ivy smiled slightly. "If you had intended to come to an arrangement, you would not have sent your Golems."

Post's eyes flashed. "I do not appreciate others meddling in my affairs," he said, almost spitting the words.

And I don't appreciate a copy of my dead husband begging me to take him back, Ivy thought – out loud she said, "Really? I couldn't tell."

"You sit here making jokes," Post said, smile twisting in amusement. "You seem blissfully unaware of what I could do to you – to your children – to Christopher."

"I'm well aware of your vicious streak, Master Post."

"Then what, Mistress? You want the Chalice for yourself?" he laughed, coldly. "You hardly seem the type."

There was a pause as Ivy studied Post. Now that she knew what he was capable of, it was chilling even to be in the same room.

"I believe you may be underestimating me, Master Post," she said softly.

He leaned closer; Ivy fought the urge to back away.

"The fire of the Chambers family burned out two generations ago," he hissed. "Do you honestly think it can be relit now?"

Ivy met his glare dead on. "It was never a flame, Master Post," she said, firmly. "And it never died."

"Such arrogance," he scoffed. "You have no power. Your family was nothing to my father, and *you* are nothing to me," he spat, all pretence at civility abandoned. "Your paltry magic isn't worth a damn! I will take the Chalice, Mistress, make no mistake, and when I do I will kill everyone in this –" He glanced around in disgust – "*fetid* place. Those without magic have no place in this world. It's no wonder your family's fortunes fell –"

"That is quite enough," said Ivy quietly, and a look of utter disbelief crossed Post's features.

He mouthed helplessly for a few moments, grasping at his throat and mouth. Angrily, he swept the tea set to the floor and banged his fist on the table, snarling something inaudible.

"I'm glad I have your full attention," Ivy said, unflustered. "You see, sir, I am not without defences. My 'paltry magic', as you call it, stands me in good stead."

If looks could kill, Ivy would have been a bubbling mess on the far wall by now. Post was apoplectic with rage and humiliation.

"Your voice will return," Ivy told him, coldly, "but until it does, *you* will listen to *me*. I am the Witch of this Manor, and I will defend those within its bounds. The *Chalice* is an exquisitely evil object, and you are an exquisitely evil man. I can see no good coming of uniting the two of you." It was Ivy's turn to narrow her eyes as she continued icily, "You have torn those who stand in your path apart, and I will not see it happen again – not here, not in my Manor. There is no place for you here."

She sat back, controlling her breathing as best as she could. The anger she felt for the rotten man in front of her was threatening to break through. It had been a long time since she had hated someone so completely.

She made a hand gesture under the table and released his voice.

"You will regret this, woman," he snarled, shaking

with rage. "I will have your head."

He thrust his cane towards her, upturning the table with an extraordinary crack – but Ivy had been ready for it.

She deflected the curse almost lazily; it flew off to the left and shattered the large glass windows of the teashop. She was on her feet in an instant, instinctively moving the furniture back with a glance.

"This is my home, Master Post," she declared, feeling Martha's power rising within her. "And you are on my *turf*."

Vines shot out of the floor, the ceiling, the fallen furniture – they snaked around the furious wizard, clamping his limbs to his body. The cane clattered to the floor and was almost immediately swallowed by the writhing mass of foliage. Post was fighting Martha with all his might, but it wasn't doing him much good. Ivy watched him struggle for a few moments, waiting for his cursing to cease. Behind the embattled wizard, Mahri and the Barracloughs were edging nearer to help. Ivy shook her head at them. She could handle this.

"The more you struggle, the tighter it will get," said Ivy, coldly.

Post immediately stopped moving. He hissed something indecipherable, but Ivy took his meaning from the tone of his voice.

"You have made an almighty mistake, Mistress Burwell," he spat, his perfect hair flying out in every direction.

"This is your one chance, Master Post," she told him. "Your 'golden opportunity', as you say. You will leave Brindleford, you will retire from the antiquities business, and you will never harm another person."

"And if I do not?" he scoffed.

"Then I will ensure that those three conditions are met," she said softly. He took her meaning.

"Release me," he commanded, and Ivy effortlessly dismissed her vines.

He brushed himself down, breathing hard. He

repaired the rips the vines had torn in his clothing with a whisper of thought.

"I was not aware you had such determination," he said, and glanced at her, some of his usual bonhomie returning. "We would make a fine team."

"Not in this lifetime," said Ivy, shortly.

Post watched her face carefully for a moment. Ivy could practically taste his desire to destroy her – but here, under the eaves of the Arcade, he couldn't hope to match her.

"Then you are in earnest?" he asked, as though he had not just tried – and failed – to kill her. "You will stand in my way?"

"To whatever end, sir," said Ivy.

"Then it will be to the death, dear lady," he said, and kissed her hand, with a flourish. He met her eyes, and Ivy could see the hatred there. "Such a pity..." He bent to collect his cane. "I did so hope we could resolve this indiscretion more amicably."

"I sincerely doubt that, Master Post," said Ivy.

A twitch of his eye betrayed him. Ivy casually clapped her hands. Around them the teashop restored itself – shards of glass flew back into their frames, melding together like new. Furniture righted itself, torn petals fell and were replaced by fresh flowers – Ivy's white porcelain tea set shot back together on the table. Peace fell over the teashop after the flurry of activity. It was as if nothing in the world had happened.

Post eyed it all with an air of mild disbelief. He really hadn't expected her to fight back – or to be able to.

"I will bid you a good day, sir," she said coldly. When he didn't move, she added, "You are no longer welcome here."

Post made a sudden movement – as if to attack her again – but appeared to think better of it.

"Mistress," he nodded angrily, and swept out of the shop.

Ivy followed him into the Arcade proper and watched him leave. Mahri and the Barracloughs joined her.

"I'm not sure showing your hand was such a good idea," Professor Barraclough observed as the dark wizard swept out of sight.

"Perhaps," said Ivy.

"He's seen your strength now," said Joanna, glaring after him. "He'll come after you all the harder."

"He was counting on our fear," said Ivy. "He thought it would make us vulnerable."

"Not so," Mahri observed, her arms tightly folded.

"No," said Ivy. "No one here will ever be controlled by fear. Not while I hold this Manor."

She strode off towards the back room of the teashop, leaving her friends staring after her.

ooo

Ivy walked alone through the darkness for the fifth time in as many nights.

She had closed the shop after Post's little demonstration of strength and spent the afternoon teaching a slightly unnerved Astrid defensive magic. Mahri had seen to the food that evening, though Ivy hadn't felt like eating. She had sat with Christopher for a while instead, forcing him to eat and refusing to tell him what had happened downstairs. She had needed time to think.

Silently, she stuck her head around Astrid's door. The girl was sleeping peacefully, a large book slumped against her chest. Ivy tiptoed over to her and pulled it gently away. Softly, she brushed Astrid's dark hair out of her eyes.

Jake was sleeping soundly as well, when she checked on him – though somehow he had managed to wriggle around so he was half out of bed, his legs dangling over the edge. After a few moments of perplexed concern, Ivy decided that he was probably comfortable as he was and simply pulled the covers over him more securely. The small boy snuggled down inside the blankets happily and Ivy chuckled.

She pulled his door to and padded over to the bookcase. A Light Orb sprang to life above her head and she squinted for a moment before picking up the simple wooden frame.

"I'm sorry, my love," she said softly. "I can't be a Burwell anymore..." she caressed the photograph of the young man in fatigues with her thumb. Gently, she pressed her lips to the frame, her eyes washed with fresh tears. With a sigh she replaced the frame on the bookshelf.

Sam's beaming face looked back up at her. Ivy smiled.

"I know," she whispered. "It's about time... But then I never did as I was told, did I?"

Heaving a great sigh, she turned away, shadows deepening as the Light Orb winked out.

Christopher was sleeping fitfully when she slipped into his room. She pressed a cool palm to his forehead and he stirred, subsiding back into sleep as she brushed her fingers through his hair.

She slipped under the covers beside him as he settled, resting her head on his shoulder.

"You're going to be okay," she whispered into the darkness, fervently hoping that this was true.

37
A Chill in the Air

Quentin Post was not a patient man.

After the ignominy of his encounter with Ivy the day before, he had been all set to plague The Vines with fire and fear – and he still would, probably – but distraction had come in the form of Rhosyn Hardwick.

She had sashayed through his door the previous evening with a wooden box and assurances that her husband had no idea where she was.

They unlocked the box together, after a candlelit meal that Post had had to grit his teeth to get through. It had been worth it. Indulging her little fantasies usually was – the woman was extremely good at removing important documents from the nest of imbeciles under Brindleford. In the years that he had worked with her she had proven herself to be deliciously ruthless. He could almost overlook her lack of magic – almost.

"It's a replica," she told him, as they pulled away the red satin cloth. "But it should give you a clearer idea of the real thing."

"It's even more grotesque than I imagined," he observed, running his fingers over the gilt surface.

Rhosyn shrugged. "Powerful wizards aren't usually interested in aesthetics," she gave him a sultry smile. "You appear to be the exception."

He smirked at her. "How long before they notice that it's missing?" he asked, turning his attention back to the goblet.

"They needn't, if you provide me with a replica," she said, speculatively. "They had some sizeable charms in place – your amulet came in handy," she said, laying it carefully on his desk. "The paperwork suggests they're going to try to switch them – it didn't say when," she added, on his sharp look.

"You will make enquiries?"

"Naturally."

ooo

"So, we're agreed then?" Ivy asked, after the general burble of discussion had died down.

"You're actually going to do this, aren't you?" said Mahri slowly.

"Yes."

The inhabitants of the Arcade – supplemented today by the Barracloughs, Constables Rake and Hardwick, and Otto Finch – were ranged around the kitchen table. They'd had to bring chairs across from the Coach Houses. Except for the subject matter, it reminded Ivy strongly of Christmases when she was very young, when the Arcade had been full of people – and of purpose.

"Well then," said Mahri, after a quick glance around the table. "You can count me in – general 'aye'?"

There was a chorus of affirmation.

"Right," said Ivy. "Astrid, will you take Jake and pack a few things, please?"

Astrid, usually the first to object to being kept out of something, nodded quietly and hurried away, her brother trailing after her. The tension in the Arcade since Post's unexpected visit had had a profound effect upon them all.

"Can you take the dogs, too?" Reggie asked.

"Victor doesn't get on very well with animals…" said Hardwick unhappily. He was pale and unshaven today, sitting quietly at the end of the table and not making eye contact with anyone.

Ivy's heart went out to the man.

"My gran will look after them," said Constable Rake, nodding. "It'll make her day."

"Thanks," said Reggie, relieved. "Will she be okay with Boscoe?"

"She'll have him eating out of her hands in no time." The two men shared a brief grin which faded too quickly in the glare of the situation.

"I think Christopher should go with the children," said Joanna Barraclough quietly.

Christopher's head came up from his chest – Ivy was fairly sure he hadn't been asleep, but it had certainly looked like it. He looked worse than ever today. It made Ivy nervous.

"No," he said, glaring blearily around him.

"No offence, old chap," said Professor Barraclough diplomatically. "You look like the Black Death warmed up."

"*No*," said Christopher in open defiance. "I'm staying. I just need something to keep me on my feet –"

He met Ivy's gaze and she nodded. Given the way he looked it probably wouldn't matter if he rested or not.

"I can give you something," she said. "We should get started," she continued, before anyone could interrupt. "If you'll excuse me I'll go and check on the children."

"I'll give you a hand with the animals," she heard Rake say, as she moved off. "Come on, Xander."

She found Astrid tersely packing a change of clothes and several books into her small backpack. Ivy sat on her bed, staring at the far wall.

"Is it going to be okay?" Astrid asked, not looking at her.

"Of course it is," said Ivy, almost automatically.

Astrid paused for a moment before reaching for her alarm clock – a gift from Reggie. "I don't believe you," she said.

Ivy looked at her and half-smiled. "The honest answer is, I don't know," she said, passing the young girl her hairbrush.

Astrid took it from her, nodding slowly.

She looked up and pinned Ivy with the uniquely penetrating gaze of a seven year old.

"Christopher's really sick, isn't he?"

"Yes," said Ivy, though her voice came out more as a whisper.

Astrid bit her lip, and it dawned on Ivy that the child was trying not to cry.

"What if he kills you?" Astrid asked, softly.

"Then the Barracloughs will look after you," said Ivy,

with as much reassurance as she could. There was no use pretending that death wasn't a possibility – she was a very intelligent girl.

She nodded her acceptance, buckling up her backpack with suddenly clumsy hands. "I don't want you to die," she whispered, and burst into angry, silent tears.

Ivy wrapped her arms around her, stroking her jet black hair. "Neither do I," she murmured.

The tears were over as quickly as they had begun, and Astrid pulled away, wiping her face.

Ivy waited until her breathing was less ragged before speaking.

"Now," she said, lifting her hand to Astrid's chin in a way that she remembered her grandmother doing, "let me look at you." She studied her for a few moments. "You seem like a fine, upstanding witch to me," she said, and a small smile crept onto Astrid's face. "You'll be polite to Victor?"

"Yes, Ivy."

"And look after Jake?"

"Always," she promised.

"And keep out of trouble?"

Astrid looked instantly dubious and Ivy laughed.

"No, I never agreed to that bit either," she said, getting to her feet. "Come on," she said, stretching out her hand. "Let's go and help your brother."

ooo

"Right chaps, you heard the man – let's get to it!"

People began shuffling about, collecting their things. It was like the end of every other day – except tonight there was an air of urgency about their movements. Conversations were hushed and hurried as people dashed to their designated stations, pulling on the police uniforms they had rather hastily put together.

Otto watched them go unhappily.

His own team were hanging back from the general evacuation, mainly so they'd be on hand to tackle any of the potential fallout. They would also be responsible for the clean-up. It wasn't something he was looking forward to.

There was just so much that could go wrong.

Beside him, Xander Hardwick checked his phone for the tenth time in as many minutes. This time it actually *had* gone off.

"They're there," he said, with some relief. "Claire's keeping her occupied."

Otto grimaced and patted the Constable on the shoulder as he trailed off. He never knew what to say to people – give him a machine or a chemical compound any day.

"See you on the other side," said Hardwick, with a brisk nod.

"Yeah... good luck."

He and Rake hurried out of the tunnel after their colleagues. They wouldn't be involved with the evacuation, either. They would be lurking in the half of Brindleford that – with any luck – wouldn't need any attention, waiting for Post to make a move. There was no way he could know *what* they were up to, but Otto was willing to bet that he'd notice they were up to something.

The best they could hope for was that it would take him a while to figure it out.

He walked pensively along the unusually silent tunnels to his laboratory. He scooped up Cat, nudging the door open with his foot.

"Not tonight," he said softly, stroking his friend's head. "I'm afraid you'll be staying here."

Cat gave a perfunctory yowl and tried to squirm out of his arms.

"I know, I know, you go your own way..." He opened the door to the store cupboard, and closed it behind him, the struggling cat still in his arms. "Here," he said, pulling down the lid of one of the boxes of supply paper and putting it on the floor. Cat stuck his nose into it experimentally; Otto pulled a packet of cat food, a bottle of water and a couple of bowls out of his lab coat. "See, you're well set up."

Cat yowled again, and Otto grimaced.

"I don't like it any more than you do, old thing…"

ooo

"I'm sorry ma'am but I'm afraid we're going to have to get you to a refugee point – at least until we find the source of the gas leak."

Arabella Jenkins peered out at the young man with an air of annoyance. She'd just got the milk to the right temperature, too. If someone was playing silly buggers there would be trouble.

"Let me see those credentials again," she barked, pulling out her reading glasses. The young man held up his identification like a shield: she read it, and frowned at him. He smiled brightly, clearly deciding that she was a bit senile.

"You've spelled 'police' wrong," she pointed out and he peered at his own badge, astonished.

Widow Jenkins looked over his shoulder. Her neighbours were being hustled out of their homes, bags with a few essentials over their shoulders.

"Gas leak, you said."

"Yes, ma'am," said the young man, almost desperately. A snowflake landed on his large, earnest nose.

Behind him, a broad-shouldered policeman whose uniform didn't quite look right lumbered over. "Everything alright?" he asked his colleague.

"Er…"

He looked up at Widow Jenkins and grinned.

"Evenin' Arabella," he said.

"Garth," she nodded. "Not a gas leak, then?"

"Not even close," he said, with a chuckle. Beside him, the younger man looked like he was about to cry.

"You can't just *tell* people!" he protested, but they both ignored him.

"Best to get to the refugee point," said Garth. "It's going to be a hairy one."

Arabella nodded. "Right you are, Garth. You take care of yourself, you hear? Looks like snow."

Garth nodded, steering his spluttering friend away by his shoulders.

She closed the door firmly behind her and went into her sparse kitchen. Slowly, she turned off the heat under the pan and stood for a moment, staring at it.

After a moment, she turned and pulled on the long, dark coat that everyone at her friendship group said made her look sinister, along with an old fedora that had belonged to her late husband. She picked up the hefty-looking stick that was leaning against the wall beside the kitchen door, flicking out the light as she moved through her house.

Her boots were on the mat where she'd left them that morning, and she sat creakily on the stairs while she laced them up. She paused with her hand on the door handle, listening to her quiet house. She walked briskly into her front room and picked up the frame that held the photographs of Flossie, their parents, and the late lamented Eric Jenkins, and tucked it into her cardigan.

Widow Jenkins locked her front door and hurried out into the snowy night.

There was work to be done.

ooo

Mahri locked her front door with a sigh. She had packed everything that might break into boxes wrapped in towels and newspapers, and stowed them snugly under the beds and the sofa in the living room, hoping that this would be enough.

Reggie was standing under the plum tree in the garden, staring up into the branches.

"Still not come down?" she asked, joining him. Snow was billowing around above the great glass ceiling.

"No, daft bugger," said Reggie. Above them, somebody squawked indignantly.

"Do you think he knows what's going on?"

"Absolutely," Reggie turned to her with a grim smile. "I think he's rather looking forward to it."

Mahri chuckled.

"If we don't make it through…" Reggie began.

"Of course we'll make it through," Mahri scoffed.

"But if we don't," Reggie insisted. "I'd just like to say, it's been an honour, Mahri Glass."

He held out his hand and Mahri took it with a smile.

"For us both, Reggie."

Side by side they strode through the quiet garden and into the main room. Joanna Barraclough had gone with Otto to see that the dogs and children were settled. Mahri had a strong suspicion that she would make a detour to her home before rejoining them, to make sure that John and Charlotte were alright. The Crooked House, as Christopher had been referring to it, was on the side of Brindleford that wasn't expecting to see any action, but only if things went *exactly* to plan.

Christopher was boxing up the last of the bottles and jars into one of the crates that Ivy had found in the storage rooms below the Coach Houses. They'd already finished with the kitchen and their own, personal breakables, and the room looked curiously empty. There was an expectant air to the whole place, as though the building was waiting, ready for the evening's work.

Mahri eyed Christopher as he dragged himself upright. There was definitely more going on there than either he or Ivy would admit – and she was willing to bet that he had confided in her young friend. She watched him cross unsteadily to the stairs to the teashop, a couple of crates following him along the top of a tangle of vines.

She sighed heavily as she helped Reggie start moving the crates back down to the store rooms. Whatever the outcome of Ivy's plan – and it sounded a little harebrained, even to Mahri – it seemed increasingly unlikely that Christopher would still be with them by Christmas. Unhappily, she pushed the thought to the back of her mind and put her weight behind the crate as Reggie hurried past with a spanner and some more mysterious plumbing parts, heading for the point where the mains gas came into the building.

ooo

Jake was clinging to Astrid's hand as though he was afraid she might disappear. It had started snowing in earnest as Constable Hardwick led them across Brindleford, and Astrid's hair was wet with the weight of it. The cavern beneath the town was weirdly empty, and the scale of what was happening had begun to dawn on Astrid as they walked between each set of abandoned desks to a staircase at the end of one of the many side tunnels. The conversation with Ivy had set her on edge and she was quiet and subdued as she followed Hardwick down the old stone steps.

It was cool down here – not unpleasantly so, as it had been outside – and the air was oddly still, as if it didn't get out much. She wondered vaguely whether they were walking to the very centre of the earth.

The corridor turned sharply at the bottom of the staircase, as if the designers had wanted to hide everything beyond it from view.

"It's all archives down here," Constable Hardwick said, over his shoulder. "Victor's little kingdom."

"How deep are we?" Astrid asked, more to keep her mind occupied than anything else.

"I'm not sure," said Hardwick, surprised at the question. "Deep enough that the bombs in the Second World War didn't make a dent. You could ask Victor – I imagine he'd know. He was probably here when it was built."

Astrid thought about this. She'd seen pictures of bomb damage in London in one of Christopher's history books. If this place could escape something like that then they must be very deep indeed.

They came to an unobtrusive door that someone at some point had painted in that institutional green that was the hallmark of 1930s government décor. It reminded Astrid solidly of the orphanage where they had been placed before their foster parents had picked them up. She felt Jake tighten his grip on her arm.

"Victor, you in?" Constable Hardwick asked, rapping lightly on the door. There was the sound of a chair scraping on a stone floor and an indistinct form appeared on the other side of the frosted glass. The door opened, and Astrid peered up into two glassy, grey eyes, set into a forbidding grey face. They surveyed her and her brother for a moment before flicking up to Constable Hardwick.

"This is Victor," he said, motioning at the tall grey man. "Victor, meet Astrid and Jake Healy – they'll be your house guests for the evening."

Victor stared at them once more, and with a motion that made Astrid feel a little unwell, gave them a thin lipped smile. She could see yellow teeth behind the dark grey lips. She suppressed the urge to shudder.

The apparition disappeared into the dimly lit room beyond and Constable Hardwick motioned for them to follow.

"On you go," he said. "I have to get to my post..." He took in Astrid's expression and knelt down in front of them. "He's alright, I promise – just a bit grumpy." He gave her a reassuring smile and continued, "He only eats tomato sandwiches, if that helps."

Not entirely sure that it did, Astrid nodded.

Summoning up her courage, she led her brother through the unobtrusive door.

"I'll see you after," Hardwick called, though Astrid wasn't sure whether it was aimed at them or at Victor.

He had retreated to one of the shelves at the back of the room and was peering at them placidly, his greenish eyes glimmering in the low light. Desperate to do anything other than meet their terrible gaze, Astrid looked around the archive. It was full of old metal shelves, filled floor to ceiling with box files and notebooks.

She felt Jake shift slightly at her side, still clutching

her arm.

"Are you dead?" he asked, his small voice sounding muffled in the papery tomb. She tensed, afraid that he had offended their host – and more afraid of what he might do to them if he had.

Victor peered at him for a moment. "Mostly," he said, in a dry, gravelly sort of voice.

"Oh," said Jake, as though he'd merely asked if Victor had a bicycle. "Do you really eat tomato sandwiches?"

Victor made a gravelly sort of noise, and after a few seconds, Astrid realised that he was chuckling.

"Mostly," he said again. "Sometimes I eat little children, too."

Jake laughed; his grip on Astrid's arm loosened a little.

"Do you promise not to eat us?" Astrid asked, trying to sound as if she was joking.

This time Victor grinned, and she could see all of his horrible, yellow teeth.

"Mostly."

ooo

Vladimir Fitzhearn looked up from his crossword. It was unusual for anyone to knock at his door this late at night. He got the odd charity collection in the summer, but as the nights drew in, callers became scarce – and that was the way he liked it these days. Concluding that it must be some ridiculously early carollers (it wasn't even December yet), he folded his paper and took his time getting to the front door.

He was nearly there when the mystery caller knocked again, louder this time. He was taken aback at the ferocity. Generally speaking, carollers and doorstep salesmen tried to be polite in this neighbourhood. Perhaps whomever it was, was lost.

Vladimir eyeballed them through the peephole, but it didn't help much – the snow was coming thick and fast now, and he was mostly able to make out a dark, coat-swaddled figure in a large fedora. He stared at it for a moment and jumped back when, to his surprise, the fedora's owner pressed their eye against the other side of the peephole.

"I know you're in there, Vladimir, the lights are all on!"

"Mrs Jenkins?" he started in surprise, and opened the door. "Come in, my dear lady – it's freezing out there!"

The apparition gratefully came inside, shaking the snow from her coat and grumbling that she wasn't as young as she used to be.

He took her fedora and disposed of it on the side table, quickly followed by her coat. She was carrying an extraordinary walking staff – almost the same height as she was and gnarled at the end. He offered to take that too, and she almost gave it to him, before hesitating.

"Better not," she said, and kept a hold of it. "Now, first things first, Vladimir –"

"My dear lady," he said, a little bit too baffled for his own liking. "'First things first' means a glass of whiskey to warm you up."

For a moment it seemed as though Mrs Jenkins was about to argue, but she followed him into his living room anyway.

"I suppose so," she said, rather gruffly. "These days the cold gets in places it has no business being – right through to the bones. Thank you."

She took the glass and took a hearty drink; the pink in her cheeks, brought out by the cold, intensified somewhat.

"Right – have you had any of these people knocking on doors and telling you there's going to be a gas leak?"

Dr Fitzhearn paused, wondering whether his friend might have been out in the cold for a little too long.

"I shall take your silence as a 'no'." Arabella Jenkins swirled the amber liquid about in the bottom of her glass a few times. "Which means whatever's about to kick off isn't expected to get this far."

"Mrs Jenkins, I have no idea what you're talking

about," he began, and he fell silent under one of her unsettlingly direct stares.

"No," she said. "I expect that you don't." There was a pause as the two friends surveyed one another, finding that they didn't know one another perhaps as well as they ought. Mrs Jenkins appeared to come to a decision. "I think you'd better pour yourself one of these, Doctor, and I'll explain."

ooo

Ivy pushed an escapee strand of hair behind her ear and tried to brush some of the chalk dust from her cheek.

It had been a long time since she'd had to do anything this complex, and never on this scale. Several times in the last few hours, as her friends moved their belongings to safety, she had wondered whether this was actually going to work, or whether she had simply gone mad.

She wouldn't have been surprised, given the way things had been going lately.

Critically, she surveyed the neatly drawn lines and arcane symbols on the floor. Getting them to continue either side of the walls had been a bit of a problem – and the bathrooms had been a little tricky – but she was reasonably confident that the whole of the Arcade was covered now. One vast arcane map for each floor, each a constellation of charms and spellwork.

Restlessly, she shoved the chalk into her pocket and brushed her hands on her jeans, leaving white, powdery streaks on her legs.

This had better work.

ooo

Something was happening, he could feel it.

Quentin Post stood at the window of his study, staring out into the snowy night.

The streets of Brindleford were too quiet, as though

they were expecting something. All along his road, people had closed their curtains and locked their doors, a feeling of unease spreading out across the town.

He tapped his fingers along the elegant window frame.

If they were intending to switch the Chalices tonight…

Abruptly, he turned and picked up the ornate telephone, dialling a number he had been careful to memorise.

There were a few moments of tense, telephonic silence before the call connected. He let it ring a few times before dropping the receiver into its cradle.

Deftly, he flicked open the concealed drawer in his desk and extracted the gauntlet. Inelegant or not, it would be useful if he ran into any members of the Court.

As he closed the clasp about his wrist, the phone began to ring.

ooo

Christopher gazed out across the snowy street, resting his head against the cool glass window of the empty shop. He'd helped Reggie secure the piano in the music shop as best as he could, and had been intending to make one final check on the books, but a wave of dizziness had sent him stumbling to the darkest room he could find. The sole unoccupied room of the Arcade was dusty, the air stale with disuse – but it was dark and quiet, and that was what he needed.

The Barracloughs had been and gone, taking with them all the supplies they would need to open the ley point out at Nadderbeck Farm. It was a bit of a long shot, but it was the only thing within about a hundred miles that had enough power to counteract (and, with any luck, destroy) the *Chalice*. Even now, he could feel someone watching the Arcade, registering the discomfort in his neck as a dull sort of memory.

It was probably one of Post's infernal creations, or a sentry from the Court. He'd managed to press the story of Post's recent visit to the Arcade out of Professor

Barraclough (though if he were honest it hadn't taken that much pressing), and had very little doubt that he'd be expecting them to make a move in the near future. The man would be a fool if he wasn't keeping a watch on the building, and Quentin Post didn't strike Christopher as a fool.

"I wondered where you'd slunk off to," said Ivy, closing the door to the empty shop behind her.

He would have turned to look at her, but it hurt his head too much. He felt her hand on his back a few moments later and smiled slightly.

"Drink this," she instructed, wafting a potion under his nose.

He looked at it blankly for a few moments, realising with mild disappointment that – for the first time since he had been bitten – he couldn't smell a thing.

"What's in it?" he asked, pulling a face at the taste.

"Don't ask," she advised. "It's usually safer."

She stuck the empty bottle in her back pocket and leaned against him, slipping an arm around his waist. Christopher pulled her closer with his good arm.

"This is completely mental, isn't it?" she asked, after a few moments of contemplative silence.

"Yes," he said.

"That's what I thought."

"But, to be fair, everything about this is mental, so I don't see why it shouldn't work out."

She smiled for a moment. "You take everything in your stride, don't you?" She rubbed his back.

For no logical reason, it made him feel a little better.

"No other way to take things, really," he mumbled, his eyes closed. "Some things just are – it doesn't matter if we like them or not, we still have to deal with them. One way or another."

He felt her nod.

"Ivy?"

"Yes?"

"Whatever happens – I just wanted to say... I'm really glad I met you."

"Me too."

ooo

There was a large amount of snow on the glass roof above the garden now, and it was drifting deeply in the streets outside. An unearthly silence had begun to descend over the town, following the evacuees to the refuge points out of harm's way. Somewhere amongst the shops and houses out there, a small army of Practitioners were stationed, lying in wait in case this all went horribly wrong.

Christopher, feeling a little stronger, reflected that this was fairly likely.

He watched as Ivy tied her hair out of the way in a business-like sort of way and took off her shoes and socks. She looked around at the three of them.

"Well," she said, after a moment.

Reggie nodded. "Yes," he said, and shook her hand. Suddenly, he smiled at her, catching her a little off guard. "My Bessie would have loved you, Ivy," he declared, and she laughed.

It echoed oddly around the garden.

"And I suspect I would have loved her, too," she said gently, letting go of his hand. She nodded curtly at Mahri, who kept folding and un-folding her arms, and glanced behind her to Christopher.

"Right..."

Delicately, she walked out across the soil to the rough centre of the garden – and of the Arcade as a whole.

"Well then, Martha," he heard her mutter as she turned away from them.

There were a few moments of absolute silence, and Christopher wondered whether anything was going to happen after all. Everything around them seemed tense, poised: he took an uncertain step forwards.

Then the silence seemed to deepen.

A shiver of cold flew up Christopher's back and out along his limbs – it seemed to ripple across the whole of the garden, rattling through the dormant plants and dead leaves. The rustling rushed inwards from the walls towards Ivy's feet – Christopher's heart seemed to contract and it was all he could do not to rush to her, however much he trusted Martha and her ability to keep Ivy safe. Not that he could have done much to help.

There was a curious sound, like tearing fabric, and a thick vine shot up through the ground and wrapped tightly around Ivy. A moment later, a second joined it – and another, and another.

Christopher watched, horrified, as his friend disappeared behind a mass of writhing foliage. The tangled swarm was getting larger by the second and he wondered how she could possibly be breathing in there – just as he was considering dragging her out of them the vines shot upwards, that eerie pale light spilling out from between them. As they gained height the deepening silence exploded with a roar. Vines were shooting out of every surface now – the air was thick with them – they twisted their way around door frames and over walls, supporting the structure of the building.

Christopher ducked as a particularly large tendril sped towards him. He straightened again, a little uncertainly, as it veered around him and ran up the wall. They were trying to avoid him, he realised.

He looked around: through the twisting mass of foliage he could just make Reggie out – sure enough, there was a space around him, maintaining itself like his own personal bubble. Mahri was nowhere to be seen, but he suspected the same would be true for her.

Martha was keeping them in mind.

An arc of blue light flashed past him, trailing a rush of air behind it. He felt the heat of it as it passed him and left him temporarily blind. He rubbed his eyes, the after-image of the arc hanging in the air between the vines.

He glanced behind him: vines were creeping over chairs and up bookcases – it was as if the Arcade had spent decades abandoned, allowing vegetation to curl over every conceivable plane. The speed of growth was unsettling.

A sudden tremor made him tense: the floor beneath him – nearly a foot thick with vines now – trembled and shook.

The tenor of the roar of the vines seemed to change and settle, then from somewhere deep beneath them came the scream of distressed masonry – Christopher staggered sideways as the building gave an almighty heave; he caught his foot in one of the enormous vines at his feet and fell to the floor.

It didn't seem keen on remaining a floor anymore, however, and bucked upwards. Panicking slightly, Christopher grabbed at one of the vines and held on with all his might.

It was going to be a bumpy ride.

ooo

Quentin Post crouched in the lee of *Ebeneezer's Gift Emporium* and ran his eyes over the trembling building. There was definitely something afoot – the sheer intensity of magic spilling out of the Arcade was having some unusual effects on the surrounding town. Behind him, two graffiti stick figures were peering up at the building along with him, probably just as astonished at suddenly being able to think and move as at the rumbling building across the road. A little further along the street an elderly pigeon that had been grazing on scraps under a bench flew off with an excited squawk, discovering that it was now barely older than a fledgling.

A couple of less fortunate birds had landed on the pavement before their companions had flown for their lives, the yolks streaking the thick snow with yellow.

If the Court got here in time he'd have to risk a direct fire fight – it would be much simpler if he could just get inside and grab the thing.

He rolled his shoulder experimentally. It was still bruised from Ivy's unexpected riposte. He wouldn't like to have to face her on her own turf again. He would have to kill her outright, and that sort of thing could get messy very quickly when it was a recognisable member of the community. People would ask questions and get in his way.

No, simpler by far if he could lure her out somehow...

The ground beneath him rumbled and he instinctively reached for the window jamb beside him.

Funny, he didn't remember any fault lines around Brindleford.

He looked up as another, particularly violent jolt ran through the urban landscape, scattering wildlife and setting off car alarms.

The Arcade was shaking, snow and masonry dust sheering off it in flurries.

With the sound of a small elephant hitting concrete what looked like the trunk of a great tree stamped onto the snow in front of him, roots piercing the snow around it, holding it steady. Another shaft-like thing formed further down the street – the dying bleats of a car alarm suggested that it hadn't found a clear spot to alight. It crunched through the metal as if it was made of paper, rocking slightly as it took the weight of the building.

A series of more distant booms and crunches suggested that at least four more limbs had sprouted around the shaking Arcade. With a great lurch – and a cracking sound that seemed to travel right through Post – the gnarled trunks straightened and began to lift the building skywards.

He felt his whole body go limp with shock; he found himself bodily leaning against the grimy door of the gift shop, staring in open-mouthed astonished as the entire building rose up on those enormous twisting limbs.

It paused for a moment, as though giddy and unused to its new, lofty position. It shook itself, scattering the remaining snow on its roof onto the buildings around it, and turned slowly, getting its bearings. It seemed to take a long time to turn, as if it was getting used to having feet instead of foundations. Post couldn't take his eyes off it.

The space it had previously been occupying looked like

a bomb had hit it – a nest of rubble and broken wiring. Water was gushing upwards through a pipe that no longer had a connection to the real world.

Then, with an almighty heave, the Arcade started forward across the roofs of Brindleford, lurching slightly, and trudged into the snowy night like some kind of huge, glittering beetle.

38
Doorway to Hell

Post roared in rage, rising out of his hiding place like a wounded lion. He leaped over what remained of the squashed car, which appeared to have formed an almost perfect moulding of metal over the cobbled pavement, chasing the lumbering giant across the town.

She was progressing ponderously, each tree-like limb moving as if in slow motion, picking her way across Brindleford almost delicately. Each step left enormous root-pocked imprints behind her in the snow. The Arcade itself seemed to be gliding across the tops of the buildings, encased in vegetation, moving softly through the treacly darkness.

Post whirled around a corner, cursing. He was having trouble keeping up with the newly mobile structure. It was moving deceptively quickly – mostly because it was so large. Everything he threw at the hulking creature was bouncing off, rebounding onto neighbouring buildings and leaving a trail of scarred masonry in its wake.

He scrambled across the square, slipping and sliding over the wet snow. He flashed past the windows of the shops, trying to calculate where the great, rumbling thing might be heading.

He was willing to bet wherever it was had something to do with the concealment of the Chalice.

Post paused to catch his breath by a roundabout in the middle of town and considered the possibility that this was the most elaborate distraction of all time. No. Nobody would be that stupid.

He squinted through the fast falling snow: he needed to slow it down...

ooo

Astrid closed her book with a sigh. She'd been staring at the same page for the better part of quarter of an hour, unable to take in any of the words.

She glanced at her brother and the zombie. Despite his terrifying appearance, Jake seemed to be getting on rather well with him. They were currently playing some racing game on a console he had unexpectedly produced from a cupboard, and Jake appeared to be winning. She suspected that Victor was letting him.

Her heart leapt into her throat as a distant crunching boom shook the archive room. Dust rained down around them for a few seconds as the three of them stared at the ceiling. Another boom shook the cavern, though this time it seemed to be coming from further away. It seemed to be echoed on the TV as the cars in the racing game crashed into a wall and burst into flames.

Ignoring the periodic showers of dust, Victor reset the game and motioned for Jake to continue.

Astrid blew the dust off her book and clutched it to her chest as the distant booms continued, trying not to think about what those booms might mean for the inhabitants of the Arcade.

She hoped they were alright…

ooo

Clinging grimly to the thick vines, Christopher tried not to look too closely at the shifting walls. The majority of things that could fall over now had, and he was beginning to relax into the great, sweeping movements of Martha's gait.

It was rather a lot like a memorable trip he'd taken across the Irish Sea as a child, in what might arguably have been a minor hurricane. Now, on top of the poisoning, he was fighting what could be a losing battle against seasickness.

The majority of the airborne vines had coalesced along the walls, floor and ceiling now, as if the rooms had been hollowed out of an old, gnarled tree. Across the garden – parts of which were still visible amongst the new undergrowth – Reggie was hanging on to the plum tree, Mahri crouching beside what used to be a garden bench.

Ivy was visible again, vines coiled about her legs and outstretched arms, that strange blue-green light spinning around her. The vines were holding her bare feet fast to the floor, as if she were a tree – the movement of the building didn't seem to be affecting her at all.

He could feel the power inside the trunk-like tendrils under his hands. It pulsed within them like a heartbeat, pushing the Arcade onwards.

There was a crash from behind him. He was just wondering what else could have fallen over when a second, louder crash made him look over his shoulder.

The main room of the Arcade was tightly bound with vines. Nothing in there could have moved.

Christopher climbed to his feet and staggered towards the sounds of breaking wood and glass coming from the front of the Arcade. Staggering across the undergrowth, he tried to anticipate the bucking movements of the building, but it wasn't easy. Several times he overbalanced, dragging himself back upright on the vines crawling up the walls. He clung to the door frame outside Ivy's study while Martha gave a particularly powerful lurch and squinted at the mass of vines at the end of the corridor, where the great windows at the front of the Arcade usually were.

There was something moving out there, like an extra layer of shadow in the darkness, just visible between the cracks in the vines. He squinted at it, and moved to get a closer look...

BANG!

The force of the crash knocked him backwards as shards of glass and lumps of gnarled wood flew past his head. His face and arms stung from tiny cuts and impacts. He pushed himself up on his elbows.

Something was coming through the window – what could have been a hand tore at the metal frame, splinters of glass sticking out of the powerful twisting limb. It was the colour of burnt umber, and roughly humanoid – parts of it kept changing shape as though it couldn't decide what shape it ought to be. The part of it that

Christopher thought was probably its head swung towards him. It split open, breaking apart into a terrible, gaping maw.

Christopher scrambled backwards as the thing roared – the sound went straight through him, like hundreds of people all screaming at once. It leapt at him, the weight of it knocking the breath from his body, pinning him to the floor.

He tried to push it back, feeling suddenly weak as the terrible mouth opened above him, inches from his face. It screamed again as he fought against its weight; a great lump of clay came off in his hand – it fell to the floor with a wet thunk.

Thick fingers closed around his throat, crushing his windpipe – he scrabbled desperately at the half-formed digits, pain spreading through his neck and chest as his body searched for air.

Purple spots formed in front of his eyes as he kicked and struggled under the inexorable weight of the Golem, his head swimming from the lack of oxygen.

He was so intent on removing the devastating grip that he watched with a sort of detached fascination as the Golem's head flattened and detached from its neck, the awful mouth deforming and stretching as it flew backwards.

The frying pan clattered to the floor by his head as Reggie shoved the bulk of the lifeless Golem off him.

Christopher gasped for air, eyes watering. The air he so desperately needed burned his lungs as Reggie pulled him to his feet. He was shouting something, but Christopher couldn't hear anything – the world had become strangely muffled, as if he was underwater. He could, however, see a second Golem climbing through the hole at the end of the corridor.

The blast of magic he aimed at it took Reggie by surprise and he stepped back. They watched, grimly, as the curse removed the majority of its upper body. It froze in position, now nothing more than a lump of lifeless clay.

"These are different than before," said Reggie gruffly, retrieving the frying pan – now quite dented.

"They don't have an *Ajna*," Christopher coughed. "He wouldn't have had time – he's had to enchant them manually. One word instruction..."

"I'm guessing it was 'kill', said Reggie, as the remains of the Golem toppled backwards. "We need to block up this hole –"

"They're coming through here!" Mahri shouted, from the other corridor – Reggie hurried off to help.

Just outside, something screamed with the force of a hundred voices.

Christopher rolled up his sleeves and crouched, ready this time.

Four misshapen arms latched onto the thick vines around the opening – two of them were trying to get in at once. The Golems hefted themselves upwards, surging and heaving against one another. Christopher sucked in a breath as one wrenched at the arm of the other.

Post really had rushed their construction: they had only been given enough sentience to identify living creatures – probably exclusively humanoids. Aside from the obstruction each was causing the other, they had no real idea that the other was there – or that they were on the same side.

He watched as they forced their way into the gap, entirely filling the window with their dense, clay bulk, fighting against one another to gain another inch. The screaming Golems twisted around one another, blocking out the driving snow. Christopher pulled magic together between his hands, bright and hot.

He waited, trying to ignore the crashes and shouts coming from the other corridor – just a little longer...

At the same moment, both constructs sensed his presence. Simultaneously, they tried to surge forward, melding seamlessly into one another to create a hideous, four-armed, two-headed creature. Christopher hit it full in the chest, pushing heat through the clay, baking it hard. He left it frozen in place, hissing as the snow outside struck its back.

He skidded around the corner and leapt at the Golem that had Reggie pinned to the wall, taking it crashing to the floor.

Mahri had one of them in the air and he rolled out of the way as she sent it crashing their way. The constructs hit each other with a sickening wet smack, deforming instantly.

"They just won't *die*!" Mahri shouted, strands of red and grey hair sticking out from her usual neat bun.

"Take the heads off," Christopher panted, as the pile of clay on the floor began to shudder and rock.

"Right," said Mahri, and made a slicing movement in the air above the constructs' joint neck. The misshapen thing rolled across the vine-clad floor as Martha swayed on.

Another horrible scream drifted up, and Christopher stuck his head out of the remains of the window.

They were moving quickly – sickeningly fast. The ground flashed below them, cars and road furniture half-buried in the thickly drifting snow. He clutched the window sill, gripped by a sudden and sickening wave of vertigo, his hair whipping about in the storm. Below them, half a dozen faceless Golems were climbing the trailing vines.

One of them had run into trouble on one of the vast, trunk-like legs that were propelling them forwards. It had become ensnared in the dense woody growth and was screaming in rage and frustration. Christopher watched as Martha gave a kick, almost in slow motion, knocking the stricken Golem to the ground.

It got to its feet and turned to climb back up the trunk when the next limb crushed it flat.

A screech to his left made him look up – one of the Golems was beating its fists against the baked remains of the two he had wedged in the window. One of their legs broke off and span off into the night. Christopher hurled a curse in his direction. Mahri joined him at the window.

"Bugger," she said.

"Yeah..."

She decapitated the nearest Golem, dropping him on the one below; the two of them tumbled away, their flight ending with a distant splash: they'd reached the river.

Ahead of them, beyond the rows of houses, lay the fields of Rouse Abbey, the ruined monastery rising like a ghostly icing sugar creation in the night. There was marsh out there, he knew, and he rather hoped Martha would know where to tread, and beyond the fields –

A feeling began in the pit of his stomach, flooding his senses. It felt like sunshine, and hot chocolate, and summer rain – and a hundred other things all at once. Like liquid happiness. He inhaled deeply, feeling stronger than he had in weeks.

A bright light spilled out of the woods at the top of the hill beyond Rouse Abbey, the trees casting deep shadows across the snow.

Beside him, Mahri hummed.

"What's going on?" Reggie called, weighing his frying pan in his hands.

"They did it," she said, appreciatively.

"They got the ley point open," Christopher told him, turning. "Can't you feel it?"

"Feel what?"

Outside, the Golems screamed. Mahri backed away from the window.

"*They* can feel it," she said. "Get ready, lads, it's a long way up that hill."

ooo

Post closed his eyes, drinking in the raw power of the magic spilling down from the crest of Nadderbeck hill.

So that was their game!

They weren't intending to hide the Chalice – they were going to destroy it!

He cursed in frustration and transported himself across the river.

The House of Vines

The Arcade was having trouble getting across, dipping its feet cautiously into the swollen river, like an overgrown cat. He had a little time.

He closed his eyes, ignoring the snow: letting it fall around him undisturbed. Post regulated his breathing, pushing his rage and any thought of revenge out of his mind. There would be time for that, soon enough.

He reached out with his empty mind, drinking in magic from the ley point and channelling it through his hands and out towards – somewhere else.

He had never been entirely certain where it existed, only that it did. He supposed others might refer to it as 'hell'. It wasn't something he had looked towards since his time at Brightwell, whiling away the dark nights with certain of his schoolmates.

They had been young and foolish then, unaware of the dangers of opening a door like this in their mind – some of his friends had suffered for months before admitting to their tutors what they had done. The Professors at Brightwell had taught them all how to form a solid image of the door – and how to keep it locked. Eventually, his classmates had stopped screaming in their sleep, and peace had largely been restored. One of the boys, a grocer's son from the other side of the valley, had had to leave the Academy. Post had seen him once, years later, being wheeled around town by his patient sister, eyes empty and staring, lips constantly moving as if in a silent, desperate prayer.

He had always wondered what he might have seen. The thought unsettled him, since the door was still there, at the back of his mind; he could feel it sometimes, waiting for him.

Even now he was uncertain that he would be able to keep *them* out. Still, desperate times called for desperate measures...

In the darkness of his mind, he approached the door – it was tall and gnarled, tight spirals curling over the blackened wood. The sound of whispering gave him pause, but he steeled himself. He was Quentin Post. With all the excess power coming from Nadderbeck Farm there was little he couldn't dispose of.

He lifted the latch.

ooo

"Bloody hell."

"You can say that again," said Joanna Barraclough, hands on hips.

She and her husband were sheltering in the lee of the ruined farm, keeping one eye on the ley point behind them and the other on the Arcade, skittering sluggishly across the snowy ground.

"I'm glad Ivy's on our side," her husband observed. "That's quite a trick."

"She won't be able to hold it for –" Joanna paused. "What is *that*?"

The land around the industrial estate – just across the river from the lumbering Arcade – had taken on a deep red tinge. It was as if the tenor of the night had changed.

A deep rumble travelled up the valley, only slightly muffled by the swiftly falling snow. The ground trembled in its wake, shaking the snow from the trees. Joanna instinctively reached for her husband. They held each other upright until the tremors passed. They subsided, leaving in their wake a deep silence as if the land itself were reeling in shock.

A tremendous roar of magic and crunching masonry rose up from Brindleford; the Barracloughs looked on, helpless in horror, as great clouds of billowing smoke rose up in front of the Arcade, enveloping the distant structure.

"Joanna," said Morton.

"Yes, dear?"

"I have a very bad feeling about this."

"Yes, dear."

ooo

The window was rapidly filling with heat and acrid smoke. Christopher reeled back from it and stumbled back into the main room where the air was cleaner, Mahri and Reggie hot on his heels.

Whatever had caused the explosion outside had obliterated several of the buildings in the industrial estate across the river. Reggie had a nasty cut on his cheek from the flying metal and all three of them were coughing and sputtering.

Christopher made a grab for the vine covered table as Martha listed dangerously to one side, trying to avoid whatever it was that had shifted so dramatically. He cast a glance at Ivy, still encased in vines and arcing light. None of this appeared to be affecting her, at least.

"That felt like an earthquake," Reggie choked. "Are we out of the river?"

Christopher nodded, and then promptly wished he hadn't. His vision blurred for a moment and he leaned more heavily on the table, head swimming. The ache in his arm and chest was impossible to ignore now, and he felt dead on his feet.

He hauled himself upright, willing the pain to the back of his mind. He had to keep fighting, just long enough to see this through. He had promises to keep.

"It has to be Post," said Mahri, brushing baked clay off her arms. "Nobody else is callous enough to blow up part of the town."

"It's a good job he missed," said Reggie, with forced cheer. Even as he said it, there was a scream from the street below. Human this time – the industrial estate hadn't been empty, after all.

It was cut off abruptly, with a horrible gurgling sound.

The three of them peered along the corridor, a dreadful sense of foreboding creeping upon them.

The remaining Golems had largely been dislodged by the explosion, giving them what they'd thought would be a moment of respite before they started to scale Martha's vine swathed legs again. Christopher edged along the corridor, Mahri and Reggie close behind.

Stripped of his wolfish sense of smell, he moved forward slowly, feeling blind and vulnerable.

There were scratching sounds outside the shattered window now, and odd grunts and whistles. As one, they stuck their heads out of the opening.

They were trampling through the remains of the industrial estate now, parts of it still ablaze. All around them were the great metal skeletons of warehouses, bent and broken from the force of a blast so powerful that the snow drifts had evaporated from the ground.

"No," breathed Mahri, staring at the ground below them. "He wouldn't. No one could be that stupid!"

"What?" asked Reggie.

Christopher followed her gaze.

The ground below them was criss-crossed with red and orange lines, spreading like veins across the concrete. Smoke hissed and billowed up where the lines met, tinges of red light showing through the black.

A strange chattering sound was drawing closer to the opening as Martha crossed the expanse of blistered metal and concrete. Christopher squinted through the smoke: shapes were moving out there, flashes of red light glinted on scales, and spines, and slick, pale skin.

"What has he done?" Reggie demanded, as Christopher plunged back into the Arcade, skidding across the vein covered floor of the main room and into the garden.

"Ivy, hurry," he shouted. "He's opened a gateway to – something – the town is swarming with imps!"

He hurried back, hoping that Ivy had got the message.

"Stay behind us," Mahri hissed at Reggie, both of them crouching part way along the dark corridor.

"With respect, Mahri," said Reggie, as Christopher joined them, "bugger that."

"We have to stop them getting to Ivy," Christopher panted, grimly. "While she's controlling Martha she's pretty much defenceless."

"Not while I'm still breathing," Mahri growled.

"I wish you'd tell me what's going on out there,"

Reggie grumbled, tightening his grip on the rather battered frying pan.

"Think of it as a portal to hell," said Christopher, tersely, listening intently to the chatters and whistles drawing closer to the window.

Reggie chuckled, and then caught his friend's expression. "Oh."

"Heartless bastard," Mahri muttered.

Christopher shook his head to clear it, his injured arm hanging uselessly at his side. There was no use concentrating on an incantation in this state, he decided. He'd just have to wing it.

A clawed hand curled around the opening, talons clicking horribly on the remains of the window frame.

Christopher held his breath, staring out at the freezing night, snow swirling lazily through the smoke. The breeze tugged at the remains of the curtains, making them billow inwards like a wraith.

Then, in what seemed like less than a second, the entire world was full of imps.

They filled the corridor from floor to ceiling, screeching and wailing. Christopher plunged into them, snarling as they clawed, and scratched, and bit at him, their spines piercing his skin as he forced them back.

Around him, he could feel Mahri's spells smacking into them and hear the occasional thwack and clang of Reggie's frying pan. He made a grab for the nearest imps but his fingers couldn't find purchase on their oily skin.

Swearing, he lashed out with his good arm, latent magic engulfing the nearest imps. They fell to the floor, variously stunned, singed, or in pieces. A few feet away, Reggie was hitting anything that moved with his frying pan; mildly concussed imps were flying in all directions, bouncing off their fellows and adding to the general confusion.

Christopher felt a hot stab of pain run through his leg and he kicked out, dislodging the imp that had bitten him. He snarled, pushing magic at it; it burst with a horrible, wet sort of popping noise. Another imp sank its teeth into the back of his neck – he screamed in pain. One of Mahri's spells made it burst into flames and it leapt away, squealing.

"There's – too – many!" Reggie shouted, between strokes.

"They're getting past!" Mahri hissed, as three of the imps tore at her hair and dress. "Get off me you little –"

She was cut off as the Arcade lurched violently to one side. Christopher stumbled, swearing.

"*Ivy!*" shouted Mahri, and tried to push through the mass of oily grey bodies. Martha wobbled dangerously, swinging upwards abruptly. It seemed to Christopher that the floor had suddenly jumped up and attacked him. He crumpled against it, imps falling all around him. Reggie had fallen backwards into Jake's room, but Mahri had been much less lucky: Christopher watched, helplessly, as she flew out of the open window, imps clinging bitterly to her body.

"*MAHRI!*" he shouted, as the Arcade lurched sickeningly back towards the earth. He scrambled to the window, throwing imps out of his way.

ooo

"Hurry *up* Kevin!"

She tapped her fingers irritably on the roof of her car, wondering if anything else in the world could move quite as slowly as a teenage boy with a grudge. "Everyone else is gone already!"

"But *Mum*! I'll miss Neighbours!"

"*Get in this bloody car right now! Do you hear me?*"

Kevin rather sulkily emerged from his front door, pulling on his trainers.

"But *Mum* –"

"It said on the news there was a gas leak – I'm not sticking around here while they fanny about trying to fix it," Stacey huffed in annoyance. Her son stopped dead halfway up the garden path, a look of horror on his round face. "I'm not falling for that, Kevin, get a bloody m—"

Her motherly encouragement died in her throat as the normally indolent teenager vaulted over the fence, rolled over the hood of her car like one of the characters from his favourite action movies and tackled her to the ground.

"KEVIN!"

"Mum! Shut up!" he shouted, pushing her behind their neighbour's wall. The look of abject terror on his face gave her pause, but anything resembling thought immediately vanished as something hit the car with the force of a small bomb.

"Wh-what was that?" she whispered.

Kevin made to peer over the top of the wall and she grabbed her son's arms.

"Don't look!"

"*Mum*," he hissed. "Gerroff —"

He ducked back behind the wall, suddenly very pale.

"What is it?"

"It..." he struggled for a moment, unable to adequately express his horror. "It looks like a giant made out of plasticine — only evil, and angry, and with no eyes."

Stacey stared at him for a moment, wondering whether the gas leak they'd been warned about had had some kind of hallucinogenic effect. The remains of the car crunched and she slid a little further down the wall. Kevin clutched at her arm as something that sounded a lot like heavy boots hit the snow beside the car like wet sandbags. The footfalls started towards them — Stacey held her breath.

They stopped on the other side of the wall and Stacey squeezed her eyes tightly shut, willing her son to stay still and quiet.

The thing behind them made a sort of sniffing noise. Stacey was certain that whatever it was would be able to hear her heart pounding in her chest. She had to get Kevin out of here —

Summoning every shred of courage she had, she forced herself to open her eyes and slowly, reluctantly looked up.

Hanging over them, leaning over the wall, was –

Her mind faltered at the sight – it just wasn't possible. The great clay creature was dented in places, pitted – as if things had been hitting it at some speed. It sniffed the air again, then, with all the speed of a glacier, turned its horrible, sightless face towards her.

It screamed, the sound seeming to come from quite far away, as if a whole chorus of nightmarish creatures were shrieking all at once. Stacey screamed too and scrambled to her feet, pulling her son upright by his coat.

A great tug brought her crashing back to the ground, winded and grasping at the scarf around her neck. The thing had the other end – it pulled it, dragging her across the snow. She watched in horror as the garden wall tumbled apart as it walked towards her.

"GET OFF MY MUM!"

Kevin, she thought, in horror, *no – run! Get out of here, leave me!*

Kevin threw a brick at the monster. It paused for a moment, picked up the brick almost ponderously and threw it back at Kevin, who ducked. The brick went *through* the van parked on the other side of the street.

Stacey scrabbled at her neck as the scarf tightened around it, cutting off her air. Distractedly, she wondered how long she could last without air – she mentally pleaded with her son to run – if she could just loosen the scarf –

With a suddenness that made her giddy, Kevin was at her side, pulling the scarf over her head. She clutched at him, gulping the frozen air and wondering how breathing could possibly hurt so much.

"Mum! Mum, are you okay? Mum..."

She managed to give him a thumbs up and he fell silent, staring at something behind her.

"H-h-how –"

"Er..."

Stacey rolled over and watched as an enormous man beat the living hell out of the clay monster, forcing it back towards the remains of the car.

"He came out of nowhere!"

They watched, numb, as the clay monster's head flew off. Its body crumpled to the floor, looking for all the world like a termite mound had just popped up on the pavement.

Strong hands hauled her to her feet. She stumbled and caught herself on Kevin, who was staring up at their rescuer.

"You alright?" he asked gruffly.

Stacey looked him up and down. He was improbably large, thickset and wearing a bobble hat; his face was rather red, probably from the effort of beating up the pile of mud behind him. He was leaning on a large piece of wood with what looked like some bent nails in the end.

"Thanks," she said, voice a little hoarse.

The giant nodded, and turned away.

Stacey watched him stride down the road in the direction of the reddish glow in the middle of town.

"Kevin," she said, thoughtfully. "Grab your cricket bat."

"You what?" he stared at his mother, dumbfounded.

She picked up the lid of the neighbour's bin and tested its weight. She nodded at the retreating back of their laconic saviour.

"Whatever's going on, I'm willing to bet that the safest place to be is going to be a few feet behind *him*."

ooo

Dr Fitzhearn clutched the wall of the council building, wondering whether he was actually having a heart attack this time. He had spent the majority of the evening running, and he hadn't realised quite how out of practise he had become.

Arabella Jenkins rounded the corner, looking quite fearsome. Her hat had come off some time before, when they had come across a cul-de-sac full of unbelievably ugly creatures, breaking windows and terrifying the residents. Arabella had simply walked into the middle of it and struck her extraordinary walking stave against the ground, and the creatures had more or less all fallen out of the air. He hadn't looked too closely at them, in case this turned out not to be a nightmare after all, but he was reasonably certain that one or two of them had melted.

"Alright?" the Widow asked him, her breath steaming in the cold night air.

He shook his head very slightly. "My dear lady, I'm really not sure what I'm doing out here," he said, trying to warm up his hands which – despite all the running – were still freezing. He wished he'd thought to bring gloves. "I'm not totally certain I'm not dreaming."

Widow Jenkins cackled. "Nobody can ever be totally certain of that." She clapped him merrily on the back.

Vladimir narrowed his eyes. "You know, I'm beginning to suspect that you're rather enjoying this."

"I am," she said, softly. "Very much. I haven't had this much fun in years."

She gazed out across the snowy town, looking like someone with questionable taste had taken an unruly Halloween decoration and stuck it on a Christmas cake.

When she turned back, it seemed to Vladimir that his friend was looking at him from across a great, dark void, full of unfathomable things.

Was it his imagination, or were her eyes a little blacker than usual?

"It is possible, Doctor, to enjoy oneself a little too much," she said, in that same, soft tone. "You are here to make sure that I don't."

ooo

Ogden Rake ducked behind a wall – he heard Xander land beside him and slide rapidly to the floor.

"That was close," his friend grumbled, batting out a small fire that had broken out on the sleeve of his coat.

Ogden nodded, peering through a crack in the wall.

The Arcade was listing badly now, lurching blindly

about the ruins of a bathroom showroom, crushing trendy shower cubicles with her large trunk-like feet and knocking over telegraph poles.

"Bloody imps," Xander muttered. "Do you think Joe got out?"

There was a rather pregnant pause as they shared a speaking look. Both men had heard the screams.

"He has two kids," Xander said, darkly.

"Maybe he got out," Ogden said, quietly. "I think Ivy's in real trouble."

He heard his friend turn, his boots scuffing in the dirt as he, too, found a hole in their makeshift shelter.

Just visible, and keeping well out of the way of Martha's enormous feet, Post hurled hex after hex at the floundering Arcade. Yellow fire blossomed on one of her legs, curling hungrily around her frame. Imps scurried away from it like ants amongst her foliage, the less fortunate falling flaming to the ground like small, screaming meteors.

"Right," said Xander, and Ogden recognised the steely note in his voice.

There was a pause as both men steadied themselves before, as one, they leapt over the wall.

Post was at the other end of what used to be a furniture shop, casting what looked like a huge net made of silver light. They hurried through the warehouse, keeping low between the sofas, many of which were on fire, ducking flaming imps.

Xander caught his eye and both men hurled curses. The first one burst around Post like a firework, snagging in the man's personal shield charm, but the other hit home. He shouted in pain as his coat caught fire in a fairly spectacular fashion.

Xander cried out as a counter-curse hit him square in the chest with a resounding crack. Ogden pressed forward, throwing his full repertoire of duelling spells in Post's general vicinity, trusting that his friend would either be alright or was already beyond his help.

He winced as a powerful counter-curse exploded in

front of him, charring the concrete: Brightwell had taught Post well. Ducking as splinters of glass embedded themselves in the twisted remains of a wall behind him, he made a mental note to have a word with the Barracloughs about appropriate levels of combat training at the Academy.

Curses crackled through the night air between them, turning the snowflakes to steam.

Ogden's shield dropped for a moment and he neatly stepped out of the way of one of Post's curses – momentarily blinded, the next one hit him in the knees. He fell to the floor, head spinning, breath knocked from his body.

Even as he scrambled to his feet Xander Hardwick was at his side.

"Good to see you up and about!" he yelled, cheerfully.

Ogden grunted, putting all his energy into disabling the dark wizard in front of them, vaguely hopeful that his kneecaps were still intact.

Parry, thrust, cast, duck, parry, jump –

Together, through a haze of smoke and sparks, they began to drive him back towards the old pump house on the edge of the river. Post must have realised he was losing ground, because the ferocity of his spell-work increased. Ogden winced as an errant hex grazed his arm – he felt the bones in his wrist and shoulder fill up with what felt like liquid ice.

The pain made his vision blur. He grunted again, throwing his weight behind his next hex. He focused on the fight – there would be time for assessing injuries later.

Parry, hex, curse, roll, parry, duck, duck –

Post was pressed up against the wall of the pump house now, deep scores in the pavement where his boots had dug in. Behind the miasma of magic, Ogden could just make out his face – it gave him considerable satisfaction to see the brief moment of panic there.

He gritted his teeth: another minute and they would have him –

Pain ripped through his upper arm, stealing his breath. He roared, the shock of it pitching him forwards. Dimly, he was aware of Post's triumphant laughter, echoing menacingly against the old stonework.

Whomever had come to Post's aid had Xander's full attention; Ogden felt him close in beside him. He grabbed his proffered arm, hauling himself upright and clutching at what he suspected was a bullet wound.

Claire Danning was stepping delicately around the burning remains of a partially melted lime green sofa, a look of carefully controlled terror on her face.

"I'm really sorry," she said, and they could hear the fear in her voice. She was clearly on the very edge of tears. "Post must have called her..."

Rhosyn stepped out of the shadows behind her, a gun pressed to the back of her friend's neck.

"It's alright Claire," said Ogden, gently. "Just keep looking at me and Xander, alright?"

She nodded fractionally.

"Rosie, just put the gun down." Xander had one hand raised, placating, towards his wife, one still covering Post. Ogden glanced behind him: the smug bastard was leaning against the wall, arms crossed. A moment of stillness amongst the chaos.

"You don't have to do this," Xander called, focus shifting entirely to Rhosyn. Ogden turned so his back was against Xander's. Post raised an eyebrow, unfolding his arms and taking a defensive stance.

"Don't even think about it, Rake!" Rhosyn shouted. "Or I'll shoot!"

"You won't shoot her, Rosie, Claire's your best friend –"

"Shut up!" she spat. Ogden felt his friend flinch.

"What are you going to do, little watch-man?" Post taunted, leaning back against the wall with an air of unconcern. "Save the girl, or save the town?"

Rake glowered at him. He began to back away, the swagger back in his step.

"Rhosyn, you don't want to do this," Claire's voice

sounded small and tremulous, barely audible over the roar of the battle above them.

"You don't know what I want," Rhosyn snapped – Ogden heard Claire stumble and guessed that she'd been pushed forwards again.

Post was still grinning, cat-like in the shadows. Rake flexed his fingers, frustrated.

"I-I thought we were friends..." Claire continued.

"You're not worth my spit!" Rhosyn sneered. Ogden heard Claire whimper as the gun was pressed more firmly into her neck. "Now, keep your stupid mouth shut."

"Don't take another step," Ogden growled – Post snickered at him.

"Or you'll do what, Constable?"

"You know what, Rhosyn," Claire said. Rake tensed, there was a new note in her voice: she sounded angry. Post appeared to have noticed, too – he had stopped a few steps away, unnaturally still. "I may be stupid, but at least I'm not a traitor."

Several things happened at once:

There was a scream and the sounds of a scuffle; Xander threw himself into the fray as Post hurled a curse in their general direction and fled into the night, leaving a considerable amount of chaos behind him.

Rake tore after him, hoping that Claire and Xander would be able to handle themselves.

39
Only Human

The snow bit at the skin on his face, already sore from the continuing onslaught of imps. Christopher screwed up his eyes as he swung out of the window, kicking and flailing at the imps swarming up the sides of the Arcade. Most of them were ignoring him as Martha lurched about the edges of the town – like him, they were more concerned with hanging on than anything else.

He slid a little further down the vine, squinted through the blizzard into the chaos below. More imps were climbing out of the red-tinged cracks that had once been the parking area of a substantial retail park. There were so many now that it seemed like the ground was moving. Streams of them were heading off into the town, small parties breaking off to tear windscreen wipers off cars and smash windows, indiscriminate in their destruction.

Small bursts of light suggested that the residents of Brindleford were assisting the Court in their enquiries. He wondered whether Charlie was down there, somewhere, keeping the peace with his big-stick-with-nails in. He rather hoped he was. He swung around, struggling to keep his grip in the biting cold.

A few metres below him, he could see one of Mahri's hiking boots poking out from amidst the foliage. Fervently hoping that her leg was still attached, he made a grab for a nearby trunk only to miss as Martha lurched off in the other direction. His heart leapt into his mouth as he slid another foot down the slippery vine, momentarily losing his grip.

A scream made him turn his head – another knot of vines flew past with what looked like a very unhappy young woman in their midst. He stared at her as she travelled through the air and vanished from sight above him.

What on earth was Martha playing at?

An imp sailed past in the opposite direction, flailing madly. Christopher followed its arc, hypnotised, until it hit a lamp post some way away and fell limply to the ground.

His stomach lurched unpleasantly as the Arcade reeled backwards. This time he got a solid grip on the foliage above Mahri. He glanced down and immediately wished he hadn't. She was sprawled in a nook above one of the vast trunk-like legs, arms and legs akimbo. There were three or four dead imps steaming gently around her.

She wasn't moving.

He dropped down beside her and moved her hair away from her face: a thin trickle of blood ran down from beneath her hairline. He pressed his fingers into her neck, praying that he would find a pulse.

Was it just below the jaw-line, or further down the throat? Visions of television dramas swam across his mind – they made it look so easy! Where, when you got right down to it, was the jugular vein, anyway?

His hands slipped on her wet skin – they were shaking too hard for him to tell whether the fragile movement he felt was her pulse or his own, wild panic. Finally, he found it: steady and strong under his fingers.

He let out the breath he hadn't even realised he was holding, dizzy with relief.

"Mahri!" he shouted, shaking her shoulder. "Mahri, wake up!"

He cast around for an easier route back up the outside of the Arcade – they couldn't stay here. Ivy needed them. Maybe he could carry her...

"Christopher?" She sounded groggy and confused, but Mahri was already pulling herself upright. "I'm getting too bloody old for this," she grumbled.

Surprising them both, Christopher pulled her into a lopsided hug. He felt oddly like crying.

"We're going to have to climb," he said, helping her to her feet in the relative calm of the nook. "Can you manage?"

"I'll have to," she said and squinted at him. "Can you?"

He grimaced.

ooo

There were just too many of them, even with Martha joining in.

All he could see was a forest of scales and fur, flashes of teeth and claws. He tried not to look too hard into their large, yellow eyes: there was murder there, and the sharp glint of insanity. The stench of the creatures was all around him, like sweaty rubber and rotten eggs. It had made him gag when they'd first surrounded him, but now his senses seemed to be shutting down in self-defence.

Reggie clung grimly to the battered frying pan, walloping anything in his reach. He had given up on trying to keep them away from Ivy, now – by the way the Arcade was lurching about, it was too late for that.

It was impossible to think about anything except the very next second. He smacked a particularly ugly specimen in the face, ignoring the one that had latched onto his leg. Two of them were trying to wrest the frying pan out of his hands; he shook them off, taking another step backwards. There was something hard behind him: a glimpse of wood told him he was backed right up against the kitchen counter.

Somewhere nearby, a woman was screaming. It cut short abruptly, and Reggie tried not to guess which of his friends it had been.

There was nowhere to go now but down into the teashop, and from the crashing sounds coming from below he suspected that that was in about the same state as the main room.

Three imps were now clinging to the frying pan, and he flailed about wildly, using their extra weight to knock out a few of their neighbours. He shouted in pain: one of them had sunk its long, sharp teeth into his wrist. He shook it off, losing his grip on the frying pan – it span away across the room, and he quickly lost sight of it in the tangle of bodies and vines.

The imps surged over him, biting and tearing at every inch they could find. He curled up, covering his head with his hands – trying to minimise the area they could reach, but it didn't do much good.

The pain of hundreds of sharp teeth took over his mind and he gritted his teeth. He couldn't last long like this. He began to inch his way towards the spiral staircase to his left, feeling his way blindly. If he was going to die here, he might as well take as many of them with him as he could – even if all he could do was squash them.

Another imp latched onto his head, its gnarled fingers curling around his throat. Reggie closed his eyes and thought of Bessie, edging nearer to the stairs – if he could just stay conscious for long enough –

Somebody was shouting nearby, but he couldn't make out the words –

He hoped they got out.

ooo

Xander hit the ground with a sickening thud, Rhosyn's body limp against him.

Dimly, he watched the vine that had plucked them out of the way of Martha's feet curl away, taking out a swathe of imps as it went.

The Arcade was overrun: somewhere nearby, someone was screaming bloody murder. He suspected that it was Claire, which at least meant she hadn't been shot as he'd struggled with Rosie.

Rosie!

He sat up, protecting his wife from the nearest imps. With a huff of frustration, he focussed on a shield charm, hoping it would hold long enough to –

He didn't know what he'd do. If Rhosyn was alive, then he'd have to arrest her, and if she wasn't...

His heart gave a horrible squeeze at the thought.

Thankfully, she groaned, and Xander sent a silent prayer to the Gods. His relief didn't last very long: as soon as she regained consciousness she pushed herself away from him and cast around for something.

The gun!

He dragged himself upright, muscles screaming in protest. Rhosyn was already on the very edge of his shield charm –

Xander spotted the gun across the room, lying just below the upturned preparation table. Could he get to it before she did?

She reached the edge of his protection and pushed through it. The change in pressure as it failed made his ears pop. Imps that had hitherto been unable to get to them swarmed towards them both – Xander swore and hurled a fireball at the nearest bunch.

Ivy wasn't going to have much of a living room left at this rate.

"Rosie! Get behind me!" he shouted, aiming spells in every conceivable direction.

But Rhosyn was ignoring him, kicking and punching her way towards the gun with single-minded abandon.

One of the creatures latched onto her back and Xander picked it off, fighting his way towards his wife. The force of the spell pushed her forwards and for a moment he lost sight of her in the morass of moving bodies. He lunged forwards, tearing imps out of the way, propelled by sheer adrenaline.

His questing fingers found her arm under a particularly bulky imp and he hauled her to her feet.

For a moment, they were fighting back to back, fending off attack from all directions. Xander set one of the nearest creatures on fire and it ran around madly, delicate flames kindling among its fellow imps. Soon Xander was at the midst of a semicircle of flaming imps – the smell of burning flesh was almost overpowering and he gagged, freezing their flailing bodies to the spot with a flick of his hand.

The imps who had backed away from the fire now pushed forward with menace, shattering their companions' bodies as they kicked and scurried forwards.

They drove Xander backwards against the stairs and abruptly he realised that Rhosyn was no longer behind him.

Desperate, he cast about the room for her, squinting through the writing bodies, calling out her name.

With a vicious burst of magic he threw the imps back. She wasn't beneath them – he could see patches of floor now, beneath the foul remnants of the imps.

She couldn't just have vanished – she didn't have magic! No matter what Post might have taught her.

A small noise from behind him gave him pause.

There were no imps in the back room of the bookshop.

Of course! he thought, suddenly. The Professors wouldn't leave the back room unprotected, no matter how efficient the Arcade usually was at repelling uninvited guests.

With sudden purpose, he kicked the nearest imp in the face and propelled himself over the railing, landing – a little unsteadily – about halfway down the stairs.

The imps above him screeched in annoyance, robbed of their prey, and followed him in a great wave. They started to dissolve just above his head, white lines forming in their flesh. They floated away, tiny flecks of silver and grey, added to the general fug of battle.

He shuddered.

Shaking off the thought that he was now breathing atomised imp, he crept down the stairs, keeping a tight hold on the rail as the Arcade bucked this way and that.

The back office was dark and cool, a small oasis of calm. Almost everything had either fallen over or rolled off its shelf – the floor was littered with books and papers in various states of repair. There was no sign of Rhosyn.

She was in there somewhere, he knew, but where? Xander closed his eyes and reached out with his mind, silently mouthing the words of the incantation. He felt his heartbeat slow, the sounds of violence above him diminishing as he built an image of the room in his mind.

His instructor at his first Court had called it Eyeball Scrying – Eyeballing for short. You let the person you were looking for come to you. Every person had a signature; some people called it an aura. If a suspect was still alive it would pulse in the quiet places like a beacon. Very useful, if you knew how to look for it. A good Practitioner could pick out a crook in an abandoned warehouse if they had the talent – but not all of them did.

Xander did. He could see them on the edge of his vision every moment of the day: people's souls spilling out into what was to him a visible spectrum, colouring his world. No matter how well concealed they were, no one could hide from that.

He readied a spell he desperately hoped he wouldn't have to use and breathed in the air of the bookshop.

He caught the slightest hint of scarlet to his left before the world lit up with pain. He clutched at his head.

"Rhoysn!" he shouted, falling back against the stairs, his carefully prepared spell shooting off and bursting against the far wall with a shower of plaster.

"NO!" she shouted, hitting him again with something hard and unforgiving. "I'M TALKING NOW!"

White spots burst across his vision as he took another blow from what looked like an iron poker.

"Rosie!" he shouted again, trying to shield his head.

"Did you think this was all I wanted from life?" she demanded between blows, sounding quite unhinged. "To be a Constable's wife? Living in that tiny two-bedroomed shit-hole, on a Constable's wage? Spending every day working for an organisation that couldn't find its own arse with both bloody hands? Pretending to be nice to runts that aren't even fit to lick my shoes?"

He tried to cast a shield between them, but his magic misfired, sending sparks up her sleeves. She beat out the flames that sprang greedily along the hem of her coat.

"I love the way we are," he mumbled, aware that he was spitting blood all over her clothes. She wouldn't be happy about that. He scrunched up his face – it was getting harder to think.

"WELL I DON'T!" she screamed, and slapped him hard about the face. "This was your dream, Alexander, not mine. You moved me up here, away from civilisation – you got me the job at the Court, working my fingers to the bone to uphold the *law*!" Rhosyn's lips curled downwards in distaste. For the first time in his life, it struck him how ugly she looked, full of anger and hate. Her beauty had simply melted away in the face of her fury. It must have been eating at her for years – all the time he had been trying to make her happy. All the time he had been happy.

How could he have missed this?

"What has the *law* ever done for me?"

The world went purple for a moment as the poker made contact with his skull. Blood was dripping down his face now, filling his eyes.

She spat in his face, "Face it Alexander, you're never going to be more than a penniless, overworked, *useless* Constable, and I want more than that – I *deserve* more than that! Quentin understands me – he sees what I'm worth. Compared to him, you're *nothing!*"

Impossible laughter welled up in his chest; he couldn't stop himself.

Quentin bloody Post.

He was going to die here, he realised. The thought didn't bother him as much as he thought it ought to. His head throbbed where Rhosyn had beaten him.

Rosie...

He ought to warn her really.

"Rosie," he gurgled, "Post doesn't play well with others – once he has what he needs you'll be expendable – a lot of the people he comes into contact with become expendable. I've seen what happened to them. Remember that orb you stole for him? He burned their souls right out of their bodies."

A flicker of doubt crossed his wife's face, and for a moment she was the woman he had fallen in love with a decade ago. She bit her lip and he reached up, cupping her face in his hand.

"He'll kill you Rosie," he told her. "And then forget you. Just like everybody else."

It was as if a light had gone out behind her eyes. He saw the rage there, and the hate. He dropped his hand.

"You'll see." She smiled, and it was quite unlike the woman he'd married: cold and frightening. "Well, you won't see, actually. You'll be dead."

She raised the poker high above her head.

Xander shut his eyes.

ooo

Bessie's face swam into his mind: the way she had been on the day they'd met, peering over the wall of her garden, her face bathed in sunlight and ringed in flowers.

I'm coming, my girl, he thought, feeling for the railing.

"GET OFF HIM YOU UGLY LITTLE BASTARDS!"

There was an almighty clang, like the gong of a bell, and the pressure around his neck stopped. He coughed, dragging much needed air into his lungs.

"*Ugly little bastards, awk!*"

The wall of imps thinned a little, and Reggie glimpsed his rescuers: a woman was striding towards him, cleaving through imps with his lost frying pan. The remains of what had probably been quite a pretty dress flew out around her, her violet hair sticking up at odd angles, like some kind of modern-day warrior woman.

"*I – said – get – off!*" she shouted, punctuating each word with a fresh swing. With some relief he spotted a flash of green – Boscoe was circling above her head and taking vicious swipes at any imps that got too close. He looked a little singed.

Reggie pulled himself upright on the counter, kicking out at the imps around his feet. He wrenched open a drawer at random and pulled out a sturdy-looking rolling pin.

"That'll do," he hissed, as another couple of imps latched onto his back. "I DON'T THINK SO!" he shouted, pain forgotten. He smacked the nearest imp in the mouth: it backed up a little, giving him room to manoeuvre.

A rush of wings told him that Boscoe had taken matters into his own talons. One of the imps on his back dropped to the ground, clutching madly at the place where his eyes had been.

Another clang removed the other imp from his shoulders and he felt the mad-woman with the frying pan put her back to his.

"I *really* hate imps!" she shouted, and Reggie had to laugh. His chest hurt. Everything hurt.

THWACK! went the rolling pin, sending another imp sailing away.

"Thanks!" he yelled, when he could breathe, swinging wildly around with the rolling pin. "I'm Reggie, by the way!"

"Claire!" *CLANG!* "Court of Miracles!"

"Thank God for that, I thought we were –" he paused to take out another couple of imps. "I thought you lot'd left us to it!"

"Don't thank him yet – I'm just a secretary! Oh, piss off you cheeky little shit!" There was a brief scream as the imp that had latched onto Claire's hair met its demise.

Reggie risked a glance backwards. "Hell of a secretary!" he hissed, as another imp snapped at his ankles.

He yelped as the world around him suddenly became incredibly hot and incredibly bright all at once: he shielded his eyes. Most of the nearby imps were crawling up the walls, trying to get as far as they could from the burning light.

Now what?

A shape strode forwards through the light, casting long shadows across the remains of the living room.

"You alright, Reggie?"

"Mahri!" he croaked. "Am I glad to see you!"

"Likewise, old thing!" She had a ball of bright, white light in her hands. Beams of it were spilling out from between her fingers. "It won't hold them for long."

"We need to get to Ivy," Christopher panted, following Mahri through the vines. "You look a right state!"

Reggie squinted at him.

The climb down to rescue Mahri hadn't done him any favours: his skin was nearly grey.

"Better than you," said Reggie, slowly, and tried not to think about how his friend's hands were shaking. Instead, he cast around for his parrot. "Boscoe!" he shouted. "Keep the imps away from Ivy!"

"*Awk!*"

They climbed through the remains of the great windows after him, Mahri carrying her fierce light with her. Already, it seemed paler – the circle of imp-free space was diminishing. Reggie could hear them screeching, just on the edge of sight.

The garden was a mess, an enormous tangle of vines and imps. The knot of foliage around Ivy was battered and torn – Reggie could see her hair and part of her arm. It was bleeding profusely.

As Mahri and the light grew closer, scattering imps, the lurching movements of the Arcade slowed and stilled. The sudden absence of it made him dizzy.

"We need to hold them off until we get to the top of the hill," Mahri said, through gritted teeth. "After that –"

After that, it wouldn't matter, one way or another.

"Ready?" Mahri asked, back to Ivy.

Reggie shared a dark look with Christopher, who appeared to be running on adrenaline alone.

He tightened his grip on the rolling pin as Mahri's light winked out.

ooo

Odgen hit the ground still running, dodging the curses Post was hurling over his shoulders. Bursts of white and yellow light scorched past his face.

Whatever had hit his shoulder was spreading painfully down his arm, filling it with ice. The bullet wound didn't help much, either.

He bellowed the words to a rather unpleasant incantation and sent it hurtling after his quarry, who ducked. The spell burst into a wall of imps, obliterating them.

Luckily, his shouts had alerted the group of figures at the centre of the room – they were clustered around a column of vegetation that practically sang with magic. This, he presumed, was Ivy. One of them broke away from the others, fighting his way over the mound of voracious gremlins surrounding them and heading straight for Post.

"Christopher! I'm surprised at you!" Post taunted, over the general clamour. He sounded a little out of breath. "I'd have thought you would have known better!"

Christopher didn't waste time on arguments, simply unleashing a torrent of inexpert but effective hexes at Post, who swore – suddenly having to focus all his energy on defence.

Ogden closed in behind him, making the onslaught two-fold.

Post – visibly sweating with the effort – redoubled his efforts, somehow repelling everything they threw at him.

The two men moved around him in a low, slow arc, keeping their attention on him as Ivy and the Arcade picked their way across the snowy fields of Rouse. The air around them began to take on a foggy hue, heavy with spent magic – it smacked of tin and iron, magic and blood.

A circle of dead imps and shrivelled vines surrounded them, unwitting victims of the mêlée, their corpses blackened with the sheer intensity of the enchantments rebounding from Post's shield charms.

The three of them were locked in a deadly stalemate, weaving intricate webs of spells at lightning speed. When they came into view, Christopher's hands were moving so fast that he could barely see them – though, now he came to think of it, the intensity of the magic he was producing was waning.

The man looked dead on his feet.

Rake gritted his teeth, forcing more energy into his spells to compensate for his friend – his voice was beginning to rasp from all the incantations – his chest pounding from the effort of maintaining his end of the onslaught.

To his surprise, Post began to lose ground, backing away across what used to be a beautiful garden. It was working! He pressed forward, feeling Christopher respond in kind – they had him now, if only they could keep him fighting, keep him –

With an almighty bellow, Post span on the spot, simultaneously removing one side of his protection and ducking out of the way. A tremendous weight hit Ogden's right shoulder, carrying him across the garden.

He landed at the foot of one of the Coach Houses, sherds of pottery from one of the window boxes raining down on him. His head span – suddenly the world seemed far too hot, far too tight – as if the air around him had decided, on a whim, that a thunderstorm was a *really* good idea.

He tried to push himself upright and overbalanced – his right arm didn't seem to be taking orders any more...

Distantly, he saw Christopher leap at Post, suddenly looking more like a large dog than a human. Everything seemed muted, somehow, like it was suddenly much less important.

His gaze fell on a shape a little way in front of him: he squinted at it, intrigued. At first he had taken it as a damaged vine, misshapen and blackened like the rest, but the more he stared at it, the less vine-like it looked. A sick feeling began to steal over him, as if there was some great joke he wasn't privy to.

He stared at it stupidly, willing his brain to make any sort of useful connection.

Moving without conscious instruction, he looked

down at himself – dully, he registered that his shirt and coat were soaked in blood. His gran was going to have a thing or two to say about that in the morning.

He gave a hoarse cry as his eyes followed the line of his coat upwards. His shoulder was smoking slightly; the stench of burnt blood washed over him.

Ogden Rake stared down at the place where his arm used to be and roared.

ooo

Surprisingly, the first thing that filtered through the fug of unconsciousness wasn't the crashing from the fight above, or even the pain – that came later. The sound that really captured his attention was the quiet series of clicks coming from the far side of the room.

Xander listened to it in utter bewilderment for a few moments. Nothing in his bedroom made that noise – and nothing in the Court, for that matter. Not that he'd fallen asleep there *that* often.

He didn't really feel like moving yet. His thoughts were sluggish and uncomplicated, and for the moment he was just fine with that.

After a few minutes, though, whatever it was that was jabbing into his spine made him try to sit up and open his eyes, and that was when the pain hit him.

It felt like a small explosion had gone off inside his skull. He retched, feeling blindly in front of him for something to hold onto.

He couldn't open his eyes – nothing seemed to be working quite right – and all the while that insistent clicking continued. It was beginning to make him nervous.

With tremendous effort, he forced his right eye open a crack: a paper-strewn table swam into view beneath his hands, and suddenly he remembered where he was.

Rosie!

The room was long and narrow, and the only light was coming from the far end of it. He squinted, but couldn't focus properly. He decided to focus on the nature of the light instead: it wasn't particularly bright and had a blueish tinge to it – more like the light that came from electronics than from magic.

He could see her shape now, dimly outlined against the far shelves. She was using her phone to illuminate a dial or something – he edged around the table, leaning heavily on it for support. His whole body felt shivery and weak.

The wall behind her seemed oddly out of place – for a start it was the only part of the room (except for the stove) not covered in books. It was glossy, diffuse: the light reflected off it oddly, like it wasn't sure it wanted to go too near to it. He screwed up his eye, trying to focus – it was gunmetal grey, he realised, with a jolt.

The vault. She was trying to open the vault!

He tried to speak, but his mouth wasn't co-operating – all that came out was a groan.

Rhosyn's head whipped round. In a second the poker was back in her hands. She looked him up and down and lowered it, laughing cruelly.

"You can barely stand," she said. "What do you think you're going to do, bleed on me?"

She turned away, dismissing him.

He reached the end of the table – his head was beginning to clear, he realised. Unfortunately for him, this brought the pain into sharper focus. He closed his eye for a moment, trying to block out the intense, consuming ache coming from every part of his head.

He forced his mouth to move. "It's not there, Rhosyn," he mumbled.

"I'm sorry, I can't hear you darling," she drawled, spinning the dial on the vault another few inches. Her cold tone made his heart constrict.

"It's not there," he said, more loudly. His voice was thick with blood and bruising; he tried to clear his throat.

"Nice try, sweetie," she scoffed. "It's not going to work."

He managed to get himself turned around, still supporting his weight on the table.

"You don't think Mistress Burwell would put it somewhere as obvious as a safe, do you?" he asked, as casually as he could.

He cast a small Light Orb behind his back. He felt it form and almost immediately wink out again. He needed to focus.

"Ivy Burwell?" she sneered. "She's nothing but a jumped-up waitress."

"That's your trouble, Rhosyn," Xander snapped, suddenly feeling all the anger he had been suppressing for the past few days well up inside him. "You only ever look at what's on the surface."

Rhosyn ignored him. With a great effort, he pushed his anger away. Anger made you stupid, reckless – what he needed now was calm, a chance to think.

If she managed to get the vault open...

He paused as a memory surfaced. Perhaps he wouldn't have to incapacitate her after all.

Xander folded his arms, keeping his tone light.

"You really don't want to open that," he said, conversationally, as the dial clicked away.

"Shut up, Alexander."

"Don't you want to know why?"

"Don't try my patience."

"*I'd* want to know why."

"This is not going to work, Alexander," she snapped. "Nothing you can say will stop me from opening this vault."

"Nothing?"

"*Nothing.*"

"Fair enough," said Xander, nonchalantly. "But don't say I didn't warn you."

There were a few minutes of relative peace in the back room, punctured only by the horrifying screeching and banging from above and the quiet clicks of the vault door.

"Hah..." Rhosyn breathed, finally finding the correct

combination.

Very carefully, Xander lowered himself to the ground and crawled under the table.

"Got it!" Rhosyn cried as the vault door gave one last, decisive sounding click. It swung open ponderously, an eerie green light spilling out.

Rhosyn reached inside, greedily, feeling around for the Chalice.

"THIEF!" screeched an unholy voice. A large, leather bound text shot out of the vault at high speed. It bounced off the table and landed on the floor, where it sat, smoking slightly. The cast iron kettle, which had been resting on the table, landed beside it with a loud thunk.

Rhosyn shot backwards, poker raised in pure terror.

"DEFILER! BOOK STEALER!"

Pale and trembling with rage, Professor Zarrubabel emerged from the vault like a demonic jack-in-the-box, his book trolley hitting the floor with an unsettling crunch. He weighed another large and clearly quite dangerous tome in his translucent hand, menacingly.

Rhosyn appeared to be frozen to the spot, mute with shock.

"HOW DARE YOU COME INTO MY SHOP!" he cried, bobbing about near the ceiling like some kind of demented airborne fishing-lure. "HOW DARE YOU SULLY THESE BOOKS WITH YOUR PRESENCE?"

He hurled the book at Rhosyn, who ducked in the nick of time. It landed on one of the chairs and promptly began eating its way through the wood.

"THIEF! MOUNTEBANK! LICKSPITTLE TROLLOP!"

He threw another book, and another, growing larger and more ferocious with every bellow.

Weeks of pent-up rage at being locked in the vault was all coming out in one, long tirade.

Under the table, Xander edged away from an indenture contract that looked like it really did mean business. Rhosyn was having to defend herself with the poker now, using it as a sort of metal rounders bat.

Every time she knocked a book away, Professor

Zarrubabel would scream in rage, possibly on behalf of the book, and hurl another at her. Slowly but surely, she was being beaten back across the room.

Suddenly, Martha stumbled; somewhere above them, a woman screamed.

Professor Zarrubabel threw the book he was holding back in the vault – it looked perfectly ordinary to Xander, but that was probably *why* it had been locked away – and shot across the floor of the bookshop to a small hatch at the other end, vanishing into it with a popping sound.

The tone of the chaos above shifted as Professor Zarrubabel emerged above their heads. Xander could hear him shrieking in rage; he almost felt sorry for the imps.

He climbed out from under the table, careful not to step on anything that might be tempted to eat him. Rhosyn was still picking herself up from a pile of ancient and deadly tomes, so he grabbed one of Christopher's book binding tools and knocked the volume that had been making short work of the chair shut.

He glanced at the title: *Reader's Digest*.

It belched. He put the fallen kettle on top of it, just in case.

"You *bastard*," Rhosyn hissed, getting unsteadily to her feet.

Xander sighed painfully. "Rhosyn Hardwick, I am arresting you under suspicion of –"

"STILL JUST A FUCKING CONSTABLE!" she screamed, running at him with the poker; he shielded himself. At that moment, the Arcade gave another great lurch and she overbalanced, falling towards the *Reader's Digest*.

Xander reached out and caught her – she beat her fists against him, driving the heel of her shoe into his foot. He gave a shout, letting go of her arms. Snatching up the poker one final time, she swung around to hit him – the Arcade shifted again, rearing up at the imps and Golems outside – Rhosyn lost her footing as the whole room began to slant upwards.

Books and furniture flew across the room – he made a grab for her hand as the floor twisted back down again, but his fingers closed around empty air – helplessly, he watched her tumble away from him, face a picture of terror as the vault door closed behind her with an almighty bang.

"ROSIE!" he shouted, scrambling over the upturned table.

He could hear her inside, even as he crawled across the book-littered floor.

"No! What are you doing? I don't want – NO!"

There was the sound of the poker hitting the metal floor of the vault; a horrible silence descended over the back room as he wrenched open the door and looked inside.

Pain blossomed in his chest that had nothing to do with his injuries.

The poker was there, at the bottom of the vault, and just one book.

He stared numbly at it for a few moments before the sounds of the battle above brought him to his senses.

With great reluctance, he turned his back on the *Atlas of Faraway Places* and hurried up the stairs.

ooo

Christopher struggled to his feet, no longer caring how wolfish he looked. He snarled as Post strode towards him, wagging a reproving finger.

His head was bursting with exhaustion. He wished the smug bastard wouldn't swagger about so damned much. It was just so *effortless*.

"Tsk tsk," Post tutted. "Naughty Christopher, you shouldn't be working for a nice respectable bookshop with a condition like *that*," he sneered, lips curling. "What would the community say? Not to mention the stain on poor Mistress Ivy's reputation – openly living with a mongrel. She'll never be able to live it down, such a shame..."

Christopher growled and leapt at him again, teeth that were currently a lot more like fangs snapping at the man – Post stepped neatly to one side and he crashed into the ground behind him. He looked up and managed to curl into a tight ball a split second before Ivy's herb shelves fell on top of him.

He groaned.

One of the shelves had hit him full in the mouth. He wiped the blood away and stared at his paw-like hand – there was a deep grey tinge to it. An odd feeling of calm stole over him. So this was what dying felt like.

Every inch of him was burning with the silver now, it wouldn't take much to finish him off. His fingers brushed against something unfamiliar amongst the vines as he tried to push the heavy shelving away. Something metal.

He scooped it up as Post's pitiless laughter approached, and tried really hard to concentrate on having useful fingers.

With a rush of air the bookshelf flew off him and crashed into the kitchen table, scattering vine covered chairs.

"Now, I'm not an unreasonable man," Post purred.

Christopher got to his knees and made a very eloquent gesture with his left hand.

"Oh, make no mistake," Post chuckled. "I'm going to kill *you*. Your kind have no place in my world – dirty, filthy things. I may, however, be more generous to Mistress Burwell – and her children."

Christopher glowered at him. If he could just keep him talking, and figure out how to keep his hands from shaking...

"If you tell me where the Chalice of Knowledge is, and help me get it, then I give you my word that Ivy and the children will live out their natural lives," said Post, carefully.

Christopher recognised an intelligently worded contract when he heard one. He glanced over Post's shoulder: Professor Zarrubabel was making a sizeable dent in the imps now, and the others were still holding out. Many of the vines had been pulled away from Ivy now, and he could see the marks on her skin where the imps had attacked her.

"What do you say, old chap?" Post asked, sweetly.

"Go to hell," croaked Christopher, and shot him in the heart.

Post staggered backwards, stumbling over the vines – he clutched at his chest, eyes wide with shock. Slowly, disbelievingly, he raised a hand to his mouth to wipe away the blood that was trickling out of the corner of his mouth.

Christopher went limp with relief. He had done it! They would be able to reach Nadderbeck Farm, and destroy the *Chalice*, and everyone would be safe –

Post started laughing. It was a horrible, gurgling sort of laugh – one that suggested that not only was the person it belonged to completely insane, but that their lungs weren't entirely intact, either. It bubbled.

Christopher stared at him, numbly, the gun slipping out of his unresisting fingers.

Something seemed to grab him by the chest and he was pulled upwards like a human rag-doll, Post cackling maniacally below.

"Didn't anyone ever tell you, Christopher?" he asked, with a voice dripping with glee. "Two hearts are better than one? Now…"

Post's face stilled, his eyes fixed on the ceiling behind Christopher. He twisted in the air, trying to see –

His heart dropped into his stomach as his eyes fell on the tangle of vines knotted in the corner, keeping the *Chalice* firmly out of everyone's reach.

"Aha," Post smiled, delicately. "Well, I won't be needing *you* any more, will I?"

Christopher caught determined movement out of the corner of his eye; he kept his face impassive as an enormous three-legged tiger came out of nowhere and swiped a powerful set of claws into Quentin Post's back.

Christopher fell to the floor with a crash and lay still, the fight knocked out of him.

The tiger leaped over his head and snarled at Post, who was white with pain and bleeding profusely. He pulled up his sleeve; Christopher saw something glinting under there – gold and blood red.

He felt hot breath on his neck as the tiger's teeth closed on his tattered jumper and lifted him out of the way. Whatever it was on Post's wrist had, silently and in a matter of seconds, left a gaping hole in the floor where he and the tiger had been only moments before.

He got a good look at the damage to Post's back as the tiger dragged him out of his reach, dropping him in the garden. Christopher met the great beast's eyes for a moment before he turned away to re-join the fight.

So, Constable Rake was a shape-shifter.

There was no time to dwell on it, however, as Post took one look at the colossal feline and hurled a curse that fizzed and spat its way through the air. For a split-second, Christopher thought he had missed.

To his horror, her realised the curse was right on target.

It hit the column of vines around Ivy with the force of a small bomb, rending the plants apart and throwing them all off their feet.

Head pounding from the force of the magical explosion, he watched – powerless – as Ivy folded up and fell slowly to the ground some feet away, like a broken toy.

40
Martha's Last Stand

"Fuck me!" Stacey cried, ducking beneath the porch of the old technical college.

Vast blocks of masonry rained down around them, crashing through windows and decapitating lamp posts. They had come up a side street in the industrial estate and were close enough now to make out the dark shape travelling high above them in the stormy darkness.

It didn't seem to be very well: it was reeling across the fields just past the very edge of the town. The buildings on this side of the river were mostly old warehouses and half-abandoned service buildings.

Which was probably a good thing, Stacey decided, as the enormous insect-like thing crashed into the old telephone exchange, taking out a healthy portion of the upper floor. She squinted at it as it tried to right itself, legs like huge tree-trunks scrabbling on the snowy ground.

"Is that – is that a *building?*" she wondered aloud.

"Who cares?" asked Kevin. "It's a menace."

"It's *'The Vines'*," the giant rumbled.

Stacey looked up at him. He hadn't said a great deal since he'd rescued them from whatever it was that had been trying to kill them, but he didn't seem to mind them following him.

"What, that naff old shopping arcade across town?" Kevin asked, staring at it.

Stacey cuffed him gently around the back of the head. "I got a lovely bunch of flowers from there once," she said, not taking her eyes off the staggering building. "Just because there isn't a games shop..."

"My friend's in there," the enormous man rumbled again. He looked very much like a man thinking about doing something very stupid.

"What are you –"

"STAND AND DELIVER!"

Stacey screamed, jumping like an electric shock had

shot through her – Kevin leapt backwards, cricket bat raised.

A fearsome apparition had appeared out of nowhere and was brandishing a large stick in their direction. Their voice seemed to go straight through Stacey, as if it wasn't quite a part of their world.

"Evening," their friend rumbled, quite unconcerned.

The stick lowered a fraction as whomever it was gave them a once over. Then the stick was retracted.

"Oh, hello Charlie," said the apparition, sounding a lot more normal. "Bloody awful weather, in't it?"

Stacey stared at it, eyes wide with shock. The sound of hurried footsteps approached and a short, rather elderly man came panting into view. He gave them an exhausted little wave of greeting and leaned heavily against the wall beside them.

"I like the snow," said Charlie, with a small shrug.

"Who're your friends?" asked the apparition. "Picking up snacks again? You'll ruin your appetite," it cackled.

Stacey swallowed hard. Suddenly, Kevin was a lot closer to his mum than he had been before.

"Arabella," the elderly man panted. "You're enjoying yourself too much."

"What?" There was a pause. "Oh yes, you're right. Thank you, Doctor."

Charlie glanced down at Stacey and Kevin. "I'm not going to eat you," he said, helpfully. Stacey wasn't altogether reassured.

A crash at the other end of the street made them all jump – suddenly the night was bristling with weapons. A group of nerdy young men were running full tilt along the other side of the road, heading for *The Vines*, which was still wobbling about in the fields. A tall, skinny specimen near the rear was yelling instructions; he noticed their little group and veered off towards them.

"Hello!" he shouted, skidding to a halt in front of them. "You chaps should be at the evacuation centre on the other side of town! There's a gas leak on!" he said brightly, while *The Vines* careened around behind him.

Stacey shared a look with the elderly chap. "You're not very good at this, are you?" she asked, bluntly.

He blinked big, innocent eyes at her.

"Come off it, Otto," said the apparition called Arabella. He turned his stunned gaze onto her. "We're not going anywhere."

"How do you know m-"

"I knew your mum growing up, and *her* mum – I'm Arabella Jenkins."

"Oh," he said, then his expression changed. "*Oh...*"

"Yes, boy, *that* Arabella Jenkins," she grinned, toothily.

"Leave him *alone,* Arabella," said her friend.

"Er – yes," said Otto, shaking himself. "In that case – I don't suppose you'd lend a hand? We're stretched a bit thin, what with the chasm into Hell and all that..." his eyes travelled across the group as a whole. "Er – that is, if you're all prac-"

Arabella cut him off. "Charlie and the doctor can hold their own," she said, with a sniff. The doctor looked a little uncertain about this. "Dunno about the others."

Charlie glanced at them again. "They're with me," he said, in a manner that suggested the matter was closed.

"Right, good," said Otto, and immediately began rummaging in a battered old canvas bag. "Er, can you hold this? Thanks – this is an experimental portable shield charm," he said, pulling a black stone on a long, leather cord out of the bag. "Might come in handy – only one, I'm afraid." He held it out expectantly.

As one, both the elderly gentleman and Stacey insisted that Kevin ought to have it. He pulled it over his head with the air of someone who thought that wearing jewellery was very uncool.

"Er..." Otto was passing all manner of unusual things to Arabella and Charlie now, from bizarre creatures in jars to pocket watches and – to Stacey's surprise – a live frog. It jumped out of Charlie's over-sized hands and hopped away into the snow.

"Aha!" he cried, triumphantly, pulling out a crossbow

and quiver full of bolts. "Knew I had this in here somewhere..."

He held it out, expectantly.

"You take it, Doc," said Stacey, giving the old man a nudge in the arm. "I'm alright with this. She waved the tree branch she'd been using as a club. "Mostly the slippery little bastards just burst, anyway."

"How kind," said the doctor, clearly uncertain.

"Here, I'll show you how it works," she pointed out the trigger and the notch where the bolt was fitted. "My ex went through a crossbow phase," she explained, on his look.

"What's that?" Kevin asked.

Otto paused. He'd been piling everything back into his bag. He lifted the large jar in his hands almost gingerly. It was full of a glittering, bright turquoise powder.

"It started off as a transport spell, but it's a little – er – unstable," he said, peering at Kevin through his spectacles.

"Unstable as in explosive?" Kevin asked, eagerly.

"Er, yes..."

"Wicked!"

"Sadly, it's a bit too fine to use," said Otto, thoughtfully. "If I could only find a suitable delivery medium..."

"You mean, something to throw it with?" Kevin asked. There was a strange light in her son's eyes that Stacey associated with the kind of video-games that her ex would buy for him, despite her argument that he was far too young for them.

"Er, yes, I suppose so."

"I think I've got an idea," said Kevin, and glanced at his mum.

"Go on then," she said, and he grinned.

"Do you reckon this building has a caretaker's office?"

ooo

"Well, that's one way to open a door," Stacey observed,

as she watched Otto and her son scramble over the wreckage. "I don't suppose you hire yourself out, say, to someone whose ex is avoiding paying child-maintenance?"

Charlie gave her a sideways sort of smile.

"I'm Stacey," she said, shifting her bin-lid shield to one side and holding out her hand.

Charlie blinked at it for a few moments before tentatively shaking it. "Charlie," he said.

"Here, Mum, hold this!" A box of lightbulbs were pressed into her hands. "Like this –" he said to Otto, gently levering the metal fitting off one of the bulbs. "You fill them with that powder, throw it at something and then – boom!"

"Boom…" Otto repeated, holding up a lightbulb. "Ingenious."

"If I were to ask how you knew this –" Stacey began.

"I saw it on the X-Box."

"This is perfect!" Otto said, with sudden enthusiasm. "Let's get them filled up!"

"You don't do work experience placements, do you?" Stacey asked, entertained.

Otto peered at her in obvious confusion.

"Never mind. Pass that jar, Kevin, I've got steadier hands."

ooo

Christopher crawled across the frigid garden, spells and imps rebounding off the battle-scarred soil around him.

Ivy was a few feet away, looking small and lost, sprawled across the hard ground. The harsh light of the magic arcing across the garden above them gave her skin an unhealthy tinge that he didn't want to think about.

Professor Zarrubabel shot past overhead, terrorising the imps and screaming profanities as Christopher inched forward, his fingers bloody from grasping at the icy soil.

The imps were ignoring them now – anything that wasn't moving a great deal couldn't really be thought of as a threat. Around them, his friends fought on with grim determination, doing anything they could to keep Quentin Post from his goal, and keeping back the Golems that had found their way back inside.

Without Ivy, he wasn't sure it would be enough.

He ought to be moving faster, he knew: the fate of Brindleford depended upon it, but beyond making sure that Ivy's heart was still beating, he couldn't bring himself to care. There wouldn't be a hell of a lot he could do about it anyway. By this point he was on borrowed time.

He groaned as he pulled himself closer to her, all his muscles protesting. His arm felt heavy and useless from the poison. The pain had gone from it, as far as he could tell, leaving behind a dull, inescapable throbbing. It felt empty, like it wasn't entirely there anymore.

It felt like a lifetime before he could even reach Ivy's hand, which was limp and cold to the touch. Christopher hauled himself forwards again, until he could roll her over.

She *was* breathing, he realised. His eyes fluttered closed for a moment in sheer relief.

"Ivy," he murmured, brushing away the lock of hair that had fallen across her eyes. "Ivy, wake up. We need you."

Ivy didn't stir.

"Come on –" he looked around: the nearest vines seemed more interested in attacking the imps than anything else, and that worried him: usually they couldn't get enough of Ivy. "Hey," he nudged a vine with his foot. It moved sluggishly away, as though it was confused.

They needed Ivy. Martha was too easily distracted from the task at hand, like a puppy that had been taken out on its first walk.

As gently as he could, Christopher pulled her into a sitting position. He pressed his forehead against hers.

"Come on, love, time to get up," he said, quietly. "You have to wake up now, Ivy. I know you're tired. Please..." He stroked her hair, gently. "Come on – look, we'll do it together."

Breathing hard, he heaved her to her feet. He swayed, for a moment, with the effort of keeping them both upright, spots forming at the edge of his vision.

"*I'm* getting too old for this," he chuckled, into her hair. It seemed oddly quiet, here at the centre of things, the battle raging on all around them – but then, that was just like Ivy, getting on with things in her own, quiet way, making the world turn around her without even knowing it.

He sighed.

"I think, on reflection," he said softly, "I would have liked to have seen Astrid and Jake grow up."

He shifted her weight to one side and reached out for the reluctant vines. They curled around his good arm ponderously.

"None of this is your fault," he pressed his lips to her forehead.

Christopher reached into himself, allowing the sounds around him to fade. He'd read about it somewhere – a fairy story maybe, in his dad's study when he was small. It was funny, really, how much he'd wanted those stories to be true. They were a lot less fun when you were living them. All it would take was a little 'push'...

His thoughts rested on his family for a moment, the way he remembered them, and hoped that they wouldn't think too poorly of him.

"Better get ready," he murmured to the vines; they seemed to understand what he was about – he could feel them moving along his arm, supporting Ivy.

He held her closely, feeling her heart beating against his chest. He paused, reluctant to let her go. Then, with one fluid instance of focus, he willed all his remaining strength to her.

ooo

Xander staggered up the last few steps and surveyed the scene with his good eye: the Arcade was in utter turmoil. The floor was littered with the corpses of imps – in some places they were piled up to knee-deep. More of their fellows were joining them as the residents struggled on. Dimly, he could just make out Christopher supporting an unconscious Ivy in the middle of the garden. They were quickly enveloped by dense, woody foliage.

One of the faceless Golems had Claire pinned to the wall. He made a move to help but Mahri got there first, neatly decapitating it with a fireball that baked it solid. Claire shattered it with what looked like an old cast iron frying pan.

The other Golems seemed to be having trouble telling the difference between imps and humans and were lumbering around in pursuit of both, adding to the general insanity.

Xander staggered and grabbed for the rail.

The Arcade shuddered to a halt, sending him flying out of the stairwell. He picked himself up from under the kitchen table which – at some point – had been flung across the room. There was a brief moment of intense disorientation as Martha turned back towards Nadderbeck Hill and *The Vines* surged forwards.

A bellow made him duck – Professor Zarrubabel zoomed past on his book trolley, wailing like a demented banshee, Reggie's parrot close behind him. He was hurling anything within reach at the imps, who were scurrying away in all directions to avoid him. The parrot was giving any escapees a hard time, scratching at their faces and pecking at their eyes.

Behind him, he spotted Post clinging to the plants near the ceiling above the kitchen. Just below him, Ogden Rake was half-transformed, snarling and hurling non-verbal hexes up at him. With a sick jolt he realised that one of his friend's arms was missing.

Xander rushed unsteadily across the room, shouting

words of power as he went. The air crackled and spat – Post had unleashed some kind of explosive magic from the bracelet at his wrist. He tugged his friend out of the way.

"We can't let him get it!" his friend hissed, words made indistinct by his over-long teeth.

They ducked again as Post tried to cut the vines around the *Chalice*, his magic rebounding in all directions. The vines responded angrily, swiping at his face and arms with inch-long thorns.

He grasped at the tawdry thing at his wrist. Xander, who had been attempting to climb up the counter tops below him, felt the magic build before it broke. He fell back in the nick of time, flinging his arms over his head for the scant protection they would provide.

The force of the explosion nearly knocked him senseless. He stared around stupidly for a few moments – his body felt leaden and slow. He seemed to be in a bubble of loud silence, as if he had been plunged underwater. He shook his head, trying to recover his hearing as wet and broken vegetation rained down on them. It steamed in places; there was a strong smell of cut grass and compost.

"No!" he heard Ogden shout, and looked up. Post was reaching for the chest containing the *Chalice*. Xander flung himself back up the counter, but it was too late – Post unleashed a creation spell, sending hundreds of stinging insects in their direction.

Xander was forced back once more, swatting and slashing at the hideous things until he was back to back with Ogden – now fully human. Nothing they threw at them seemed to make a blind bit of difference: their bodies were slick and black, like volcanic glass. Their wings and stings were sharp as a knife blade – in minutes the two Constables were covered in cuts and gashes, their skin slick with blood.

It was all that Xander could do to keep them away from his face.

Above them, a triumphant cry went up.

The wooden chest hit the ground a few feet away, somehow still intact.

Post laughed aloud as he raised the *Chalice* aloft.

"It's a *book*!" he cried. "Well, no wonder you couldn't keep your hands off – what are you – no! NO!"

Xander looked up: there was a flash beyond the cloud of Obsidian Hornets – Post screamed.

The insects changed direction, following a shock of green and grey feathers. The parrot shot skywards, gaining enough height to really make his next attack count. He dropped like a stone towards Post, who wasn't fast enough – Boscoe's claws closed around the *Chalice* and snatched it out of Post's reach. The Obsidian Hornets, chasing the parrot at some speed, didn't have time to change direction: they slammed into Post with sickening force, spraying blood across the kitchen.

He screamed in agony and shattered his own creations, scrambling madly across the ruined Arcade in pursuit of the African Grey.

ooo

"Why is it always *bloody* imps?" Professor Barraclough panted, repelling another wave of them as they scrambled up the hill.

"There are those half-formed Golem things, too," Joanna called, engaged in her own firefight across the lane. "Urgh – they don't have faces!"

The mindless clay creatures lumbered slowly up the hill, drawn by the power of the ley point.

"They're making time again!" his wife shouted.

Morton glanced over the heads of the nearest fiends. Sure enough, the Arcade was climbing up the hill, doggedly pursued by the imps spilling out of the ruined industrial estate. They were close enough now to feel the great stump-like footsteps crashing into the ground. The noise was incredible.

"Come on!" Morton hissed, concentrating on removing as many imps as he could.

To his surprise, the ones in front of him exploded with a little more force than he had intended.

"Wha-"

"Sorry!" someone shouted, from the woods to his left.

"Watch your aim, Kevin!"

"Sorry Mum!"

"Evening Professor," said a voice, some feet above his head. The light from the ley point was momentarily blocked out.

"Oh, hello Charlie – what are you doing here?"

"Kevin borrowed a truck."

"And if I *ever* find out where you learned to do that, young man!"

"*Mum!*"

The night on their side of the fence was suddenly alive with people. Morton risked a glance behind him: ten or fifteen Court Technomancers were clambering out of a battered Eddie Stobart lorry. There were deep gashes along its green liveried side and one of the wing mirrors was hanging off.

"We took a shortcut," said Charlie, following his gaze.

Somewhere in the distance, he could hear Otto Finch shouting instructions to his team: they were lining up along the fence line, hurling spells and small glass grenades into the encroaching horde. He suddenly felt a little out of place.

"Got another batch for you, Mr Finch!" someone shouted. There was a responding shout from the front line and a small, wiry shape dashed past him. "Careful with those, Kevin!"

"Right you are, Doc!"

"Dr Fitzhearn!" Morton sputtered, recognising the voice. "What on Earth –?"

"It's a long story, Professor," said the diminutive doctor, deftly plugging the top of a small, glass bulb full of blue powder. The woman beside him was carefully pouring powder into more of them. Both looked like they had quite recently been running for their lives.

"Right, Professor," barked the Widow Jenkins,

appearing noiselessly at his shoulder in an entirely unsettling way. "What do you need?"

He stared at her for a moment before collecting himself.

"We need to hold the ley point until Ivy can get close enough," he said. Widow Jenkins nodded briskly. "If too many of that lot get through it'll close early."

"I can do that," rumbled Charlie. He strode off into the midst of the Golems, merrily smacking them this way and that with his big-stick-with-nails-on.

"Just what are we throwing in there?" Arabella Jenkins asked, giving the Professor a hard look.

"Something that Quentin Post is prepared to kill for," he told her, and watched her expression change into one of abject loathing.

"*Right*," she hissed, and she, too strode into the fray.

"It seems like all of Brindleford is up in arms tonight," Joanna observed, getting her breath back a few feet away.

"Not long now," he said, patting her on the shoulder.

"I just hope they're alright in there..." Joanna trailed off, staring at the sky. "Is that –?"

Somewhere above them, something gave an urgent screech. Professor Barraclough fumbled with his monocle, trying to fit it to his eye. There was another high pitched squawk, and a shape detached itself from the Arcade, flying high above her.

"BOSCOE!" Joanna shouted, jumping to her feet. She waved her arms to catch his attention. "BOSCOE! DOWN HERE!"

He squawked again and shot across the night sky, veering away from the light as a hundred glittering insects hurtled after him. Lit by the ley point, they looked like the tail of a comet.

"Hornets," Professor Barraclough realised and hurled a freezing spell at them; the swarm scattered, some falling away – the others came back together, a little more disorganised than before. Behind them, the Arcade lumbered stubbornly up the hill, squashing imps and making the ground shake.

"He's got something in his talons!" Joanna said, pointing.

She was right. Boscoe was carrying extra weight – and a lot of it, if the way the hornets were catching up was anything to go by.

"He's got the *Chalice*!" he shouted, aiming another curse at the Hornets as they crested another arc.

"HERE, BOSCOE!" Joanna screamed. "DROP IT DOWN HERE!"

But Boscoe was ignoring her. He wheeled around the stand of trees, momentarily passing out of sight behind the old farm buildings. He shot out the other side, pursued by a much smaller cluster of Obsidian Hornets.

He cried shrilly, too far away for them to make out any words.

"GET BACK HERE YOU INTERFERING FEATHERBRAINED BASTARD!"

Quentin Post was climbing out of the Arcade, hexes and the occasional imp bursting around him. His handsome features were lacerated and bloody – even at this distance Morton could see the man's murderous expression.

He slid down one of the trailing vines and leapt to the ground, sprinting towards the ley point and hexing everything within reach.

Professor Barraclough raced to intercede as Post drew level with Widow Jenkins. The old witch, seeing that her spells were having little effect, smacked him in the sternum with her staff. For a moment, Morton lost sight of him amongst the imps –

An expanding ring of fire roared through the crowd, throwing the Widow back. He could hear her swearing, somewhere in the scrum.

He pressed forward, towards the centre of the spell – the smell of burning flesh seared his throat and nostrils, making him gag. Post was at the centre of it, fighting off one of his own Golems. It boiled away to nothing as he reached them; Post was running on pure rage now.

Swiftly, Professor Barraclough wove a net of magic between his hands and threw it at Post. It tangled around him like a web of light, tightening as the dark wizard struggled.

Above them, Boscoe flew higher, still pursued by the Hornets. They were gaining on him now, tired as he was from carrying the Chalice.

He could hear Joanna shouting at the bird, somewhere behind him.

Post ripped through the gossamer threads like they were spider-webs. He reached for something on his wrist – it glinted in the flashes of light from the skirmish around them. Professor Barraclough's heart leapt into his mouth as he realised what it was – he cast a hasty shield charm as the gauntlet's power was unleashed.

He flew through the air, skimming over the tops of the imps and landed with a thump that winded him, despite the shield charm. Professor Barraclough scrambled off a small mound of squashed imps and ran back towards the ley point, dodging between the Arcade's enormous feet.

Flashes of red and white by the fence line at the Farm suggested that Post had run into a little trouble with the Technomancers.

A screech made him tear his eyes from the furore at the fence line and he looked up in time to see Boscoe spiralling towards the ley point at some speed. He wheeled swiftly back up, flapping hard. The comet tail of Hornets fell away, shooting downwards after a dark shape, tumbling downwards –

The night lit up with magic – it shot high into the sky, spilling out across the hill. The snow rapidly evaporated around them, steam shrouding the top of Nadderbeck Hill. Boscoe was nowhere to be seen.

Then the screaming started: a piercing cry that rose and fell on the wind. It put the fear of God into the imps, which started climbing over each other in their hurry to escape.

Professor Barraclough fell to his knees with the power of it; he covered his ears as best as he could. It was so loud they could probably hear it in the next county.

The first voice was joined by a second – then a third – as the pages of the *Chalice of Knowledge* burned in the magical fire. Above the wailing was another sound: a hundred voices were speaking at once, in a disjointed chorus of language. There were whispers and shouts, snatches of song, groans of desperation, cries of triumph and grief, words of power.

Their thoughts and desires – preserved for so many centuries in ink and blood – finally faded in the searing heat of pure magic.

Amongst the chaos, he could see Quentin Post bellowing in impotent rage. He sprinted into the woods, clearly with the intention of rescuing the *Chalice*, already fully in the thrall of his coveted treasure.

Professor Barraclough staggered up the hill towards his wife. She was dragging an unconscious Technomancer towards the Eddie Stobart lorry. Her scarf was tied around her head, covering her ears.

He took the man's other arm and helped lift him over the stile.

The air around the farm was foggy with magic. The warm light above them was almost white now, tiny flecks of colour the only hint that anything might be caught within it.

The Vines had stopped at the top of the hill and was waiting with palpable expectation, imps scuttling out of every opening, trying to get away from the *Chalice's* baleful wails.

Then, as suddenly as it had started, the screaming ceased; the light faded with it, rendering everyone temporarily blind and deaf.

"Is it over?" Dr Fitzhearn shouted as they reached the truck. He was bandaging Widow Jenkins' arm and ignoring her obvious protests.

"What the bloody hell is going on?" the woman in the lorry demanded.

"I think so," Joanna shouted back, over the buzzing in everybody's ears. She turned to the woman. "We just killed one of the most dangerous books ever written."

"How do you kill a book?" the woman wondered aloud.

"Well, Boscoe did," said Professor Barraclough, as his hearing returned to normal.

Joanna grimaced.

"And he paid for it – the plume from the ley point caught him on the wing," she said. "He'd have burned up in seconds."

Professor Barraclough pulled off his hat, greatly saddened.

"Reggie will be heart-broken."

"You mean that parrot?"

He turned to find a teenage boy eyeing him quizzically. He was about to respond when Quentin Post burst from the trees some metres away, screaming like a madman and running towards their group, murder in his eyes.

The demented wizard began to cast, and Professor Barraclough saw that one of his arms ended in a bloody stump, burned clean off when he'd plunged it into the ley point, trying to rescue the *Chalice*.

There was a swift rearrangement of practitioners around non-practitioners as he sprinted towards them.

He skidded to a halt a few metres away, puce with rage.

"YOU DID THIS!" he screamed. "YOU TOOK IT FROM ME! THE CHALICE WAS MINE!"

He was close enough now that Morton could see his eyes: they were pitch black. The man was so consumed with dark magic and vengeance that not even the whites were visible. His tirade continued. Shield spells sprung up all around them as the magic Post was gathering around him became palpable. While he still wore the gauntlet there wasn't a great deal they could do to him. Professor Barraclough steeled himself for the oncoming assault.

"I'LL MAKE YOU PAY! I'LL –"

But they never found out what he'd do. At that moment, the sky appeared to fall. With quiet deliberation, the Arcade dropped like a stone, right on top of Quentin Post.

There was a sickening crunching noise as she settled against the ground. Professor Barraclough stared up at the Arcade as a hush fell over the farm.

"Eurgh," said the woman from the lorry.

"Yes," said Joanna, faintly.

"Well," Otto chirped, brightly. "At least that will save us some paperwork!"

A great cracking sound echoed up from the valley below, making them jump – without Post's mind to sustain it, the chasm had closed, the imps around them melting away into a sort of oily black liquid that seeped into the snowy ground, vanishing from sight.

One of them ran past Professor Barraclough in utter terror, the colour draining from every part of its body as it, too, seeped away into the snow.

A shadow passed overhead and Morton looked up.

"Boscoe!" he exclaimed, stunned. "You're alive!"

"That's what I was trying to tell you!" said Kevin, with exasperated impatience. "He flew right out of it like a jet fighter, half on fire – then he hit the snow!"

"Bloody good show, old chap," murmured the Professor, as Boscoe landed on Charlie's bobble hat, showering him with smouldering feathers.

Boscoe made a tired sort of croaking noise, and that was that.

ooo

Ivy groaned.

Every part of her body felt bruised, used up. She was terribly thirsty.

Even her hair hurt.

She cracked open an eye. It was dark in the garden of the Arcade, and still snowing. It fell gently on her face, muffling sound. She blinked the snowflakes away, opening the other eye. She was on her back, she realised, lying on thick vines. One of them stroked at her hand

and she patted it absently.

"I'm okay," she murmured. "Just tired."

She lay there for a few minutes, her mind blissfully empty, until the snow really started to annoy her and she rolled onto her side – moaning as her body protested. Bleakly, she looked at the ruins of her home and garden. The past few hours had not been kind. People were moving around in the Arcade proper, but they were blurry and indistinct.

Her gaze fell on the shape beside her, half-hidden beneath leaves and snow.

Something about it bothered her, but she couldn't place it. Whatever it was, it was covered in attractive blue flowers.

She reached out to touch one of them, but it dodged away from her hand. Ivy frowned. There was something oddly disquieting about the flowers, too.

She wondered where Christopher was.

Ivy reached out for another of the flowers and it darted away from her fingers; one of the vines that were lying so thickly over the mound gave her hand a sharp slap.

She swore, sucking her knuckles.

"What are you playing at, you daft thing?" she wondered aloud. "Why won't you..."

Ivy froze, staring at the flouncy azure petals.

She looked again at the vine covered mound beside her.

"Christopher?" She pulled at the nearest vines, brushing away the snow. As soon as she pulled away a tendril another moved into its place. She felt sick. "Get off him!" she demanded. They ignored her. "Please! Just let me see his face –"

Sluggishly, some of the vines receded, revealing Christopher's head and neck. There was a dark silver stain around his mouth – it ran along his jaw and down his neck, following the line of his jugular vein. Ivy ran her fingers along it, her hands numb and shaking.

His skin was slick with snow, and he was cold – too

cold.

"Christopher..." she whispered.

He was slumped on his side, shivering violently. She stroked his hair; it was wet and lank against his forehead.

"It's alright," she said softly. "Everything's going to be fine. I'm right here, Christopher – don't give up... *Please* don't give up..."

She closed her eyes and, for the first time since her father had died, she prayed. She prayed to anyone that might listen, silently begging that Christopher would be alright – that the aconite would draw out the poison – that the aconite wouldn't just kill him.

"Ivy?"

She felt a hand on her shoulder.

"I'm alright, Reggie," she said, wiping away the tears that had accumulated at the very end of her nose. "Is everyone okay?"

There was a pause where she suspected Reggie was considering whether to include Christopher's condition in his assessment.

"A few of us are in a bad way," he said. "Mahri and Joanna are ordering people around – er, we're using the kitchen as a makeshift first aid tent. We picked up some passengers at the ley point. No deaths..." there was a pause, and she guessed that he was looking at Christopher again. "So far."

She watched his eyes slide to the ground to her left.

"He's still breathing," she said softly.

"Is he going to – be alright?" Reggie asked, gently.

"I don't..."

"Ivy..."

Ivy whirled around – Christopher was stirring within his toxic cocoon. She fell to her knees as the wolfsbane receded. She heard Reggie's footsteps retreating through the snow.

"Is everyone okay?" he asked. The shivering was much milder now, and the dark stain around his lips was fading.

"More or less," she told him, gently.

"How did we…?"

"I'll tell you when you're stronger." She brushed his fringe out of his eyes. "How do you feel?"

"Alive…?"

Ivy laughed, tightly clasping his hand in hers. "That's a good start. Let me look at your hand."

He gave her his other hand and she unwrapped the bandages. He frowned at his arm, confused.

"It doesn't hurt," he said, surprised. "What happened?"

Ivy smiled. "Martha took matters into her own hands," she said. "When you gave up your energy to keep us going she must have taken the opportunity to cover you in aconite."

Hope bloomed in Christopher's face. "Aconite?" he asked, almost breathlessly.

Ivy pulled the last of the bandages away. She laughed out loud. "It's healed."

"What, really?" Christopher stared at his own hand, running a finger over the thin, right angled scar – the only reminder of the poison that had so recently been flooding his bloodstream.

"You're going to be alright," she beamed, feeling lighter than she had in months.

"I am," he said, wonderingly, and laughed.

He sat up and pulled Ivy into a tight hug. "I'm going to be fine…" he said, into her hair.

Ivy felt oddly giddy, sitting in the snow with him, laughing like a couple of children. Christopher beamed at her.

"You are the most beautiful person I have ever met," he said, that playful smile playing around his lips. "Inside and out."

Ivy's heart did a funny little wobble that she didn't altogether dislike. She didn't have any idea what to say to him, so she kissed him instead, hoping he'd get the message.

He pulled back slightly and tucked a curl of hair gently

behind her ear.

"Hi," she said, almost shyly.

"Hi..." he replied, a broad grin spreading over his features.

"When you two have finished canoodling, we could really use a hand in here!" someone shouted, from the remains of the living room.

Ivy made out the commanding form of the Widow Jenkins and gave her a wave to show that they'd heard.

"What a mess," Christopher observed, as they got shakily to their feet.

"We'll sort it out," said Ivy, taking his hand. "Together."

Epilogue

It had taken quite a long time to get Martha to settle down after her adventure, but once they'd hooked up the electricity and water again, and apologised profusely to the very confused gas man, things began to pick up.

The children had been escorted up from the Court by a man who looked like he'd been fossilised and Otto, whose cat was now more-or-less permanently attached to his head. They had clung to Ivy and Christopher like they hadn't seen them in months.

The Arcade was, for lack of a better word, wrecked. They'd covered the hole in the roof with a shield charm and an illusion, to save too many questions, and decided to worry about the rest of it later. As soon as it had become clear that they were more in the way than needed in the triage unit that had taken over the kitchen, Christopher and Professor Barraclough had vanished downstairs to the bookshop to assess the damage.

That had been three weeks ago, and the shops at least were beginning to get back to normal.

The local (and then national) press had decided, probably with a little nudge from the Court of Miracles, that the whole episode had been the result of a gas explosion. There was a local enquiry being run into how hallucinatory gas had found its way beneath the town, and almost every practitioner in the area had to stop themselves sniggering whenever it came on the news.

ooo

It wasn't as if Ivy had actually *decided* to have a party.

Charlie had turned up one morning with a toolbox and a Christmas tree, and had helped salvage what they could of the furniture. They'd phoned everyone they could think of and stuck the Christmas tree up in the garden.

Their odd assortment of friends had trickled back to

the Arcade, still injured, most of them, but bearing large quantities of food and followed by a trail of family members who were curious to see what their new Witch was like.

Christopher could tell it made Ivy uncomfortable, so he stayed close to her all night, while Ogden Rake's gran shook his hand over and over, thanking him for making sure that her grandson had come home – or at least, most of him.

She appeared to have absorbed Hardwick into her gregarious family, which Christopher thought was a good thing. Getting over Rosie was going to take a long time.

He couldn't imagine losing Ivy the same way.

He'd danced with her in the snow around the Christmas tree, dodging children and puppies (all of whom seemed to have made friends) and ignoring everyone else. Ivy's laughing face was far too distracting. As the dancing descended into a snowball fight – probably started by Stacey's son, Kevin, but enthusiastically continued by everyone else – they had slipped back inside. Mahri had ushered Astrid outside into the chaos, telling her that this was exactly the sort of thing that a young Witch needed to experience.

Reggie, Xander Hardwick and Ogden Rake, still nursing their injuries, were drinking quietly on one of the sofas. Ivy went over to speak with them and Christopher watched her, fondly.

Certain that she was holding her own in the midst of the throng, he snuck away at a quiet moment to break the rule he had set for himself when he'd first been bitten – well, it was Christmas Eve, after all.

He held his breath while it rang – the one phone number that he knew by heart.

"Mum? It's me, Christopher..."

The House of Vines

Acknowledgements

This book has been a part of my life now for the better part of half a decade, in which I have fallen in and out of love with it many times. It is unsurprising, therefore, that many people have helped me bring it to life. Enormous thanks must go to the following people:

First and foremost, I have to thank my patient husband, who is the worst critic in the world in terms of never giving usable feedback, but who nonetheless has supported me throughout the whole process. He has helped me out of word-blindness, fixed formatting issues and made me cups of tea like a champ. I would not have made it this far without you, Niall, nor would I have had half as much fun, so thank you!

Immense thanks must go to my fellow editors and ghost writers at Coleman Editing, who are always there to bounce ideas off and spot typos.

Fellow authors and co-conspirators, Jessica Grace Coleman and G. Burton, who are always up for a bit of plotting and very kindly read through the final proofs for me. You two have pulled me out of plot holes and boosted my confidence, so much. Thank you!

Mum, for telling me that it wasn't as awful as I thought it might be and putting up with all the punctuation.

The many lovely people who have read through chapters or the whole work over the years and been enthusiastic about it when they were done. These lovelies include – but are by no means limited to – Krystyna McGurk, Rowena Thomson, Louise Smith, Eirini Steerlorb, Clare Keogh, Riley Coles, Mina Lofthouse and Jamie Barnett. Tremendous thanks!

Liz Hearson, who always comes up with awesome illustrations, despite my often vague waffling! Every time I get a message from you, my day brightens up a little. You rock!

For designing The Mysterium symbol, helping me use

drawing software and laughing at my plot, Carl Mitchell.

Once again, James at www.goonwrite.com has put together a gorgeous cover for this book – thank you again!

The Superstars, whose group and anthologies I curate, for keeping me from going mad in the period before publishing this, and teaching me things about writing I didn't know I didn't know.

There are many others who have helped The House of Vines on its way, and I thank you all. I've probably forgotten half of you, but in your honour, Liz has prepared something rather special, which you'll find on the following page.

Last, but not least, I want to thank you, dear reader. Books only come to life when they are read!

The House of Vines

About the Author

Lauren K. Nixon

An ex-archaeologist enjoying life in the slow-lane, Lauren K. Nixon is an indie author fascinated by everyday magic. She is the author of numerous short stories, *The Fox and the Fool* and the *Chambers Magic* series. Happily, there are many things to keep her occupied, and when she's not writing or curating the Short Story Superstars club she can be found gardening, singing, crafting, reading, laughing uproariously at nothing, playing the fool with Shipley Little Theatre and playing board games.

You can find out more about her writing, and the weird stuff she finds herself researching, over at her website: www.laurenknixon.com

About the Artist

Liz Hearson

"Is that a really big sheep or are aliens smaller than we thought?"

Printed in Poland
by Amazon Fulfillment
Poland Sp. z o.o., Wrocław